The Broken System

A BUDDING SCIENTIST IN A FANTASY WORLD

BOOK 3

THE BROKEN SYSTEM

A C ASWELL

Podium

Podium

THE BROKEN SYSTEM

<h1 style="text-align:center">Chapter 1</h1>

Illa, retired [Warmage], leader of the town of Cyra, and former mentor of a young [Scientist] named Alice, looked at the air around her and suppressed a surge of frustration.

{Detect Danger}, a perk from her [Warmage] class, was ringing an alarm in the back of her mind. It wasn't the immediate alarm she felt when she was about to die—but she still knew that something was wrong. Something dangerous was coming, and sooner or later, it would reach her. Not for the first time, Illa wished the perk was a bit more specific. Illa knew danger was approaching, but she had no idea *what* the danger was. All she knew was that it existed.

At first, Illa had wondered if another group of [Assassins] from the Sigmusi Colonia was coming to kill her. While most of the [Assassins] and [Spies] in southern Illvaria had been removed by Allira at the beginning of spring, it was entirely possible that a few remained. If that was true, Illa was a prime target for assassination.

She remembered writing a reminder to the head of her [Guards] to investigate Cyra for any potential assassination attempts. While some [Assassins] could slip by, the head of her [Guard] had perks specialized in finding hidden threats.

Her [Guards] had found nothing.

This had sent Illa into an even deeper level of worry and confusion. Her [Guards] had found nothing, and the sense of danger hadn't eased, even though it *should* have decreased once she started preparing for potential [Assassins]. After all, it was much harder to assassinate somebody who was on guard, and in the middle of a well-fortified town full of [Guards] actively trying to weed out [Assassins]. Normally, the level of danger detected by her perk should have weakened, even if the [Assassins] weren't caught.

This was when Illa started to realize she had gone in the wrong direction. The threat likely wasn't from [Assassins] at all, but something else.

Illa's next guess was that a disaster was about to befall the town of Cyra. A monster swarm could prove just as disastrous as an [Assassin] if handled poorly.

However, none of the [Scouts] had picked up any unusual activity in the woods surrounding Illvaria.

This was when Illa started to feel more worried. She had, grudgingly, swapped out some of her [Charisma]-boosting enchantments and put on more protective items. It never hurt to be prepared. However, even that didn't ease the constant twinge of anxiety created by her perk. No matter what Illa did, she couldn't pinpoint the danger. If she didn't know what the threat was, she couldn't take countermeasures against it.

Illa shuffled uneasily as she thought of the futility of the last few weeks. Then her mind drifted toward a rather unusual girl she had met several months ago. The girl had been named Alice, and she had been obsessed with scientific experiments and learning. Most of Alice's experiments hadn't been very impressive, but with her out-of-the-box thinking and her experiences as an {Outworlder}, the girl had refreshed her understanding of magic.

As far as she knew, Alice had been taken on by the Immortal of Spells and Seeds, Ethan, as his latest apprentice a few months ago. Clearly her experiments had come quite far, if an Immortal had taken an interest in them.

Perhaps Alice or her mentor knew something about the current situation? As far as Illa knew, Alice still had some goodwill toward Illa after leaving Cyra—one of the reasons Illa always tried to treat her business associates well. If Alice was willing to ask her new mentor for advice, Illa would be able to tap into the intelligence network of an Immortal. However, if Illa wanted to ask an Immortal for a favor, even indirectly, she would need to do things formally. That meant showing up personally and asking for help.

Illa looked at the town of Cyra again and felt a stab of hesitation in her heart.

She didn't like the idea of being away from her town for long. However, the sense of uneasiness in her heart, and the prickling warnings of future danger from her perk, simply wouldn't go away. The more time passed, the worse it became. If Illa left, she would be gone for a few weeks, possibly a month. That was a lot of time to spend asking someone who might not be able to help her.

Illa gritted her teeth. The years she had spent mired in politics and on a battlefield warred within her, before her instincts as a former [Soldier] won out.

When something was wrong, she needed to move. Otherwise, she might end up on the wrong side of a [Thermal Mage]'s heat explosion—or, in this case, caught in the midst of a catastrophe with no preparations whatsoever. Right now, Illa's instincts were screaming at her. She felt that she should contact Alice *now*. The sooner the better.

Even if Illa wasn't certain that this was the best move, she would trust her instincts again. Illa quickly summoned her [Combat Maid], and her old friend.

"Ellia, let the other mages know that I'm going north. I felt something weird a few hours ago, and no matter what I do, I can't seem to shake off the warning signals from my perk. I can't figure out what the problem is, so I'm going to seek more information. While I'm gone, I want you to take care of the town." Illa handed Ellia her personal token. "I trust you more than anyone else. If it's a problem you can't manage, hire a [Messenger] to get in contact with me as fast as possible. For smaller problems, handle them as you see fit."

"Me?"

Illa didn't hesitate for a moment as she nodded and gave her old friend a wry grin. "I trust you the most. I know you won't let me down." Illa's grin deepened.

The [Combat Maid] sighed. "I'll do my best to hold down the fort, my lady. Come back safely, and make sure that your trip is fruitful."

Illa nodded, and the two started to make more specific preparations for her departure.

Alice sat on her bed as her mind raced furiously. She scanned a few of the reports that Ethan, her mentor and one of the Immortals of Illvaria, had given her. She tried not to worry, and failed.

The collapse of the System was a problem. An incomprehensibly massive problem. One that even an Immortal, one of the unaging, nearly invincible demigods of this world, would struggle to handle. And most of them didn't even know what was going on.

Less than a day ago, the System itself had winked out of existence. The System that, as far as Alice could tell, was responsible for keeping most of the humans on this planet alive. It did a huge variety of critical things, such as helping people survive mana baptisms, keeping their minds from being eroded by mana, and giving people the strength to resist monsters.

Even though less than twenty-four hours had passed since the collapse of the System, Ethan had already confirmed that nobody was surviving mana baptisms anymore. Mana baptisms were risky at the best of times—after all, absorbing mana in order to grow a new organ without breaking the human body was dangerous. However, the System had always helped people survive the process. With it gone, the danger level had escalated an entire order of magnitude.

She took another look at her status screen in hopes that it would tell her something new. That somehow, she would find an error, or a glitch, or . . . *something* that would help her understand what was going on.

Name: Alice Verianna	Age: 16
Strength: 115→117 (122%)	Perception: 137→139 (165%)
Dexterity: 115→119 (124%)	Intelligence: 167→169 (128%)
Endurance: 130→134 (121%)	Willpower: 148→150 (108→109%)
Charisma: 130→132 (107%)	Magic: 161→164 (122%)
Primary classes: 6/6	Survivor: 54→56

	Explorer of Magic: 71→75
	Scholar: 54→56
	Scientist: 55→58
	Kinetic Manabinder: 41
	Careful Enchanter: 27
Evolved classes: 2	Student of Kinetic Magic: 25 (Apprentice) Enchanter: 25
Secondary classes: 2	Fisherwoman: 3 Student: 8→9 Student of Organic Magic: 11 Courtier: 0→1
Perks:	**Survivor Perks:** Foraging (Survivor 5) Microbe Resistance (Survivor 10) Extremophile (Survivor 15) Camouflaged (Survivor 20) Enhanced Training (Survivor 30) Moderate Tissue Regeneration (Survivor 40) Adrenaline Rush (Survivor 45) Extended Organics (Survivor 50) Enhanced Senses (Tier 2) (Survivor 55) **Explorer of Magic Perks:** Enhanced Regeneration (Explorer of Magic 10) Seeds of Magic (Explorer of Magic 25) Broken Seed (Upgraded) (Explorer of Magic 35) Expanding Comprehension (Tier 2) (Explorer of Magic 55) Combat Seed (Tier 2) (Explorer of Magic 60) Intuitive Magic Modeling (Tier 2) (Explorer of Magic 65) Seeds of Ambition (Tier 2) (Explorer of Magic 75) **Scholar Perks:** Enhanced Memory (Scholar 5) Accelerated Thinking (Scholar 15 (-5)) Rhetorical Flourish (Scholar 20) Photographic Memory (Scholar 25) Improved Multitasking (Scholar 30) Scholar of Magic (Scholar 35)

	Lesser Organic Vision (Scholar 40) Delve Into the Arcane (Scholar 50) Sleep Reading (Tier 2) (Scholar 55) **Scientist Perks:** Precise Mana Measurement (Scientist 5) Sample Collection (Scientist 10) Safety Analysis (Scientist 20) Shared Memory (Scientist 25) Advanced Mana Measurement (Scientist 30) Degraded Seed Slot (Scientist 35) For Science! (Scientist 45) The Science of Mana Deprivation (Scientist 50) Speed Experimentation (Tier 2) (Scientist 55) **Kinetic Mage Perks:** Object Control (Student of Kinetic Magic 5) Above-Average Mana Sight (Student of Kinetic Magic 10) Folds of Magic (Student of Kinetic Magic 15) Split Mind (Student of Kinetic Magic 20) Improved Object Control (Sensory Enhancement) (Student of Kinetic Magic 25) Mana's Binding (Kinetic Manabinder 5) Enhanced Focus (Kinetic Manabinder 10) Vastly Improved Kinetic Vision (Kinetic Manabinder 15) Overclock (Kinetic Manabinder 20) Kinetic Enchanting (Kinetic Manabinder 25) Reflection (Kinetic Manabinder 30) Kinetic Tendrils (Kinetic Manabinder 35) Speed Analysis (Kinetic Manabinder 40) **Enchanter Perks:** Enchanter's Vision (Apprentice Enchanter 5) Monstrous Enchanting (Apprentice Enchanter 10) Faster Enchanting (Apprentice Enchanter 15) Faster Mana Regeneration (Apprentice Enchanter 20) Speed Enchanting (Apprentice Enchanter 25) Repurposing (Careful Enchanter 5) Blueprint (Careful Enchanter 10)

	Enchanter's Basic Magic Seed (Careful Enchanter 15) Pride of a Craftswoman (Careful Enchanter 20) Enchanter's Armory (Careful Enchanter 25) **Organic Mage Perks:** Improved Organic Manipulation (Organic Mage 5)
Skills	**Academic Skills:** English (Language Proficiency): 100 Illvarian (Language Proficiency): 100 Sigmusi (Language Proficiency): 7 Russian (Language Proficiency): 1 Verinthian (Language Proficiency): 0→1 Basic Mathematics: 123 Intermediate Mathematics: 79 Advanced Mathematics: 19 Basic Human Biology: 38 Mana Biology: 11 **Magic Skills:** Kinetic Manipulation: 70 Mana Control: 52 Mana Precision: 53 Kinetic Force: 51 Projectile Awareness : 32 Divided Attention: 34 Basic Enchanting: 31 Broken Mana Purification: 22 Mana Filtering: 24 Seed Formation: 19 **Crafting Skills:** Weaving: 27 Woodworking: 28 Cooking: 12 Stoneworking: 11 **Physical Skills:** Dodge: 31 Etiquette: 0→21 Spearmanship: 19 Sprinting: 22 Riding: 0→15

	Climbing: 9 Fishing: 9 Digging: 8 Stealth: 4 Basic Medicine: 3 Dancing: 0→6
Magic Seed: 3/3 (unused seed has 15% conversion rat. max) (Note to self: The electromagnetic magic seed is {Degraded Seed Slot}. For that seed, perks = no, achievements = yes) (Final slot is one where Alice keeps trying and failing to make a System seed)	Kinetic seed (145%)→154% Healing mana seed (23%)→55% (Deactivated—you may link this to a perk if desired!) Electromagnetic seed (15%)
Lesser Magic Seeds (Base max 25%, achievements now apply as usual)	Display seed (11%) Organic seed (68%)→74% (6% Exp. Comp.) Pure mana seed (36%)→44% (8%→12% Exp. Comp.)
Achievements:	Outworlder (Rarity: 10)
	Seeker of Truth (IV) (Rarity: 10)
	Baptized by Broken Mana (Rarity: 6)
	Survivor of Winter (Rarity: 3)
	Monstrous Encounter (Rarity: 1)
	Monster Slayer (III) (Rarity: 2)
	Well Trained (Rarity: 4)
	Murderer (Rarity: 4)
	Bookworm (Rarity: 3)
	Kinetic Manabinder (Rarity N/A)
	Careful Enchanter (Rarity N/A)
	Capable Enchanter (Rarity: 5)
	Seed Creator (Rarity: 8)
	Scientific Discoveries (II)→(III) (Rarity N/A)
	Immortal's Apprentice at the Battle Against the Society (Rarity: 4)
	Legendary Healer (Rarity: 7)

Unfortunately, her status screen looked normal. If Alice ignored the fact that System mana in her surroundings had disappeared, she wouldn't even have known something was wrong. The only upside was the fact that the System mana in her body seemed to be working just fine. If *that* had turned off, most humans on the planet would have been eaten by monsters within hours—if their own biology didn't break and kill everyone first, or their class mana didn't overwrite their personality and devour them alive.

Alice thought about the moment she had seen the System blink out of existence, and shivered.

The System had been getting weaker for months. It had been growing more and more glitchy, but Alice hadn't really thought about what would happen if the whole thing shut off. It had just been a disaster scenario she thought about in her idle time, a scary but unlikely possibility. And now it was a reality.

Alice had a hard time imagining what the consequences would be. Since the System was so integral to human life on this planet, Alice knew one thing for sure: The System collapsing was *very bad* for the people of this world.

Luckily, her studies hadn't been entirely in vain. In the day she had spent studying her status screen, she had started to notice a few peculiarities that hadn't been there before. Normally, when she tried to examine System mana, the System was . . . less than cooperative. Even though System mana was present in a wide variety of things, from every single class seed in her body to her status screen, it actively avoided being caught in a small space, touched by other people's mana, or studied in any way, shape, or form. The System seemed to be actively designed to prevent other people from interacting with it or learning about it.

After the System's collapse, System mana no longer avoided her attempts to study it. She had even tried adding some display mana to her class seeds, just to see what happened when she tried to look at them without System interference. Interestingly enough, adding display mana to her class seeds now gave her weird, nonsensical strings of binary numbers, none of which she could make heads or tails of.

However, none of Alice's discoveries were useful for solving the root problem: the collapse of the System. If that wasn't fixed, no amount of scientific discovery would keep humanity alive in this world. Worse, Alice couldn't study real System mana anymore, because it was gone. The System mana in her body was the *only* thing she could analyze. While both types of rainbow mana came from the System, Alice knew there were some differences in composition and design between the two. She just hoped those differences wouldn't screw her over while she tried to examine the System.

Alice looked at her door and furrowed her brows.

She had never spoken about her studies of the System; after all, she was afraid of stepping on the toes of this world's religion. The Church of the System worshipped the System as its god: If Alice had publicly announced that she was studying the god of one of this world's two major religions, or that she was relatively certain this world's "god" wasn't sentient, she suspected that she would be burned at the stake the following week. As tolerant as this world's religion seemed to be, Alice really didn't want to push things.

However, that had been her mindset *before* the System had disappeared into thin air. If nothing was done, kingdoms would collapse soon. Children would find themselves twisted by the class-related mana they absorbed. Mages would experience all sorts of strange problems, and many of them would be lethal. It would become nearly impossible to fend off monsters as humans grew weaker and monsters remained the same.

She took a deep breath, thinking about the possible consequences of her next action. She had already trusted Ethan with most of her other secrets, and the Immortal who had taken her on as an apprentice had never betrayed her confidence. As far as she could tell, he was trustworthy. Alice couldn't handle all this alone.

Perhaps it was time to discuss the nature of the System with Ethan.

Alice took a deep breath to steady her nerves and stepped out of her room. If Ethan knew about the current situation, he would be able to help her work through the best follow-up actions. Alice's research wasn't just a personal hobby anymore, or a potential fix to obscure problems that *might* appear someday in the far-off future. Now, Alice's research was a crucial link to whatever catastrophes were about to appear in the world. Alice wasn't willing to stay quiet when her research might be critical to the survival of millions of people.

Alice took one final deep breath, stepped out, and made her way to Ethan's office.

<h1 style="text-align:center">Chapter 2</h1>

I mmortal Ethan, I would like to talk about my research," Alice said after Ethan invited her in and she made sure there weren't any nearby [Servants]. "I feel that it will be extremely relevant in the coming days, which is why I'm willing to talk about it. However, I would also like to keep it a secret—if the Society of Starry Eyes learns about my studies, I feel that they would stop at nothing to hunt me down. And honestly, while I'm not sure what the Church of the System's stance on this is, I think it would be best to avoid treading on their toes. Just in case."

Ethan paused for a moment, giving Alice a curious look. Then, he solemnly nodded. "I understand. I'll respect your wish to keep this secret." After saying that, a bubble of rainbow mana flickered into existence around the two. "I've set up my anti-eavesdropping perk, so you can speak freely now."

At the back of her mind, Alice noted that, despite the System being down, Ethan seemed to have no problem using his perks. Alice also hadn't had any real issues running her own perks or looking at her status screen or anything of the sort. If other people were having the same experience, that was valuable information about the collapse of the System.

Fortunately, things like status screens, classes, and perks didn't seem to need any connection to the System to keep working. Of course, there might be problems with status screens and perks that Alice simply hadn't noticed yet. She hadn't leveled up or gained any new perks since the System had shut off, so she would need to see how the collapse impacted those things. Of course, Alice really hoped that leveling up and gaining new perks still worked: If it was still possible to get new perks and levels frequently, it would make fixing this mess much easier. Alice felt that she could dissect and understand how the System had worked even with the tools she had currently available—but it would probably take years of research and investigation. She had no idea whether she had that kind of time anymore.

However, while it was a good thing that not everything had collapsed, it also made it much harder for Alice to prove that something was horribly wrong. Alice really hoped that Ethan was willing to trust her, because if he wasn't, she would need to wait until things got worse before bringing this topic back to his attention. In that time, an awful lot of people might get hurt or die.

"As you already know, I'm focused on research. Most of my perks are related to research, I have quite a number of research classes, and most of my notable achievements are related to research."

"Indeed," Ethan acknowledged.

"Well, the biggest thing I've focused on is researching the System itself."

"Why are you researching the System?" Ethan seemed baffled. "I never took you as an aspiring [Priest of the System]. I always figured you were most interested in being a mage. All your research and actions so far seem to support this idea. Or is there some sort of connection I'm not seeing here?" Then his eyes seemed to light up. "Wait, is this about that Boris boy? Now that I think about it, you often claimed to be researching mana itself, but you seemed oddly focused on Boris. He unlocked his status screen early. You also mentioned at the time that you had been looking into how mana and status screens interacted with each other . . ." Ethan gave Alice a quizzical look. "So is your real focus of research the System and its connection to mana? I see . . ." Ethan trailed off, looking a lot more thoughtful now. "If that's the case . . . are mana and the System really intertwined enough to make it into an entire focus of research? Hmm . . ." Ethan seemed to enter a daze before he nodded to himself. "That actually treads on quite a few toes. It's some sort of . . . union between the beliefs of the Church of Mana and the Church of the System." He turned back toward Alice. "What have you found? Elaborate."

Alice shrugged. "Honestly, mana and the System are far more intertwined than most people think. Do you recall what I mentioned about my previous world? The kind of environment that existed there?"

"You mentioned that there was no mana and no System, either, yes?"

Alice nodded. "Yes. When I came to this world, I found magic and the System very interesting. So I spent a lot of my time researching both. I spent a great deal of time trying to figure out what magic was, how it worked, how it could possibly exist, and the rules it operated on . . ."

Ethan seemed to realize what she was going to say even before Alice finished speaking.

"And the other half of your time was devoted to figuring out what the System was, how it worked, how it could exist, and what rules it operated on?" His face grew a little bit more troubled.

"I see. I've . . . never heard of anyone researching the System itself. I don't think the church has an official stance on people researching the System. After all, nobody has *done* it before. Sure, plenty of people have studied things like faster ways to level up, or how to optimize perks more effectively. The church doesn't frown upon that kind of research at all; in fact, most [Priests] actively encourage it. They regard it as 'observing the will of the divine.' Hmm . . . Now that I think about it, the church's holy text does mention a time before the System. I just never thought much about it before. So perhaps your research is less offensive to the church than you think." He shook his head. "But you're right. I have no idea how they would react, and it's probably best not to test their reaction if we have a choice in the matter."

Alice felt a bit relieved. Ethan had mentioned *we* instead of *you*. Even though Alice's secret was potentially dangerous, he wasn't abandoning her.

"Why bring this up now?" Ethan asked.

"Because of a few of my perks and achievements, I can see the System mana."

"System mana?" Ethan gave Alice a blank look. "The System actually has mana?" Ethan glanced at the space in front of him for a moment, seeming as if he was looking at his status screen, and then glanced at Alice again with a confused and intrigued expression.

Alice nodded. "System mana. In all parts of the world, rainbow-colored mana exists. It seems to be the way that the System does everything, from giving people classes to assisting with mana baptisms and everything else it's responsible for."

Ethan gave Alice a slightly more blank look. "So the Church of the System is . . . a church worshipping a bunch of mana?" He paused, his expression simply growing more vacant as he looked at Alice, and then he shook his head.

"Does that mean that, at the end of the day, the Church of Mana and the Church of the System really are worshipping different forms of the same thing? What a strange idea." The corners of Ethan's lips rose, and Alice realized that he was actu-ally grinning in amusement. "I wonder what would happen if they realized that, for all their centuries of arguing, both are the same." Then Ethan sighed. "Well, I imagine they would probably just keep arguing. Once different groups of people dislike each other enough, even reality isn't enough to stop them from believing the other side is comprised of people who are crazy and irrational. Facts stopped being a part of their conflict before I was born, and that was centuries ago." Ethan paused. "Still, it's an interesting thing to know."

"That's not the important part, either," said Alice, swallowing nervously as she finally reached the main topic of conversation. "Yesterday, while I was investigating that artifact, the System mana that's *always* present just . . . disappeared."

"Disappeared?" Ethan's amused grin evaporated. "What does that mean?"

"A lot of things," said Alice. "None of them good. At least, if my understanding of what the System is and what it does is correct. Do you mind if I use {Shared Memory} on you? It's the perk that I used before, when I was showing you memories of my home world. I want to show you a few observations I've made about what System mana is and what it does. I think it'll help provide some context on why I'm so worried."

Ethan didn't hesitate before stretching out his arm toward Alice. "Go ahead."

Alice grabbed Ethan's wrist and then activated her perk.

First, she showed Ethan an image of the System mana during a mana baptism. In the memory Alice showed, the System's mana was trying to prevent the mana from destroying a person's nerves and arteries while the mana baptism formed a mage core behind the person's heart. She had seen multiple people go through their mana baptism recently. Finding an example of the System interacting with a baptism was easy. After she showed Ethan the image, Ethan pulled his arm back for a moment, giving the air around him an increasingly strange look.

"So the System is involved in mana baptisms . . ." said Ethan. "I wasn't aware there was so much happening behind the scenes. Most attempts to understand mana baptisms have failed." Then Ethan stopped scanning the air around him and turned back toward Alice.

"In that case, I can see how studying the System and studying mana baptisms go hand in hand. I suppose your idea was to take what the System is doing and then improve it?" He sounded interested. "I can also see why improving upon mana baptisms is so difficult. If even the System struggles with it, and most people can't even see what the System is doing, then it's nearly impossible. Especially since the memory you showed me also showed the mana baptism dragging in nearby mana and converting it to the same type of mana that started the baptism. Any type of mana, such as organic mana, would simply join the mana whirlpool. It would make the problem worse rather than providing a solution." Ethan fell deeper into thought. "I wonder why System mana doesn't get dragged into the mana baptism . . ."

"I haven't figured that out yet," said Alice. "But that's not the point I was trying to make. I was trying to show you one of the things that we don't even think about, which the System is responsible for. If the System's mana is gone, mana baptisms are about to become far more lethal."

"That is quite a problem," Ethan said. "I haven't had any reports of mana baptisms being *unusually* lethal in the past twenty-four hours. That being said, the base survival rate is only 4 percent to begin with. It's hard to notice if the odds get even worse, at least within a short time frame."

Alice nodded. "Keep an eye out for me, would you? That would be valuable data."

Ethan nodded as well. "What else did you want to show me?"

Alice grabbed Ethan's arm again. She showed him the way the System condensed a class seed, the way a class seed seemed to absorb problematic kinds of mana and convert it into levels and perks, the way the System helped people form magic seeds, and the way the System filtered mana for people who were increasing their stats. All the strange but important functions of daily life that the System helped make possible. Along with those images, Alice also showed a few other more dangerous experiments she had performed on herself, such as the time she had tried forming a class seed incorrectly and had nearly had her personality erased by mana before the System helped her get everything back under control.

Ethan remained quiet, only occasionally stopping to process what Alice had shown him. When he saw Alice's memory of almost having her personality erased, he winced and spent nearly a minute rubbing his temples before the two continued. Finally, Alice got to the most critical scene.

"This is what I saw yesterday," said Alice, showing Ethan the image of the System mana vanishing.

Ethan crossed his arms and bit his lip. His eyes started to scan the air in front of his face, the telltale sign he was looking at his status screen. Ethan sighed.

"Based on your memories, I have some guesses. But what do you think will happen now? You've obviously studied this topic far longer and in greater depth than I have."

"Unless the System fixes itself, things are going to get very bad. The System is responsible for too many things. Mana baptisms are about to become even more lethal. Creating new magic seeds might become dangerous, especially for those who don't know how to form one without System aid."

Ethan rubbed his chin in thought. "You can form a magic seed without System assistance? I didn't see that in the memories you shared."

Alice shrugged. "I did it once, as an experiment. But it's very difficult, and very easy to mess up and hurt yourself. The only reason I was willing to try it out was because I have some perks to fix any problems that come up."

Ethan gave Alice a perplexed look. "While it's useful now . . . why did you work on forming magic seeds without the System to begin with? It seems like a very odd project to devote time to."

"I want to create a magic seed based on System mana," said Alice, grinning a bit. Despite how dire the circumstances were, she still felt a little bit of excitement when she thought about her favorite research project and goal. "The System is unwilling to let people make System magic seeds, and seems to actively block attempts to copy it. So I practiced forming seeds in areas without System mana. The idea was to create a System seed while outside the System's area of authority."

Ethan grimaced. "Thank you for sharing this information with me. I have a few things I should start setting up *now*, since the System's disappearance is so potentially catastrophic. When you treated Boris, you gave him an enchanted item that isolated him from the environmental mana, right? Given what I just saw, I imagine it was to prevent him from obtaining more [Farmer] mana, thus safeguarding his mind? That might be a good direction to focus on for now. I'll also let people know that forming new magic seeds might be dangerous. Would a copy of the enchanted item you gave Boris work for everyone, do you think?"

Alice paused, thinking about it. "I'm pretty sure that would help people in Boris's situation, at least. It would be a good solution to children unlocking access to problematic mana types before they're ready. Which, if I'm not mistaken, will probably start happening quite soon." The System seemed to normally keep children from unlocking their status screens by maintaining a kind of bubble around them. Now that the System was gone, children would have no protection against personality erosion from mana. That was a good first problem to address.

Ethan nodded. "I'll have some of the [Enchanters] under me start mass-producing similar designs. While I am not sure if we can hit the quantity we will need in the coming days, it'll be a start. In the meantime, your research will be vital for untangling this mess. For now, don't set foot outside my manor without me—if the Society has any idea what you've been researching, they'll stop at nothing to drag you away." Ethan shook his head. "If they learn about your experiments, I wouldn't be surprised if every single living member of the Society moved to Illvaria to lay siege to the capital, no matter how suicidal that would be. You're now in greater danger of being kidnapped or assassinated than the royal family, which is . . . an accomplishment. Do you understand?"

Alice nodded.

Ethan relaxed a little bit. "Good. I'm going to look into a few things. I'll see if I can get any hints about whether the System collapsing is regional or whether it's gone from the entire world."

That was a very good idea, and one that Alice hadn't thought about. The System was gone from Metsel, but was it gone from the rest of Illvaria? Was the System gone in the rest of the world, too? She was glad that she could tap into Ethan's network now—little bits of information like that might prove invaluable to her research.

"If you need anything at all for your research, let me know immediately. If the System's collapse is a worldwide event and things are as bad as you're afraid they are, your research might save millions of lives. Are there any other people that can assist you?"

"Cecilia, my best friend," said Alice. "She's the one who taught me enchanting, and she's helped me with a lot of my experiments. She has some achievements that help her see what's going on, even if most of them are downgraded copies of mine."

Ethan nodded. "I'll have a [Hidden Guard] watch over her for now, since she seems determined to make her own way. If things get worse, I'll step up the security. It would be catastrophic if she were targeted."

Ethan dissolved the perk isolating the two from their surroundings. After that, he seemed to hesitate for a moment and turned back toward Alice, as if wondering if he should say something further.

Before he could, however, a [Servant] knocked on the door to the office. Ethan opened the door. The [Servant] seemed startled when he saw Alice, but then his attention returned to Ethan.

"Honored Immortal, a message from your honored mother," said the [Servant].

He handed Ethan a report before scurrying away.

Ethan quickly opened the letter, and his frown deepened.

"It seems that your fears are correct," he said as he scanned the letter. "Five hours ago, a group of mages who work for my mother injured themselves while forming new magic seeds. None of her organic mages can make heads or tails of the issue, and she asked me if I understood what was going on. She thinks it's a plague," Ethan said before he sighed. "It might be a good idea to take a look. Since you're the only one who can see System mana and investigate what's going on, your presence would be very helpful. Are you willing to come along?"

Alice nodded.

"Then let's go."

<h1 style="text-align:center">Chapter 3</h1>

The two made their way out of Ethan's manor and headed toward the infirmary where the mages were located. Ten high-level [Guards] tagged along in case the Society attacked them. Alice felt nervous as she walked through the streets.

In the past, Alice hadn't needed anything more than her [Hidden Guard] when she traveled around the capital. This time, even though Ethan and her [Hidden Guard] were both here, Ethan still brought more high-level [Guards] with them. Alice had already known that her research would make her a valuable target for the Society of Starry Eyes, but she had underestimated how seriously Ethan took the matter.

Alice wondered if this would continue.

Once again, Alice felt the pressure of the Society of Starry Eyes. Even though they weren't present, they were there. Watching. Waiting.

Alice wondered how long it would take her to become strong enough to fight off the Society on her own. She practiced fighting a few times a week at the Magic Academy, and from time to time Ethan had given her small tips about how to improve her combat abilities. However, those always took a back seat compared to her research—and that was even more true now that the System had collapsed.

Alice sighed. There was too much to do and she didn't have enough time in a day.

Alice was distracted from her musings when she felt someone watching her. The perk she had recently combined in her [Survivor] class, {Enhanced Senses}, was quietly needling at her, letting her know that someone was looking at her.

The perk confirmed what Alice had already suspected—the watcher didn't have good intentions. The feeling that they gave her was different from before she had combined her previous perks into {Enhanced Senses}, when she could only sense when someone was watching her and felt hostility toward her. Now, Alice could distinctly sense that the eyes felt greedy and careful, like the eyes of a thief looking at a painting they were planning to steal. She also felt her perk feed her information about the watcher's strength.

Alice shivered.

The pair of eyes watching her felt dangerous. They were obviously very high level, at least compared to her. They probably had a combat- or assassination-focused class.

She found herself reaching for her magic tendrils, although she managed to restrain her urge a moment later.

"Ethan," she whispered, feeling her anxiety spike more and more with each passing moment. "Someone is watching me."

"I know, I can feel them," whispered Ethan as a rainbow shield of mana sprang up around them and blocked their conversation. "Try to relax and don't tip them off. I want to see if I can get a little information about who they are. If they're from the Society, it'll mean the Society knows something and is targeting you. If they aren't part of the Society, I want to know why they're following you. Just pretend they aren't there."

Alice relaxed a little bit. If Ethan knew about the enemy and was monitoring them, then she shouldn't be in danger right now.

However, seeing another person stalking her was a good reminder of something else.

Now that the System was collapsing, the Society of Starry Eyes had likely started to notice *something* was wrong. Since they ran unethical magic experiments all the time, they would notice oddities in magic sooner than others. Once the Society realized that something was wrong, they would grow desperate to acquire information. Desperate people were more likely to take stupid risks. That wasn't limited to the Society, either. If people realized Alice knew something and wasn't sharing, she would be in an even more dangerous position than she already was.

Despite the fact that she was the disciple of an Immortal and traveling with one of the most powerful people in the country, there was already someone following her with bad intentions. That would get worse and worse as time went on, until Alice showed that she was entirely capable of handling herself even without protection.

Ethan and the [Guards] ignored the hostile watcher, and after a few minutes of walking, Alice felt the eyes on her disappear. If anything, that made her feel more nervous. Had they noticed that she was aware of them and used some method to make their presence disappear? Had they gone back to report to their superiors? What if Ethan's [Spies] didn't figure out who they were and why they were? What if they brought back a large group of enemies?

Alice felt her nerves tighten even more and forced herself to take a deep breath.

She started trying to run through what she knew about herself as a way of calming her anxiety. *Even on my own, I'm not defenseless. Right now, I'm standing next to an Immortal. I'm surrounded by high-level [Guards]. There is no safer place on the planet right now. I just need to trust my allies.*

Alice straightened her back and did her best to look unperturbed. There wasn't much she could do now but remain alert.

Not long after the stalker disappeared, the group arrived at their destination. Alice did her best to put the hostile eyes out of her mind and started looking at the mages who were ill.

To the side, an [Organic Mage] had a helpless expression on his face as he looked at the patients. Two more [Organic Mages] were trying to pump mana into the lungs of some of the patients. The [Organic Mage] who was standing to the side looking helpless had bone-deep exhaustion etched into his face. It was obvious that he had drained himself dry trying to heal the patients and was out of mana.

On the table lay three mages. All three of them had malformed magic seeds in the middle of their bodies and looked incredibly ill. If Alice were back in her original world, she would have assumed that the people in front of her were suffering some chronic illness. Their skin was as pale as a ghost, and their lips were bloodless. Two of them were coughing every so often, and occasionally reddish-pink goop dribbled out of their mouths.

Alice frowned.

When she had formed her own magic seeds without the help of the System, she had usually destroyed any malformed seeds she made less than an hour later. After all, her {Safety Analysis} perk usually informed her that keeping the magic seed around would be dangerous. However, according to Ethan's information, the mages had formed their messed-up magic seeds less than a day ago. It should have taken much longer for them to get sick. The only other case she could think of where a magic seed had been malformed was Samantha, and it had taken her around a week to start suffering.

These three mages had deteriorated far more quickly than they should have. Was this a symptom of the System's breakdown, or some other factor?

Either way, the situation was dire. Alice could only break one person's faulty magic seed at a time, and then she would need to wait four days before she could break another. She had no way to cure all three today, and she had no idea how long the other two would last.

Choosing which of the three patients would live was a horrible decision, and one that Alice didn't want to make. Worse, this was the first day after the collapse of the System. Would she have to face more and more problems like this in the future? The System had broken down, so there was no way it could help people form magic seeds anymore. Even though word would spread that forming magic seeds was dangerous, there was no way for that information to spread throughout Illvaria instantly. There was nothing equivalent to the internet here.

How many people were going to get hurt before people stopped forming magic seeds?

Alice moved closer to the nearest patient. The mage was still conscious, unlike the other two, although he seemed to be in great pain. He looked to be in his midtwenties and around level sixty. Perhaps due to his high level, he looked to be in slightly better shape than the other two.

He coughed violently every few seconds, and each racking cough sounded miserable. As Alice approached, he briefly focused on her before another fit of coughing distracted him.

"Give me consent to use perks and achievements on you. I need them if I'm going to figure out what's wrong and how to fix it," said Alice.

The man coughed again before he managed to squeeze out a single word. "Okay."

The moment she had consent, Alice activated {Lesser Organic Vision} and her regular vision to look at the man's chest, where his mage core should be located. She wanted as much information as she could get.

Then she rubbed her forehead in frustration.

The issues were indeed located in the man's mage core, but they were different from what she had expected.

The man's mage core, which all mages condensed after being born or after surviving their mana baptism, was a mess. It looked like a chaotic whirlpool of kinetic mana, which swirled around his body like a messy mosaic of light.

This was creating a rather odd effect on the flesh surrounding the man's mage core. The man's malformed kinetic seed was clearly different from Samantha's.

The kinetic seed in the man's mage core was applying kinetic force in completely random directions every few seconds. The one and only reason the man was still alive was because the core was tapping itself out of mana almost every second, meaning it had no time to build up a big enough push to crush the man's internal organs or rip his body apart. Trying to fully heal the man in his current state was useless. After all, even if Alice could heal his injured organs and stitch everything back together, his failed magic seed would turn everything back into mush within an hour or two. Healing could stave off death but couldn't fix the real problem.

There was another problem with what she was seeing, though. One that made her far more worried.

When Alice had tried forming a magic seed without the help of the System, she had messed up several times. Through that process, every time she made a mistake, she would have fairly similar symptoms to the man in front of her. She would start to feel sick, and she usually scrapped the seed right afterward.

However, she was pretty sure the man's magic seed was malformed in a way that was *different* from the problems Alice had experienced. When Alice felt sick from a malformed seed, she felt kind of like she wanted to puke. The man showed no signs of nausea, and Alice was pretty sure her own malformed magic seeds had never gone haywire and started attacking her body, either. The man's symptoms were different from what she had experienced, and what Samantha had experienced.

That gave Alice a sneaking suspicion that every malformed magic seed was different from the others. Which also meant that healers would need to create different, specialized treatment plans for every patient like this—a daunting task at the best of times, and several times harder if things got as bad as Alice expected them to.

If things got worse, the Illvarian medical system would get overloaded in days.

Alice glanced at the other two ill mages to see if she could confirm her suspicions.

Sure enough, the problems in their bodies were slightly different. The other man who had tried to form a kinetic seed seemed to have accidentally mixed his magic seed with a few other kinds of mana. Instead of a pure kinetic seed, the man had combined his seed with organic mana and pure mana. This had created an issue where his seed was trying to *convert his body* into kinetic force. The fact that physical flesh and kinetic energy were completely different things didn't seem to be stopping his magic seed from trying. He was the only mage who wasn't coughing out blood, and this was because his lungs and heart looked like Swiss cheese. If it weren't for the fact that the people of this world had [Endurance] stats that made them stronger than most Olympic athletes at home, this man would have died already. Even *with* his remarkable [Endurance], he looked like he could die at any minute. The [Organic Mages] in the room weren't even trying to heal him anymore. Either his magic seed was blocking their healing somehow, or they had given up.

Alice turned her eyes to the final patient—a woman with a malformed organic seed. Her lungs were filling up with some sort of fleshy soup. Her magic seed kept creating more and more pointless flesh inside her lungs, for reasons Alice couldn't identify.

Worse, her magic seed wasn't acquiring the raw materials for this soup from its own mana production. It seemed to be harvesting random bits of her body, especially near her shoulders and stomach. Several parts of her organs had already been chewed up by her magic seed and randomly added to her lungs, and at some point, part of her stomach lining had also been consumed. This had made a bad situation worse, because now her stomach acid was liquefying other internal organs.

Alice glanced at her perks and thought of {Broken Seed} again. She could activate the perk once every four days, meaning she could save one of the three patients.

What could she do for the other two?

The woman with an organic seed filling up her lungs would probably die soon. The [Organic Mages] treating her were running out of mana, and her death would be incredibly agonizing. Both men with kinetic magic seeds would also die horrific deaths if she didn't help them.

She had an easy way to treat one person, but the other two would die if she didn't have a solution.

Alice felt her brain scrabbling for an idea. Moments later, she latched on to her pure and organic mana seeds. She was missing a *lot* of components of System mana. But the people in front of her had no time to waste.

"Can you save all three?" Ethan whispered, using his perk to keep their conversation private.

"I can save one easily," Alice said. "The other two might die before my perk can be reactivated."

Ethan paused, and then nodded. "First of all, don't feel guilty if you can't save the other two. It looks like all three would die without your intervention, so no matter what happens, you don't have to feel bad about the results. That being said, do you have any ideas at all that could save the other two?"

Alice hesitated. She had absolutely no certainty at all that her next idea would work, and she strongly suspected that she might fail miserably. Her odds of succeeding were probably several times lower than the odds of surviving a mana baptism.

But it was also obvious that this couldn't continue. All three patients would die within a day if she let them be. Her perk cooldown was four days, meaning that if she didn't try, two of the three patients would die today.

"I have an idea. I'm going to try straightening out their magic seeds using my pure magic seed and my organic magic seed," said Alice. "Or I'll try copying whatever my perk is doing to break their magic seeds. Both ideas seem like they would help."

Ethan paused. "I know this will be hard for you, and you might not succeed. But good luck. Whether you try to fix their magic seeds or copy what your perk is doing, I believe that you can do it."

Alice nodded and resolutely strode up to the man whose magic seed was the most deadly, the one who had mixed his kinetic seed with pure mana and organic mana. She laid her hands on his arm and utilized {Broken Seed}. Luckily, it seemed that the man had given anyone trying to heal him blanket permission before he passed out.

The magic seed shattered as Alice carefully watched what her perk was doing, trying to figure out some way, any way to replicate it and help the other two patients before they died. Alice saw a few level-up notifications appear out of the corner of her eye, but she blinked them away. She was happy to see that leveling up still worked, despite the lack of System infrastructure, but she had more important problems to deal with. Such as the fact that she had no clue what her perk had actually done, and no idea how to copy it. Whatever it was doing was so complicated that Alice had no hope of replicating it, at least not within a short period of time.

There was no simple solution to heal the other two patients. She was on her own. Stepping toward the man with the malformed kinetic magic seed, Alice felt her lips tighten into a grim line.

The easy part was over. It was time to see if she could perform a miracle.

CHAPTER 4

She laid a finger on the second patient's stomach. As she did, she tried her best to think of the man as a patient rather than a real, living person.

Alice felt something foreign prod at her emotions, and a moment later, several of her emotions felt lessened. Their influence on her mind didn't quite disappear, but they became less noisy, as if someone had turned their volume down. It took her a moment to realize what had happened. Ethan had activated his perk, the same one he had used when they had rescued Samantha. It was slowly deadening her emotions, allowing her to focus on the task at hand. Even though she would usually remove any perk that influenced her emotions immediately, Alice decided to leave it for now. She needed focus, and her nerves were not helping. She turned toward Ethan.

"Tell me if you want me to turn it off," he said.

"Keep it on."

Then she turned back toward the patient.

Trying to save someone when she had no idea what to do was terrifying. Every time she even thought of taking an action, her mind screamed at her that she might be about to kill them by accident. So, she needed to think of the patient as a collection of things instead of a person. The patient was a series of moving organs, muscles, and mana. Not a breathing person with thoughts and feelings. She tried to pretend that the person in front of her was a machine, and thought back to her time spent working on robots when she was still on Earth. She found a sort of comforting numbness in the thought.

The person in front of her was just a machine. A collection of moving parts. Right now, some of those parts were broken. She had to figure out what was wrong and fix it before the machine broke.

Just parts she needed to fix and nothing else.

Her mana tendrils drilled into the patient.

Then Alice realized something.

Something that she should have realized earlier.

She thought about the way mage cores and mana inside a body interacted with each other, and then about something else she had heard in the past.

Mages who had their mage cores cut out would lose the ability to use magic, but they survived the process. People could even have their mage cores regrown in the future by someone with the right perks. Cutting out someone's mage core was a semicommon way to handle mage prisoners.

Would that work here, to keep the patient alive?

"Ethan, can you slice out the patient's mage core?" asked Alice. "Your precision is higher than mine, and I don't want to accidentally cut into the heart."

Ethan immediately took a decorative iron ornament from the corner of the room and turned toward the [Organic Mage] who was originally in charge of healing the patients. "Do you mind if I break this?"

"Go ahead, Honored Immortal," said the [Organic Mage].

Ethan immediately used kinetic magic to shave down the sides of the metal ornament, turning it into a makeshift scalpel. Then Ethan cut out the patient's mage core, used his mana to lift the lump of flesh out of the man's body, and healed the rest of the damage with his organic mana.

Alice glanced at the man's body and waited to see what changed. Had her idea worked? It should be good enough to spare his life.

A moment later, Alice frowned.

Something was wrong, but she couldn't quite tell what it was. However, chunks of mana flesh inside the patient's body were starting to glow brighter and dimmer, seemingly at random. That shouldn't be happening.

Alice started tearing through her memories as she tried to figure out what was happening.

Her mind flashed back to the first successful mana baptism she had observed after getting all her relevant sight-related perks built.

As each chunk of muscle fiber, nerves, and flesh was linked up with the new mage core, it lit up, glowing with mana as Tavi's body adjusted to its new organ. The mage core flashed several times with rainbow and pure mana before its near-blinding glow started to fade away, replaced with the ordinary, dull light of a mage core with no seeds in it. Another few strings of mana flesh and nerves linked everything with Tavi's brain, creating new clusters of nerves before his brain also flashed with rainbow mana. Finally, the rainbow and pure mana surrounding Tavi started to disappear.

Alice remembered that she had grinned at the sight.

Despite her worst fears, Tavi's mana baptism had been successful.

Alice suddenly got a very bad feeling.

Did the mage core do more than just regulate magic seeds? What if the way it linked up to all the strange muscle fibers and mana flesh was important? Perhaps the System normally stepped in to fix that problem once a mage core was removed. However, the System was gone now.

She jammed her magic tendrils into the patient's body.

If the System wasn't around, she needed to do it herself. Otherwise, the patient would die. She wasn't quite sure what was happening, but she knew for sure that it was bad.

The patient's eyes flicked open. He gasped in pain, and Alice started trying to use a mixture of organic and pure mana to soothe the trembling mana flesh in the patient's body. She paid closer attention in hopes of finding a way to keep everything under control.

After several seconds of observation, she noticed that only some patches of mana flesh were reacting. The mana flesh that was going haywire was vomiting out huge amounts of mana and then randomly sucking in mana a few seconds later—almost like it was breathing. Alice tried to use her mana tendrils to control the strange mana reactions of the man's mana flesh and noticed that, with the help of her pure mana, she could make the bizarre reaction stop.

Unfortunately, Alice had nowhere near enough mana to fix everything. Trying to interfere with a living organism cost a huge amount of mana, and Alice didn't have enough mana to fix even half of the patient's organs.

Alice started to feel desperate.

Clearly, there *was* some sort of System interaction that made the body counterbalance whatever happened when a mage core was cut out. She had no idea whether it was a quick fix or a complicated solution: She had never noticed anything happen to mages from the Society of Starry Eyes if their mage cores were cut out. Was it something she had simply never noticed, or was it something incredibly tiny that happened in their body with System help? Was it a different issue entirely?

The man's body spasmed again as Alice furiously thought of potential solutions, and with a heave and a shudder, something inside him broke.

Several of the chunks of reacting mana flesh stopped working. Blood started to clot in every chunk of mana flesh, and at the same time, the man's entire body began to try to absorb huge amounts of mana for no discernible reason.

"Ethan! Help me stabilize the mana and mana flesh in his body!" yelled Alice.

"Got it," he said, and immediately plunged his mana tendrils into the patient's body.

A moment later, Ethan turned a brilliant rainbow color for a moment as he activated a perk. And then another one hundred mana tendrils appeared and joined the previous forty.

Alice sent her own mana tendrils into the patient's body and began pumping small amounts of pure and organic mana into the problematic chunks of flesh. However, the mana costs still made the endeavor hopeless. Alice's eyes settled on Ethan, and then she realized there might be a solution to her problem. While Alice had nowhere near enough tendrils and mana to stabilize the man, Ethan had far more than he needed. Unfortunately, Ethan didn't have a pure mana seed, meaning that Alice was still the one doing a huge chunk of the work. However, she could offload all the organic mana usage onto him, which would let her focus on the parts only she could take care of. He could also keep the patient more stable while Alice searched for a better solution. The man's heart, lungs, and brain were especially important, and also in especially bad shape.

"Ethan, help me," Alice said as she started directing him to stabilize a few of the man's organs. With the two of them working together, the man's condition started to stabilize, although it was still desperate.

While Ethan held the man's organs together, Alice went from one chunk of mana flesh to the next, stabilizing each one in the man's major organs. For now, she still didn't know what she was doing, so every chunk of mana flesh was treated by putting some amount of pressure on it, trying to stop each contraction from doing anything at all. She just hoped that she was helping instead of making things worse.

Luckily, her efforts bore fruit. After five minutes, Alice's mana was nearly bottomed out, but the man's heart, lungs, and brain were no longer on the verge of popping. The man's arms and legs had basically collapsed, and Alice suspected they would need to be regrown later—but the man was alive, at least. Regrowing limbs wasn't too hard in this world, so there were far worse outcomes.

Of course, Alice's patch job wasn't perfect—even after each chunk of mana flesh settled down it would still occasionally pulse erratically. However, he was still alive.

Alice breathed a sigh of relief.

There were remaining problems in his body that Alice and Ethan had completely failed to address, because Alice had no idea what the System usually did when someone lost a mage core.

But despite the errors, the man was alive.

However, Alice was now almost completely out of pure mana.

She looked at the second patient and felt panic start to build up.

She could now confirm that cutting out the patient's mage core wouldn't save them. She also couldn't calm all the mana flesh in the female patient's body. She was basically out of pure mana. She couldn't even keep the woman's heart, brain, and lungs safe.

She took a deep, shuddering breath and felt Ethan's perk start to kick in more strongly, tamping down her rising panic.

She wasn't sure whether she could heal the second patient, but she needed to try. Nobody else could pick up the slack if she failed.

Alice started using her mana sight to more carefully analyze what was going on inside the woman's body. She would need to try something different to heal the second patient. {Intuitive Magic Modeling} fed Alice very basic information, helping her understand more of what was happening in the woman's magic seed. However, Alice had woefully little information to work with. For the first time, she wished that she had studied her own flawed seeds in more detail instead of destroying them immediately.

She gritted her teeth and tried to focus on what {Broken Seed} had done to the first patient. She needed to do the same thing, but without the System helping her. And she barely had any pure mana left, meaning she needed to somehow fix the problems with the woman's body using only her organic mana.

She knew that it was possible to recreate what System mana did. After all, the System was built from mana. The question was whether she could do it before the patient died.

She took a deep breath and plunged her mana tendrils into the final patient's body.

She tried to poke at the malformed magic seed with her pure mana. If she could touch the malformed magic seed with her mana tendrils, her plan was to try to unwind it using what little remained of her pure mana.

She was hoping, she could unravel the magic seed as if it were a knotted-up thread. Her magic tendrils made their way toward the mage core, getting ready to start activating Alice's pure mana.

And then they bounced off the mage core, accomplishing absolutely nothing.

When she stuck her mana tendril into the woman's mage core, it felt like she had hit a brick wall. The rest of the woman's flesh had felt like very thick mud when she tried to push her mana tendrils through it: It resisted her, but didn't totally shut down the movement of her mana.

However, the mage core felt like a major barrier.

Alice resisted the urge to curse.

She didn't have the mana to mess around and try to figure out a solution to this problem. In total, she had a maximum of 121 Mariums of organic mana and seventy-two Mariums of pure mana to work with. But that was her mana maximum; she had probably spent somewhere between fifty and sixty Mariums of pure mana trying to heal the first patient.

And just now, Alice had lost a big chunk of her organic mana just to push her mana tendrils close to the patient's heart.

Alice grimaced and then started probing the outside of the mage core again. She searched for a weak point in the barrier around it but couldn't find one. The woman's mage core was like a hard plastic shell that wrapped itself tightly around her magic seeds. Alice couldn't find a way in unless she just cracked the whole thing open. She suspected shattering that shell would have bad consequences.

What was she supposed to do here? If she couldn't get into the mage core, she couldn't fix the problem. If she let the woman be, she would also die. Trying to cut out the mage core would kill the woman. She had no idea how to fix this.

Alice hesitated for another moment before she pushed her mana tendrils into the woman's mage core, punching through the strange barrier around it.

Around ten Mariums of organic mana vanished into thin air as she ripped apart the mana barrier. More Mariums drained away every single second she pushed her mana tendrils into the woman's body. Mana leaked out of Alice like air rushing out of a punctured spaceship.

Alice felt her heart leap into her throat. She moved quickly, trying to take advantage of the moment the wrap around the woman's mage core collapsed. However, before she could even touch the magic seed, something strange happened: All the mana in the woman's body dimmed for a moment.

And then the woman's mage core started absorbing mana nonstop. Alice's eyes widened as it started to look like the woman was going through another mana baptism. *This is bad*, Alice thought as she started to panic. She used several mana tendrils to force the mana near the patient's body away.

One of Alice's seven mana tendrils finally contacted the magic seed she needed to remove. Alice tried to keep her focus on her goal. If she destroyed the magic seed, she could hopefully fix whatever else was going wrong.

At this point, Alice could only pray that was the case.

However, something *crunched* when Alice tried to pull apart the magic seed. Alice wasn't quite sure what she had messed up, but something was broken beyond repair. Worse, her attempt at fixing things hadn't made the magic seed disappear. Instead, it now looked brittle, as if it were made of glass.

The woman's body stopped trying to absorb mana. Then all her magic seeds suddenly went haywire. They started tossing around mana left and right, as if they were boats being tossed about by a hurricane.

Ethan immediately used a kinetic tendril to drag Alice out of the way, and then grabbed every single bulky object in the area and used them to isolate the woman from the rest of the room.

Alice's eyes widened.

And then the woman's body detonated like a bomb, sending her organs and limbs flying into Ethan's hastily erected barrier.

Alice gasped in shock and, after the sound ended, pried away Ethan's shield using some kinetic mana.

Inside Ethan's shield were the remains of a corpse. There was absolutely no way to save the woman anymore. There was barely anything *left* of the woman besides chunks of meat.

Alice felt her hands start to shake.

Even though Alice had been trying to heal the woman, even though she had done what she felt was best, the woman had died. And it was undeniable that Alice's attempted intervention had killed her faster instead of healing her. She would have died in less than a day either way, but Alice still felt sick.

Alice felt numb horror start to wash over her. She felt Ethan's perk start to grow in intensity, but it wasn't enough to fully remove her emotions.

"Process your emotions later," said Ethan. "Remember, these two were dead if you didn't help them. You were trying to resuscitate a corpse. There is no shame in failing. You succeeded in saving one patient. He'll need more attention from a healer later—but you stabilized his condition." He gently patted Alice's shoulder as Alice tried to work off the numb horror from the woman's splattered remains.

Ethan sighed. "Take a few minutes. You seem like you need them. Then look back at the first patient and try to see if there are any remaining problems. You know more about this subject than I do, so you're going to need to help with any follow-up issues." Alice nodded and moved over to the wall. Ethan's perk was still deadening her emotions, which *helped*, but Alice was already dreading the moment she would need to process her emotions in full.

Luckily, it wasn't time to do that yet. After Alice's emotions settled, she moved numbly back toward the first patient. His malformed kinetic seed was no longer jostling his bones and organs around, and he looked . . . at least sort of like a healthy person. There were still splotches of pale and damaged skin and tissue in and outside of his body, and his arms looked like wax. Alice was pretty sure they had already stopped working entirely. However, his torso and head looked at least somewhat healthy. She started carefully inspecting the man using her perks, before she sighed.

"I think that his muscles are going to be in a lot of pain, and it might be impossible for him to walk around. Keeping him unconscious is probably the best thing to do—I imagine he's going to be in horrific pain if he's awake." She turned toward Ethan. "Can we come back tomorrow?"

Ethan nodded. "I was planning on it. We can try to stabilize him more and see if any other complications come up once you're rested and have a little more mana to work with."

He gently patted her head.

"Take a deep breath and calm down," said Ethan. "You kept one alive. You didn't kill a person today—you saved a person's life when they should have died, and you tried your hardest to save the other one. Take pride in that."

Alice nodded and felt a breath escape her lungs.

She still felt awful, but she had done what she could.

A few moments later, mana began to swarm toward her body.

CHAPTER 5

As mana flowed into her, Alice focused on her System messages. She needed a distraction from the corpse lying in the other room—and the System was one of the best distractions. It was her first time leveling up since the collapse of the System. She was worried that something would go wrong, and so she half expected to find a line of glitch signs instead of a normal System message. She took a close look at her new System messages as she sat in another room of the clinic, one blessedly free of stark reminders of her failure.

You have leveled up!
Scientist 58→60, Explorer of Magic 75→76, Student of Organic Magic 11→17

Alice's shoulders slumped in relief. It seemed that her classes had still gained experience normally. When she gained a level, she usually saw the System first filter the mana in her environment before it was absorbed by her class fractals. This time the System wasn't around, so it couldn't filter her mana. Despite the System's absence, however, the process hadn't changed much.

Then she scratched her head in confusion.

If she could gain levels with or without the System's purification efforts, why did the System go through so much effort to purify mana right before people leveled up? What was the point? Alice started paying closer attention to her own body, as well as the mana inside it, in hopes of finding an answer.

As she watched mana slowly work its way through her body and toward her class fractals, {Intuitive Magic Modeling} informed Alice that the types of mana going through her body weren't quite as pure as she had thought. There were small chunks of other mana attached to the main types of mana she was absorbing. Her [Scientist] mana, for example, had some chunks of [Scholar] mana attached to it, possibly because [Scholars] and [Scientists] were similar in this world. The [Scientist] mana she had absorbed was around 80 percent pure [Scientist] mana and 20 percent other types. The [Scholar] mana she had absorbed faced a similar problem.

Once the bits of [Scholar] and [Scientist] mana reached the class fractals in her brain, each class fractal absorbed *most* of the mana correctly, but the extra bits of mana got stuck. It was kind of like seeing a giant piece of food get stuck in a drainpipe: It just sat there, unable to move. What did that actually *mean*? Would she lose the ability to level up if her class fractals got entirely clogged with the wrong types of mana?

Furthermore, a few minutes after the chunks of extra mana got stuck, Alice felt a subtle inclination to behave more like a [Scientist] and a [Scholar], as well as a subtle inclination to behave more like a . . . [Doctor]? Alice felt even more confused, until she took a closer look and realized there was some [Doctor] mana mixed into the [Scientist] mana she had just absorbed. It was a very small amount, so the behavioral change was very minor, and Alice could easily squash it. Even so, it was concerning.

Alice reached for her pure mana seeds to see if she could somehow drag each bit of mana over to its correct class fractal. Unfortunately, her head started pounding right afterward. She had used too much mana treating the patients, and she was totally out now.

Alice winced and shook her head before moving on to her other System notifications. The external influence on her personality was minor, so she doubted it would be a problem to wait a few hours to recover some pure mana before she tried again. She didn't think this problem was actually that hard to solve; she just needed to manually reroute each mana type toward the correct class seed. The [Doctor] mana was harder to fix, because she didn't have a [Doctor] class, but she would figure that out later. For now, she ignored it and continued examining her System notifications.

Scientific Discoveries (Rarity: N/A) III→IV
An achievement created by the For Science! perk. It currently has four successful experiments catalogeds. Upon reaching five experiments, this achievement will receive a beneficial upgrade.
+20% class experience for all research-related classes (per tier of the achievement), +5% bonus to mental attribute growth (per tier of the achievement)

Alice felt her relief get stronger as she noticed her {Scientific Discoveries} achievement upgrade with no weird complications or issues. However, her relief was short-lived. Moments later, Alice saw . . . a rather odd blob of mana. It looked similar to the mana that appeared whenever she got a new achievement.

And just like the other types of mana she had seen, it looked impure. Alice sighed. She had relaxed too early. There was something wrong with her achievement as well.

After a few minutes of aimless drifting through her body, Alice saw the new blob of mana start bouncing off her muscles and bones. It looked like a drunk squirrel trying and failing to scamper up a tree.

Alice wondered what was going on, and then, in a fit of inspiration, connected a mana tendril to the strange clump of mana and started using display mana. If it worked the way she thought it would, her display mana would let her understand what the clump of mana was supposed to do.

Normally, Alice might have worried that the display mana would show her incorrect information. However, as far as Alice could tell, display mana would never actually let her lie about part of her status screen. Even when Alice had deliberately tried to give herself fake level-up notifications during her initial testing, it had never worked. She had been able to make System messages that displayed the words *level up*, but no matter what she tried, the System messages would show her correct level.

In other words, if Alice used display mana to look at the System notifications for her new, messed-up achievement, she should be able to get some idea of what was going on.

It worked, and moments later, Alice started examining a rather unique set of System notifications.

Legendary Healer (Rarity: 7)→SD??SD@#$@ (This achievement cannot be upgraded. Error!
Legendary Healer (Rarity: 7)→SD??SD@#$@ (This achievement cannot be upgraded. Error!
Legendary Healer (Rarity: 7)→SD??SD@#$@ (This achievement cannot be upgraded. Error!
Connecting to main server to find resolution for issue . . . failed. Connection cannot be established.
?@#%(#)@$@#()(@#$ @#$*# @#$@#($ @#((!)%#(!@$#)*^T$_#@ @#_ (@#_$*

Alice blinked at the increasingly bizarre System notification. Then she started to worry.

A moment later, the clump of mana started to sink into her muscles and bones.

Error resolved. (Rarity: 4)
Y0^ h@ve cu**d a mEEEEdic(((((l c*(Sn which kn***# how to. Y((*U.
@#*$&# @#*$(&@#$ @#$*()@#$ @#)(*@#$(@# @#)(@#$*@

A new achievement appeared on her status screen.

Its name was {Error Resolved}, and it was a rarity-four achievement. It was incomprehensible.

Alice worried if her status screen had just permanently glitched out. If her achievement was glitched out . . . what happened?

Right as she was starting to seriously worry about what would happen next, Alice noticed that the achievement {Error Resolved} was beginning to change again.

The mana in her body was still attached to her muscles and bones, but after a few minutes, it started to detach itself. A moment later, it started moving back toward her mage core. The System notification changed again.

Creative Healer (Rarity: 4)
You have used multiple magic seeds to heal patient, and _____used magic seeds beyond the b@sic healing seeds, such such such such such @s your P*^e magic seed.
Organic Magic Seed Conversion RaTTTTio: +10%, mana capacity for ALL seeds +5%

While this was better than a set of illegible error messages, Alice still felt worried when she saw the new version of her achievement.

The weird glitch words and spelling errors in the achievement had decreased, but they hadn't disappeared entirely. And even more oddly, Alice could still *see* the achievement hovering around in her body. It wasn't . . . *quite* right. It didn't look like other achievements.

She shifted uneasily and examined the achievement more closely. At the back of her mind, she kept hoping that the achievement would keep modifying itself until it became normal again. Even if it might waste an opportunity to learn more, Alice didn't like the idea of having uncontrolled mana that exhibited unusual behavior inside her body.

Several seconds passed, as Alice hoped the error would finish resolving itself. Nothing happened.

Alice grimaced and then decided to look on the bright side. There were a few bits of the achievement that looked a bit scrambled, but it didn't look like the achievement was totally ruined. As long as it didn't influence her personality or hurt her, Alice had plenty of tools to deal with weird System errors: Out of all the people on this planet, Alice was one of the only ones that could understand the problem. Since she still had {Moderate Tissue Regeneration}, she could also handle minor health issues. She just needed to stay calm, use her perks to observe the situation, and learn more once her pure mana seed was ready.

Alice tried to examine her magic seeds, doing her best to determine whether they had any problems. After all, her new achievement interacted with her magic seeds, and there was a small risk that they might explode and turn her into jelly.

Even weirder, if she tried to look at her new achievement the normal way, by opening her status screen and then focusing on her new achievement, she still saw nothing. There was obviously still something wrong with the new achievement.

However, when Alice investigated her magic seeds, she realized that all of them *had* expanded slightly. Nowhere near the amount they were supposed to expand, but they had still clearly improved. Alice estimated that her magic seeds had increased their conversion ratio by about 2 to 3 percent each. Her organic mana seed had also gotten a 7 percent boost out of the 15 percent boost it was supposed to receive. She was missing about half of the benefits her new achievement was supposed to give her. She didn't see any signs of them going crazy or threatening to explode and kill her. Losing a few of the benefits she was supposed to have sucked, but right now Alice was just grateful that her messed-up achievement wasn't dangerous.

Alice felt her empty pure magic seed again and tried not to shiver in fear. Even if she didn't see anything dangerous right now, she was still worried. She wished she could recover her pure mana instantly so that she could investigate her magic seeds for any problems.

At least she finally had some idea what the collapse of the System meant. She made a mental note to have Ethan keep an eye out for any similar problems. Perhaps the Church of the System would be a good place to collect more data? After all, that was the first place most people would go if they encountered status screen error messages.

How the church responded to the System collapsing would also be a good indicator of whether working with them to quell the chaos was a good idea. If the church handled the crisis well, it might be a good opportunity to help soothe people's minds and distribute ways to handle the crisis.

She took a deep breath, managed to calm herself down, and focused on her new perk selection. She had just reached level sixty in [Scientist], and it was a good opportunity to check how perk selection worked now that the System was gone.

Of course, the first thing she did was run a few checks with {Safety Analysis}. Now that the System wasn't around to keep her safe if she messed up, Alice had to be extra careful with every single action she took.

Alice got a slightly fragmented response back. Messing with perks apparently wasn't *completely* safe, but it also wasn't incredibly dangerous. It was just . . . mildly dangerous. Alice got the feeling that it was similar to sticking her hand on a hot stove: It would hurt, and she might burn herself—however, no matter what happened, it shouldn't threaten her life or her sense of self. At least, that was the rough impression she got from the perk.

Alice gritted her teeth and decided to push on. If she wanted to fix the System and deal with whatever was happening to the world right now, she needed more perks. If her new perks were just like her new achievement, they would probably be weaker than they should be and might leave behind some weird medical complications she would need to sort out later. However, the alternative was to keep working with only the tools she currently had available to her—and Alice suspected that was far more dangerous than taking a few calculated risks right now. Society wasn't falling apart *yet*, but with the System gone, it was only a matter of time.

True to Alice's fears, her perk selection screen looked far more messed up than before.

Perk Selection:——(missing entry)
?????????
Perk Selection:——(missing entry)
?????????
Perk Selection:——(missing entry)
?????????
Perk Selection: Combine Perks
(Add perks here)

What in the world was she supposed to make of *this?* This was just . . . nonsense. Alice waited, hoping that the words would rearrange themselves the way her achievement had. Nothing happened.

After several seconds of fruitless waiting, she decided to try poking her messed-up status screen with display mana and see if that clarified what her perks were supposed to be.

To her surprise, it worked. Kind of.

Perk Selection:——Contact with main System lost. Loading from last previous record . . . **Perk_Name: Study_????** **Requirements: HOsT meets requirements. Scientist level 60+**
Grants better study. **Increases Intelligence????.**
Perk Selection:——Contact with main System lost. Loading from last previous record . . . **Perk_Name: Learn_Magic** **Requirements: Host Meets Requirements: Achievement Requireemnt Meeet.** **Scentist level 60+**
Better Learn Magic. Gooder sleep learn. Increase learning Intelligence by by **by Number_amount.**
Perk Selection:——Contact with main System lost. Loading from last previous record . . .
Perk_Name: Memory_Other
Requirements: Creative Shared Memory. Stat Requirement. Level **Requireemnt. Scientist level 60+**
Learn_from_other memories. No violation of core tenet.

Core Tenet_Free/Will.
Perk Selection: Combine Perks
(Add Perks here)

Alice could definitely still get *some* idea what each new perk did based on the current text, but the exact details were hard to figure out. Even more frustrating, every single perk required display mana for Alice to even read this messy, grammatically inconsistent version of the perk-selection screen. Even with display mana, Alice was beginning to get the feeling that she was missing some other component that the System used in conjunction with display mana to make sentences more comprehensible.

Alice distinctly remembered that the System had shown her a status screen entirely in English the moment she arrived on this world, after all. This was before the System even figured out what English *was* and created a language skill for it. However, when Alice used display mana, she could only show System messages in English or Illvarian, since those were the two languages she was fluent in. Her System messages did not automatically translate themselves for the reader with just display mana.

Alice rubbed her chin thoughtfully as she wondered what she was missing. A moment later, she sighed and shook her head. At least for now, she had a semi-functional status screen. That was probably more than everyone else had. Alice started looking at her perk-combination options instead—after all, perk combination was usually more valuable than taking a new one. She discovered that perk combination had far fewer glitches than new perks did.

Of course, her perk-combination options were still subject to the broken grammar and weird System glitches. However, she had a much better idea what each option did, which was a relief.

After a few minutes of thinking, Alice decided that she was going to combine two perks instead of taking a new one. Two of the three new [Scientist] perks actually seemed somewhat appealing: Learn_Magic and Memory_Other were, as far as she could tell, perks that would let her use {Sleep Reading} to learn magic, and a perk that would let her read other people's memories and experience an enhanced learning effect. She probably needed the other person's permission to use the perk, but she was willing to bet Ethan would let her observe some memories of his own training: He seemed pretty committed to the idea of raising a new Immortal, and this was definitely something that would help her improve. Even if Ethan wasn't willing to share his own memories, Alice doubted Ethan would have a hard time finding a teacher who was willing to share their memories, if the pay was good enough.

Both perks sounded useful. However, Alice had noticed a rather curious (and possibly critical) perk that she could create by combining two others. It was an option that hadn't existed in her perk combinations at level fifty-five, but even though the grammar was a bit broken, Alice was still pretty sure she knew what it would do. So she combined the perks.

The first perk she decided to sacrifice was {The Science of Mana Deprivation}.

The Science of Mana Deprivation
Requirements: Scientist level 50 or higher, Intelligence 150 or higher, must have extensively experimented with mana and lack of mana and its effects on other creatures and/or oneself, Magic 150 or higher, pure mana seed (or similar seed) present

You may use your mana tendrils to interfere with mana, allowing you to create manaless fields at will, given enough time, or otherwise allowing you to prevent mana from interfering with your experiments.
Note 1: The farther away the mana is, the more difficult and mentally draining it will be to activate this perk. It is advised you use this on areas near you.
Note 2: Please remember that interfering with mana controlled by other people will be far more mentally taxing than manipulating the same amount of mana would be if it were uncontrolled.

Alice loved {The Science of Mana Deprivation}. It was a perk that didn't *sound* amazing, but the most powerful component was the fact that it let her mess with other perks and System mana. It could let Alice deflect or deactivate perks that other people tried to use in her surroundings, assuming she had fast enough reflexes.

However, it also had several shortcomings right now. Most notably, it couldn't interact with most kinds of mana besides perks, because it required her to spend a fair amount of mental energy and pure mana, and it was very mentally exhausting to actually create things like manaless fields, despite that being the main use of the perk. Finally, the perk struggled to interact with other people, as well as higher-level perks (something that Alice had discovered during a testing session when Ethan had graciously helped her). Right now, Alice wanted a fast and easy way to turn off *all* kinds of mana—even if that mana was inside other people. It would be the most effective way to treat problems like going nuts because one's mana hadn't been absorbed by a class seed. It would have also helped a *lot* when trying to treat the final patient earlier.

This was why she had decided to combine it with another perk to get the result she wanted. For the second component of perk combination, Alice decided to throw in {Degraded Seed Slot}.

Degraded Seed Slot
Requirements: Scientist level 35 or higher, Explorer of Magic class available, Magic at 100 or higher, have all magic seed slots taken, use magic seeds themselves as a source of experiments and inspiration for new advancements

<table>
<tr><td>You gain a magic seed slot with a maximum 5% mana conversion ratio. This magic seed cannot be boosted by other perks and can never be combined with other perks. (It can still be influenced by other things, such as achievements.)</td></tr>
</table>

Frankly, Alice didn't have much use for this perk anymore. She generated two new magic seeds a month, and she had practiced creating magic seeds without the System. A perk giving her one low-quality magic seed was just not that important after she gained the {Seeds of Ambition} perk.

Thus, Alice stuffed the two together and nervously watched as the System combined them, hoping it didn't mess up and cause some sort of disaster.

Before hitting the "combine" button, Alice did a final check with her {Safety Analysis} perk, just to make sure she wasn't about to screw herself over. After confirming it was safe, Alice activated the perk combination.

<table>
<tr><td>**Perk_Name: No_Mana**
Perk costs: Degraded Seed Slot + The Science of Mana Deprivation</td></tr>
<tr><td>You create a No_Magic magic seed. This seed seed seed can deactivate_____ (Get_Var: missing) delete mana.
Warning: Without permission, it's harder you modify_____ seed of magic for @nother peeerson.</td></tr>
</table>

Shortly after she combined the two perks, Alice felt a new magic seed start to form in her mage core. This seed was the first magic seed she had formed directly as a result of a perk existing, instead of just having a magic seed slot granted to her. Instead of Alice needing to concentrate on a specific idea and then absorb mana to make a magic seed, this time her class fractal took over the process entirely, as it dragged in mana and converted it into a specific concept. Which was probably why Alice could do this safely: The System was still doing the dangerous bits for her, even if the mainframe of the System was down.

A few moments later, Alice had an entirely new magic seed. One that was, apparently, called a No_Magic magic seed. Alice suspected the name was slightly off, but as long as the magic seed itself worked, it would be fine.

Then Alice tried poking herself in her arm, right next to some of her mana muscles, and used a small wisp of mana from her new magic seed.

To her delight, she felt the very small muscle boost she had barely been aware of fall away for a moment. This new type of mana could deactivate chunks of the System. She would need to test its limitations later on, but that was incredibly valuable both for handling emergency healing and in the middle of a fight. Alice took one final look at the room where she had tried and failed to treat one of the afflicted Mages. She hesitated for a moment as memories of a woman's body exploding like a bomb flashed through her mind. She let out a deep breath. She had gained a new perk, one that might help the still-suffering mage across the hall. Her head still hurt, and Alice didn't feel ready to do much of anything right now, but there was a patient that needed her.

She stepped back into the room. She looked at Ethan and the remaining [Organic Mage], both of whom nodded in her direction before turning their focus back to the other patient. Alice sucked in another deep breath then joined them.

The final patient still had several patches of skin growing out of control. Alice attempted to use the sliver of mana from her new seed to deactivate some of the writhing flesh growing out the man's ruined arms, and while he hadn't stabilized completely by the time the mana was spent, there was at least some noticeable improvement.

After some estimation, Alice deduced the seed had around a 30 percent mana conversion ratio. Not amazing, but not terrible, either.

She grinned to herself. At the very least, she had a way to treat patients a little more effectively now. She could deactivate magic seeds that were going haywire and possibly delete mana that wasn't properly integrated with a class seed. She could finally treat patients like Boris completely, instead of just giving him a ring to stave off the worsening of his illness. It was nowhere near enough to handle the problems caused by the collapse of the System, even in a country as small as Illvaria, but it was a good start.

"Alice, are you done?" asked Ethan. "If so, we should go back for now."

Alice nodded and then gave the corpse of the woman she had failed to heal one last, sad glance.

If she'd had access to her new perk before she had started treatment, she would have been able to keep the woman alive. But she hadn't reached the right level until after the woman died.

She sighed and then followed Ethan as the two of them left the building.

Chapter 6

Neither Alice nor Ethan said much on the way back to Ethan's manor. Instead, Alice stewed in her thoughts. Images of the woman she had failed to save kept reappearing in her mind, like flickers of a dying star drifting through the cosmos. Alice sighed, and for a moment, she almost wished that Ethan's emotion-deadening perk would return. Then Alice shook her head.

Trying to run from her emotions certainly wouldn't make things better.

"Ethan? Do you think there's anything I could have done better?" she asked after a few minutes of contemplation.

Ethan paused for a moment, then reactivated his anti-eavesdropping perk.

"Alice, a lot of [Organic Mages] and [Doctors] start to lose confidence when their first patient dies. Especially in smaller towns and villages, where medical perks and [Organic Mages] are scarce, meaning that patients can't always get timely care. In those areas, many people involved in medicine lose a patient.

"I don't think you should put such a heavy burden on yourself. Keep in mind, you only have an apprentice healer's license right now, and you're not even an adult yet. You're . . . what, level twenty in your [Organic Mage] class?"

"Level seventeen," said Alice. "And it's a secondary class."

Ethan nodded. "So not even a real level seventeen. You're basically a level-five [Organic Mage], for most intents and purposes. Even so, you managed to save the lives of two of your patients when I'm sure nobody else could have.

"These people were dead without your intervention. You did everything you possibly could. You're doing a lot of good." He gently reached down and patted Alice's shoulder a few times. "Don't worry too much about what happened. You lost a patient, but it was due to factors out of your control. You're doing a good job. Much better than I did when I was learning organic magic." Ethan gave her a gentle smile.

"Did you ever lose a patient?" Alice asked despite herself.

Ethan paused, and for a moment, a dark grimace caused his lips to twist into an ugly frown. Then he sighed.

"I did. When I was younger, I was, to put it bluntly, arrogant. I was a young mage, the child of two Immortals, and I was making excellent progress toward Immortality. I thought that I couldn't do anything wrong and that every action I took was a guaranteed success. I tried to treat a rather complicated issue when I was lower level than I should have been, and . . . well, I messed up," he said. He shook his head. "I don't want to say anything else about the issue, but it was a big wake-up call for me. I slowed down a bit in leveling and started thinking about how to improve, both as a person and a mage. I . . . admit that I also didn't practice using my organic magic for almost an entire decade after the incident. Obviously, I can use it just fine now, but it's something I deeply regret to this day." He sighed. "At least your patient died because of factors you had no control over. I have no excuse." Then he gave Alice another more relaxed grin, although there was a distant shadow behind his smile.

"So you're not alone. I've also lost patients before. And while I lost mine because I was arrogant, you lost yours because you didn't have enough mana. Your reason for losing a patient is far better than mine. All right?"

Alice hesitated for a moment before she nodded. Ethan smiled. A moment later, the rainbow mana in their surroundings disappeared and the group started moving again. Alice thought about Ethan's words.

The fact that Ethan had lost a patient as well oddly made her feel better. She was used to seeing Ethan as nearly invincible. Most Immortals that were old enough seemed to be nearly omnipotent, at least within their respective classes. The idea that Ethan, a mage focused on combat magic and, to a lesser extent, things like organic magic, had still lost a patient . . . well, the idea was foreign to her. But it also made it seem more normal to lose a patient, in an odd way.

She wasn't happy that the woman had died. But she also realized that she hadn't had a way to save her in the first place. Perhaps if she had made different choices during her perk selections and lived a wildly different life since coming to this world, she could have produced a different outcome. But she had done her absolute best.

The incident wasn't entirely behind her, but she could at least push it behind her for now.

She would never forget the woman she had failed to save—later, she would ask Ethan to look up every single detail about the woman's life, history, and who she had been. She wanted to know who the woman was and whom she could have been if she had lived today. Alice felt that was the best way she could honor the woman's death. But that would come later. For now, Alice just wanted to function again, and she also wanted to go to the mansion and sleep like the dead for several hours.

Sadly, once they arrived at Ethan's manor, Alice realized she would have to put sleep off for a bit. She needed to report what she had observed to Ethan so that he could spend some time brainstorming what her observations meant. So even though she was exhausted, she hauled herself to Ethan's office and told him everything.

She discussed her experiments on the System, System mana, and how this world's magic worked. She hoped Ethan could use that information to save at least a few more people, and he would know what to warn them about.

The moment Alice was done explaining her experiments on the System in detail, she asked Ethan to keep an eye on the Church of the System for her. It was one of the first places where the collapse of the System would become evident, and Alice suspected the church would be swarmed with suffering people sooner or later.

Then she stumbled to her room and collapsed onto her bed.

She was asleep before her head hit the pillow.

Several hours passed. Normally, Alice used the time while she was asleep to dive into her dream library using {Sleep Reading} and learn more about the world around her. But today, Alice felt exhausted. She decided to read a few lighthearted adventure stories she had lying around in her storage perk instead. Since her dream library was entirely contained in her imagination, Alice also created a nice cup of tea and a cozy reading chair to relax in.

Just as she reached the climax of the first story she was reading, she was abruptly yanked out of her dream library and back into reality. It took her a moment to realize what had just happened—a massive burst of mana had ripped through the world like a crack of lightning. Alice spent a few moments trying to process the sheer madness of what was happening in the world around her before her mind finally caught up with the situation.

Mana was in chaos. The previously calm night air was now filled with distorted, jagged lines of rainbow mana. Alice was used to seeing rainbow mana exist in her surroundings: After all, the System was usually present everywhere.

However, right now, the System was broken. There hadn't been any System mana in Alice's surroundings for nearly thirty-six hours. Normally, Alice would have found the return of the System comforting. However, this System mana didn't look anything like what Alice was used to seeing.

The System mana Alice saw right now looked more like someone had taken a giant bucket of paint and then spilled it onto the continent. Massive spikes of rainbow mana stretched into the sky and other patches of air were bereft of System mana. Instead of the organized flow she was used to, the System looked like a giant patchwork quilt.

The chaotic and terrifying sight only lasted for a minute before it started to peter out. Chunks of System mana vanished from her surroundings as if they were being scrubbed out of reality itself. Alice, finally realizing that it must be some sort of aftereffect of the System collapsing, peeled her eyes open to memorize every single detail. She needed to seize the opportunity to grasp any information she could. Her feelings could wait; the information she needed could not.

The deluge of rainbow mana lasted for thirty more seconds before it started to fade. Alice frowned as she watched the flickers of rainbow mana dwindle into nothing. She couldn't quite put her finger on it, but the way the System mana was shaped reminded her of something. However, she hadn't quite managed to pinpoint it before the System mana faded. Alice sighed. Whatever she'd noticed, it would have to wait. She needed more information, but she had no way to obtain it right now.

Then she checked her status screen.

The short-lived spurt of System mana had been rather unexpected, but Alice harbored hope that it had changed something on her status screen. If it had, she would have an easier time pinpointing the consequences of losing the System. Perhaps it would even fix the glitched-out name of her most recent perk.

Of course, if the burst of System mana had somehow messed up her status screen, Alice also wanted to know as soon as possible. That way she could start preparing countermeasures.

Her newest perk still had a name that looked more like an error message than a real name. The description was still filled with grammatical issues. Nothing had changed. Alice felt a burst of frustration. The System was still just as broken as before, and she hadn't obtained any new information. She gritted her teeth before she took a few breaths to calm herself down.

She needed to focus on what she could do right now. Not failed hopes that the world would fix itself. She decided to take her pure mana seed and try to sort out the clogged bits of mana attached to her class seeds. She still vividly remembered that there was a bit of [Scientist] mana stuck to her [Scholar] class seed, and a bit of [Scholar] mana stuck to her [Scientist] class seed, along with a few miscellaneous types of mana. As far as Alice could tell, it almost looked like it was inhibiting the mana absorption of her class seeds.

That was something that she would need to fix sooner or later. It would also take her mind off her emotions.

Thus, after several checks using {Safety Analysis}, Alice tried to create a pair of tweezers with her pure mana. She wanted to use her pure mana seed to pick up the clogged bits of mana and then shove it into the correct magic seed.

It took several minutes of fiddling around to get it right, but eventually, Alice succeeded in picking up a few chunks of [Scholar] mana that had tried to integrate with the wrong class seed. The biggest issue was that mana proved unexpectedly slippery inside her body. Every time she tried to grab the bits of disorganized mana, they ended up sliding out of her grasp. Even more frustrating was that the tactile senses provided by her mana tendrils were very vague, making the whole endeavor about ten times harder than it needed to be.

Eventually, Alice used all seven of her mana tendrils to create a kind of net that she used to trap the disorganized mana. It took a great deal of time and concentration, and she accidentally dropped the bits several times, but eventually, she succeeded in dragging the [Scholar] mana over to the correct seed.

There, she ran into another problem.

Much like a clogged drainpipe, now that Alice's [Scholar] mana seed had a bunch of the wrong kind of mana stuck to it, it simply didn't want to absorb the [Scholar] mana. Instead, the class seed was insistently trying to suck up all the nearby [Scientist] mana and completely ignoring the mana it was supposed to deal with.

Alice felt the urge to throw something at her class seed.

If she had to create an opening in her other clogged-up magic seed, that would make this already ludicrous task even more difficult. Not to mention, her pure mana reserves were starting to run low. Alice was anxious to make some real progress before her mana ran out.

Alice started to rush, which only made things worse. Every time she dropped the chunk of displaced mana, it would get dragged back to the wrong seed, which would continue to fruitlessly try to absorb it. Every time she messed up, she had to start over.

She resisted the urge to growl in frustration after her tenth failure. Once again, Alice split off three of her mana tendrils to keep the chunk of [Scholar] mana next to the [Scholar] seed, and then used the other four mana tendrils to try to grab the [Scientist] mana that was clogging up the seed. Perhaps it was skill—or, more likely, it might have been pure luck. Either way, this time, Alice managed to shift the [Scientist] mana out of the way *just* long enough for her to shove the [Scholar] mana into the correct seed.

The class seed greedily absorbed the correct kind of mana, and Alice let out a sigh of relief. Even though she was still in an awful mood, at least she had accomplished *something* worthwhile today.

You have leveled up!
Scholar: 56→57

Alice blinked in surprise, then grinned. She had suspected that having her class seeds get clogged up with the wrong type of mana would create problems when it came to leveling up. It was nice to have her suspicions confirmed.

Now that her [Scientist] seed had far less [Scholar] mana clogging it up, it proved far easier to stuff some [Scientist] mana into the correct seed. Alice started shifting her mana around, until, halfway through moving another chunk of [Scientist] mana over, she ran out of pure mana.

Instantly, the chunk of [Scientist] mana was dragged back toward her [Scholar] seed, where it once again got stuck. Most frustrating of all, Alice could still see multiple chunks of [Doctor] mana and a few other types still floating around her body. They were much smaller and weren't really a big problem yet, but Alice suspected they would become an issue if she didn't deal with them eventually. But she didn't have a [Doctor] class seed, meaning Alice had nowhere she could put the [Doctor] mana. And as she had already discovered while trying to move around the [Scholar] mana, anytime she wasn't actively pushing mana away, it would fly right back to its starting position. Meaning she couldn't just push it out of her body.

A few moments later, another few globs of mana from her surroundings started to flow toward her class seeds. Most of it was [Explorer of Magic] mana. That made sense. After all, Alice *had* just created a new, innovative use for her pure mana.

You have leveled up!
Explorer of Magic 76→77

Along with her extra [Explorer of Magic] mana, a few new types of unidentified mana swarmed toward her class seed. Alice resisted the urge to curse as they *also* got stuck.

Apparently, in addition to one level in [Explorer of Magic], Alice had gained some mana for two classes she had never heard of, called [Pure Mana Manipulator] and [Esoteric Mage], as well as some more misplaced [Scientist] mana. Some of the [Scientist] mana had gone to her [Scientist] seed, but some had tried to enter her clogged-up [Scholar] seed, and even more was now stuck to her [Explorer of Magic] seed. Alice felt deeply irritated. She had been rewarded for her hard work with more class levels . . . and the reward had just undone all her hard work.

Alice felt an increasingly large headache start to form. She took a few deep breaths and tried to quell the rising irritation. Annoyance was not a *productive* emotion, and she hated feeling it, but after everything else that had happened today, it was just so *easy* to be frustrated by small problems. She took a final deep breath and focused on her new observations.

At the very least, Alice had gained more information. She was now mostly certain that the System had originally sorted out mana somehow—after all, Alice had never seen this problem before the System collapsed. *Something* must have been fixing it, and since the System had just collapsed, it was highly likely the two occurrences were related.

Of course, there was also a small chance that Alice was falling into a post hoc, ergo propter hoc logical fallacy. She would try to verify her assumptions more later. But at the very least, her theory seemed valid.

Along with that, Alice had a few new assumptions she could work with. Alice now suspected that any time anyone did *any* action that was related to a specific idea, they would get a huge hodgepodge of different mana types. For example, if someone healed someone, they would get a bunch of different kinds of mana: [Organic Mage] mana, [Doctor] mana, and perhaps a few other similar kinds of mana, because those were the classes people associated with healing. Despite that fact, when the System was still around, most people didn't have dozens or hundreds of classes. It was pretty unusual for someone to have more than ten in total, even if they dipped into a few secondary classes for some extra perks.

Why was this the case?

It was likely because the System converted various similar kinds of mana into one specific kind of mana, thus concentrating people's benefits into a few categories they could make the most use of. This might also be why most classes had specific unlock conditions. By design, the System was meant to share information about what classes people *could* unlock. Then they would take specific actions to unlock the class they wanted, which was a way of signaling to the System what perks they wanted in the future. There might be restrictions on what the System could transform different mana types into, but Alice suspected she had a rough idea how the whole process was supposed to work.

Of course, there were still some oddities with this theory. Alice had looked it up before and knew for a fact that nobody had ever observed a decrease in leveling speed for their classes, even if they had several similar classes. If somebody had twenty different research-related classes and then made a new discovery, each class would level up just as quickly as if the person only had one research-related class. However, Alice also knew that magic didn't follow the law of conservation of energy, so maybe she was thinking too much in terms of energy conservation.

Either way, at least for now, she had to find a way to copy the System's filtering ability. She had a huge amount of mana her class seeds couldn't absorb properly, and if she didn't find a way to deal with it, it would cause issues for her mental stability sooner or later. Especially right now, when she already felt bad, she didn't feel like trying to manage an increasingly strong desire to act like a [Doctor] or an [Esoteric Mage].

The biggest question was what kind of magic seed she needed to properly convert mana from one type to another. She spent several minutes tossing ideas around, trying to figure out what magic seed she could form with {Seeds of Ambition} once the perk came off cooldown in about a week.

As she was lost in her thoughts, she heard a sudden crash in the distance. It was loud enough that it threw her out of her thoughts, and she immediately started scanning out her window.

Moments later, Alice began to pick up increasingly noticeable clanging and scratching sounds as metal clashed against metal in the distance.

She frowned.

Something was very wrong.

She immediately started preparing her magic tendrils. The metal ringing against metal *could* be some [Guards] training, but it was late at night. Would [Guards] really train well past midnight?

Suddenly, Alice thought of the hostile gaze that had been centered on her earlier that day, and a chill ran down her spine.

She wasn't entirely sure if the manor was under attack yet. However, she suddenly felt as if the night was filled with hidden eyes, hungrily gazing at her from the distance.

She quickly moved away from her window and toward the hallway.

Alice wasn't terrible in a fight, but she wasn't great, either. If something bad was happening, the first thing she needed to do was find Ethan or her [Hidden Guard]. Preferably both.

As she moved through the corridors, the sound of metal clashing against metal became louder. Someone was attacking the manor, and they were getting closer by the second.

CHAPTER 7

Alice felt her heart leap into her throat before the fruits of her training started to kick in. When Ethan had taken her to fight a Society base with the army, Alice had grown used to the sounds of magic and metal clashing. Ethan had also constantly quizzed her about what to do when things went wrong. Combined with combat training from the Magic Academy, Alice had at least some instincts to fall back on.

The first thing she realized was that she wasn't a great fighter. She was okay at best. She needed to find someone stronger and link up with them. The most logical person to find was Ethan himself.

She sprinted down the halls of Ethan's manor and toward his study. Unfortunately, despite her exceptional [Dexterity] stat that would put an Olympic athlete's running speed to shame, she wasn't fast enough to escape the battle.

As Alice was rounding a corner, she stumbled upon two mages fighting with a [Guard].

One of them noticed her and yelled something in a language Alice didn't recognize. The gaze of the other mage jerked toward her. Then both Society mages flooded their bodies with organic mana.

[Organic Mages], thought Alice.

Alice immediately realized that the two had been conserving mana against the [Guard].

They weren't conserving it anymore.

One of the two mages continued to fight the [Guard] while the other charged toward her.

A moment later, {Enhanced Senses} kicked in.

Time seemed to slow down. It wasn't quite as drastic as the boost from {Adrenaline Rush}, but Alice's perception of where her enemies were and what they were doing also increased significantly. At the same time, Alice felt a certain awareness of the strength of her two enemies. Her mind spun as she searched for a way to survive.

I'm thinking faster than they are right now. The moment {Enhanced Senses} and {Adrenaline Rush} end, I'll be too slow to fight. Wait, I can still use {Speed Experimentation} to give me another speed boost. Maybe that will let me deal with them before I'm out of perks?

Alice reached toward everything in her surroundings and ripped up four floorboards with her mana tendrils. Then she quickly used her remaining three tendrils to turn the floorboards into sharpened stakes by shaving off the ends, and fired them at the charging [Organic Mage].

The man lit up with rainbow mana, and suddenly, his movements stopped looking like they were in slow motion.

He's using a perk similar to {Adrenaline Rush}, she realized.

The man sprouted three mana tendrils of his own and channeled kinetic mana through them.

Before she could react, he ripped a painting off the wall and hurled it at Alice's projectiles. He managed to knock two of the sharpened floorboards off course before he stopped the other two dead in their tracks with his kinetic magic.

Alice launched a second wave of sharpened floorboards at the man, hoping that anything would connect. He deflected two of them, but he missed the other two, and they tore into his torso. Rainbow mana surged through his body, and then he sped up *again*.

Alice felt {Adrenaline Rush} kick in as the man appeared *behind* her. She couldn't tell if he'd teleported or simply sped up well beyond her perception, but she didn't have time to think. The man's fist descended toward the back of her head like a meteor, but under the influence of {Enhanced Senses} and {Adrenaline Rush}, Alice could process his motions, if barely.

Alice tossed a bit of display mana into {Speed Experimentation} to boost herself even more by convincing herself that she was experimenting with how her new No_Magic seed worked in a fight.

Then, with the help of {Extended Organics}, one of her mana tendrils popped into existence behind her and drilled into the man's arm. She activated her No_Magic seed.

The man's body slowed down. In a tenth of a second, the man went from moving so quickly that Alice could barely see him to crawling through the air like a snail. The organic and rainbow mana in his body dissipated. At the same time, Alice felt her No_Magic magic seed start to bleed mana at a ridiculous rate.

Alice's new perk could deactivate magic, even inside someone else's body. But trying to push against the innate magic resistance of another person was causing her to leak mana like a pipe that had been sliced in half.

Alice immediately dematerialized more of her mana tendrils before rebuilding them right next to the attacking mage. This time, she didn't try to force her mana into the man's body. She latched on to his sleeve and then tried to pick him up and slam him to the ground. His sleeve negated Alice's mana, and she bit back a curse. It must be enchanted to ward off external mana.

Alice whipped a beaded bracelet out of her storage perk and activated the enchantment on it, right as the man showed signs of reacting to her attacks.

All the beads on the bracelet propelled themselves into the man's face, forcing him back as he screamed in pain. However, she hadn't inflicted a lethal wound. She had torn up one of his eyes, but he was already healing.

Alice felt the man reach for more organic mana to heal himself. Alice dug the tendril deeper into his body. Her No_Magic mana reserves started to deplete even more quickly, but the man's healing stopped. The man continued to struggle and thrash, but he hadn't managed to land a solid hit on her.

With her remaining six mana tendrils, Alice prepared another spray of sharpened floorboards. She needed this man out of the fight *now*, because her perks were about to expire. Her No_Magic seed was also nearly out of mana, and the [Guard] seemed to be losing the fight with the other mage.

Before she could finish off the first mage, she saw the other [Organic Mage] use a perk. His muscles swelled up, and Alice felt a hint of danger. Then the [Organic Mage] used his bare fist to punch through the [Guard]'s armor and hammer him in the head, knocking the [Guard] out.

Alice felt {Adrenaline Rush} wear off. The mana she had poured into {Speed Experimentation} started to peter out. Her perception of time started to revert to normal, and her exceptional processing speed and bullet time disappeared. Only {Enhanced Senses} was left.

Rainbow mana started to flow toward the fallen [Guard]'s head. He wasn't dead. The second mage had turned his attention toward Alice. Unfortunately, the [Guard]'s survival didn't help her much. The [Guard] wasn't going to be rejoining the fight anytime soon, and Alice hadn't finished off her mage.

Alice focused on {Speed Experimentation} again and tossed in some organic mana. She wasn't very proficient in using it in combat, and she needed to keep her bullet time up if she didn't want to die. {Speed Experimentation} clicked into place again.

As the second mage leaped toward her, Alice sent her floorboard volley at him. As much as she wanted to finish off the first mage, if she did that she would probably go down, and who knew what would happen after that. The [Organic Mage] dodged out of the way with contemptuous ease, and a split second later, he was nearly touching her.

Then the [Organic Mage]'s eyes widened in surprise as Alice made the floorboards launch him away like a miniature catapult. The man slammed into the wall and bounced off before leaping back to his feet. However, that gave Alice just enough time to turn her attention back to the first [Organic Mage].

He had taken advantage of her distraction and managed to flop away from her, temporarily breaking contact with her mana tendrils. This had given him a quick window to heal himself, free from the influence of her No_Magic mana. Alice took a step closer to him, and her mana tendrils disappeared and reappeared before drilling into the man's body again.

Before she could do more than reapply her No_Magic mana, Alice felt her world light up with pain as the man's fist connected with her head. The world swam, and Alice fought off a surge of nausea. If the man's organic mana hadn't been disabled, that punch might have knocked her out or killed her. Even without mana, her head *hurt*.

Alice tried the catapult trick on the first mage to repel him before he punched her again. However, the man sidestepped her attempt, then stepped forward for another swing.

Alice felt her No_Magic mana finally run out. Organic mana started to surge through the man's body again, and Alice's stomach clenched in fear.

Alice sent another spray of sharpened shrapnel into the [Organic Mage]'s skull. This time, it connected. The organic mana in his body tried to reach his brain and heal him, but the massive wooden spike in his skull blocked him. He struggled a few times and then went still. The mana in his body winked out like a light bulb dying.

He was dead.

The [Guard], conscious again, stood up just in time to intercept the other [Organic Mage]. Alice wanted to cry in relief, even though the world was still swimming. The [Guard] had rejoined the fight far faster than she had thought was possible. The [Organic Mage] backed off after his ally died. He glared at Alice, as if he wanted to eat her alive—and then he started running away.

Alice quickly realized that he was out of organic mana. She had thought he was conserving mana earlier, but it was clear that the [Guard] had put up a better fight than she thought. The second mage wasn't in good condition anymore.

A sharpened floorboard to the head ended any potential threat he still represented before he could escape.

Then Alice sagged to the floor, feeling a mixture of pain and relief. Her head still hurt, but the room's sickening tilting and twisting had finally stopped. At least for now, there weren't any enemies nearby, either.

She had been forced to use almost all her perks and abilities, but she had survived. She lay against the wall for nearly a minute and went over the fight again in her head.

The two attackers had been around level sixty in their primary classes. They had clearly optimized some of their abilities for combat. If Alice had been less prepared, she might have died.

"Are you all right?" she asked the [Guard]. She was running low on most kinds of mana, but she could still spare some organic mana to heal any injuries he might have sustained. She also still had {Moderate Tissue Regeneration} to heal herself later, if she needed it.

"I should be asking you that. Fuck," said the [Guard], grimacing. "My ribs hurt, and I think one might be cracked, but my perk healed most of it. That bastard hit like a fucking building."

"Don't fight against my mana," Alice said. "I don't have any perks like {Patient's Consent}, and I can't heal complicated injuries, but I can heal basic wounds like cracked bones."

The [Guard] hesitated, as if he were wondering whether Alice would screw up and kill him, before he reluctantly nodded.

Alice shoved a mana tendril into the [Guard]'s chest and started healing his cracked ribs. She didn't manage to completely patch up the injury, but she helped his body speed up the healing process a bit and made the pain and damage lesser. Unfortunately, she ran out of mana partway through the job.

"Thank you, Lady Alice," the [Guard] said after she did what she could. "I can at least move around more easily now."

The two quickly scanned the hallway for other enemies, but didn't see any.

"Lady Alice, are you looking for Honored Immortal Ethan? I believe that he would want you to find him as soon as possible," said the [Guard] after a few moments. "I was originally trying to reach your location, but it seems I was the one in need of protection instead of you." The [Guard] chuckled grimly.

Alice nodded. "Do you know where Ethan is? We should meet up with him as fast as possible."

"He was moving between the first and second floors, last I knew. The attackers seemed surprised the Honored Immortal was still present, so he's taking the opportunity to ambush them."

Alice decided to wait instead of meeting up with Ethan. If Ethan was in the middle of a big fight, she might distract him if she went over right now. She had burned through most of her best perks during the fight, and rushing through potentially dangerous areas in hopes of finding her highly mobile mentor would be foolish. It was better to hunker down and wait.

The two of them struggled to their feet before confirming that the nearest room was empty. There was a big hole in the door, but it would do well enough as a shelter. The [Guard] helped barricade the door and then the two waited.

After a few minutes, Alice saw another group of [Guards] moving through the corridor. One was sporting a rather large hole in his guts, although he was still moving around just fine, and another was Alice's [Hidden Guard]. He was currently missing an arm, which made Alice wince. Even if regenerating limbs wasn't too hard in this world, it was still a sign of how hard he had fought. Alice and the [Guard] had been lucky. If some of the stronger opponents had attacked them instead, Alice would probably have been at the mercy of the Society.

Alice and the [Guard] let them in, then rebarricaded the door and continued to wait.

The [Guards] and Alice's [Hidden Guard] grouped up around her in tense silence, keeping a wary eye on the hole in the door.

The sounds of fighting started to die down as the minutes passed. Alice's [Guards] never stopped being wary of their surroundings, but no other enemies found them. Several minutes later, Ethan walked into the room. His eyes immediately flicked toward Alice, and some of the tension bled away from his shoulders.

"Good, you're still alive," he said, immediately striding over to Alice. "Are you injured? I have a lot of organic mana left over."

"I should be fine," said Alice. "Just a few bruises and a nasty headache."

"I'm glad you had the sense to leave your room—the attackers were targeting you. They managed to get into it and ransack it, and a few seemed rather high level. I didn't even manage to kill all of them," he said with a grimace. "The person who was watching you earlier seems to have been some sort of decoy. They led my [Spies] to what I thought was a Society base, but it was a trap. I'm still not sure how they managed to fool the [Spy]'s perks so well—that shouldn't be possible at his level," said Ethan, looking more than a little disturbed. "Something I'll need to investigate later."

Then he turned toward Alice's [Hidden Guard] and the others who had been protecting Alice. "All of you did well in protecting my apprentice. I'll personally heal your injuries in a moment, and I'll give you a generous bonus tomorrow. Well done," he said, extending a few mana tendrils toward the injured [Guards]. A few moments later, all their injuries were wiped away by Ethan's organic mana. Ethan also extended a tendril toward Alice and cleaned up her headache and bruises. The [Guards] looked much more relieved when all their injuries were healed.

"Go help the other [Guards] check the manor for any hidden enemies," said Ethan.

The [Guards] dispersed. Ethan's rainbow perk shimmered into existence, preventing outsiders from eavesdropping as he spoke again. "This attack is very troubling. The attackers seemed to have been very focused on you. They either know something, or they're desperate." He sighed. "Either way, it's not good that the attackers were willing to attack an Immortal's manor in the middle of the city."

"Were they from the Society?" Alice asked.

"Almost certainly."

Alice glanced at the splatters of blood in the hallway where she and the [Guard] had fought against the attacking mages, and then nodded. She and Ethan both knew the Society would want to capture her if they were aware of Alice's research into the System. Was this a sign that they knew something?

They *had* to know that she knew something. Otherwise there was no way they would throw a huge batch of mages at her.

"Did you have any research notes lying around in your room?" Ethan asked, breaking Alice out of her thoughts.

"I have a good memory perk. I don't usually write things down anymore," said Alice. "I used to, when I first arrived in this world, but these days, my memory is the best notebook I have available."

Ethan nodded. "Good. They won't be able to steal any of your notes, then."

The two fell silent, as both considered the implications of the attack tonight. Alice felt a wave of cold anxiety worm its way into her stomach as she realized the truth. The Society was coming. At the same time, she felt a strange sense of . . . relief?

She was startled once she realized that she felt relieved. It was such a strange emotion to feel after confirming that the Society of Starry Eyes was now targeting her, and it took her a few moments to figure out why she felt that way.

Since the moment she had learned about this world's situation, she had been worried that the Society would target her. She had spent almost every single moment aware that if her research was known, the Society would come. Every single move she took was careful, and she was always afraid that someone would find out more than they should know.

And now it didn't matter. During the tea party a few days ago, Ethan's mother had said that it probably didn't matter whether Ethan and Alice tried to cover up the fact that she was a researcher and not a combat mage.

Alice now understood why. The Society was targeting her already.

It was a terrifying situation, but at the same time, Alice didn't have to be worried about whether the Society *might* target her anymore.

She now knew for a fact that they knew *something*. And they were coming.

Chapter 8

Before she went to sleep, Alice dealt with the process of filtering her mana and leveling up.

You have leveled up!
Survivor: 56→58, Kinetic Manabinder: 41→42

Both her [Kinetic Manabinder] and [Survivor] class seeds had gotten clogged up, meaning that if Alice wanted to level up again, she would need to unclog them. Unfortunately, Alice had no pure mana left right now, and some of the types of mana stuck to her class seeds were classes she didn't have a seed for. So she'd have to wait for a while to deal with the leftover chunks of [Survivor] mana stuck to her [Kinetic Manabinder] class and the [Kinetic Manabinder] mana stuck to her [Survivor] class seed, as well as the oddball mana types still stuck to her other seeds. She was probably missing at least one level in [Kinetic Manabinder], possibly two. None of it would be fixed until she had the time and mana to resolve the issue.

She sighed in frustration before she looked over her other System notifications.

Through training, you have increased an attribute!
Magic: 164→165, Endurance: 134→135

The point in [Endurance] must have come from the fight with the [Organic Mage]. Alice was beginning to appreciate just how much her [Endurance] stat helped her, despite how painful and exhausting it was to train the stat. If it hadn't been so high, she might have been more seriously injured.

She also noticed that, unlike her class seeds, her attributes didn't cause any noticeable clogging when they converted themselves into mana flesh. However, her body seemed to have a harder time digesting the new mana and turning it into mana flesh. Alice suspected that she had probably gotten slightly less progress toward improving her attributes than she should have. It wouldn't have been enough to boost her up another point in any of her attributes, but if she didn't figure out how to deal with the issue, she would certainly notice the effects over time. However, it wasn't a big deal. She would fix it if she could, but it was certainly not a priority.

Alice felt the urge to rub her temples in annoyance.

She really needed to fix her class seeds and mana filtration somehow. She would look into it when {Seeds of Ambition}'s cooldown ended next week. There was probably some way to do it using just pure mana manipulation, and Alice vaguely recalled seeing [Seed Boosters] use a few mana-filtering fractals before the class went extinct. Those *might* fix her problem, but Alice wasn't skilled enough at mana manipulation to replicate those fractals yet. And there was probably a filtration magic seed that would do the same job with far less effort, and probably produce far better results as well.

After finally looking over her System notifications, Alice went back to sleep.

The next day, Alice had a quick breakfast before Ethan called her into his study and handed her a stack of reports.

Alice scanned one report after another and started frowning. What she had read didn't make sense. The attack on Ethan's manor hadn't been an isolated case. Several towns and cities that could get news to the capital quickly had sent reports of Society attacks on other important researchers. An extensive number of Society mages were reported to be involved in four of the attacks. Three of the heavily targeted mages had been kidnapped in their sleep. The final mage had managed to flee for his life and made it to the [Guard], who protected him successfully against the attackers.

Alice had originally thought that the Society knew something about her research. She had assumed that perhaps they knew she was researching the System, or perhaps that she was from Earth, and had launched an attack against her because of that.

However, while the Society clearly knew *something*, she wasn't the only one being targeted. They were targeting every single mage with good levels in research-based classes, it seemed. They were looking for *some* sort of information, and they were desperate enough that they didn't care what they risked.

Society attacks on almost a dozen mages over the course of a night was very unusual. For most of its existence, the Society had remained hidden. It launched attacks against others, but those attacks were always controlled and infrequent. Launching an all-out attack like this made it far more likely that the Society would expose more bases . . . and also ensure that Illvaria had a reason to focus on the Society instead of the recolonization effort. Why had the Society done such a thing? The Society was behaving as if it had no sense of self-preservation at all—completely at odds with how it had operated in the past.

"What do you make of all this?" asked Ethan, putting the reports back on his desk before turning to Alice. He seemed genuinely curious rather than as if he was testing her.

"Well . . . I doubt all these people were secretly researching System mana," said Alice. "The rarity of the achievements I've gotten for studying System mana strongly implies that it's an unusual subject. And the Society is clearly desperate to find out *something*. Otherwise, they wouldn't have done something so dangerous. What were these mages studying? If we can figure that out, maybe we can figure out what the Society is so desperate to learn."

Ethan paused for a moment as he consulted some of the papers he had been thumbing through on his desk. A moment later, he grimaced. "Two of them had dimensional mana research licenses, and two others were focused on pure mana and how it interacts with other forms of mana. The less heavily targeted mages seem to have a much more scattered set of research focuses, but they were mostly aligned with different types of pure mana research."

Alice nodded thoughtfully. "The branches of research from the four most heavily targeted mages are very clearly in line with the Society's interests. But their actions make no sense to me, even if they could get valuable information from this. If a real war between Illvaria and the Society broke out, the Society would lose. Right?"

Ethan nodded. "The Society is not capable of winning an outright war with another nation. They are powerful but also scattered across the continent, and they lack the military cohesion or raw forces needed to overthrow even a smaller country." Ethan paused. "Well, unless you count some of the really small nations in the Shil Confederacy. But nobody likes the Society, so the moment they took over even a small country, Illvaria would unite with the rest of the Shil Confederacy to root them out. So I'm also baffled. The Society is acting in such a way as to potentially help unite the entire Shil Confederacy in taking action against them. If they wish to survive the next year or two, they *shouldn't* be behaving like this. They're picking a fight they can't win with no regards for how much it will cost them."

"Do they know anything about the System collapsing?" asked Alice, trying to suppress a quiver of fear in her voice. "If so, the Society might also be desperate . . ."

Ethan looked concerned as well. "That . . . is a scary thought. I don't know what the Society would do if they knew for sure that something was terribly wrong with the world. I also don't know how they could possibly have obtained that information—without a mixture of perks and achievements as unique as yours, I suspect learning that information would be nigh impossible, at least right now." Ethan shook his head. "I'm afraid I don't know, either. The Society is acting like a beehive that was lit on fire, and I don't know why."

The two stared at the stack of reports in silence.

"I suppose we just don't have enough information to work with," said Alice. At the same time, she couldn't help but think of the Society base that she and Ethan had attacked a few months ago.

During that battle, they had recovered a wide variety of research notes. Some were about the Society's devotion to researching floods of dimensional mana.

The Society was mostly comprised of [Organic Mages] who wanted to do human experimentation. The Society had dimensional magic researchers, but they seemed to be a minority.

Despite that fact, the leaders of the Society of Starry Eyes had been forcing the members of the illegal mage society to devote an absurd amount of resources and time to studying the strange floods of dimensional mana that had been appearing recently. It was a decision that was terrible for the long-term growth of the Society of Starry Eyes, much like last night's attacks on prominent Illvarian mages.

Perhaps something had gone wrong when it came to dimensional mana? Alice hadn't had time to form a dimensional mana seed yet, but she had a license for it now. Combined with the strange village disappearance that she and Ethan had investigated a few weeks ago, Alice started to wonder if the Society had noticed something else. A piece of the puzzle she hadn't noticed yet. Maybe the System collapsing had caused some other problem with dimensional mana and the Society was reacting to that?

Alice quickly outlined her thoughts to Ethan, who thought for a moment and then nodded.

"It seems likely," he said with a sigh. "I'll see if any of my [Spies] or anyone from the crown estate has found a lead on another Society base. If we can steal more of their research notes, we could probably learn more." He shook his head and then scanned the reports again. Then he rubbed his forehead in frustration and turned back toward Alice. "That reminds me. We need to bring Miss Cecilia to the manor *now*. Frankly, you're too valuable, and the Society is clearly targeting you. I will also be tripling the [Guard] here and finding a few more [Hidden Guards] for you *and* Cecilia. If the Society's actions are this erratic, your safety needs to come before everything else. That includes the safety of your friends. I don't want to end up in a hostage situation."

Alice paused. She didn't like the idea of forcing her best friend in this world to come to the manor. Not to mention, Cecilia's classes were all devoted to making enchantments and running a shop. If she was placed in protective custody, her leveling speed would suffer. Alice's odds of reaching Immortality were pretty good. If she became an Immortal, she didn't want her best friend in this world to die of old age. It would be better if the two of them became Immortals together.

But at the same time, Cecilia needed to survive in order to reach Immortality. With the Society of Starry Eyes going nuts, there was no guarantee that Cecilia would be safe without the protection of an Immortal.

Finally, she nodded.

"Bring her here," said Alice.

Ethan quickly called over a few [Guards] and gave them orders. The [Guards] left. Then the two waited. Alice felt bad for taking away Cecilia's right to make decisions on her own, but she also didn't want to find out that her friend was dead or had been kidnapped by the Society, either. About an hour and a half later, the two [Guards] returned, along with Cecilia.

"Alice?" said Cecilia, nodding. "You missed board game night yesterday. Today, some [Guards] showed up and said I needed to come with them and meet you. What's going on?"

Alice winced. She had forgotten about board game night. Not that she would have changed her actions either way—the lives of the mages she healed yesterday mattered more than playing board games with her friends. But she still felt bad that she had forgotten to send word, at least. She handed Cecilia the stack of reports she and Ethan had been reading through.

Cecilia started scanning, and her face started to turn whiter and whiter as she read.

"Uhh . . . this is . . ." Cecilia shuddered before she glanced at Ethan. "This is quite scary. Am I here for protection?"

"Yes," said Alice. "Ethan and I are worried that the Society may target you to get to me. I know that having your freedom taken away won't feel great, but . . ."

"Don't worry, I get it," said Cecilia. "After reading this, I'm not exactly enthusiastic about wandering around without a platoon of [Guards], either. I value my freedom, but getting kidnapped and tortured definitely isn't on my to-do list. I heard about what Samantha went through."

Alice relaxed. She had been worried Cecilia would object, but she seemed to be taking it in stride.

Then Ethan looked at Cecilia, and Alice could see a hint of disapproval in his gaze.

"I'm glad that you're willing to analyze the situation and make the best decision. Now . . . I hear that you knew about my apprentice's research into the System?"

Cecilia's gaze turned blank for a moment, and her eyes flicked toward Alice. "You told him?"

Alice nodded. "We'll talk about that in a bit. This week has been . . . very chaotic. And terrifying."

Cecilia turned back toward Ethan and shivered under his gaze. "Yes, Honored Immortal, Alice has told me about her research, and I have participated in it," she said. "Alice originally asked me for help with creating enchanted items. Nowadays, she doesn't really need my help, but we still talk about her research from time to time."

"Have you told anyone else about Alice's research?" asked Ethan.

"I haven't, Honored Immortal. I would never betray my friend's confidence like that, and Alice's research might get her hunted down by the Society if they learn about it. I'm not a fool."

Ethan gazed at Cecilia for a few moments and then nodded. The disapproval in his eyes faded.

"That's good to hear. I thought it was unlikely that you were the one that got Alice targeted, but I needed to make sure."

Cecilia shrugged. "Do you have any guesses why the Society is going crazy?" she asked. "Their actions are inconsistent with their own long-term survival. This doesn't look like a crazy plan that will get their organization exceptional benefits if it succeeds . . . it looks more like the Society has just randomly decided to destroy itself."

Alice paused and then reached her hand out. "We don't know. All we have is a rough guess, which is that the Society might have seen something else go wrong. Something related to dimensional mana. Or maybe they know something about the System collapsing."

Cecilia's eyes widened. "The System *collapsing*? What do you mean?" Alice held out her hand.

"I want to use {Shared Memory} to show you something. Are you willing to let me use it on you?"

"Go ahead." Cecilia looked uneasy but held out her hand to touch Alice's.

Alice shared the memory of the System and its mana collapsing into thin air.

Cecilia turned even paler than before.

"When did this happen?"

"A few days ago."

"That's . . . fuck. No wonder you said this week has been chaotic." She paused. "So . . . the two reasons that the Society seems to have lost its mind are both horrible. Either the Society knows about System mana, meaning that they are targeting you because you know more about System mana . . . or they have discovered some sort of horrifying secret about dimensional mana and are freaking out. Both options are awful." Cecilia shuddered.

"It certainly appears that way," said Ethan. "Of course, even if our assumptions are wrong, the Society acting like an enraged hornets' nest is still a problem."

"At the very least, I doubt they discovered my research specifically," said Alice. "They're probably just targeting me because I'm a research-oriented mage. If an Immortal took me as an apprentice because of my research, there's obviously something special about it. They might not know much more than that."

"What about Alice's classmates?" Cecilia asked. "The ones that come to board game night every week might get targeted as well."

"I instructed Alice's Magic Academy to up their security quite a bit once I realized just how dangerous her research is," said Ethan. "I will probably need to upgrade it a few more times, but I don't know if the Society would be quite as keen to target the classmates Alice is close to. They seem like far lower-priority targets." Ethan paused and then narrowed his eyes. "However, ultimately, while I intend to scale up the defenses in the city, defending alone will not protect everyone. The

Society dared to attack an Immortal's manor in the middle of the city. They attacked my apprentice. There will be consequences," Ethan said, his voice practically a growl. Then the ice-cold rage in his eyes dissipated. He turned back toward Cecilia and adopted a somewhat gentle expression, as if the earlier suspicion toward Cecilia and anger toward the Society had been a lie.

Cecilia absorbed Ethan's words for a moment and then sighed softly. "I suppose that's everything, then. Should I go and pack my things?"

"I'll send a few [Guards] to grab everything for you, if you don't mind. No sense in having you wander around the city right now."

Cecilia nodded, and Ethan summoned a few more [Guards] before sending them to retrieve Cecilia's stuff. When the [Guard] returned, Alice helped Cecilia move to a room right next to her own new room—her old room had been trashed during the Society attack. The two of them were located down the hall from Ethan's study, where he spent most of his time.

Less than five hours later, another report came.

True to one of Alice's earlier suspicions, people were now flocking to churches of the System and trying to figure out what the heck was wrong with their status screens. While Ethan had given orders for [Enchanters] to start manufacturing as many antimana rings as possible, many, *many* children were unlocking their status screens far before they were supposed to, and people were beginning to notice.

It had been a few days since the System disappeared. And the first effects were finally starting to ripple through Illvarian society.

The collapse of the System, and its effects, was now fully underway in Illvaria.

Chapter 9

Alice spent the next day observing the Church of the System's reaction to the unfolding crisis. Ethan excused her from attending the Magic Academy, which at this point was a relief—as much as Alice actually *liked* school, she had other priorities right now. She also took the time to use pure mana and unclog what parts of her class seeds she could unclog, although it was a very frustrating and tiring process.

You have leveled up!
Kinetic Manabinder: 42→44

Alice learned that nearly two levels of [Kinetic Manabinder] had been stuck trying to integrate with the wrong class seeds, although none of her other classes leveled up after the unclogging process. Unlike [Kinetic Manabinder], those classes hadn't had enough mana lying around for another level.

Seeing so much mana clogging up her class seeds made Alice nervous for more than one reason, though. Alice had tools to combat her class seeds getting clogged up, but even with those tools, she found it difficult to stay on top of her class seeds and mana. How much worse would it be for other people who didn't have her array of perks and achievements to deal with this problem? How many other cities and countries had someone who could even find a part of the problem and fix it? If she didn't have {Lesser Organic Vision} and {Intuitive Magic Modeling}, Alice would have been unable to even maintain her own class seeds. How long before other people became lunatics controlled by their class mana?

Alice sighed.

At the very least, Ethan's subordinates and the [Enchanters] at the palace had been working to churn out mana-blocking rings. The number of rings they could make at once was pitiful compared to the population of Illvaria, and the problem was worsened by the lack of mages with pure mana seeds. Pure mana just wasn't a very useful seed for most mages. However, even if the quantity was lacking, at least there were *some* preventative measures available for people.

Still, the supply was completely inadequate. Worse, Alice herself knew that blocking external mana from entering someone was only a temporary solution. It would stop people from being afflicted with class mana–related madness, but it would also prevent them from leveling up—meaning that they would never be able to improve their abilities in a meaningful way. If she never found a way to solve the problem, once all the adults died off, humanity would perish as monsters overran every nation in the world. Trying to figure out how badly society would be affected by this crisis made Alice's head hurt.

She took a deep breath and worked her way through a breathing exercise to calm herself down. At the very least, rings were being made. Even if the supply would be nowhere near what was needed, it was better than nothing.

A moment later, a new thought occurred to her. *Am I being selfish by only leveling up myself? I have the ability to help other people using my magic seeds and my achievements. Should I be going from door to door and helping people, like a volunteer doctor or something?* Part of her knew that the thought was ridiculous, since there were so many people about to be in trouble and she had such limited mana reserves. But once the thought entered her head, she couldn't get it out.

Alice sighed before she got up and went to find Ethan. Answering dumb questions was the role he had taken on when he accepted Alice as an apprentice, at least in her mind. He could be a sounding board for her worries.

It didn't take long to find him. After Alice explained her stray thought, Alice would have sworn that Ethan rolled his eyes at her, although she wasn't sure if it was a trick of the light or not.

"Alice. There are probably at least a hundred million people on this planet. You have the mana reserves to help . . . what, five or ten a day? At that rate, you wouldn't even make an impact on Metsel, let alone the entire planet. I know that you'd also get some levels from doing so, but . . . this crisis is probably going to spiral more and more out of control with each passing day. If you spend your time trying to stave off a few problems for a random selection of patients, we'll lose any chance to resolve the greater crisis before it gets worse. If you want to help people, do more research and find a permanent solution. Don't worry so much about working yourself to the bone to help a few people. Once you level up some more, get a few more perks, and find a way to fix the System, you'll have a way to help *everyone.*"

Alice had to admit, Ethan's words felt a bit harsh . . . but they also made sense.

She made her way back to her room and tried to figure out what tools she needed to fix the System. After a few moments of thought, Alice came to a new conclusion.

Right now she needed to find ways to resolve issues on a much, much wider scale. For that to happen, there needed to be people besides just her working on solutions—and enchantments seemed like the way to go right now. Alice was probably the only person in the world who could design the enchantments the world needed to survive this mess—but once she had a template, she could hand the blueprint off to Ethan's [Enchanters] and tell them to get moving. For Alice to design a better blueprint, she needed to level up her [Enchanter] class a bit more.

With her next course of action set, and a suitable way to work off some of her anxiety and guilt, Alice started churning out mana-blocking rings as well as restocking her kinetic bracelets. Since the Society could attack her at any moment, she wanted to have as many disposable magic items on hand as possible.

You have leveled up!
Careful Enchanter: 27→29

Finally, on Tuesday, as Alice ditched school for the second day in a row, reports started coming in, which Ethan immediately passed along to Alice. After reading the reports, Alice felt a strange mixture of depression and frustration.

There were several smaller churches dedicated to the System in Metsel. After all, the capital had over a hundred thousand people living in it. It would be impossible for one church to cover everyone's needs. However, there was still one main church that all the other churches in Illvaria took orders from. Unfortunately, the leader of the Illvarian main church had melted down after the System went silent.

The head [Priest of the System] had retreated to his quarters yesterday in wake of the strange, garbled perks and status screens that were starting to show up. He had not emerged since then. He had not issued any words of comfort to the believers in the System, or come up with any idea why the System had suddenly glitched out, or even told people to "have faith." Instead, as more and more people stopped by the Church of the System to ask what was happening, the head of the Church of the System was having his own crisis of faith.

In other words, in the wake of bad news, the first person who should have stepped up to start helping people had collapsed like a house of cards.

In the absence of the head of the Church of the System, the local [Priests of the System] had started going in very different directions. Some had been shaken by the collapse of the head priest and had followed suit. They also withdrew from public life and effectively shut down.

Another group of [Priests] had started claiming that the System was testing the faith of its followers. An extreme subgroup of this faction had even started demanding that the world appease the System, although they didn't seem to have any idea how to do that. Some of them started taking advantage of their position to put forth some truly bizarre ideas, such as the notion that the System was about to usher in a golden age of prosperity for those who remained true to the faith.

The exact responses from [Priests] in the second category were all over the place, and most contradicted each other.

Finally, a third major group of [Priests of the System] tried to sidestep the issue until they got more information. They didn't state that this was a test of faith, and they also didn't melt down. Instead, based on the reports on Ethan's desk, they seemed to be waiting for something. They focused on doing whatever they could to help the people who came to their churches. They continued to help witness {Trade Agreements} between people, convert primary classes into secondary classes, and swap out perks. In Alice's eyes, it seemed like they were waiting for actual news before making a judgment.

The first two groups of [Priests] seemed hard to work with. People who melted down in a crisis were unreliable, and as much as Alice sympathized with their fear and anxiety, they were supposed to be community leaders. If people saw their community leader breaking down, that would make their anxiety and fear worse, not better. In short, they were useless. The second kind of [Priest of the System] also seemed hard to work with; people who just started making stuff up when things started going wrong seemed dangerous to her. Maybe Ethan could figure out a way to work with them, but Alice had no idea what to do with them.

The third group of people, however, seemed like logical targets for cooperation. At the very least, they were still providing aid to people where they could, and they hadn't started making stuff up, either.

Thus, once the [Servants] of the manor finished sending Alice reports on behalf of Ethan, Alice decided it was time to start organizing. She moved to Ethan's study and then started by outlining what she had tried so far regarding System mana and classes—especially the fact that she had been successful in swapping out which mana was absorbed by which seed. Now that several days had passed without her getting sick or having anything go catastrophically wrong, Alice was pretty sure she was on the right track. Her method for curing mana clogs wasn't harmful, at least. After Alice outlined all her progress and discoveries, she asked Ethan to arrange a meeting with the third group of [Priests of the System].

"Are you sure?" asked Ethan. "Exposing your research into the System *probably* won't be the end of the world, but . . . the Society will definitely target you if word gets out."

"They're already targeting me, aren't they?" Alice paused. A moment later, she had an idea. "If you tried to pass off my research as your own, would anyone even believe it?"

"I doubt it," said Ethan as he immediately shut her idea down. "I'm known as an Immortal who specializes in combat. What you've done is so far beyond my research abilities that nobody with a brain would think I was behind it. Since you're already known for being focused on research, people could probably put two and two together pretty quickly."

Alice grimaced before she tightened her fists in determination. The idea of the Society coming after her with even greater intensity was scary, but . . . She wasn't going to just sit around while millions of people suffered or died because of her inaction. "Then I've decided. The Society is coming for me either way. If they come, then let them come," she said. Then she did her best to grin at Ethan, in order to mask the terror she felt. "Besides, I have a powerful and competent Immortal protecting me!"

Ethan looked thoughtfully at her and grinned. "I'll certainly try my best." Then, his expression became more serious. "But the attack on the manor a few days ago should show you that while I'm strong, I'm far from perfect, especially because I can't be everywhere at once."

"While it's impossible for you to perfectly protect me, I also don't think sitting around and doing nothing is an option, either. The crisis is already upon us, and burying our head in the sand isn't going to fix it," said Alice. "Besides, the crisis is only going to get worse. The mana-clogging issue already caught me off guard. Who knows what other problems I've overlooked that will spring up later?

"Realistically, I'm not even sure if I have the tools to keep *myself* safe from the collapse of the System. I can use pure mana to fix clogged class seeds, and I can probably create a new magic seed to deal with the problem better once I have another seed slot available. However, I need to keep growing or I'll eventually get hit by a problem I'm not ready for. Then I'll die. Perks are the best way to acquire ways to handle new problems, so if I stagnate, I'm already doomed." Alice shrugged. "Working with these [Priests of the System] will help me mitigate the impact of the System's collapse while still minimizing risk. They can help spread word about the System in a way most people will trust and believe, and they are unlikely to be infiltrated by Society spies because the Society is comprised mostly of mages and [Priests of the System] are almost never mages," said Alice.

Ethan sighed. "I'm glad that you have such firm resolve, although it's unfortunate that this might expose you to danger you aren't ready for." Then he smiled. "On the bright side, saving millions of people from the effects of the collapse of the System should give you some amazing achievements if you succeed. If you don't get killed by the Society, this should single-handedly guarantee that you'll become an Immortal. Will Cecilia be helping you explain your research?"

Alice paused. She hadn't thought of including Cecilia in her conversation with the [Priests]. "Should she come?" she asked.

Ethan shrugged. "The Society might not target her if she doesn't publicly help you. On the other hand, if Cecilia helps mitigate the impact of the collapse of the System, she would also get some achievements out of it. Right now, her odds of reaching Immortality are atrocious. I would guess that she has maybe a 2 percent chance right now. And that's including future help that I assume you will give her. As compared to you, where I would currently put your odds of reaching

Immortality at something like 80 percent—if you don't get killed or kidnapped by the Society first. It's up to you."

"I don't think I'm qualified to make decisions for Cecilia," said Alice. "I'll bring it up with her, though, and see how she feels. She should decide whether she's willing to bear the risks associated with this," said Alice. "Being targeted by the Society is nothing to scoff at. But if she does help me, she could make my life much easier. She actually understands my research, and I trust her. Those are huge upsides to consider, especially when I'm already short on manpower."

"Fair enough," said Ethan. "I'll arrange a meeting with the [Priests] for tomorrow. Let me know whether Cecilia will be part of that meeting by tonight."

Alice nodded.

"One more thing," said Ethan. "I suspect you already know this, but . . . for now, you should probably drop any plans of attending the academy. With everything happening right now, I don't think I trust the academy to keep you safe—and I also suspect that you have other problems to worry about. It's your choice, but that's my advice."

Alice sighed. Part of her had already known that she wouldn't be returning to the Magic Academy anytime soon. Part of her felt regretful. She had fought tooth and nail to get in, but only got to spend one semester attending classes before moving on. In a way, it felt strange that something she worked so hard for would be sidelined so easily. On the other hand, she definitely needed to focus on the crisis. At the same time, this reflected how much her position in the world had changed. At the start of summer, she had been unimportant enough that she could barely get a sponsor to help her attend a magic academy. Now she was arranging meetings with a third of the [Priests of the System] in Metsel and was the apprentice of an Immortal.

Life was strange.

Alice shook her head, brushing her thoughts away, and started walking toward Cecilia's room.

After she knocked on the door, Cecilia opened it and gave Alice a quick glance.

"Come in," she said.

Alice entered the room and observed Cecilia for a moment. Alice wasn't sure what she would choose to do . . . but she certainly knew what she *hoped* Cecilia would do. What if Cecilia said no?

What if Cecilia said yes and then got hurt by the Society? How would Alice live with herself afterward?

She took a deep breath and pushed away her erratic thoughts. Alice didn't have the right to make decisions for Cecilia. She would present all the facts, share her opinion, and let Cecilia decide. If she tried to control Cecilia's actions, she would no longer be treating her friend as an equal.

"Cecilia, how do you feel about helping me wrangle some [Priests of the System]? I need their help to start controlling this crisis."

Cecilia looked baffled. "What does that have to do with me? I mean, I'm willing to help you, but . . . what can I even help you with?"

Alice started out by outlining why she felt Cecilia would be a good fit—Cecilia's understanding of Alice's research, Alice's trust in Cecilia, and the fact that Alice needed trustworthy help right now. She also outlined the dangers—reprisal from the Society and public scrutiny. Finally, Alice hesitated for a moment before she presented the last bits of her reasoning.

"I think it's a good chance to potentially reach Immortality," said Alice. "It would give you an excellent achievement. I don't know if you want to reach Immortality, but if you're willing to do so . . . I'd be happier if I had a friend by my side as we work toward Immortality together."

Cecilia seemed to consider Alice's words, mulling them over. Eventually, she sighed and then smiled awkwardly at Alice.

"All right. I'll do it. I never thought I'd have a friend trying so hard to push me toward Immortality, but if you have so many things you need my help with . . . who am I to say no?"

Chapter 10

Ethan, Alice, and Cecilia walked into the room filled with [Priests of the System] while Alice tried to stifle her anxiety. There were forty-one [Priests] here. Far more than Alice was used to addressing. Of course, Alice had already known who was going to attend. In fact, Ethan had made Alice analyze the list of people who were invited as practice for assessing security risks and dangers. However, there was a difference between knowing she was about to speak to a crowd of strangers and actually doing it.

Even worse was the knowledge that, while unlikely, she might have made a mistake when analyzing who should or shouldn't be invited to the meeting. Every person here could, at least theoretically, be an [Assassin] from the Sigmusi or another neighboring nation sent to deal with Alice before she reached Immortality. They could also be informants for the Society of Starry Eyes; while the Society wasn't known for their infiltration abilities, Alice doubted that they had no informants in Illvaria. Money could make some people do anything, after all.

Ethan had spent a very long time discussing the dangers of inviting a large group near her, especially when Alice was still rather low level in her combat classes, and now that she was looking at a room full of people, Alice couldn't help but think back to his warnings. Still, this had to be done.

Alice shook her head and banished her anxiety. She was right next to Ethan, and she had {Adrenaline Rush} to fall back on if something went wrong. She needed to focus. It was time to tell the Church of the System about her research and hope that they didn't take it as badly as the Catholic Church on Earth had when people started asking inconvenient questions. Even that wasn't likely: After all, it would take monumental courage to start raising metaphorical pitchforks against the apprentice of an Immortal, especially when Ethan was very visibly standing with her. The biggest barrier standing in her way . . . was herself.

She stepped to the front of the room, along with Cecilia.

Upon looking at the [Priests], for a moment, Alice had the bizarre impression that she was holding a press conference, even though there weren't any cameras or reporters present.

"Ahem," said Alice as she tried to clear her throat. "It's nice to see you all, and thank you for coming here. As many of you have noticed, the System is behaving oddly."

She saw a few [Priests of the System] nod or wince.

One of the [Priests] had a slightly more unusual reaction. Instead of wincing or nodding like the others, she gave Alice a dubious look before Alice could continue speaking.

"No disrespect to the apprentice of an Honored Immortal, but . . . why are you giving this speech?" asked the irritable-looking [Priest]. "I imagine you're quite accomplished for your age, but I had heard that you were combat-specialized, and I also imagine that you're probably only a bit better than a regular adult right now. You're . . . what, seventeen? Most of Ethan's apprentices over the centuries were about level fifty at your age, according to church records. That's pretty impressive for your age, but that doesn't make you qualified to hold this discussion. Shouldn't the person who did the research present it?"

The [Priest of the System] narrowed her eyes at . . . Ethan?

Why would the [Priest of the System] look at Ethan? And why did she seem so irritated?

A few moments later, it clicked inside her mind.

Ethan had a large group of mages and researchers under his command. Ethan was also well-known for trying to propel new apprentices into Immortality and had gone through several rounds of failed apprentices already. Doing impressive things would cause the System to give people achievements, many of which would boost someone's leveling speed. Giving this speech was probably worth an achievement, or at least some progress toward one.

This woman thought that Ethan had gotten a huge number of mages and researchers to do all the legwork and then had Alice take credit for their work in order to earn an achievement. She likely thought that Ethan was treating the collapse of the System as an opportunity to let Alice level up instead of the horrifying disaster that it was. Since she was also a [Priest] who probably cared about her religion, someone treating the malfunction of her god as an opportunity to earn levels probably rubbed her the wrong way.

Alice felt a strange urge to laugh bubble up in her chest for a moment. She and Ethan had talked about how obvious it would be to most people that she was research-focused. They had discussed how anyone who was paying attention would know that Alice was probably the brains behind any research Ethan presented and how trying to hide was pointless at this stage.

The Society's actions even backed up this belief—they had accurately identified Alice as the real problem and then tried to kidnap her. However, that didn't mean that everyone had extensively researched her before now. Alice found it a little amusing that the potential allies in this room were the last people to realize that Alice was almost entirely research-oriented instead of combat-oriented.

"If you're asking about my qualifications, I'm already above level seventy-five in my primary class, which is research-based, and I also have multiple achievements that are rarity seven or higher. These were earned without Honored Immortal Ethan's help. I have indeed gotten more resources and opportunities since becoming Honored Immortal Ethan's apprentice, but I got here with my own hard work . . . and some luck, of course. The research I am presenting today is almost entirely mine." Alice paused and glanced at Cecilia. "Though I did have some help from a friend."

"Is that true?" asked the [Priest of the System], turning to Ethan for clarification. The woman's eyes squinted in a very particular way, as if she was using a lie-detection perk.

However, no rainbow mana flashed in her eyes, leaving Alice feeling even more amused. The woman was bluffing. A few [Priests] *did* have lie-detection perks activated, but several more were just making "I'm detecting lies right now" faces. Alice supposed it made sense—if people thought that you were using a lie-detection perk, it was almost as good as actually having the perk—as long as no one called your bluff.

Ethan nodded. "All her words are true," he said, gesturing toward Cecilia and Alice. "My apprentice is a very talented researcher, and she is the most qualified person in Illvaria to lead this discussion."

The woman squinted at Ethan for a few more seconds before she sighed. She looked somewhat mollified as she turned back toward Alice and Cecilia. Alice noticed that the [Priests of the System] with lie-detection perks seemed far more interested in Alice than before. The other [Priests] were glancing at the ones with real lie-detection perks out of the corners of their eyes, as if they were trying to gauge their reactions. Alice felt even more amused. Did the [Priests] have some sort of system worked out? Did they have an agreement to help the [Priests] without lie-detection perks help pretend that they had them? That was . . . an amusing way to handle bluffs and lies.

"My apologies, apprentice of Honored Immortal Ethan. Ah . . . I suppose I should also apologize to your friend?" the woman asked as she looked at Cecilia.

Alice internally winced.

Ethan had treated this crisis with all the seriousness it deserved. However, Alice had, in a way, done exactly what the woman was irritated by—used the crisis as an opportunity to boost Cecilia's leveling speed. Of course, Alice's guilt was assuaged by the fact that Cecilia had genuinely been integral to some of her early research. Presenting Cecilia at this meeting would do more than just boost her leveling speed—it would also show that Cecilia was an alternate person that people could talk to and ask questions if Alice was busy with her research. Alice *was* using this crisis as a way to pump up Cecilia's levels—but she was also trying to establish a group of people who could work together to resolve the crisis, and Cecilia deserved a place in that group of people.

Alice cleared her thoughts and continued speaking. She could think about all this later.

"I wanted to meet all of you today in order to discuss two things. First, I wanted to commend you. When the System collapsed, you didn't fall into a panic or start making crazy claims. Instead, all of you kept a level head and tried to help the people where you could," said Alice. "That tells me that you can be trusted to help resolve this crisis."

Complimenting the people gathered here was a good place to start, right? Alice wasn't that familiar with public speaking yet, but she was pretty sure it wasn't a bad idea, at least. Alice needed to engage in *some* form of diplomacy to succeed here, and complimenting people was never a bad thing.

Alice also noticed a bit of [Courtier] mana float into her body, although the mana was mixed with a few other things, such as [Orator]. The amount was minor enough that she decided to ignore it. It wouldn't hurt her as long as she paid attention to it.

"I have information about the collapse of the System to share. To discuss it in further detail, I first need to talk about my research. For a long time, I've been fascinated by the System. To the best of my understanding, nobody has ever done a proper, in-depth analysis of how the System works. At least, not from the perspective of mana. Sure, there have been plenty of people who examined the System from the perspective of religion—trying to figure out the System's intentions and why it does what it does, and how to better follow its will," said Alice, trying very hard not to make a face at her own words.

She was 90 percent sure the System was a nonsentient, nonsapient clump of mana or some sort of enchantment. This made it very hard for her to take the "will of the System" seriously. But if Alice said that, the [Priests of the System] in this room might very well walk out before she even finished talking.

"The method the System uses to interact with us is a bit more understandable, at least from my studies and my perspective as a mage. After all, things like status screens, perk descriptions, and so on must require a lot of effort to maintain. That always made me wonder how everything works behind the scenes," said Alice.

She saw a few [Priests] start to blink in confusion. It didn't look like they were angry, but it looked like they were preparing to *get* angry in the near future. A few of them started shooting daggers at Alice with their eyes.

A different [Priest of the System] chose that moment to speak up.

"Why did you assume that the System needs a how at all? The System is a god—it makes sense that it would be able to do things impossible for us to understand," said the man. "Even Immortals are not so close to the System that they can understand its workings or its will."

"I simply felt that the System might have some way it used to bridge the gap between us and its almighty workings," said Alice.

"But isn't that questioning the divine will of the System?" asked the [Priest of the System], frowning at Alice. "It isn't our place to question how the System works—we need only work hard."

"I believe the System approves of my actions," said Alice as she tried not to frown. She was getting too bogged down in theology—that wasn't the focus here, nor was it why she had brought these people together. But if she didn't answer well, they wouldn't work with her at all. She resisted the urge to sigh.

"As a reward for my continued experiments, the System granted me a special achievement. It wouldn't have done that if it didn't feel that my research had value." Alice noticed that the [Priest of the System] who had previously been frowning and arguing with her had relaxed. She felt a sigh of relief almost escape her lips. It looked like she had finally found a good enough argument that she had pacified some of them. Since the [Priests] believed that the System was a sentient, sapient god, Alice claiming that she had discovered a new type of mana called System mana would probably go over poorly. However, if she first mentioned that the System itself had granted her the ability to see System mana as a reward for her hard work, it would imply the System approved of her research. In that case, if they continued questioning her, the [Priests] would be the ones questioning the will of the System—not her.

"This achievement allows me to see a new kind of mana—one that most people, as far as I'm aware, are completely unable to see," said Alice. "I've taken to calling it System mana, and what it does is allow me to see *how* the System works. Every single time somebody uses a perk, they access some of the System mana in their body to do so. Every time the System grants someone a point in a stat or skill, the System mana in the air reacts to the mana in their surroundings, entering their body and giving them the reward for their hard work. It seems that this is the bridge the System uses to close the gap between itself and its believers.

"I've kept this research to myself and a close circle of friends for a long time. However, as many of you have noticed, the System has been behaving oddly ever since a few days ago. That is because the System mana in the air around us simply disappeared for some reason. Something is interfering with the bridge the System uses to communicate with us, and this is likely the reason why things have become so . . . odd recently."

A few of the [Priests of the System] gave Alice blank looks, as if they were trying to process what she had said. A few of the other [Priests] started to look at the air around them, as if they were trying to see the missing System mana and figure out where it had gone. A few other [Priests] placed their hands on their temples and fell into deep thought. Alice also noticed four [Priests] were frowning at her again. Before she could focus on the frowning [Priests], a different [Priest] interrupted her.

"What does that mean?" asked an older man with brown-gray hair and a long, well-kept beard. This one seemed more horrified than upset. Alice spent a moment glancing at his face, trying to figure out whether he was horrified at Alice's actions or at the situation. After a brief moment of hesitation, Alice decided to hope it was the latter.

"I suspect it is the reason that the status screens started to get weird recently. I would like to say that this is a lot worse than one might expect: The System didn't JUST create our status screens and System notifications—it also did a lot of other very important things. For example, the System helped people form magic seeds—and without the System, trying to form a magic seed is very difficult. Cecilia can tell you a bit more about this," said Alice, gesturing toward Cecilia.

Cecilia had also formed a magic seed without the help of the System in order to get the achievement for it. Naturally, this meant that this was the best topic for Cecilia to talk about if Alice wanted to help Cecilia get a good achievement. However, before Alice could step back and let Cecilia take over the conversation, one of the [Priests of the System] who had been frowning at her stood up and pointed at Alice, looking like he was about to explode.

"Did you make the System mana disappear? Did you *do* something with your studies? If you dared to experiment on the System itself—"

Ethan glared at the man, and rainbow mana flashed across Ethan's eyes.

The man's face turned white as Ethan glared at him. "My apprentice did not do a thing to harm the world, or Illvaria, or the System. She is currently placing her life at risk in order to save people's lives. The Society has already attacked her once, and after today, they will certainly do so again. If you have a problem with that, you may leave."

The man shut up.

Alice hesitated for a moment before she added in a few final words of her own.

"I've only observed and only did so via the gifts the System itself gave me. I have never taken a step beyond that." She waited a few more seconds, to see if anyone objected, before she gestured for Cecilia to start her own speech.

Cecilia, who seemed a bit rattled by the aggressive stance of the [Priest] who had spoken, took a moment to compose herself. Then she stepped forward and began detailing her attempts to form a magic seed without the help of the System— first detailing how the two had cut off the System mana from their surroundings, and then talking about their actual successes. Of course, Cecilia minimized Alice's presence in the research—just as Alice had asked her to do. If it seemed like Alice was the biggest driver of Cecilia's research, it would defeat the purpose of Cecilia's presence here—to establish that Cecilia was part of Alice's research team but also capable of doing things on her own. Once Cecilia finished talking about forming magic seeds without help from the System, Alice stepped back in and talked about the mage who had recently died while she was trying to help her keep control of their messed-up mana flesh. Her voice caught in her throat a few times, but Alice managed to push forward.

"Excuse me, Cecilia, but may I ask why you were trying so hard to form a magic seed without help of the System?" asked one of the [Priests of the System]. Once again, a few of the [Priests] were frowning, although they were different ones this time, and they seemed far more civil than the last man.

"I felt it was reasonably likely that the System would give me a nice achievement for doing so," said Cecilia, not mentioning the fact that she was confident about this because Alice had gotten a valuable achievement of her own before Cecilia had even started trying. {Seed Creator} was a rarity-eight achievement, and while Cecilia had gotten a much weaker version of the achievement, it was Cecilia's best as far as Alice knew. "The resulting achievement has some value in combat, so I would prefer not to discuss the details, but it was indeed quite high rarity and rather helpful for my future."

Some of the [Priests] looked mollified. While it still seemed like a few [Priests of the System] were merely trying to keep their tempers in check, most of them looked thoughtful and interested instead of angry and suspicious.

Alice stepped forward again and began talking about class mana—and how, now that the System wasn't present in the world, unfiltered class mana might forcibly warp people's personalities or mess with them if it wasn't properly filtered and dealt with.

After a few more moments of thought, one of the concerned-looking [Priests] spoke up.

"What do you propose we do about this?"

"I think it wouldn't be a bad idea if we start talking about cutting off mana and how to manage the strange instincts people will start to have in the near future. It's also probably not a bad idea to encourage people to buy mana-blocking rings, since some [Enchanters] under Ethan have been manufacturing them since the moment we realized the System had disappeared. And I would also really appreciate it if any mages with open seeds that were part of your churches came to see Cecilia or me so that we can help them get pure mana seeds," said Alice. "I can help some with perk selections as well, since I know that most people can't even see descriptions for perk choices anymore—though I would prefer if priority is given to mages, who are likely to get seed slots. That would help alleviate some of our production problems and help us as we attempt to cure and assist more people."

The [Priests of the System] discussed Alice's requests and suggestions between themselves for a while.

After some discussion, many of them agreed to her requests, apart from the few [Priests of the System] who still looked angry and suspicious. Alice decided to memorize their names and faces and mention them later to Ethan. She didn't think they would cause any trouble—but it was best to keep an eye on them, just in case.

Alice didn't want to hurt people who hadn't done anything, and having Ethan send watchers after some people still felt like it was violating a few of her old world's ideas about privacy. However, Alice also didn't fancy someone alerting the Society and getting her assassinated, either.

Despite the potential for troublemakers, Alice was still satisfied with the number of [Priests] who were working with her instead of against her. Many of them were discussing how to implement Alice's suggestions and were willing to help, and that was good enough for now.

The first step to quell the chaos following the collapse of the System had been taken.

Chapter 11

In the days after the meeting with the [Priests of the System], Alice had numerous smaller meetings with the most cooperative [Priests] as she helped clarify what she had discovered and how to use that information to help people.

Most of the [Priests] seemed open to further discussion, which was a relief. Apart from the few who had seemed disgusted with her research into the System, most of the [Priests] were focused on helping people. A few of the [Priests] *had* expressed concern about whether Alice had done any human experimentation, but reading through a list of statements under lie-detection perks had assuaged their worries. The cooperation wasn't perfect—Alice could tell that a few of the [Priests of the System] still didn't necessarily approve of her research. However, they were willing to put it aside for the sake of the bigger picture. She could live with that.

The thirty-eight cooperative [Priests] also seemed more than happy to spread a limited version of Alice's information to the people who frequented their church.

While the [Priests] and Ethan had both agreed that telling people absolutely everything was a bad idea, the [Priests], Ethan, Cecilia, and Alice worked out a doctored version of the truth to spread to anyone who would listen.

First, the [Priests] who were keen to work with Alice publicly acknowledged that the System was "damaged" right now. They wouldn't get very far by denying the reality in front of people's eyes, so they had decided that being honest was important. However, they didn't give anything remotely resembling a full picture of how System mana worked and why it had disappeared. Instead, the [Priests] claimed that the System was "testing the faith of the people" in these times. They also acknowledged that until the System was operating at full capacity again, things like mana-blocking rings would help to mitigate the impact of its collapse.

Alice wasn't necessarily happy that so many of the [Priests] pushed a "the System is testing us" narrative, but at the very least, they were helping her spread information that people needed to know to stay safe. In Alice's mind, helping people was more important. If the Church of the System felt a need to add a religious narrative to this information, then . . . well, it wasn't her preference, but so be it.

The [Priests] also revealed the existence of class mana and taught people about the help the System used to give when forming magic seeds, in order to ensure that other mages didn't hurt themselves trying to form magic seeds when they had no clue what they were doing. This fact was something the [Priests] spread far and wide. They seemed gleeful to learn just how critical the System was to mages everywhere—although they were slightly less pleased to hash out the exact details of how class seeds worked.

Giving as many people as possible this information ensured that people were aware of the danger of mana exposure and prevented much of the danger people faced after the collapse of the System. It would take time for this information to spread beyond Metsel, but Alice hoped that word would spread fast enough to prevent people from endangering themselves by accident.

Apart from that, with Ethan and several [Guards], Alice and Cecilia also met with a few mages who had the potential to be useful. They had classes that gave them lots of magic seed slots and had at least one perk choice they hadn't used yet. Alice and Cecilia quickly came to an agreement with those mages: They would help the mages form pure mana seeds, and in exchange, those mages would help produce more antimana rings and any other enchantments they created in the future. Perhaps the mages were motivated by morality—or perhaps by Ethan's generous wages. Either way, Alice was glad to see a way to actually fight back against the crisis. Once they came to an agreement, Alice used her display mana to help them choose their perks. After that, Cecilia started walking them through how she had formed a magic seed without the help of the System. It would take a while before they were ready, but Cecilia could at least guide them through the process. It was the biggest part of the project Cecilia could help with, and it was also a load off Alice's shoulders.

Of course, when the mages in question actually started forming seeds, Alice would need to be ready to shatter their magic seeds if something went wrong. But at least for now, Cecilia could lead them through visualization exercises and teach them the basics. Alice also stepped in once a day to use {Shared Memory} to share her own experiences with forming magic seeds without the help of the System. It wouldn't completely cover the experience these mages would be missing, but Alice hoped that within a week or two the mages would be ready to form their pure mana seeds.

Apart from the cooperative [Priests], there were still the few remaining disgruntled [Priests] to deal with as well, in addition to the attention some other people were starting to pay to the [Priests].

Ethan had [Spies] keep a close eye on the three [Priests] who were less willing to play along with Alice's program. He also started keeping an eye on every single person who fought against claims that the System was damaged or weakened—few in number though they were. Keeping an eye on people dissatisfied with Alice's program was a massive drain on manpower, but it did prevent at least one attempt to slip information to the Society from one of the disgruntled [Priests of the System]. It also made it clear to Alice just how much Ethan was giving to keep her safe during the crisis. The monthly cost of his spy network probably exceeded all the money Alice had *seen* since entering this world.

The [Priests of the System] who were willing to work with Alice also assisted her in keeping an eye on the city. They started sending reports and pages of statistics about how people were reacting, what classes and perks they had available, and whose behavior was starting to turn . . . *odd* after the collapse of the System. It was a huge help for Alice. Even if the [Priests] might not have the memory or mana-sensing perks she had, they could still gauge how quickly some of their more well-known members were growing and help Alice gauge how quickly people were losing their minds. It wasn't the most precise information ever, but it was good enough. With this information, Alice was able to start checking some of her previous assumptions and guesses about how the broken System would interact with things like people's leveling speed, personality corrosion, and the impact of achievements.

Alice didn't even have to go over the data by herself. Ethan had pulled together a team of high-level [Mathematicians] and [Analysts] to go over any information collected by the [Priests of the System]. They were tied to secrecy with a mixture of agreements, contracts, and even more absurd wages—but they were under Alice's command and tasked specifically with looking over information the [Priests of the System] had gathered. Alice still went through the information on her own—but she didn't have to do all the work, which made her life infinitely easier.

By going through these mounds of information, Alice found another way to combat the collapse of the System—one that she hadn't recognized before, although it made a lot of sense once she found it out. Alice could now confirm that the [Willpower] stat actively fought against personality corrosion. The higher one's [Willpower] stat, the lower the influence of unfiltered class mana on one's mind and personality. This was reassuring for Alice—evidently, the System hadn't left people with no defenses against its collapse, even though people were still screwed in the long run. So long as someone had a high [Willpower] stat, they had a way to push back against losing themselves.

Combined with the increasing awareness of people regarding the catastrophe, the church started sponsoring [Willpower] training for anyone who showed up. Alice even specially watched a few of them, to make sure there weren't any surprise problems with increasing attributes or with the training itself.

The exact nature of these [Willpower] training sessions varied from one church to another. Some of the more extreme churches subjected people to relatively painful situations, while forcing people to work through the pain to accomplish some sort of ultimately unimportant task. It still made Alice flinch a bit when she thought about people being explicitly subjected to pain and discomfort for the purpose of training, even if the people participating knew exactly what they were getting into. However, she didn't say anything—even if it made her uncomfortable, she didn't have the right to take away people's choices, and these people were volunteering for the treatment.

Most churches chose much less extreme methods, though. They subjected people to highly distracting environments instead of outright painful ones—such as doing math problems while loud and disruptive noises constantly echoed through the church.

Apart from that, through the information the churches managed to collect, Alice confirmed that the errors in the achievement she'd obtained after the collapse of the System wasn't unique to her. When Alice had gotten {Creative Healer}, she hadn't been entirely sure what to make of it, since it looked so different from achievements obtained before the collapse of the System. The fact that the achievement only gave her 50 percent of the correct boost only reinforced her confusion.

Every single other person who got an achievement had the same problem—they were only getting a fraction of what they were supposed to get from new achievements. Most people noticed that they got somewhere between 40 and 60 percent of the bonus they were supposed to. The [Analysts] and [Mathematicians] Ethan had hired claimed that it seemed to correspond to what the achievement did. People that got an achievement that had odd effects usually had a weaker buff. Their new abilities would be about 40 percent of what they were supposed to be. On the other hand, those who got raw attribute boosts usually had 60 percent of their achievement's expected boost. Achievements like {Creative Healer}, which dealt with things like mana, or that had unusual effects on stats usually fell between the two numbers. It was harder to quantify how much the leveling speed component of achievements was impacted, since there hadn't been enough time to collect data yet, but Alice suspected those probably worked at about 60 percent of what they claimed to do, much like other number-related achievements. The [Priests of the System] had promised to keep an eye on people with similar achievements and let her know what they could find, although it wasn't a priority.

For now, Alice theorized that giving people new perk-adjacent abilities via achievement was more complex than strengthening someone's muscles, which was why they were more prone to messing up. Alice wanted to fix her achievements at some point, but for now she only had one broken achievement, and it didn't seem to be causing any immediate problems.

The reforms that Alice had pushed for were helpful—but they were far from the universal boosts to human survival she had been hoping for. The response of churches they hadn't set up a working relationship with was anemic. The churches led by other [Priests of the System] had three different types of responses. One group supported the actions of Alice's cooperating churches and hopped onto her program after a day or two. The second group of [Priests] still hadn't recovered enough to do anything—those churches were starting to lose visitors, because people were nervous and nobody wanted to go to a place that didn't have answers for them. The final category of [Priests] decried any claim that the System had fallen or was damaged in any way, shape, or form. They had taken to calling Alice all sorts of unsavory names, and most were on Ethan's watch list.

The third group was the most annoying and seemed to be merging with the group of churches that had started making absurd claims once the System collapsed. Alice had the distinct impression that these people were going to be a major headache in the future, but Ethan had promised he would take care of them. Alice was more than happy to fob that task off to Ethan. Wrangling stubborn people had never been her strong suit. Even though it probably would have been valuable experience for when she became an Immortal, Alice would be happy to learn how to manage people when the planet wasn't in the middle of an extinction event.

Over the course of the week, she and Ethan had also had more time to check on the man Alice and Ethan had only partially healed and had found that whatever was going wrong with his mana flesh it wasn't getting better on its own. They spent a bit of time each day stabilizing more of his mana flesh, which did seem to at least moderately reduce his pain and the severity of his injuries. After several days of treatment, the injured patient could now move around after the [Doctors] applied some painkilling perks—which were quite rare, since [Organic Mages] usually just healed problems away.

This treatment work also led to a few levels in Alice's [Student of Organic Magic] class.

You have leveled up!
Student of Organic Magic: 17→22

If circumstances were different, Alice would have felt excited by how quickly [Student of Organic Magic] was growing, despite being a secondary class. With all her achievements and other modifiers stacked together, as well as the current circumstances, the class was leveling up more quickly than main classes usually did. However, given the circumstances, Alice just felt depressed when she saw how quickly her healing class was gaining levels. When healing was this badly needed, it was *never* a good thing.

Alice didn't have to think too much about which perk she would take once she used her display mana to figure out what her new perks did.

> Perk Selection:——Contact with main System lost. Loading from last previous record . . .
> Perk_Name: Patient's_Yes
> Requirements: Host Meets Requirements: Achievement Organic Level 10 (Error: secondary class need_Level20 or seed implosion. Requirement met!)
>
> Cheaper heal when patient yes. Perk fail on malicious magic—must use user benevolent intent or no perk.

The broken grammar in the System message was still hard for Alice to adjust to, but she was pretty sure this perk was one of the many, many variations of {Patient's Consent} that [Organic Mages] had access to. It was one of the most valuable perks that [Organic Mages] who wanted to heal people could get, because it made healing *much* cheaper as long as the patient agreed to be healed. Most versions of {Patient's Consent} could knock the penalty for pushing mana into another living being down by somewhere between 20 percent and 50 percent, depending on how limiting the requirements for the perk were and how high level the perk was. After testing it on the patient, Alice had confirmed that her perk was close to 25 percent, which was on the lower end. However, a 25 percent reduction in mana cost to heal future patients was huge, and with the help of the perk, Alice was finally able to finish stabilizing the patient's mana flesh the following day.

This greatly reduced the pain the patient suffered, although it didn't remove it completely. But at the very least, the man could walk around again and live life without constant infusions of painkilling perks—which was a huge step up. Alice just hoped she could find a better solution to the damage left behind by her healing attempt.

On Saturday, after a week of Alice's excused absence from her classes, analyzing the movements of the church, and running through data with Ethan's [Mathematicians] and [Analysts], something Alice had been waiting for was finally ready.

Her {Seeds of Ambition} perk finally came off cooldown—which meant that Alice had work to do.

She needed a way to clear out the personality-altering mana that had started building up in her body and clogging up her class seeds.

Alice's best guess for how to do that was to create some kind of magic seed built around mana conversion. For now, Alice was planning on focusing on the idea of mana filtration.

So, the moment her perk came off cooldown, Alice spammed {Safety Analysis}, and after confirming it was fine, she started going through the usual process of making a magic seed without the help of the System, this time with a focus on creating a magic seed that could convert one type of mana into another with ease.

She spent a few hours carefully thinking about exactly what image she was planning on using to build the seed, and exactly what she needed out of it. Then she got started.

She almost expected something to go horribly wrong. In the week after the System had collapsed, Alice had gone through a slowly escalating series of problems, all of which needed to be dealt with before they spiraled out of control. So part of her expected that something would just fail to work while she made her new magic seed.

Nothing went wrong, much to Alice's surprise.

Alice spent several minutes after she finished just using {Safety Analysis} over and over again, trying to figure out if she had missed something. Finally, she accepted that things had actually gone according to plan. That made her smile. At least *something* wasn't going horribly wrong after the collapse of the System. Then Alice started filtering the mana types stuck to her class seeds.

[Doctor] mana became [Student of Organic Magic] mana. Newly built-up [Scholar] mana became [Scientist] mana. [Scientist] mana became [Scholar] mana. All the miscellaneous types of mana that Alice had collected over the past week melted away as she converted them into appropriate mana types.

She was gratified to see that her new magic seed was doing exactly what it was supposed to—and she was equally pleased to see a new wave of level-up notifications.

You have leveled up!
Survivor: 58→59, Student of Organic Magic: 22→24, Scholar: 57→58

The leftover chunks of mana weren't quite enough to level up all her classes, and they didn't bring her to a point where she unlocked any new perks. However, four of her classes were now only one level away from getting a new perk, which made Alice very excited. Soon, she would have a new wave of perks to pick that would help her solve the numerous problems she was facing.

As an added bonus, moments after Alice finished dealing with all the leftover mana, a final wave of mana came and rushed toward her [Explorer of Magic] class fractal. After Alice used her filtration seed to convert all the [Scholar], [Arcane Researcher], and [Organic Mage] mana into [Explorer of Magic] mana, she just got one final level.

You have leveled up!
Explorer of Magic: 77→78

The levels in that class were still excruciatingly slow right now, but the boost she had gotten from Ethan's mother at the tea party, as well as the fruits of her own hard work, were beginning to pay off.

After that, Alice spent several minutes thinking about what she wanted to do with her second mana seed before she settled on dimensional mana.

Less than a month ago, she and Ethan had gone to a village that had been strangely flooded with broken dimensional mana. The Society was also one of the major institutions in the world that focused on studying dimensional mana, and for some reason they were losing their minds recently.

That seemed like pretty good evidence that there might be something going horribly wrong with dimensional mana, somewhere in the world.

Alice also had a license to form a dimensional magic seed lying around, although she hadn't taken advantage of it yet.

Besides, if Alice ever wanted to go back home, she definitely needed to understand how dimensional mana worked.

Those seemed like pretty good arguments to prioritize making a dimensional magic seed over anything else. If a crisis involving dimensional mana popped up, Alice wanted to have some way to respond to it.

Therefore, with a mixture of excitement and nervousness, Alice finally started forming a dimensional magic seed for her second magic seed of the month.

CHAPTER 12

Alice had always wondered why dimensional mana behaved the way it did. She had heard, multiple times, of the tragedy of Allenheim—where a bunch of dimensional mages had effectively nuked their kingdom with dimensional mana by accident. The idea of doing the same worried her—although she also couldn't deny how *useful* dimensional mana could be for her future.

Because of this, she had spent quite a while trying to figure out why the tragedy of Allenheim had happened. Her most recent theory, and the one that she favored the most, was that any objects, including air molecules, that passed through a portal would start to infect any mana they came in contact with, much like a virus. After passing through a portal, this air would eventually stop infecting other types of mana—but the damage would already be done by that point. That was Alice's first guess.

Her second idea was that perhaps mana itself became broken while passing through any portal. She was pretty sure that mana *did* naturally pass through portals. That wouldn't explain why dimensional broken mana had such a ridiculous cascading effect, but if the mana itself became infectious, much like her first theory, perhaps this theory would make sense. Alice felt that this theory had a few holes in it, but it was still worth double-checking.

Her third idea was that portals warped mana that existed near them simply by virtue of existing. This would be a little strange, because most mana didn't have any sort of area of effect as far as Alice could tell. Mana changed what it touched but left everything else alone. However, dimensional broken mana had already proven that it was unusual in a wide variety of ways—and it also made sense for dimensional mana to ignore things like distance in a way other mana types might not. Alice felt like this idea was a bit of a stretch, but for the sake of proper analysis, she had still included it in her ideas list.

Since Alice had only seen dimensional mana a few times so far, she wasn't sure which of the three theories was correct. It was also possible that all three were wrong and Alice was overlooking something.

Either way, Alice was eager to finally put it to the test. Since the broken mana part of dimensional mana was what made it so dangerous, Alice needed to have an idea of what caused broken dimensional mana to form before she could start really studying it.

Figuring out how dimensional broken mana worked might also help Alice protect herself against any Society teleportation in the future—and whatever was causing the Society to freak out. So there was a lot more than just Alice's curiosity at stake right now.

After Alice used {Seeds of Ambition} to create a new dimensional seed, she waited a few hours for her new magic seed to form some mana. Then she informed Ethan that she was going to be experimenting with dimensional mana, in case she messed up and created a problem that Ethan needed to help resolve. Even though Alice didn't think she would mess up that badly, there was no sense in taking risks with other people's lives. Having someone to watch over her tests and step in if something went wrong was a good idea when using something as dangerous as dimensional mana, even though {Safety Analysis} had already claimed that the tests she wanted to run were probably fine.

After Alice outlined the tests she wanted to perform and her reasoning, Ethan gave her the green light to start. He brought her to one of the testing rooms in the mansion, which was already enchanted to keep broken mana contained. After that, he settled into a comfortable-looking seat while Alice started her test.

The first thing Alice tried was opening a small portal between two spots in the room, just to observe what happened.

Alice quickly realized that opening a portal was much harder than she had thought it would be.

When she tried to use dimensional mana, it felt like she was trying to pry apart a steel mesh using her mana. She had imagined that opening a portal would be as easy as using other types of magic, but this felt more like a fight against reality. Alice pulled her mana back. What was this resistance based on? Did the size of the portal change how hard it was to open? The shape? The distance between each end of the portal?

Alice started running a few smaller tests. The conclusion she came to was that the size of the portal *and* the distance both changed the difficulty of opening a portal. A smaller portal was easier to open, and a portal with a smaller distance between each end was also easier to open. The bigger and longer distance a portal became, the harder and more expensive it was to open.

For her further tests, Alice decided to stick with thumb-size portals that only teleported things a few centimeters. It was the most cost-effective way to handle her tests, at least for now. Once she got her first portal open and then tossed a pen from one side to the other, she realized something else. The portal didn't take any extra mana to actually teleport things. Portals cost quite a bit to open and had a small maintenance cost—but they cost nothing to use. The portal also didn't seem to have any kind of delay between an object teleporting through it. In fact, if she stuck a pen halfway through the portal, she would end up with a pen that looked like it had been split in half. She absently wondered what would happen if she closed the portal right now. Would the pen get cut in half, as though split by a sword? Would the pen get *ripped* in half, flinging both sides of the pen in opposite directions? Or would something else happen? Alice decided not to try it, since {Safety Analysis} gave her a few minor warning signals when she thought about it.

The second thing Alice noticed was the broken mana. After a few minutes of observation, Alice decided that both her first and second hypotheses were probably correct. When Alice created a mana filter to let air pass through the portal *without* any accompanying mana, the mana on the other side of the portal still turned into dimensional broken mana after a few seconds. The same thing occurred when mana passed through a portal with no accompanying air. In short, both mana and air could act as a virulent form of broken dimensional mana—once something passed through the portal, it would start spreading broken dimensional mana for several seconds until the object returned to normal.

Alice mused that if one made a longer-range portal, the difference in air pressure would probably accelerate the process of air molecules passing through the portal, causing one side to suddenly break out into a massive flood of broken dimensional mana. Any countermeasures taken to handle the normal spread of broken dimensional mana would probably have to be adjusted based on a variety of factors, such as air pressure, distance, and several other things. The tragedy of Allenheim had probably happened because people failed to take this into account, although Alice was ultimately just guessing. Meanwhile, even if Alice created a massive difference in mana concentration on each end of her portal, it didn't cause mana to flood through the portal. In other words, unlike air, mana didn't seem to react to pressure differences at all—which kind of confused Alice, but she decided to just accept it at face value for now.

After testing what actually caused the mana in the air to turn into dimensional broken mana, Alice moved on to chucking more normal objects through the portal, to see what happened. Alice was vaguely hoping to find some objects that didn't become sources of broken mana after passing through a portal. If she could find a material that didn't turn infectious, she would learn a lot more about *why* objects became problematic after teleportation.

First, Alice tried tossing a few copper paupers through the portal, to see if they ALSO infected the air around them with dimensional broken mana.

Alice quickly confirmed that, for some reason, some coins would start infecting the air around them with dimensional broken mana, while other coins did not.

Alice had no idea what the difference was. Her first guess was that maybe some of the coins had different metal contents and that somehow influenced which coins started spewing broken dimensional mana. So she tried standardizing her tests by using a few pieces of pure iron that Ethan had lying around from some centuries-old enchanting project he had started and then forgotten about.

After Alice tried tossing those through the portal, they also seemed to have a completely random chance of infecting the mana around them with dimensional broken mana.

Standardizing how long the pieces of pure iron were exposed to the portals still resulted in seemingly random results. Changing how hard she threw the pieces of iron through the portal didn't change the randomness of her results. Changing the amount of mana they were exposed to *still* produced random results.

Throwing the *same piece of iron* through the portal over and over again had random results. There was no consistent pattern—i.e., it starts breaking mana every third throw—or anything to that effect. It was more like randomly rolling the dice anytime something passed through the portal. The more Alice thought about her tests, the more deeply confused she felt. Especially after she noticed something even *more* odd.

Only whole objects were impacted by her tests. A piece of pure iron was either entirely infectious or entirely noninfectious. Every single piece would either infect mana or fail to do so—even if it was cut into much smaller pieces right after it became "infectious." Alice suspected that she would observe the same thing even if she somehow cut the iron down into individual molecules. She had no idea *why* this was happening, though. It didn't seem to make any sense.

Eventually, Alice tried banging her head against the plates of pure iron before throwing them through the portal. She didn't think that would actually give her any new information, she was just frustrated after an hour of testing that seemed to produce totally random results.

Predictably, banging her head against the metal before throwing it through the portal also produced seemingly random test results.

At this point, Alice decided to seek outside help. She looked at Ethan, in hopes that maybe he could figure out what she was doing wrong.

Ethan gave her an unhelpful shrug. Alice felt tempted to scream into a pillow for a few minutes but pushed down the urge.

She tried several more things, but no matter what she attempted, she just couldn't figure out what rules actually governed dimensional broken mana production. The one and only consistent result she got was that it seemed random.

Not to mention, cleaning up all the broken mana in the area so that she could get a clear view of what was happening was becoming quite irritating. Anything that passed through a portal had around a 40 percent chance of becoming infectious, and only returned to normal anywhere from two seconds to two minutes afterward. The duration of an item's infectivity was *also* random, but at this point, Alice was growing numb to the utter incomprehensibleness of the whole thing.

After another twenty minutes of testing things with a portal the size of her thumb, Alice ran out of dimensional mana, and all she'd learned was that she had a headache.

Was this what the physicists who discovered quantum physics had felt like?

"Find anything interesting?" asked Ethan.

Alice was about to seriously answer the question before she realized that Ethan's voice had a rather playful edge to it. Instead of responding, she gave him her best intimidating glare. Ethan actually laughed.

"Don't worry. If dimensional mana was easy to study, other countries would have lifted the ban on dimensional mana studies years ago. The fact that the ban has lasted as long as it has is proof of how complex and unusual its behavior is."

Alice didn't feel any better at all after Ethan's words. Just because other people had failed to solve a mystery didn't mean that she felt better after spending over an hour to get no useful information.

She decided to take her mind off her unsuccessful first foray into dimensional mana experimentation by looking at her System notifications. Of course, she first converted all her mana into appropriate classes, to make sure she didn't lose any of her hard-earned levels, or face external influences on her personality. She got a couple attributes from the tests as well as a few scattered levels, which was *something*, at least.

You have leveled up!
Scientist: 60→62, Scholar: 58→60

Sadly, despite doing an entirely new experiment, as well as benefiting from Ethan's mother's boost, Alice still didn't get enough XP for another level of [Explorer of Magic].

Alice also noticed, with some concern, that there was now a fair amount of [Dimensional Mage] mana floating around inside her body. Luckily, after a few minutes of worrying, Alice realized that even though her [Dimensional Mage] mana wasn't sticking to any nearby class seeds, unlike all the other mana she had gathered while leveling up her classes, it was still similar to [Explorer of Magic]. Or at least, she hoped it was. It *might* be possible to just . . . convert it into [Explorer of Magic] mana, even though Alice had noticed it was hard to convert mana into other types of mana that were highly dissimilar.

After a quick confirmation with {Safety Analysis}, Alice tried something new. She started using her filtration magic seed to whittle away at the [Dimensional Mage] mana by converting it into [Explorer of Magic] mana. Even though the efficiency was horrible and half of the mana vanished into thin air, Alice managed to successfully convert one type of mana into another.

Alice sighed and kneaded her forehead in a mixture of frustration and relief. She was no closer to understanding this madness than before, but at the very least further experimentation wasn't a risk to her health or her mind. Unfortunately, even post–mana filtration, Alice was *still* stuck at the same level in [Explorer of Magic]. She was finally starting to understand why so many people struggled to reach Immortality. The penalty to leveling speed after level seventy-five was *brutal.*

Then, as Alice was thinking about the way she had converted [Dimensional Mage] mana into [Explorer of Magic] mana, an idea hit her. It wasn't related to her own status screen—instead, she started thinking about all the problems caused by the disappearance of the System.

Currently, it was a huge problem if people got more class mana, because their class seeds were getting clogged up. But what if Alice could create an enchantment out of her filtration mana that solved this problem?

Alice could turn [Dimensional Mage] mana into [Explorer of Magic] mana. With some hard work, she could make an enchantment to do the same thing.

This would create ways to actually resolve problems for the citizens of this world. Right now, her best solution was to block off environmental mana, but that also meant people couldn't level up and grow. A filtration ring would remove this problem. Even better, this would make one ring capable of keeping smaller communities safe, thus meaning each ring could cover far more ground than one mana-blocking ring.

After all, people didn't need to have any problematic mana wiped out immediately. Most people could probably last a few months before class mana became a problem. If Alice's idea worked out, people might just be able to wear a [Farmer] ring once a month to get all their pending levels, clear out the mana harming their mind, and then get back to work in the fields. Not only would it solve all the health problems associated with too much buildup of the wrong mana type, but it would also let people keep leveling up, AND it would take far fewer resources and much less time than making a mana-blocking ring for everyone in Illvaria.

The mana-blocking rings would still probably be better choices for young children, since the System restricted children from gaining access to their classes until the age of six, but at the very least, adults would have a way to progress safely again.

Of course, Alice also realized that she would run into a few problems if she wanted to implement her new idea.

First, all enchantments needed three things: a power source (usually a monster core), a material that could contain instructions that an enchanter programmed into the material, and, finally, an [Enchanter] with the right magic seed to bring everything together.

Power sources weren't that hard to find—even spidercrabs had monster cores packed to the brim with mana. Sure, they wouldn't be attuned to the right type of mana, meaning the enchantment would wear out faster—but that wasn't a huge problem. Even if people needed to replace the rings more often, they would still work just as well to keep them safe.

However, the other two things would still be major problems. Alice had no idea where to find materials that could memorize filtration mana instructions, and Alice was also the only filtration mana mage that she knew of.

Alice frowned. Just because she was the only mage with a filtration seed didn't mean that was an ironclad law of the universe. Cecilia already understood a lot of Alice's experiments and research. If she spent several days helping Cecilia learn about filtration mana, Cecilia could probably form a filtration magic seed. Come to think of it, Cecilia was also training several mages on how to form a pure mana magic seed. Those mages had [Enchanter] classes, an open seed slot, and a willingness to work with Alice and Cecilia. Perhaps she could get them to form filtration magic seeds instead of pure mana magic seeds?

Admittedly, the fact that they had never seen or heard of filtration mana before today would make it far harder for them to conceptualize and build the magic seeds, compared to pure mana magic seeds, which were already well-known, even if they were uncommon. However, that wasn't an unresolvable issue.

It was something worth trying, at least. She made a mental note to let Cecilia know about her new idea and then walked over to Ethan to discuss her failed dimensional mana experiments and her new request to look for weird enchanting materials. Maybe some [Adventurers] or [Enchanters] could scrounge something up that worked with filtration mana. It was worth a shot.

Alice now had yet another project to work on. And this one might actually be a game-changer that started solving the problem, instead of just mitigating damage. It was nice to know that she had gotten something out of her dimensional mana experiments besides a massive headache.

Chapter 13

After spending several seconds thinking about her new idea to resolve class mana, Alice took a moment to settle her new perk from [Scholar]. After all, she had reached level sixty in the class during her broken mana experiments—it was time to get a new perk.

Alice scanned her new perk and perk combination options.

After a few moments, she felt a flicker of disappointment.

She had been hoping that one of her new perk choices or combinations would help her restore the System and its mana, or help her with enchanting. After all, Alice's new idea for a ring enchantment was far more complex than the previous enchantments she had created. Having a perk that made the process easier would have gone a long way toward speeding up production.

Unfortunately, she didn't find any perks that directly impacted her enchanting or her experiments with System mana. That didn't mean her perk combinations were devoid of good options—just that none of them met her two most critical needs. Alice sighed and checked back over her perk combination options. Finally, she decided to sacrifice {Delve Into the Arcane} and {Enhanced Memory} for a new perk.

Delve Into the Arcane **Requirements: Scholar level 50 or higher, Magic 150 or higher, Intelligence 100 or higher, some sort of perk that gives you the ability to learn information, rarity-eight or higher achievement related to magic and research**
If you have spent at least an hour learning about magic within the past twenty-four hours, your mana regeneration rate is increased by 100 percent (this multiplier takes effect AFTER accounting for all other perks you have that multiplies mana regeneration, working multiplicatively instead of additively).

Alice had leaned into {Delve Into the Arcane} to help fuel the mana she needed for her experiments for quite a while, and to some extent, she still relied on it. In fact, considering the fact that she spent eight hours a day reading while she was asleep, she found it easier than ever to trigger the perk's activation conditions.

However, she was also starting to run into limitations on how useful mana regeneration was. Right now, her biggest limitations weren't mana-based—they were limitations imposed by her lack of knowledge and research time, or limitations on perk uses. {Broken Seed}, for example, could only be used every four days, and {Seeds of Ambition} could only be used once a month. Right now, Alice had several magic seeds she wanted to try forming and no way to make them all quickly.

Therefore, even though losing {Delve Into the Arcane} would sting, it was a bearable loss. And the text Alice had seen for her new perk combination seemed promising enough that she was willing to lose the perk.

The other perk Alice was losing was much less of a struggle.

<table>
<tr><td>

Enhanced Memory
Requirements: Scholar level 5 or higher, Intelligence 100 or greater

</td></tr>
<tr><td>

Greatly improves your ability to remember information.

</td></tr>
</table>

As for {Improved Memory}, {Photographic Memory} was simply a much better version of the same perk. Alice felt absolutely nothing at the prospect of losing it and probably wouldn't even notice that it was gone.

So, without further hesitation, Alice combined the perks into something new.

<table>
<tr><td>

Perk Naaaame: Delve_Memories
Perk costs: Delve Into the Arcane + Improved Memory
Perk_Synergy detected: Sleep Reading

</td></tr>
<tr><td>

Vastly improved understanding while using remembering. Can level, analyze, and improve magic better.
Synergy detected_ Sleep Reading.
Add_Text Synergy.

</td></tr>
</table>

Ah yes, the ever-enlightening "Add_text synergy," Alice thought sarcastically. Even with the help of display mana, she had no idea what half of the perk's text *meant*.

Fortunately, this time, the System didn't leave her perk in a *totally* incomprehensible state. As if sensing Alice's puzzlement, the perk started to shift around until the least understandable part of the text—the "Add_Text Synergy"—resolved itself into clearer words. It still looked like an English teacher's worst nightmare, but at least Alice could understand what it was supposed to say.

<table>
<tr><td>

Perk Naaaame: Delve_Memories
Perk costs: Delve Into the Arcane + Improved Memory
Perk_Synergy detected: Sleep Reading

</td></tr>
</table>

Vastly improved understanding while using remembering. Can level, analyze, and improve magic better.

While {Sleep Reading}, can use objects you remember. Leveling speed improved by Get_Number while sleep reading. Experiments and enchantments very accurate while sleep.

As her perk rewrote itself in front of her eyes, Alice also took the opportunity to observe what the System mana inside of her body was doing.

The chunks of the System that were still active in her [Scholar] class fractal had started breaking down and rearranging themselves. As she watched, {Intuitive Magic Modeling} caught sight of a new type of mana, operating purely within her class seeds. She wasn't entirely sure what type of mana it was, but as far as she could tell it was something like meaning mana, or perhaps correction mana. It felt like it leaned a bit into both of those concepts—almost as if it was capable of correcting information from display mana, but also like it was meant to interact with something else on a deeper level.

Alice was reminded of the fact that people were normally able to read their perks without help, no matter what language they spoke. Alice herself had been able to read her System screen the moment she arrived in this world, despite not speaking a single local language. But ever since the System collapsed, unless Alice used her display mana, all she saw when looking at perk options was a glitched-out System box that said, "Perk Selection:——(missing entry)." This pushed things in the exact opposite direction—instead of *everyone* being able to read a System message no matter what, *no one* could read a System message. Perhaps whatever the System was using to make itself understood had vanished along with the collapse of the System, and that was why perk-selection screens were glitched out?

In addition, Alice realized that the fake System messages she could create using display mana didn't contain any sort of auto-translate feature. Alice could create System messages in English or Illvarian, but if someone who spoke a different language appeared in front of her, she would have no way to make her display mana fix their bugged perk-selection screen. The System could ignore language boundaries, but Alice couldn't. That was an obvious sign that she was missing something.

Perhaps this new mana type filled in the gaps that she had been missing? It was something to test next time she could make a new magic seed. Unfortunately, Alice had no way to get more magic seed slots right now.

After she finished selecting her new perk, she turned toward Ethan, who hadn't moved since Alice had started messing with her status screen.

"Thank you for watching over me while I tested things," said Alice.

"That's what I'm here for," said Ethan. "Besides, as much as I think it's unlikely that you'll blow yourself up or recreate the tragedy of Allenheim in my basement, there's no sense in tempting fate."

Alice nodded. "I had a new idea about how to potentially address the collapse of the System. I believe I already mentioned how I was using filtration mana to correct my class seeds. I've started thinking that maybe this can be reproduced on a larger scale, perhaps using enchantments. If we could create a few rings that can filter class mana for people, we could resolve the class-mana issue with some level of efficiency. Even more importantly, people can survive with some personality corruption for a while—meaning that one ring could help dozens of people." Alice started detailing her idea for how to automate the mana-filtration process as they walked toward the exit. Ethan nodded along as Alice discussed the problems that needed to be solved for her plan to work, as well as the potential benefits. Once she was done talking, Ethan grinned.

"It's a good idea, and it has a reasonable chance of working if we can figure out solutions to the problems you mentioned. Since you need an enchanting material that can record instructions from filtration mana, I'll look into any mysterious enchanting materials that people have found over the years. There might be something that reacts with System mana that someone has lying around in their shop inventory or something. I'll also see if anyone has access to an enchanting perk that lets them create the kind of material you need. It'll take some time, but I'll see what I can find," he said as the two of them climbed the stairs.

With their conversation finished, Alice thanked Ethan again before she went to her room to take a nap and play with her new perk. Since it synergized with {Sleep Reading}, Alice wanted to see if anything had changed while using the {Sleep Reading} perk. It didn't take her long to fall asleep.

Within her dream, Alice returned to her usual dream library. However, unlike before, the dream library had a new addition to it. It was a giant room filled with every enchanting material Alice had ever interacted with.

Alice grinned.

Perhaps she had been too pessimistic when she lamented the lack of enchantment-boosting perks during her [Scholar] perk selection.

Alice strode toward the new room. At the same time, another memory bubbled up. An idea on top of an idea.

There had been a few times, recently, where Alice had wondered if she wasn't using her {Sleep Reading} ability to its full potential. However, with the System's collapse, she hadn't found time to experiment with her perk more. She had spent almost every moment in her dream library looking up information that she felt would be useful to her or Cecilia. She had learned a lot about pure mana, and how it could be used to filter other kinds of mana, as well as historical records of changes the System had made over the years.

However, now that Alice had her new enchanting room added to her dream library, and had had the issue brought to her attention once more, she started to think about what her new perk did and the ways she might have been failing to use her old perk.

She pulled up the description for {Sleep Reading} again, to see if she had missed something.

<table>
<tr><td>

Sleep Reading
Perk costs: Lesser Reduced Sleep Requirement + Super Speed-Reading

</td></tr>
<tr><td>

Any time you are asleep, so long as you are close to or touching a book and have permission to read it from the owner of that book, you may read it in your dreams. This will not affect your sleep, meaning you will still be fully rested after a night of sleep, and all the speed and comprehension bonuses offered previously by {Super Speed-Reading} will still apply while you are asleep.
Note: Any books stored in any storage perks you have are considered touching you at all times for the purposes of this perk.

</td></tr>
</table>

She squinted at every single letter of text and rubbed her chin in thought.

Now that she was explicitly looking for exploits, she started to realize that there really might be a few things she could do with this perk that weren't explicitly outlined.

So far, she had used this perk to gather background information and data as efficiently as possible. But what if she used her dream library as a brainstorming area?

Her perk specified that she could read books in her dreams, but it was also obvious that the perk actively let her lucid dream as much as she wanted to. After all, Alice had imagined up this giant, comfortable library, and the perk let her walk around in the space to pick up books and look at them, even though that wasn't explicitly reading. She could even drink a nice cup of tea and conjure up a few snacks if she wanted to. The perk didn't seem to stop her from doing things like that.

What if she took that even further? What if she went on an enchanting spree in her dreams? In the first place, Alice had taken the {Blueprint} perk at level ten for [Careful Enchanter]. She looked up the description for {Blueprint} again to see if she could do anything with it while asleep.

<table>
<tr><td>

Blueprint
Requirements: Careful Enchanter level 10 or higher, Intelligence 150 or higher

</td></tr>
<tr><td>

You may create up to three different blueprints in your memory by carefully imagining each enchanting material you wish to add to the enchantment and then imagining what kind of instruction you wish to add to each enchanting material.
You will be able to get some sense of how well the enchantment will work in practice—and you will also be less likely to make mistakes when making a physical copy of a blueprint if you spend a larger amount of time on making the item.
Note: You can freely delete old blueprints, but some amount of mental taxation will occur. Frequent use may cause headaches or migraines, so it is advised not to delete blueprints too frequently.

</td></tr>
</table>

Alice nodded thoughtfully to herself.

She felt that she could probably have also been brainstorming and using some other perks during the time she spent asleep.

Of course, now that she could see enchanting materials in her sleep, she could do experiments even while she slept.

She looked at the new enchanting room and grinned.

She didn't know exactly what materials she would be working with when she tried to make her mana-filtering rings, since right now Alice had no knowledge of any enchanting materials that could work with System mana. Her new perk specified that it would only let her interact with materials she *remembered*. Meaning that she needed to have had contact with an enchanting material first.

However, she was pretty sure she could design new enchantments in her dreams now using materials she had already had contact with. If she liked a particular design, she could save it into her {Blueprint} perk, making it easier to replicate in reality. She could probably also test what new materials were capable of in her dreams. Her new perk also implied that she would now have a boosted leveling speed in her dreams, making it easier to get new perks and making the whole process even easier.

Alice took a step into her new dream enchanting workshop and took a few materials off the wall. Just as she had expected, they behaved exactly like they did in real life—leaving her free to mess with materials and practice enchanting as she pleased.

Even better, while she was asleep, she didn't seem to be spending any of her real mana on the enchanting experiments. She would have to wake up to check if she really was leveling up her enchanting classes efficiently this way, but at least so far, Alice was pretty sure she had hit the jackpot with her new perk.

She just needed to find a material that could use filtration mana and she could put her class-rings idea into practice. She now had an easy and efficient way to test new materials.

Alice felt herself getting more and more excited as she started messing with her enchanting materials, and in the span of a few minutes, got lost in her work.

Illa Weissarus stepped down from her ship and onto the dock with a sigh. The news that she had come across as she was sailing toward Metsel was *not* promising. All the passengers that had boarded the boat were discussing strange things— things like the System making mistakes. More recently, they were talking about [Willpower] training, or the [Priests] of the Church of the System going mad, among other things. The closer she got to Metsel, the more people seemed to have heard similar, equally troubling rumors.

Illa was usually skilled at picking out which information was accurate and which was worthless. Ever since she had started delving into politics, it had become something of a necessity. However, she usually picked out useful information by comparing it to what she already knew and figuring out what made sense. Right now . . . nothing made sense.

People were scared, and a strange tension hung in the air. However, pulling useful information out of the whirlpool of anxiety and rumors was hard to do.

Illa dearly hoped that was simply because [Messengers] hadn't reached most parts of the kingdom yet. If there was *no* official news, it would imply that the ruling estates of Illvaria didn't understand the problem—which was even more terrifying than the notion of a catastrophe befalling the nation.

She strolled through the streets of the little dock town she had landed in before she decided to spend a few hours chatting with some patrons in a tavern. Drunk people passed information far more easily than people who were sober, after all.

She took a few steps into the first decent-looking tavern she saw and spent a few moments relaxing as the nostalgic scent of alcohol hit her nose. She wondered how long it had been since she last stepped into a tavern. She had used to go out with a few friends every week during her time in the army, whenever they could sneak away from the barracks for a few hours. However, once she transitioned from the front lines to politics, she had never found the time to just sit in a tavern and relax the way she used to.

"Hello there, Lady Mage!" said a [Waiter] after she took a seat near the center of the room. It was harder to notice the strain in his voice than it had been with some other people, but Illa could still detect an edge to his demeanor that most professionals wouldn't normally show. "What can I get for you?"

"A mug of ale, please," Illa said as she pushed away her nostalgia. She was here to learn, not to reminisce.

The [Waiter] quickly got her a mug of ale, and Illa felt a little bit of the stress and frustration melt away after taking a few sips of cheap-tasting swill. It tasted foul. Which, frankly, was what Illa preferred if she was drinking alcohol. The point of drinking was to get drunk, not to taste good.

After that, Illa simply settled down to relax and listen in on conversations. Luckily, unlike the scattered, ambiguous information she had collected during her journey north, the people this close to the capital seemed to have much better information.

"—say that the church is trying to raise people's [Willpower]. If your [Willpower] is too low compared to . . . something about ambient mana, or something, your personality will start to get warped by your classes. Not sure what the heck anyone means by 'ambient mana,' since they don't seem to be talking about the pure mana in the air around us, but I don't like the idea of my personality—"

"—heard that the apprentice of Honored Immortal Ethan discovered it. I heard she was a combat mage, but I didn't really pay much attention. The guy who claimed she was a combat mage must have been drunk. She's clearly a researcher, if she found—"

"—Society is openly at war with the Shil Confederacy! They *have* to be, with the way they're openly attacking people!"

"—something about perks is wrong. All my perks just look like error messages when I go to the perk-selection screen. My daughter got her first couple achievements last weekend when I brought her and a few of her friends to kill some spidercrabs, and they didn't get the stat boost they should have! With both perks and achievements getting weird—"

"—and the high [Priest] of the System church collapsed, or so they say. Hasn't seen anyone since—"

"—[Farmer] Edmund hasn't spoken with anyone since yesterday. He just keeps throwing seeds onto the ground over and over again. It's the wrong season to sow seeds, and I know for a fact he isn't high enough level to ignore seasons yet. I can't tell if this is some sort of version of the personality-warping the . . . uhh . . . 'ambient class mana' stuff causes, but something's wrong with his head right now. Maybe if we get him to a church—"

Illa spent nearly two hours collecting conversation fragments and stringing information together before she got a solid idea of what was happening.

It seemed that the System was truly collapsing, at least in some limited way. The Church of the System had mixed responses to the crisis, but it looked like at least *somebody* knew what was going on and was trying to organize a response to it.

And the more she listened, the more Illa was certain that the person who understood this madness was her former apprentice, Alice.

Illa grinned as she finished up her last tankard of ale, paid, and left to continue moving toward the capital.

Chapter 14

Alice woke up from her nap with an excited grin and spent several seconds thinking about what she had learned during her experiments in her dream library.

She'd spent the first few hours getting used to how the dream library enchanting workshop operated—what she could do in it, the best way to test new enchantments, and so on. During that time, she had made several discoveries.

It hadn't been immediately obvious, but as Alice continued to test things out, she noticed that she understood things *better* when she spent a few moments reflecting on them after reading them. That had always been the case, of course—but the difference was far more extreme than before. Previously, reflecting on something she had just learned might improve Alice's understanding a bit as she tried to connect this knowledge to her previous base of knowledge—but now it felt like adding a supercomputer to her thinking process. She could learn things several times faster and more efficiently when she reflected, compared to what she learned in the moment.

In addition, while thinking about experiments she had recently done, she would get certain instincts and flashes of insight that she wouldn't normally have about what the answer was, which had proven exceptionally useful when trying to figure out which enchanting materials she wanted to pay more attention to.

Unfortunately, her newly improved understanding and instincts still couldn't help her figure out what the heck was up with dimensional mana, which made Alice wonder whether it worked in a way similar to quantum physics—it might actually *be* random.

{Delve_Memories}, or whatever the perk was really called, was a useful boost to Alice's comprehension and her experiments, and she was happy to have it.

After Alice got used to using her new perk, she had knuckled down and focused on material testing. Cecilia had already retrieved most of her shop's inventory, and before Alice had gone to sleep, Cecilia had lent all her miscellaneous enchanting materials to Alice in case one of them proved useful. As a result, Alice had been able to try out a few things during her dream workshop experiments. Those tests had mixed results. Unfortunately, Alice hadn't found any materials that synergized with filtration mana. However, she *had* found a few chunks of tree bark that accepted instructions from display mana. The material clearly wasn't the optimal material for handling display mana, since Alice got a strange feeling that the material was resisting her attempts to inject display mana into it—but even if it wasn't a perfect conductor, it still worked. That was good enough for her.

The material in question was a gray-colored type of tree bark that Cecilia had acquired back in Cyra.

Alice hadn't originally been focused on display mana. After all, filtration mana was what could actually solve the class-mana madness—it was clearly the priority. However, during her time in the dream library, Alice had realized that display mana was also surprisingly useful. Right now, Alice was personally assisting all the mages Cecilia was training during their perk-selection process. This was workable for now but wasn't really a good long-term solution. Furthermore, if Cecilia managed to increase the number of [Enchanters] who were working with them, Alice would eventually run into time and energy limitations.

Those [Enchanters] were critical to helping with relief efforts, so the training of new [Enchanters] couldn't be stopped. However, Alice also needed to spend as little time and mana on them as possible. Display mana rings were an obvious and useful solution.

That was the only major discovery Alice had from her first night of testing, but discoveries weren't the only thing she had gained. Spending several hours knee-deep in enchanting materials and blueprints had also given her some [Careful Enchanter] mana.

Not only could she learn new things by testing enchanting materials in her dreams, but she was getting XP for it—and at a much faster rate than when she was awake. The boost was probably somewhere between a 50 percent and 100 percent XP boost—likely due to a mixture of her new perk's influence and the fact that she didn't have to pay attention to mana expenditure while she was dreaming.

It had even been enough to tip [Careful Enchanter] up to the next level, despite the fact that she had only put in one night of work.

You have leveled up!
Careful Enchanter: 29→30

Her progress had also brought Alice up to another perk level. Alice briefly considered grabbing a new perk immediately before she decided to ask Ethan for advice. After all, she might need her new perk to help her compensate for the lack of enchanting materials, or boost her speed, or do something completely different depending on the situation. She could also ask Cecilia where she had gotten the tree bark so they could find more.

She headed for Cecilia's room, where she found the other girl sitting at her desk, buried in paperwork.

Alice tried not to chuckle at the sight. Ever since the collapse of the System and the start of the pure mana mage project, Cecilia had nearly as much paperwork to manage per day as Ethan. [Mathematicians] and [Data Analysts] could only work their way through so much of the information, and since Alice and Cecilia were the only two who could pore over the data and figure out what was important, Cecilia had taken on a role similar to an [Assistant] for Alice. Alice really appreciated her friend helping her deal with organization and paperwork, but the sight of Cecilia sitting at her desk poring over papers was also one she found endlessly amusing.

Alice spent a few moments grinning to herself before she stepped into the room.

"Cecilia, do you have a moment?" she asked.

Cecilia quickly put down a document and turned toward Alice.

"I can spare a few minutes," said Cecilia, quietly shoving her paperwork as far away from her as possible.

"Do you remember a certain kind of enchanting material that you had in your shop in Cyra? It's something you gave me last night—a kind of ashy bark that was heavier than it looked. Do you know where you got those pieces of tree bark?"

Cecilia frowned. "Can you describe them in more detail? There are a lot of enchanting materials that fit that description."

"I have a better idea," Alice said after a few moments of thought. "Can I just share the memory of the item I want?"

"Sure."

Alice grabbed Cecilia's wrist and shoved the memory of the bark she wanted into Cecilia's mind.

Cecilia pondered this for a few moments and sighed. "I bought it from a few [Adventurers] who were scavenging in an area near the outskirts of Cyra. They asked me if I wanted more, but I didn't end up buying more than a few samples. My perks claimed that the materials were good with informational mana, so I thought they might be interesting—more importantly, they were cheap. I never actually found a good use for it; my magic seeds aren't very compatible. I was planning to sell it for a markup in Metsel, but no one bought it." Cecilia pouted a bit at that. "I can give you the rest of what I have, but I can't get more unless we find those [Adventurers]. Since they lived in Cyra and not Metsel . . . that might be a problem."

"It was from near Cyra, you say?" said Alice, frustrated. Shipments from Cyra to Metsel happened pretty regularly—it only took a week of travel by boat, and enchanting materials were lucrative. That was one of the biggest reasons the recolonization effort was happening in the first place—the higher density of enchanting materials there.

Unfortunately, shipments of materials were easy to come by in normal times, and times were far from normal right now.

Worse, it didn't sound like Cyra even had a stable source of the bark she wanted. It would take a lot of effort to get a proper supply line going, and Alice wasn't sure how long that would take or what unexpected problems would crop up.

Still, Alice desperately needed access to enchanting materials. Even if a display mana ring was a lower priority than filtration mana enchantments, it was also much simpler to set up and could help people mitigate the immediate aftershocks of the System collapse. As long as people could choose perks again, Alice suspected that all sorts of people would start to invent their own solutions to at least some of the problems Illvaria would soon experience.

She sighed. Since it seemed unlikely that she would have access to renewable quantities of that particular bark in the near future, she would need to ask Ethan if he had any solutions. If he had a way to copy the properties of the bark or knew of a different material she could use, that would work out. If he didn't, Alice might instead need to see if her new perk choices from [Careful Enchanter] offered some sort of solution.

"Help me get those few chunks of bark, please. I need them," said Alice.

"Just ask one of the [Guards] where my shop inventory is and tell them to get the contents of the sixth green box," said Cecilia. "The bark is in there, along with a few other enchanting materials. The bark should be in the fourth compartment. I labeled them."

"Got it," said Alice. It was quick work to get a [Guard] to retrieve the enchanting materials she wanted, and then she made her way to Ethan's study.

"Illa Weissarus?" asked Ethan. "You mean the retired [Warmage] who taught Alice before she moved to Metsel?"

Naturally, Ethan had done an in-depth investigation of Illa's past after he had taken in Alice as an apprentice. He'd initially been rather familiar with Illa, since he had hoped that she would become another Immortal, but he'd stopped paying attention to her after she got married and went into politics. Everyone's choices were their own to make, but Ethan had always felt it was a shame the woman wasn't pushing toward Immortality anymore.

What he had *not* expected was for one of his [Spies] to let him know that Illa was now approaching his manor. What was Illa doing in Metsel? Given the collapse of the System, Ethan had assumed Illa would be busy putting out fires in her territory. Surely she had noticed the problems by now—Illa had always been competent. If the woman didn't even look after the land she was in charge of, why was she wasting her potential trying to found a barony?

Ethan realized that perhaps he was thinking about it incorrectly. The woman might have heard that there was more information in the capital and came here to collect data. Illa might even know that Alice was one of the bigger sources of information about the current crisis and perhaps she wanted firsthand information.

Although, if that was the case, Illa's arrival would be strangely timed. The System had collapsed barely a week ago, so Illa would have needed to start moving toward Metsel almost immediately after. Either Illa had a way to speed up her movement, or she was exceptionally good at sensing trouble and how to resolve it . . .

Ethan thought about it for a few moments, trying to figure out if Illa had ever had a reason to pick up a powerful movement-based perk, and then shrugged. Ultimately, it didn't really matter. She probably wanted to see her old apprentice. Ethan didn't see anything wrong with that, as long as Alice was willing to see Illa again. Illa might also want to see *him*, which he didn't mind, either. Ethan normally wouldn't make time to see a minor noble from southern Illvaria, but he was perfectly willing to make time for the former mentor of his current apprentice. Especially now that the System had collapsed—Illa's influence in the South might help quell some of the chaos there.

"If Illa stops by the manor, make sure she's who she claims she is. Have several people with lie-detection perks verify it, just in case a [Spy] or an [Organic Mage] is impersonating Illa," said Ethan, giving his [Spy] a nod. "If she is who she claims she is, I'm willing to see her."

"Understood, Honored Immortal," the [Spy] said before she left the room. A few moments later, the [Spy] moved around a corner and Ethan lost track of her.

Ethan quickly got back to his paperwork, until a few minutes later, when there were several knocks on the door.

He quickly activated {Pervasive Perception}, allowing him to see past most lower-level disguise perks and track nearby physical objects, and quickly confirmed that Alice was on the other side of the door.

"Come in," said Ethan.

Alice opened the door and gave Ethan a quick nod before she started speaking. "Ethan, do you have a few minutes? I had an idea for how to start the System-enchanting rings project I mentioned yesterday, but I ran into a few issues. I also want some advice on perk selection."

"What do you need?" asked Ethan, trying not to feel a little burst of excitement when Alice mentioned that she *already* had an idea for how to start.

When Alice had mentioned that she wanted to enchant rings with filtration mana, Ethan had thought it was a good idea. However, he hadn't expected her to find a way to implement the idea for quite a while; after all, doing tests and making new enchantments could take a team of lower-level researchers months, and even higher-level [Scholars] and [Scientists] would need weeks. Alice had even more obstacles in her way, because she was working with an unknown type of mana. For Alice to have made any progress at all in just a day was rather impressive.

When Alice had talked about her origins, Ethan had found it ludicrous that somebody could reach level seventy-five in less than a year. Now that he knew Alice better, he felt it would have been ludicrous if she *hadn't* reached this point within five years of her arrival.

"I found an enchanting material that can work with display mana. It isn't quite the filtration mana ring that I wanted to make, at least not yet. However, I did realize that there is another major area of concern that we need to address, which is letting people actually see what new perks they can take. This can allow people to reshape their build a little bit even while the System is down—which is critical for allowing people to adapt to the collapse of the System and allow the workforce of Illvaria to start managing the crisis on their own," said Alice. "The problem is acquiring more of the material . . ."

Alice quickly began detailing the conversation she had just had with Cecilia while Ethan nodded along in thought.

"I'm still assembling my own samples of enchanting materials. They should be ready in another day or two," said Ethan. "In the meantime . . . you say that the enchanting material comes from southern Illvaria? Specifically Cyra, the town run by Illa Weissarus?"

Alice nodded.

Ethan felt a grin tugging at his lips.

Illa just so happened to be in town right now. And Cecilia was apparently going to get a sample of the material that Alice needed, which would make it very easy for Illa to see what was needed and possibly help work out a supply route of some sort.

Ethan felt that all the puzzle pieces for how to solve the enchantment problem were assembling themselves right in front of his eyes.

Chapter 15

Honored Immortal Ethan, Lady Illa is at the door. She has requested to see you and her former student," said someone from outside Ethan's study, startling Alice out of her discussion with Ethan.

"Illa?" said Alice, suddenly feeling very confused. She wasn't sure why Illa would come to Metsel. Didn't she have a town to run?

Alice turned toward Ethan, but instead of explaining anything, Ethan just looked at her and grinned.

Alice glared at Ethan, and he burst into laughter. "You need to work on controlling your facial expressions, Alice. You're a bit too easy to read. Though I also admit, they are quite funny. To answer your unspoken question, yes, the woman outside is your mentor from Cyra. I haven't directly confirmed why she's here, but I assume it's due to the collapse of the System. She must have sensed something and has come here to ask you for more details." Ethan grinned. "There's a reason she lived through so many close scrapes in the military. She has good instincts. This time, it seems those instincts led right to you."

Alice mulled over Ethan's words. During her time in Cyra, she had proven how interested she was in mana and the System. Heck, Alice had explicitly told Illa about the achievement she had gotten for observing the interaction between attributes and mana. Even if Alice hadn't outright said she was studying the System, it wouldn't be very hard for Illa to put two and two together. The moment Illa caught wind of Alice's cooperation with the Church of the System, she would realize Alice knew something. From there, it made sense for Illa to come here. Illa had moved faster than seemed logical—but there were plenty of perks that might explain that.

"Are you willing to meet with her?" asked Ethan, breaking Alice out of her thoughts. "I think the meeting would be beneficial, but it's still your choice," he said. "I intend to speak with her, of course. I want to talk with her about her observations and ask her how she got here so quickly. But you can make your own decisions."

Alice thought about it. *Was* she willing to meet with Illa?

It would have been much harder for Alice to adapt to this world without Illa's intervention. She'd also been fair, if pragmatic, in her dealings with Alice—she had never left Alice in a situation she didn't understand. She was forthcoming about danger and benefit alike. She had even raised Alice's payment during the expedition to see the broken mana zone outside Cyra once it became clear that Alice was in more danger than expected.

"I'd be happy to see her again," said Alice after she finished thinking.

"Good," said Ethan, giving Alice a curious look. "Well, potentially good. Why did you agree? I was hoping you would say yes, but I still want to hear your reasoning."

"I was thinking about the potential for getting enchanting materials, and the fact that the previous cooperation I had with Illa turned out well. Illa is fair and easy to work with," said Alice. "She also has direct access to several southern trade routes, and she is located in the South. A lot of Illvaria's enchanting materials used to come from the South. Therefore, Illa is in a great position to supply us with enchanting materials, which I currently need. I know that you said that you would have a set of sample enchanting materials for me to work with tomorrow, but getting access to more raw materials faster and in larger quantities could be critical to halting damage from the crisis."

Ethan grinned so widely that he reminded Alice of the Cheshire cat. "I'm very glad that some of my lessons are sinking in."

Ethan notified a [Servant] to show Illa into the room. A short time later, Illa Weissarus was led into the room by a [Maid], who bowed at Ethan and departed. Illa gave Alice and Ethan curious glances.

"Honored Immortal Ethan," said Illa, giving Ethan a respectful nod. "I thank you for being willing to meet with me, and allowing me to see my old [Student]."

Then she turned back toward Alice, and Alice saw a brief moment of confusion on Illa's face, as if she wasn't quite sure how to address Alice now. Ultimately, she gave Alice a quick nod. "Lady Alice," said Illa. "I am glad to see that you are doing well." Then Alice saw a little bit of the pragmatism and bluntness that had characterized all her interactions with Illa fade away, and Illa gave her a cheeky grin. "Perhaps saying you're doing well is an understatement. Honored Immortal Ethan does not take in many apprentices per century, and I imagine that you've leveled quite significantly if you caught his attention. The way you sit is much more poised as well. Is your [Dexterity] simply much higher than before? Or have you taken some kind of {Etiquette} lessons?" Illa's grin widened. "Either way, quite impressive."

Alice felt a hint of pride as Illa mentioned her leveling progress and the strides she had made over the past six months. When she had left Cyra, her highest-level class had been level forty-seven. She had already felt decent about her progress at that time—after all, the average adult in Illvaria was somewhere between level forty and sixty. For Alice to reach the same level in only a few months was a testament to her hard work, even if she knew that a lot of her success came from the {Outworlder} achievement and her education from Earth.

However, Alice's status screen had grown leaps and bounds since the last time Illa had seen her.

Alice's highest-level class was now level seventy-eight. Level seventy-five was already considered the level of an elite craftsmen or warrior and was a level few people ever reached. It was only when seeing Illa again and thinking about her progress over the past several months that Alice could truly feel how much she had grown in a short six months. She had come a long way from being a scared teenager in the Illvarian forest.

Of course, as much as Alice was happy to see her levels steadily increasing, she also felt the urge to wince. Almost every action that Alice had taken recently fit her [Explorer of Magic] class like a glove. Despite that fact, she had only gained three levels in the class recently. If it had been before she reached level seventy-five, Alice was willing to bet she would have gained six or seven levels in [Explorer of Magic] instead of three. The stretch of levels between seventy-five and one hundred was going to be an incredible slog.

"I'm indeed doing very well," said Alice, pushing her thoughts aside as she smiled at Illa. Then, feeling just a little bit cheeky, she gave Illa a slightly more mischievous grin. Since Illa was dropping a bit of formality around her, it felt right to do the same. "I might even be at a higher level than you now." Then Alice laughed. "Thank you for all the work and time you put into training me when I was in Cyra and had no connections or abilities to fall back on."

Illa chuckled. "A sixteen-year-old who might be higher level than me . . . that would really be something." Then she shook her head. "We both benefited from your actions in Cyra. You don't need to thank me—your current state is a result of your own hard work and passion. I only served as a footnote in your efforts along the way."

Then the mirth slowly faded from her face. "Now, for the reason I came here. A little over a week ago, I got a very strange feeling, as if something important had vanished into thin air. Shortly after that, people started to notice oddities regarding their status screens. People couldn't read their new perks anymore, achievements started to incorporate strange glitch symbols into their words, and last I heard, there are also issues with mages forming new magic seeds." Illa frowned. "The last one is harder to verify, since there aren't that many mages forming new magic seeds on a daily basis. But I am greatly concerned by these changes." She squinted at Alice like a wolf eyeing its prey. "I would greatly appreciate more information, and I think you have it."

Alice glanced at Ethan, who simply gave her a curious look. Alice wondered why Ethan hadn't given her any suggestions. It took her a few moments before she realized Ethan was testing something. Perhaps he wanted to see how well she handled this interaction?

Or perhaps he wants to see how I handle negotiations in general, thought Alice, frowning. Illa had something that Alice needed. Illa had also come all this way to see Alice, so she certainly wanted the information Alice had.

Or at least, Illa *had* wanted that information. Alice and Ethan had gone to a decent amount of effort to get more people informed about the current state of affairs, and even if they weren't giving people all available information, they were still making a large part of Alice's research results available to everyone. Illa had likely already found some of this information during basic investigation into the city.

Alice resisted the urge to sigh. If Ethan *was* testing how well she tried to bargain with Illa, her position would definitely be weakened by these facts. Of course, Illa wouldn't give her a terrible deal—after all, Alice was confident in Illa's long-term planning abilities, and it was obvious that dealing with the current crisis was a priority for everyone. But that didn't mean it was fair to ask Illa to spend huge amounts of time and manpower helping to solve the current crisis without being compensated for her time and effort, either.

Alice sighed. She had been in a vastly inferior bargaining position the last time she was in Cyra, and almost all her deals with Illa had been from a bad negotiating position. Illa had still treated her fairly, but that didn't mean the same thing would happen here.

Now, she needed to bargain with her former mentor from a very different position. This was also the most free-form test Ethan had given her so far. Usually he asked her how she should respond to something and would then give her the answer right afterward. This time, she needed to do this on her own.

"I do, indeed, know quite a bit about the current situation. I'm in the midst of developing countermeasures for it at this very moment, in fact," said Alice. "For this, I would very much appreciate some help from you."

"Oh?" said Illa, sounding genuinely surprised. "What can I offer to the apprentice of an Immortal? I'm sure you have much better tutors available if you want training for magic or combat, and Immortal Ethan certainly has more resources than me when it comes to experiments . . ." Illa trailed off, giving Ethan a curious glance.

"I need enchanting materials. Specifically, I need a material with certain properties, but I haven't found anything suitable yet. I also want a specific kind of tree bark that Cecilia purchased in your town several months ago. Will you permit me to use a certain perk to share an image of what I'm looking for?"

Illa hesitated for a very long moment, eyeing both Alice and Ethan, before she nodded. Alice grabbed Illa's wrist and used {Shared Memories}. After a few moments of processing, Illa nodded at Alice, indicating that she could continue.

"As for the unknown enchanting material I need, I am looking for something compatible with a new type of mana I've been using. The mana type is . . . somewhat similar to pure mana, but it has a few different characteristics. It needs to work with filtration mana. Its similarity to pure mana gives us a starting point for searching, but there are a few differences as well . . ." Alice started describing what she perceived filtration mana to be and what she needed from her materials, while Illa nodded.

"So you want an enchanting material. I suppose that in exchange, you're willing to give me *real* information on whatever is happening to the System?" said Illa, giving Alice a grin.

Alice hesitated and then nodded. She couldn't give Illa ALL the information she had uncovered, but she could certainly share more.

"I'm afraid that's not good enough as a trade," said Illa. "I want to know more, but it's also obvious that you're taking efforts to spread this information far and wide. I would like a little bit more out of this deal. After all, you're asking me to tie up a bunch of my own funds and manpower to find weird enchanting materials. That'll be very expensive, and I need to keep my town intact through all this. Otherwise, there will be no point to this deal for me."

"I don't recall you having any [Enchanters] in the South since Cecilia left," said Alice, after some thought. "Meaning that a lot of the testing and enchantment-related perk usage will have to come from our end. You'll be using far less manpower than you claim you'll be spending on my task. Unless you've lured another [Enchanter] to your town who has information-related mana, or perks that let them gather the information we need?"

"I have found a replacement, yes," said Illa, grinning. "It cost me a pretty penny, as well as a sponsorship for one of the woman's children at a magic academy. However, since I have an [Enchanter], I would, indeed, be spending the time and resources on your task. If nothing else, she's going to need to sort through all the materials that MIGHT be useful. [Adventurers] tend to only be able to identify whether an item has enchanting potential or not—nothing more detailed than that. An [Enchanter] double-checking those materials will save you hours of work. Surely you see the need to compensate me for this?"

Alice tried to think. Illa probably still wanted information, and Alice could give her some valuable information that wasn't available to the public. But what else could she offer?

As if sensing Alice's thoughts, Illa leaned a little bit closer. "I'll tell you what I want," said Illa. "In addition to information, I want first priority for whatever you're making with your enchanting materials. I don't know *exactly* why you need them, but I'm pretty sure it's related to solving the current crisis. I want you to prioritize Cyra as the first town that gets access to these solutions the moment they're implemented."

Alice thought about it. That was . . . fair. Probably. Especially if Cyra turned into the main supplier for Alice's enchanting needs, keeping Cyra stable would ensure that future supply shipments weren't disrupted. By becoming a useful component for solving the current crisis, Illa was basically guaranteeing that Alice would help keep the town safe and protected until the crisis was over.

Alice looked at Ethan, who simply shrugged.

"I think I would probably need to prioritize the capital first," Alice said after some hesitation. "But after that, I could put Cyra as the next priority for crisis solutions?"

Illa thought about it for a moment and then nodded. "That's reasonable. I accept."

A deal was struck.

Chapter 16

After the negotiations between Alice and Illa ended, there was a strange pause in the conversation. Alice hadn't seen Illa in *months*, and it felt like a lifetime ago. The negotiations had given her a topic to focus on, but now that it was over . . . Alice felt unsure how to proceed.

After several seconds of silence, Illa spoke up.

"Now that we've hammered out a plan for the future . . . You say you might be higher level than me? I see that times have been even better for you than I expected."

Alice resisted the urge to victoriously cackle like a witch. Seeing Illa really brought her progression speed into a new light, and Alice felt proud of what she had accomplished. She would need to avoid giving specific numbers, but she could probably chat about her progress.

"I'm pretty high level now," Alice said. That was vague enough that it wouldn't give Illa a complete picture of her current status, but would still allow Alice to talk a bit about how far she had come. To Alice's side, Ethan grinned and then nodded silently.

Illa glanced at Ethan, and then she also started grinning.

"If even Ethan believes you've reached a high level, you must be level sixty-five at minimum. Perhaps even over level seventy-five? The levels after level seventy-five are very slow, so you're unlikely to be much higher than that," Illa said before she grimaced. For a moment, Alice was reminded of the fact that Illa herself was likely stuck in the levels between seventy-five and one hundred. "I know I'm not your mentor anymore, but I feel it's important to remind you about that anyway. Don't be discouraged and just keep going. You'll make progress eventually."

Alice tried not to wince. She had definitely noticed how hard it was to gain levels in [Explorer of Magic] these days. Even if she took actions directly focused on improving the class, it still barely budged.

"I'm surprised by how much you've grown. You've been in this world for a year, right? And yet, despite only accessing the System for a year, you've come so far."

"Yeah, I've been here about a year," said Alice. "I don't remember the exact date I came here, since I didn't have my memory perks back then—but it should have been about twelve months ago."

Illa chuckled. "So I've almost been surpassed by a kid in a year," she said before shaking her head ruefully. "Well, either way . . . I'm glad for you. I never thought you would reach this far, especially considering your late start. I thought it would take a miracle for you to catch up to people who were born on this planet. Somehow, you've already more than caught up, though."

Then Illa turned back toward Ethan. "So how exactly are we going to do this, logistically? The easiest way for you to handle this would be to simply let me return to Cyra, and I'll start sending shipments of enchanting materials up north. But that also risks a few things—most notably, I might spend months searching for materials and find nothing useful. We did already talk about my [Enchanter], and she'll certainly be helping out—but there's only so much she can do when trying to test compatibility for a mana type she doesn't understand or have access to. At high enough levels that might not be a problem, but she's average level for an adult."

Ethan sighed. "There are a few ways we can handle this. The first way is to head to Cyra ourselves and directly process and test ingredients on the spot after your [Enchanter] removes materials that are wholly irrelevant. We could also leave things to you or send over some decent [Enchanters] to help speed things along. I personally favor sending over some members of the military and a few [Enchanters], but . . . Alice, would it be faster if you did the testing? Keep in mind that this will necessitate us actually traveling to Cyra—but it will likely make the actual testing process much faster and more effective. What do you think?"

Alice thought about her as-yet unchosen [Careful Enchanter] perk, as well as her new ability to test enchanting in her dreams. The fact that she could process information incredibly quickly now, as well as her effectively unlimited mana while testing things out in her dreams, would definitely make it much faster and easier to test enchanting materials herself. Alice finally popped open her options for [Careful Enchanter] to see if that changed her decision in any meaningful way.

"Lemme look at some perk options for a moment," said Alice. "I've been holding off since I wasn't sure what I needed until now, and I wanted to ask for advice. However, I think I know what I want now."

"Take your time," said Ethan. "You should choose your perks carefully. We can wait a few minutes. If you have any other questions, feel free to ask me as well."

Alice nodded and started scanning her perk options while using display mana to get actual perk descriptions.

The first option she saw wasn't particularly impressive: It made any monster core that she personally added to an enchantment slowly recharge itself. This was nice, since it would save a great deal of monster cores in the long run. However, Alice didn't think it was anywhere near high priority, given the current situation.

It saved a bit of money, but Ethan was covering her material costs anyway. She had bigger problems than the budget.

The second perk choice was a bit more interesting. Rather than make monster cores recharge themselves, it made Alice's enchantments slowly repair themselves. However, it still wasn't *that* impressive. Wear and tear was a common problem for enchanted items, but it still usually took years before it mattered. It wasn't useful enough to take right now.

The third and fourth perks were far more interesting.

Perk Name: Get_Text: Error
Perk Reqs: Perception greater than 100, Level 30+ Class_Name
Perk gives user option to process better. Learn enchanting material property fast!
Perk Name: Seed Enchanting
Give information to user: Relate class seeds to enchantments. Instincts for class seed enchantments. Error: System-related perks must remain hidden. Hide Perk_Option 4. Hiding failed. Seeking main server to rectify error . . . cannot connect to main server. @#)(*$@%*()@&#$ @#)($*@#$()#@ @#$)(@*#

A few moments later, the fourth perk's error messages disappeared, leaving a much simpler perk behind.

Perk Name: Seed Enchanting **Requirements: Level 30+ Enchanter_Class_Quality_Enchanter,** **Perception______, {Outworlder} Achievement, {Seeker of Truth} _Or_** **Equivalent_ Achievement ____**
Give information to user: Relate class seeds to enchantments. Instincts for class seed enchantments.

The third perk, {Get_Text: Error}, was almost exactly what she was looking for. It looked like it let her understand the properties of enchanting materials more quickly, which perfectly fit her current needs. It was only a level-thirty perk, so it probably wasn't anything *too* impressive, but it was still a step in the right direction. Combined with Alice's ability to analyze enchanting materials in her dreams, this would drastically speed up her testing.

However, perk four looked like it was related to how enchantments and class seeds interacted. This *greatly* interested Alice.

Alice hesitated for a few moments. The perk with the unknown name was exactly what she needed right now. It would make identifying enchanting materials that she desperately needed easier, faster, and more efficient. It would assist her in managing all her current problems.

On the other hand, the reason Alice had advanced as far as she had was mostly because she had stuck to things that interested her and improved her main focus. In most cases, this meant studying how the System worked. Figuring out how the System worked was also the most important thing she could do if she wanted to actually solve the current crisis rather than just managing some of the aftereffects and running damage control.

And a perk that the System was supposed to remove, but failed to because the System was down?

That was *definitely* something that interested her. It might even offer new information. It was a bit more of a gamble, but Alice felt it was too big of an opportunity to miss.

Alice didn't hesitate long before she decided to pick {Seed Enchanting}.

A moment later, her class fractal twitched and writhed for a moment before tendrils of rainbow mana reached out of her brain, searching for . . . something.

It was as if it was trying to connect to the System and failing.

Finding nothing, her class seed started to connect with . . . the mana in the atmosphere?

Alice had never seen *this* happen before.

The mana in the air surged toward her class fractal. Alice felt a spike of fear. She started preparing her pure mana seed and her No_Mana magic seed to isolate herself from the atmospheric mana. However, before she did anything, she had a flash of insight and used {Safety Analysis}.

{Safety Analysis} claimed that there was no danger in this situation. It was . . . fine. Alice stopped panicking and, after some hesitation, let the mana in her surroundings connect with her.

Moments later, Alice was barraged with a wave of mental images and ideas, similar to the first time she had tried forming a class seed with a magic seed slot. She could see something appear in her mind, like a blurred mosaic. As seconds continued to pass by, the image in her mind became clearer and clearer until she could finally make out what she was seeing.

She saw layer upon layer of enchantments. Every single enchantment was almost identical, but also slightly different from the one before it. The layers of enchantments were massive—the entire enchantment was bigger than most of the cities back on Earth, and so large in scope that it utterly dwarfed cities of this dimension. Each enchantment processed information at speeds that rivaled a supercomputer from Earth. Even trying to mentally track what was happening in the image made Alice feel dizzy.

For a moment, Alice simply felt bewildered. However, her confusion was quickly replaced with surprise as she realized that she felt a strange familiarity with this image. The way some parts of the enchantments were layered together, and especially the rainbow color of mana darting in and out of various subcomponents of the enchantment . . . it all felt *very* familiar.

It reminded her of the System.

At first, Alice thought she was seeing things—but the more she looked at it, the more she suspected she was looking at the System. That was, the core of the System. The center of it all.

It took Alice several more seconds to realize that the System seemed rather . . . *physical* in nature. It wasn't some law of reality that she was looking at, or some metaphysical construct, or anything of the sort.

It was a concrete, physical enchantment housed . . . somewhere. Or at least, that was what it looked like to her.

Alice's mind reeled from the weight of her newest suspicion. The System had a PHYSICAL COMPONENT to it. Not just the rainbow mana she had seen in the air around her—there was a physical building somewhere and the System was located inside it. If she knew where it was, she could literally walk into the System.

Which wasn't something Alice was entirely prepared for, even though in hindsight, it seemed quite obvious. The System clearly followed the same laws of magic as everything else—it was just very well designed to exploit the laws of magic and help humans in this world. Still, the idea that Alice could just walk into the System and start poking around was baffling. What would happen if someone just cut a wire inside the System? Would the whole thing implode?

A moment later, the System disappeared. What if the reason the System had vanished was because of the exact scenario she had just thought of? Or what if a monster had gotten inside and started eating the System? The System *had* to be processing ludicrous amounts of mana every second. If a monster managed to get inside, that seemed like a good explanation for why things had suddenly gone so wrong.

After several seconds of wild speculation, Alice finally jolted herself out of her chaotic thoughts. She didn't have enough information to make any conclusions yet—in fact, she didn't have enough information to do ANYTHING. Right now, she needed to observe the other information packed into her new perk.

The information that the System had a physical location was very important, but until Alice knew where the System was, she couldn't do much. She delved more deeply into the riot of images and ideas contained within the perk. This time, she saw that a lot of the System's enchantments were giant blobs of different kinds of mana, mixing together seamlessly. Different bits of mana often drifted from one enchantment to another, almost as if they were motes of living energy that knew exactly where they were needed.

A few moments later, Alice saw an image of a person approach the edge of the System. She saw their bones, their tendons, their organs, and their muscles being besieged by mana. This wasn't the chaotic but controlled mana of the System: It was a barrage of [Farmer] mana. Alice watched in mute comprehension as the mana swarmed toward the brain of the image, starting to erode the personhood of the fake person with every second . . .

Then the System reached out a tendril of rainbow mana toward the [Farmer]'s body, leaving behind a seed made of rainbow mana. A moment later, the chaotic mana stilled, forming into a bundle of mana etched into the [Farmer]'s brain. The [Farmer] mana no longer besieged the person's body—instead, it was all absorbed into the mark of rainbow mana. Alice realized that the rainbow mana had allowed the human brain to work like an enchanting material. It had somehow created a strange mixture of an enchantment, a class seed, and . . . *something* else which absorbed mana to create and enhance classes.

Moments later, the mark of rainbow mana seemed to condense, almost like matter being sucked into a black hole. The mark of rainbow mana erupted a few moments later, like roots sprouting from a seed, and turned into a new [Farmer] class seed.

The System had just used the human brain and ambient mana as enchanting materials to construct a class seed. The moment the class seed was finished, the mana in the body's person seemed to light up for a moment, although Alice wasn't quite sure why. Then Alice's view was dragged toward the newly created class seed. Alice saw mana start to run through it, and through some quirk of how her new perk worked, she *understood*.

The class seed truly was a magic seed, just like the kinetic mana one buried in her mage core. However, it was very different from a real magic seed. It needed far more mana to do the same amount of magic, making it far worse than a real mage in mana expenditure. However, the class seed had two oddities that differentiated it from a regular magic seed.

First, it vacuumed up problematic mana from the body, compressing it inside itself and using it to boost the strength of the magic seed. With the assistance of the perk, Alice could see that the class seed could *theoretically* grow without limits, although the denser the mana was inside the class seed, the more difficult it would become for the seed to grow. This was likely why people had a harder and harder time leveling up as they grew higher. It also lined up with all the other observations that Alice had made about class seeds so far.

The second thing that Alice noticed was a lot more interesting. For some reason, class seeds were less volatile and potentially harmful for their user. Ninety-six percent of would-be mages died during mana baptisms, but nobody had ever gotten hurt from acquiring a class.

As Alice was mulling over what she had seen, she felt the vision start to fade and she was pulled back to reality again.

Alice blinked. She finally had some guess as to how she could create a class seed.

Out of curiosity, she tried checking with {Safety Analysis} to see if she could safely make a new class seed for herself. She got back the mental equivalent of a giant siren blaring at full volume. {Safety Analysis} thought her plan was a *terrible* idea.

Alice sighed.

At the very least, she had a bunch of new ideas to think about. The idea of using human organs as an enchanting material was . . . novel. Especially since human organs weren't naturally enchanting materials at all, apart from the mage core.

Then Alice thought about something else. She had felt for quite a while that there was something familiar about System mana. Now that Alice was explicitly thinking about it, she remembered an old perk. She had occasionally used it to improve her enchantments but had often struggled to make the time she needed to maximize the value of the perk. However . . .

Kinetic Enchanting
Requirements: Kinetic Manabinder level 25 or higher

If you interact with an enchanting material for an extended period of time while focusing on this perk, you may permanently increase the number of instructions the enchanting material can remember by one. This extra instruction may ONLY be used to increase its memory for kinetic enchantments, and the material must already have some affinity with kinetic mana or the perk will not work.
This can only be used on a given material once, and will fail if other similar perks, achievements, or any other effects have already been used on it.

If at level twenty-five, she had gotten a perk that let her add the capacity for extra instructions to an enchanting material . . . Perhaps it was somehow similar to the way the System itself made class seeds? The System *had* turned a man's brain into an enchanting material. It was strikingly similar to the basis for how {Kinetic Enchanting} worked.

It also made Alice think of the way rainbow mana from the System had always been present. No matter where she had looked, she had *always* seen a flood of System mana, back when the System was still functional. Perhaps that *also* had some sort of similarity to {Kinetic Enchanting}. What if the System had turned air itself into an enchanting material, and then used that as a sort of . . . communication relay between the System and the humans of this world? Another flash of insight lit up Alice's mind as she finally realized why the System enchantments she saw floating in the air around her looked familiar.

They were paired enchantments.

The System had probably turned the entire atmosphere of this world into a paired enchantment. As long as someone interacted with *air* in the world, the System would see them and connect with them. This System was actually slightly less perfect than it might appear to be—after all, Alice had already confirmed that if she locked herself in a manaless room, the System would no longer be able to reach her. However, for most scenarios, the System had created an effective way to reach every human being on this planet. Especially since the System actively hid its nature from the world, making it very hard for someone to intentionally lock someone else out of the System.

In other words, normally one wouldn't create an environment without System mana unless they knew what they were doing. Nobody was ever supposed to know what they were doing.

Either way, she had gotten a huge amount of useful information and ideas from her new perk. Even though the perk didn't seem to do much else besides provide her with that one vision trip, similar to the perk she had eventually turned into {Expanding Comprehension}, Alice was more than happy with the perk she had taken.

After she finished thinking, Alice returned to the present and looked at her mentor and Illa, who were still waiting for her. As she looked at them, Alice realized something else that she had missed during her perk-induced vision trip.

Alice still had no idea how to solve her current problems. She had gotten all sorts of inspiration for how to start making class seeds, but she hadn't gotten a specific, concrete boost to her abilities from her new perk. She would eventually be able to transform her new inspiration and ideas into something amazing, but the perk wasn't going to contribute to her current needs very much. Alice sighed.

Chapter 17

After Alice finished processing the information from her new perk, she took a few moments to focus on the present again.

Originally, she had been wondering if there was a reason to go to Cyra with Ethan. It would represent a huge time commitment, and she would lose contact with the Church of the System in Metsel, which she had been making good strides with. She would also suffer some delay in gathering more information. Metsel was the capital of Illvaria, which also meant that most information in the kingdom was readily available here—whereas Cyra was a frontier town, with far weaker communication infrastructure.

However, it would also mean that Alice would be present in person to test enchanting materials. Did she provide anything that Ethan's subordinates couldn't make up for? The question Alice needed to answer was whether going to Cyra would save or cost her more time.

Alice hesitated, mulling over her options.

Right now, the cooperation Alice had established with the churches of the System mostly boiled down to the church sending along potential [Enchanters] for Cecilia to train. However, the number of [Enchanters] she and Cecilia could train at once was limited—after all, Alice still needed to have {Broken Seed} ready to rescue each [Enchanter] if they messed up while making a new magic seed. Therefore, they wouldn't really be losing that much training time for new [Enchanters] if they left.

On the other hand, going to Cyra seemed like a reasonable way to resolve the enchanting material problem faster. The [Enchanter] who lived in Cyra wouldn't be able to test for everything Alice needed—after all, they likely didn't have a display mana or filtration mana. Ethan's subordinates would have the exact same problem. Any subordinates Ethan sent to Cyra would need to approve a box of materials for Alice to test, send it to Metsel, wait for her to approve certain materials, send that message BACK to Cyra, and then both sides would need to somehow coordinate a way to get those materials back to Metsel en masse. This added in a two-week delay to ANY communication or problem-solving attempt *per message*. Higher-level

[Messengers] could reduce this problem, but they would not be able to resolve it entirely.

A multiweek delay for every message sent was a *huge* amount of time to lose while trying to combat an unfolding crisis. Alice still had things she could do in Metsel, but when she thought about the potential time lost from remaining in Metsel, she started to think it was a better idea to go to Cyra herself.

"I think it's best if we go south for a while," said Alice, finally turning her attention back to Ethan. "Assuming that all the enchanting materials you provide me with later fail, of course. If we find a material that meets my needs, we'll reassess. But assuming we don't find anything, we'll have an easier time doing things personally instead of via subordinate in Cyra. We should collect a few final reports and supplies before going, and I want to run a magic seed test before we go, but I think that the time it would take to send messages to and from Cyra would be an unacceptable delay right now." Alice paused to collect her thoughts. "Also, I have something I need to speak with you about later."

Ethan's eyes narrowed for a moment before he nodded. At Alice's final comment, Illa gave Alice an appraising look before she tactfully ignored it.

"That sounds reasonable," said Ethan. "As long as you're sure that heading to Cyra is the best path, I'll make it happen. You also mentioned magic seed testing?"

"Yes. {Broken Seed}'s cooldown is going to be a big factor in how fast my plans proceed, so I want to be using it the instant I can. I'm going to have the most promising of Cecilia's [Enchanters] try forming a magic seed without the System, and I'll remove it if it starts to catastrophically fail. With enough practice, they'll succeed," said Alice.

"Very well," Ethan said after a few moments.

"If you two are planning to go to Cyra and bringing along a contingent of important mages, I will excuse myself. I need to send a few messages to prepare for your arrival," said Illa. "Honored Immortal, Lady Alice, thank you for being willing to see me. I know that this must be a very busy time for you, and I appreciate you taking time to meet with me and discuss the future anyway. May we find a solution to this crisis as soon as possible."

Ethan nodded, and a few moments later, Illa left.

Afterward, Alice waited a few moments.

"Are we alone?" asked Alice.

Ethan paused and then motioned toward the wall.

A [Spy] that Alice had somehow failed to notice melted out of the wall and quickly left the room before Ethan turned back toward her. "We are now," he said. "What did you need to talk about?"

"It's *very important*," said Alice, doing her best to emphasize her words as much as possible. "When I picked my last perk, I saw something . . . interesting. Let me show you," she said before extending a hand toward Ethan.

Ethan seemed to realize what she wanted, and a moment later, stretched out a finger. "Go for it," he said. Alice grabbed his finger and activated {Shared Memory}, showing Ethan what she had seen while using her newest perk.

After seeing Alice's memories, Ethan frowned.

"That is . . . not what I expected to see," he said, finally. "The System has . . . a physical body? That idea is very . . . I don't . . ." For once, the Immortal had no coherent response.

Alice felt a sudden urge to laugh. She didn't see Ethan at a loss for words very often, and she was rather enjoying seeing him so baffled for once.

After several seconds of long, drawn-out thought, Ethan shook his head.

"For now, tell *no one* about this," he said. "Besides Cecilia. She is trustworthy and might be able to offer useful insight. Mention it to no one else. Considering what has happened recently with the System collapsing, we can infer that something has probably gone wrong at the System's mainframe. We should also find the System's physical framework as soon as possible and see if we can figure out what's wrong. We'll talk about this more in a few days, after I look through the available data and have something more useful to think about. All right?"

Alice nodded. The idea of the System having a physical framework was quite an unusual perspective for a society that worshipped the System like a god. It was also very possible to abuse this knowledge, if someone with bad intentions wanted to manipulate the System itself. She had hesitated to even tell Ethan about it. If the System was a massive enchantment, the way Alice suspected it was, perhaps there was some way to manipulate levels, perks, and achievements as well. Alice didn't *think* that could be done, based on her understanding of how class mana and attributes worked—but it was better to be safe instead of sorry.

The two of them sat in silence for a few more minutes as Ethan simply processed the information Alice had given him.

Finally, the two of them left Ethan's office.

Alice left to find Cecilia and update her on their plan to go to Cyra. Afterward, Alice retired to her room for a bit to decompress and wait for Cecilia's [Enchanter]. A few hours later, Cecilia let Alice know that the most promising [Enchanter] had come to the manor. Alice, Cecilia, and a few [Guards] went to meet them.

"So this is the most promising mage?" asked Alice, looking at the middle-aged man sitting in front of her.

"Yes, he is," said Cecilia. "I don't think he will actually succeed on the first try, but he has a good grasp on what we need. I've drilled every single scrap of information I have about the process and the mana type in question into him. He has the best chance to succeed out of all the mages I'm training."

Alice nodded and gave the man a curious glance. He seemed to be about level sixty, which was a bit above average, but he didn't seem to have any other outstanding characteristics. When he saw Alice, he gave her a respectful nod.

"Are you planning on forming a pure mana seed or a display mana seed?" Alice asked.

"I am going to try forming a display magic seed, Lady Alice," said the man.

"Oh?" said Alice. She had only started talking about possibly expanding the use of display mana recently. Had Cecilia already integrated it into her lesson plans?

She turned toward Cecilia, who gave her a grin.

"I did my best to generalize my lessons about forming magic seeds without the help of the System," said Cecilia. "I figure that we're going to need a lot of weird enchantments to get through all this. Pure magic seeds are useful, but they're only a stopgap measure. So I focused more on the actual process of forming magic seeds." Cecilia grinned. "Of course, I have also done a few more specialized lessons on certain kinds of mana. Right now, I'm running them through introductions on what pure mana seeds, display mana seeds, and filtration magic seeds look like. That way, the moment you find compatible enchanting materials, we can start the mass production of the enchantments we need. I'm trying to make sure there are as few delays as possible from my side."

Alice nodded.

"On that note, I have an idea," said Cecilia. "Before we start, I think you should use {Shared Memory} and show this man what forming a magic seed looks like. {Shared Memory} has exceptional potential as a teaching tool, and we aren't utilizing that perk to its full potential yet."

Alice paused. It felt very personal to share her memories, so she had only shared them with people she was close to until now. However, these were definitely extenuating circumstances. Alice sighed, pushed down a wave of discomfort, and nodded. People's safety came first. "That's a good idea," she said before she turned back to the middle-aged mage. "Give me your hand, and give me permission to share some memories with you."

The mage extended his hand toward her. "I give you permission to show me your memories," he said.

Alice grabbed his wrist and used {Shared Memory} to share her recollection of creating a magic seed without the help of the System. She also showcased a few of her failures, as well as her usage of {Broken Seed}, so that the mage knew what to expect.

The mage spent several minutes sorting through his thoughts and Alice's memories before he finally nodded. "I think I'm ready to start, Lady Alice. I give you permission to destroy any of my magic seeds as needed within the next hour. Thank you for watching over me."

"It's what I'm here for," she said. "You can start."

The man closed his eyes in concentration and started pulling in mana from his surroundings.

Alice carefully started assembling the mana fractals for mana filtration, the same way she had done when she herself was forming her electromagnetic seed without the help of the System. It probably wouldn't be enough for the man to succeed, but Alice still wanted to give him every possible chance of success. If the mage actually managed to form a display magic seed today, Alice wouldn't need to use {Broken Seed} on him—which meant that someone else could try to form a new magic seed today. In theory, if everyone formed a magic seed safely on their first try, Alice wouldn't need to use {Broken Seed} at all. Of course, that was a pipe dream, but she could hope.

The man drew in the mana Alice had filtered as if he were a sponge soaking up water. For several minutes, Alice and Cecilia watched in tense silence as the man tried to compact mana inside his mage core.

Seconds passed by as pieces of mana flesh and the mana in his mage core reacted to each other, slowly arranging themselves into a magic seed. However, as Alice watched, she started to frown. The magic seed he was forming didn't look quite right. Despite the memories Alice had shared with the man, despite the classes he had spent trying to understand the nature of seed formation and display mana, the man's magic seed was clearly flawed.

Alice used {Safety Analysis} and confirmed that the seed was dangerous. She let him spend a few more minutes trying and failing to form his magic seed, to get him the most learning experience she could, and then shattered the magic seed before it could start actually harming him.

The man blinked before opening his eyes and sighing.

"My apologies, Lady Alice," he said.

Alice shrugged. She had been hoping to get lucky, but she hadn't really expected it.

"Not bad for a first attempt," she said. "Keep it up. You'll get it within a few tries."

The man nodded and left.

It seemed that luck was not on their side this time.

A day later, Alice looked at the massive tray of enchanting materials in front of her and grinned. Ethan had managed to put together a huge number of enchanting materials in just a day. Such was the influence of an Immortal.

She also noticed that at least a few of the enchanting materials seemed to be covered in rainbow mana. This wasn't because the material was compatible with System mana—it was because one or more perks had been applied to the material to change its innate properties. Having only recently thought about the {Kinetic Enchanting} perk from her [Kinetic Manabinder] class, and how it allowed Alice to improve the maximum capacity of enchanting materials, Alice suspected that these materials were probably man-made. That was a direction Alice hadn't thought of before, but she decided to ask Ethan to send some subordinates on a quest to get more man-made materials. She doubted any of them would fit her needs, but if they *could* have [Enchanters] manufacture the right materials, it would save a lot of time and effort.

After that, Alice turned her attention back to the materials Ethan had acquired. They were sorted into rows based on how easy it was to acquire more. The enchanting materials at the top, while not exactly common, were at least possible to acquire more of on short notice, but the materials near the bottom of the case were rare oddities from far-off lands, or man-made materials created by incredibly high-level people. In other words, she needed to start testing from the top and work her way down and hope that something less rare worked.

She sighed before stuffing it all into her storage perk and then going to sleep.

It was time to do some dream testing.

It only took Alice a few moments to reappear in the dream library and make her way to the enchanting room.

The first material Alice tested was a kind of white plant. Frankly, it looked like a human finger bone, and it took Alice a few moments to confirm that the item wasn't an *actual* finger. After confirming she wasn't holding part of a human skeleton, Alice tried injecting a little bit of filtration mana into it, and then a bit of display mana into it, before shaking her head.

This material was useless.

The next item was a type of reddish-green moss. It looked almost like someone had bled onto a patch of moss and then dunked it into water to try to clean it off.

This one also didn't work.

Alice simply continued working. Like a machine, she grabbed one material after another, injected the relevant types of mana into it, and tossed it aside after confirming it was useless.

The first forty-two test materials were all completely unable to interact with the necessary kinds of mana. However, when Alice got to the first artificially made enchanting material, she was pleasantly surprised to see that it was able to hold on to some filtration mana. It was far from an ideal conductor of that type of mana, but it was at least somewhat viable as a backup. She still hoped to find something better, but it was better than nothing. She grinned to herself.

The material was several rows down, so it wouldn't be easy to acquire more of, but it was far better than what she had expected to find, which was nothing at all.

Alice continued testing materials but unfortunately found only a few other useful materials. The only other material she found that was usable was *also* artificially made and was considerably more compatible with her desired mana types than material forty-two. This material was an amber-colored rock, and it was material 147 out of 162. It was an artificial material that could hold four enchanting instructions instead of one, and was somewhat compatible with both display and filtration mana. However, it seemed to require multiple specific combination perks—meaning that only one person in the capital could produce more of it. Hardly a viable source of mass production for enchantments.

Alice sighed.

At least it was better than nothing, for now.

After that, Alice started toying with the actual process of creating a filtration enchantment with both of the compatible materials. After all, figuring out how to create an enchantment that actually did what she wanted it to do would be a slow, difficult process. Alice wasn't bad at creating enchantments, but she wasn't amazing, either. Unfortunately, the enchantments she needed to create were especially complicated. First, Alice needed to get the enchantment to find and hook up with the appropriate magic seed. Getting an unintelligent enchantment to find the correct magic seed was surprisingly difficult, and by the time she woke up, Alice was far from accomplishing even this first step.

She woke up feeling rather frustrated by how poorly her first attempts at creating a filtration ring had gone, but she also felt relieved. At the very least, there were a few materials that she could use to start implementing her enchantment plan. They might be rare and hard to make, but it was better than no options at all.

After that, she quickly rubbed the sleep out of her eyes, got dressed, and went to meet Ethan.

None of the readily available enchanting materials in the capital were usable. That meant they needed to find something else. It was time to head back to Cyra, where she had begun her journey in this world.

Chapter 18

One day later, Alice, Cecilia, Illa, Ethan, and the five mages Cecilia was training set off toward Cyra. The last day had mostly been filled with packing bags and storage perks. Even though Ethan and Illa were both competent combat mages, it was never a bad idea to have more eyes to deal with threats, especially since the Society of Starry Eyes might strike again at any time.

During that packing session, Alice also found time to bring Illa up to date on her intelligence about the System. While Alice didn't tell Illa that the System had a real, physical mainframe somewhere in the world, she told Illa most of the other information she had gathered during her months of hard work and experimentation.

After everyone was ready, the group boarded a metal ship that Ethan's mother had, at one point in time, used to level up her [Admiral] class and subsequently stuffed into a storage perk. The ship had been created by Doll, Illvaria's fifth Immortal, and was more suited for deep-sea travel rather than river travel. However, thanks to Doll's exceptional craftsmanship, as well as a healthy number of high-level perks, the ship could handle the various depths.

The group of [Guards], mages, and Ethan boarded the ship, along with a crew of hastily assembled [Sailors] and [Soldiers]. Then the boat lurched into motion, far faster than Alice had expected. It was clear that this trip to Cyra would be *much* faster than her original trip to Metsel—the boat was somehow churning through the water at a speed that really shouldn't have been possible without magic or modern technology. Alice spent a few minutes observing the strange, perk-boosted motion of the ship before she went below deck to help teach Cecilia's [Enchanters]. She might as well make use of the time they were stuck on the boat.

The first three days of the journey were uneventful. Alice tested ways to make her enchantments work while she was asleep, and when she was awake, she helped train Cecilia's [Enchanters]. When the group needed a break, they played board games. Illa even joined them for a few games, much to Ethan's amusement.

On the fourth day of travel, Alice and Cecilia once again sat down with the mage who had nearly succeeded in forming a seed without the System's aid last time.

Unlike the first time, this time the middle-aged man succeeded in forming a magic seed without the System's help. It was a near thing—Alice was pretty sure the magic seed the man had formed *barely* worked. It probably had all sorts of issues, such as leaking broken mana everywhere, having problems regenerating mana efficiently, and other general issues. However, the seed wasn't harmful to the man. {Safety Analysis} didn't detect any problems with it, and he didn't feel any discomfort, either. Furthermore, once the man finished forming a seed, Alice got a surprising achievement.

You have gained an achievement!
System_Teacher (Rarity:7)
You have le@rned and ta__ught about collapse of System, and its imp@ct on the world. YYYYY have taken variety _____ other steps to mitigate the impact. Of the collapse of the System.
++50% class experience for all main classes that research, +15% class experience for all secondary classes that researrch, +100% teaching experience classes.   Support from the SY@@@TEM increased more.   Error—cannot connect to mainframe of System. Support from System weakened.

Alice allowed herself a small smile.

Plus 50 percent experience points for research-based classes was certainly nice. Since achievements were weakened due to the collapse of the System, Alice was probably getting something closer to plus 25 percent instead, but it was still better to have it than not. Unfortunately, that was probably where her benefits from this new achievement ended. She didn't have any classes that could take advantage of the 15 percent boost to secondary classes focused on research, and she didn't have the [Teacher] class to benefit from the boost to [Teacher] progress, either. Still, the achievement was a nice boost to her growth speed.

However, the "Support from the System increased more" line caused Alice to raise an eyebrow.

When Alice had first arrived in this world, she had gotten the {Outworlder} achievement, which stated that Alice got "increased support from the System." Alice had never figured out what that meant. Did it make it easier for her to see and interact with System mana, compared to other people? Did it somehow make it easier for Alice's body to adapt to mana, thus improving her survival odds during a mana baptism? Was it some sort of hidden leveling speed boost that enhanced her attribute and leveling growth? Did it make it easier to acquire achievements? Or was it something else entirely?

She had no idea.

Alice spent several minutes trying to find something different in her Status Screen, but her ability to interact with mana felt exactly the same as before.

Her body also felt exactly the same as before. Her magic seeds hadn't changed and neither had her class seeds.

After thirty minutes of searching, she gave up and concluded she would just have to keep an eye out for any changes.

As she was making no progress determining what "support from the System" meant, she returned to the original issue: the [Enchanter]'s display mana seed. His partial success put Alice and Cecilia in an interesting position.

On one hand, keeping {Broken Seed} ready for any potential problems made a great deal of sense. It would let the man safely experiment with his seed and immediately give the two a way to fix things if stuff started going wrong. However, it also meant that Alice's perk was tied up preparing for an eventuality that might not be relevant—and in the meantime, they would be wasting time on the perk's cooldown. Given how important {Broken Seed} was right now, that was a potentially massive waste of resources they could scarcely afford to lose. Alternately, they could let the man experiment with his new magic seed for a while and then break it down. They could also just leave it be and hope for the best while getting the next mage started immediately. Alice knew that the man's new magic seed was rather inefficient, but it might be worth accepting that a perfect magic seed was unlikely, given the circumstances. The mages might just have to accept partial successes until Alice found a better way to handle the loss of the System.

Alice and Cecilia debated the right course of action for a while and ultimately decided to have the mage keep his magic seed for twenty-four hours before they broke it. He would hopefully create his final display mana seed next time. Even though it meant that Alice would waste a day of cooldown of {Broken Seed}, it seemed like the best way to keep Cecilia's students safe while still meeting their needs for the future.

The next twenty-four hours were largely consumed with Alice and Cecilia observing the mage as he messed with his magic seed. He tested how quickly it regenerated mana, how effectively he could use it without producing broken mana, and how well his version of display mana did its job and allowed people to view perks.

The three of them quickly realized that the new magic seed was horrendously inefficient—perhaps 70 percent of its mana turned into broken mana. However, the magic seed seemed to have almost normal mana regeneration, oddly enough. Most importantly, it did its job just fine. Apart from the atrocious broken mana production, the mana worked just like it was supposed to. Alice was glad that they had decided to help the man rebuild his seed one more time—it would be very hard for him to work effectively with such low efficiency.

Before breaking down the man's seed, Alice decided to test something after verifying that it wasn't a terrible idea using {Safety Analysis}.

One of Cecilia's other [Enchanters] had reached a breaking point for a perk in a different class. Alice wanted to see if there were any differences in perk descriptions if different people used display mana to look at the perk. So she asked the other mage to look at the man's perks and then used her own display mana to do the same. Then she had the mage [Student] record what he saw.

The man was able to see the perk descriptions for his new perks, regardless of whether Alice or the other mage used display mana. However, there were small, subtle differences in word choice based on which mage helped him.

Alice's version of the bugged-out first [Student] perk looked like this:

Fast_Learnor
Requirements: Student level 10 or more, Intelligence 100 or greater
Increases learn_experience speed for all class by 5%.

Meanwhile, when the other mage used his display mana seed to help the younger mage view his [Student] perks, the result was subtly different.

Sp@@d Learner
Requirements: Student level 10 greater, 100 or greater Int@#$nce
Increases g@#$th by 5% for classes.

The actual *meaning* of the perk was the same—it increased leveling speed by 5 percent for all classes. However, Alice found the minor differences in how the perk was displayed to be fascinating.

When she used her perk, the glitched-out parts of the perk tended to be random underscore signs and abbreviated grammar. Meanwhile, the middle-aged mage still had glitchy perk descriptions, but the specific glitches were different. The name of the perk was also different depending on whether Alice or the middle-aged mage was translating the perk.

It was a small but interesting difference that Alice suspected originated from two different understandings of what mana and the System were and how they worked. Alice, being from Earth and having some familiarity with computers and coding, tended to visualize the System as something more like an incredibly complex magic computer. This likely lent itself toward more coding-esque abbreviations for glitches in perk descriptions. Meanwhile, the mage from this world tended to view the System as a more of a . . . divine entity. Even if some of that view had been shaken by recent events, it probably wasn't possible to totally shake off a lifetime of beliefs in only a week or two.

The difference in the perk translations served as another hint that display mana was deeply tied to the mage using it. This further highlighted one of Alice's earlier assumptions—that the System had some way of translating *meanings* into words, instead of just translating things for the viewer.

After that experiment, Alice helped the middle-aged mage shatter his defective magic seed. Alice actually had a slight hope that she would also get a few System rewards when the man formed a proper magic seed—specifically, she hoped to finally get the fifth tier of {Scientific Discoveries}. The perk mentioned that she would get some kind of extra benefit at the fifth stage, and she had been stuck at the fourth stage of the perk for a while now.

Another day passed. The group was nearing Cyra when something unusual happened.

As Alice and Cecilia were quietly finishing up another round of the most recent board game, Alice saw a spigot of rainbow mana wash through the world. She had noticed another random wave of rainbow mana over a week ago, right before the Society had attacked Ethan's manor.

She wasn't quite sure what to make of it. The wave of mana didn't seem to be doing . . . much of anything, really. Now that Alice knew there was a physical System mainframe somewhere in the world, she suspected the System was probably just vomiting energy into the atmosphere as it glitched out. Even so, she paid very close attention to the giant wave of rainbow mana. Even if she didn't understand everything she was looking at, she hoped that she could get more information from observing it.

Sadly, the glitchy rainbow mana was too chaotic. Alice couldn't pick out any meaningful information from it. She still memorized everything she saw, but at least right now, she simply didn't have the skill to make use of her observations.

At least, that was Alice's thought until she heard Cecilia's awed gasp.

"Is that what the System always looks like?" asked Cecilia. "It looks a bit different than I thought it would, based on your memories."

Alice blinked and then turned toward Cecilia.

"Wait, what?" asked Alice. "What do you mean?"

"The giant wave of rainbow mana," said Cecilia. "Is that what the System always looks like?"

Alice felt rather surprised. This was the first time someone other than her had seen System mana, at least without her help. The idea that someone else would actually *see* System mana was strange.

"You can see it?" asked Alice.

Cecilia shrugged. "I guess?" she said. "This is the first time I've ever seen it outside of your memories, but I definitely see a giant cloud of rainbow mana surrounding us right now."

Alice glanced at Cecilia, then back at the rainbow mana.

Cecilia seeing the System and its mana wasn't necessarily a bad thing. Cecilia was a friend Alice trusted and a useful ally. However, the fact that other people might have also seen the System was a cause for concern. It showed that the deterioration of the System was even more severe than she had feared.

"Well, as someone more experienced in enchantments than me . . . do you have any guesses where the System's mainframe might be?" asked Alice, trying to push aside her fears for the moment. "I can't find any clues about the physical location of the System based on that giant wave of rainbow mana, but as an experienced [Enchanter], do you have any ideas?"

Cecilia sighed and shook her head. "None. It's too complex for me to understand."

Alice sighed but nodded.

"Hold on, let me see if other people saw it, too," she said before making her way out of the cabin.

She started moving through the boat, listening in on other people as they talked. And to Alice's growing concern, she could hear other mages talking about the wave of mana they had just seen.

Clearly, she and Cecilia weren't the only ones who had noticed the System mana this time. Everyone had seen it.

Something about that idea bothered her, beyond just the fact that the System was clearly deteriorating more and more. However, the exact problem wasn't springing to mind immediately.

Deep within the woods of Illvaria, pack after pack of monsters hungrily tore into the air in front of them where a giant feast of mana had suddenly appeared without warning. It had only appeared for a few minutes, but they had still eaten a great deal in that time.

The mana had been rainbow in color. The monsters had never seen such a strange kind of mana before. If they had the intelligence to care, they probably would have found the situation quite bizarre.

However, monsters weren't particularly intelligent.

All they knew was hunger and desire. With the sudden, miraculous feast of rainbow mana appearing in front of them, they didn't think about how the mana had appeared or why.

They simply ate.

Of course, this phenomenon wasn't limited to the monsters in Illvaria.

Throughout the world, mages were wondering why a random tidal wave of rainbow mana had suddenly appeared in the air in front of them.

And all the monsters in the world were busy gorging themselves.

CHAPTER 19

The group docked in Cyra less than a day later. Alice was actually looking forward to seeing what had become of her first stopping point in this world. She had changed so much since her days in Cyra, and Alice wondered if Cyra had also changed.

She also felt a bit nostalgic for her time in Cyra. Even though not all her memories were good, she had met Cecilia and learned magic under Illa here. She had learned the basics of enchanting here. She had started to study the System here. In many respects, Alice's time in Cyra was the foundation of who she had become since arriving in this world.

After the boat docked, the [Guards] quickly fanned out and double-checked the area for suspicious activity. After several minutes of perks, checks, and patrols, the travelers were finally allowed to disembark and Alice got her first good look at Cyra.

The streets were still well maintained and ordered. Alice could see that the strange, wooden streets that had baffled her when she came to this world were still intact and covered in perk-induced rainbow mana.

The population seemed to have shrunk—likely as a result of the chaos ensuing from the collapse of the System. Alice wondered if they had moved away, or if they had met a worse fate, and tried not to think about it.

Even though the population had decreased, Cyra was far from deserted. There were still several hundred permanent residents in the little town, by Alice's rough estimate. For a frontier town that had been established only a few years ago, the number of inhabitants was still quite impressive.

Furthermore, the town looked a lot more finished than before. The dock was fully constructed now and had clearly been built with shipping quantity in mind. There was even a small entertainment and shopping district surrounding the dock, where people who had just sailed up or down the river could relax or shop for goods after unloading their merchandise. The wall surrounding the town was also higher and thicker than before, and the rainbow mana inside the wall was more densely packed.

Ethan took a glance around and nodded in approval. "This town is quite well developed, considering when it was founded," he said.

Illa smiled at Ethan's praise.

"We should head to the city lord's residence," she said. "I would like to rest and eat a hot meal."

Ethan nodded, and the group started heading toward Illa's residence.

As they walked, Alice kept an alert eye on her surroundings.

Even if the [Guards] hadn't noticed any problems, Alice knew that there were always ways to fool people if one's level was high enough. If she managed to become an Immortal in the future, she would need to get used to relying on herself for protection. There was only so much that low-level [Guards] could do, after all. The more time Alice spent with Ethan, the more she was getting used to thinking about what she would need to do as an Immortal.

Luckily, nothing disrupted their journey. Alice had been half expecting the Society of Starry Eyes to somehow show up, but at least so far, there hadn't been any signs of the hostile mage organization.

After the group arrived at Illa's manor, Alice came face-to-face with a person she vaguely remembered—Illa's [Maid], Ellia. Now that Alice's perception was better than before, she noted that Ellia actually had several rather . . . interesting abilities. She moved with a grace that stood out, now that Alice had a better idea of what a normal citizen looked like. When she had first come to this world, everyone had seemed superhuman, so Ellia hadn't stood out much. However, now that she could see Ellia again, she realized that the [Maid] moved far more quickly than even most [Soldiers] managed. Alice's eyes narrowed a bit in curiosity—perhaps there was more to Ellia than she had seen the first time she passed through Cyra?

"My lady," said Ellia, giving Illa a courteous curtsy before she gave Ethan an even deeper curtsy. Finally, she gave Alice a curtsy as well—which Alice noted, with some amusement, was about the same depth as the one Ellia had given to Illa. Despite having no formal title or land, Alice now apparently ranked the same as a decorated war hero with a noninheritable title and a town that was nearly large enough to grant Illa a formal, inheritable title as well.

"Ellia. I'm glad to see that the town looks well," said Illa, giving Ellia a grin and a brief hug. "Have you already prepared rooms for everyone?"

"Of course, my lady."

Illa nodded. "Please see them to their rooms, then."

Ellia led the group toward a suite of rooms located on the uppermost floor of Illa's manor. They were clearly prepared to receive guests. After directing Alice's group toward the guest rooms, Ellia left in order to lead the [Guards] toward the barracks.

As Alice entered the room Ellia had pointed her toward, she noted, with some amusement, that Illa had kept the same room that Alice had previously stayed in ready for her. If she closed her eyes, she could almost pretend that nothing at all had happened—that she had never left Cyra and gone to Metsel, that she had never taken an Immortal as her teacher, that the System had never collapsed.

So much was familiar, and at the same time, so much was different.

Alice couldn't help but reflect again on all the things that had changed since she left Cyra.

She was happy with who she had become since coming to this world. When she had arrived from Earth, she had been a scared and lost Earthling who could barely survive in this frightening, wondrous world. While she still missed her family and friends from home and hoped that she would be able to return someday, she wasn't the same person she had been before. If Alice was asked whether she would be willing to return home and never come back to this world, she didn't think she would say yes anymore. All her experiences in this world had caused her to grow into someone new. In many respects, she had become a part of this world as much as she had been a part of Earth.

With that thought, Alice drifted off to sleep. She found herself back in her dream library and spent the rest of the night trying to figure out how to get her enchantment to work. She had a smile on her lips as she worked.

The next day, Alice found herself standing in front of a large group of people along with Ethan and Illa.

On Earth, Alice had heard stories about these people, but she had yet to interact with them. It was a group of people Alice had fantasized about once upon a time. It was also a group of people who were far more disappointing in reality than in stories. In stories, [Adventurers] usually led the charge on dragons, pursued the pinnacle of human strength, and scoured fantastical places for treasure and mysteries. In reality, [Adventurers] were mostly people who wandered into the wilderness, tried to dodge monsters, and found rare enchanting materials or monster cores before fleeing back to civilization. Few [Adventurers] actually fought dragons or pursued the pinnacle of human strength.

However, Alice had to admit, she was still excited when she saw a massive crowd of [Adventurers] assembled outside Illa's manor.

"All right, all of you are here today for a few reasons," said Illa. She glanced at Alice and Ethan for a moment. "First of all, as you may have noticed, things have gotten . . . weird lately. In a lot of ways."

"Like when our status screens started glitching out and offering total nonsense as perk choices, or when that giant burst of rainbow mana popped into existence out of nowhere yesterday?" said one of the [Adventurers].

A few other [Adventurers] chuckled at that, while several more looked confused. Illa nodded.

"Indeed. I have news about that, as well as information given to me by Lady Alice that I will share later. This should help protect you and your friends from danger in these trying times. However, in order to find real solutions, we will need your help.

"All of you are accomplished [Adventurers], and I'm sure you've found plenty of odd and potentially useful enchanting materials over the years," Illa continued. "Now, Immortal Ethan and his apprentice, Alice, need a great deal of enchanting materials—especially those that can be acquired in large quantities and can interact with certain special kinds of mana that are related to information and mana filtration."

At the mention of *Immortal* Ethan, a few [Adventurers] who were slower on the uptake suddenly widened their eyes and glanced at Ethan again, as if they were seeing him for the first time. A few others gave Alice curious glances, as if they were trying to figure out what made Alice special enough to be an Immortal's apprentice.

"In exchange for your help, Immortal Ethan and I have discussed an appropriate reward, and we've determined that five hundred gold suns is appropriate for the most successful find. Keep in mind, the ability to grow or extract the resource en masse is the most important thing here. A material that is slightly inferior but can be mined in ten times the quantity will be valued more highly," said Illa. Then she gestured toward Alice. "Lady Alice will be in charge of testing the materials and determining whether or not an enchanting material meets the mana-compatibility requirements, while I will be in charge of determining whether the material can be harvested on a larger scale." Illa paused. "Of course, smaller rewards are available for materials that are useful but don't have sufficient quantity. They may not be exactly what we need right now, but they are certainly still useful."

The [Adventurers] started to focus more and more intently on what Illa said. It was obvious that they were very interested in the rewards proposed by Illa. Five hundred gold suns was an unimaginable amount of wealth for most people. Alice's education for an entire year in a magic academy had cost forty gold suns. Five hundred gold suns was enough to change someone's life. However, Illa wasn't done yet.

"In addition, we are also looking for a certain kind of tree bark, which I've had an [Artist] draw a picture of. Anyone who can figure out where this type of tree bark grows can also get a reward of thirty gold suns . . ." Illa said.

"Can you let me see that picture?" asked one of the [Adventurers].

Illa immediately handed the piece of paper over and then started distributing extra copies of the drawing.

"I believe I've seen this before," said one of the [Adventurers] after a few moments. "I can mark the spot on a map, if you have one that covers the nearby area."

"Oh? Already?" said Illa, sounding pleasantly surprised. "All right, mark it. I'll send a few [Scouts] to examine the area, and if your claim can be verified, I'll give you the reward."

A [Cartographer] led the [Adventurer] to another room, where Alice could see the two of them start messing with a larger sheet of paper.

After the first [Adventurer] spoke up, there was silence for a while. Then the [Adventurers] started looking at Alice with fervent expressions.

"You're the one in charge of figuring out if any weird enchanting materials meet the criteria for the reward, right?" asked one.

Alice nodded.

The [Adventurer] grinned. "I have a few weird materials at my home. Can you wait half an hour for me to get them and come back?"

Alice nodded. "I expect to stay in this manor until a stable source of enchanting materials is found." Alice glanced at Illa for a moment. "If you have any materials you want to submit to me . . . give them to Illa. She will turn them in to me afterward?" Alice said. The last half of her statement came across as more of a question than a statement, since she wasn't sure if that would ruin Illa's schedule or something. Illa, however, simply nodded.

"That works for me," she said.

The [Adventurers] nodded and started breaking into groups of twos and threes. Then, much to Alice's amusement, she saw a few [Adventurers] dash out of the manor, as if the reward money depended on how quickly they could run.

Alice resisted the urge to chuckle.

Illa turned toward Alice.

"Once they get back, I'll send any relevant materials to your room after a few [Guards] make sure there aren't any poisons or other dangers mixed into the materials. You can check them afterward and then tell me if any of the objects meet your needs. After that, I'll do follow-up questions about the mass extraction of the material. Does that work for you?"

"Yes."

Illa nodded. "Good. I'll leave you to it," she said.

Alice quickly retreated to her room before she went back to sleep so that she could keep testing her enchantments.

Alice was occasionally woken up by a [Maid] bringing more enchanting materials for testing purposes, which Alice constantly crammed into her storage perk before going back to sleep. She spent most of the next two days in her dream library, with the occasional meal or bathroom break slipped in to get some exercise. Sadly, after two days, none of the enchanting materials so far had met her needs. Her progress in creating a prototype enchantment setup had made some progress, which blunted the sting of not finding what she had come here for.

Alice had discovered that if an enchantment could remember at least three instructions related to pure mana, she could get the stupid enchantment to locate the right type of magic seed. One instruction was to locate the human body, the next found certain *types* of mana cluster, and then the third one checked the magic seed to make sure it was a class seed and not a magic seed.

She just needed to figure out how to locate the correct class each time and ignore other class fractals. Then she needed to get the actual filtration part of the enchantment working . . . in short, Alice still had a very long way to go. But at least she was making progress.

The [Adventurer] who had claimed to know the location of the tree bark Alice wanted had come through, at least. There was a decently large grove of trees with the correct type of bark about three hours away from the city. While it was a long walk, the bark was plentiful enough that it could meet Alice's immediate needs, even if it would probably only serve as a piece of the final enchantment.

As Alice was thinking about enchanting materials, she heard someone gently but firmly rap on her door. Alice frowned and opened it. On the other side of the door, she saw the [Maid] Ellia, looking anxious.

"Lady Alice, Honored Immortal Ethan and Lady Illa request your presence," she said. "It's an emergency. A large swarm of monsters is attacking the city walls."

Chapter 20

Alice stood on the walls of Cyra and looked at the monster swarm in the distance. She could see a pack of giant wolves lobbing fireballs at the wooden wall, where they crashed against the matrix of perks keeping the wall stable and intact. Their bodies were half hidden by the trees, making it easy for them to dodge the stray arrows and missiles that the other mages on the walls were throwing at them. While some wolves occasionally fell, the number that died each second was alarmingly low compared to how quickly the perks maintaining the wall were weakening. Worse, the mages on the wall had limited mana, and it was dwindling with each passing minute.

However, the wolves weren't the most worrying part. That was because they weren't alone. In the trees, Alice could see a pack of Lovecraftian crows eyeing the walls. The horrifying creatures had two extra eyes on each of their wings, and their torsos looked almost like mirrors rather than any sort of biological component. She had no idea what type of monster the crows were, but they looked unnerving.

The prospect of monster species cooperating was new and terrifying. Every time Alice had seen two different species of monster near each other, they'd tried to eat each other. Now, for the first time in recorded history, two monster species were working together to break into Cyra and eat the people there.

Alice narrowed her eyes and turned toward Ethan, a few meters away, and Illa, who was directing the [Archers] and mages.

"The wolves are trying to burn down the wall," Ethan said. "They'll eventually punch through the antifire perks and light the wall up. The crows haven't taken action yet, but it feels like they're waiting for something." He turned toward Illa. "What do you think?"

"Well, they seem to be working together. Worse, they are staying out of range and using the trees for cover instead of just charging. This is not how monsters usually behave. Do you see any alphas? If we can take them out, the monsters might stop using tactics. I hope," said Illa, her face scrunched in concentration.

After a moment, Alice focused on her mana-related senses and started scanning the area as well.

Normally, monster alphas were pretty easy to notice. They were bigger than their subordinates and they usually sat in the center of their pack. After several seconds of searching, Alice shook her head.

"I can't find any monster alphas," she said.

"How long can the wooden walls last?" asked Ethan.

"Fifteen to twenty minutes before their perks fail. Maybe half an hour if we thin out the swarm enough. Assuming the crows don't do anything, at least," Illa replied. "{Locate the Commander} isn't finding any monster alphas. I can feel my perk activating, but nothing is happening. It's like . . . Alice, that rainbow mana cascade that we saw a few days ago—it looks like the mana that you've spent so much time studying, right?"

"It's System mana, yes."

Illa simply took Alice's words in stride, nodding as she looked over the monsters.

"The feeling I'm getting from my perk is similar to a battle I participated in when I was still in the army. There was a [Nomad Commander] I tried to locate and remove early in the fight. He specialized in stealth and movement perks, and he was a massive pain in the neck. Eventually, one of my [Assassins] managed to {Locate Target} and cut him down. But my perk kept failing to find the [Nomad Commander], even though I could feel it activating each time."

"Is your perk high level?"

"No. It's actually intended to find my *own* commander. I just got creative and started using it to locate enemy commanders, too, but it's a level-twenty perk. Nothing special. My old [Commander] made all the [Soldiers] grab it and then taught us a bunch of signals. We knew that 'if the [Commander] moves west a lot, swap to ranged attacks and start harassing,' for example. If he needed to move for other reasons, he would disguise his location from perks. However, the problem is that monsters *shouldn't* have a defense against this perk," said Illa. "I've found it pretty useful for hunting down any spidercrab alphas that pop up too close to the farms. The fact that it isn't working right now only makes me more uneasy."

The wolf alpha and crow alpha were shielding themselves against Illa's searching perk?

Alice started wondering if the alphas for these monsters specialized in stealth, in addition to the fire attacks of the wolves. Or perhaps the crow alpha, wherever it was, was cloaking itself and the wolf alpha? She had no idea what kind of magic the crow monsters could use, but some sort of stealth-related magic would make sense. Alice found herself dearly hoping that this was some sort of innate, biological ability that some of the monsters here had, because she had a sinking feeling that there might be other ways that monsters could cloak themselves against Illa's perk. And all those methods would be *far* worse for humanity as a whole.

As if to corroborate Alice's fears, a moment later, she saw something that sent chills down her spine.

One of the monsters pulsed with a type of mana none of its brethren had.

The monster didn't use rainbow mana. Not a single fleck of the mana inside its body resembled the insanely complex, detailed constructions that the System routinely created. However, it still faintly reminded Alice of the System, even if it was drastically simplified. It only took Alice a few seconds to realize what she was looking at: The unique monstrous wolf had some kind of knockoff perk.

Even if it was a knockoff, the sight of it still sent alarm bells ringing in Alice's mind. A monster had a perk. That was *terrifying*.

She scrambled to identify what the monster's perk did. Fortunately, the way it worked seemed obvious after a few minutes of observation. The perk enhanced its magic somehow. Every time one of its fireballs hit the wooden wall, it looked far more concentrated and controlled than the attacks of its brethren. Even though the creature didn't use any more mana than the other wolves surrounding it, it was managing to do much more damage because its fireballs were more condensed than the other attackers'.

Without thinking, Alice immediately reached into her storage perk and grabbed one of her enchanted bracelets. Several of the bracelet's stone beads were filled to the brim with kinetic and organic mana. They were enchantments Alice had made for her own use—they would fly like bullets toward any target she had, accelerate again in midair, and then use organic mana to rend and tear whatever flesh they came into contact with.

She activated the beads on the bracelet, and they seemed to vanish as they tore through the air and toward the wolf. Before it could duck behind a tree for cover, Alice's beads ripped into its stomach and head.

The monster died instantly, along with two other nearby wolves. For a moment, Alice felt a surge of triumph in her chest—before a fourth wolf nearby lit up with a different perk. This one had some combination of fire mana and organic mana in its body. Alice shuddered as she saw the monster use *organic* mana. Monsters shouldn't have access to organic mana at all—it was usually exclusive to humans.

Before Alice had time to react, the monster seemed to speed up. Its movements were eerily similar to Alice's own when she used {Adrenaline Rush}, as the monster dodged the blood and remaining beads from Alice's attack. It looked at Alice and gave Alice a knowing smirk with its tiny, all-too-intelligent eyes. Alice felt {Enhanced Senses} mark the location of the creature like a giant beacon, alerting her to its exact position.

A moment later, the wolf froze as Ethan flung a pebble at it at nearly the speed of sound. It ripped through the creature's brain with a massive boom and turned the creature's body into paste.

But even though the creature had died, Alice didn't feel at ease.

Two of the wolves had used knockoff perks. Monsters shouldn't be using perks at all. Monsters didn't have access to the System. The entire reason humans could thrive on this planet was because they had the System and monsters didn't. Even then, humans hadn't conquered this world—the Western Continent was firmly outside the reach of humans here.

Now monsters were using perks *and* displaying the ability to cooperate with each other.

Alice felt fear sprout in her stomach like a vile seed. Was this some sort of unusual mutation, caused by monsters absorbing a great deal of mana? Was she reading too much into things? Or were her fears correct—had monsters somehow accessed the System?

Alice decided that the moment this attack ended, she would have Ethan get her some spidercrabs and see what happened when they absorbed enough mana. But for now, she needed to report what she had seen. She turned toward Ethan and Illa.

"The monsters are using some sort of facsimile perks," said Alice. "They appear inferior to proper perks, but they are similar in nature."

Illa's face whitened, while Ethan grimaced.

"Monsters with *perks*?" said Illa.

Ethan took a deep breath before he shook his head. "That . . . is quite dangerous. I was originally hoping you'd get a few levels out of this in a fairly safe environment, but I'm taking action," he said as he shot an apologetic glance toward Alice. "If monsters are using perks, I don't want an unpredictable component of the battlefield to kill you by mistake."

Ethan's magic tendrils tore out of his body before they reached for one of the buckets of stones the mages on the wall had been using as ammunition.

A few moments later, Ethan began launching volleys of stones at the horde of monsters. Not every single stone connected with its target—a fair number collided with trees. However, Ethan's status as an Immortal clearly wasn't for show, either. Each second, a dozen more fire wolves dropped dead as the stones slammed into the wolves and turned them into paste.

After a few seconds of stunned silence from the monster side, the crows took action.

Suddenly, Alice's vision twisted. Instead of seeing the forest when she looked beyond the wall, she saw an illusory mirror image of herself and the others standing on the wall. Ethan's volley of stones vanished into thin air. Another second passed, and then all of Ethan's projectiles reappeared—but this time they were hurtling straight toward Alice, Ethan, and Illa.

A burst of rainbow mana flooded Ethan's body. His forty mana tendrils turned into 140 and surged out to intercept the stones. Then he activated his electromagnetic seed and a bolt of lightning cracked through the sky like a whip.

The strange mirror image of Alice and the others shattered, and the burst of lightning ripped through a nearby wolf. The other wolves reacted immediately, backing away from the smoking corpse of their packmate. A few moments later, Alice saw Ethan toss another lightning bolt at a nearby wolf—which *somehow* deflected it with its own magic. Apparently, lightning was close enough to fire that the wolves could control it.

Experimentally, Ethan heated up a few of the stones with his thermal seed, until they became closer to magma than proper stone, and then tried tossing them at the crows. Much like the lightning bolts, the wolves redirected the globs of magma toward the wall. A moment later, the crows recreated the mirror image of the wall, and the wolves neatly deflected Ethan's next lightning bolt.

The monsters were definitely working together. The crows were handling physical attacks and the wolves were handling light and heat-based attacks. A few moments after the mirror wall was reestablished, the wolves began cautiously peppering the wall with fireballs again.

Before Alice could stew in her dread any further, Ethan suddenly grinned, and most of his magic tendrils reached toward the ground. Normally, any magic performed more than a meter away from somebody required exponentially more mana to activate than before, getting worse the larger the distance was.

But Ethan didn't seem to care about that at all as the grass outside the wall started to ripple and slither. In seconds, the ground turned into a giant wave of snakelike vines, which then lunged toward the mirror. A moment later, the vines vanished—and Alice heard wolves and crows shriek in terror. The mirror vanished, and Alice saw a picture of pure carnage on the other side of the wall . . .

The wolves fired several blasts of fire at the vines, but the vines didn't even slow down. The wolves and crows finally seemed to realize they were outmatched and started howling at each other. Alice squinted at the fragmented, ruined reflection that still hovered in the air in front of the forest and wondered why the giant mirror stopped the stones but not the grass and vines.

"Whatever they're doing, it can't stop living things or nonphysical objects," said Ethan, seeing her confusion. "Not sure why, but that's what my perk is telling me."

As Alice watched in awe, the pack of wolves and their crow allies turned and began fleeing back into the forest, leaving Alice feeling unnerved.

"They're running away?" she said.

Monsters did sometimes flee from a fight, but it was rare. When monsters were in packs, fleeing became so rare it was practically nonexistent. Yet, right before her eyes, an entire pack of monsters was fleeing.

Ethan started launching volleys of stones at them again as they fled, and the [Archers] and other mages quickly joined in. Several monsters fell, but others managed to flee into the cover of the trees.

Ethan grimaced. "Down a lot of mana," he said. "But at least we got rid of them." He glanced at the forest before turning toward Illa. "Any chance you have the forces to pursue?"

Illa glanced at the [Archers] and mages assembled on the wall and then shook her head. "Too many of them left. The monsters have already shown remarkable intelligence. If they resort to ambush tactics, or another monster swarm attacks the town, the results could be catastrophic. I don't think it's worth pursuing given my forces." Illa sighed and shrugged. "There just aren't enough people in Cyra to support a big army."

"Figures," Ethan said with a sigh. "Alice, you're our System expert. What do you make of the monsters this time? This all happened right after that giant burst of rainbow mana. Any connection there?"

"Well . . . probably. My best guess is that when the monsters came into contact with raw, uncontrolled System mana for the first time a few days ago, *something* happened. The monsters are using perks, which they've never done before, and they're also using tactics, at least on a rudimentary level. Normally, a monster swarm wouldn't flee unless the pack leader died, but this time the monsters fled without us even seeing a monster alpha." Alice shivered. "If the monsters changed because of their contact with System mana, I suspect that this isn't a problem localized to Cyra. It looks like the collapse of the System has left us with even more problems to deal with."

Ethan frowned. "That is . . . concerning." Then his gaze turned thoughtful. "You said that monsters might have reacted to the System mana floating in the air a few days ago. But you aren't sure, right? Do you think it's possible to try exposing some spidercrabs to System mana and see if they also pick up a few perks? It might give us valuable data, and it would only take me a few days to get some spidercrabs ready for testing." Alice felt some of her fear dissipate as Ethan returned her focus to experiments. She had *never* seen monsters acquire perks before . . . but she also wasn't a combat-oriented mage. She would leave the matters of tactics and [Soldiers] to the experts and focus on her research. She would help wherever she could, but there were limits to what she could do alone.

"Get me a few spidercrabs. I'll see what I can learn from them," said Alice.

Chapter 21

As the last remnants of the monster swarm disappeared into the forest, the incident came to an end. However, even though the two monster swarms had withdrawn from Cyra, they didn't withdraw from Alice's mind.

Monsters had worked *with* each other. Monsters had used facsimile perks during a fight. Alice wasn't sure which of those pieces of information was more terrifying, but combined, they spoke of an entirely new threat to humanity. After learning that there was *yet another* deadly threat to the human species in this world, Alice was starting to feel exhausted. Even keeping track of all the different ways people were in danger felt like a full-time job to her.

After the trio returned to Illa's manor, Alice threw herself onto her bed and tried to calm down. Everything was just starting to feel like it was too much for her. Every single time she started working on a solution to one problem, another problem appeared. Every time she took a step forward, it felt like she was five steps behind. Every single solution needed days or weeks to execute, while new crises appeared like the heads of a hydra. Alice kept searching and hoping for some sort of magic bullet that would cure the whole situation, but unless she found a way to restore the System tomorrow, she had no idea how to fix everything.

For a few moments, Alice simply lay on her bed and stared at the ceiling, trying to find some sense of inner peace as she grappled with the frustration of yet another crisis to solve. Then, for the first time, Alice curled up and cried in bed. She felt overwhelmed, and she needed some time to just . . . not think for a while.

After several minutes, Alice started pulling herself back together. She took a quick look in the mirror to make sure she didn't look like a mess. Even if her companions might understand, she knew what Ethan would say if he saw her walking around with puffy eyes. She was a potential Immortal, and one of the key researchers combating the crisis. If it looked like Alice was losing hope, it would lead to morale issues they couldn't afford.

So Alice took a few minutes to collect herself before she left her room to find Ethan. Even if she wasn't feeling great, she still needed to convey any information she could gather to someone who knew what to do with it. It only took her a minute to make her way to his room before knocking on the door.

"Alice. Come in," said Ethan, his voice flat and controlled.

Alice opened the door and saw that Ethan looked far more composed than she did. He had several pieces of paper in front of him, which, Alice realized with some surprise, seemed to list the combat classes and perks of several people in Cyra.

This certainly caught Alice off guard. People usually guarded their combat information very closely. Yet, right in front of Ethan, the combat information of thirty [Guards] from Cyra was neatly laid out. Some of them had scouting-related perks. Some of them had direct combat-related perks. Some of them had antimagic perks. Ethan even had detailed explanations of the uses each [Guard] had found for their skill set.

"Combat information?" asked Alice. "From [Spies]?"

"No, from the [Soldiers] themselves," said Ethan.

"Really? I mean, if people were advertising noncombat abilities, that would make sense, but why did they give you their combat information?" Alice still didn't quite believe it.

Ethan chuckled.

"Before you reached the walls, some people noticed a few other odd monsters—there were three more that [Adventurers] and other [Guards] have seen over the past twenty-four hours. One had a self-healing ability, another had access to an unusual mana type, and the final one was abnormally physically strong. I shared your speculation that the monsters are using knockoff System perks with the [Guards], and they had *quite* the reaction. Plenty of [Guards] have family members who live in town, after all, and people are worried that things will get worse.

"I need as much information as possible to help keep things under control, so I asked Illa to persuade her [Guards] to share information with me. She came through," said Ethan. "This also helps me figure out which [Guards] should be responsible for overseeing the harvest of the bark we need, as well as any other enchanting materials. Normally, [Guards] just give a general overview of what they're good at to their [Commanders], but with exact descriptions from the [Guards], we can put together more efficient teams. Of course, not all the [Guards] shared their information, but about half of them cooperated." Ethan shrugged. "Honestly, it's more than I was expecting."

Alice nodded, but Ethan's words brought to mind *another* problem that she needed to think about.

Enchantment materials were going to be harder than ever to come across. Now that monsters were more dangerous, finding and harvesting new enchanting materials was about to get far more complicated. After all, anyone in the woods probably needed [Guards] to keep them and their cargo safe.

Worse, supplies might not be the only problem the empowered monster swarms would pose. [Messengers] would also have a harder time delivering messages, slowing down the information lifeline vital to Illvaria's effectiveness as a country.

Alice felt her stress and frustration start to build up again, and she took a few deep breaths to calm herself. If she started crying in Ethan's room, Alice would die of embarrassment. Ethan looked at Alice for a moment and frowned.

"Are you all right?" he asked.

"Just stressed out," said Alice, resisting the urge to rub her forehead in frustration. "There are too many things going wrong at once. When I first arrived on this world, I thought the System was weird and fascinating, and I enjoyed exploring it. But now, it feels like something new goes wrong every day. I wish the System hadn't just . . . disappeared like this." Alice shook her head as she tried to quell another wave of waterworks. "Anyway, I'll get back to it. I still need to keep working on that enchantment."

Ethan looked at Alice for a moment and then sighed. "Alice . . . while the centuries have changed a lot about how I perceive the world, I haven't forgotten what it's like to feel frustrated or stressed. Today, we learned a new, important piece of information—but that information isn't directly related to you. Don't forget, you're a *researcher*. Leave things like tactics and military matters to people like me and Illa. Tell us what you observe and then let us handle the rest. Don't try to solve every problem." Ethan paused and scanned Alice's face before he focused on her eyes for a moment. "Your eyes look puffy. How about you take the rest of the day off? Take some time to settle your mental state and then get back to it."

"What?" Alice asked.

"I didn't bring a [Psychologist] with us to help treat mental issues, but . . . I believe that at some point you mentioned having a few acquaintances in Cyra, right? One was named . . . Milo, I think? And the local [Priest]? You'll have more to do soon enough anyway—it won't take me too long to round up some spidercrabs for your testing. Until then, go relax. Consider that an order from me, as your mentor," Ethan said as the corners of his lips quirked upward. "Don't forget, you're not alone. Illa and I and other people are also working to solve this crisis. We're here to help you. Cecilia's mages will help you handle enchantment-related stuff. You're a part of a team, not the sole person responsible for saving the world."

Alice paused, then nodded. Ethan was right. She was still trying to do an awful lot of different things on her own—which was probably part of the reason why she felt so stressed out and frustrated. No matter how many minutes and hours she had in a day, it would never be enough if she didn't rely on other people. Alice had already found a way to use her perks to get a full twenty-four hours of work done every single day. Of those, Alice spent about twenty of them working, with one to two hours of pleasure reading and two hours of meals, bathroom breaks, and other bodily necessities set aside. There really wasn't much left that Alice could use in a given day to work on the crisis—unless she stopped needing food in the near future.

"I'll go visit my acquaintances," she said after a few moments. Ethan gave her an encouraging smile, and Alice left Illa's manor.

Even though it had been months since Alice was last in Cyra, thanks to her memory-boosting perks, she still perfectly remembered the way to the Church of the System, and also remembered where Milo usually worked.

Alice decided to find Milo first. She had always enjoyed chatting with the simple [Kinetic Mage], and seeing him again might be good for her mind.

She searched through town for a while, and asked several passersby if they had seen Milo. It took her nearly fifteen minutes to track him down.

"Sir Milo!" said Alice the moment she saw him.

"Lady Alice," he said, giving her an easy grin. "It's been . . . months, hasn't it? I was glad to hear that you were doing so well last time you sent a letter." Milo chuckled. "I didn't think I'd see you in person so soon, though. It's almost as surprising as when you told me you had become an apprentice of an Immortal. Funny how life works sometimes, isn't it?"

"Indeed," said Alice, feeling a bit of weight fall off her shoulders. She checked the road and guessed, with some surprise, where Milo was going. "Are you heading to the Church of the System right now?"

"I am. I wanted to borrow the holy book for a while—I know that recently, it's been hard to see our perks properly, but I still like to look at the higher-rarity achievements sometimes. I doubt I'll ever actually get one, but it's nice to dream about it, you know?" said Milo, before laughing. "Not that I'm eager to try. Most of those high-rarity achievements that are even sort of related to my specialties also have incredibly deadly acquisition requirements. I don't want to die."

Alice nodded, right as they finally arrived at the door to the church. Alice took a look around. The walls of the church seemed a bit less vividly painted than when she was last in Cyra, but the depictions of various Immortals using impressive perks were still as clear as before.

Now that Alice had met three of Illvaria's six Immortals, she was pretty sure she could at least vaguely recognize a few of the paintings. The Immortal drawn on the outer wall of the church using magic tendrils to heal someone looked kind of like Ethan, and another of the paintings of a woman singing looked like Allira. Of course, the resemblance wasn't perfect—but it was close enough that Alice could tell the paintings were at least influenced by the Immortals in question.

Alice took a deep breath and then stepped into the church with Milo.

There weren't any other people in the church besides the other person Alice wanted to see—a [Priest of the System] Alice knew well.

"Father Friedheim," said Alice.

"Lady Alice! It has been . . . quite a few months now." Father Friedheim gave Alice a warm smile. "I'm glad to see that life in the capital agrees with you so well. I've heard about your exploits. Becoming the apprentice of an Immortal is no easy feat." Then he turned toward Milo. "Sir Milo. It is good to see you as well. Are you here to see the book of the System again?"

Milo gave Father Friedheim a friendly nod.

Father Friedheim turned back toward Alice. "You should tell me more about how you've been doing in the capital! I'd love to hear the story firsthand, if you're willing to share it!"

Alice nodded, and gave Father Friedheim a slightly strained grin. "It was a bit . . . stressful. It involved a Society attack and a few near scrapes with death, but I'm glad Honored Immortal Ethan opted to take me under his wing. I just find myself quite short on time these days."

Father Friedheim laughed. "Being short on time is the curse of those searching for their path within the System. The System demands much from us in exchange for the blessings it gives. But this excellence is what defines potential Immortals from the rest. One cannot get anything without first putting in hard work and effort, after all." His eyes shone. "I hear that you have been overcoming a different trial as well? I hear you've been instrumental in illuminating the System's trial."

"System's . . . trial?" asked Alice.

Father Friedheim nodded eagerly. "The System's trial. The fact that, currently, our status screens display gibberish when we try to pick a new perk, and that mages are in danger if they form a new seed, and monsters have grown stronger. All of them must be trials of the System," Father Friedheim said.

Alice felt a little bit surprised by Father Friedheim's interpretation. He seemed to approve of Alice's work and progress toward reaching Immortality. At the same time, he also didn't seem to take the current crisis very seriously and didn't seem to mind Alice's research. She wasn't sure what to make of that.

"So . . . how do you feel about my . . . studies?" asked Alice, more curious than afraid.

"I've heard from several reliable sources that the System itself has approved of your research," said Father Friedheim, giving Alice an amused look. "It gave you an achievement for it, no? If even the System itself approves of your actions, who am I to question it? Though I do think you're misunderstanding the current situation. The System is surely giving people more room to grow without its benevolence. I fail to understand whether this is a trial given to the world by the System, so that we may grow stronger because of it, or whether this is a warning to us. That is for the System to know and for us to discover. But I have no feelings about your research, unlike some *other* people who are less perceptive." Father Friedheim sighed. "It is a shame some are so misguided by their faith and fail to see the truth before our very eyes, but . . . that is life sometimes. Either way, I'm glad to see you again. Come, tell me about your time in Metsel. I will make some tea." He turned toward Milo. "Would you like some, too? If Lady Alice is going to have a cup of tea and chat for a while, you should join us."

At Father Friedheim's words, Alice felt herself relax a bit. She had never been particularly religious—on Earth, she had been an atheist, and that hadn't really changed since coming to Luliv. Alice felt the existence of the System was indisputable, but she didn't really feel that it was a god.

But even though Alice wasn't religious, Father Friedheim had still given her a fair amount of emotional support during her first few weeks in Cyra. She was surprised to learn how relieved she felt that the [Priest] didn't disapprove of her research.

Milo gave Father Friedheim a nod, and Alice and Milo quickly seated themselves at a table in one of the side rooms, obviously meant for entertaining guests.

The three settled down over a few cups of tea, and Alice started telling Father Friedheim and Milo about her studies in the Magic Academy, her run-ins with the Society of Starry Eyes, and her time learning under Immortal Ethan. Father Friedheim seemed fascinated by Alice's stories, as well as her attempts to make mana baptisms safer. When Alice spoke about her time in the Magic Academy, Milo seemed to be caught up in his own memories of the past. At the end of Alice's story about rescuing Samantha from the Society, Milo gave her a gentle grin and an approving nod.

"You did a pretty good job, Lady Alice. It takes a lot of guts to put yourself in danger to help a friend."

Eventually, Alice ran out of stories, so Milo and Father Friedheim began telling her about what she had missed in Cyra. Eventually, Alice pulled a board game out of her storage perk, and the three played a round before it grew dark.

As Alice walked back toward Illa's manor, she reflected that it hadn't been a very productive day, but she felt less tense and stressed out. All in all, it had been good to take a break.

Chapter 22

After spending the rest of the day with Milo and Father Friedheim, Alice felt refreshed. She followed it up by spending her time in her dream library reading another autobiography doubling as an adventure novel, about one of the [Kings] of the Central Continent, and woke up feeling better than ever. After breakfast, Alice started reading over the reports Ethan had left for her.

Through letters and reports, Ethan's information network had confirmed that two other towns in southern Illvaria had been attacked by intelligent, organized monster swarms. One of the two had successfully driven off the newly upgraded monsters, while the other town was still fighting. Both towns had included reports of monsters with "unusual" abilities, which made Alice's stomach sink. Monsters accessing System perks wasn't unique to Cyra. It was a worldwide phenomenon.

The second thing that Ethan's reports told her of was far more unusual. One of the [Scouts] from a nearby town had noticed a small horde of monsters in the woods staring at a tree, as if they were studying it. The [Scout] had felt that the behavior of the monsters was unusual, so he had sat around to watch.

However, as the monsters watched the tree . . . the tree slowly started to decay and warp. Not as if it were dying, or as if it were being influenced by magic somehow. Instead, according to the report, it was more like the tree had been shrinking or fizzling out of existence. The [Scout] hadn't been able to detect the monsters using any sort of magic on the tree, despite having a perk specialized in detecting creatures using magic nearby.

Afterward, with a fizzling sound, the tree had popped like a grenade from Earth, sending wooden shrapnel everywhere. The monster horde had fled the scene and started avoiding other nearby trees. Anytime they strayed too close to another tree, it *also* exploded.

This report left Alice scratching her head.

Was a monster misusing a perk somehow and accidentally causing the trees to explode? Or perhaps the trees had some sort of potential as enchanting materials, and the monsters were somehow setting off a sort of . . . magical reaction? Or perhaps an [Enchanter] had just rigged the trees to explode for some reason? Alice had absolutely no idea what the report meant—it seemed like total nonsense. Since Alice had no clue what to make of it, she could only keep an eye out for similar ones. The [Scout] hadn't taken any samples from the tree shrapnel, which was a shame—Alice would have loved to see if it could help her figure out why the trees were exploding.

Underneath the pile of reports, Ethan had also left her a note informing her that he had secured a few spidercrabs for testing purposes. They were now locked in cages in Illa's storage room, ready for Alice's tests.

After looking through the reports, she thought about what she needed to do next. She had two major issues she wanted to focus on.

First, she still needed to develop enchantments to prevent humans from falling into mana madness. This couldn't be delayed—it was a ticking time bomb that would eventually hit every human on this planet if nothing was done to stop it.

She realized that she would need to hand part of that job to the mages she and Cecilia were training. The entire point of their training was to make Alice's job easier, and it was high time she let them start contributing to the current crisis. All five of the mages had been selected because they were good at enchanting, and right now, Alice's biggest problem was *designing* the enchantment she needed. After all, the harvesting operations for the necessary enchanting materials hadn't really gotten underway yet.

The mages she and Cecilia were teaching might not be able to actually use filtration mana yet . . . but they could still do some of the legwork for designing filtration-related enchantments. Alice found Cecilia and let her know what she needed, and Cecilia promised to get her [Enchanters] to start working on it.

After that, Alice got to work on her new self-appointed task.

She needed to figure out what was wrong with monsters. Ethan had come through and gotten her test subjects, and unlike human test subjects, Alice had no problems using monsters as living guinea pigs. She found a few [Guards] to come along with her, just in case something went wrong, then made her way to the room where the spidercrabs were stored and gave them a scan. None of them seemed unusual in any way.

A moment later, Alice tried creating a bit of rainbow mana using one of her perks, and then frowned. She had originally been planning to just take some rainbow mana from a perk and push it toward the spidercrabs, but trying to maneuver the rainbow mana proved ridiculously challenging. She had a sneaking suspicion that this method wouldn't work.

Where else could she get System mana?

A moment later, Alice's eyes lit up. She turned to one of the [Guards].

"Hey, could you go tell Ethan to get me a big pile of low-quality System-enchantment items? Just random stuff that gives an attribute or two," she said.

"Oh, and ask him for some random enchanting materials, too. Nothing special—just low-quality stuff that nobody will miss if it gets destroyed."

The [Guard] saluted her before running out of the room.

An hour later, Alice had a giant pile of System-enchantment clothes and low-quality enchanting materials. Most of the clothes gave minor boosts to the wearer, such as plus-one [Strength] or [Dexterity]. Alice also had a few pieces of clothing that had regular perks applied to them, just like the skirt she had purchased in Cyra all those months ago that covered wardrobe malfunctions. These ones just made the clothes slightly tougher and more stain-resistant. However, Alice was mostly curious to see if these perks would induce some kind of special change in the monstrous test subjects.

Alice spent a few moments reviewing her plans before she committed to taking action.

There were two things she wanted to test.

First, she wanted to see what happened when monsters were exposed to System mana. She just hoped that her substitute forms of System mana would work for her tests.

Second, the report about the mysterious exploding trees had gotten Alice thinking. She wasn't sure what to make of the incident, but her first guess was that monsters could try to enchant objects now. She would try tossing enchanting materials at the spidercrabs and see if anything happened. The second test was riddled with problems, and if nothing happened, it would more than likely be because Alice had made an error somewhere—but right now, she had so little information that silly mistakes were inevitable anyway. She would just try tossing materials around and see if anything worked, and reassess if she ran out of weird ideas.

After Alice finished running over her plans, she dragged one of the spidercrabs out of its cage using kinetic magic. The spidercrab thrashed and squirmed wildly, but its innate mana resistance meant little to Alice. The difference in mana quantity was too vast for the creature to overcome.

Then, before Alice tried stuffing an enchanted shirt down its throat, she got another idea. She couldn't just toss System enchantments directly at the spidercrabs by borrowing mana from her perks, but she *did* have another way to replicate the System. She had seen, and even recreated, a few basic System mana fractals using her own abilities before, after all. Specifically, Alice had managed to create a mana-filtration fractal, back when she was trying to create a magic seed without the help of the System.

She decided to try that first, *then* start cramming clothes down the spidercrab's throat. She quickly built another mana-filtration fractal. It was missing several types of mana and couldn't really be considered a proper recreation of the System fractal. Alice also skipped a few steps, just in case the spidercrab managed to somehow learn something from the fractal by eating it. If the spidercrab ate her messed-up fractal and then grew stronger, Alice wanted the creature to be as weak as possible.

The spidercrab completely ignored the dysfunctional System fractal, which *really* confused Alice. Most monsters went after the nearest source of mana like moths to a flame. How could a monster *ignore* a nearby source of mana? This was . . . odd.

Alice created a *proper* mana fractal and shoved it toward the spidercrab. This time, the creature consumed it normally—and then its stomach started to swell up like a balloon. The mana inside the creature's stomach started to change, and for a brief moment, it faintly resembled the mana fractal Alice had created. However, there were also a huge number of differences.

As she watched, the creature's stomach continued to expand.

The monster started futilely kicking the floor, scrabbling with its spidery legs as the top half of its body grew larger and more distorted . . . before it stopped.

Instead of a normal spidercrab, the creature in front of Alice now resembled a fleshy balloon.

This result was *not* the outcome Alice expected.

She observed the creature for a few minutes but didn't notice any further changes. The creature kept awkwardly thrashing about, and if it weren't for the violence and hunger in the creature's eyes, Alice might have felt sorry for it.

She observed the creature for several minutes to see if the spidercrab had gained any new abilities. However, apart from its grotesque, twisted appearance, it still didn't seem much different from a regular spidercrab. Eventually, she put it out of its misery before inspecting its corpse. Then Alice froze as she realized the spidercrab's corpse was *quite* unusual.

All monsters had monster cores—it seemed to be the organ they used to interact with and store mana, and it was basically required for a monster to keep living. However, the spidercrab's monster core was swollen, much like its body had been.

Alice frowned. This was *also* unexpected. Was it something she could replicate with the other spidercrabs? She dragged over another spidercrab and repeated the experiment with another mana-filtration fractal. Just like the first time, she started out with a broken mana fractal, which this spidercrab ignored as if it didn't exist at all. This puzzled Alice—but the monster ate the second, functioning mana fractal, just like the first spidercrab had. Then, just like with the first spidercrab, the upper half of its body ballooned as its monster core started to swell.

Alice shrugged and left the spidercrab alive this time. She dragged over a third test subject. This time, Alice tried feeding it the skirt with an anti-stain perk. Then Alice tried dumping some dye on that spidercrab, as well as another random spidercrab, to see if the first spidercrab had become more resistant to stains. She noticed that the test spidercrab seemed somewhat less covered in dye afterward, although it was subtle.

Right as Alice finished inspecting both monsters, Ethan entered the room. He glanced at her test subjects, which were now rather unfortunate shades of orange, and tried not to laugh.

"Have you found anything?" he asked.

"I . . . THINK that monsters now adopt characteristics from whatever mana they come in contact with," said Alice. "I can't think about *why* that would be the case, but it seems to be true."

"Is that so?" said Ethan. "I don't recall monsters ever displaying this kind of adaptability before."

Alice nodded. "Neither do I. This spidercrab seems more stain resistant after it ate a skirt with a stain-resistance perk. I have yet to see whether other spidercrabs can replicate the feat, and I also wonder if this adaptation only happens with certain types of perks. However, either way, the situation is quite concerning."

"What do you have left to test with the spidercrabs?" asked Ethan.

"Just normal minor stat-boosting System enchantments," she said.

Ethan eyed the small pile of minor rings Alice had assembled, before he sighed. "Hopefully that test proves less worrying," he said. "Though at least we have some idea why the monsters have started using perks recently."

Alice threw a ring of plus-one strength at a different spidercrab.

The spidercrab didn't react to the enchanted ring at first. It was as if it couldn't see the System mana at all. It simply continued to thrash and try to escape.

Very curious.

Alice recalled that several months ago, when Allira had led a fight against some vinebears, some of the vinebears had tried to eat Allira's illusion of a town. However, in most cases that Alice had observed, monsters acted as if they didn't see the System at all. After the attack on Cyra two days ago, Alice had assumed that monsters were now able to see the System's mana 24-7. The previous spidercrab test subject had eaten the stain-proof skirt quickly enough. However, this spidercrab was acting as if it couldn't see the System-enchanted ring at all. This was quite unusual.

After several seconds of the spidercrab not reacting, Alice became irritated. She picked up the ring using kinetic magic and rammed it down the spidercrab's throat.

The creature shrieked in agony as Alice accidentally shoved the ring a *bit* too hard into its throat and broke a few things. Luckily, she didn't accidentally kill the creature. The spidercrab tried to screech at her, but with its throat half ruined, the spidercrab sounded more like it was gargling than screeching.

Alice didn't give up and continued trying to shove the ring down the creature's throat.

After a few minutes of wrangling, Alice finally managed to get the ring into the creature's digestive tract.

The monster continued lunging toward Alice for a few moments. Then it sat down, almost as if it needed to think for a while.

Inside the creature's body, Alice could see mana start to squirm and change. The mana started to warp, almost as if it were trying to replicate the mana of the ring Alice had just stuffed into it.

Alice brightened up, expecting that she would soon see a monster with slightly higher physical strength than normal.

However, the mana in the creature's body seemed slightly *off*. It started twitching and squirming, and the joints and muscles in its spidery limbs started to swell. The creature started thrashing and screeching at Alice for several more moments before it collapsed to the floor, unconscious.

Alice watched the spidercrab with great curiosity. The creature didn't seem to be improving quite as directly as she assumed it would. After seeing the monster swarm that had attacked Cyra, and seeing the stain-resistant spidercrab, Alice had somewhat expected the monster to instantly grow stronger. Instead, it had fallen into a coma, and she wasn't certain whether it was upgrading or dying. Clearly, the ability for monsters to upgrade themselves was a lot less omnipotent than she had imagined. A few moments later, she confirmed that the spidercrab wasn't improving—it was dying. She waited a few more minutes to see if anything changed, but ten minutes later, the creature was dead.

This left Alice scratching her head in confusion again.

Why did some monster upgrades seem to work while some failed? The spidercrab that had eaten a stain-resistant skirt was now resistant to being dyed different colors. The spidercrab that had been fed a strength ring had died. Was it because she had accidentally ruined its throat while feeding it? Alice tried the same experiment again with another spider crab, but she was more careful this time. The result did not change. The new spidercrab *also* died. What was the difference here?

Furthermore, why had monsters changed so much over the past few days? Before the collapse of the System, monsters hadn't had the ability to upgrade themselves by eating strange mana constructs. Now they could. What caused this change?

Alice sighed and rubbed her temples. She tried tossing the pile of enchanted materials at the spidercrabs to see if they did anything with them, and a few of her surviving test subjects walked over and started trying to gnaw at them. However, after a few seconds of trying and failing to eat a few metal ores with some mild potential for holding thermal enchantments, the spidercrabs lost interest and went back to trying to escape their cages and eat her. Nothing else happened.

Alice sighed.

She felt like she had learned something, at least, but she was also left even more confused about what had changed and why.

CHAPTER 23

After Alice's experiment was over, she returned to her room in order to handle her System notifications. Alice hadn't discovered anything revolutionary, beyond the fact that monsters reacted to some kinds of System mana and ignored others, but she still hoped to get a perk or two out of it. Before filtering her mana, she first summarized all the information she had gathered into a note for Ethan, then had a [Servant] deliver it. Alice hadn't learned very much useful information yet, but Ethan might still discover something.

Then Alice focused on her rewards. First, she used her filtration magic seed to purify all the clogged-up mana stuck in her class seeds, and then she used display mana to look at her new System notifications . . .

You have leveled up!
Scientist: 62→65, Scholar: 60→62, Survivor: 59→60

Apart from her new levels, there was one more notification that Alice was very pleased to see.

Scientific Discoveries (Rarity: N/A) IV→V
An achievement created by the For Science! perk. It currently has five successful experiments cataloged. Upon reaching five experiments, this achievement will receive a beneficial upgrade.
+20% class experience for all research-related classes (per tier of the achievement), +5% bonus to mental attribute growth (per tier of the achievement)

When Alice saw the second System notification, she grinned.

A long time ago, Alice had picked up a rather interesting perk.

> **For Science!**
> **Requirements: Scientist level 45 or higher**
>
> Whenever you successfully complete an experiment related to science or magic that you do not already know the results of (with reasonable certainty), you gain a permanent increase of 20% in leveling speed for all research-related classes. You will also gain a permanent 5% bonus to the attribute growth of all mental stats. (This will be added to your status screen as an achievement named {Scientific Discoveries Rarity: N/A}. Upon reaching five completed experiments, an additional beneficial effect will be added to the achievement.)

When Alice had taken the perk, she had wondered what the beneficial effect of the upgrade would be. She had not expected that it would take very long to reach rank five, considering how often she did experiments, but the perk's definition of an experiment had proven hard to nail down. Still, after several months of hard work, Alice could finally see the perk's upgraded version.

A few moments later, Alice saw a new System notification pop up.

> **Upgrade requirements met. {Scientific Discoveries} achievement reconstruction in progress.**

Alice was more than a little surprised to see that this System message didn't have any of the broken grammar or glitch signs she was getting used to. It looked exactly like the old System messages—complete, concise, and translated directly into English for her. Perhaps the notification for this upgrade had been created a long time ago and then stored somehow for future use? Since Alice didn't see any odd streams of System mana in her surroundings, that was her best guess for why the perk wasn't gibberish.

A few moments later, a new System notification appeared.

> **Upgrade Complete**
> **In Pursuit of Science**
>
> An achievement created by the For Science! perk. It has reached max tier and cannot improve anymore.
> +100% class experience for all research-related classes, +25% bonus to mental attribute growth.
>
> As a final benefit to this perk, you may choose one of the perks for any research- or science-related class and upgrade it.
> Perk must be a Tier 1 or Tier 2 and be below level 75.

Alice blinked at her new notification and then grinned.

The ability to upgrade a perk was quite rare. Alice had only gotten one other opportunity to upgrade a perk so far. Getting another chance was very exciting.

Alice started thinking about which perk she wanted to upgrade, and immediately thought of one—a perk that she currently needed to use repeatedly but that simply had too long of a cooldown, especially considering how useful it was in helping to resolve the current crisis.

{Seeds of Ambition} was the perk that let her create two new magic seeds a month. Right now, Alice needed an absolutely insane number of magic seeds if she wanted to replicate the System. Currently, she still needed a magic seed for math mana, so that she could finally add it to her version of System mana. She also needed a magic seed for meaning mana, or something of the sort, because it helped her System notifications work the way they were supposed to. She also had a few magic seeds that she had lost access to while she was combining perks and had simply never had the time to regain access to. There were also other components of System mana that Alice knew existed, even if she had yet to identify them.

Alice hoped that upgrading {Seeds of Ambition} would solve this problem.

She double-checked the new menu in her status screen that had been created after her achievement finished upgrading, and started scrolling through a long list of perks she could improve. Alice double-checked that she wasn't missing some other amazing upgrade, before she zeroed in on {Seeds of Ambition} and activated the upgrade. It took a few moments for her perk to rebuild itself.

<table>
<tr><td>Seeds of Ambition (upgraded)
Perk costs: Three Seeds + Seedy Ambitions sacrificed to create this perk.</td></tr>
<tr><td>Two times a month, you can create an inferior magic seed with a maximum mana conversion ratio of 30%.
The seed-creation rules from {Seedy Ambitions} are applied to this perk.
However, achievements may now apply to the inferior magic seeds as they would to other magic seeds.
Once a month, you may combine two of your inferior magic seeds.</td></tr>
</table>

Alice frowned. She had been expecting the perk to improve in a slightly different way. She had expected the perk to increase her mana seeds per month. Instead, the perk now let her combine two different magic seeds once a month. Was that useful?

A moment later, Alice relaxed. The System clearly combined a lot of different types of mana together. This perk upgrade would hopefully let her do the same. It wasn't the upgrade she had been expecting, but it was clearly useful. She decided to use it that very moment, to see how it worked in practice. She took a look at her magic seeds. She had five lesser magic seeds right now.

Lesser Magic Seeds (Base max 30%, achievements now apply as usual)	Display seed 14%/16% Organic seed 77%/79% (6% Exp. Comp.) Pure mana seed 47%/49% (12% Exp. Comp.) Filtration seed 37%/40% Dimensional seed 37%/40%

Alice also wanted to test something else—something she hadn't thought about until now but that *might* let her ignore one of the bigger limitations her enchantments had been facing. This was the limitation on the number of instructions a given enchanting material could remember. If Alice got lucky, combined magic seeds might only count for a single instruction slot, allowing her to cram lots more information into each enchantment she made.

After all, if the System was using *air* as a way to carry its instructions around the world, it had obviously circumvented the limitations most enchantments faced. At first, Alice assumed that the System used some sort of crazy set of perks to increase the instruction limit of everything it touched. But perhaps it cheated the limitations of enchanting materials in a different way, by combining different types of mana together? Or perhaps it employed both solutions at the same time, by enhancing the instruction limit of everything it touched *and* compounding instructions somehow.

Alice shrugged. In any case, it was worth testing.

Alice decided to combine display mana and filtration mana first. If her theory about sidestepping enchantment instruction limitations was correct, those two were the most immediately useful ways to create knockoff System components. She made sure that {Safety Analysis} wasn't blaring any alarm bells at her first, and then activated the new component of {Seeds of Ambition}.

For a few moments, Alice felt as if her entire torso was heating up.

Then two different kinds of mana merged inside her mind. It was an indescribably odd sensation, akin to having two different limbs suddenly fuse together as one. A few moments later, Alice had a completely new kind of magic seed.

Lesser Magic Seeds (Base max 30%, achievements now apply as usual)	Compound seed 1 (Display/Filtration) 54%/56% Organic seed 77%/79% (6% Exp. Comp.) Pure mana seed 47%/49% (12% Exp. Comp.) Dimensional seed 40%

Alice was more than slightly amused to see that the new magic seed didn't have a proper name. It was just Compound Seed 1. She was also very interested in seeing what had happened to the mana conversion ratio of the two magic seeds. Originally, she had a mana conversion ratio of 16 percent for her display seed, and 40 percent for her filtration magic seed. She had assumed that the new magic seed would take the average of the two numbers and end up with a mana conversion ratio of 28 percent. Perhaps a bit less, since {Creative Healer} still wasn't properly applying its bonuses to her magic storage capacity. However, instead, the two numbers had been added together, giving Alice a much larger pool of mana to work with. It also meant that some of Alice's achievements that boosted the mana conversion ratio of different mana seeds were now applying multiple times to the same seed. Alice wasn't sure exactly how that worked, or if it would continue to be the case if she acquired more achievements with similar rewards. However, the strange interaction between achievements and her new magic seed was certainly appreciated.

Alice noticed that a few [Explorer of Magic], [Scholar], and miscellaneous wisps of mana had gotten stuck in her [Explorer of Magic] class seed while she was interacting with her status screen. It would serve as a nice experiment to see what her new magic seed could do.

Alice filtered the mana using her new magic seed. It worked just like before. However, there was something rather different once she finished.

Normally, Alice's fake System messages didn't really bear much resemblance to the System in how they worked. Sure, Alice could create a System message that looked kind of like the original System messages—but Alice had never really understood how the System knew when to send things like level-up notifications.

But this time, as Alice filtered the incredibly tiny amount of [Explorer of Magic] mana that had tried to bond with her seed, she got a System notification.

You have leveled up!
Explorer of Magic: 78→78

Some of the text for Alice's new System notification was nonsense. She hadn't leveled up—she had gone from level seventy-eight to level seventy-eight. In other words, no advancement at all had occurred.

However, the display mana was accurately reporting Alice's level the moment she filtered her mana now. In other words, the two different kinds of mana were now communicating with each other. Alice's filtration mana had helped her filter all the mana into [Explorer of Magic] mana and then sent that information to her display mana so that it could be turned into a System message. Alice sensed that she *could* stop this from happening—but she was glad to see what combining two different magic seeds did.

Alice smiled.

She was now very curious to see if this worked for other things. Specifically, Alice wanted to see if her new magic seed would automatically translate other types of System messages. During her experimentation with her new mana type, a few wisps of [Scientist] mana had drifted over. Alice tried filtering it.

<table>
<tr><td>You have leveled up!</td></tr>
<tr><td>Scientist: 65→65</td></tr>
</table>

Alice tried opening her perks list . . . and gasped in surprise.

Alice saw the usual System screen for leveling up appear . . . and along with it, Alice saw her perk-selection screen open as usual.

However, even when Alice stopped using her Compound Seed 1, the perks that she had unlocked didn't suddenly turn into gibberish. Instead, all the perks and perk-combination options that Alice had unlocked after leveling up remained the same, even when Alice stopped actively using mana to translate it.

In other words, unlike before, the perks that were unlocked through Alice's mana usage now *stayed* translated. They still didn't have whatever feature the System used to translate messages even for people who didn't speak the local language, but it was still an improvement.

Alice grinned.

This discovery *also* attracted a few wisps of [Explorer of Magic] mana. This time, when Alice filtered them, she got a nice System notification.

<table>
<tr><td>You have leveled up!</td></tr>
<tr><td>Explorer of Magic: 78→79</td></tr>
</table>

Getting levels in her primary class still felt slow, compared to the breakneck leveling speed Alice was used to. Still, she was making progress—and that was satisfying in its own right. Alice felt satisfied with her upgrades today. She had gotten another level in [Explorer of Magic], upgraded {Seeds of Ambition}, gotten two new perk slots, and started interacting with compound seeds.

Then Alice turned toward her two perk slots. She was more than slightly surprised by the fact that [Survivor] had leveled up, considering the fact that Alice had done basically nothing related to survival. However, since Alice had at least some insight into how classes worked behind the scenes, and how they seemed to be related to beliefs, Alice eventually came up with a theory for why she had gotten a level in [Survivor].

Experimenting with monsters was probably perceived as dangerous by most people, even if those monsters were just spidercrabs. After the events of the past few days, Alice suspected that people were much more afraid of monsters than before—thus boosting any experience gains she got related to monsters. At least, that was Alice's best guess for why she had gotten levels in [Survivor]. The fact that classes and beliefs were so deeply intertwined still surprised her sometimes, but she was starting to get the hang of how things worked.

Alice frowned.

People's understanding of the world around them. Monsters. Inconsistency.

Something about all those ideas started pulling at Alice's brain, and she started thinking.

According to the Church of the System, monsters were supposed to be the expressions of humanity's laziness, the greatest human sin.

Alice hadn't found any concrete ideas about what this actually *meant*, and nobody else seemed to, either. Alice had always just taken it as church nonsense and ignored it. But a huge chunk of this world's population followed the Church of the System. Classes reacted to beliefs.

What if other types of magic *also* reacted to beliefs? A long time ago, when Alice and Ethan had rescued Samantha from a base of the Society of Starry Eyes, she had gotten an achievement for the battle. The description for {Immortal's Apprentice at the Battle Against the Society} described Alice as a *combat* mage, despite that being wholly inaccurate.

What if monsters were *also* somewhat defined by people's expectations?

What if the System somehow stopped things from reacting to people's expectations and enforced some kind of rigid, underlying reality? Such as keeping beliefs from *actually* turning monsters into incarnations of humanity's laziness?

If that was true, then the oddities in monster behavior might be because the System had stopped suppressing this interaction. Or perhaps the System had limited monsters in some other way before it had collapsed. Since the System only seemed to help humans, Alice was pretty sure the System was explicitly pro-human. It wouldn't seem out of place for the System to weaken monsters on this planet in order to give humans an extra layer of advantages. Preventing monsters from suddenly mutating and getting new abilities left and right based on people's understanding of them definitely seemed like something the System would do.

If Alice's second hypothesis was correct instead, then perhaps the ability for monsters to consume different mana structures and improve themselves wasn't new.

Perhaps it was one that monsters had always had before the System, and just regained.

Alice sighed. She had a lot more tests to run with monsters if she wanted to figure out what was going on behind the scenes.

Then she turned back toward her System notifications.

She still had two perks to choose.

First, Alice looked at her new [Survivor] perk choices. [Survivor] was the closest she had to a combat class, and Alice needed to find a way to defend herself against

Society attacks and monster attacks. Ethan couldn't keep her safe forever—especially with the recent changes to monsters and the behavior of the Society. She checked the newly unlocked perks but didn't see anything particularly appealing. So she turned her attention back to the perk-combination screen.

She had a rather hard choice to make.

Alice had three relatively good perks from her [Survivor] class that she was thinking about combining. The rest of her perks were either extremely situational, such as {Extremophile}, which let her survive in much hotter or colder weather, or were so vital to Alice's continued survival that she was afraid of messing with them, such as {Microbe Resistance}. Combining {Microbe Resistance} with anything seemed like a monumentally bad idea when Alice's immune system was built for a different planet and its ecosystem.

However, Alice still had three perks that were useful and had good synergy when combined.

<table>
<tr><td>Moderate Tissue Regeneration
Requirements: Survivor level 40 or higher, Endurance 100 or greater</td></tr>
<tr><td>Once per day, you may regenerate a great deal of damaged tissue and internal organ matter, healing you from even potentially fatal wounds or missing parts of limbs (hand size or smaller). May only be used once per day.
Increases the effect of the Endurance stat by 10%.
(Note: If you lose an entire arm, this perk WILL help you eventually recover the lost limb, but it will take several days.)
(Note: Regenerating large amounts of organic matter also requires proper nutrients. Each time you use this perk, you will need to eat a great deal more afterward.)
(Note: It is impossible to recover from destruction of the brain, regardless of method used. If your brain is damaged enough, recovery is impossible.)</td></tr>
</table>

{Moderate Tissue Regeneration} was one of the perks that Alice used to keep herself safe when things went wrong. That usually mattered the most when she was running tests on herself, but she had always been aware of the perk's uses in combat as well.

This perk *could* be replaced entirely with organic mana, but only if Alice was skilled enough to do so. At least right now, Alice was more likely to kill herself than heal herself if she tried that. Thus, this perk was still useful, although its usefulness decreased with every day as Alice got more proficient in wielding organic mana. It was worth considering combining.

Alice looked at the perk's combination with the other two perks and confirmed that both options looked good and kept some form of self-regeneration.

The next perk Alice looked at was {Adrenaline Rush}.

<table>
<tr><td>

Adrenaline Rush

Requirements: Survivor level 45 or higher, two or more perks related to perceiving the world around you have already been taken within the Survivor class at an earlier level, Perception 125 or higher, Magic 100 or higher

</td></tr>
<tr><td>

At any point in time, if you are highly likely to die or potentially die within the next five seconds, your perception of time will speed up significantly for five seconds. Your Dexterity, Endurance, Magic, and Perception stats will have their effectiveness increased by 100% for these five seconds. This skill may only be used once per week.

Note: This perk consumes a fair number of calories to activate. It is advised to eat a large meal whenever it is used.

</td></tr>
</table>

{Adrenaline Rush} was Alice's best combat perk. It gave her advanced warning when something was about to seriously hurt her, and it also synergized so well with the combat style of [Kinetic Mages] that Alice felt nearly invincible whenever she used it. Of course, the perk also had the downside of only being active for five seconds and then needing a full week to recover. Normally, Alice wouldn't have considered combining the perk with anything at all, unless the result would be spectacular, because it was just so powerful. But both of the combination perks that used {Adrenaline Rush} as one of the ingredients seemed to keep a lot of the perk's original properties, while solving some of its problems, such as cooldown time.

Finally, Alice considered {Extended Organics}.

<table>
<tr><td>

Extended Organics

Requirements: Survivor level 50 or higher, Endurance 100 or higher, Magic 125 or higher

</td></tr>
<tr><td>

The area to which you will naturally apply resistance against magic is extended by three meters. Your body's natural resistance to mana is greatly enhanced. This can be turned off. This does not apply inside other objects. This area is also counted as inside your body for the sake of other magic-related perks you control, allowing you to extend magic tendrils from anywhere in this space without the need to form a tendril and move it outside your body, or use any point within this three-meter range to form tendrils before moving them elsewhere.

</td></tr>
</table>

{Extended Organics} was probably *supposed* to be used as a shield against other mages messing with one's biology. After all, while all living beings had an innate resistance against foreign mana, that didn't mean that it was impossible to overcome. On the very first day at the Magic Academy, Alice had seen one of her teachers rip a monster in half using raw kinetic magic, because his mana had simply overwhelmed the creature's defenses. This perk made it much harder to overcome her natural resistances and prevented other people from messing with Alice's clothes, which was a common tactic in battles between [Kinetic Mages].

Alice, admittedly, did not use this perk for its intended purpose very often. She instead used it to give her magic tendrils greater range and mobility. The ability to instantly break down and re-form a magic tendril within her range made it possible for her to teleport her magic tendrils around at the speed of thought, and the fact that the perk worked within three meters also extended her tendril range quite significantly. Alice didn't want to lose this perk, either, but the combination perks looked quite appealing.

Alice sighed and continued thinking about her choice for several minutes. It was hard to decide what she wanted. But a choice had to be made.

Eventually, Alice chose to combine {Extended Organics} and {Moderate Tissue Regeneration}.

Extended Tissues

Perk_Costs: Extended Organics + Moderate Tissue Regeneration sacrificed to create this perk.

At all times_ tissues are one meter bigger (pseudo-body—not expanded flesh, but mana).
Within_body_(pseudo-body), self and allies heal fast. (passive effect.)
Magic tendrils extend from pseudo-body like normal body.
Once per day, regenerate much more. (Can focus self or friend.)

Alice blinked. The messy grammar, which Alice had been vaguely hoping she was now free from, had returned, which was unfortunate. However, it wasn't too hard to figure out what her new perk did.

{Extended Organics} had shrunk a bit, dropping from three meters to one meter. That was a shame, but not the end of the world. In exchange, Alice now had a weaker version of {Moderate Tissue Regeneration} active at all times, and she could heal anyone within one meter of herself. Alice gave herself a very small cut on her arm to test the effect of her new passive healing aura and confirmed that her new perk was drastically speeding up her natural healing process. It would probably take about ten minutes to heal that scratch, which wasn't quite the super-human regeneration Alice had been imagining, given that she had only given herself a paper cut. Still, it made Alice far more resilient against death, since if she were out of mana and bleeding out, this perk would still work. Its ability to heal allies within a meter was also useful, since it didn't cost mana. Finally, once per day, Alice could resort to a much more powerful version of her supercharged healing, which was exactly what {Moderate Tissue Regeneration} had previously offered her. Overall, Alice was happy with her new perk.

She did wish the passive healing effect was stronger, but perhaps in the future she would have a chance to strengthen it. Alice knew that past level seventy-five, instead of just combining perks from the same class, one could combine perks from OTHER classes, too. That meant that once she got [Explorer of Magic] to level eighty, she could potentially strengthen this perk again if she didn't have a better idea for what to do with her perk slot.

Then Alice shook her head, pushing away her daydreams about how powerful her future perks *might* be. Alice hadn't reached that point yet, and she had a lot of other problems she needed to solve right now. She focused on her final reward for her previous experiment.

She still needed to pick a perk for [Scientist].

The first thing Alice started wondering was what would happen to the {In Pursuit of Science} achievement if Alice combined the {For Science!} perk with something else. Alice had already upgraded {In Pursuit of Science} to its maximum level, and she wasn't sure if the perk was just free combination fodder, or if deleting it would disable {In Pursuit of Science} and all its related upgrades.

Luckily, Alice didn't have to just sit around and guess. She had an Immortal nearby who would be happy to answer her questions.

Alice quickly found Ethan and inquired about the results of combining a perk like {For Science!}. He informed Alice that if she combined the {For Science!} perk with something else, the achievement she had acquired with the perk, as well as any accompanying upgrades derived from it, would deactivate. That shut down her ambition to use {For Science!} as perk-combination fuel. Instead, she started looking at her other perks from [Scientist].

{Precise Mana Measurement} was just an inferior version of {Advanced Mana Measurement}, so Alice would be happy to toss it for something more useful. {Sample Collection} was Alice's only storage perk, and Alice was extremely fond of being able to cart around a few weeks' worth of food and water, as well as a rather large library and several different kinds of enchanting materials. Having things readily available was too convenient to lose.

{Shared Memory} was another perk Alice *could* use for perk combination, but she was reluctant to do so. It was very useful as a teaching tool and a way to share knowledge. Which meant, at the end of the day, that the only perk Alice was really happy to use for perk combination was {Precise Mana Measurement}. Alice sighed. She couldn't exactly start a perk combination with only one perk, so it looked like she was taking a new perk this time. After checking, she saw two options that looked useful.

The first perk was one she probably would have killed for a few months ago, but it was now far, far less useful.

<table>
<tr><td>

Mana Testing
Requirements: Scientist level 65 or higher, Intelligence 100 or higher, at least three achievements rarity five or above that are related to testing or experimenting with mana

</td></tr>
<tr><td>

Gain_ability to take a chunk of mana. Trap it in storage perk. Use as experimental fodder, and using other perks to understanding mana easier use on mana.

</td></tr>
</table>

Alice resisted the urge to throw something.

Now that the System mana Alice was so eager to study was no longer easily accessible in the air around her, she got a perk that would allow her to trap some mana and easily analyze it?

Alice tried not to tear her hair out in frustration, and took a few deep, calming breaths. Even though the System was gone, the perk still had uses. After all, there were System enchantments available everywhere. Even if the System mana in a class seed or System enchantment was a bit different from the world-covering System mana that Alice yearned to study, both were different types that came from the same source. This perk would also be useful if another flood of System mana appeared and Alice managed to capture some of it in time. The other perk Alice was looking at was {Science's Mana}.

<table>
<tr><td>

Science's Mana
Requirements: Scientist level 65 or higher, Intelligence 150 or higher, enchanter class at level 25 or higher, create at least three enchantments of your own design

</td></tr>
<tr><td>

Make System enchantment for item. Must be related to a perk you already have from the research classes, or attributes_thought association with science. (Intelligence, Willpower, Perception.)

</td></tr>
</table>

This perk was less immediately relevant to Alice's goals, but it had serious potential. Right now, Alice was trying to find ways to help people by mass-producing enchantments that replicated the System's functions. Having a perk that let her make System enchantments would potentially teach her something valuable about enchantments, or give her a way to sidestep some of the snags she had run into.

Alice thought about her choices. One had the potential to let her break down System mana, at least in some form. It would help her understand some of the components of System mana more effectively, making it easier for her to replicate the System down the line. However, this would still run into the problem of magic seed production. Alice could make two new magic seeds per month, and if she discovered more types of System mana, that wouldn't let her create them any more quickly than before.

By contrast, the ability to form System enchantments was a bit more interesting. Alice rather liked the idea of being able to create System enchantments. After all, they could temporarily grant the wearer a perk from another class. Usually these perks were pretty low level, so they didn't matter very much. However, if she could find a way to share, say, {Broken Seed}, she could potentially resolve some of the problems she had run into *very* quickly. It was a long shot, but it seemed like something worth trying.

After mulling over the best- and worst-case scenarios for both perks, she decided that {Science's Mana} had too much potential to ignore. Even if creating more copies of {Broken Seed} didn't work out, learning System enchanting would be useful. Besides, Alice was already discovering new components of System mana on her own as she experimented and improved, so {Mana Testing} was a lot less useful than it first appeared to be. After selecting her new perk, Alice smiled as she watched it form inside her.

It was time to experiment with System enchanting.

CHAPTER 24

To start off her System-enchanting experiments, Alice had a [Maid] fetch a few iron rings. It only took twenty minutes for a crate to be delivered to her room. After securing her experimental supplies, Alice pulled out her first iron ring and inspected it.

She had never created a System enchantment before, and she hadn't had any opportunities to observe other people create System enchantments, either. Alice had devoted most of her time to studying traditional and consumable enchantments. This was unfortunate, because it meant Alice had no idea how to actually use her new perk. All she had was a vague feeling given by the perk itself—but she lacked precise understanding of how to accomplish her goals.

Alice sighed and eyed the container of iron rings. If she didn't succeed the first time, she had plenty of materials to use for her next attempt.

For her first System enchantment, Alice decided to try enchanting a ring of plus-one [Intelligence]. It was one of the simplest enchantments Alice could add, and she wanted to get an idea of how the perk worked before she tried anything complicated.

She started out by trying to visualize what she wanted the ring to do, then fed {Science's Mana} some mana. Alice wasn't quite sure how to make a System enchantment, so she was hoping that the perk would just automate the process if she gave it some resources.

This did not work. It only took Alice a few seconds to realize why. System enchantments were primarily used by people who weren't magically gifted. In other words, she shouldn't be trying to create a System enchantment with mana at all—there was a completely different process involved. Sadly, Alice's perk-granted instincts didn't tell her much beyond informing her what she had done wrong.

Alice tried holding the ring closer to her face and squinted at the band of metal. This time, she tried concentrating on what intelligence *meant*. She wanted whoever was wearing the ring to have a faster and more nimble mind and a better understanding of the world around them. She wanted their memory to improve. She wanted the mind of the wearer to become faster and less prone to making careless mistakes.

Alice concentrated on her vision of what she wanted, held the ring in her hand, and waited. Nothing happened. Alice sighed, wondering what she was doing wrong. A few moments later, she realized that she didn't have to puzzle this out on her own. There were plenty of other people in Cyra who had access to System-enchanting perks and could help her. After all, System enchantments were offered to most crafting classes beyond level fifty, and they were popular perk picks.

Alice exited her room and looked for a [Butler] to help her find a [Tailor] or [Blacksmith] who could help her out. Instead of a [Butler], the first person Alice ran into this time was Illa.

"Lady Illa," said Alice.

"Lady Alice. It is a pleasure to see you again. I hear your experiments on the spidercrabs went well?" asked Illa. "Ethan gave me a few pages of potentially useful information that you discovered."

Alice nodded. "It went well enough. I wanted to ask for some more resources for a new experiment now. Could you get someone with a System-enchanting perk to come help me? I have a System-enchanting perk that I wish to experiment with, but I'm not sure how to operate it. The perk's description hasn't helped me much."

Illa paused and then nodded. "I'll get someone to bring over one of the town [Tailors]. There is a level-sixty [Tailor] named Tallie who should be more than willing to help you for a decent price. I can cover her fees, as thanks for the information you found yesterday. Will that suffice?"

"Yes. Thank you, Lady Illa," said Alice.

"I'll have her sent to the room you used for spidercrab testing, then," said Illa.

Alice nodded and returned to her testing room.

She noticed that the corpses of the spidercrabs hadn't been cleaned up yet. Perhaps the [Maids] thought they still held value for Alice? She hadn't actually clarified much to them beyond requesting they not interfere with the room, after all. As a result, the room stank. Alice sighed and reached a kinetic tendril toward one of the spidercrab corpses. No reason to pick it up with her physical hands and get blood all over herself.

However, as Alice touched the corpse of the spidercrab, something interesting happened. She felt her mana tendril sink into the spidercrab shell far more easily than it usually did. It was as if the shell was more willing to accept mana than usual.

Interesting. Alice wondered if the spidercrab corpses had any sort of value as enchanting materials. She decided to test it in the dream library later, where she would have access to infinite mana. For now, she went back to thinking about System enchantments.

Some time later, someone knocked on the door to her testing room.

"Come in!" yelled Alice.

A moment later, a tall woman in her midforties with decent [Charisma], black hair, and an easy smile stepped into the room before giving Alice a close inspection.

"I assume you're the one I'm supposed to help, Lady Mage?" said the woman. "My name is Tallie. It's a pleasure to make your acquaintance."

Alice nodded. "Thank you for coming, Tallie. I'm Alice. I need help getting System enchanting to work. I got a perk for it, but I can't figure out how to use it."

Tallie nodded. "Never taught a mage how to make an enchantment before. What specifically are you trying to make? That makes a pretty big difference in how you need to approach a System enchantment."

"It does?" asked Alice.

Tallie nodded. "Did your perk not have a description about how to activate it?"

Alice shook her head. "With how messed up System descriptions are these days, maybe my perk was supposed to come with a more detailed set of instructions, but I didn't get very many details."

Tallie winced. "That's rough. It's normal for a System-enchanting perk to have a paragraph or two discussing how you're supposed to operate the perk. There are some similarities in the way a [Blacksmith] makes a System enchantment and the way a [Tailor] makes one, but there are also many differences.

"As a [Tailor], my System-enchantment perk requires that I focus on a certain concept while stitching threads together to create a piece of clothing. The more cloth is changed or added before I lose concentration, and the better I focus, the better the System enchantment turns out. It also helps if I am doing something related to whatever enchantment I'm trying to make, although that isn't always practical. It's exceptionally easy to add an enchantment for [Dexterity], since it already requires nimble fingers to sew and weave. Similarly, if I want to make a System enchantment related to [Strength], it helps if I tie some weights to my hands while I work." Tallie shrugged again. "On the other hand, trying to be charismatic while sewing is . . . difficult. It usually requires you to multitask, perhaps by singing to an audience while sewing or finding some other way to make sewing a social activity. It can be done, obviously, but it's hard."

Alice pursed her lips in thought. Given what she knew about how class seeds worked, it did make sense. Alice was becoming more and more aware of the fact that a *lot* of System-related mana constructs responded to how people conceptualized things.

"Tallie, just making sure, you can add a System enchantment to anything, right?" asked Alice. She was pretty sure she already knew the answer to this question, but there was no harm in double-checking.

"Depends on the specific perk you're using, but in theory, anything can become a System enchantment. I can use any type of cloth to make System enchantments— even leftover dirty rags from the garbage, if I felt like it. It doesn't matter what material I use." Tallie made a face. "Not that I would do that, obviously. But you get the idea."

Alice nodded. Consumable and traditional enchantments all required special materials to get started, while System enchantments could work with anything. While Alice knew of a few perks, such as {Kinetic Enchanting}, that allowed one to add instruction slots to materials, Alice wondered whether System enchantments worked by adding an extra instruction slot to a material or circumvented the problem entirely. That was something she looked forward to observing more closely.

Alice fell into thought. Tallie enchanted things by sewing them or manipulating their cloth components. That meant that the way someone added a class enchantment to a material was heavily related to their class. How would a [Scientist] add a System enchantment to something?

The first thing that came to mind was one of the stereotypes from home. In the stereotype, [Scientists] spent all day pouring various fluids from one flask into another in some sort of nonsensical chemistry experiment. Even though it seemed ridiculous, if Alice needed to align her actions with the concept of whatever she was trying to add to her enchanted items, leaning into stereotypes should work. If it didn't, she would try writing a scientific paper or reading a book.

"Are there any other things to keep in mind?" asked Alice. "Could you show me the process of creating a System enchantment?"

"Things to keep in mind? Well, I don't know what you're trying to accomplish, but something worth remembering is that the process of imbuing an item with a perk is different from an attribute," said the [Tailor]. "You'll need to sort of . . . feed the perk into your System-enchanting perk while you go through your usual enchanting process. It's kind of hard to describe the feeling, so I'll try to guide you through it, if you pay for another lesson. I can also show you the process of creating a System enchantment, even though I have no idea what you would learn from that."

Alice quickly nodded. Tallie requested a few sewing needles, some bolts of cloth, measuring tapes, and a variety of other tools, along with some mirrors and colorful objects. Once everything arrived, she got to work.

Alice watched as Tallie frowned in concentration before she started tailoring the bolts of cloth to fit the figure of an imaginary person. It took her a few minutes before Alice realized that Tallie was creating a dress. After the very basics of the dress had gained their shape, Tallie took one of the mirrors and set it in front of the half-formed dress before setting up another mirror to view the dress from a different angle. Then, without explaining a thing, she got back to work, sewing and stitching parts of the dress together while taking a few moments to admire her work every so often.

Alice started to notice that every second Tallie worked, little bits of rainbow-colored mana leaked into the dress. Most of the bits of rainbow mana looked like regular perk usage—but oddly enough, even when Tallie stopped to admire her work, rainbow mana *still* left her body and surged into the dress. Those bits of rainbow mana, in particular, looked like they were slowly forming a System enchantment contained within the dress.

Alice was used to the System working like a filter for mana that already existed, but in this case, Alice was instead reminded of steeping tea leaves in hot water. Rather than filtering what was already there, it seemed more like the System fractals Tallie had created were slowly infusing rainbow mana into the dress itself.

After about two hours, Tallie wiped the sweat away from her forehead before grinning at Alice.

"Done, Lady Mage. This is a dress that gives the wearer six points of [Charisma]," she said. "Charisma is usually a social activity, but it's also related to beauty—which is why I kept admiring the dress through the mirrors. By admiring how beautiful my work was, I could connect with the concept of [Charisma] and infuse it into the dress. It feels a bit narcissistic, but it does work. Does that make sense?"

"Thank you for the help, [Tailor] Tallie. That makes the process much easier to understand," said Alice.

Tallie grinned before she stifled a yawn. "I'm quite tired, so I don't think I'm up to teaching you any more today. Sorry, but I need to take a nap. I hope you found this useful. If you need my services, feel free to contact me again!" Tallie gave Alice another smile, and after a few more pleasantries, she left.

Once Tallie left, Alice looked at all the iron rings and sighed.

After a few moments of thought, Alice discarded the iron rings and asked for the [Maid] to get her a few sets of glass goggles. On Earth, chemists often wore goggles to keep dangerous fumes and chemicals out of their eyes. Of course, on Earth those were usually made of plastic, but Alice figured that as long as it looked close enough it was probably fine.

Once the goggles arrived, Alice started reading a book. At the same time, she started thinking about the nature of intelligence and tried to push that idea into her goggles entirely through her perk.

It wasn't *entirely* successful, but Alice could at least see some traces of rainbow mana exit her body and flow into the goggles, even if they were few and far between.

Alice was encouraged by her partial success and kept going for a few hours. But she became increasingly aware that something wasn't *quite* right about her method of adding a System enchantment to the goggles.

Perhaps reading a book was more scholarly than scientific?

Alice tried again. This time she got a piece of paper and started copying a paper she had submitted to the Magic Academy a few months ago. Science had a lot to do with testing, verifying, and sharing the results of experiments and ideas, so Alice hoped that writing a paper for peer review would get the perk working.

This time proved quite a bit more successful, and after she finished copying her scientific paper, Alice saw System mana start to flow out of her body and toward her goggles. It was interesting to watch. Rather than mana being filtered and shoved into an item, the way Alice had expected a System enchantment to work based on observing Tallie, it looked more like her body had created a tiny new System fractal. Then the System fractal floated over to her hand before exiting her body entirely and stamping itself onto her goggles. This new fractal stamp started pulling more rainbow mana out of her body, as if it were using it as an energy source to finish constructing itself. A few moments later, the fractal finished building itself and the entire process came to an end. Alice now had a pair of goggles that would raise her [Intelligence] by one point.

Alice felt as if she had just run a marathon. It seemed that her new perk had a stamina-related cost, perhaps as a way to compensate for its lack of mana cost.

While it hadn't been a perfect trial run, Alice had still gotten her new System-enchantment perk working and had created her first System enchantment. It was another step in the right direction.

Alice yawned. She understood why Tallie had left right after creating her System enchantment—she was also tired. She walked out of the room and found a [Maid], completely forgetting to store a spidercrab corpse in her storage perk.

"Keep the spidercrab corpses preserved for me, and make sure everyone else knows not to mess with them," Alice said before another thought occurred to her. "Actually, bring the [Enchanters] that shell and tell them to experiment with it to figure out what it does. I'll also . . ." Alice yawned and shook her head. "I'll also run some tests later." The [Maid] nodded as Alice stumbled toward her room. She barely remembered to deal with the clogged bits of class mana in her class seed before she went to sleep.

You have leveled up!
Careful Enchanter: 30→32

CHAPTER 25

While Alice was asleep, she found herself in her dream library, as usual. Naturally, this was a perfect opportunity to run a few tests with the spidercrab corpse that she had grabbed before retiring for the night. With unlimited mana available in her dreams, Alice could run tests to her heart's content and none of it would impact her actual enchantment production or battle readiness.

Then she realized that she had actually forgotten to grab one of the spidercrab corpses and stuff it into her storage perk. Her dream library had a lot of functions now that multiple perks were feeding into it. However, it still needed a physical testing material to be in her storage perk before she could interact with it. In other words, she had no way to test her new research materials during her sleep, and she also couldn't use the unlimited mana from her dreams to test things right now.

Perhaps she had been more tired than she thought. Making such an obvious mistake frustrated Alice, but now that she was asleep, she didn't have a way to wake back up. Alice had always been a heavy sleeper, and her dream library didn't have a way to sidestep that problem.

After realizing this, Alice sighed and took it as a sign that she really had been overwhelmed by stress. After some hesitation, she spent the night reading adventure stories and trying to relax. It wasn't the most productive night she'd ever had, but it did reduce some of the mounting pressure she felt. As much as Alice tried to be efficient and solve every single problem related to the System's collapse, she was still human. She had been relying on perks and force of will to sustain her work efficiency, but even that had its limits. She decided to spend the night restoring her mental state. Some light reading would do the trick.

She found an interesting-looking biography about the Immortal who had established the Shil Confederacy, and started reading.

The next day, after a quick breakfast, Alice rushed to the testing room. She had spent eight hours relaxing and needed to get back to work. The spidercrab corpses had been left untouched in the corner of the room, as Alice had requested, apart from the single shell she had sent to the [Enchanters] for testing purposes. She quickly double-checked with one of the [Maids] and found that the [Enchanters] hadn't had time to poke at the spidercrab shell yet—they were scheduled to do so in a few hours. Alice decided it was better to have two independent groups poke at the shells instead of lumping it all together as one big test, so she stepped toward the remaining shells and prepared another round of experiments.

Alice gave the spidercrab corpses one last check with {Safety Analysis} to make sure she wasn't about to blow herself up. Then she poked the corpses with her mana again. She wanted to see if the properties of spidercrab shells changed after the spidercrabs copied their knockoff System perks.

Alice held her breath as she started trying to use the spidercrab shells as enchanting materials by imprinting instructions onto them. Alice tried to create enchantments that would show someone a basic System message when they touched the shell, because the enchantment itself didn't matter. All that mattered was whether the corpses had changed or not. Spidercrab shells were normally useless as enchanting materials, so if these shells accepted her mana at all, it would mean something had changed. She also made sure to use her compound mana, to ensure that the spidercrab shells could accept both filtration and display mana.

Alice's eyes widened as she felt her mana sink into the spidercrab shell, patterning itself on the enchantment that she had been trying to create. She stepped closer to the shell and touched it with her hand.

She saw mana surge out of the spidercrab core, and a moment later, a System message appeared in front of her.

Through testing, you have created a System message!
Test

Alice started cackling like a crazy witch. It took her several seconds to regain control of herself before she glanced at the spidercrab shell again and smiled like a madman.

Alice hadn't been sure whether the tree bark Ethan had secured a supply of would accept her new compound mana. She hadn't thought to test it yet. However, she could *definitely* confirm that the spidercrab shell had just accepted a display mana enchantment to create a System message. In other words . . . it could accept mana from her compound mana seed. That meant Alice could start creating enchantments to handle the emergency. She still had no way to keep up with the number of enchantments Illvaria would need, of course—there were too many people, and she was just one person. But at the very least, Alice could finally get started on production. The sooner she got started, the faster people could level up and pick perks to help navigate the crisis. With any luck, this could create a snowball effect that kept the country stable even if the world kept spiraling out of control.

The spidercrab shells didn't *just* let Alice start getting the snowball rolling, either. One of the two biggest bottlenecks in enchantment production was finding the right enchantment material. Spidercrab shells could obviously accept display mana, which meant that she had just found a good, easy-to-produce material she could make rings out of. Feeding a spidercrab an item enhanced by a perk wasn't that hard, and spidercrabs were almost literally everywhere. While it would still be hard to get enough [Enchanters] to meet demand, Cecilia was already working on solving that problem. She had found a path forward.

Then Alice frowned. Since she had a compound mana type now, she hadn't actually tested whether the spidercrab shells would accept normal kinds of mana, such as filtration mana. She also had not tested whether spidercrab shells could accept multiple mana types at once. Display mana enchantments were important for her future plants—but filtration mana was even more important, since it could handle the problems caused by class-mana madness. She still needed to see what this material was capable of.

Alice tried focusing on her new compound magic seed and extracting *only* filtration mana. Alice felt filtration mana slowly drain out of her compound magic seed, unaccompanied by the display mana she had connected it to.

Then she tried to create a basic enchantment using a different spidercrab shell. This one was designed to filter a few miscellaneous types of ambient mana into pure mana, since the enchantment was just a proof-of-concept test.

Alice felt the mana try to sink into the spidercrab shell . . . and then bounce off, as if it had run into a brick wall.

Alice's earlier delight faded away, replaced with a feeling of worry. If the spidercrab shell only accepted compound mana, this would *not* be a suitable solution for Illvaria. Alice hadn't heard of anyone else using compound magic seeds, which meant they were rare.

Alice tried shoving more filtration mana into the spidercrab shell, but once again, the mana failed to take root. Alice tried shoving the compound mana type into a new spidercrab shell, more out of frustration than any hope it would accomplish something . . . and it *also* bounced off.

Alice felt her anxiety melt away, replaced by pure confusion.

Why was one spidercrab shell accepting her compound mana while another one wasn't? Was the original spidercrab shell that Alice had tested just a fluke?

Alice grabbed a third spidercrab shell and tried shoving pure filtration mana into it. This time, unlike with the second spidercrab corpse, the mana sank in perfectly. However, Alice noticed that the filtration enchantment she had just created was different from the compound enchantment she had created with the first spidercrab shell. The enchantment had succeeded, but barely.

She tried testing the enchantment. The enchantment did exactly what it was supposed to, filtering the mana in the air around it into a slightly purer form.

However, it was *very* leaky. It was spewing broken mana into the air like a burst water pipe. Alice looked at it for a few moments before she started to relax again.

The enchantment being leaky wasn't a big deal. Her biggest concern was the potential inability for spidercrab shells to accept more normal enchantments. Another spidercrab shell working alleviated this fear. However, Alice was still confused. Of the three spidercrab shells she had tested, two accepted compound enchantments just fine, while a third had rejected all forms of enchantment, like a normal spidercrab shell.

She glanced at the remaining spidercrab corpses and shoved them all into her storage perk before she quickly ran back to her room and took a nap, with instructions to a [Maid] to wake her up in an hour.

In her dreams, Alice started experimenting again.

She discovered that if a shell accepted compound mana, it would also accept pure filtration or pure display mana. Every spidercrab shell accepted either all the components of her compound magic seed or none of them. There was no other outcome. She also noticed that enchantments created from single types of mana were consistently more leaky and less efficient than compound enchantments.

Alice supposed that made sense. The spidercrabs had adapted to System mana, not one particular component of System mana. Types of mana that were closer to System mana would thus match the spidercrab shell's adopted pattern better.

But the difference wasn't that severe. Her compound enchantments lost about 30 percent of their mana as broken mana, while filtration or display mana enchantments lost around 40 percent. It was a huge amount of waste, but luckily, broken mana was one of the easiest problems for mages to deal with. Any mage could remove broken mana once they learned the right method.

After Alice finished her experiments, she was still left confused about what distinguished one type of spidercrab shell from the other. Why did some spidercrab corpses accept compound mana instructions now while some didn't?

Eventually, the [Maid] woke Alice up and she rushed back to the testing room. She wanted to get to the bottom of this new oddity.

Alice had several more rounds of spidercrabs brought to the testing room. The first thing she did was run a control trial. If regular spidercrabs that hadn't adapted to System mana could also be used as enchanting materials, she would need to revise her thinking somewhat.

However, none of her control spidercrabs left behind useful enchanting materials. Just like the spidercrabs from before the collapse of the System, the spidercrabs that hadn't interacted with System mana left behind corpses that couldn't be used for enchanting.

After Alice verified this with a few more rounds of testing, she went back to experimenting on enhanced spidercrabs. Since most of the spidercrabs in the area were unchanged by the collapse of the System, Alice had to manually empower each of her test subjects. After they absorbed the System mana and created their knockoff perks, Alice killed them and tested their shells.

Just like the first batch of test subjects, some spidercrab shells accepted compound mana, while others didn't. This was despite the fact that *all* the spidercrabs had successfully copied a System perk when exposed to the same conditions.

Alice went back to the same [Maid] and again told her to wake her in an hour. The [Maid] gave Alice a very strange look but acknowledged Alice's request. Alice went back to sleep again and used her dream library to test the next few batches of spidercrab shells.

The altered spidercrab shells accepted compound magic, pure mana, and organic mana but did *not* accept No_Magic mana from the seed Alice had gotten via the {No_Mana} perk. Alice was starting to strongly suspect that the spidercrab shells only accepted components of System mana—in other words, the closer a type of mana was to System mana, the more easily the spidercrab corpses would accept it. Unfortunately, her tests didn't tell her why some spidercrab shells became useful while others were useless. Alice did at least confirm the chance of a spidercrab shell becoming useful. If Alice fed a spidercrab a piece of perk-enhanced clothing, it had a 30 percent chance of turning into an enchanting material afterward. It seemed to be entirely random whether this happened or not.

Even though she had no idea what separated these two types of spidercrab shell, Alice had confirmed that spidercrabs sometimes turned into enchanting materials. This information was critical. She had found a way to solve the material shortage. It wasn't perfect, since the enchantments created afterward would be leaky and inefficient, and they would wear out more quickly than most enchantments would. Still, any solution was better than no solution. When Alice was woken up by the [Maid] again, she dashed out of her room, found Ethan, and dragged him into her testing room to show off what she had found.

Ethan sat there as Alice ran through her new discovery, sometimes nodding approvingly and sometimes giving the spidercrab corpses curious looks. Finally, Ethan grinned.

"Well done!" said Ethan. "This is incredibly useful. I was originally thinking that the monsters growing more intelligent and getting access to knockoff perks was another catastrophe piled on top of the others. It looks like you've found a way to turn this catastrophe into a blessing in disguise. It won't fix *everything*, but it will definitely help. I believe I already told you about monster farms and how they were used to farm monster cores, right?"

Alice scoured her memory. A few moments later, she recalled Ethan mentioning people using ranches to raise monsters, similar to the same way people on Earth grew cattle and pigs, and then slaughtering the monsters for their mana cores. They weren't common, because monsters were dangerous, but some people still did it.

"I remember you mentioning it," said Alice, after a few moments.

"Well, I'll have a few of my subordinates go to some of the nearby ranches and have the ranchers there start producing batches of spidercrab shells. I probably won't even need to incentivize the ranchers much. This is one of the problems money *can* solve. Heck, they might even figure out why some spidercrab shells are useful while the rest aren't. After all, if they figure that out, they might be able to boost their income," Ethan said as he chuckled. "After all, their entire class is built around analyzing and making use of monsters. They're much better equipped to get that kind of information than you are."

Alice thought about it for a moment and then nodded. She definitely didn't feel the need to waste a perk and a bunch of time on this. If people with more specialized classes could solve this mystery, that was fine with her.

Ethan patted her on the shoulder. "Well done. I'll get that started. How long do you think it'll be until the mages you and Cecilia are training are ready to start producing enchantments?"

"The mages we're training are getting better, but the cooldown for my {Broken Seed} perk is still proving to be a major bottleneck," said Alice. "The failure rate for producing magic seeds without the help of the System is a lot higher than expected as well. Honestly, I'm not sure how long it will take before we can get production for the right enchantments off the ground," said Alice. "I will need to check in with the [Enchanters] again to give you a more accurate timeline. Still, I don't think basic production is *too* far away. I think we'll start out by creating an enchantment that lets people fix the [Enchanter] class. That way, we can recruit more [Enchanters] and further boost production."

Ethan nodded. "That makes sense." Then he grinned. "If this goes well, you should get a pretty good achievement for getting this whole production line started."

Alice also nodded. She still hadn't quite figured out what the deal with achievements was, or how to fix them yet, but even if achievements only gave half their benefits right now, it was something to look forward to.

After that, Ethan left and Alice went to check on Cecilia's [Enchanters].

With any luck, they would have been able to use their own perks to create a blueprint for Alice to work with when creating enchantments. If that happened, perhaps they could take the biggest step toward solving this crisis so far.

Chapter 26

As Alice walked out of the experiment room, she took a moment to purify her mana and then checked her System notifications.

You have leveled up!
Careful Enchanter : 32→34, Scientist: 65→66

With the levels she had gained, Alice was only one away from her next perk in [Careful Enchanter].

There were no other interesting notifications, so Alice closed the System screen and continued walking. After a few minutes, she found Cecilia and asked her to bring over the [Enchanter] who had successfully formed a seed. Now that the supply problem was dealt with, it was time to deal with the other half of her logistical needs.

Ten minutes later, Cecilia returned with the [Enchanter].

"Have you made any progress in creating the enchantments we need?" asked Alice.

"We've made some good progress," said the man. "We have three different blueprints for enchantments that we think will work. They all do slightly different things. We also tried to model them off the materials we already know we'll have available—that is, the tree bark and the spidercrab shell you sent us. They probably waste a lot of mana, but we used various perks to confirm these enchantments can work. We can always update the blueprints once we get more experience with these types of mana."

Alice gave the man a big thumbs-up. He, along with Cecilia and the other [Enchanters], had come through. Without needing to handle everything herself, a working model of a class mana–fixing ring had been delivered right to her and examined using several perks that she herself didn't have access to.

The [Enchanter] handed Alice three stacks of paper, each of which contained a detailed list of perks that went into each enchantment, what each perk did, diagrams of how to build the framework for each enchantment, and a step-by-step process for how to put everything together. There were even suggestions for alternate perks that could fill in some gaps, in case one [Enchanter] couldn't help with the process for whatever reason.

Alice skimmed the three designs before returning to the first stack to give it a closer look. The first diagram was an all-in-one enchantment to fix both class seeds and the garbled System messages. It used both display and filtration mana and also pure mana to find the System fractal it was supposed to straighten up. It was actually quite similar to Alice's attempted design, but the [Enchanters] had added in a few parts she didn't understand. Alice ran through the enchantment using {Safety Analysis} and confirmed that it should work. It even looked like the enchantment would find the correct class seed to modify, though Alice didn't understand how.

Unfortunately, the design would only work for one specific type of class, and that class would need to be decided during the ring-creation process. Once a ring was made, it would allow someone to filter only one type of mana. That wasn't the end of the world, since Alice had already suspected this design flaw would crop up, but realizing the [Enchanters] hadn't found a solution was still a bit disheartening.

The second proposed enchantment just fixed one's System notifications. It used only display mana and, as a result, it was much simpler and easier to produce. It was also optimized to use the tree bark Alice had found in Ethan's pile of materials. This enchantment did nothing to help with class-mana madness, but it would let people choose perks again.

The third and final proposed ring used filtration and pure mana. It would straighten out the System mana related to the [Enchanter] class, much like the first ring. Unlike the first version of the enchantment, it wouldn't fix System notifications. This didn't reduce the difficulty of producing the enchantment much—but Alice suspected the first ring would require something like her compound mana to fix the production process. The second and third enchantments were much more practical solutions to the current crisis, while the first all-in-one enchantment was basically only practical for her to produce.

Alice also noticed that the first and third enchantments also had a few enchantment components that she had never seen before. Alice squinted at the unfamiliar components before she turned to the [Enchanter].

"What are these?" she asked, pointing them out in the diagram.

"This mana construct is an enchantment instruction that helps an enchantment detect things. It's usually added via one of a number of perks that are offered to [Enchanters] who have a pure mana seed. The most common variants let you detect when another mage uses magic of some sort, before activating the other enchantments—basically, it's used to create traps for other mages. One of us has it because the military buys them in bulk every raiding season. We reconfigured it to find the class seeds you were talking about. We still need to do some tests to make sure it works, but our perks say it's okay.

"We tried to find a way to remove the need for the perk in question, but unfortunately, we couldn't create a viable design. For now, I recommend getting more [Enchanters] who have the correct perks," said the [Enchanter]. Alice sighed but nodded.

Unfortunately, Alice did NOT have the perk the [Enchanter] had mentioned. This made Alice feel quite annoyed, although she supposed she might be able to rush the last level in her enchanting class with a few days of hard work and some luck.

She turned back toward the [Enchanter]. "Do you think it's likely you can put the second and third models into production with your team once you get the right seeds?" she asked, glancing back toward the display-mana enchantment that used tree bark as its primary material.

"We could, Lady Alice," said the man. "We can probably make twenty or thirty a day per person, given adequate materials and some time to familiarize ourselves with the production process."

Alice nodded. "The tree bark should start coming in soon. The monsters have been slowing down retrieval of the needed materials, but with the help of higher-level [Soldiers] and [Guards], harvesting is still happening, last I heard. The spider-crab shells will also alleviate supply problems. Are you ready to get enchanting once we have the materials?"

"Of course, Lady Alice," said the [Enchanter]. Alice smiled. They were taking another step toward solving the crisis.

Alice's grin grew wider.

All she needed to do now was wait for the materials to start rolling in and then set Cecilia's mages to work. As long as nothing went wrong, they were about to reach their goal in Cyra.

Alice had to admit, she was kind of looking forward to returning to Metsel. Seeing Illa and reminiscing about the start of her journey had been interesting, and securing the enchanting materials here had been important. Alice had discovered things that she probably wouldn't have if she had remained in Metsel. But she missed the abundance of materials, books, and manpower in the capital. She also missed the ability to give time-consuming calculations to Ethan's [Mathematicians] to deal with.

Alice sighed, thinking about the last little bits of cleanup they had to do in Cyra and then gave the [Enchanter] another encouraging grin.

The two exchanged a few more pleasantries. Then she returned to her room and went to sleep.

The next day, Ethan sent some [Messengers] to the nearby monster ranches. Three of the seven ranches near Cyra were more than happy to swap production to spidercrab shells. They also started mass-importing System enchantments with weak perks attached to them.

The other four ranches were completely unable to do so. This wasn't because the owners were against earning more money, or unwilling to help with the current crisis. Instead, it was because the owners had vanished into thin air and the monsters they had been raising had escaped. The [Messengers] also reported that farms near these ranches were heavily damaged and a few [Farmers] had vanished into thin air or reported being attacked. It was a stark reminder that Alice couldn't save everyone, no matter how hard she tried.

Living away from other people was dangerous in this world, but in the past, as long as one had a certain ability to defend themselves, it was still possible to live far away from towns and cities. Surviving such conditions could even boost leveling speed, assuming one didn't turn into monster chow. Many higher-level [Farmers] even did so as a way to chase their hopes for a brighter future. But with the collapse of the System, the sudden empowerment of monsters, and the myriad of other problems assailing the world right now, living away from other people was more dangerous than ever. Even the monster ranches that were still operating had requested Ethan's help in hiring a few reliable [Guards] to keep them safe—and had mentioned that if they didn't get any help, they would rather abandon their ranches.

Apart from that, one of the [Messengers] had also given Ethan a rather odd report that he passed along to Alice. While the [Messenger] was avoiding a monster swarm, several monsters had simply vanished into thin air. They hadn't camouflaged themselves or fled from the battlefield or anything like that. They just disappeared.

Alice wasn't quite sure what to make of that incident. Perhaps the monsters had gotten some kind of perk that was related to dimensional mana? It seemed like the most likely reason for monsters to vanish. The [Messenger] didn't have any sort of mana-sight ability, so Alice's information on the subject was limited.

Apart from that, nothing else of note happened that day. Alice simply got to work testing enchantment blueprints. Even if she didn't have the right perk, Alice wanted to see if she could create some kind of workaround for it, since it would make it far easier to mass-produce the most useful enchantments.

Unfortunately, she spent several hours trying and failing to create the mana-detection instruction that the [Enchanters] had included in their blueprint. Trying to create a mana construct that sensed other mana constructs was *very hard*, and Alice just couldn't do it properly. She could see why people relied on a System perk to create this particular enchanting instruction. Trying to create it manually was like trying to juggle with one hand, draw a portrait with another, and solve a complicated math equation all at once.

Luckily, at the end of the day, Alice's hard work was rewarded, even if it wasn't in quite the way she'd been hoping for.

You have leveled up!
Careful Enchanter : 34→35

Alice had a vague hope that she might figure out how to make the enchantment on her own instead of needing a perk to do it. However, the creation of this enchantment was just too dire and important for Alice to waste time. Since the System had offered her a chance to get the perk she needed, she had immediately checked to see if she had it. Luckily, it was available.

Mana Detection
REQUire: Enchanter_Careful 35, Intelligence 100 or more,   **var: Magic_seed = pure, conversion ratio = 30% or higher**
Effect: Use pure mana to detect things in enchants. Detection costs one instruction slot. Use on an enchantment is hard, costs mental energy. Sleep if overuse.

Alice sighed but took the perk. After all, it wasn't likely that she would figure out the incredibly complex and convoluted mana construct on her own. Frankly, Alice hadn't held much hope to begin with—she had just been hoping for the best.

Cecilia's [Enchanter] also took the day to familiarize himself with the tree-bark enchantment. At the end of the day, Alice's {Broken Seed} perk was finally ready to use again, so she helped another mage work on forming a magic seed. He succeeded, leaving Cecilia's [Enchanters] with one filtration and one display magic seed. The group broke out into celebration after the man succeeded. Alice gifted the man her pair of plus-one [Intelligence] goggles. She wished she could have gifted the man a pair of goggles that gave him access to the {Broken Seed} perk, but after how hard it had been to get her {Science's Mana} perk working yesterday, Alice realized two things.

First, she had been *way* too optimistic about what she could accomplish with a System-enchanting perk. It was incredibly stamina-draining to use, and Alice desperately needed to manage dozens of different things at once.

Furthermore, after her failure to replace the {Mana Detection} perk earlier today, Alice realized that her fundamental skills as an [Enchanter] were still on the weaker side. She needed to focus on improving before she could even think about imprinting the {Broken Seed} perk onto a new piece of equipment—if she could even find the time to learn everything she needed to. Alice hated to admit it, but it was also possible that she might not be able to succeed at all, or at least within a reasonable time frame.

That wouldn't stop her from practicing her enchantments, though.

The next day, by combining a spidercrab shell and the tree bark they were harvesting en masse, Alice cobbled together the first working class-fixing ring. It would fix the class mana for any [Enchanter] who wore it, as long as the ring had a monster core to power it.

Right after she completed the enchantment, Alice looked at her work and frowned. She was a bit hesitant to actually test the enchantment on a human, since it could be dangerous. {Safety Analysis} claimed that touching it wouldn't pose a problem, but Alice felt very nervous as she and the other [Enchanters] checked her work.

Before Alice could say anything, the [Enchanter] who had helped her put together the enchantment volunteered as a test subject. When he touched the spidercrab shell, contrary to Alice's fears, nothing bad happened. His mana was purified properly, and his class seed absorbed it without any issues.

The enchantment was successful. It could be used to start addressing Illvaria's critical needs.

Alice and the other [Enchanters] celebrated their first successful product before they started churning out more of them. Alice managed to make six enchantments that day—which wasn't as many as she had hoped for, but perhaps it was the most realistic outcome given her total unfamiliarity with the enchantment.

Unfortunately, since the ranches hadn't gotten their first shipments back to Cyra yet, Alice ran out of enchanting materials after that and was forced to twiddle her thumbs for the rest of the day.

On the third day since Alice had gotten the enchanting blueprints, the first big shipments of tree bark finally came in. A few more scattered spidercrab shells were also shipped in, although the number wasn't quite enough to meet her needs yet.

Alice, Cecilia's mages, and Ethan assembled to test the implementation of the new enchantments.

Alice had already tested the first enchantment model and had gotten it working properly. Now they just needed to test the simplified enchantments and see if they could start mass-producing them.

After a few failed attempts at making the bark rings, the [Enchanter] with the display magic seed successfully created a copy of the second enchantment design, allowing the wearer to see their perk choices again. Furthermore, the mage with the filtration magic seed successfully made an alternate version of the class-filtration enchantment. Instead of fixing the [Enchanter] class, this one would fix the [Farmer] class—which was vital, because every country needed [Farmers] to avoid starvation.

Both enchantments had been successfully created by Alice, Cecilia, and Cecilia's team of [Enchanters] in Cyra. They had even successfully created an alternate version of the class mana–filtering enchantment, proving that it was possible to do with only a little adjustment.

As if to celebrate the group's success, after a few moments, Alice got a new achievement.

You have___achievement!
First_Steps (I) (Rarity: 6)
You have taken the first steps toward_solve catastrophe and created foundation to succeed where succeeding is important.
+50% growth speed enchanter classes, +20% growth speed all classes, +50% growth speed healing classes. With one_month time, var: enchanting material instructions can be increased by one (just hold item in storage perk to activate). Can only work on five items at a time, takes one month to finish.

CHAPTER 27

So we're leaving Cyra soon?" Alice asked before she stuffed a forkful of eggs into her mouth.

Ethan nodded. "With the supply lines for enchanting materials established, everything seems to be moving in the right direction. I think it's time to go," he said, taking a sip of tea.

"How long until we leave?" asked Alice.

"A few days, probably," Ethan said before taking a bite of sausage. "I would like to spend another day or two making sure the next few groups of [Adventurers] can safely harvest the tree bark and then return, and I would like to confirm the [Guards] are keeping the monster ranches safe. It would also be good to check the next few batches of test products from the ranches, in case something goes wrong," said Ethan. "I don't think production will suddenly run into problems, but you never know."

Alice nodded. Ethan smiled before his gaze suddenly turned a lot more serious.

"Make sure to prepare for danger during the journey back to Metsel. We don't know enough about these new, intelligent monsters to know if they hold grudges. If they do, the group that attacked Cyra and escaped last week might attack us again. The Society could also make another move."

"I understand," Alice said as she tried not to shiver. The idea of being hunted down by an army of intelligent monsters was . . . horrifying. Luckily, she would be under the protection of an Immortal, which at least somewhat blunted her fear.

"Well then, let's let Illa know when we'll be leaving. Say goodbye to anyone you'll miss, and be ready to leave in a few days."

Murim, Illvaria's sixth Immortal, stared at the land before him and scratched his beard in disbelief. The sight in front of him was something he normally would have loved to see, but right now, it was unsettling.

The land was *wrong*. It didn't look like most land did after powerful monsters fought nearby. Instead, it looked as if the very world itself had broken somehow.

Fragments of land floated in the air like bits of water spilled from a giant's cup, caught in the middle of falling to the earth. Patches of water flowed upriver instead of downstream, as if gravity had decided to turn itself off in the area. The land itself occasionally flickered and distorted, tangling and untangling itself like a ball of yarn being played with by a cat. Anytime Murim wasn't looking at a particular patch of land, he would sometimes notice that the world had *shifted* when he wasn't looking at it. That, more than anything else, set Murim's teeth on edge. As an [Explorer], nothing made him more nervous than losing track of the area he was exploring.

The mana in the area was also far denser than Murim had ever seen before, even this far south. The Mana Wastes were normally quite rich in mana—however, over the past week, the mana had grown more and more dense. It was now four times denser than it had been a month ago. Worse, the density was still increasing. The local monsters hadn't quite caught up to the new levels of mana yet, but Murim knew it was just a matter of time before this area became hundreds of times more dangerous than before.

Murim frowned. He was confident in his survival skills. As one of the highest-level [Explorers] on the entire Southern Continent, he could escape or fight off most monsters. Of course, Murim had never ventured onto the Western Continent—he was interested in exploring, but he wasn't suicidal. But he was confident that nobody had a better grasp of the Mana Wastes of the Southern Continent than him. He *thrived* in places where no other human had set foot before.

But the messed-up, jumbled land and ridiculous mana density was different. Murim had never seen anything like this before.

Murim looked at the shifting landmasses and floating bits of rock before shuddering.

Most landmasses had a certain kind of logic to them. Despite the incredible mana density of the South, despite the horrifying monsters that could rip apart squads of [Soldiers] in moments, and despite the totally unmapped wilderness, the southernmost reaches of the continent had never seemed . . . unstable to Murim before. Dangerous, wild, and uncharted, yes, but everything had always felt logical to him. As long as he played by the rules and didn't do anything stupid, he had always been confident that he could survive. Now, things just felt wrong.

Should he keep exploring anyway?

Part of Murim's heart yearned to keep going. The rush of each new discovery was what drove him to keep pushing. The thrill of outwitting monsters and discovering new sights that nobody had witnessed before brought him joy. It was a thrill that few people would understand, but Murim loved every new sight and area that he came across.

And then, as Murim was debating exploring the far messier and less stable South, he heard an unearthly screeching in the distance. It didn't even sound like a proper monster this time. It sounded like someone had taken most of the monsters in the world, stuck them into a grinding bowl, and then tried to stir them all together. The cacophony was unimaginable.

{Threat Detection} started blaring, and he felt another shiver run down his spine.

He finally made up his mind. Exploration was wonderful, but he didn't want to die yet. He turned back north, away from the monster, and started sprinting. His stealth-related perks snapped into place, shielding him from the view of almost everything. A regular person wouldn't even see him as he ran by. As an Immortal with exceptional physical stats, he could run nonstop for hours before getting winded, and he could travel without sleep for days thanks to his high [Endurance].

As he ran, he started to think about the last time he had been in Illvaria. It had been . . . perhaps a decade now? Two?

He shook his head. It was easy to lose track since he spent so much more time in the wilderness than in civilization. Murim just hoped that whatever had changed recently hadn't spread into the civilized lands of the Southern Continent. If the geography, gravity, and mana of the entire world itself was imploding, Murim wasn't sure there would be anything to return to. He was looking forward to a nice mug of ale and some time with old friends once he returned to civilization, and he definitely didn't want to find his homeland reduced to a pile of corpses and monsters, the way it had been after the war with the Sigmusi. He still felt guilty about missing that mess, and he hoped this wouldn't be a repeat of that incident.

{Perfect Cartographer} started to help him track all the newly rearranged geographical features of the South, and {Undying Explorer} helped him keep his footing, avoid danger, and survive the dangerous levels of mana as he traveled. As he ran, the terrain continued to shift everywhere he wasn't looking. He ignored it. Or, at least, he tried to. However, his perks gave him a constant, unnerving set of updates about a rather disturbing fact: The path from his current location to the nearest Illvarian city kept changing. It was very subtle, but it almost felt like his location was shifting when he wasn't paying attention—almost as if he were trapped in the maze of a dimensional mage gone mad.

This idea unnerved Murim the most—his perks should have made getting lost about as likely as jumping to the moon. An Immortal [Explorer] should not get turned around while moving—it was his area of expertise, and the idea that the land was confusing him pricked at his pride. But it also reaffirmed that Murim needed to leave the Mana Wastes *right now*, before the situation got even worse.

After nearly a day of running, Murim checked the time and the distance he had traveled before nodding to himself. Even though the land was changing and he occasionally had to move around the territory of larger and more powerful monsters, he was still making good progress.

At this rate, it wouldn't be more than a week or two before he returned to Illvaria.

The last few days in Cyra were dominated by reports, paperwork, and chaos, as Alice and Ethan tried to settle every problem related to monster ranches and how to get everything shipped back to Metsel. Ethan did most of the work—but he made sure Alice understood every detail about his *paperwork* as training for the future. It was . . . not very pleasant, although Alice could now navigate basic Illvarian bureaucracy. Something that, sadly, even Immortals had to deal with on a regular basis. Apparently, the magical middle ages still had an abundance of annoying forms to fill out.

After several hours of paper wrangling, Alice was pretty sure she had figured out how everything was supposed to be filled out, and Ethan had double-checked all her work.

All the [Guards] had reached the monster ranches they needed to defend, the cash flow to pay the [Monster Ranchers] had been arranged, and plans to deliver everything to Metsel had been finalized.

The first batch of materials from the [Monster Ranchers] had also come in, along with a few theories about what made some spidercrabs useful enchanting materials while others were worthless. Apparently, the age of the spidercrab seemed to influence the shell after its death. Younger spidercrabs would turn into useful enchanting materials for Alice's purposes, while older ones did not. The spidercrab ranchers hadn't pinned down an exact age range yet, but three of the four monster ranches seemed to have similar results so far. Which at least let Alice put one question to rest.

After completing all the paperwork, Alice also noticed that a completely new kind of mana had built up in her body. It was a very, very minor amount, and Alice had originally intended to simply convert it into another class's kind of mana . . . until she found that she couldn't.

It took Alice several minutes of careful probing before she realized that the new mana type seemed to be [Bureaucrat] mana, or perhaps [Administrator] mana. There were a lot of kinds of mana jumbled together, but they all sounded related to paperwork and government forms.

This revelation made Alice frown.

So far, she had found that she could convert similar kinds of mana into each other—[Kinetic Brawler] and [Kinetic Mage] mana could generally be converted into [Kinetic Manabinder] mana, and similarly, mana types for research-based classes could usually be converted into [Scientist], [Scholar], or [Explorer of Magic] mana without any issues. However, this was the first time Alice had confirmed that if a mana type was too different, it couldn't be converted into another type of mana.

Alice didn't have any classes related to paperwork or bureaucracy. The closest classes she had were [Courtier] and [Scholar], but [Courtier] was mostly related to the concept of comporting oneself as a [Noble] at parties and social events. Alice had checked through the class's known perks, most of which helped with things like dancing, etiquette, and conversations—there wasn't much of a relationship with paperwork and forms. Similarly, [Scholar] was related to research and was too far removed from government forms for Alice to convert the [Bureaucrat] mana into [Scholar] mana.

Alice sighed. This realization added yet another layer of complexity and problems to how she needed to behave until the System was fixed. If Alice got too much [Bureaucrat] mana, she wouldn't be able to solve the collapse of the System. She would be too busy behaving like a [Bureaucrat]. In short, Alice needed to avoid doing things that were *too* different from her classes until she found a way to fix class-seed creation, or boosted her ability to convert one form of mana into another.

The amount of mana that had built up in her body was tiny, so it wouldn't have much of an effect on her. But it definitely sounded an alarm bell in Alice's mind. She also decided to mention her new discovery to Ethan so that he could warn other people about this danger.

On their final day in Cyra, Illa hosted a small banquet to celebrate everyone's accomplishments. Alice was also pretty sure Illa wanted to display the fact that she was on speaking terms with an Immortal to the other mages and people of Cyra. Since the stability of Illa's town was now critical for Illvaria as a whole, Alice rolled her eyes at the pageantry but didn't say anything.

A few of the mages Alice had previously met showed up to the banquet. She hadn't seen most of them in months, and she also hadn't thought about them very much. They were just work colleagues, after all. She didn't know them very well. She still made some time to say hello and catch up, though. Apart from them, Milo and Father Friedheim also attended the banquet, and Alice ended up spending most of the night chatting with them and saying goodbye.

Alice's {Etiquette} skill still got a bit of a workout during the second half of the banquet, as she greeted and interacted with the mages in town and introduced herself to a few new people. However, most of the mages seemed more focused on Ethan—which suited Alice just fine. She was glad to dodge the most annoying parts of the banquet and hang out with the people she actually liked.

By the end of the meeting, Alice had gained a level in [Courtier] and {Etiquette}, much to her own surprise. She had expected [Courtier] to sit at level one for a very, very long time, considering how much she disliked parties and socializing with [Nobles].

You have leveled up!
Courtier: 1→2

Through training, you have increased a skill!
Etiquette: 21→22

Afterward, the group departed from Cyra in the same boat they had come in.

The boat sailed unimpeded up the river for two days, while Alice and Cecilia got to work teaching the [Enchanters] as much as they could about the System-related magic seeds they wanted to popularize. Another mage successfully formed a display mana seed during the boat ride home, meaning that it would be easier to start mass-producing the status screen and perk-viewing rings once they arrived back in Metsel. The mages were having a harder time grasping filtration mana, but Cecilia's [Enchanters] were still making good progress. Near midnight on the third day of the journey back toward Metsel, as Alice and Ethan were discussing plans about what to do when they returned, Ethan froze and commanded the boat to slow to a halt.

"Alice," he said. "Things are urgent. I think the Society, or the Sigmusi Colonia, has sent multiple near-Immortals to kidnap or kill you. They're close."

CHAPTER 28

Alice felt like someone had dumped a bucket of ice water on her.

She'd hoped the Society would back off after the attack last month, when they had thrown several agents at Ethan's manor and suffered a massive defeat. They had infuriated the Illvarian government last time and exposed a few research bases during the attack. Taking more actions would only make it worse for the Society's overall position.

Unfortunately, the Society didn't seem to care. It only took Alice a few seconds to figure out why. Her actions in the last few weeks had been very eye-catching. She had found a way to reduce the impact of the System's collapse through enchantments, identified several of the root problems people were facing, had used the Church of the System to spread that information, and had even helped the church set up [Willpower]-training programs. All these things indicated that Alice had a solid understanding of what the System was and how its collapse had changed the world. For the Society, Alice was practically waving a giant neon sign around saying, "I'm a very high-priority target!"

Still, she hadn't expected the Society to throw caution to the wind and attack Ethan, backed up by a small army of [Guards] and [Soldiers]. Alice wasn't a slouch in combat, either, even if she wasn't spectacular. The Society *should* have been nervous about trying to attack her. Which was likely why they had invested near-Immortals into the attack.

Her heart thudded like it wanted to leap out of her body, and her palms felt cold and sweaty.

"How many enemies are there? How powerful are they?" asked Alice, hoping that Ethan could dispel some of her mounting terror.

"I can see thirty people," said Ethan. "Two near-Immortals, and twenty-eight more standard spellcasters, according to my perception perks. I don't see any full Immortals, although it's entirely possible that one of them is using a disguise perk that I can't detect," said Ethan. "I'm not specialized in scouting, after all."

Alice's heart started beating even more furiously. Two near-Immortal-level enemies. A potential hidden Immortal. That seemed far beyond what they could handle on the boat.

"Can you fight them?" asked Alice.

"I should be able to," said Ethan, although he sounded less certain than usual. "If they don't have a build specialized in countering mine, two near-Immortals are manageable for me. That being said, if they didn't think they stood a chance, they wouldn't attack us. The situation is already dangerous. Keep an eye out for any anomalies."

Alice gritted her teeth, scanning every single perk in her status screen that might be useful in a fight.

{Adrenaline Rush}. {Enhanced Senses}. {Extended Tissues}. {Combat Seed}, which Alice hadn't needed to make use of outside of training sessions for a while. {No_Mana}. {Reflection}. Various sight- and senses-related perks from [Kinetic Manabinder] that let her track objects moving near her. Finally, {Enchanter's Armory} to enhance her enchanted items.

She had a lot of perks available. Even so, it seemed pitiful and inadequate when she thought about what a near-Immortal would have.

When fighting alongside Ethan, Alice had seen him use forty magic tendrils comfortably. When he activated a temporary boost, he could increase that number by one hundred mana tendrils, for a total of 140. He probably had other tricks, too—he had simply never needed to use them.

Alice had a measly seven mana tendrils. While under the effects of {Adrenaline Rush}, she could make those seven mana tendrils as good as a few dozen from a normal mage—but there was an upper limit to what she could accomplish. Ethan had crushed her in every training session. If a near-Immortal was only half as strong as Ethan, Alice would still be utterly dominated during a fight. Even staying safe would be impossible. Worse, in higher-level combat, Alice was still very dependent on perks like {Adrenaline Rush} to level the playing field—and those perks had very short time limits before they lost effect.

"How many soldiers are with us?" she asked.

"About fifty [Guards] with above-average levels, including your [Hidden Guard]. We also have Cecilia's five [Enchanters], although they're not very proficient in combat," said Ethan. "I also brought along twenty combat mages. At least in theory, we have an advantage in strength. That makes me even more nervous, since it's likely the real threat is hidden."

"How long do we have until they reach us?"

"Maybe ten minutes? Or a bit less."

She hadn't felt this scared in a long time. The attack on Ethan's manor had felt frightening, but at the same time, Alice had known that Ethan would probably be able to control the situation. After all, they were in the middle of the city, and the Society's reinforcements had already lost when they failed to locate her. The attack on the Society base hadn't felt very dangerous to Alice, either, since Ethan had been the one initiating the attack with an entire army at his back.

This was the first fight Alice really thought she might lose, even after becoming an Immortal's apprentice. She felt her shoulders start to shake—not violently, but she could feel the fear and tension clawing at her nerves. Ethan seemed to notice and gave her a comforting pat on the shoulder.

"Look—the situation isn't desperate yet, just dangerous. I'm still here, and I can probably handle one of the two near-Immortals easily. Just keep an eye out for whatever tricks they have up their sleeves. If we can identify that, we'll win. All right?"

Alice hoped that Ethan wasn't just trying to make her feel better. She nodded.

"Do you want to join the fight or hide in your cabin?" Ethan asked after a few moments.

Alice started to say that she wanted to hide, before she paused.

The situation was dangerous for Ethan and the other soldiers. Alice was afraid. She didn't want to fight. She didn't like violence. But was hiding really the correct answer here?

Realistically, Alice wasn't a weak combatant anymore. She could be considered above average. She was never going to have the combat potential of someone who had five classes dedicated to fighting, but she could inflict a bit of damage before {Adrenaline Rush} ran out and she had to retreat. Any contribution she made to the battlefield could be the difference between winning and losing. Besides, if the group lost, Alice's outcome would be miserable. Ultimately, this fight was to protect her. Not to mention, Cecilia was on this boat, too. Alice didn't want to see her best friend get hurt. If she helped, the odds of Cecilia dying were much lower.

Even though Alice wanted to hide in her cabin and wait for the danger to pass, she would fight.

"I'll fight with the troops," said Alice.

Ethan's eyes shone a bit, and he nodded. "Good choice. I would have done the same, although I think both choices would have been reasonable in this situation. Just make sure to stay safe. On this boat, you are the most valuable person. If you die, all this is for nothing," he said.

Alice nodded. A moment later, Ethan dashed toward where the other soldiers were housed. Alice trailed behind him and, a moment later, darted toward Cecilia's room. Cecilia took a few seconds to wake up, even after Alice told her that they were under attack, but quickly got her enchantments ready. When the two returned to the deck, they found several [Guards] strapping on their armor and weapons. They wore grim, determined expressions as they prepared for battle.

Several people quickly ran to the deck of the ship, where they could get the clearest view of their surroundings.

Alice scanned the area, relying on her unusually high [Perception] to try to make out the approaching enemies. However, her vision wasn't good enough to mimic night vision, and the mana sources were too far away. Luckily, the [Scouts] were better at their job than Alice was.

"I can see several people over there," said a [Scout], pointing northwest toward the shore. "There are a few hiding behind those trees. Does anyone have other observations?"

"I think I can see a few people that have mana on them, although I only have a basic {Mana Sense} perk, and they're quite far away. I think we can confirm Honored Immortal Ethan's earlier statement—almost all of them seem to be mages. I can sense a few that aren't, though," said another man, standing a bit farther away.

Alice frowned.

Not all of them were mages?

All members of the Society of Starry Eyes that she knew of were mages. If there were nonmages mixed in, it either meant they had hired mercenaries who were willing to attack an Immortal, or that someone else was helping the Society attack the boat. Alice was relieved to know that all the people attacking them wouldn't be mages, at least. Mages were usually stronger than other combat classes at the same level, so facing fewer of them was a good thing. However, if the Society had managed to fill in some of the roles they were usually missing, then the overall danger of the group might still be higher than usual. After all, when Alice joined the attack on the Society base, she had been able to tell that the enemy lacked an effective system of command. Their [Kinetic Mages] had been placed too far away from the [Organic Mages] to defend them against missiles, and they had only tried to correct this oversight halfway through the battle. The Society mages had also fled once things looked bad enough. This implied the Society had no competent [Generals] or [Commanders].

If the Society was working with another organization, they might have corrected this flaw.

"The nonmages who came with the Society have a certain level of organization that I would expect from the military," said Ethan, and his lips tightened into a grimace. "They don't look like [Mercenaries] at all. I wonder who is providing troops for the Society . . ." Ethan trailed off, before he glared at one of the distant ambushers. "It's probably the Sigmusi. I can't think of anyone else who would work with the Society."

Ethan turned toward the [Guards] on the deck of the ship, as well as the mages who were now assembling themselves behind the [Guards].

"All right, I want the [Kinetic Mages] to start spacing themselves out between the [Guards]. Deal with any projectiles likely to kill the [Guards] on deck. We need to handle a few volleys. I plan to clear out the trees they're using for cover to make things a bit easier. Also—" Ethan's words were cut off as his mana tendrils sprang out of his body. A moment later, Alice saw Ethan produce a large number of enchanted rocks and attach them to his tendrils.

Every single rock had five instructions. For a consumable missile to have five enchantments in it was a completely absurd display of wealth. But Ethan didn't seem to care about the extravagance of his actions. He launched the first wave of rocks toward the Society and the Sigmusi, ripping apart trees and shattering several missiles that had been heading toward the Illvarian troops. Alice was faintly reminded of artillery shells from home—every single rock that hit a tree somehow shredded the tree into nonexistence with a flare of organic mana. A few of these bursts of organic mana even clipped hostile archers, maiming or killing them outright.

"Don't engage yet, unless you have good perks for long-range attacks," said Ethan, his previously concerned tone starting to evaporate. Instead of concern, his voice started to take on a different quality.

Icy determination.

Alice saw that Ethan hadn't cleared out every missile that was heading toward the Illvarians. She spotted a few arrows filled with rainbow mana still heading toward the boat. The Illvarian [Kinetic Mages] responded when the missiles grew close enough and blocked the wave of arrows with their mana tendrils. A few arrows slipped through this web of protective magic tendrils, as the arrows literally zigzagged in midair and dodged the mages. Two Illvarian [Guards] died as arrows sank into them.

Ethan grimaced, but Alice noticed a lot of the trees that the Society had been using for cover had been destroyed by Ethan's rocks.

"Shots are much clearer now. Shoot," said Ethan.

The Illvarian [Guards] who had bows and useful perks released their first wave of arrows at the enemy. Many of them were deflected by the Society's magic tendrils—but Alice heard a distant scream, and another far-off blob of rainbow mana fizzled out of existence.

Then some of the distant patches of rainbow mana flickered, and Alice saw four different patches of dimensional mana start to fizzle into existence on the boat.

Alice and the other Illvarian mages started hurriedly purifying the dimensional broken mana, and at the same time, Alice used her own dimensional seed to plug up the portals that had just been opened. She had never tried closing a portal manually before. Luckily, she succeeded on her first try, cutting down the first wave of portals. The Society immediately tried to open up a second wave of portals, but all three portals were located right next to Alice. She immediately shut them down and smiled.

Moments later, the third wave of portals opened, and a wave of knives and arrows shot out. However, Alice had bought the Illvarians enough time to respond. Several [Archers] shot at the portals, sending arrows right back at the attackers. Alice joined in by spraying several of her consumable bracelet beads at the portals. She wasn't sure how successful her attack was, but a few moments later, a few distant blobs of rainbow mana flickered out of existence, followed by remote screams.

Meanwhile, on the other side of the boat, the waves of missiles and arrows continued to fly back and forth between the Illvarians and the Society. Ethan and the two near-Immortals seemed locked into a desperate game of whack-a-mole, except every failure meant a [Guard] or mage died.

Meanwhile, the Society attackers on the shore started to creep closer to the Illvarian boat, using the few remaining trees for cover. Despite their losses, they seemed determined to press forward.

A few moments later, Alice identified two people who had incredibly dense mana in their bodies. They stepped forward. One of them had a kinetic and a dimensional magic seed, while the other was a pure [Organic Mage]. Alice sucked in a breath of frigid air.

The two people attacking them weren't Immortals, but they were *very* close. Alice could only see a little bit of nonmana flesh left on their bodies. It wouldn't be surprising if they became fully fledged Immortals in a decade or two, even if they didn't work particularly hard.

The first near-Immortal was already locked into a projectile battle with Ethan and was just barely managing to hold off the Illvarian Immortal's storm of dangerous missiles and enchanted objects. Meanwhile, the Society [Organic Mage] seemed far more reluctant to engage and was instead looking for an opportunity.

Alice aimed another bracelet of enchanted beads, and was prepared to start peppering the Society lines with her own missiles, when she froze.

Just out of sight, Alice could see a new person appear. And unlike the two near-Immortals that were attacking the boat already, this person was a walking cloud of solidified mana. There wasn't a single bit of nonmana flesh left in their body. It only took Alice a moment to realize what that meant.

The Society hadn't brought two near-Immortals to attack her.

They had brought two near-Immortals and an actual Immortal.

CHAPTER 29

“Ethan,” hissed Alice as her heart hammered against her ribs. She had found the Society's trump card. “I see a hostile Immortal.”

Ethan scanned the area and frowned. “Are you sure?” he asked as he deflected another wave of missiles.

“I can see their mana, even though I can't see their actual body,” said Alice. “With the way their mana looks, they *have* to be an Immortal.”

Ethan's frown grew deeper. “A stealth-based Immortal. I only recall the Society having one Immortal, and that guy definitely isn't focused on stealth. Either the Society recently had another person ascend to Immortality, one that I know absolutely nothing about, or . . .” Ethan trailed off before he snorted. “No, it's probably Emilia. She's an [Assassin] and [Blade Dancer] from the Sigmusi Colonia, and one of their eight Immortals. She has rather strange perks, from what I know—they aren't necessarily optimized for her role as an [Assassin]. Instead, many are optimized to counter my father's perks. She has tried to assassinate him a few times over the past century.” Ethan grimaced. “This is going to be difficult.”

Alice felt her heart beat even faster. If Ethan thought the situation was difficult, things must be truly dire.

“So you can track Emilia?” Ethan asked after a split second of silence.

Alice nodded.

“Keep an eye on her, and let me know when she gets within thirty meters of the boat. She's a melee fighter, so I don't have to worry about her until she gets close. But I need you to let me know when she's in range,” said Ethan. “Have you noticed anything else odd, or is Emilia their trump card?”

Alice examined the battlefield again, taking in the entire scene as she searched for any other anomalies. Of the original fifty Illvarian [Guards] and twenty combat mages, perhaps forty-five [Guards] and seventeen mages were still alive. Most of the living were still in fighting condition. Cecilia and her five [Enchanters] were also part of the battle, although they were huddled near the back, hurling enchanted items into combat when an opportune moment arrived.

Of the thirty regular attackers, perhaps ten had died already. Ethan was keeping the two near-Immortals distracted, so the attackers were suffering. However, once the enemy Immortal joined the fray, the situation would collapse. The Illvarian side suffered from a major deficit in high-level combatants right now.

Alice didn't see any other surprises, thankfully. That meant they *only* needed to find a way to fend off an Immortal to keep the battlefield under control.

"I don't see any other abnormalities," said Alice. Then she paused and eyed Emilia again. "Emilia seems to be wearing armor and daggers with System enchantments attached to them. I don't know what they do."

"That's probably her custom armor set," said Ethan. "She always wears it when she fights. It boosts her [Dexterity] and [Strength] and covers up a few weaknesses in her stealth perks. At least, we're pretty sure that's what it does." Ethan nodded to himself, and he seemed slightly less nervous than before. "Keep an eye on Emilia and assist on the main battlefield when you can. Let me know if something important happens." Then Ethan turned his attention back to the battle.

Alice nodded.

Another portal ripped its way open in the middle of the boat a few moments later, and Alice immediately started cleaning the broken mana that it spewed out. She also tried to help close the portal, but this one felt far sturdier than the previous wave of portals. It was as if it was reinforced by a perk. Before anyone else could respond to the portal, an arrow ripped out of it and hit a [Guard] a few meters to her left.

Blood sprayed onto her face as the [Guard] gurgled and clutched the arrow in his throat. She simply stared at the [Guard], hoping that the passive healing effect of {Extended Tissues} would somehow keep the [Guard] alive, but a moment later, the rainbow mana surging out of {Extended Tissues} shut off. There was nothing left to heal anymore.

Some part of Alice's brain numbly processed the portal finally snapping shut as another mage tossed something through the portal and a mage in the distance screamed. However, the warm blood on her face was too distracting for her to focus entirely on the battlefield around her.

Ethan cursed again, even as his mana tendrils continued to desperately deflect waves of arrows and missiles. "Alice, try to take out the dimensional mages if you can. There are too many things to keep track of at once. We need to lower the number of variables on their side. I have a perk that could help if the dimensional mages are out of the picture. I need to get rid of at least one of the three powerful combatants before they finish positioning themselves." There was a determined light in Ethan's eyes, and he looked grim and focused in a way Alice had never seen before. Alice eyed Emilia, who was creeping closer to the boat, and nodded. She wasn't sure if she could deal with the [Dimensional Mages]—but if she failed, she would either die or suffer horribly.

"I'll handle it," said Alice. She was surprised by the determination and confidence in her own voice.

She scanned the attackers again, and this time she searched for the telltale hint of purple mana unique to [Dimensional Mages]. It was still hard to pick out, since she was trying to look at magic seeds from a massive distance, but as the enemy closed in it grew easier and easier to see things.

Another portal on the boat opened near one of the other Illvarian mages. This time, Alice did her best to ignore it. She needed to trust that the other mages and [Guards] could handle some problems on their own.

Instead, she focused her vision on the enemies in the distance and hoped to find the enemy dimensional mages. This time, she caught a small flicker of purple mana out of the corner of her eye. It was only there for an instant before it disappeared, but it was enough. She whirled toward the source.

There, she saw a mage with a purple magic seed hiding behind a tree. Standing right next to him was a pair of people who Alice assumed were [Archers]. She had found her first target. After a few moments, Alice smiled grimly. The Society mages liked using portals to attack. She decided to return the favor. She reached for her dimensional mana and opened a portal right next to the Society mage.

The mage and the two [Archers] froze in shock.

Alice immediately layered a small amount of No_Magic mana onto all the beads on several bracelets, and then unloaded all of them through the portal.

Every single bracelet took one mana tendril to activate and had twenty beads on it. Alice had seven tendrils. The No_Magic mana Alice had layered onto the beads would make it even harder for people to block the magic beads, and {Enchanter's Armory} would boost their effects even more. For a brief moment, Alice resembled Ethan—she sent 140 projectiles toward her enemy in a single attack.

Then Alice immediately reached into her storage perk and got the next set of bracelets ready. Before the first round of projectiles connected, she sent another wave of beads at her targets. One of the three blobs of rainbow mana winked out of existence. However, Alice saw a portal pop open in the distance. One end was right in front of the projectiles she had launched, and the other was opened directly in front of her.

Her eyes widened in surprise, but {Adrenaline Rush} didn't activate for some reason.

Right as Alice started panicking, she saw the portal suddenly vanish.

It took her a moment to realize what had happened.

Alice's beads were resistant to the mana from other mages, thanks to her No_Magic mana and the enchantment she had layered onto them. {Enchanter's Armory} had enhanced the strength of the first enchantment she had put onto her beads, which made it hard for other mages to manipulate them. With all these effects stacked on top of each other, Alice's enchanted beads had ripped through the hostile portal as if it weren't even there.

A second later, Alice saw the other two globs of rainbow mana disappear. The first [Dimensional Mage], as well as two nearby [Archers], were dead.

"One down," said Alice.

"Interesting," said Ethan as he watched her work. "I didn't realize you could do that. Can you do it again?"

"Yes," said Alice.

Ethan grinned. "Change of plans. When I say so, toss a few of those antimagic beads where I tell you to. It'll work just as well as removing the other [Dimensional Mages]."

"Got it," said Alice, and went back to observing the battlefield. A few seconds later, the near-Immortal [Organic Mage] from the Society started dashing toward the shore of the river, plowing through trees as if they were imitating a bulldozer. At the same time, the stealthy Immortal circled the boat by walking on water as if it were solid land. Rainbow mana flickered through her body as she leaped off a wave. She appeared to be moving toward the [Guards] at Alice's back.

"The [Assassin] is behind us!" said Alice. "The near-Immortal's charge is a distraction."

"Got it," said Ethan. His eyes flicked back toward the stern of the boat. "When the time comes, grab Cecilia and her [Enchanters] and bring them to my side. We can't afford to lose them." Then Ethan reached into the air in front of him, and pulled out . . . a sword?

Alice had no idea why Ethan was holding a sword. Wasn't he a mage?

Even though Alice was confused, she quickly realized that the sword was a masterpiece. There was an incredible amount of System mana inside it, and it also had a traditional enchantment intertwined with the System enchantment—in other words, it could boost the user AND activate a more traditionally magical effect. The traditional enchantment seemed to be focused on kinetic and thermal mana, although Alice couldn't tell what it did.

Ethan grinned. "One of Doll's best early works. It was originally my father's, but he gave it to me for my two hundredth birthday. He has a better one now." Then the grin on Ethan's face faded as he glanced at the [Organic Mage] dashing toward the shoreline. "When I count to three, shoot a round of antimagic beads at that [Organic Mage], then grab Cecilia. Got it?"

"Got it," said Alice.

"One, two, three!" said Ethan, before he swung the sword down.

Alice immediately pumped a few bracelets full of No_Magic mana and then shot them at the [Organic Mage]. Right as the beads reached the halfway point, a giant beam of fire, heat, and light leaped out of the sword, as if the sun itself had jumped from the blade and was trying to kill the enemy.

The battlefield lit up for a moment, as if Ethan's slash had dispelled the darkness of nighttime and returned the world to midday. Alice blinked tears out of her eyes just in time to see two portals open up in front of the giant beam of death.

Alice's beads ripped through the portals as if they were made of paper, and the flash of light crashed into the [Organic Mage].

The man screamed in agony. Alice could tell that his perks were somehow keeping him alive. But Ethan didn't let up. Before the [Organic Mage] could recover, waves of enchanted items surged toward him while the other near-Immortal dashed out of cover and tried to help his ally. The [Kinetic Mage] managed to stop most of Ethan's enchantment swarm right as Alice finally turned toward Cecilia and started sprinting.

The blob of hidden rainbow mana suddenly sped up as the Immortal's gait changed from a regular human's sprint to a speed that could rival a sports car. Alice looked at the approaching blob of rainbow mana and tried not to shudder in fear. No matter what she had prepared, no matter how much she had trained, Alice knew she wasn't ready to fight an Immortal yet. And there weren't enough [Guards] on the boat to fend off an Immortal, either. Everything would come down to how successful Ethan's gambit was.

"Cecilia, go to Ethan's side!" Alice yelled, trying to make herself heard over the sound of battle. She turned to the [Enchanters]. "You guys come along, too!"

The [Enchanters], as well as Cecilia, looked a bit baffled, but Alice had gotten close enough that they could hear her, at least. Their eyes darted fearfully to the dark, moonlit wilderness beyond the boat before they dashed toward Ethan.

"An Immortal is charging toward the back of the boat," Alice whispered to Cecilia once the other girl got closer to her. "Ethan wants you close by, just in case."

"An *Immortal*?" said Cecilia as her expression turned white with fear. She and the [Enchanters] sped up. Within moments, the group had reached Ethan's side. Alice looked at the battlefield again.

The [Organic Mage] *still* wasn't dead, somehow. Ethan had managed to embed three different consumable enchantments into the man's skull, and Alice could see rainbow mana coursing through the enchantments as they tried to rip the man apart. Despite the multiple wounds that should have been lethal, the man's perks were keeping him alive. The [Kinetic Mage] was still desperately trying to fend off Ethan's attacks, and he and Ethan had both used temporary perks to boost their combat ability. Ethan was wielding 140 different magic tendrils and firing a storm of items at the enemy, but the opposing [Kinetic Mage] had created a wall of crackling rainbow mana that kept him and his companion safe. Alice took in the spectacle of an Immortal and two near-Immortals fighting for a moment before she saw a bolt of lightning rip through the darkness toward her.

She tried to deflect it using one of her magic tendrils—only to discover that lightning was not a physical object and her mana types could not interact with it. She felt {Adrenaline Rush} on the verge of activating—but before the perk could turn itself on, Ethan flung a rod of enchanted metal right in front of the lightning bolt. The lightning bolt veered toward the metal rod as the gleaming iron glowed with mana, before the iron rod sucked up the electricity and began to glow.

Ethan caught the metal rod with another magic tendril before he flung it at the rainbow wall. The metal rod exploded like a bomb the moment it made contact, spewing metal fragments and captured electricity into its surroundings. The rainbow wall didn't even budge as the explosion crashed into it, and Alice and Cecilia ducked below the ship's railing as metal fragments zipped through the air. Alice caught a few of the ones that flew over her head before they could kill nearby [Guards] and mages.

"Fuck," muttered Ethan. "I was hoping that would work."

Alice turned around to check on Emilia and saw that the rainbow-colored patch of mana was perhaps five seconds away from boarding.

"Emilia is about to board the boat," Alice said.

Ethan gave the injured near-Immortal a look of frustration and disgust before he whipped another round of consumable enchantments out of his storage perk and fired them at the man. The first few consumable enchantments also exploded when they touched the rainbow wall, which *finally* destroyed it.

The [Kinetic Mage]'s eyes widened, and he tried to drag the [Organic Mage] out of the line of fire with a magic tendril. It didn't matter. The enchanted items turned in midair to keep following their target, almost as if they were heat-seeking missiles.

The [Kinetic Mage] created another shimmering wall of rainbow mana, and all of Ethan's consumable enchantments exploded as they made contact with the wall. However, the second wall of rainbow mana still held. Ethan grimaced.

Alice, seeing an opportunity, empowered a round of beads with No_Magic mana again and fired them toward the shimmering rainbow wall.

The rainbow wall cracked under Alice's attack, and then parts of it collapsed. It didn't completely shatter the way the first wall had—but it was pockmarked and weakened.

"Damaged it," said Alice as she let loose with another spray of enchanted items. She was almost out of bracelets, so she hoped Ethan closed out the fight soon.

Before Alice could get her hopes up, the [Kinetic Mage]'s wall repaired itself.

"I don't have time for this," said Ethan. He whirled back toward the injured Society [Organic Mage] one last time, and then for a moment, Alice felt a crackle of energy stir in her surroundings.

Rainbow mana exploded out of Ethan's body like a thick fog, reaching toward absolutely everything in their surroundings. Trees, pieces of metal and cloth vibrated in response to Ethan's mana, and for a moment, Alice felt like every physical object within a hundred meters was under Ethan's control.

Then, like an enraged nest of hornets, almost every physical object in Ethan's surroundings flung itself toward the injured [Organic Mage] and his [Kinetic Mage] protector. Only the Illvarian boat was spared. A storm of wood, bones, a few unlucky enemy combatants, and metal closed in on the men from a variety of angles.

The Society [Kinetic Mage] tried to fend off the wave of items with another rainbow wall, but Ethan's attack just came from too many directions at once. The [Kinetic Mage]'s shield missed nearly a third of the projectiles.

Another shield of rainbow mana sprang up around the [Kinetic Mage], keeping him safe.

The [Organic Mage] turned into Swiss cheese. Dozens of items ripped through him, and the perks in his body *finally* ran out of energy, killing the resilient mage once and for all.

And while Alice and Ethan were distracted, Emilia leaped over the railing of the boat and beheaded nearly twenty [Guards] and four combat mages in five seconds flat. Alice still couldn't see the woman's face, since her stealth perk was still on.

Alice's heart clenched.

One of the three major threats the Society had sent their way was finally dead. Ethan had been forced to spend one of his most powerful perks to deal with him.

But the most dangerous threat was now on the boat and decimating their defensive lines.

Alice felt her heartbeat accelerate even more as she stared at the Illvarian corpses on the other side of the deck.

Perhaps half of the ordinary attackers had dropped, while about half of the Illvarian troops were still alive. With an Immortal and near-Immortal still prepared to fight against Ethan, Alice did not like her odds right now.

Alice felt the anxiety grip her thoughts more and more tightly as the rainbow mana turned toward her. Then more rainbow mana flared inside Emilia's body, and she rushed toward Alice at a speed that defied imagination. Despite the fact that Alice could *see* Emilia's mana, she couldn't see the woman's physical body or hear a sound. All she could hear was the deafening silence of the dead [Guards] and mages on the other side of the boat.

As if something had broken, the terror in her heart gave way to anger. If she wanted to keep her freedom, she needed to do something *now*. Ethan's attention was fixed on the deck, but he wasn't looking at Emilia—he was looking near her. He couldn't see her. [Kinetic Mages] relied on pinpoint precision to fight. Emilia's invisibility was a huge problem for Ethan's fighting style.

Alice's mind spun in circles until she found a desperate solution.

Alice pushed her magic tendrils toward Emilia and felt them strain as they got farther away. Emilia was too far for Alice to mess with her clothes or weapons directly. The twenty meters between the bow and stern of the boat had never felt so huge. Another desperate idea flashed through her mind, and Alice opened a portal right in front of her. The other end of the portal opened up a few meters in front of Emilia. Alice hoped that her idea would work.

Alice focused on {Extended Organics}, the perk that let her treat any air within a few meters of her as part of her body. Then she glanced through the portal and hoped that the perk would work from this distance. She tried to form a magic tendril right on top of Emilia and saw one spring into existence.

It worked. Alice could extend the range of her magic tendrils in basically any direction with creative use of dimensional mana.

She could feel the portal she had opened straining a bit as it tried to make sense of what Alice was doing. But even though the portal was straining and eating far more mana than usual, it was still hundreds of times more efficient than just extending a magic tendril dozens of meters away.

Alice only realized it now, but dimensional mana opened a whole new layer of efficiency in combat. Most [Kinetic Mages] could only influence nearby objects, but portals and {Extended Organics} could totally change that.

Alice stuck a bracelet at the end of her tendril. She aimed the bracelet right at Emilia's brain and then activated the enchantments. Twenty magic beads tore through the air.

With contemptuous ease, Emilia dodged out of the way like a ghost. She had missed, and Emilia knew Alice could track her now.

Emilia continued sprinting toward Alice, although the woman started dodging and weaving as she approached. It slowed her down, but Alice knew the Immortal would still be on her in seconds.

Alice snapped her portal shut as she felt a new wave of panic surge through her body. She wanted the threat *gone*.

"Ethan!" yelled Alice, hoping he would figure out where Emilia was and help her. She didn't bother with portals this time—she just started throwing bracelets at Emilia, praying that they would hit, or at least slow Emilia down. Ethan joined in Alice's offensive—but he wasn't aiming directly at Emilia, just throwing things in her general direction. Emilia's invisibility perk was too troublesome. Ethan still didn't know where she was.

Alice finally realized that Emilia's perk wasn't *just* invisibility. Instead, it seemed almost like it selectively messed with one target's vision, making it even harder for them to pinpoint and attack the perk user.

Alice needed to get Emilia's perk deactivated somehow. Ethan couldn't fight without his vision. How could she do that?

Perks were impossible to deactivate externally.

Unless . . .

Alice thought of another desperate gamble. She opened a new portal and then materialized a small mana tendril right in front of Emilia.

Then Alice dumped almost all her No_Magic mana into the air, creating a small cloud of mana that stopped perks from working. Something pushed against Alice's mana for a moment as Emilia dashed into the area, before Alice saw something bright red flash into existence for a moment. It wasn't much, but Alice could see part of Emilia for a brief moment. Ethan's eyes flickered directly toward the spot where Emilia was standing. In a flash, dozens of enchanted items flew toward the area, cutting off almost any path of retreat Emilia could take. Arrows made of crystal, enchanted rocks, and glass vials filled with orange liquid screamed through the air as they flew toward Emilia.

At the same time, Alice felt something latch on to her clothes and fling her away.

Alice screamed as she was suddenly catapulted into the sky before she realized that Ethan was moving her out of the way. A moment later, Alice found herself back on her feet, with Ethan now between her and Emilia.

Meanwhile, Emilia desperately tried to weave through Ethan's storm of attacks, like a raindrop dancing in a hurricane. It was like she could see the future—even though Ethan's attacks looked impossible to dodge, Emilia somehow found a way around almost every single one.

Luckily, Ethan seemed to know how good Emilia's dodging abilities were. Several of the flasks of orange liquid shattered in midair. The moment the liquid exited its container, it burned like napalm. Emilia shrieked as Ethan finally hit the damned Immortal with an attack. As she darted out of the way, the strange crystals exploded, sending shrapnel tearing through the air. A few Illvarian [Guards] also groaned in pain as they were caught in the aftereffects, but clearly, Ethan couldn't protect them right now. Unfortunately, Emilia managed to use her daggers to swat those pieces of shrapnel out of the air along with the crystal arrows. However, Ethan had managed to slow her charge down, and parts of her body were on fire now. For a moment, he stopped Emilia.

And then Alice's injection of No_Magic mana ran out. Ethan's attacks grew erratic again, and with a surge of rainbow mana, the fire on Emilia's body disappeared. Emilia staggered back a few steps before she turned toward Alice and dashed.

Alice felt the despair in her heart grow heavier.

How was she supposed to fight something like this?

Emilia was so *fast*. So agile. Hitting her was nearly impossible. She moved like a gymnast with no bones in her body, and Ethan couldn't even *locate* the woman without Alice's help.

Alice was discovering just how strange and terrifying Immortals could become with the right perks. Alice flung a final round of beads at Emilia, then reached for another bracelet and realized she was out of ammo. The woman danced around the beads, barely even slowing down as she neared Alice. Ethan fired at the spot Alice had attacked, but Emilia was already gone. When Emilia was five meters away, Alice decided on a last, desperate plan. She strained her magic tendrils to go as far as she could push them and tried to reach *inside* Emilia's body.

Alice still felt like she was pushing her mana through a steel wall, but desperation gave her the strength to push her mana forward. She barely managed to push her magic tendril a few centimeters into Emilia's body before Emilia's innate magic resistance shut her down. It was enough.

Alice shoved every single Marium of No_Magic mana directly into Emilia's body.

Alice felt something crack, as if she had just tried to stuff a glass beaker into a hydraulic press.

The rainbow-colored blob of mana a few meters away suddenly fizzled and sparked, as if something had gone horribly wrong inside it.

Alice hoped, for a brief moment, that perhaps No_Magic mana had some sort of lethal effect on Immortals. They were made of mana, so perhaps No_Magic mana could kill them on the spot.

This hope was quickly dashed as Emilia staggered out of thin air. For the first time, Alice could actually *see* her opponent as more than a blob of mana.

Emilia had short, neatly trimmed black hair that peeked out of the back of her helmet. She wore bright red armor that was so colorful that Alice could scarcely believe Emilia was invisible moments ago. Alice could only see a few traces of Emilia's skin through the eyeholes in the woman's helmet. The woman's cold, piercing eyes gazed at Alice like a wolf eyeing a rabbit. She held two short swords in her hands. Each weapon was packed with enough mana to send shivers down Alice's spine.

The moment ended. Emilia glared at Alice and raised her short swords. Ethan launched another volley of objects at Emilia, but her limbs contorted and blurred as she spun out of every attack. Rainbow mana shivered in Emilia's heart . . . and then did nothing. It was almost as if the rainbow mana in Emilia's body was asleep. Whatever perks Emilia was trying to activate, they weren't able to push through the No_Magic mana Alice had injected into her body, at least not yet. However, the No_Magic mana was rapidly dissipating—it would only last a few more seconds.

A crystal arrow nicked the edge of Emilia's armor and tore through it as if it were wet paper. Somehow, Emilia bent out of the way before the arrow could graze her skin. Another round of crystal shrapnel tore through Emilia's position, but she dodged every single piece of it.

The woman's body flickered with rainbow mana again, and this time, the No_Magic mana in her body ran out. Emilia smiled viciously and took a simple step forward. For a moment, it was as if space itself bent. Alice felt a prickle of danger as she realized that she had *failed*. This was the end. Space itself was bending, and even {Adrenaline Rush} wasn't going to be enough. There was no way Alice could keep up with Emilia's speed, not with a low-level [Survivor] perk.

And then, something broke. Space remained contorted for a brief moment, and it almost looked like Emilia existed in two places at once. She was standing in her original position, and she was also standing right next to Alice, her hands stretched out toward Alice's hair as she tried to grab her. Then both images snapped out of existence, and Emilia stumbled as she appeared between the images. The perk had failed to fully activate.

Ethan didn't miss that opportunity.

He pulled the sword out of his storage again and slashed at the air. The rest of the mana in the sword drained away, and rainbow mana cascaded through his body.

Alice saw the world dim, as if someone had turned off the moon. She felt a flash of heat, raising the temperature to a nearly unbearable level. {Extremophile} fought and lost against the ridiculous burst of heat.

The air around Ethan, Emilia, and Alice crackled with energy, and then Alice saw a miniature implosion of heat and electricity spring into existence right on top of Emilia, like a supernova collapsing inward with the unnerving Immortal at its core. Right on its heels was the second burst of light and heat that sprang out of Ethan's sword.

Emilia's body flashed rainbow, and Alice saw Emilia grab a dagger from her belt and throw it at Alice. Alice felt {Adrenaline Rush} finally activate as the dagger spun toward her, twinkling with rainbow mana.

Alice tried to reach out and teleport the dagger away, but came up empty. She had apparently burned through the rest of her dimensional mana earlier in the fight.

Instead, Alice tried to shove the dagger away using kinetic magic—but found that it felt like trying to push a mountain. It was impossibly heavy and impossibly hard to manipulate.

Alice reached for one of her perks and activated {Reflection}.

To her shock, the perk activated without any problems. The dagger instantly reversed directions, heading right back toward the woman who had thrown it.

Emilia's eyes widened in surprise, right as a storm of fire and electricity ripped into her body.

The dagger flashed rainbow again, and all the mana inside it surged toward Emilia the moment it touched her. A moment later, Emilia teleported away from Ethan's attack and the dagger shattered. Emilia smelled like burned toast, and some of her armor had turned into charcoal. Unfortunately, she was alive and well. Worse, she had somehow teleported the moment she touched her dagger.

Somehow, she had swapped places with her dagger.

"Annoying bitch, aren't you?" she said as she glared at Alice.

Ethan snorted. Organic mana flared inside his mage core, and then he dashed forward. For a moment, he was nearly as fast as Emilia. He flung himself at the Sigmusi Immortal. Emilia smiled at Ethan, and her body flickered with rainbow mana again. She took one *perfect step*, like a dancer in a ballroom, and somehow, she was right in front of Alice, while Ethan missed the woman completely.

Emilia smiled and reached toward Alice.

Alice felt {Enhanced Senses} activate on top of {Adrenaline Rush}, and everyone *finally* slowed down enough that she could track what was happening again. Emilia's hand approached her neck, as if the Immortal wanted to choke her unconscious and then drag her away.

Alice desperately tried to figure out a way out of this.

She couldn't move fast enough to escape.

She couldn't fling herself away using her kinetic magic—she wouldn't move fast enough.

None of her perks would let her dodge Emilia. The woman was so much faster than Alice that it would be like trying to outrun a photon.

She didn't have enough dimensional mana left to teleport herself away.

As Alice started to despair, a portal ripped itself open in midair, and Ethan appeared in front of Alice. Emilia's eyes widened . . . and then she grinned. Her body flickered again, and suddenly there was a pair of daggers in Ethan's stomach.

Her grin turned into an expression of shock when Ethan completely ignored the daggers and gave Emilia a bone-crushing hug. Organic mana swarmed toward the two daggers planted into his intestines, and Alice could see that the mana there was fighting with *something*. It was almost like Emilia's daggers carried some sort of incredibly virulent poison—but Ethan's organic mana was holding it back.

Ethan started to squeeze, and Emilia desperately whipped another dagger out of her storage and tried to stab Ethan with it. But she couldn't maneuver her arms very well anymore, so she instead dropped the dagger by accident, causing it to barely nick Ethan's skin. The organic mana in Ethan's body surged toward the new wound, quickly repairing whatever damage had been done.

A moment later, a new storm of enchanted and unenchanted items swept toward her and Ethan, and Alice realized the hostile Society mages had finally joined the battle. The near-Immortal [Kinetic Mage] was trying to buy time for Emilia to free herself. Alice felt the urge to scream, either in fear or frustration. She looked at Ethan and Emilia, then gritted her teeth and turned toward the storm of items flying toward them. Her body felt like it was moving in slow motion—both of her bullet-time perks made the rest of the world seem like it was barely moving. Alice realized she needed to buy Ethan more time.

Right as {Adrenaline Rush} was about to end, she saw an opportunity.

A pair of vials that were packed to the brim with enchantments flew toward her. Alice still had two more uses of {Reflect} left, and the vials looked similar to the magic napalm Ethan had used earlier.

Alice hit both vials of liquid with {Reflect}, then activated {Combat Seed} to ensure the daggers would shred other mana they came in contact with. It wasn't quite as effective as No_Magic mana, but it would have to do.

Then Alice used {Extended Organics} and the last dribbles of {Adrenaline Rush} and {Enhanced Senses} to fend off as much of the wave of attacks as she could manage. She blocked nowhere near all the attacks—but she did manage to deflect a lot of them. A moment later, the vials were caught by the near-Immortal's magic tendrils, and he sent them right back toward the fight. Alice had totally failed to return the attack to its origin. But she had bought time.

Alice heard a wet cracking sound as Emilia's spine broke like a twig. A moment later, rainbow mana surged through the area, and Emilia's body spun unnaturally through the air, like a ballerina animated by a puppeteer. In a way Alice's brain somehow failed to comprehend at all, she slipped out of Ethan's grasp and appeared on the railing of the ship.

She shot Alice a hateful glare as another surge of rainbow mana rebuilt her shattered spine. Then the woman turned back toward the Society's decimated forces . . . and then she jumped off the railing, soaring back toward the forest at an impossible speed.

Ethan tried to hit her with several more rounds of projectiles as the woman fled, but he seemed to have a hard time pinpointing her exact location again. None of his attacks hit. The Society [Kinetic Mage] seemed to realize the plan had failed and started fleeing as well. Ethan tried to hit the [Kinetic Mage] with another round of attacks but couldn't get anything through the other man's rock-solid defense. A few moments later, the two high-level enemy combatants escaped the battlefield and returned to the forest.

Ethan coughed wetly a few times before, to Alice's shock, he took the Sun Knight's old sword back out of his storage perk and then beheaded himself. His old body, no longer supplied with Ethan's organic mana, rapidly succumbed to Emilia's poison and collapsed into a pile of black mush.

Meanwhile, a new body sprouted from Ethan's head in the span of a few seconds. Before Ethan's head even hit the ground, he had a brand-new body.

"That was very dangerous," Ethan said. "I managed to force her to use her second life, but I was pretty close to death as well. If I hadn't had my second life from my Immortality achievement, I don't know if I would have survived that poison. It was . . . something."

"Is there any chance we can pursue them?" asked Alice.

Ethan sighed. "Normally, I would try. But both Emilia and I were forced to use our second lives, and I'm honestly not sure who would kill who if I chased her down. It's not worth the risk. She fled because she's unwilling to risk her life on this endeavor. She wants to get paid but doesn't want to potentially die. Similarly, I'm not willing to risk your safety to hunt her down." Ethan grinned, although it turned into a grimace as he looked at his own body. "I wish I had another perk or two. If I had just another three levels, maybe I could have killed her . . ." Ethan shook his head in disappointment.

Alice winced. Letting Emilia go after she had nearly kidnapped her felt bad. But Alice wasn't naive enough to think Ethan was invincible. This fight could have easily gone the other way. Ethan had barely squeaked out a victory this time. She had no idea if they could do it again while pursuing Emilia and the surviving Society mages into the woods. It was best to take this victory for what it was—Alice and Cecilia were still alive and unkidnapped, and Ethan was safe.

They had won.

CHAPTER 30

After the battle finished, Alice checked how many people had survived. Fewer than she'd thought.

Half of the [Guards] and mages had died, and one of Cecilia's [Enchanters] had also been killed. Alice hadn't even noticed—which made her feel even worse. The [Enchanter] who had died wasn't one of the ones who had gained a new magic seed, which made Alice feel relieved—and then she felt even guiltier.

After that, Alice decided to do what little healing she could with her organic mana, while also giving {Extended Tissues} a chance to boost everyone's healing speed. She had the [Guards] who were moderately injured group up, and she sat among them while she treated more manageable injuries with her own organic mana. While Alice didn't do anything revolutionary, she managed to stabilize a few [Guards] until more experienced healers got to them.

Once the injured were taken care of, Alice took one look at the mana built up around her class seeds, looked at all the various System notifications she had gotten during the battle, and firmly decided that it could all wait until tomorrow.

With that, Alice returned to her quarters and passed out. That night, in her dreams, she focused entirely on some light adventure novels.

The next day, Alice was in a much better mental state, so after purifying all the mana stuck to her class seeds, she finally got around to looking at her System notifications.

The first, and most prominent notification, was a new achievement.

You have g@ined an acccccchievement!
Battle With an Immortal (Rarity: 9)
You have fought against an Immortal and successfully weakened them ___#@$___ dying.

> +50% growth sp_speed combat_classes, +20% effect of M@gic, Dexterity, and
> Endurance stats
> +200% boost to Surrrvvor class level speed.
> The next time you get/acquire/absorb a perk from the Survivor class, you may
> choose an EXTRA perk, equal to a level-50 Survivor perk.

Alice studied the text of her newest achievement, and despite the flawed grammar, she grinned to herself.

During the fight with Emilia and the Society near-Immortals, there were several times she was sure she would be captured. However, at the very least, the reward had been equally high. The achievement not only boosted the leveling speed of Alice's only combat class, [Survivor], by 250 percent in total, it also gave her an extra perk in [Survivor], which would make it easier to survive future attacks of similar intensity.

Especially after the fight, Alice was eager to grow stronger. She had seen Ethan get hurt for the first time during that battle, and that sight had convinced Alice that there was never enough preparation. Even Immortals needed to be ready for catastrophes to fall out of the sky.

Ethan had nearly killed Emilia, and only the revival ability most Immortals shared had kept her alive. Similarly, Ethan had needed to *behead* himself to get rid of Emilia's magic poison. Both Emilia and Ethan had been forced to use their extra lives to get out of the fight intact—and while Ethan had said that the extra life of most Immortals was often useless, right now Alice was thinking about how dangerous those fights had been *even with an extra life.*

If Alice didn't want to get assassinated after she became an Immortal, she would need to be capable of fighting off people like Emilia, because last night had shown her, once again, that Immortals were far from invincible.

Alice checked her level increases next. The first class seed she unclogged was [Survivor].

> **You have leveled up!**
>
> **Survivor: 60→68**

Alice stepped back in shock.

She had gone straight from level sixty to sixty-eight in ONE FIGHT. Of course, once Alice reflected on the fight, it made more sense. It had been desperate. One Immortal versus an Immortal and two near-Immortals were terrible odds. There hadn't been very many normal troops on the battlefield, so consequently, the fight had mostly been dominated by high-level combatants. Ethan had relied on the Sun Knight's old sword to turn things around, and he had still been forced to use his

Immortal regeneration just to escape the aftereffects of the battle. The group hadn't even managed to kill the opposing Immortal.

But, much like with the achievement, the rewards for surviving were excellent.

Alice put off the perk selection for [Survivor] until she was done unclogging her seeds. She grinned and moved to her next System notification.

You have leveled up!

Explorer of Magic: 79→81

Alice was a little disappointed that she had only gained two levels after the ridiculous number she had gotten in [Survivor]. Still, two levels finally let her take her first post–level-seventy-five perk, which was pretty nice.

It also meant that Alice had a lot of new options for what to do with her next perk slot. If she wanted to, she could combine two tier-one perks. Alternately, she could now combine an [Explorer of Magic] perk with a perk from a completely different class if she felt like it. This opened up a massive number of possibilities—and created an equally high amount of choice paralysis.

Alice decided that if Ethan was willing to, she would consult with him before taking her first level-seventy-five perk. An Immortal would probably have decent advice on what she was lacking and needed to improve.

Especially after the battle, Alice definitely wanted to boost her self-defense abilities more. Combining something from [Explorer of Magic] and [Survivor] seemed reasonable to her, if Ethan didn't advise against it.

You have leveled up!

Kinetic Manabinder: 44→51

Alice grinned. Two more perk choices. She now had five to spend. She had used a fair amount of kinetic mana during the fight, and since it had been against an Immortal, she was glad to see that it had paid off. After that, Alice checked through her two final System notifications.

You have leveled up!

Careful Enchanter : 35→36, Student of Organic Magic: 24→25 (Max) (Class Evolution Available)

Alice was a bit surprised to see that [Careful Enchanter] had gotten any levels at all. Apparently, flinging around her own homemade enchantments in the middle of a dangerous battle gave the class a bit of progress.

On the other hand, Alice had emptied weeks of work into a battle against an Immortal and had still only gotten a single level in [Careful Enchanter]. Clearly, combat with her own enchantments helped, but not much. Alice shrugged. She hadn't really expected any levels in that class at all, so anything was better than nothing.

Finally, Alice had gotten her final level in her secondary class [Student of Organic Magic]. It was ready for class evolution. Alice had probably gained the final level while she was healing the [Guards]. She wasn't actually sure how being a secondary class would impact the benefits she got from evolving it, and she also wasn't sure if the System *could* process a class evolution right now.

She decided to wait until they got back to Metsel before taking a look at her class-evolution options for [Student of Organic Magic], to see if anyone had reported the System glitching out when trying to evolve classes. It had been nearly a month since the System collapsed, so by now, someone *must* have tried it. Alice would wait to see if there were any problems before she proceeded.

With all her postbattle levels processed, Alice turned her attention to her perks. She started out by looking at her new level-fifty [Survivor] perk. She quickly noticed that the level-fifty perk options for [Survivor] were different than when she had originally reached level fifty. She had four options to choose from.

Two of them weren't particularly appealing, and had a lot more to do with surviving lack of food and water. They would let Alice go literal years without eating or drinking—but Alice had a storage perk now, so she wasn't worried about running out of food or water. She was already carting around several weeks of supplies, just in case she got randomly teleported to another dimension again. Those two perks would probably never see use if she grabbed them.

The other two perks were more in line with what she wanted—ways to either flee or fight against a greater threat.

Speedy ________

Requirements: Survivor level 50 or higher, Endurance 125 or higher, Dexterity 125 or higher

Once per day, if you in danger, physical speed_____improved several times for ten seconds, especially your balance and running abilities, as well as _____ fly with kinetic magic.

In short, this perk allowed Alice to flee from bigger threats. Alice would have preferred something that helped her win a fight against an Immortal instead, but she thought this was still worth considering.

Alice spent a few minutes giving the perk serious thought. Alice didn't like fighting. Running away wasn't a bad option.

But after some thinking, Alice reluctantly ignored the perk.

If she cared about nothing, that might work. But Alice had friends that she couldn't bring with her if she relied on this perk to survive. Last night, if Alice had this perk, she might have had an easier time fleeing—but Cecilia wouldn't have been any better off, and running away might have caused Ethan to lose the fight. In that case, Alice would have been hunted in the woods by an Immortal and several hostile combatants, which sounded unlikely to end in her favor. Alice wasn't willing to abandon her friends to save herself. That meant she needed ways to fight back rather than ways to flee.

So she turned toward her remaining [Survivor] perk.

<table>
<tr><td>

Dimensional___Survivor
Requirements: Survivor level 50 or higher, have dimensional seed, {Outworlder} achievement (or similar achievement), have 150 Magic stat___ greater than and 100 Endurance

</td></tr>
<tr><td>

Your ability to use magic tendrils through portals and command over portals is enhanced drastically. Increases dimensional mana seed ratio by 20% to give you more mana. Your portals less broken mana.

</td></tr>
</table>

During the previous fight, Alice had discovered that using magic tendrils through portals let her ignore a lot of the range limitations that mages usually had to deal with. Most mages couldn't move or interact with objects more than a few meters away from them, because the mana cost and difficulty of doing so was crushing. Portals didn't completely obviate this problem, since portals still seemed to become more expensive the farther away each end was. However, it still made it *much* easier to become a long-range mage. This perk promised to reduce the problems inherent to that strategy. After some hesitation, she took {Dimensional ____ Survivor}.

She felt her dimensional magic seed expand, from a mana conversion ratio of 40 percent to 60 percent. She experimentally opened a few small portals and confirmed that they leaked about 30 percent less broken mana than before. They were still horrendously leaky abominations—but the perk at least minimized the problem.

Most importantly, Alice found it easier than ever to use {Extended Organics} through a portal. Before, Alice had still struggled to balance the mana cost of manipulating items that were too far away, but now she felt that her range had expanded from thirty meters to around sixty. After that, Alice looked at her level-sixty-five [Survivor] perk.

She originally thought that she was going to be picking a new perk—after all, she couldn't figure out how to combine any of her perks into something usable.

However, just to be safe, Alice scanned her new perks and then also looked at all the perk combinations she could make—and found something useful.

A very long time ago, Alice had taken the perk {Camouflaged} in order to avoid monster attacks. It had proven rather useful when Alice had fled to Cyra. After that, the perk had never been used again. She simply didn't get any value out of a minor camouflage effect in the middle of a human city.

Camouflaged
Requirements: Survivor level 20 or higher

While staying still, dramatically increases your ability to blend into the environment, making creatures around you much less likely to notice you.
This can be turned off.

But apparently, the result of combining it with her newest perk had a rather interesting result.

Alice only hesitated for a few more moments before she combined {Camouflaged} and {Dimensional ___ Survival}.

Dimensional Camouflage
Perkkkkkkk Co$t: Camouflaged + Dimensional ___ Survivor sacrificed to create this perk.

Your ability to use magic tendrils through portals and command over portals is enhanced drastically. For a small price of mana, you may make portals only work ONE WAY—and for an extra mana cost, you may drastically reduce broken mana leakage through the portal.

One of the biggest weaknesses of the Society mages who used portals in combat was the potential for return fire. She had seen plenty of Society mages get killed by an [Archer] firing an arrow into a portal right after it opened. Alice had been aware that this might be a problem if she started using portals in her combat style, but she hadn't had a good solution for it.

Now, her new perk would solve that problem. She had lost the 20 percent boost to her dimensional magic seed, dropping it back from 60 percent to 40 percent. However, the trade-off was more than worth it.

Finally finished with her [Survivor] perks, Alice turned toward her [Kinetic Manabinder] perks.

This one wasn't too hard to figure out. Alice wanted to improve her combat abilities, and the best way to do that was to get access to more mana tendrils. One of the perk options did exactly that, while the others looked more focused on enchantments. Alice just wanted raw combat efficiency right now.

> **Kinetic Combatant**
> **Requirements: Kinetic Manabinder level 45 or higher, Magic 100 or greater**
>
> Increase the number ______ tendrils you can control by two.

She almost immediately selected this perk. With this upgrade, Alice's controlled magic tendrils increased from seven to nine. Alice's final perk choice was a fair bit more interesting, because there were two perk options worth considering.

> **Tendri____ of Kinetic.Mage**
> **Requirements: Kinetic Manabinder level 50 or higher, kinetic seed at 120% or more**
>
> You get six more magic tendrils, BUT these tendrils can ONLY be used to control ______ Get_Mana: resolved: kinetic mana. They may not be used for other types of mana at all.

Alice found this to be a pretty desirable perk. Getting four more tendrils would increase her count to thirteen. It wouldn't be a world-shattering increase, but it would certainly be worth a lot in a fight. Ethan had a natural tendril count of forty. If Alice could get to thirteen, she would essentially be at one-third of Ethan's base combat prowess.

Of course, it looked like Ethan had a LOT of limited-use perks. Alice still vividly remembered the implosion of light and heat he had nearly fried Emilia with, as well as the perk that gave him an extra one hundred magic tendrils, and the other crazy one-use abilities he activated during the battle. Still, Alice felt that pushing to forty magic tendrils was a good long-term goal if she didn't find other, higher priorities to pursue instead.

The other perk option was similarly useful, but in a different way.

> **Burst of Kinetic __________**
> **Requirements: Kinetic Manabinder level 50 or or or _______, h@ve more than five magic tendrils, Magic 150 or greater**
>
> Once per day, you get ten temporary magic tendrils. They last five ?????
> (Error: Get_Unit_)
> 300 seconds _ convert to ___ minutes _ Error!

The perk was simple and to the point, but it was a perk that Alice would get a lot of use out of in fights. She had seven tendrils right now, and more than doubling that number for five minutes would usually be enough time for a potential fight with an [Assassin]—which was exactly what Alice was most afraid of right now.

Alice thought about the two perks for a few moments before she opted to take {Tendri_____ of Kinetic.Mage}. She felt that she still needed to improve her baseline combat abilities more before she worried about limited-use perks. Then, once she finished selecting her new perks, she went to find Ethan and Cecilia. She wanted to talk with Ethan about her first post–seventy-five perk, and maybe get some advice. But before that, she wanted to see how Cecilia was doing after the fight.

CHAPTER 31

Cecilia was in her cabin. When she entered, Alice had expected Cecilia to look rattled, afraid, or concerned. Instead, the girl seemed oddly cheerful, all things considered.

"Cecilia?" asked Alice.

"Alice! Come in!" said Cecilia as she strode over and gave Alice a very brief hug before closing the door.

"Sorry I didn't come earlier. I was busy handling level notifications," said Alice. "How are you doing?"

Cecilia shuffled, and for a moment, Alice could see something beneath Cecilia's outwardly cheerful demeanor. A hidden sense of loss. Then it vanished as Cecilia shook her head.

"I'm fine," she said. "People die sometimes. I didn't even know most of the [Guards] or mages that died. I only knew Morgan, the [Enchanter] who died, and only for a few weeks. We can recruit someone else to take their place."

"Even if you know someone for less than a month, you can still grieve for them," said Alice, trying to be gentle.

Cecilia sighed. Some of the forced joy in her face disappeared, and she looked at Alice. "I . . . don't feel great. Someone I've been teaching died in front of me. All because of the Sigmusi Colonia. *Again*. I just . . ." Cecilia sighed. Then to Alice's surprise, Cecilia opened her arms up again and wrapped Alice in another hug.

Alice realized that this was the most obvious sign that something was wrong. Cecilia had *hugged* Alice. Not just once, but twice.

Alice didn't really like hugs very much. She occasionally hugged her friends and family, but it wasn't something she did *often*. Perhaps once every few weeks, or when someone she cared about was having a particularly bad day, she would give them a hug, but it wasn't something Alice really enjoyed. Cecilia seemed to have picked up on this shortly after she got to know Alice, and so she had never forced Alice into a hug. But the first thing Cecilia had done when Alice walked into her room was demand a hug.

Alice awkwardly hugged her friend and added in her best attempt at a comforting shoulder pat.

Cecilia finally crumbled and started softly crying into Alice's shoulder.

"I just . . . can't believe he's gone. The Sigmusi took my father from me, and now, when it felt like things were under control again, someone died. It was *also* because of the Sigmusi." For a moment, Cecilia's breathing ratcheted up in intensity, and Alice thought she was going to take in a great, heaving sob. But Cecilia stopped herself a moment later. "System, I'm a mess now." Cecilia's face oscillated between depression and hatred, back and forth for several seconds, before she sighed.

"I'm really all right now, Alice. Thanks for checking up on me and being here. I needed it."

Alice patted her friend on the back a few more times. "I'm sorry that this happened. It's unfair that you've seen so much death." Alice paused and then sighed.

The two spent several minutes just sitting there, in comfortable silence, as they worked out their emotions after the battle. Finally, Cecilia seemed to perk up a bit.

"So, why did you come here? I imagine it wasn't just to check up on me—though if that was your only reason, thank you. I appreciate it."

"Well, there were two reasons. The first one was to check up on you. The second was an offer—if you want, I can use my filtration seed to help you deal with your pending level-up notifications, the same way I handle my own mana filtration problems."

"I'd be happy to get some help with my class seeds, then. I have no idea how many levels I should have gotten that are stuck, but I do know I am not leveling up at all right now for any class besides [Enchanter]."

Alice nodded and then started looking at Cecilia's class seeds. She noticed a fair amount of mana stuck to Cecilia's various class seeds, much like they had been for Alice. Cecilia's [Enchanter] class seed had no clogging issues, likely due to the fact that she was wearing one of the enchanted rings.

However, Alice also noticed that Cecilia had picked up four levels of a different class—one Alice was tempted to call [Warmage]. Cecilia didn't have any class seeds similar enough for her to convert the [Warmage] mana into something she could use. [Kinetic Mage] was a bit too different for the conversion. Alice frowned.

That was . . . not good. Alice needed to figure out how to form new class seeds as soon as possible. Unfortunately, she had no idea how to do that. Alice sighed and decided not to think about it for now. Cecilia should be able to fend off the mental corrosion from four levels of [Warmage] without too much difficulty. She just needed to make sure she could get rid of the problem before it grew.

Alice handled the rest of Cecilia's unfiltered class mana before she gave Cecilia a few warnings about her [Warmage] mana. Alice made a mental note to do that for the rest of the [Guards] and [Enchanters] once she finished consulting with

Ethan. The men on the boat had put their lives in danger to keep Alice safe. The least she could do was help solve their class mana–related issues. Alice's new combined class seed let her generate a lot more filtration mana, so she could start helping others when she had a spare moment.

"Thanks. I got a couple more levels," said Cecilia.

"You're my friend. I'm happy to help you when I can."

Cecilia smiled. The two chatted for several more minutes before Alice got up to find Ethan.

It didn't take much time for Alice to find Ethan's room. Unlike Cecilia, he didn't seem bothered by the attack. He *did* seem tired, though, so Alice decided to get right to the point.

"Ethan, I wanted some advice on perks," said Alice.

"Oh? Are you getting your first post–level-seventy-five perk?" asked Ethan. "At least you got a few benefits out of the mess last night."

Alice resisted the urge to flinch. Was his accurate guess some benefit of Ethan's long life, or just a result of his attention to his apprentice?

"Yes, I'm preparing to take my first post–seventy-five perk," said Alice.

"Are you sure asking me is a good idea? I don't know as much about research as you do. You've gotten this far on your own, which is a pretty strong recommendation for whatever build you're going for."

"I wanted to ask about a combat perk, not a research-oriented perk," said Alice.

"Really? I thought your main class was research-oriented?" Ethan said, sounding increasingly confused.

"It is," said Alice. "But the attack last night made me very nervous. I want to be more prepared if something like this happens again."

Ethan looked at Alice's expression before he rubbed his chin thoughtfully.

"I can see why it was scary, and I can also see where you're coming from. Are you sure this is the right way to address it? The collapse of the System is still underway, and if you spend too much of your efforts and perks on keeping yourself safe from violence, you might not be able to handle the collapse of the System. [Organic Mages] have always saved more lives than [Kinetic Mages], even during wartime," said Ethan.

Alice paused. Ethan made a good point. After the fight last night, especially after seeing Ethan *behead* himself to handle Emilia's daggers, Alice felt scared. Her decision about her next perk was a reaction to that. Was reacting really the right thing to do?

Both from the perspective of her own personal desires, and for the sake of the people who were harmed by the collapse of the System, Alice needed to figure out how to handle the current crisis. Nobody else could do what she was doing. [Explorer of Magic] was also the best class for getting new tools to handle the collapse of the System.

Ethan continued speaking while Alice fell into thought.

"I think that your build should ultimately be decided by you—but you should think carefully about whether you want to invest your perk into improving your combat ability or your research ability. Last night was almost a disaster, and I intend to make sure it doesn't happen again. But you should also keep in mind that the collapse of the System will impact you, too. You need to strike a careful balance when you select perks, or else you won't be able to protect yourself or anyone else." Ethan grimaced. "You should also keep in mind that the difference one perk will make in future fights against Immortals is limited. The impact of a new research perk could make all the difference in handling the current crisis." Then Ethan did his best to give her a reassuring smile. "But you should still pick whatever you think is best. This is my advice, but your build is your own."

Alice thought about Ethan's advice and then nodded. She still wanted Ethan's assessment of what she was missing as a combatant, but he also made a good point: Dealing with the collapse of the System was her first priority. She could always get more perks to protect herself once she had finished handling the System—she would have all eternity to work on her combat ability afterward. She only had a few months to fix the System before the entire world imploded.

Alice still wanted advice on what she could improve, so she asked Ethan to give her a few less-perk-oriented tips. Ethan went through a few finer details of the way Alice had fought the previous night, discussing various problems she'd had during the fight—the way that Alice had tried to essentially short-circuit Emilia's perks using mana had barely worked because she had misjudged how much mana it would take, for example. While it had bought Ethan a bit of time to really hammer her with attacks, Alice had also been caught off guard by how quickly Emilia had shrugged it off, which Ethan noted was due to Alice's lack of experience using perks in combat.

A lot of Alice's issues came down to lack of practice, which wasn't really something she could fix overnight, but Ethan still gave her some advice on what she could work on. After the conversation, she returned to her own cabin and started sorting through her perks.

The first thing Alice noticed was that the interface for tier-two perk combinations was cluttered. There were far, far more options than there had been for tier-one perk combinations. The ability to combine any [Explorer of Magic] perk with any other perk she had meant that the number of combinations was dizzying.

Furthermore, the collapse of the System seemed to have completely short-circuited its ability to predict the results of combining tier-two perks from different classes. Alice was pretty used to the System at least giving her a few hints about what a combination would do, but while the System had been able to help with those predictions between levels fifty-five and seventy-five, it seemed clueless now. In other words, Alice was going off her intuition and the months she had spent studying how the System worked.

After sorting through several different lists and thinking about how perks would probably interact with each other, Alice came up with three different perk combinations.

{Adrenaline Rush} and {Combat Seed} would probably make for a potent combination if Alice decided to try to make a combat perk, after all. Alice distinctly remembered how useless she had felt in the fight once {Adrenaline Rush} had ended yesterday, and Ethan had noted that making {Adrenaline Rush} a perk she could activate more often would help Alice a lot in higher-level combat. In fights between Immortals, one side would usually win if they had overwhelming speed—which was why [Dexterity] was one of the stats combat-oriented Immortals tended to emphasize training, regardless of their combat style. Improving {Adrenaline Rush} would allow Alice to handle this. She wasn't quite sure what {Combat Seed} would do for the combination . . . but it would probably give her something useful. Perhaps it would help Alice shut down other people's magic or perk use while {Adrenaline Rush} was in effect?

That was the best option she could think of for a combat-oriented perk. The other combinations she thought of were strictly research-oriented. The first thing that Alice thought of when thinking of research-oriented perks was {Seeds of Ambition}. Right now, Alice was held back by the limited number of magic seeds she had access to. She still hadn't been able to build a math or meaning magic seed. To get everything integrated into a magic seed and get more magic seeds, Alice could feed {Seeds of Ambition} another sacrificial perk to boost its seed-production speed. This was probably one of Alice's most immediate ways to address problems induced by the collapse of the System.

Alice's final idea was to combine something with {Expanding Comprehension} to boost her actual understanding of the System and its mana. She wasn't quite sure what it would do for her immediately, but the perk could very well give her some crucial insight that would speed up her attempts to resolve the situation or otherwise fix everything. It was a bit more of a gamble, because Alice wasn't sure if {Expanding Comprehension} *could* give her any more useful insight on the situation, and she also wasn't sure if combining it with another perk would somehow break the previous benefits she had extracted. However, it could provide her with a way of fixing things more effectively and easily if the perk combination *did* work the way she hoped. It would probably combine with {Intuitive Magic Modeling} pretty well if she decided to go that route.

So Alice could see three major paths forward: the pure research route of combining {Expanding Comprehension} and {Intuitive Mana Modeling}, which would give her the most information, but provide the least actual solutions to her current problems. The accelerated System seed route, which involved combining {Seeds of Ambition} with {Science's Mana} or a different perk in order to boost her magic seed production rate. Alice also thought that combining her new System-enchanting perk with the perk that she hoped would eventually create a System magic seed would create something amazing. And finally, if Alice wanted to focus purely on combat potential, she could slam {Adrenaline Rush} and {Combat Seed} together and hope for the best.

Those were her best options, at least in her mind.

Alice spent several minutes thinking over her options before she discarded the combat route. Ethan's reasoning made sense, and Alice also knew that she wasn't really that good at combat compared to other people her level. She could beat people who were lower level than her, but at the end of the day, Alice's ability to contribute to a higher-level fight was limited, and that wasn't going to change until she had a few decades to knuckle down and train up some real combat classes. In other words, it would need to happen after the System was fixed. For the immediate future, Alice was going to be reliant on Ethan and Illvaria's [Soldiers] if she wanted to stay alive and unhurt. No action she could take would change that right now, even if she spent this perk boosting her combat abilities.

After that, she debated whether it was better to create more magic seeds or to gather more information. That choice was hard to make, because a huge part of her was screaming to take the pure research perk. The entire reason she had started down this path was because she loved learning.

Unfortunately, Alice eventually decided in favor of boosting her magic seed production. System mana was obviously an amalgamation of several different types of mana. If Alice wanted to replicate or repair the System, she needed to have the right magic seeds available. No amount of understanding could change that fact. She needed to get her magic seeds ready first, then find the right way to use them via experimentation. That was the fastest and most stable path forward.

And so, with a sigh, Alice put aside the research route and resolved to take it at level eighty-five if she didn't have a better plan by then. Then she spent a few more moments thinking about what secondary perk she wanted to sacrifice.

The first was obviously {Seeds of Ambition}.

Seeds of Ambition
Perk costs: Three Seeds + Seedy Ambitions sacrificed to create this perk.
Two times a month, you can create an inferior magic seed with a maximum mana conversion ratio of 30%.   (Since this perk has been upgraded, you may now also combine two magic seeds once per month.)   The seed-creation rules from {Seedy Ambitions} are applied to this perk.   However, achievements may now apply to the inferior magic seeds as they would to other magic seeds.

The second perk, however, was a much more interesting question. Alice scrolled through the list of other perks she could sacrifice until she found one that seemed suitable for her needs.

<table>
<tr><td>
Science's Mana
Requirements: Scientist level 65 or higher, Intelligence 150 or higher, enchanter class at level 25 or higher, create at least three enchantments of your own design
</td></tr>
<tr><td>
Make System enchantment for item. Must be related to a perk you already have from the research classes, or attributes_thought association with science. (Intelligence, Willpower, Perception.)
</td></tr>
</table>

{Science's Mana} was probably the correct choice. She had originally hoped that it would be easy to create new System enchantments . . . and Alice definitely *could* create things that boosted [Intelligence] by a point or two. However, after learning how difficult it was to infuse a perk into an item, especially a perk such as {Broken Seed}, Alice decided to give up on the dream of mass-producing {Broken Seed} perks. She was too far away from that goal to reach it before the collapse of the System killed everyone, and she had already gotten the actual information related to System enchantments she wanted. Thus, {Science's Mana} was the ideal perk for sacrificial fodder now. It made her feel a bit bad, but Alice combined {Seeds of Ambition} and {Science's Mana}.

Mana started to swirl around her, far more than Alice had been anticipating, and the mana in Alice's body started to surge.

For a moment, Alice wondered if she had made a horrible mistake. Perhaps the System breaking down had caused perks above level seventy-five to malfunction? Alice spent a few seconds mentally kicking herself for rushing her perk choice. She had assumed it was safe because every other perk so far had been safe, but with the System down, she should have double-checked whether this would cause any problems. At the very least, she should have used {Safety Analysis}.

Before she had more time to worry, she felt something inside her *twist*.

Alice felt a myriad of bizarre sensations.

She could suddenly *taste* what it felt like to conduct an experiment. She could smell mana. She could hear curiosity. Every single sense blended together in a chaotic mixture of concepts, smells, sounds, and tastes.

A few moments later, Alice realized that these strange sensations weren't random. Each and every one of them was associated with the concept of being a [Scientist] or an [Explorer of Magic].

Time passed as the sensations continued, while Alice tried to make sense of everything. The strange barrage of sensations nearly overwhelmed her ability to think, but after a few moments, Alice managed to regain control.

Once she wrenched control of her thoughts back, the first thing she did was use her {Lesser Organic Vision} and mana sense to look inside herself. To her surprise, she could see her [Explorer of Magic] and [Scientist] class fractals orbiting each other. Rainbow mana flowed between them as they expanded like miniature nebulae.

Much like the first time Alice had learned about the true nature of classes, she felt the concepts of being a [Scientist] and being an [Explorer of Magic] start to flood through her mind. However, the sensation was considerably muted compared to the time Alice had nearly lost her sense of self. It was equivalent to the mental pressure of ten levels of unfiltered mana instead of an overwhelming barrage of information. Meanwhile, her body started sucking in mana like a black hole, draining her cabin of mana in seconds.

Then the class fractals that were located in her brain started to stretch *into* each other, and all the neurons between those two class fractals started to glow with mana. The glow intensified until the System mana inside those class fractals did . . . *something*.

A moment later, Alice felt more *complete* than before.

It was the strangest sensation she had ever felt—but at the same time Alice felt more like herself than ever before. The dull thrumming of mana pushing against her mind and body, which had been growing more pressing since the collapse of the System, started to disappear. The concepts corroding her sense of self vanished. It was like she had been dreaming and had woken up and forgotten what she was dreaming about.

In addition to this sudden clarity, Alice could see a very small part of her biology had changed. Instead of regular flesh, it was now composed of a type of mana Alice had never seen before. She was *sorely* tempted to call it "Alice mana." It was a mana that constituted the most fundamental aspect of who *Alice* was.

No, thought Alice as she investigated the new type of mana more closely. It wasn't mana built off who *she* was.

It was mana that was built off what *other people* thought of her.

It was as if every single person who had ever heard of her had a very small image of who she was, living in their mind, and the tiny chunk of mana flesh was trying to press that idea of *Alice* into her, overriding the real person behind the image.

Alice felt a spike of fear before she realized something else.

The Immortals didn't have this type of mana in their body. Ethan didn't have "Ethan mana" inside him. Allira didn't have "Allira mana" inside her, either. Their bodies were mostly made of mana, and that mana was constantly transforming back into their bodies—but Alice didn't think that the mana-based bodies most Immortals had altered their minds. Instead, Immortals were constantly transforming into themselves—not some stereotyped or perceived version of who they were, but just . . . themselves. What was the difference here?

The most obvious assumption was that this was some kind of inherent problem that all higher-level people had. Perhaps the System had some sort of solution to this problem, which Alice didn't have access to because she had created her first post–seventy-five perk after the System collapsed.

When Alice had tried to form a class seed in a magic seed slot, she had realized that classes were probably constructed out of the beliefs of other people. What people felt an [Explorer of Magic] *was* influenced by what people with the class needed to do in order to level up—and, similarly, what perks the class could obtain.

Based on that fact, it seemed that beliefs interacted with mana and the System on a deeper, more fundamental level. Beliefs warped the System and the way it worked. What did that mean?

Originally, Alice thought the System just surveyed people when creating new classes somehow. Perhaps it had some kind of hidden threshold built in, where whenever enough people recognized a new job, such as [Blacksmith], that job would be created. This would actually be ingenious design—it ensured that classes for every common job existed, and furthermore, that those classes would always have perks relevant to what the users of those classes needed.

However, the strip of Alice mana in her body had been created while the System was down. In other words, the Alice mana here wasn't a result of the System surveying people's beliefs and then making use of it. It was a direct result of the way mana itself worked. Alice also remembered that in the past, the System had given her an error message, because personality warping was a "core violation" of the System. Immortals didn't seem to be constantly changing based on the way people perceived them, but Alice was now experiencing a small amount of personality warping based on other people's perception of her.

This also implied that beliefs might literally warp reality somehow, at least when it interacted with mana.

In fact, now that Alice thought about it, there were other signs that beliefs could change reality. For example, Alice's achievement {Immortal's Apprentice at the Battle Against the Society}. She pulled it up again, just to double-check the wording.

Immortal's Apprentice at the Battle Against the Society (Rarity: 4)
As a talented combat-specialized mage who is apprenticed to Ethan, the Immortal of Spells and Seeds, you participated in one of the battles between Illvaria and the Society of Starry Eyes and played a notable role in securing victory for your side. Even if you didn't distinguish yourself as an MVP of the battle, you performed above and beyond what would be expected of you for your age group.
+30% class experience to your primary magic-related class [Explorer of Magic], +15% class experience to all kinetic magic–related classes. The effect of the {Divided Attention} skill is increased by approximately 50%.

The achievement *explicitly mentioned* that Alice was a combat-specialized mage, even though it was abundantly obvious that Alice was a research-focused mage. She had found the wording of the achievement odd at the time, but now Alice understood. People's assumptions about Alice's abilities and personality had been turned into an achievement by the System—and perhaps, in the process of turning these beliefs into an achievement, the System had somehow removed any potential for the mana to change who Alice was. Just like the System did with class mana.

The more Alice thought about it, the more she felt that her new assumption was correct. There were a lot of ways that she could test her theory, but Alice wasn't even sure if she should. If someone else realized that the System could be manipulated based on other people's beliefs, how long would it be until some madman forced a nation to believe he was a god? If it worked, it would throw the world into chaos.

Alice wondered how much mana could change the world around her, if enough people believed something to be true.

If people stopped believing that gravity existed, would everything on the planet float around as if they were in space? If people developed weird beliefs about how atoms worked, would the laws of physics implode? How much could belief actually affect?

At the same time, Alice started wondering how much the System did behind the scenes to manage all this. There were just too many ways that belief altering reality could and *should* backfire spectacularly. Humans were too curious about the world around them, and too prone to making up explanations to satisfy that curiosity. That mindset had created all sorts of religions back on Earth. If beliefs could alter reality, then the laws of physics should have collapsed and killed everyone. However, people were still alive on this planet. In other words, something had worked to curtail this influence.

Alice eyed the System mana in her brain.

Was *that* the ultimate purpose of the System? To lock human beliefs down before they interfered with reality?

Come to think of it, several very weird incidents had been reported to her while she had been in Cyra. She wasn't sure if those incidents were related to her new theory or not—but she distinctly recalled that a bunch of trees had exploded for no reason while some [Scouts] had been tracking down monsters. Alice hadn't been sure what to make of the exploding trees when she had first heard of them, but now she wondered if beliefs were somehow bending the laws of physics that governed those trees or something like that. She would need to ask Ethan if the locals in that area had any peculiar beliefs regarding trees—if they did, it might help Alice shed some light on all the weird things that had gone wrong ever since the System collapsed.

If the System really did have some sort of locking mechanism that prevented human or monster beliefs from breaking down the laws of reality and killing everyone, Alice *needed* to get that part of the System fixed or replaced. If she didn't, tomorrow all the important rules about how atoms worked might get swapped out and turn every atom on the planet into a nuclear bomb or something.

Alice took a deep breath and tried to slow down her spinning thoughts. Even if she now realized just how dangerous life without the System was, she doubted the world was going to explode tomorrow. It probably took time for belief to influence other things, and there might be other limiting factors at play. Since the world hadn't imploded moments after the System disappeared, the laws of physics were probably less volatile than she feared. She shook off her fearful thoughts and instead focused on her new perk.

After she hit the switch and tried to combine the two perks, Alice had apparently gotten a new System message. She hadn't noticed it due to all the other chaos, but now that she was checking her backlog of messages, this one stood out as glaringly obvious—and worrying.

Perk Combination in Progress.

Combining {Science's Mana} and {Seeds of Ambition}.

Error—{Science's Mana} judged to be misnamed. Cannot find correct name—please reestablish connection to main server.

No connection can be found. Searching user's memories for a suitable name . . .

{Science's Mana} renamed {Scientific System}.

Proceeding with combination process.

(Due to increased assistance/authority/recognition from the System and multiple achievements related to exploring and understanding the System, as well as the desires of the creator, perk direction is influenced.)

(Perk direction is banned.)

(System removing upgrade to find a suitable replacement upgrade.)

(System cannot be accessed. Not enough processing power present in class fractals. Error.)

(No suitable replacement upgrades found. Continuing with original path.)

Finally, after that rather worrying set of System messages, Alice got the perk she had been waiting for.

System's Ambition (Tier 3 perk)

Perk cost: Scientific System + Seeds of Ambition sacrificed to create this perk.

Once per month, you may create and synthesize four seeds. If they are added to your S_yst@m seed, then each synthesis will also increase seed mana conversion ratio by a further 10%. If not added to your System seed, these magic seeds are instead categorized as inferior seeds, meaning that they cannot be influenced by other perks or achievements.

Seeds will add 30% to mana conversion ratio at maximum.

Due to influence of other upgrades, magic seeds created by {System's Ambition} can be influenced by perks.

Due to influence of other upgr@des, magic seeds created by {System's Ambition} can be influenced by achievements.

The first thing Alice noticed was the fact that {Science's Mana} had changed to {Scientific System} during the perk-combination process. Alice had always figured that the name {Science's Mana} was probably a glitch—a lot of the names in the System, as well as the spelling and grammar, had gotten messed up after the collapse of the System, after all. There was a lot more trial and error involved in figuring out what a new perk did than before. Alice thought it was interesting that the "correct" name had reappeared during the perk-combination process, although it wasn't that important.

The second thing Alice noticed was a System message she had never seen before. The message about "perk combination in progress."

When Alice had combined {Science's Mana} and {Seeds of Ambition}, she had felt like she was *more* than before. As if something about her very nature, her very existence, had changed. She felt as if she had taken some very important, critical step forward.

The System seemed to reflect that—the System message about combining perks, upgrading them based on her achievements and her own behavior, and the various checks the System seemed to have gone through reflected the fact that the System seemed to be personalizing upgrades after level seventy-five, at least to some extent. When Alice had checked the perk list from the book of the Church of the System, it hadn't had many perks listed after level seventy-five. It was now obvious why—if each perk was personalized, any record of what perk combinations resulted in would be, at best, a loose guideline for what might happen.

At least in this specific case, the System collapsing worked in Alice's favor. The System had tried to prevent Alice from getting a certain perk upgrade direction and replace it with a suitable alternate upgrade. Alice suspected it was an attempt to prevent people from discovering and exploring the System. Since the System was down, this replacement attempt had failed.

It was also the very first time Alice had seen "increased help from the System" impact anything at all. Alice had spent about a year wondering what in the world "increased help from the System" did. It was mentioned in {Outworlder} that she had it, but she had never, at any point in time, figured out what it actually meant.

Now, for the first time, it actually came up in a System message Alice suspected she hadn't been supposed to see.

Alice wasn't entirely sure what to make of that, so for now, she just noted it. There would be more time to experiment with the benefits of the {Outworlder} achievement in the future, and to see if it cropped up *every* time Alice got a post–level-seventy-five perk. But she finally had some hint about what the weirdest part of her first achievement did.

The moment Alice finished scanning her new perk, she noticed that the perk was asking her to designate a seed—or, at least, Alice was pretty sure that was what it wanted her to do. She checked the perk's wording again and noticed that it would give her extra benefits if she added seeds to her System seed.

In other words, Alice needed to point at one of her seeds and tell the perk it was her System seed, or at least it would be in the future. Alice selected her combined filtration/display magic seed. She had already been working on turning it into a System magic seed, and she saw no reason to change that. Then Alice checked her new perk and found that, sadly, it was still on cooldown. She got the feeling that she needed to wait about a week to use it again—which she was pretty sure was less time than she originally had before {Seeds of Ambition} would be ready.

Alice rubbed her temples in frustration as she thought about her new speculations and then decided to go lie down and see if she could get some sleep.

She needed some time to think about what had just happened and find a way to prove or disprove her new speculation and defend her mind against the influence of Alice mana. She had developed plenty of other ways to fight back against the erosion of her willpower in the past—she just needed to cement what she planned to do this time and how to do so without hurting herself. The Alice mana wasn't what worried her, because Alice was confident she could find a solution.

Instead, as she went to sleep, she thought about whether the laws of physics would implode tomorrow. The collapse of the System had always felt terrifying, but now it felt dozens of times more dangerous than ever before.

Chapter 32

After some hesitation, Alice decided to ask Ethan what to do about the potentially unstable laws of physics. In some ways, telling anyone was a terrible idea, because knowledge of the instability would further destabilize them. However, Alice also needed a way to verify her theory. Ethan was well situated to gather information through his information network—without making the problem worse.

Despite her trust in her friends, Alice decided not to tell Cecilia about her latest discovery. As much as she didn't like the idea of keeping information from Cecilia, this was a crisis that literally got worse the more people knew about it. Unless someone had the ability to do something about it, Alice decided not to inform them.

Alice made her way back to Ethan's office and told him about her theory. Part of her was hoping that he could disprove her new hypothesis. Instead, Ethan fell into thought after Alice finished speaking.

After two minutes of silence, Alice couldn't bear it any longer.

"Do you think it's correct or not?" asked Alice.

"I have no idea," Ethan said. "It seems plausible." Alice's heart sank. "I will get my information network to look into *interesting* occurrences and see if I can gather more data. Unfortunately, the fact that I can't tell my informants what to look out for makes it harder to get information." Ethan gave Alice a careful look. "I will say that most Immortals know that achievements seem to be based on other people's beliefs. Do *you* think this theory is correct?"

Alice nodded. "It's more of a sneaking suspicion on my part—but it seems to line up with other things I've observed. I still need more information, though."

"Let's keep an eye out for other information and act as if spreading this theory could make the planet implode," said Ethan, frowning. "Either way, our priority remains the same—fix or replace the System. We just need to keep a closer eye on public opinion than expected. I can ask Allira to handle that—her build is well suited for it."

Alice felt relieved that managing public opinion wouldn't fall on her. She had enough on her plate already.

"Is there anything else you need to talk about?" asked Ethan.

"I had a rather troubling encounter with a new type of mana," said Alice. She went on to describe the newly discovered "Alice mana" and how it might influence her.

Ethan seemed quite worried at that. "Do you have a way to stave off the influence of Alice mana?"

Alice sighed. "I'm pretty confident that I'll find a solution. But when we get back to Metsel, do you mind if I study you a bit more? This is obviously a problem that all Immortals *should* have to deal with—but I don't see any Ethan mana inside your body. In other words, you don't seem to be influenced by other people's opinions of you. After all, most people think you're some sort of amazing master of magic, and yet according to Elder Sujia, you accidentally blew up your training facility once when you were teaching her. It seems to be evidence that your personality and abilities remain your own rather than becoming an amalgamation of other people's perceptions."

Ethan's eyebrows rose in surprise. "She told you that story?"

Alice nodded. "The first time I met her. When we were gathering [Soldiers] to rescue Samantha."

Ethan actually snorted before he nodded. "Then you think the System somehow solved this problem for Immortals?"

Alice nodded.

"Then when we get back to Metsel, you can take a look and see if you can figure anything out. It's best to wait until then, though. We have half a week left before we reach Metsel, and we're down a lot of [Guards] and combatants. I don't think that Emilia will make a second attempt, but I want to keep my guard up just in case," said Ethan.

"Sounds good," said Alice. "Alice mana is far from an urgent problem, so I can deal with it for now."

"Just be careful," said Ethan. "And let me know the *moment* you start to feel odd or notice an issue."

With that, Alice left Ethan's cabin.

Alice kept a close eye on their surroundings for the four days it took to reach the capital, in hopes that her vision-boosting abilities would let her spot Emilia if she made another attempt. Fortunately, the Sigmusi Immortal never reappeared. While Alice felt sure that the Society would stir up trouble again eventually, it seemed like they needed time to recover.

As the boat docked near Metsel, Alice breathed a sigh of relief. A fresh group of [Guards] was waiting to replace the dead. This group had about a hundred people in it, ten of whom were level seventy-five or above. Alice was happy to see higher-level [Guards] after what had happened during the trip.

After reorganizing the [Guards], Ethan and Alice proceeded to one of the cooperative churches of the System, where Alice got an update on how things had gone in her absence.

First of all, the [Willpower] training was starting to produce noticeable results. According to the church's records, the average [Willpower] of most churchgoers was a few points higher than before.

Second, while it wasn't common yet, some people were starting to lose their minds to class-mana madness. People with the lowest [Willpower] were displaying the same symptoms that Boris originally had: They were obsessively following the behavior of their class and were losing their sense of self as the days passed by. Many were family members who had tried to keep the affected people safe based on the knowledge Alice had passed around. Even so, it would be hard to address all the cases—so far, Cecilia's [Enchanters] and Alice only had a small number of enchantments that could fix these problems, while the number of people in need was swelling like a balloon.

The only upside was that these cases motivated people to focus even more on [Willpower] training. Seeing people start to lose their mind had naturally disturbed others, making them more proactive about protecting themselves and their families.

Third, a few people *had* evolved their classes. Naturally, they couldn't see anything in their status screens, due to the collapse of display mana. After Cecilia's [Enchanters] lent one of the display rings to the church, they were able to confirm a few interesting differences. The first person to evolve their class was evolving from an [Apprentice Farmer] to a regular [Farmer]. The moment he finished evolving his class, the accumulated mana instantly pushed him to level five, where he made a rather interesting discovery. He had gotten a completely different set of perks than the ones recorded in the book of the church. They were weaker than they should've been. The perks were more built around what he wanted, but had less overall effect. At level five, one of the regular perk options gave a 3 percent boost to the effect of the [Strength] and [Endurance] stats. This wasn't anything particularly crazy—it was just a flat percentage boost. The [Farmer] who had evolved his class valued [Endurance] quite a bit more than [Strength]. His version of this perk had similar text and a similar description, but it gave a 4 percent [Endurance] boost and no [Strength] boost at all. The perk was more overtly tailored to his needs and interests—but it lost more than it had gained in the process.

Accompanying this perk choice had been a System message written entirely in binary and garbled Illvarian, which the [Farmer] hadn't been able to understand once he removed the ring for testing purposes. Some of the words that the [Farmer] had been able to translate were "localized perk source," "optimization algorithm lost," and "no connection." The [Farmer] hadn't been sure what to make of those messages, but Alice had a pretty good guess what had happened. She guessed that before the collapse, whenever someone evolved their class, the class seed would download information from the mainframe of the System. It would then use that to optimize the perks that person could acquire in the future by referencing the best perks the System had and then copying the blueprints.

Without the mainframe of the System, the class seeds were probably using limited computing power to try to cobble together their own perk blueprints instead.

The [Farmer] in question also noted that his achievement for evolving a class had gone wrong, as had his perk selections. One of the benefits of a class evolution was that everyone got an achievement each time they leveled up a class, which gave them a few minor benefits. Through some testing, the [Farmer] confirmed that, just like every other achievement, it had taken a massive hit in effectiveness.

Both of these issues made Alice less eager to evolve her [Student of Organic Magic] class. Even if it was just a secondary class, losing around 50 to 60 percent of the benefits of an evolution would sting.

On the other hand, Alice was pretty sure that she could solve the problems posed by the collapse of the System *eventually*. She just needed to figure out how achievements worked, find a way to straighten them out, fix everyone's class fractals, figure out how to prevent Alice mana from replacing her personality, and prevent the laws of physics from imploding. A small, easy-to-accomplish to-do list.

Alice sighed, before making up her mind.

She had no idea when, or if, she would be able to fix the broken System in its entirety. Losing 50 to 60 percent of the benefits of her class evolution would sting—but watching the process would give her more information. Alice had watched what had happened the other two times she had evolved a class, and she had a perfect memory to allow her to double-check the differences.

Besides, Alice felt that if or when she fixed or replaced the System, it would be possible to fix all the inefficiencies and errors in her status screen. Evolving her [Student of Organic Magic] class was going to waste some of her potential gains, but she could recover them later. And improving her abilities *now* would make it easier to fix everything.

With her mind made up, Alice returned to Ethan's manor again and then looked at her evolution options for [Student of Organic Magic].

> **Congratulations! You have unlocked a class evolution for the class: Student of Organic Magic. Listed below are options for what you can evolve your class into. You may only choose one, so please make your decision after thinking carefully about the future.**

Organic mage: The most traditional advancement for Students of Organic Magic. Organic mages have a wide variety of perk options available and can learn almost anything. Be it combat, research, or enchanting, this class trades away the power and precision other class evolutions might offer in exchange for a wide and versatile selection of perks.
Unlocked as a result of: Having the Student of Organic Magic class at level 25.

Increases effect of Magic attribute by 10%. Increases effect of Endurance attribute by 10%. Your organic magic seed will have its mana conversion efficiency improved by 10%. You will gain a moderate boost to your instinctive ability to use organic magic, improving the speed and effectiveness with which you wield it.

Alice looked at her first evolution option before she shrugged. It was just a generic evolution with no real strengths or weaknesses. She looked at the next option.

Organic Spearman: An organic mage who specializes in close-quarters combat, especially their ability to boost their own strength and heal themselves in the middle of a fight. An Organic Spearman is a nightmare for regular soldiers to fight against.
Unlocked as a result of: Having the Student of Organic Magic class at level 25, having a spearmanship skill at level 10 or higher, have engaged in battle with both monsters and humans several times, have worked with a military unit at least once.

Increases effect of Magic, Endurance, Strength, and Dexterity attributes by 10%.

Alice eyed the [Organic Spearman] evolution for a few more moments. She still wasn't particularly thrilled at the idea of close-quarters combat—but on the other hand, being prepared for the worst wasn't a terrible decision. The class would directly boost her combat abilities, which Alice found appealing, and it would cover one of Alice's major weaknesses.

But after a few moments of consideration, Alice decided against it. Most of her combat strength still relied on her kinetic magic—and this was a secondary class, so Alice wasn't going to be getting very many perks from it. The class just wasn't good enough to assist her without some powerful perks to lean on. Thus, she tossed the evolution option into her mental trash bin.

Legendary Organic Mage: An organic mage who specializes in healing others, at the cost of the perks that boost physical abilities that other organic mages have. A Legendary Organic Mage is willing to heal others no matter how ridiculous their methods might be.

This particular class variant is only offered to those who have made exceptional contributions to the field of studying and healing the human body, despite their low level.

Unlocked as a result of: Having the Student of Organic Magic class at level 25, having the Creative Healer achievement (or something similar), having the Legendary Healer achievement (or something similar), having at least two skills related to healing or human biology at level 20 or higher, having the {Basic Medicine} skill.

Increases effect of Magic attribute by 50%. Classes related to research will get a leveling-speed boost based on how often and how effectively you have used those classes for healing, with a maximum 50% boost to leveling speed. The mana conversion ratio of all seeds is increased by 5%. All skills related to healing or biology level up 100% faster. Your innate ability to heal the human body without accidentally causing harm is amplified considerably, making it much harder for you to make mistakes and harm or maim your patients.

Alice grinned.

This was more like it.

The fact that the class had rarity-seven and rarity-four achievements as pre-requisites for the upgrade was rather appealing, and the boost Alice would get was exceptional.

She usually didn't think a lot about smaller attribute effect boosts—but a 50 percent boost to her magic attribute would be huge even if she got no other bonuses. Magic was her most used attribute, and Alice really didn't think that would change any time soon. A 50 percent boost would increase the effect of her magic stat from 142 percent to 192 percent, which was a pretty substantial increase. Then the class also offered her a boost to skill-leveling speed and mana conversion ratio for her magic seeds, *and* a small leveling-speed boost for her research-related classes if Alice used them for healing.

Alice was pretty sure that boost would be active most of the time, depending on what the class considered "healing." As long as her work to stymie the chaos of the collapse counted, the boost would always be active.

Alice checked her final class notification to see if it topped [Legendary Organic Mage].

Regenerating Lab Rat: An organic mage who specializes in using organic magic to heal themselves. Unlike most researchers who delve into forbidden topics of research, rather than using others as test subjects, you have instead opted to use *yourself* as a test subject. This class will help you survive your own mad experiments and perhaps undo whatever damage you've done to your body along the way.

Unlocked as a result of: Having the Student of Organic Magic class at level 25, having the Creative Healer achievement (or something similar), frequently using yourself as a test subject for your experiments.
Increases effect of Magic attribute by 30%. Increases effect of Endurance attribute by 20%. Your innate instincts when trying to heal even the strangest of magic-related problems is increased moderately, but only when attempting to treat yourself. You gain knowledge and retain it more quickly when using yourself as a test subject.

Alice squinted at the last option.

In a very, very weird way, it was a bit tempting, because Alice knew herself well. She definitely wouldn't stop experimenting with magic, and she only had one human test subject she felt okay using.

On the other hand, it only helped her heal problems in her own body, and it didn't provide anywhere near the bonuses of [Legendary Organic Mage], which probably also had better perk selections. If Alice didn't have [Legendary Organic Mage], she might have actually chosen [Regenerating Lab Rat], but it just seemed much worse than her other option.

Alice finished checking through her evolution options and selected [Legendary Organic Mage]. The mana in her surroundings seemed to swirl around, and at the same time, one of the class seeds near Alice's heart burst with rainbow mana . . . but as Alice had expected, due to the fact that there was no rainbow mana in her surroundings, the evolution of her [Student of Organic Magic] class felt like it was missing something. She watched as the class seed tried to compensate for this before it failed, leaving an incomplete class seed behind.

A few moments later, the seed flashed with rainbow mana, just like every other magic seed Alice had seen. Unlike the other, completed class seeds, the class seed flashed with mana again every ten seconds.

Curious, Alice stuck a tendril of display mana into the seed and checked to see if there were any hidden System messages associated with the seed.

Perk database not found. Using local, derivative perk options.
Scanning . . . please wait.
Perk database not found. Cannot update. Trying again in 10 seconds . . .

After about thirty seconds, Alice realized that the System message was just repeating, again and again.

Alice sighed, but then shrugged and nodded to herself. That was about what she had expected, honestly. She had already known that her perk options would be messed up until the System was back online. She was relieved to know that her class seed was constantly trying to update itself. It confirmed that she could fix the class seed's perk selections whenever she fixed the System.

After Alice finished gathering information and dealing with her class evolution, she and Ethan left the Church of the System. At Ethan's manor, they found a royal [Messenger] waiting for them.

"Lady Alice, Honored Immortal Ethan, the [King] of Illvaria has requested your presence in three days."

<h1 style="text-align:center">CHAPTER 33</h1>

After receiving news from the royal [Messenger], Alice felt very nervous. She had only met one other member of the royal family, and she hadn't exactly enjoyed trying to interact with the unfavored [Princess]. Ethan had told the girl off, which had rescued Alice from the awkward situation, but Alice's reticence to interact with royalty had still increased after the event. Alice enjoyed researching more than talking to people with secular authority.

Ethan, perhaps seeing Alice freeze up, gave the [Messenger] a quick nod. "Understood. We have discoveries to report to the crown estate anyway."

Alice finally unfroze and gave the [Messenger] a somewhat stiff nod. {Etiquette} helped her force the words out of her lips, despite her nerves.

"I understand."

The [Messenger] nodded and left.

Ethan patted Alice on the shoulder.

"Relax. Meeting with members of the crown estate is an inevitability as an Immortal, and the current [King] isn't too bad. He's a bit ambitious, but he's willing to listen to reason and moderate his actions when needed. Otherwise, Illvaria would have crumbled under the financial and manpower consumption of the recolonization project. Just think of it as meeting an administrator who you have to report progress and information to."

Alice nodded and suppressed her nerves. If Ethan felt so relaxed, she would do her best to calm down. She didn't really want to do anything that felt nerve-racking and anxiety-inducing—but on the other hand, when Alice tried to think about it from the [King]'s perspective, she could understand why this meeting was happening.

The [King] trying to get to the bottom of why his country was imploding seemed quite reasonable to her. Alice was someone who best understood what was happening, and she and Ethan had made this fact rather public when she started gathering the support of the church. It was only logical for the [King] to ask her to come and explain what was going on.

After she and Ethan entered the manor, she quickly returned to her room. And then, for the first time in a while, she examined her full status screen.

The first thing she noticed was that, at some point in time, she had reached 120 [Strength]. All of her attributes were now 120 or above. The {Outworlder} achievement was no longer going to provide her with any boosts to attribute training speed. It had once provided a variety of useful benefits, but many of them were limited to classes and stats below a certain level. It had boosted primary classes below level fifty, secondary classes below level ten, and attributes below 120. Alice thought about it for a moment before she shrugged and finished scanning.

She could see several perks and skills that would be useful when interacting with the [King] of Illvaria—but they didn't ease her nerves completely. She would have preferred to see a much higher-level {Etiquette} skill, or perhaps a few perks from [Courtier].

She decided it might not be a bad idea to grind {Etiquette} for the next few days.

But first, Alice had a few things to do.

Her newest perk, {System's Ambition}, had just come off cooldown. Alice wanted to use it immediately—adding four magic seeds to her compound magic seed sounded amazing.

Alice started out with a round of {Safety Analysis}, just to make sure that she wasn't about to kill herself by accident, then got to work.

The first seed she decided to create was a math magic seed. Alice only had three mana types that she was totally sure were part of System mana that she didn't have access to right now, so she figured she might as well start with one of those.

The math magic seed creation went smoothly—Alice was more than capable of handling the creation of a simple magic seed without the System, especially one that she understood quite well.

When Alice fused the math seed into her System seed, she felt something that hadn't been there before.

It felt as if there was a connection between the three types of mana present in her compound seed. It was as if the three types of magic in her seed weren't just three different types of mana that happened to share a seed slot. Instead, it felt like something fundamental to their nature was slowly growing.

Alice frowned at her System seed and spent several minutes prodding at it, but she couldn't figure out what that feeling meant or how to use it. At least, not yet.

Alice sighed and ran several ideas through {Safety Analysis} before she started thinking about her next seed. She knew for sure that organic and pure mana were also part of System mana, so they might be good candidates for integration into the compound seed.

She was also pretty sure that "meaning" mana, or something like that, was a component of System mana. After all, the System had somehow shown her understandable System messages without understanding English.

Alice had also been thinking about *other* parts of the System recently. Parts that should, logically, be part of the entire framework of System mana. Since System mana was composed of so many different types of smaller mana, all working together, Alice was recently starting to suspect that there was some sort of mana that worked to keep everything else functioning. Perhaps it was a type of mana that served as a core for how everything worked, or perhaps it just let different kinds of mana communicate.

Alice also suspected that there was some sort of mana in play that locked down the laws of physics, or somehow acted as an intermediary between human beliefs and the laws of physics. She had no idea what that mana could be, though, so she had no way to integrate it into her compound seed.

Alice found herself overwhelmed by choices. It was hard to decide which magic seed to integrate into her System seed next. Mathematics mana had seemed like a good way to start, since the System itself was built off RPG mechanics, and those were basically giant blocks of math and numbers. That was the only easy choice. She stared at her status screen in frustration and decided to try another experiment, to see if she could find any obvious flaws or needs she had but couldn't address. She would need Ethan's help, so she walked to his office.

"Are you ready for me to observe you?" asked Alice. "I want to deal with Alice mana sooner rather than later."

Ethan smiled and then pointed at a chair near his desk. "You can sit there and observe me while I deal with some paperwork. Let me know if you need me to do anything more specific, like sit still or use magic or anything like that. I'll put your needs above the paperwork as needed."

"You can work on your paperwork for now," said Alice. "I'll let you know if I need a different kind of data."

Alice took a seat and then started slowly examining Ethan as he analyzed documents.

True to her suspicions, Ethan didn't seem to have a single speck of Ethan mana in his body. His body was composed almost entirely of mana flesh, and it did, indeed, look kind of like Ethan was a cloud of mana constantly transforming into itself. But Ethan definitely hadn't been overwritten by Ethan mana—he was still fundamentally himself. This was completely different from the people who were suffering the symptoms of class-mana madness. The System clearly had some way to deal with problems like Alice mana. The question was *how*.

"Would you let me use some perks to poke around inside your body?" asked Alice.

"I grant you full permission to use any perks that help you perceive the inside of my body," Ethan said without looking up from the letter he was writing.

Alice touched Ethan's arm and then used {Lesser Organic Vision} and every single mana-viewing perk she had available to start investigating Ethan's organs.

What does the System do to manage Ethan mana? It must do something with it. It isn't a kind of mana that can just be filtered into a class, the way some types of mana can be converted into each other. I tried that already with Alice mana, and it didn't work. It also shouldn't be possible to just transfer it out of the body. When I broke my [Fisherwoman] class seed and then went fishing, I immediately got all my [Fisherwoman] mana back. That indicates that you pick up a certain default level of mana when you do related actions. Since Ethan is always being Ethan, any System attempts to make a bubble and lock out Ethan mana should have failed when the System collapsed. The System doesn't block the mana, and doesn't filter it . . . hmm . . .

Alice continued probing Ethan's body, trying to figure out how the System managed the Ethan mana that he should have inevitably built up.

And after several minutes of careful searching, Alice made a discovery.

Embedded in the core of Ethan's brain was a tiny little gemstone-like object made of mana. It was almost impossible for her to notice, even with Ethan willingly letting her inspect him, because it was so small. It had a variety of smaller facets to it, all of which were made of mana. These facets weren't equal in length: Some were small, some large, and some medium size. It looked like a tiny, poorly cut jewel made of System mana, but Alice could see a lot of smaller types of mana attached to it as well. Alice couldn't see it well enough to inspect its composition, and it was too small for {Intuitive Magic Modeling} to analyze in detail.

But one thing Alice *could* confirm was that there was a great deal of Ethan mana inside the little crystal.

Ah. So that's what the System does with Ethan mana, thought Alice.

She started inspecting her own brain using her perks, and now that she knew where to look, she confirmed that she also had a tiny mana gem embedded in her brain. It was even smaller than Ethan's mana gem. Unlike Ethan's little mana gemstone, it didn't have any Alice mana inside it.

What are you? Alice wondered as she continued to inspect the gemstone.

Sadly, her vision just wasn't precise enough to inspect the little gemstone yet. She needed access to a better vision-enhancing perk, or some way to zoom in.

On the bright side, at least Alice knew where to look for solutions now.

Alice decided to hold off on using her other three opportunities to make magic seeds until her perk was closer to refreshing or she made any new discoveries. But for now, she had a path to keep researching. And she also needed to prepare for a meeting with the [King].

C H A P T E R 3 4

Alice spent the next three days analyzing mana gems. The first thing she did was ask Cecilia if she could investigate her brain, to see if Cecilia also had a mana gem in her head.

She did not. Or, at the very least, Alice couldn't find one. There was a chance that it was too small—after all, even the one inside her own brain was too small for her to find without knowing where to look. Regardless, Alice wasn't able to analyze Cecilia's mana gem because she couldn't find it.

Upon failing to find Cecilia's mana gem, Alice started thinking. She had a sneaking suspicion that Cecilia truly didn't have a mana gem, and moreover, she had a guess about why that was the case. Just to make sure, she asked Cecilia what level her highest class was at.

Cecilia was now at level sixty-three in [Enchanter], which had overtaken her [Merchant] class. This matched Alice's new theory—that only people above level seventy-five had mana gems.

To gather more data, Alice asked Ethan for help. Ethan had several [Guards], [Soldiers], and other assorted professions come in and let Alice check them. Through these tests, Alice learned two things.

First, as far as she could tell, anyone below level eighty did not seem to have a mana gem in their brain. It seemed that the mana gem appeared at level eighty, not seventy-five.

Second, Alice confirmed that the mana gems were truly linked to level, not to tier-three perks or anything of the sort. If a target of observation had merged two tier-two perks together into a tier-three perk, they had a mana gem. If they had just taken a new perk at level eighty, or made another tier-two perk, they also had a mana gem in their brain—although it was much smaller.

In other words, the way that one handled their perks made a significant difference in the size of the mana gem but didn't influence the *existence* of the mana gem. This made Alice lean toward the theory that people below level eighty still had mana gems; they just weren't large enough to observe in detail. Alice hoped that whenever she reached level eighty-five in [Explorer of Magic], she would get a better way to check on smaller mana constructs so that she could confirm this theory.

As Alice observed these mana gems, she also confirmed that anyone who had reached level eighty before the collapse of the System had a bunch of person mana stuck in their mana gem. Alice's first observation target that Ethan hired, Ollie the [Hairstylist], had a small amount of Ollie mana in his mana gem. Martha the [Commander] had a large amount of Martha mana in her mana gem. Mark the [Knight], who had just reached level eighty, was in the same position as Alice—he had a small amount of Mark mana running rampant in his body.

This confirmed Alice's suspicion from earlier: The System clearly had a built-in mechanism to deal with person mana—but now that the System was down, Alice hadn't benefited from it. She would need to find a way to deal with it before it became dangerous.

When Alice asked the Church of the System and Ethan if anyone else had similar problems to her own, both did a little bit of searching. It took some time to find someone else who had reached level eighty after the collapse, but two people were found.

Similar to her, they had a moderate amount of person mana stuck inside their brains, and complained about minor amounts of personality corrosion. They had less person mana in their brain than Alice did—but all three of them had similar problems.

Alice next wondered whether filtration mana could stuff the Alice mana in her head into her mana gem. Unfortunately, this didn't work. Every time Alice tried to cram Alice mana inside her mana gem, it felt like she was trying to stuff liquid through a solid wall—she was clearly doing it incorrectly.

After that, Alice revised her plan. Her primary class was [Explorer of Magic], and Alice felt that the class was tailor-made to handle the problem. With another tier-three perk, she would hopefully have a better solution for Alice mana.

Since she was out of both ideas and time, Alice spent the rest of the day preparing for her audience with the [King]. With Ethan's help, she got her {Etiquette} teacher back, as well as a large number of books on {Etiquette}. After three days of cramming, Alice's {Etiquette} skill had grown significantly.

Through training, you have increased a skill!
Etiquette: 22→28

After her days of research and cramming last-minute {Etiquette} training into her brain, it was time to meet the [King]. The next day, after breakfast, Ethan led her to the palace while Alice tried to look confident. This meeting with the [King] of Illvaria felt much more intimidating than the tea party Ethan had brought her to a month ago.

There were a large number of [Guards] scattered throughout the hallways of the palace, which was a distinct contrast to a month ago. When Alice and Ethan had attended the second [Princess]'s tea party, there had only been an occasional [Guard] patrol on duty.

Eventually, the two arrived at the audience chamber. They were almost immediately let in by the [Guards] stationed outside the door.

Once they entered the audience chamber, Alice saw an older man sitting on a throne and a beautiful girl sitting on a much smaller throne to the side. The throne room itself was different from what Alice had expected. The royal meeting chamber was a tapestry of rainbow mana that faintly resembled the web of a spider. Each wall of the room shimmered faintly, making the entire room look both radiant and chaotic to Alice's mana vision. Although she wasn't quite sure what most of the perks did, she suspected that at least some of them strengthened the [King] and made it hard to assassinate him inside this room.

The man sitting on the throne appeared to be in his early forties. Since Alice knew the [King] was nearly fifty, it was clear that the [King] barely benefited from any aging speed reductions.

Based on the rainbow mana in his body, Alice estimated that the [King] was level fifty-five. Since most inherited seats of power tended to favor the child with the highest level compared to their age, Alice wondered how he had gotten the throne. Had he not had any siblings to compete with, or were they even worse than the [King] was? The man's level wasn't *bad*, but it certainly wasn't impressive.

Alice decided that it was none of her business and turned her attention to the woman sitting on a smaller throne in the room.

At first glance, Alice wondered if the woman might be the [Queen]—but a closer inspection revealed that the woman was far younger than the [King]. Alice knew the [King] and [Queen] were the same age. Also, there was a very strong family resemblance. Alice searched her memory, and a few moments later, she recalled Ethan mentioning that the first [Princess] was very favored by the [King] and likely to be the next monarch. She also recalled Ethan speculating that the first [Princess] might be higher level than the current [King].

A quick glance let Alice confirm that the woman *was* higher level than the [King]—she was about level sixty. Alice was struck by the strange notion that, despite being older than the second [Princess], the first [Princess] actually looked younger.

The first [Princess] wore a long dress that had a massive System enchantment on it. Alice estimated that it gave her around fifty points in stats, divided between [Charisma] and [Intelligence]. The first [Princess] gave Alice and Ethan both clear, measured looks before she dipped her head toward Ethan slightly. The [King], interestingly enough, did the same, although a moment later, Ethan gave the [King] a much deeper bow.

Alice's brain kick-started itself as she remembered the proper etiquette for handling Illvarian monarchs. She gave the [King] a respectful curtsy, which the [King] acknowledged with another nod.

"Immortal Ethan sees Your Majesty," said Ethan.

"Alice, mage of Illvaria, sees Your Majesty," Alice said.

With the formalities complete, the [King] gave Ethan a strained smile.

"Immortal Ethan. It has been a long time since we last saw you," said the [King]. "I wish that we had met again in better circumstances, but as you know, the current state of the kingdom is quite troubling."

"Indeed, Your Majesty," said Ethan. "There are new problems cropping up left and right, and every second it feels like ten more appear."

The [King] grimaced. "We hear that you and your apprentice have had a hand in cleaning up at least some of this mess?"

Ethan smiled ruefully. "Mostly my apprentice. Her skill set is exceptionally well suited to help understand the problem. She has been doing a lot of the research that has helped others keep the situation under control."

The [King] gave Alice a more appraising look, and the [Princess] followed suit. A few moments later, the [King] gave Alice a more friendly smile.

"We've heard quite a bit about you, Lady Alice."

Alice tried not to shuffle awkwardly.

"I wish to keep as many people safe as possible," Alice said, once it became clear that the [King] expected her to respond.

The [King] gave Alice a more curious look. "Is that so? I don't detect any lies, but I'm surprised to hear that's one of the things that motivates you. I suppose the easy levels that come from solving a crisis like this have nothing to do with it?"

Alice blushed.

"I would do it either way, but I'm definitely happier to work for a reward," she said. Something about the way the [King] spoke to her felt strange. She had expected him to be more . . . formal. Instead, it almost felt like he was trying to reduce the formality and {Etiquette} required for the meeting as much as possible. Was this because the [King] knew that she had only learned a bit of {Etiquette}, and was tailoring the meeting to her needs? If so, he was acting surprisingly considerate.

Before Alice could focus on that thought, the [King] moved to yet another topic.

"I also heard that you were attacked by Emilia last week?"

Alice shuddered. "Yes, Your Majesty. During the boat ride back to Cyra, Immortal Emilia attacked our boat."

The [King] pursed his lips in disgust. "So the Sigmusi sent an Immortal after you." Alice could see worry on his face as well as frustration.

The [Princess] touched the [King]'s shoulder, and he shook himself out of his thoughts. He turned back toward Alice.

"It must have been frightening, encountering a hostile Immortal when you are still so far away from Immortality. We hope that you were not terribly injured during the fight?"

"It was terrifying, but I'm not hurt," said Alice. "I saw perks that I don't understand being tossed around on a battlefield I had no hope of surviving on my own. I must say, it is not an experience I am eager to repeat."

As the [King] nodded, his eyes remained fixed on Alice. She had the strange sensation of being stared at by an unwavering block of iron before the [Princess] touched the [King]'s shoulder again.

This time, Alice saw a flicker of rainbow mana pass between the two of them, which she assumed was some sort of perk to relay messages. She studied the flicker of rainbow mana with interest, but it disappeared too quickly for her to get a good look at it.

"We're curious, Alice. What do you make of this crisis? It's obvious that you know quite a bit about it. What is the root cause of all this? What are we to make of your claims that the deity most Illvarians worship is malfunctioning?"

Alice swallowed. She felt a certain weight attached to this question that she hadn't felt earlier. She spent a brief moment wondering whether the monarch of Illvaria was religious. A few members of the Church of the System hadn't taken Alice's claims very well, although most of them had been willing to put aside religious dogma in the face of the crisis. Alice also hadn't divulged all her thoughts on the matter, such as her belief that the System was neither sapient nor sentient.

If the [King] was religious, speaking the truth might be dangerous. But Alice wasn't in the habit of lying. She cleared her throat and tried to swallow down a lump of anxiety.

"I would like to point out the decisive evidence that the System is malfunctioning. There are many recent instances of the System not working properly. Children are getting their status screens too early. People's class mana is overwriting their personality. Perk selections don't have any text if people don't have a way to fix it," Alice started, eyeing the [King].

The [King] nodded as Alice went into more detail on each type of incident. Contrary to Alice's fears, he didn't lash out or contradict her as she spoke, simply letting her present all the oddities she had encountered. Finally, the [King] turned back toward Ethan.

"What do you think, Ethan?"

"At least for now, I'd say that Lady Alice has proven her understanding of the situation," Ethan said as he quirked the corners of his lips upward. "Not only that, but my apprentice has found ways to counteract some of the problems posed by the collapse of the System. I'm sure you are already aware of the supply line established between Metsel and Cyra, and how important the enchanting materials and enchantments involved are."

The [King] returned Ethan's strange half smile.

"Do you think that there is anyone better positioned than Alice in the kingdom to handle all this?"

"I don't. I can confidently say that Alice is the best positioned in Illvaria to handle this crisis, and possibly, the best positioned in the world." Ethan's half smile had turned into a full-blown grin, though Alice wasn't sure why.

The [King] eyed Alice thoughtfully again, and this time, she could see a slight twinkle in his eyes.

"Then perhaps we should move to the real reason we called you here, Lady Alice."

"The real reason for this meeting?" Alice asked as her brain short-circuited.

When she had learned the [King] wanted to see her, she had thought the [King] wanted to consult with her due to her understanding of the crisis. After all, the System breaking had introduced an avalanche of problems for the kingdom to face. Alice had been a little surprised that the [King] knew of her existence, but she *was* the apprentice of an Immortal. That probably gave her a lot of extra visibility.

"Indeed, Lady Alice," said the [King]. The twinkle in his eyes grew stronger with each word he spoke. Alice suspected that the man was enjoying catching her by surprise. "We have some things we wished to request of you, and some boons to aid you in your efforts. Your character has met our expectations, and your understanding of the crisis is sufficient."

"All right? I mean, your subject hears your request," Alice said as she scrabbled for the shreds of {Etiquette} she had crammed into her head over the past days.

"We wish to preface this meeting with a statement," said the [King] as the twinkle faded from his eyes. "The collapse of the System is extremely dangerous. We estimate that within a year at most, most of the population will go mad. This is based on the analysis from several perks and [Mathematicians] at work. There may be some variance in these estimates, but the collapse of Illvaria is inevitable if this crisis is not nipped in the bud."

Alice nodded. She didn't have a perfect idea of how long this world had left, but she definitely agreed that this crisis would destroy humanity if it wasn't handled. Things might last longer in Illvaria now that she had distributed class-mana fixing rings, but the rest of the world didn't have that advantage.

Sure, Cecilia's [Enchanters] were now at work creating rings to fix the [Enchanter] class, and Ethan had also started getting other [Enchanters] in the kingdom to make antimana rings for stopgap measures. Despite their efforts, the production of enchanted rings was insufficient. Illvaria had somewhere between one and two million residents—there was no way the [Enchanters] could make enough rings for everyone. It was also taking too long to get people the right magic seeds for boosting production.

The [King], heedless of Alice's internal musings, continued speaking.

"This crisis worries us. As much as we hate to admit that the System could struggle, we are not so foolish as to deny the evidence in front of our eyes." The [King] looked at Alice. "So we have two things to bestow upon you and one thing to request."

"First of all, we hereby raise you to the rank of an honorary [Baroness]. It does not carry the benefit of any land, much like all other mage-noble titles. But you will receive the other benefits according to your new station." The [King] paused. "This is what you deserve for establishing countermeasures for the crisis and securing the enchanting materials from the South. A few have trickled into Metsel already, and the preliminary results are promising." Then the [King] paused, glancing at Alice. "One thing to keep in mind is that mage-noble titles will *not* pass on to any children or family members you may have. If you want a hereditary [Noble] title, you will need to work harder."

Alice just barely managed to resist the urge to shrug. She didn't have any kids. She had never been particularly interested in romance, either. Unless that changed, she doubted she would ever care about whether her title was hereditary.

"The second thing we want to bestow upon you is a title, of sorts."

Hadn't the [King] just given her a title?

"This title comes with certain conditions," said the [King], heedless of Alice's confusion. "We believe that the collapse of the System has the potential to inflict great harm upon the people of Illvaria . . . and we need someone who is able to advise us on how to counteract those problems."

Alice felt a little bit better. At least her suspicions about the purpose of this meeting hadn't been totally wrong. The [King] *had* called her here to address the collapse of the System. He was just more focused on giving her tools to help *her* handle the problem—which was fine. As long as the [King] was trying to help her, Alice was more than happy to keep working hard.

"What specifically would this adviser position entail? What are the benefits?" asked Alice. Even if she did want to help people, she had been doing fine with Ethan's help. Working directly for the [King] might prove more of a hindrance than a boon, depending on the circumstances.

"Let's talk about compensation first," said the [King]. "According to Ethan, you are already paid a generous amount?"

"Yes, Your Majesty," said Alice. Ethan currently paid her about thirty golden suns a month. He also handled most of her expenses. She was staying in his manor to be safer from [Assassins] and the Society, which meant she didn't need to pay for rent, food, or protection. Ethan also paid for her [Teachers], and Alice didn't have enough time for entertainment beyond some light reading when she was in her dream library. Essentially, she didn't have much use for money right now.

"In that case, we have three different offers for you. First of all, we could give you proper compensation in the form of money. Say . . . one hundred golden suns a month? This amount of money would be quite reasonable as a reward for someone who has managed to discover so much critical information. Especially given the very limited time frame and resources you have had available to do all this."

"What are the other offers?" asked Alice.

"Well, based on our understanding of your personality, we doubt this one will appeal to you . . . but if you're interested, we can make it happen," said the [King]. "As a reward for your previous actions, as well as your agreement to our conditions, we could make you a *real* [Baroness], with land. Your mage-noble title would be converted into a proper [Noble] title. The crown has several smaller baronies and counties that could be given to you, so if you *do* wish to own land, we could certainly find something that suits you." The [King]'s expression grew sour a moment later. "Some members of the [Noble] estate might object to that, but we can force it through, if you wish."

Alice shuddered. Being a [Baroness] sounded more like a nightmare than a reward. Alice could just imagine how much time she would waste trying to administer her territory, handle political discussions, meet with other [Nobles], and manage finances. Not to mention how weird it would be. Alice had accepted that this world had nobility, but Earth hadn't had [Nobles] with real power since before Alice was born. She wasn't ready to become part of the feudal system.

The [King] seemed to see Alice's rejection of this offer from her expression. He chuckled.

"It seems that you're not interested. Very well then, moving on to the offer we think you would actually be interested in. We could give you *and* your [Enchanter] friend the titles of {Royal Crisis Analyst} and {Royal Enchanter Trainer}. Do note that the title of {Royal Crisis Analyst} will be bestowed upon you regardless, but we are offering to help your friend out. We would also be willing to hire a few [Royal Tutors] to help train your friend once this mess is over. It would amplify her leveling speed significantly."

Alice blinked in confusion.

Why would giving Cecilia an honorary title matter to her? She didn't care that much about what other people thought of her and Cecilia. Sure, having a few official-sounding titles would be nice, since it would help her get through bureaucracy. Alice still remembered how long it had taken to get her dimensional study license approved. But she wasn't sure if this offer mattered to her. Did Cecilia have some sort of burning desire to be recognized as a royal adviser that Alice didn't know about?

The [King] seemed to see Alice's confusion. He turned to Ethan, and Ethan cleared his throat.

"Ahem . . . Alice, you may not be aware of this, but there are a lot of royal titles that double as achievements. These achievements can only be bestowed by a monarch, and there is a specific perk needed to be able to bestow them. Only one copy of each title can exist at the same time, and only a certain number of royal titles can be bestowed at once. Currently, there are twenty-three royal titles distributed in Illvaria," said Ethan. "The [King] is offering you a mostly permanent boost to leveling speed along with a few other benefits. He is also offering the same to Cecilia. The titles can be taken away, of course—but there are penalties associated with removing a title that was already bestowed, so it isn't an action taken lightly. Most [Kings] and [Emperors] avoid taking away official titles unless someone breaks a whole lot of laws or betrays the country."

That was interesting. She had been thinking since she hit level seventy-five about how to accelerate her leveling speed, and the fact that the achievements from the System were on the fritz meant it was harder to acquire new leveling-speed boosts. Alice definitely wouldn't mind something to speed the process along. Having a way to help Cecilia reach Immortality also sounded great to her. Alice's first priority was to resolve the collapse of the System, and her second priority was to stay safe . . . but Cecilia reaching Immortality was probably her third priority right now.

"What kinds of bonuses does this achievement grant?" asked Alice.

"Well, I have one of the royal titles. It gives me a 100 percent boost to leveling classes that are related to both combat and magic. Most royal titles also have some miscellaneous benefits related to what specific title you get, such as an extra combat or crafting perk. They're usually about equal to a level seventy perk, though they can be a bit stronger or weaker depending on the specific title and level of the [King] bestowing the achievement." Ethan shrugged, seemingly uncaring that the gesture was a slight breach of {Etiquette}. "It's nothing world-changing, but you and Cecilia can use every little bit of help you can get, right?"

Alice nodded. Every boost to leveling speed was greatly appreciated right now. She wanted to hit level eighty-five in [Explorer of Magic] as fast as possible so that she could finally fix the Alice mana problem, and perhaps the class seeds problem as well.

Alice understood that Cecilia hadn't really earned a royal title from the [King]. She had contributed a little bit to solving this crisis, but most of her actions built on Alice's discoveries and work. Giving Cecilia a title was of dubious value to both Illvaria and the crown.

Alice didn't care. She wanted her friend to live.

"What are the conditions for accepting the title?" asked Alice.

"First, you need to actually act as an adviser for us," said the [King]. "We want to keep the people of Illvaria safe, but we can't do that if we don't know the intimate details of the problems we're facing. So we expect you to share the underlying information about how and why you act the way you do."

Alice winced. That would require that she reveal at least some of her studies of the System.

On the other hand, the System had collapsed, people were being warped by the mana in the world around them, and monsters were gaining intelligence. Perhaps questioning the System wouldn't be quite as inflammatory now as it would have been a few months ago.

Alice sighed and then nodded.

The [King] smiled.

"For this purpose, we would require that you meet with us or send documents and letters at least once every three days to discuss your findings and proposed solutions. If you leave Metsel or Illvaria and cannot send these messages or meet with us, we require that you at least discuss everything you know about the collapse of the System, and discuss potential solutions. We're willing to implement most solutions we feel are reasonable, and given the unfolding crisis, the estates are a lot more cooperative than usual. Effective solutions require information to be useful, though," said the [King].

Alice thought about it for a moment. That wasn't too bad. Attending a meeting with the [King] to explain what was going on made sense, and afterward, Alice could just return to solving—

"There will be other people at these meetings as well, of course. A few of our other [Advisers], as well as other people, such as the [Minister of Finance], will be critical to forming policies for Illvaria as a whole. We would need you to be able to present information and evidence confirming its authenticity so that we can build policies around it."

Alice tried not to wince. There went her dream of a simple, quick meeting.

"I have {Shared Memories}. Is that enough for evidence?"

The [King] thought about it for a few moments before he nodded. "That would be acceptable. We would appreciate it if you had everything written down as well, though. While it seems like you have invested heavily in memory perks, most people have not."

"I accept your conditions," said Alice. "And I would like the title for myself and Cecilia as the reward."

"We thought you might appreciate that offer the most," said the [King] as his smile grew wider. "I hereby name you {Royal Crisis Analyst}."

A moment later, mana surged toward Alice, and a few seconds later, a System notification popped up.

You have gained an achievement!
Royal Crisis Analyst (Rarity: N/A)
Named by king. Appoint. Chosen to analyze crisis.
++80% class experience for classes that analyze the crisis Collapse of the System. Perception stat +20% effect. You g@in ability to sense places where crisis hits harder than others within country_Illvaria, and some perception of relevaaaaaaant areas of interest.
Note: Due to the influence of the {Outworlder} and {Seeker of Truth} achievements, some extra information is revealed.

Alice blinked as the new achievement settled into her body. The way the mana from the achievement moved into her body also felt slightly different than before. She turned her eyesight inward using {Lesser Organic Vision} and noticed that a lot of the mana from this new achievement was making its way toward her head. There, Alice lost sight of it—it was moving a little bit too fast, and she was also distracted reading her new achievement.

But most distracting of all, a moment later, Alice felt a very new, very weird sensation. It was a very, very weak sense of *where* people were succumbing to problems caused by the System collapse.

In a very limited way, Alice felt like she could sense all of Illvaria now. Some villages were filled with people who were starting to succumb to their class mana. Other people had been ripped apart by armies of intelligent, coordinated monsters. Alice couldn't detect the exact location of these crises or detect specific details. Still, she could probably pinpoint rough locations of these crises on a map with some careful estimation and focus. Considering the fact that her vision extended all the way across Illvaria, that was quite impressive.

Finally, Alice also sensed . . . something. Something far to the northwest that felt important to her.

A place relevant to the crisis . . .

The fact that the System had a physical mainframe somewhere, which she had discovered when she gained her {Seed Enchanting} perk.

Alice had been baffled about the right way to track down the System's location after she learned that it existed. After all, this planet was just as big as Earth, and Alice had no way of knowing where the System's mainframe was. It could be under the ocean, in the sky, or even in the center of the planet. It could even be on the moon, and she would be none the wiser.

But now, Alice had the very distinct feeling that something important was to the northwest, even if the exact location was vague.

Alice had a very, very strong suspicion that she knew what that important thing was.

Chapter 35

After bestowing on Alice her new royal title, the [King] said that Cecilia would be called upon for her own royal title that evening. Then he shooed Alice and Ethan out of the throne room.

Once they got back to Ethan's manor, Alice told Ethan about the information her new perk had given her. Even now, Alice could feel as if *something* northwest of Illvaria was calling to her. However, northwest of Illvaria was the Sigmusi Empire—which Alice was unwilling to enter alone. In other words, Ethan would need to help her if she wanted to make use of this information.

"So you think that the mainframe of the System is in the Northwest somewhere?" Ethan asked after Alice finished explaining.

Alice nodded. "I could be wrong, but it seems plausible. If I'm right, this could be an opportunity to fix everything. Right now I can help people survive the loss of the System—but if I could repair the source, everything would be fixed."

Ethan frowned.

"I'm glad that you have an idea for how to fix all this, but the direction is quite unfortunate. How far away is it? Does your achievement tell you?"

"It doesn't, sadly. I only know that it's far away—likely far beyond Illvaria's borders."

Ethan's expression grew darker. "There are only a few places northwest of Illvaria, and *all* of them are problematic. The first place your achievement could be leading you to is somewhere in the Sigmusi Colonia. In which case, if we wanted to investigate it, we would need to enter the Sigmusi Colonia's territory. Asking them for passage sounds like an *awful* idea. Just a week ago, one of their Immortals tried to either kidnap or assassinate you. Waltzing into their territory is just asking for them to try again.

"The Sigmusi Colonia's territory extends all the way to the western and northern coasts of the Southern Continent.

"The second place the achievement could be leading you toward is the Western Continent, which is filled with the world's most powerful monsters. The Western

Continent is nearly untouched because humans can't survive there unless they are already very powerful. There are no colonies or towns there, because children would surely become monster food. Only Immortals are strong enough to explore the wilderness of the Western Continent.

"The final place your achievement could be leading you toward is underwater. Not to mention, that particular region of the ocean is right between the Sigmusi Colonia and the Sigmusi Imperia, meaning it's right in the middle of their naval region."

Alice winced. Every single one of those locations sounded frustrating to access and investigate.

"Without submarines, I can definitely see why operating underwater would be a major hassle," said Alice as she thought of the possibility of the System being underwater. Maybe there was some way to get around the problem of breathing and moving underwater with enchantments?

As Alice was lost in her thoughts, Ethan started speaking again.

"When your perk gave you a glimpse of the mainframe of the System, did you see any hints that would indicate whether the System was underground, underwater, or perhaps flying in the sky somewhere?"

"I think the System is underground," she said, then paused. "Though the mainframe *could* also be on another celestial body, such as the moon, if the moon is northwest of here . . ."

"The moon is most definitely not northwest of here right now," said Ethan. "According to most [Scholar] estimations of the moon's orbit, at this moment it should be a bit to the south, and also on the other side of the planet. Your perk should lead you almost straight down in that case."

"So much for that idea, then," said Alice. She felt a bit of relief at Ethan's words.

Trying to figure out how to land on the moon had been incredibly difficult for her own world, and that was with industrial-scale production and excellent understanding of physics and engineering. Alice had zero confidence that she could manage the same thing in this world, even with magic. Not to mention, Alice had no idea if there were any differences between outer space in this dimension versus her home dimension. For all Alice knew, in this dimension, space could be infested with some sort of horrifying void monster species that could devour stars or something. Space was not a place she wanted to visit until she had a much better understanding of the universe here.

Ethan also seemed relieved that they wouldn't need to recreate the moon mission, although he still seemed frustrated. "So it's either on the ocean floor or surrounded by enemies." Ethan sighed before falling more deeply in thought.

"Well, the possibility of the System being located on the Western Continent seems likely, at least to me. After all, the Western Continent is mostly unexplored by humanity. Based on what you've told me about the System, it must emit a ridiculous amount of mana on a day-to-day basis. The Western Continent is known to have some of the densest mana on the planet. Given how powerful the monsters there are, it would be very hard for anyone to accidentally intrude upon the System. After all, even a team of Immortals could easily lose their lives while exploring the Western Continent." Ethan paused, looking thoughtful. "It would be a very clever way to prevent someone from breaking into the System's mainframe as well. You would need some way to prevent monsters from getting into the System, but if you found a way to accomplish that, the System would be totally inaccessible. If I were the creator of the System, that's where I would put it."

Alice frowned. "How easy is it to sail to the Western Continent from Illvaria? Or to get to the ocean northwest of the Southern Continent?" she asked.

Ethan laughed bitterly. "Not very. The Sigmusi would definitely see it as an opportunity, and we have no way to keep you safe on the ocean. Illvaria isn't exactly a big naval power. Even during the golden age of Illvaria, when the southern region was fully under control, we only had a few ports. Now, we don't even have a settled coastline. Apart from my mother's boat, and merchant vessels built for river travel, Illvaria doesn't have any way to get into the ocean at all. My mother is probably the highest-level [Admiral] in the country, and she's probably only level fifty or sixty in the class," said Ethan.

"So no matter where the System is . . . we still don't have an easy way to access it?" asked Alice, resisting the urge to ball her fists in frustration. The possible location of the mainframe of the System was an amazing clue. If Alice had access to it, it might be possible to fix everything. But based on Ethan's words, the easiest solution to the crisis was inaccessible.

"Is there any chance we could . . . I don't know, sail around the Sigmusi Colonia's navy? Or hide from them while searching? Even if we don't have a navy to work with, if it's just a single ship, maybe they won't notice us?" Alice asked.

"Trying to sail around the Sigmusi Colonia's navy would be difficult," said Ethan. "Unless they get much weaker. Though I suppose if the crisis goes on for long enough, and for some reason Illvaria is less badly hit by the collapse of the System, there might eventually be a window of opportunity. Even so, it would be risky. The Sigmusi Colonia is mainly focused on exporting raw materials to the heartland of the country. To ship all that material back to the Central Continent, and protect it from [Pirates] and the navies of other nations, the Sigmusi navy is excellent. It's arguably the best in the world." Ethan paused. "Although a few other nations could give them a run for their money, especially if they work together. But that's not relevant for this situation. If you go on the ocean using Illvaria's navy, you'll be basically unprotected, in a region controlled by a nation that practices slavery and is actively targeting you. I suppose [Kinetic Mages] *do* have a big advantage in naval warfare, and Illvaria is known for its mages . . ." Ethan rubbed his chin in thought. "I'll consider it, but at least right now I don't like our odds."

"Maybe we could convince them to help us?" asked Alice. "The collapse of the System affects everyone, and without it getting fixed, the Sigmusi Colonia is ultimately going to suffer just as much as Illvaria." Alice was disgusted by the Sigmusi Colonia, but if their help was needed to save the world, she would still do it. The world was at stake, after all.

"They would probably betray us and use it as a way to kidnap you. A near-Immortal is *always* a prime target—especially since you're so focused on research. Your self-defense skills are above average for a regular combatant, but nowhere near high enough to keep yourself safe. Furthermore, you're a bit young and . . . kindhearted," said Ethan, although it sounded like he had been about to say something else. "The Sigmusi would see you as an easy target."

Ethan's words sent a shiver of horror down her spine. The Society of Starry Eyes stalking her and waiting to strike was terrifying enough. Alice didn't need to send herself into a situation where she would be targeted and have almost no protection.

"Is there any way that we could use other nations to pressure the Sigmusi into helping us pass by their naval region?" asked Alice. "You mentioned that a few other nations could give the Sigmusi navy a run for its money. I don't know much about diplomacy, but surely other countries are also worried about the collapse of the System. If other nations with functioning navies work together to put pressure on the Sigmusi, maybe we could search the Western Continent and the ocean freely?"

Ethan paused to think about it.

"If the System's mainframe is indeed on the Western Continent, or underwater, that *might* work. I don't know how hard it would be to wrangle international support for your passage through the area. My mother, Allira, and the crown estate tend to be most involved in international diplomacy, while my father and I manage the military side of things. But I can say that to get other nations to help, we would need a good reason for them to do so. Exposing the fact that the System has a physical mainframe could be dangerous. I shudder to think what the Sigmusi, or *any* nation, would do with the System if they had unrestricted access to its control center. Even Illvaria might abuse access to the System, given enough time," said Ethan. "So far we've mostly had good rulers, but there were a few that were incompetent. They might have acted with bad intentions if my father hadn't been around to keep them in check. Who can say whether something will go wrong somewhere down the line? This is knowledge that should never be shared outside of a very small circle of people."

Alice thought about it and then sighed in agreement. Even if a nation with excellent intentions got access to the System, it would still be a ticking time bomb. What if they tried to study the System and broke something? What if they messed with the way the System designed classes and added in some sort of mandatory subservience perk that affected everyone? What if the System got tied up in some sort of internal factional dispute? Alice had no idea what someone could *do* with unrestricted access to the System, but she doubted it would end well.

In other words, it was best to keep the team of people who explored and studied the mainframe of the System small. After this incident was resolved, it would be best if they never spoke of it again. While Alice loved spreading knowledge, knowledge of how to break the enchantment that kept humanity alive on this planet wasn't something other people needed.

But that also limited her options even more.

Alice sighed in frustration.

"Is there any way at all we could get into Sigmusi territory, to start looking around?" asked Alice, hoping that Ethan had some sort of solution she hadn't thought of yet.

"Unless we declare war on the Sigmusi, then successfully conquer the country, I doubt it. I don't fancy our odds against them in a war right now. Also, wars take time."

Alice sighed.

She absently grabbed a world map and started scanning it, hoping to find something that was northwest but wasn't one of the three locations Ethan had mentioned. Maybe looking at the map would provide Alice with some sort of inspiration?

There were no good locations for the System to be in. Every single one was problematic and hard to access.

The only thing Alice got out of looking at the map was a vague guess about an alternate location for the mainframe. Alice felt that Ethan's argument about its location made sense. The Western Continent was a logical place for it to be.

However, there was one other obvious spot where the System might be located.

Far to the northwest, there was a place that was renowned for being incredibly rich in mana. It was a massive shipping hazard, and it was filled with monsters. In fact, Alice had heard about it before during her time in the Magic Academy— she just hadn't considered it important, and so she had ignored it.

"The Maelstrom," said Alice, looking at the large plot of ocean marked on the map. There were even a few small islands noted to exist in the middle of the Maelstrom—although much like the Western Continent, nobody had ever explored them. The dense mana and powerful monsters drove off any would-be [Explorers].

Ethan paused and looked at the map in front of Alice. Finally, he nodded.

"The Maelstrom would also make sense. I think the Western Continent is a better candidate for the location of the System, but the Maelstrom would be my second guess," he said.

Then Ethan sighed.

"Unfortunately, the Maelstrom is located right between the Sigmusi Colonia and the Sigmusi Imperia. Regardless of the location, we don't have enough information to make plans. We also have massive roadblocks in our way." Ethan shook his head in frustration.

"I guess we'll just have to keep doing what we've been doing, then." Alice pushed down the feeling of bitterness rising in her heart as she sighed and left.

She spent a lot of time that night thinking about how to proceed, now that the most obvious paths forward were blocked off, but couldn't think of an easy solution, even during the extra thinking time afforded to her by the {Sleep Reading} perk.

When she woke up the next morning, at breakfast, she was surprised to see Ethan was in a rather jovial mood. Before she could ask, Ethan grinned at her.

"You're lucky. Trying to find the mainframe of the System might not be as hopeless as I thought. The sixth Immortal of Illvaria returned to Metsel last night."

CHAPTER 36

When Alice had heard that she was about to meet with another of Illvaria's Immortals, she had expected to meet him at a fancy dinner or a [Noble] tea party. After all, Illvarian Immortals were wealthy and had high status in the country.

Instead, Murim had asked them to meet him in a pub. It wasn't even a fancy pub. It reeked of alcohol and grease. The few [Waiters] and [Waitresses] in the bar weren't particularly attractive, despite the fact that their class should emphasize [Charisma]. That meant they had abnormally low levels in their class. Alice checked the level of the servers and confirmed that most of them were below level forty.

The building wasn't even well lit. The walls were the color of urine. The only real compliment Alice had for the establishment was that, despite the smell and sound, all the seats looked clean. Though that was probably due to a cleaning perk rather than diligence on the part of the business.

After entering the building, Ethan raised a wooden token high enough for the [Bartender] behind the counter to see it. The [Bartender] gestured toward a staircase with a bored expression. Ethan and Alice ascended in silence, entering a private room. Alice carefully inspected her seat and the table before she sat down, just to make sure she wasn't about to sit on anything gross. Luckily, whatever cleaning perk was at work keeping the rest of the building neat had kept the chair spotless.

"Is this really where we're supposed to meet Murim?" asked Alice. Even though Ethan had said that Murim disliked formality, this was still outside of Alice's expectations.

Ethan sighed, and then nodded. "Almost certainly. The [Waitresses] match Murim's preferences quite well . . ."

"The [Waitresses]?"

"Slightly over thirty and kind of sallow-faced," said Ethan, shrugging. Alice's confusion only deepened. She wasn't sure why Ethan had mentioned the [Waitresses] to begin with.

"Murim has a thing for [Waitresses]," said Ethan. "But the problem is, his type is unconventional. You know how [Charisma] directly influences how attractive you are, right?" Alice nodded. "Well, there's also a saying that beauty is in the eye of the beholder. There are some facial features that are considered almost universally attractive. You know, symmetry, smooth skin, things like that. But there are always a few people who are attracted to very different facial features. Those people would either need to find others with high [Charisma] and similar beauty standards, or find people whose [Charisma] hasn't changed their body too much. So Murim hangs out in pubs and bars like this one, where the [Waitresses] are typically more than happy to be swept about by a highly attractive and wealthy Immortal for a few months. Then he says goodbye and leaves for several decades before returning to civilization again. He always informs them what the relationship will be like before they go anywhere, so it's not like he's tricking them." Alice felt her cheeks warm when she realized what Ethan meant.

"I don't know if it's really the perfect way to handle the stress of being in the wilderness for years on end," said Ethan thoughtfully. "But everyone's life is their own to live. And he does genuinely seem to love his lifestyle, even if I find it baffling. To each their own, I guess."

"Are the [Waitresses] the only criteria for a meeting spot?" asked Alice incredulously.

"No." Ethan chuckled. "Murim is also a massive alcoholic, and he isn't quite as conventionally wealthy as most Immortals. After all, Murim's exploration doesn't produce much that other people have a use for. The [King] still pays him a decent salary, since he's an Immortal, but frankly, the crown has no use for any of the maps Murim returns with. Nonmages would just die of mana poisoning if they tried to explore the lands he spends most of his time in. So Murim probably chose this pub because it sells large quantities of cheap liquor. With the [Endurance] of an Immortal who has a survival-oriented class, he certainly needs a lot of alcohol if he wants to get drunk."

Alice felt an oncoming headache, but pushed it down. How Murim lived his life had nothing to do with her, as long as he wasn't hurting anyone else in the process. Though she *did* wonder if this information changed how she should interact with him.

The two sat in silence. Alice started to get lost in her thoughts as the minutes ticked by. The agreed-upon meeting time came and went.

About ten minutes after the meeting was supposed to start, there was still no sign of the other Immortal.

Alice started to feel worried.

Has something happened to him? Why isn't he here yet? Did something go wrong with the class seeds in his body, causing him to lose control of himself? I haven't seen any similar signs in Ethan, but just because Ethan is avoiding most of the fallout from the collapse of the System doesn't mean every other Immortal is. Alice started to panic as she thought of bad possibilities.

Class-mana madness wasn't the only danger. Had the Society attacked him? Or a Sigmusi [Assassin]? Alice vividly recalled the fight with Emilia. Now that humans across the world were weakened and in danger, it would be the perfect opportunity for someone to take advantage of the chaos. Alice could definitely imagine the Sigmusi trying to find a way to weaken their neighbors while everyone was trying to handle the fallout from the crisis. Alice felt the anxiety start to build up, and she absently touched a few of the enchanted bracelets she had fastened to her wrist. Should they go out and look for him?

Just as Alice was entertaining thoughts about what would happen if they really fought against a hostile [Assassin] in the heart of Metsel, the door opened with a loud crash. Alice felt a wave of mixed relief and irritation break over her as she looked at the man who had entered the room.

The man, much like other Immortals, was a walking cloud of mana. He looked to be slightly lower level than Ethan. He was on the shorter side, and stood at perhaps 160 centimeters tall. He had dark black hair that looked like ink. His muscles were well defined, and every single step he took carried the [Dexterity] and grace of someone who had stats well beyond a normal human's. He had an easy, confident smile. The man was also stunningly handsome. It was nowhere near Allira's level of beauty, but he had clearly invested time and energy into his appearance.

Murim's exceptional charm was undermined by the horrid reek of alcohol clinging to every single orifice. It was so bad that it overshadowed the smell of alcohol emitted by the rest of the building. There were dark bags under the man's eyes that spoke of exhaustion, and Alice was pretty sure there was a very, very small smear of lipstick just below the man's chin. It looked like someone had tried to rub it off with their fingers but failed.

At the very least, Alice was now sure that the man hadn't been attacked in the middle of the capital. The stubborn little lipstick smear just below his chin definitely hadn't come from a fight.

As if he didn't notice the reek of booze clinging to him, he gave Ethan a wide grin when he saw him.

"Ethan! It's been a long time! How have you been?" asked the man, raising a hand in greeting.

"Murim. I've been doing well. Just teaching my newest apprentice," said Ethan. "How about you? How have your travels gone?" Ethan acted as if there was nothing unusual about the man's appearance or entrance. Despite some hesitation, Alice decided to act the same way.

"Tell me about it," said Murim, grimacing. "My last exploration turned into a total mess. Things have been getting very weird recently."

A moment later, Ethan awkwardly gestured toward Murim's neck. Alice quietly breathed a sigh of relief. The smear of lipstick was very distracting.

"Oh, did I miss a spot?" Murim asked, before wiping his neck with the hem of his sleeve. The stubborn lipstick smear disappeared. "Thanks."

"So you found another one?" Ethan asked after a few moments.

Murim nodded. "Yeah. She seemed nice, and we ended up getting along well. When I leave, would you mind keeping an eye on her for a bit? I don't want any trouble to come her way."

"I'll handle it," Ethan said with a resigned roll of his eyes. "I wish you would just clean up your own messes, though." He spoke as if this was routine for him. Maybe it *was* routine for him.

Murim shrugged. "I do my best to leave people in a good position, but it's hard. I can't stand being stuck in one place for too long."

Ethan rubbed his forehead, and for a moment, Alice wondered if even Ethan was stumped by Murim's response. Ethan sighed again. "How long were you originally planning on staying in Metsel?" he asked.

"Well, that's a good question," said Murim. "Normally I hang out for a month or two and then leave once I've had some time to relax. This time, I want to stay out of the Mana Wastes until things calm down a bit. As I mentioned earlier, things got . . . very weird down there. How about you? Speaking of finding another one, I see that you've picked up yet another apprentice."

Ethan smiled. "I have indeed! She's very promising. I think her odds are incredibly high!"

Murim shrugged. "Is that what matters? The success of the student?"

Ethan looked thoughtful. "I suppose that's part of it. Honestly, I've found that I do enjoy teaching itself . . . but I want my students to succeed. That's normal, isn't it?"

"Perhaps. But honestly, I think all of you just don't get it," said Murim. "People die sometimes. Someone dying of old age should mean that you treasure what time you have with them more. You shouldn't fear connecting with people just because they might die. Does the fact that Elder Sujia will die of old age someday cheapen the time you spent teaching her?"

Ethan shook his head. "I still cherish her as a student. But I can't stand the fact that she won't live. It's too painful to know that in just a decade or two, she'll be gone." His voice carried the stubbornness of a set of wheels, cycling through the same, well-worn rut for the hundredth time.

Murim rolled his eyes. "With that attitude, maybe in a few centuries you'll be like Doll and never leave your house. I really feel that you'd be happier if you just appreciated the *now* more. I only spend a few months with each girl, but that doesn't diminish our time spent together. We make each other happy for a while and then go our separate ways. I never forget anyone I've loved, even if we part ways right afterward. If I was as afraid of connecting with people as you, Doll, and your mother are, I would never have any beautiful memories." Murim shook his head before he sighed and looked at Alice.

"Before we go any further, I have to ask, is this meeting for business or just to talk?" asked Murim. "Not that I don't appreciate the occasional conversation, and I also enjoy debating philosophy with you. But you don't usually bring your apprentices along."

"Sadly, we have business to attend to," Ethan said. "First of all, let me formally introduce you to my newest apprentice. Her name is Alice, and she's currently sixteen."

"Nice to meet you, Alice," said Murim, giving Alice a nod. "I haven't seen any of Ethan's apprentices be so young in quite a while. Are you biologically sixteen or chronologically sixteen?"

"Both," said Alice. "I didn't really level up very much before I became a mage, but after I survived my baptism, my leveling speed skyrocketed."

"A magic enthusiast, then?" asked Murim. "Well, it's risky to undergo a baptism, but it seems to have worked out for you. As long as you can stand by your own decisions, regardless of whether you live or die, you've lived a good life. I've always admired the determination of people who undergo mana baptisms, even if it seems insane to me."

Alice decided not to reveal the fact that she had undergone her baptism entirely by accident.

"More importantly, she's also someone who has researched the current crisis in great detail," said Ethan, saving Alice from trying to figure out what to say.

"Is that so?" asked Murim. "What exactly *is* going on? I've seen how messed up the Mana Wastes have become, and I've also heard that a few people have lost their minds recently. Is all this even the same crisis? It seems more like a bunch of bad things are happening all at once for no reason." Alice almost asked how "messed up" the Mana Wastes had gotten but decided to hold off on questioning Murim until later.

"If you went to any Church of the System, you could get a full, detailed report of the most recent events concerning the System," said Ethan. "But the short answer is that I have no idea whether the oddities of the Mana Wastes and the crisis are connected."

Murim shrugged. "I'm not religious. The System exists, but the only god I worship is the green woods and the night sky. Why would I go to a church?"

"Fair," Ethan said after a moment. "Well, in any case, the current crisis is . . . complex. My apprentice can fill you in. Alice?"

Alice cleared her throat and then started introducing Murim to the collapse of the System. Since he didn't seem like the kind of person who would appreciate a long, detailed list of theories, Alice did her best to shorten the crisis down to a quick and dirty explanation.

Finally, after Alice's explanation, Murim rubbed his temples.

"So if I'm getting this right, you're basically saying that the System is a giant enchantment. Now that it broke, everyone is fucked. Is that right?"

"Essentially."

"I knew there was something funny about worshipping the System as a god," said Murim. "Back when she was alive, my ma always said I was a smarter cookie than I seemed to be." Murim grinned. "Glad to see that I can prove her right today." Then Murim frowned. "But I don't see how this relates to me. I don't have a magic seed, and at this point, I'm an Immortal. I have an achievement that makes me totally immune to mana poisoning, so I have no way to force a mana baptism. Even if I *could* undergo a mana baptism, I wouldn't. The odds of survival are too low, and I don't want to be a mage. How am I involved in this mess?"

"Well, it's like this," said Ethan. "Alice has a few theories about where the System might be. That is to say, a central mainframe of the System."

"Ah." Murim seemed to understand where the conversation was going now. "So you're saying that there is a physical location where the System might be, and you want me to locate it?"

Alice nodded. "If it's possible for you to find it, that would be really useful. I might be able to fix this mess if I have access to the mainframe of the System."

Murim seemed intrigued now. "What are the potential locations?"

"Either the Sigmusi Colonia, underwater, the Maelstrom, or the Western Continent. No matter what location it's in, it should be northwest of Illvaria. But I don't know how far to the northwest it is."

Murim burst out laughing. "You don't pick easy targets, do you?" He shook his head as if he found the entire situation hilarious. "Well, I'm up for a challenge." His grin grew wider and wider until it looked almost inhuman how far his lips stretched. "If it's the Western Continent, there's no way I can explore it. That area is too dangerous, even for me. But I can at least investigate the northwest edges of the Southern Continent and tell you what I find. How about you tell me everything you know and I'll see what I can do? I'm confident in my ability to sneak around the Sigmusi Colonia for a month or two and get away undetected."

Alice and Murim conversed for nearly an hour afterward, with Alice giving Murim every scrap of information she could about the System's mainframe and potential locations.

Afterward, Ethan and Murim discussed payment and other final details before they struck a deal.

Murim would search for the System mainframe for her.

Chapter 37

After the conversation with Murim, Alice and Ethan returned to the manor. As they walked, Alice looked over her status screen.

The [King]'s achievement had given her a rough idea where the System might be, but Alice couldn't take advantage of that information yet. Murim was her only chance to narrow down its physical location. If he failed, Alice had no idea how to get to the mainframe, so she put that train of thought aside for now.

Alice's other attempts to quell the chaos of the collapse were going better. Cecilia's [Enchanters] were successfully forming new magic seeds, and rings to filter mana for people were now fully in production. The [Enchanters] had recently even given her a proposal for expanding the group. Alice didn't think that things were moving fast enough on that front, but they were at least progressing.

Now it was time to think about what to do next.

There were still several problems to solve. Alice mana was a threat that she didn't know how to remedy. Achievements were still broken. Intelligent monster swarms were devastating smaller towns around the country. Class-mana madness wasn't being solved quickly enough to keep up with the rate at which people lost their minds. The recent actions of the Sigmusi and the Society were also worrying. Broken achievements were a minor inconvenience, although Alice did want to fix them at some point. Finally, Alice needed to figure out how to make new class seeds.

She massaged her forehead in frustration as the two rounded the corner to Ethan's manor.

What problem should she tackle next? What problems *could* she tackle? Right now, Alice had no idea how to speed up production of enchanted rings that cured class-mana madness. The biggest problem was production capacity, and Alice was more of a researcher than a proper [Enchanter]. Monster armies . . . really weren't a problem Alice understood how to tackle, either. That would have to be something she left to Ethan and Illvaria's other military leaders. Similarly, Alice wasn't going to be capable of defending herself against the Society or the Sigmusi anytime soon.

While she wanted to learn how to defend herself eventually, she was stuck relying on Ethan and her [Guards] for now.

After much thought, Alice decided to focus on Alice mana. Unfortunately, she wasn't sure how to handle that problem. Realistically, she needed to be level eighty-five to look at Alice mana. That was when she would be able to fuse {Expanding Comprehension} and {Intuitive Magic Modeling} to get a better analysis perk. That meant Alice needed to get four levels in [Explorer of Magic].

How was she supposed to get four more levels in [Explorer of Magic]?

Just a few days ago, she had been thinking about what mana types *must* be part of System mana. She had made a list of magic types she could create. She hadn't used three of her four magic seed creations for the month yet, because Alice had been hoping for a bigger hint about what she needed next. The moment Alice used the first magic seed combination, she had felt the perk start ticking toward its cooldown, so she hadn't felt a need to make a hasty decision for the final choices yet. Unfortunately, the meeting with the [King], as well as her discussion with Ethan, hadn't really shed any light on what kinds of mana she needed next.

Still, Alice needed levels. Adding new types of mana to her compound magic seed would probably help with that, since it would open up new experiments.

What did she need? Alice was pretty sure pure mana, organic mana, meaning mana, and possibly some sort of core mana were parts of the System. Alice had no idea what else she was missing, so she decided to stick with what she knew she needed first.

First, Alice decided to focus on a meaning mana seed. Alice spent several minutes running various questions through {Safety Analysis} before she got started.

The process for creating a meaning mana magic seed was unusual. Alice didn't perfectly understand the type of mana she was trying to create, which made it much harder than typical seed creation.

It ended up taking several minutes of effort, and once it was built, Alice felt that she might have botched the construction. That part of her compound magic seed started leaking horrendous amounts of mana the moment she used it.

Still, even though it wasn't perfect, it wasn't a safety hazard. Even though Alice was tempted to destroy that fragment of her compound seed, after thinking it over, she decided to leave it. She had very limited uses of her seed-creation perk and {Broken Seed}, and she couldn't waste either.

Alice spent a few more seconds going over the changes in her System seed, trying to see if anything felt different than before. She distinctly remembered that after she had created a math magic seed, she had felt like her integrated magic seed had gained something . . . more. Something crucial to what the System was.

This time, she didn't get the same sensation.

Alice frowned.

She had been hoping for that sensation to return, because it might have given her more hints about what it was. Unfortunately, her hope ended up fruitless.

Alice sighed and decided to try again with another magic seed once she tested out her new mana type. If at first she didn't succeed, she just needed to keep trying. She used some of her newly made meaning mana, along with her display mana, to look at one of her perks, and see if the translation of the System message changed. First, she checked the regular translation for the perk.

<table>
<tr><td>

Perk Naaaame: Delve_Memories
Perk costs: Delve Into the Arcane + Improved Memory
Perk_Synergy detected: Sleep Reading

</td></tr>
<tr><td>

Vastly improved understanding while using remembering. Can level, analyze, and improve magic better.
While {Sleep Reading}, can use objects you remember. Leveling speed improved by Get_Number while sleep reading. Experiments and enchantments very accurate while sleep.

</td></tr>
</table>

The description for {Delve_Memories} looked like a mess. It had been a bit hard to figure out what the perk did before she used it.

With the addition of meaning mana, the perk looked a lot like System messages from before the collapse.

<table>
<tr><td>

Memory Experimentation (Tier 2 perk, level 60 Scholar of Magic)
Perk costs: Delve Into the Arcane + Improved Memory sacrificed to create this perk.
Perk synergizes with {Sleep Reading}

</td></tr>
<tr><td>

Your ability to understand things is drastically improved if you are analyzing a memory. Your magic stat and all associated skills improve 20% faster.
While {Sleep Reading}, you can experiment with objects that you remember the existence of and which you have been in contact with during the last twenty-four hours. (Contact can take place either physically or through any of your perks/magic.) Any experiments you conduct while using {Sleep Reading} will obtain accurate results, as if they were real objects. You can experiment with mana and objects while {Sleep Reading} freely (especially for enchanting purposes).
Warning: You cannot subject items to experiments you are incapable of recreating in the real world. For example, if you want to see what would happen if you threw an item into a black hole, you must have the item and have a way of throwing said item into a black hole in real life.

</td></tr>
</table>

Alice grinned.

Ever since the System had collapsed, every System message that Alice had seen had been in Illvarian. That was fine—Alice was now just as fluent in Illvarian as a native speaker. Still, seeing the System work the way it originally did was comforting.

Still, Alice was disappointed that she hadn't gotten any clues about the weird sensation she had felt when creating math mana. She spent a few minutes filtering [Explorer of Magic] mana but didn't get a level out of it. Based on how much mana it had taken to reach level eighty-one, Alice guessed that she had gotten about a quarter of a level from creating her magic seed. There was a lot of work left to be done.

The next magic seed she decided to create was pure mana. Since the System was so involved in mana filtration, pure mana must be pretty important. Not to mention, Alice had a lot of experience utilizing pure mana. Some of her earliest enchantments had been made using it. It would be easy to create another copy and integrate it into her compound seed.

Alice got started. A minute later, she had another pure magic seed, which fused into her compound seed a few seconds later. Alice grinned.

Just like when she had created and integrated her math magic seed, Alice felt as if the System seed in her body had gained something *more*. Something integral to its existence.

This time, Alice got a clearer idea of what exactly had changed.

The System seed in her body was more *communicative* than before.

The System did a lot of different things—and most of those things involved multiple kinds of mana. For example, in the process of helping someone survive a mana baptism, the System needed to help filter mana in the patient's surroundings, heal the disconnected nerves and chunks of flesh, and help the person put their newly forming mage core into the correct spot. That was just the surface of what the System did.

How did the System know where each organ was supposed to go? How did it know what type of mana the patient needed? How did the System even know "hey, there's a person undergoing a mana baptism right here"?

Alice now had a rough idea.

Pure mana, math mana, and a few other types of mana acted as the core of System mana. They did something that other parts of the System didn't handle— they input information into the System. Pure mana and math mana had other functions, but one of the most critical parts of the System was that these types of mana acted as "eyes" for the System. Pure mana was able to sense mana fluctuations around the world, and tell the System, "Hey, this person is forming a [Farmer] seed." Without pure mana to feed this information to the System, it would have no way of detecting what kind of class mana someone had in their body, and thus no way of figuring out what the follow-up steps were.

Math mana was responsible for backing up this information, serving as a kind of double-check for various things the System needed to be aware of. For example, [Farmer] magic seeds were always located next to people's hearts. Math mana seemed to be responsible for figuring out "where is the patient's heart?" and relaying that information to the System. It also seemed to evaluate any information given by pure mana. For example, if only one one-thousandth of a Marium of [Farmer] mana was present in someone's body, it obviously didn't make sense to build a [Farmer] magic seed for them. Math mana was responsible for figuring out when something was too small to bother dealing with.

Alice was probably missing a lot of information, but that was what she had managed to glean from the faint feeling of completion in her System magic seed. It gave her a much better idea of how to proceed.

As it turned out, one of Alice's earlier assumptions was correct. She had mostly been speculating earlier, but when she had formed her first magic seed, she had assumed that there was some sort of core type of mana that helped the System actually work. She just hadn't realized that there wasn't *one* type of core mana— instead, several different types of mana worked together as a core framework for the System.

It was a clever solution to the problem of getting nonsapient mana to do things carefully and effectively.

Alice checked her experience again and was sad to see that she *still* hadn't gotten to level eighty-two in [Explorer of Magic] yet. She was probably close, but apparently her actions weren't enough to push her over the edge.

She had one more magic seed left to build.

Alice spent several minutes thinking about whether she wanted to stick to her original plan or try something else . . .

I could also make an organic magic seed and then feed it to the System seed . . . but I'm not sure if that's the best option. There must *be something more useful I can make. Organic magic being integrated into my System seed would probably help me make mana flesh, among other things . . . but right now, stats seem to be working well enough, even without the input of the System. Best to put out the immediate fires and focus on actual problems.*

Alice started dreaming up the most outlandish ideas she could think of involving System mana, just to see if she found any new mana types that would be helpful and that she needed.

Artificial intelligence mana was tossed out by {Safety Analysis} immediately. Alice was pretty sure it wasn't part of System mana, but it had seemed worth checking. Programming mana didn't work, either, at least when Alice conceptualized it as a way to rewrite reality entirely using willpower. Thinking mana was also ruled out by her perk. After going through a few dozen variations on "intelligence" or "programming," Alice finally found something useful.

Communication mana.

During her brainstorming session, Alice had started to wonder what let math mana give information to pure mana. There must be *something* that allowed math mana to relay its findings to other parts of the System. Right now, her magic seed was trying to communicate with itself, but it felt like the communication was very slow and clumsy. Having communication mana act as a dedicated messenger seemed like it would help the seed work better. {Safety Analysis} gave her the green light when she thought about integrating it into her System seed, so Alice decided to go for it.

Alice confirmed that this was a better idea than her original plan, then formed her final magic seed for the month. After several minutes of hard work, she created a communication mana magic seed. Just like Alice had expected, her System seed felt *much* more complete now. The previously slow and clumsy communication between math mana and pure mana started to feel very clean and efficient.

She decided to run a new test. She extended a mana tendril outward before placing it against a big copper coin she had found in a corner of the hallway and funneled some System mana through her tendril.

A few moments later, she noticed that the different kinds of mana in her tendril were all interacting with each other. The math mana in her magic seed was giving Alice random numbers, while the display mana and meaning mana translated those numbers into useful information.

Alice was bombarded by a wave of information.

Suddenly, Alice had a very accurate understanding of the mana inside the copper coin. Alice still had {Advanced Mana Measurement} to tell her the number of Mariums of mana in a given object or area. But now she had far more detailed information than ever before. She knew exactly how the mana distribution in the copper coin looked. She could tell that near the center of the coin, the mana was slightly more concentrated. Alice watched in fascination as mana swirled inside the coin. She was intimately aware of where each fraction of a Marium of mana was and could even see the concentration of mana in the coin change by minute fractions of a Marium each second.

Her math mana worked with her pure mana to analyze and measure every single Marium of mana in her view. Her communication mana fed that information to her display mana and meaning mana. Those two kinds of mana then worked together to create a packet of information and sent it to Alice's brain. Alice's brain unpacked that information and interpreted it. It was a coherent set of systems layered on top of each other to create accurate information within a fraction of a second. It happened without any input from perks or external measuring devices. They weren't needed for System mana to operate.

Alice smiled. With her test complete, Alice shut off the mana tendril as a massive headache formed behind her eyes.

Unlike the mainframe of the System, Alice had a regular human brain. She had gained a lot of points in [Intelligence] since coming to this world, and so she could process way more information per second than a normal human being should be able to—but there was still a limit.

The amount of information her new magic seed was feeding her was far greater than what her brain was able to process. Alice suspected that if she didn't shut the magic seed off, her head might explode.

I need to create some sort of filter for information, thought Alice, grimacing as she rubbed her forehead. Sadly, she hadn't thought about this when creating her filtration magic seed, so that seed was entirely concentrated on filtering mana. Perhaps she needed an *information filtration* magic seed? Or something like that? Something to think about next month.

After her headache got better, Alice checked her levels.

You have leveled up!
Explorer of Magic : 81→83

She had been very close to level eighty-two before she started her experiment, but finally figuring out how the core of System mana worked had clearly been worth quite a bit of experience. She went to sleep satisfied with her progress.

CHAPTER 38

During the time she spent in her mental library while asleep, Alice had an idea. The biggest bottleneck on enchantment production was the number of [Enchanters]. Alice used {Broken Seed} to allow [Enchanters] to get new magic seeds safely. However, she could only use the perk once every four days. She had originally hoped to solve this problem with {System's Mana} but had deemed the endeavor to be unlikely to succeed in a reasonable time frame. The amount of effort and experience needed to make her idea a reality was far too high in comparison to her abilities and learning speed, and time was ticking away as more and more fell to class-mana madness. For this reason, she had abandoned the perk and used it as fodder for a combination.

But Alice realized that she might have a different way to approach this problem. Creating System enchantments via perk was difficult for her, since she was very unused to creating them. That didn't mean she couldn't make System enchantments, though. After all, if the System could do something, that implied it was possible to do the exact same thing without the System—it was just more difficult.

If that was the case, what if Alice tried to make a System enchantment without any relevant perks?

Alice doubted her idea would work. But trying to succeed might net her a few levels in [Explorer of Magic]. If she *did* succeed, it would be a huge boost to enchantment production, and even failure would get her some benefits.

She was much less familiar with System enchantments than with normal enchantments, so she spent several minutes reviewing her memories of her first System enchantment. She hadn't made extensive use of {Science's Mana} before she had combined it with {Seeds of Ambition} to create {System's Ambition}, but she had still gotten a lesson from Tallie the [Tailor] to understand System enchantments. She remembered that System enchantments relied a lot on doing something related to a certain idea while using the perk. So she started thinking about what it meant to destroy a magic seed without harming the wearer. She also summoned a few dream copies of enchanting materials and then used mana to destroy them over and over again. In the real world, this would be absurdly wasteful—but since Alice was in her dream library, she didn't care about wasting mana or materials. Nothing was real here anyway.

Then Alice spent several hours staring at an iron ring and trying to replicate what her perk had done.

Unsurprisingly, Alice's first attempts were disastrous. System enchantments were *complicated*. They were far more difficult to create than regular enchantments.

A System enchantment basically had a bunch of mana inside it that operated according to similar rules to the System seeds. Lots of different kinds of mana worked together to create one absurdly complicated effect. To replicate that, Alice would need to somehow make an ordinary material accept a huge influx of mana while also making those different types of mana communicate with each other.

Alice was beginning to understand why having a bunch of different mana types fused together into one magic seed was important. With the right perks or materials, it was far simpler to combine multiple types of mana into one instruction slot in an enchanting material. It was far from perfect, but she could at least somewhat understand what was going on behind the scenes. Sadly, Alice's System seed wasn't developed enough yet. She was still missing several mana types, so she had no way of replicating the effects of System mana in a ring.

This didn't disappoint Alice very much, since she hadn't really expected to succeed. However, she still wanted to get as many [Explorer of Magic] levels as possible. So Alice started getting creative.

She couldn't replicate what the System was doing, but it was possible to approach things from a completely different angle. She didn't need to perfectly copy the System, anyway. She just needed to get a solution that worked and didn't harm the user.

Alice turned toward artifacts next. As far as she knew, an artifact was essentially a massive enchantment that had artificial magic seeds stapled into it. Maybe there was a way to make an artificial magic seed replicate the effects of her [Explorer of Magic] class? Her next several attempts failed miserably, but at the very least, Alice had a new idea to try out when she woke up. Sadly, her experiments during her dreams didn't get her any new levels, which had been her original goal, but she had accumulated quite a bit more [Explorer of Magic] mana. She was closer to level eighty-five, at least.

Once she finished breakfast, Alice rushed to Ethan's office to ask whether it was possible to see Illvaria's canal-creating artifact again. Considering Alice's new position, it was very easy to get permission from the palace. Later that day, Alice and Ethan found themselves once again sitting in front of the artifact that controlled Illvaria's southern canal system.

The first thing Alice studied was the nature of the artifact. When Alice had first observed the artifact that controlled the rivers of southern Illvaria, she had noticed that it seemed to work via a set of artificial magic seeds. The main one was related to water, and the other one was related to dirt. Finally, several tendrils extended out of the room and into the distance to relay mana between the artifact and the canals themselves. Alice also noticed that the artificial magic seeds the artifact relied on to function somewhat resembled class seeds. Alice grinned. Hopefully, that meant she was heading in the right direction.

The System had started collapsing while she was in the middle of studying the artifact the last time she was here, so she had been somewhat panicked. This time she didn't have that problem, making it easier to focus and learn.

Alice watched as the artifact worked. Every few seconds, a pulse of System mana traveled through one of the tendrils toward the large metal pillar at the core of the artifact. Then the metal pillar sent a pulse of mana back into the distance through one of the massive mana tendrils.

Now that she had managed to create a half-baked System seed, she could see how some parts of the System mana were feeding information to the artifact. Math mana, pure mana, and a few unknown types of mana fed packets of data to the core of the artifact. They seemed to be delivering information about things like the location of each canal, the soil near it, and a bunch of geological information that Alice couldn't interpret.

The artifact did far more than she first thought. It didn't just maintain the shapes of the canals in southern Illvaria. It somehow monitored the soil composition of the entire region, then used the canal system to restock nutrients when they were depleted. It was an all-in-one farm-management enchantment that covered the entire southern half of the country.

Still, even though Alice was glad that she could understand more about how the System tendrils worked, she was struggling to figure out how she would create an artificial magic seed. This would be needed to create an artifact. Besides, Alice was very interested in artificial magic seeds for other reasons besides her half-baked attempt to farm a few [Explorer of Magic] levels. The System clearly had some way of creating magic seeds for people when they gained a class. Alice might get a better understanding of the System if she tried to create artificial magic seeds as well.

After ten more minutes of trying and failing to learn anything new, Alice gave up. She turned to her side. If she couldn't recreate an artifact on her own, the easiest way to fix things was just to ask the creator of the artifact.

"Ethan, who created this artifact?" she asked.

"It was created by Demor, an [Enchanter] from one of the other Shil Confederacy member nations called Morendia," said Ethan. "Morendia is one of the medium-strength nations that Illvaria is on decent terms with. After all, the Shil Confederacy might work together against outside threats, but most nations in the confederacy are also perfectly happy to invade their neighbors if given the opportunity. This creates a rather chaotic web of smaller alliances that the member states take part in, but I digress. The point is, at the time this artifact was created, Illvaria and Morendia were allied, and the Illvarian [King] of the time was rather invested in the creation of magic artifacts that could guarantee the prosperity of Illvaria for future generations. Since the South was so important economically, but so difficult to keep fed, this artifact was created. To accomplish this, he paid Demor a good deal of money," said Ethan.

"Is it possible to contact Demor and ask him a bit about the theory behind artifacts?" asked Alice. "I'm trying to see if there's a way to give other people access to my {Broken Seed} perk. I don't think it'll work, but I also need information about artificial magic seeds for other reasons. Specifically, I need to figure out how to make class seeds. Learning more about artifacts might help me."

Ethan thought for a few seconds before he nodded. "It's probably possible. The alliance between Illvaria and Morendia isn't as strong as it used to be, but our nations are still on good terms. Illvaria and Morendia are also geographically distant from each other, so they don't have any territory that both nations dispute the ownership of. They are far away, but close enough that they can still work together during wars."

Alice nodded. "So we can invite Demor over here for a few lessons?"

Ethan frowned.

"Well . . . that might be difficult. You see, the collapse of the System is almost certainly being felt by every nation on the planet right now. Nations that are weaker are more likely to turtle up and hide in their territory . . . which makes it more likely that [Enchanters] and other non-combat-oriented Immortals won't leave their country for any reason. At least, I suspect that's what will happen if we ask him to come here."

Alice grimaced. "Is there no other way?"

"How important is this to you?"

"Very."

Ethan stroked his chin in thought. "I'll send a few letters by the fastest [Messengers] we have available, but . . . how do you feel about traveling to another country?"

CHAPTER 39

After four days of riding, Alice was convinced that the smell of horse had seeped into her very bones. At least the riding lesson from Elder Sujia, as well as her high [Endurance], had kept her from suffering the muscle cramps and soreness she had experienced last time.

Of course, Alice's natural [Endurance] wasn't quite high enough to accomplish this. Before leaving Metsel, Ethan had gone to borrow a piece of armor from Doll, since Doll generally didn't see people who weren't Immortals. Not even if she was making equipment for them.

A day after Ethan had left to place an order, he returned with a full suit of metal armor. The armor's torso *almost* looked like a breastplate, but there were distinct differences. For one, it looked like it was some sort of hybrid between a long-sleeved shirt and actual armor—which confused Alice quite a bit. She didn't know much about armor, but she was pretty sure this wasn't what it was supposed to look like. Inside of the shirt, there were also a bunch of complicated-looking straps and latches. Alice had no idea how to put it on. It was also swimming in System mana, making Alice wonder just how many System enchantments Doll had stuffed into the metal.

When she gave the shirt a baffled look, Ethan had grinned.

"Don't worry," Ethan had said. "It's one of her better works in the last few decades. Put it on."

When Alice had touched the armor, she realized that her concern about how all the latches and straps worked was irrelevant. The moment she touched it, the suit of armor started rippling, almost as if she had touched a pool of water. Then it had swarmed across her body and all the straps and latches had just . . . clicked into place.

A few moments later, Alice saw System mana spread throughout her body. Then she started feeling more *solid*. Almost as if her skin had been rebuilt out of iron.

"Ethan . . . how much [Endurance] did I just get?" asked Alice.

"A hundred points," said Ethan, causing Alice to blink in shock. She had heard that Doll was Illvaria's best craftsman, since she was an Immortal [Blacksmith] and [Tailor]. But one hundred points from a shirt was insane. "It also gives you the {Resilient Body} perk, which makes your skin harder to bruise, cut, or pierce. In most cases it's similar to a 10 percent increase to your [Endurance] stat—but it's not entirely the same. It doesn't provide the same temperature and disease resistance that raw endurance does, and it also won't help against things like lightning or fire. Electromagnetic mages aren't exactly common, but they do still sometimes make their way onto battlefields."

Alice had looked at the armor, opened her mouth, and then closed it.

One hundred points of [Endurance] from a suit of enchanted armor was way more than she had expected. The extra perk on top of the extra hundred stat points was even more ludicrous. While it didn't quite double Alice's [Endurance] stat . . . it got pretty close. After the gradual improvements in Alice's stats due to training and hard work accumulating over time, her [Endurance] was currently sitting at 138, before factoring in stat effectiveness. With her new armor, Alice had 238 [Endurance].

Of course, that wasn't the only precaution Ethan had taken this time. He had done away with most of the entourage of [Guards] that had followed them around last time. According to him, they were useful in a fight—but they also forced the group to move slowly. Instead, when the group had prepared to leave Metsel, Allira, Immortal of Song and Shadow, joined them.

Alice hadn't seen Allira since her time in Cyra—but she vividly remembered how she'd decimated a pack of vinebears with her voice.

The final member of their group was Cecilia. She had extensively tested the best of her [Enchanters] and deemed them able to manage the newly recruited [Enchanters] for the time the journey was expected to take. Of course, the [Enchanters] wouldn't have any way to utilize {Broken Seed}, meaning they wouldn't be forming any new magic seeds. However, at the very least, they could produce some rings for the use of the country and select new perks. The [Enchanters] they had trained so far would keep getting more efficient over time, even if their numbers wouldn't grow much.

When Cecilia and Alice had seen Allira, she had seemed rather surprised to see them as well.

"Your name was Alice, right? And you were Cecilia?" Allira asked upon seeing the two of them. "Well, it's a small world. Didn't think I'd see the two of you again so soon."

After Allira had joined the group, they'd started traveling east.

For four days, the group had traveled on horseback. Ethan and Allira had taken care of night watch, which was the only time the group stopped to rest. Cecilia looked like she wanted to flop over and die, and Alice sympathized with that feeling. Even though her abnormally high [Endurance] kept her physical exhaustion low, she was still mentally drained after fourteen hours in the saddle each day.

"I see the border fort up ahead," said Ethan, breaking Alice out of her rumination on the past four days. Alice spent a few seconds trying to jolt herself back into awareness of the present before she looked up.

Ahead of the group, she saw a large fort made of wood and stone. System mana crackled in its walls and towers, and several hundred troops manned the walls. All of them were dressed in well-polished metal armor—although Alice noted that only some of the armor had System enchantments on it. Just outside the fort, the [Soldiers] had dug several rows of ditches, with a few narrow wooden bridges spanning them. The bridges looked like they could easily be destroyed in a pinch, if needed.

"Polished armor," said Allira before snorting softly. "They must have a lot of free time if they're polishing their armor."

Ethan chuckled softly but didn't say anything else.

"Are the eastern forts of Illvaria not well-liked?" asked Alice.

Ethan snorted. "None of the other member states of the Shil Confederacy are likely to invade Illvaria. Our immediate neighbors wouldn't mind us being humbled a bit, but we act as the front lines between the Shil Confederacy and the Sigmusi. Nobody wants our military weakened enough for the Sigmusi to invade, and so our eastern borders are safe. Since that's the case, the eastern forts have become a place to stick [Soldiers] who have problems. The people here might lack discipline, or they might level up slowly or have personality issues that aren't severe enough for actual punishment but disqualify them from the battlefield. Or maybe their [Commander] wants them to go learn a few life lessons before returning to the front lines." Ethan shrugged. "Either way, don't expect much from this fort. There isn't much substance to the troops here."

Alice felt thoughtful after hearing Ethan's words. It was one of the first times that Ethan had spoken poorly of some members of Illvaria's military.

As the group approached the border of Illvaria, there was a stir as some of the soldiers shifted around. Alice noted, with some amusement, that it looked like there were still [Soldiers] in the fort. They were doing their best to . . . polish their armor? It was hard to tell, since Alice was relying on her mana senses, but that was what it looked like.

She also confirmed Ethan's words as she started to get a better look at the [Soldiers]. The highest-level [Soldiers] she saw were only level forty-five, and the majority were only level thirty or thirty-five. Most military units that she heard of in the north had a core of level-fifty [Soldiers], backed by some elites around level seventy or eighty. The [Soldiers] of this fort were severely underleveled.

A few moments later, Alice saw a man rush toward one of the towers. She realized that he was the [Commander] of the fort, based on the rank insignia on his shoulder. He had enchanted gear, but he was only level fifty.

Despite Ethan's derisive words earlier, he gave the man a brief nod before speaking.

"Hail! Have the replacement horses been prepared? Ours are about to drop," Ethan said, giving the group's current rides a few dubious looks. The four days of travel had been even harder on the mounts than their riders.

"They are ready for your use, Honored Immortals," said the [Commander]. "Would you like to tour the fort and rest awhile?"

"That won't be necessary. We need to keep moving," said Ethan. The [Commander] hesitated for a moment, as if disappointed, before he gestured to the side of the fort. There, another group of horses was ready for them.

"Then have a safe journey, Honored Immortals," said the [Commander]. After a [Stable Hand] led their old horses into the stables and helped get the new horses saddled up, the group kept moving. As the group rode beyond the fort, Alice got her first glimpse of her second nation in this world, and one of the member-nations of the Shil Confederacy. Sendria was the country just east of Illvaria, and according to Ethan, it was below average in terms of military strength for a Confederacy member. She was surprised by the stark contrast between Illvarian and Sendrian lands. She hadn't been expecting the terrain to change much, since that was how geography worked on Earth. Instead, the difference was highly visible. Illvaria's lands weren't particularly poor or barren, but they weren't exceptionally fertile, either. In contrast, Sendria was a carpet of greenery. There was a certain unkemptness to the plants, as if they hadn't been cared for or managed recently.

"Why is the land here so different?" asked Cecilia. Alice was relieved to know that she wasn't the only confused one.

"There are a lot of differences here," said Ethan. "First of all, perks. A [King]'s perks often influence themselves at lower levels, and even at the middle levels. They might boost a [King]'s intellect, or wit, or help them stay aware of their surroundings. A [King] might even end up with a lot of social skills to help manage the [Nobles] of the country. But at higher levels, the influence of a high-level [King] becomes more obvious. A high-level [King] can do things like {Search the Kingdom for Talent}, which allows them to find people with great potential or skill and teaches them how to best entice them to join the court. Sendria had a [Teacher] who nearly hit Immortality a few generations ago. Although the [Teacher] fell short and died of old age, he left behind a legacy of other high-level [Teachers]. Those [Teachers] train each new generation of [Teachers] as well as the other people in the kingdom, creating a positive feedback loop for the average level of the country.

"The abnormal soil fertility is the influence of [Farmers] who are, on average, a few levels higher than in Illvaria. When an entire group of people has a notably higher average level, the effect becomes very obvious." Ethan frowned. "Although the unkemptness of the land is odd. I wonder why the [Soldiers] at the fort didn't report this. They can *see* this from the fort, so it's not like they are unable to see what's happening here." Ethan grimaced and then looked at the [Soldiers] they had left behind again. He didn't say anything else.

"Is Sendria ruled by an Immortal [King]?" Alice asked. She remembered Ethan mentioning that many powerful nations had Immortal rulers.

"The country is ruled by [Queen] Cendaria, an Immortal who is two and a half centuries old." Ethan frowned. "She is not on the best of terms with Illvaria. She also likes to rub in the fact that a little country like hers has an Immortal [Queen], while Illvaria does not have an Immortal ruler. Of course, she's also the *only* Immortal in her country, while Illvaria has six Immortals."

"Will she make problems for us?" asked Alice. Alice had already been on the receiving end of multiple assassination or kidnapping attempts, and she wasn't eager to face more.

Ethan shook his head. "I wouldn't have traveled through her territory if I thought she was going to be a problem. While Cendaria isn't on the best terms with Illvaria, she honors oaths and treaties. She has some sort of perk that only works if she upholds bargains. It was probably the result of combining {Honorable Treaty} with some other perk at level seventy-five. Either way, she doesn't break agreements easily. Perks with a drawback tend to have bigger upsides, and {Honorable Treaty} is very restrictive, even if it's also incredibly powerful. While she and Illvaria have their disagreements, she is still a member of the Shil Confederacy. When I sent a [Messenger] asking her for passage, she agreed and guaranteed our safety within her lands. I had a few [Scholars] comb the exact wording of the message, just to make sure there weren't any hidden traps. We should be fine here."

Alice felt relieved at Ethan's words. It wasn't an absolute guarantee of her safety, but it was impossible to achieve absolute safety even in the best of times. With the intelligent and strengthened monster hordes running around, and the aftershocks of the System's collapse, a perk-backed guarantee of safety was good enough.

"Let's hurry up," said Ethan. "I don't like the way these lands look, and we still have two more countries to pass through." Ethan paused. "Well . . . three. But one of them is basically only a country by technicality." Alice wondered what Ethan meant but decided to ask when it was actually relevant. Instead, the four continued moving through the overly green countryside.

Alice noticed, as the group kept traveling onward, that there weren't any [Farmers] tending the fields. Many of the regions they passed through showed the same signs of recent neglect that they had seen earlier, and a few had signs of battle. A few villages even looked like they had been razed to the ground, while others showed signs of the villagers packing up and leaving in a hurry.

Ethan and Allira grimaced as they passed the fourth abandoned village in a row.

"The monster hordes are hitting Sendria a lot harder than they hit Illvaria," said Allira after looking at the messed-up houses and bloodstains. "I'm surprised that Cendaria has let it get this bad."

Ethan nodded. "I knew that Sendria's military was weaker than Illvaria's, but the difference shouldn't be this significant. Odd."

Alice grimaced.

She might have been more sheltered from the monster hordes than she had thought. She had assumed that Illvaria had the problem under control and figured other countries were also managing. But the abandoned and destroyed villages they had encountered painted a different picture.

It only took Alice a few minutes to realize why. The monster hordes were bad enough on their own. Coupled with most of the citizens gradually losing their minds, and all the other cascading problems caused by the collapse of the System, perhaps the monsters were more unmanageable than she had thought. Alice's influence on the situation in Illvaria might have been even more significant than she realized.

"Let's hope the same thing doesn't happen to Illvaria," Allira said.

Then the group continued traveling onward. Two hours later, they came upon something Alice had been half dreading and half expecting.

"I see a monster horde," said Allira. "Around two hundred. Maybe two fifty."

"What kind?" asked Ethan.

"Glimmerspren," said Allira. "I don't see any villagers left in the area. We can take the horde, even if some have a few extra perks. Glimmerspren have no way to shut off their sense of hearing, so I have a great matchup against them."

It took Alice a few seconds, but she remembered the term *Glimmerspren*. It was one of the monsters she had learned about during her monster biology class. Glimmerspren were creatures that faintly resembled crows but had the rather unique trait of folding in and out of sight based on light level. In dim light, they were easy to spot, but in full light or darkness, they were almost impossible to see. They had the ability to fire metallic feathers at targets with fairly high accuracy.

"Glimmerspren . . ." said Ethan thoughtfully before he turned toward Alice. "Normally, I would take this as an opportunity for you to train a bit before stepping in. You'll need to be able to defend yourself eventually, and we won't lose that much time if you fight for half an hour or so before we move on. But with times being what they are, I'll leave the choice up to you. What do you think?"

Alice thought about it. Two hundred and fifty monsters was more than she could handle, but with two Immortals behind her, she would be safe. This might also help her build up a few levels for when an actual emergency happened. Besides, Alice was full on basically all her mana types, and most of her classes required mana expenditure to grow. Maybe creative magic use during a fight would push her closer to level eighty-five in [Explorer of Magic]?

"How about I try what I can, and then you step in once I start getting overwhelmed?" asked Alice, trying not to grimace. She couldn't believe that she was heading *toward* a fight.

Ethan's shoulders relaxed, as if he had been worried Alice would say no. "I'm glad you're taking the chance to improve," he said. Alice realized she had walked straight into another one of Ethan's training scenarios. Still, she got off her horse and stepped toward the monster horde that had invaded the village.

Chapter 40

As Alice approached the nearest monsters, she felt her heart hammer in her chest. However, her mind became calm. She needed a few levels in [Explorer of Magic]. For that to happen, Alice needed to use magic creatively during the fight.

Glimmerspren were the ideal monster for Alice to do some experimentation midfight. Their primary weapons were their metallic feathers, which kinetic magic could easily handle. The only other advantage glimmerspren had was the fact that they were hard to spot. This didn't pose a problem for her, since Alice could see mana. In other words, this was a fight she should never lose unless she screwed up. She could afford to take some risks here, as long as she didn't try anything too risky.

Alice thought for several seconds. She had always wondered how the System actually built class seeds, and unlike with humans, Alice had no qualms about using monsters as test subjects, which made them ideal for running some risky experiments on. The tests might not be perfectly analogous to building class seeds in humans—but it might give her an idea where to start, at least.

Even if the data Alice got wasn't very useful, she would still probably get a few levels in [Explorer of Magic] from it. After all, it was an interesting experiment that would teach Alice more about mana.

Alice started thinking about what class seeds were. The System constantly helped people form class seeds, so it was obviously possible to assist another creature in forming a class seed—she just needed to figure out the right method.

Alice took a few stones and fired them into the air with kinetic magic. It didn't take her long to beat a few glimmerspren out of the sky. Alice spent a few seconds verifying that the creatures were unable to hurt her before ducking under a spray of metal feathers. Alice snorted and ripped the wings off the glimmerspren that had nearly forced an activation of {Adrenaline Rush}. Then Alice realized there was no reason to leave *any* of the glimmerspren with their wings intact, so she destroyed all their wings before dragging the monsters toward her.

Then Alice spent a few seconds examining the biology of one of the glimmer-spren. How was she supposed to force a creature to develop a class seed? Alice shrugged and decided to try the simplest way. She doubted it would work, but she might learn something from the experiment failing.

She started focusing on what kinetic energy *was*, almost as if she were trying to form a kinetic magic seed. Then she took a huge amount of kinetic energy and crammed it into the monster's body.

The monster core in the glimmerspren's body drank up the mana greedily. Alice frowned. The monster's core would be more of a problem than she thought. Humans didn't have any organ analogous to monster cores, so the monster core would massively skew her test results.

Alice sighed. She had already known these tests would be dubious, but the obstacles were even more frustrating than she'd expected. She tried again. This time she also used her pure mana seed to block off her mana from the monster's core. The monster's flesh and mana pushed back against Alice's as it tried to fight off her intrusion. Unfortunately for the monster, Alice had far more mana than it did. She bulldozed the monster's mana resistance with brute force. In moments, she had completely cut off the flow of mana to the monster's core.

The monster started spasming, much like how a fish would react after being dragged out of water. As Alice watched the monster struggle, she realized she was going about this the wrong way. Monsters died when their flow of mana was cut off, and if she continued this way, Alice would definitely kill this creature. She had thought most monsters took around ten minutes to die—but she didn't think the glimmerspren in front of her would last that long. She hesitated before she decided to keep pushing forward. She stuffed more and more kinetic mana into the creature's heart while preventing its monster core from absorbing any of her mana. Without the monster core's interference, the kinetic mana started to rampage throughout the monster's body. The monster's blood vessels and internal organs quickly started to tear themselves to pieces, and then the creature's body imploded.

Alice stared at the monster mash she had created. That was *not* what she had expected to happen. She started wondering if she would learn anything at all from this experiment. The difference between humans and monsters was just too significant. The unique facets of monster biology were ruining her experiments.

She sighed and dragged over the second monster. She just wanted a level in [Explorer of Magic]. Surely this line of experiments could at least get her that much. She still needed to get a closer look at the mana gem inside her brain, and that wasn't going to happen until level eighty-five.

Before Alice started on her second test subject, she spent a few moments going over what she had learned. Once she cut off the mana core, it seemed like monsters lost any ability to regulate mana in their body. If she wanted to do any tests, the monster's core needed to help regulate what she was doing. However, if Alice dumped a bunch of mana into a monster's body *without* controlling the mana core, it would eat up all her mana. What was she supposed to do?

She got another idea and started a new test. She started stuffing kinetic mana into the monster's body again, but this time, Alice tightly leashed every drop of mana she released, to make sure the monster core couldn't take control of her mana . . .

Or at least she tried to. She lost control instantly. The mana she had stuffed into the glimmerspren's body was consumed by the monster core in seconds. Alice sighed in frustration.

Monster cores were too efficient. Fighting against one felt like trying to swim up a waterfall. If she didn't cut the monster core off entirely, there was no way she could keep her experiment going, since the core would absorb all mana from its surroundings.

Monster cores devoured mana from their surroundings?

Alice spent a moment checking her memories about the differences between magic seeds and class seeds. She distinctly remembered that one of the biggest differences was the fact that class seeds could devour mana from their surroundings and then use that mana to grow and improve.

Monster cores seemed to do the exact same thing. In the first place, it was a well-known fact that monsters that ate enough mana would eventually undergo a massive change in size and power, becoming a monster alpha. They would then lead their lesser brethren on a rampage until they were put down.

A monster turning into an alpha seemed awfully similar to someone leveling up, now that Alice thought about it. Had she been looking at things the wrong way? What if class seeds weren't based on magic seeds, the way she assumed they were? What if they were some kind of hybrid between a magic seed and a monster core?

Alice had spent a very long time believing that class seeds were just magic seeds with a few tweaks. Since the System was almost certainly artificial, and mages predated the System, Alice had assumed that the System creator(s) had found a way to create upgraded magic seeds via the System. What if she had gotten the origin of classes wrong?

As she grew more convinced that her hypothesis might have merit, Alice was struck by a new idea. She already knew what a human leveling up looked like. What did a monster evolving into a monster alpha look like? If the two things looked similar, she would have some verification that she was onto something.

She turned back toward the others, who were watching as Alice messed with the monsters, and signaled toward Ethan.

"Are you done already? You should have much more left in you than this, even if you want to play it safe," said Ethan.

Alice shook her head.

"I have an idea," she said. "I want to observe a monster as it becomes a monster alpha. I am trying to figure out if monster cores are the basis for how class seeds work. If they are, I might be able to get more information about class seeds by observing a few monster alphas."

Ethan looked thoughtful. "All right, your idea has merit. Even if it turns out to be wrong, we won't lose much, and if it turns out to be correct, we could gain a whole lot of information. Do you need my help?"

Alice nodded. "Can you force-feed this monster a lot of mana? I don't have the mana reserves to trigger a monster turning into an alpha."

Ethan grinned. "As an Immortal who specializes in magic . . . I *absolutely* have enough mana. You just want me to shove raw mana into its body, right?"

Alice nodded.

Ethan grabbed the monster Alice had been experimenting on and then started cramming mana into it. Alice saw hundreds of Mariums pour into the creature, helping its monster core grow richer and more dense each second. But hundreds of Mariums weren't enough to prompt the creature to evolve. Alice's eyes widened as the number of Mariums Ethan shoved into the creature exceeded one thousand. Then two thousand.

At about three thousand Mariums, Alice started to wonder how high Ethan's magic stat was. Three thousand Mariums was a number that Alice had a hard time wrapping her head around. It just seemed so utterly ridiculous that it was hard to think about.

Finally, at four thousand Mariums, Alice saw something start to change.

"Stop," she said, and Ethan snapped off the flow of mana. A few moments later, Alice saw the monster's core start to glow, like a shining beacon of energy. The core also expanded from the size of a peanut to the size of a golf ball over the next five minutes. As it grew, mana also poured out of the core and into the rest of the monster's body. As she observed the situation, Alice realized that the *type* of mana in the monster's body was changing.

Originally, there had been two kinds of magic seed present in the monster's core. One type had looked pretty similar to kinetic magic, although it hadn't been entirely the same. Alice suspected it was the mana that glimmerspren used to launch feathers at people. The other type of mana had been some sort of optical camouflage–based mana type. Alice had never seen that type of mana before, but she was pretty sure it was related to optical illusions.

Now there was a third type of mana present. It looked like a mixture of organic mana and pure mana, but with other concepts mixed in that Alice couldn't identify. The third type of mana felt *wrong* to her in a way that was hard to express in words.

This mixture of mana flooded the monster's body, swirling around it as it started to interact with the monster's muscles, bones, and organs. As more minutes slowly ticked by, Alice noticed that the monster's body was getting bigger. Its muscles and bones were becoming more defined, and its monster core continued to grow brighter.

Alice blinked in surprise. Usually, when people got new perks, their class fractal just got a little bit brighter and more defined. It definitely didn't look like *this*. This looked more like a mana baptism than a class fractal.

A few moments later, Alice saw something else start to appear in her surroundings. Something that was even more unexpected.

It almost seemed like a paired enchantment was forming between the monster Ethan had forced into an evolution and the other glimmerspren she had captured for testing purposes.

Why did the monsters resemble a paired enchantment now? Alice was baffled. It almost seemed like the monster was creating a constant, endless set of links between it and the other glimmerspren in its surroundings. A few moments later, Alice realized what was happening.

Monster alphas were known to be able to command their ordinary brethren. Obviously, they needed to have some method of communicating and controlling their kin. That must be what Alice was seeing right now.

Moments later, the new monster alpha hissed, and Alice saw tendrils of magic writhe inside the creature's body before clawing their way toward its surroundings. At the same time, the monster core in its body started to flash with glimmers of rainbow mana in a pale imitation of the System. A few moments later, the monster's core flickered again, and Alice recognized with some surprise that it was an imitation of *her* mana—and Ethan's.

She blinked in recognition as she realized the monster was somehow copying some sort of perk using the knockoff System mana.

Unfortunately, the creature was growing too dangerous. Alice fired a pebble through the creature's brain, killing it instantly. As much as she wanted more data, she wasn't going to give the creature time to potentially fight back and kill her. If the monster was copying a System perk, Alice might get caught off guard and die. Alice heard a few System notifications go off, but she ignored them for now as she turned toward her next test subject. Her curiosity was fully invoked now. She needed more data.

She turned toward the third glimmerspren. The creature was still wriggling around, even though it had no wings. She glanced at Ethan.

"Do you have enough mana to make this one into an alpha as well?"

"I can make one more, but I don't want to make a third alpha. Even for me, this is a lot of mana, and I need to keep some for an emergency."

"Understood," said Alice. In that case, she had to make this test count. Ethan started infusing the final glimmerspren with mana. Alice crossed her fingers and hoped that this one wouldn't also develop a perk, since perks were unpredictable and dangerous. Even if she lost the opportunity to conduct more tests, if this monster also developed a perk, Alice would kill it on the spot.

Just like the last test subject, the glimmerspren's body started shimmering with mana. The two kinds of mana present in its monster core flashed and pulsed, and at the same time, a new type of mana started to spread throughout its body.

The monster core in its body started pulsing with rainbow mana, then a few unidentified types of mana, then Ethan's organic mana. Thankfully, this time the monster didn't start developing a perk. Five minutes passed as the monster's body changed. Then ten minutes. After twenty minutes, Alice started frowning.

Why aren't there any paired enchantments forming this time? Alice wondered. When the second test subject had started to turn into a monster alpha, it had only taken fifteen minutes for the creature to start forming pseudo-paired enchantments with the final test subject. This time, twenty minutes had passed, but she hadn't seen a single pseudo-paired enchantment. What was the difference here? A few moments later, Alice realized the difference: There were no nearby monsters anymore. While monster alphas could influence most nearby monsters, they didn't have infinite range. Theoretically, most of the nearby glimmerspren should be in range of this monster alpha—but perhaps its range expanded as it changed from a regular monster into an alpha. This would line up with all her observations so far. The second test subject had only been a few meters away from the third test subject, which would allow them to form a connection the moment it started forming paired enchantments. By contrast, for this glimmerspren, there were no nearby glimmerspren to connect with. The next closest glimmerspren was still a few hundred meters away.

Alice thought of a new question. What would happen if she reintroduced the newly created glimmerspren alpha to the monster swarm? The original monster swarm already *had* an alpha. How did the mana of two different monster alphas interact with each other? Obviously, the two alphas would try to eat each other— but what did their connection look like before one of them died?

Then Alice realized the two monster alphas might not kill each other. It seemed pretty obvious that mutual slaughter had been the norm *before* the destruction of the System—but the monster swarms cooperating in Cyra indicated that times had changed. Even if monster alphas usually ate each other, that might not be true now.

In these circumstances, awakening another monster alpha and letting it loose upon the world seemed irresponsible. Alice felt a bit regretful but decided to do the wise thing instead of the interesting thing.

However, collecting *no* data seemed like it would be too much of a waste. She wouldn't let the two monster alphas near each other, but a few glimmerspren should be harmless, right?

She spent a few moments scanning their surroundings before she turned toward Allira. "Honored Immortal, would it be possible to bring over a few more test subjects? Their condition doesn't matter."

Allira looked at the evolving monster alpha for a few moments before she shrugged. "Sure. Give me a moment," she said before hopping into the nearby woods. Alice heard Allira start singing an upbeat ballad. A minute later, the song cut off, and Allira returned with five more wingless glimmerspren.

Alice double-checked the monsters and discovered that one of them had a perk. She killed that one, then started placing the remaining glimmerspren around the clearing. She laid the first glimmerspren one meter away from the evolving alpha. The second one ten meters away. The third was placed twenty meters away, and the final test subject was placed forty meters away. After she finished setting down the glimmerspren, Alice waited.

The first glimmerspren, the one closest to the alpha, started forming a connection with the half-baked alpha glimmerspren right after she set it down. Alice noted that her earlier observation was correct—the two monster cores really did look like paired enchantments after a few minutes.

About a minute later, the glimmerspren that was ten meters away started to undergo a similar process. The glimmerspren that were twenty and forty meters away didn't respond to the new alpha, which made Alice smile. It seemed her other hypothesis was also correct: Monster alphas started out with very limited communication range, which then expanded as they finished their evolution. She stopped paying attention to the twenty- and forty-meter glimmerspren and focused back on the two that were already connected to the alpha.

After some inspection, Alice realized that the ability for a monster alpha to issue commands to other members of its species wasn't as one-sided as she had believed. The two glimmerspren she was observing seemed to receive something from the alpha in exchange for their subservience. It was hard to tell exactly what the monster alpha was giving them, but it looked like a stream of mana. As the monsters absorbed this stream of mana, it looked like their cores were changing, although the difference was subtle. As their cores changed, the two glimmerspren started to absorb more mana from their surroundings with each second. Alice had to use her Marium-measuring perks to confirm this improvement in "digestion speed," but after a few minutes of observation, Alice confirmed that she was correct. Monsters under the command of an alpha started to absorb mana faster as the connection stabilized. Alice also noticed that the monster that was physically closer to the glimmerspren was more affected.

In other words, monsters don't just mimic and adapt to new sources of mana that they encounter—they also mimic each other, thought Alice.

With that minor mystery solved, Alice turned back toward the alpha itself, and was astonished. The monster alpha seemed to be nearly finished evolving. The irregular types of mana in the monster core had started to disappear, leaving only the original two types of mana.

Most interestingly, after evolution, the glimmerspren's monster core had started to resemble a magic seed more strongly than before. It was still very distinctly a monster core, but the speed it absorbed nearby mana had *decreased*, unlike its underlings'. This was incredibly confusing for Alice. Monsters constantly consumed mana. This was a fundamental fact of life—it was one of the most well-known facts in the world. Monsters used mana the same way humans used oxygen. In Alice's mind, a monster alpha should have used *more* mana, just like someone would breathe heavily after doing heavy exercise. But she was faced with the exact opposite situation, which caught her off guard.

"Ethan, has anyone ever verified whether monster *alphas* suffocate once you cut them off from mana?" asked Alice. She also started searching her own memories for any similar studies that she might have read in the school library. She recalled hearing studies talk about experiments performed on monsters, but she didn't remember seeing that many performed on monster alphas specifically.

Ethan frowned. "A few? Not many, though. Most studies just assume that monster alphas are bigger and smarter versions of the same monster. They never demonstrate any particularly unique capabilities. Apart from the link between monster alphas and their subordinates, of course, but that's likely similar to the way paired enchantments work. At least, that's the commonly accepted scholarly theory right now."

Alice blushed. She had just spent several minutes thinking that she had discovered something new, but at least part of her discovery was already common knowledge. Ethan didn't seem to notice her blushing as he continued speaking.

"There *are* a few theories that suggest some monster species produce wildly different results when they evolve into alphas. Spidercrabs are the most commonly used test subject, since they aren't really a danger to researchers. Spidercrab alphas definitely die of mana deprivation if you cut them off from mana, at least. It's not certain whether this is true for every monster species."

Alice tried to push her theories about paired enchantments out of her mind as she focused on the differences in monster species. In hindsight, it should have been obvious that different species of monster grew differently. After all, they were completely different animals with different body shapes and needs. Due to her time in this world, Alice had gotten used to lumping monsters together as one giant species.

Alice shook her head and focused on her experiment again. She could mull over the differences between monster species later. Right now, what she wanted to do was examine the monster core/magic seed in more detail.

She continued investigating the alpha's core. After a few minutes of probing, Alice noticed something interesting. The monster core seemed to be multiplying all the mana it absorbed, somehow. It wasn't quite the same as a human magic seed, which seemed to create energy from nothing at all. Instead, any time mana entered the core, it suddenly grew more dense, despite the volume of mana not changing at all. If the monster core absorbed five Mariums of mana, after the monster's core finished absorbing it, it became about fifteen Mariums of mana.

It was still creating energy from nothing, as far as Alice could tell. But it needed a source to keep going, unlike magic seeds. Alice wondered whether it was possible for a monster core to just release some of the mana inside it before reintegrating it again—but regardless of whether it was possible or not, the monster in front of her did not do so.

Alice continued watching the new monster alpha to see if it did anything else that surprised her. The creature continued flopping around like a fish out of water for another ten minutes. However, the only other thing she noticed was the communication range of the new monster gradually expanding as it linked up with the other two test subjects.

This time, Alice noticed that the other monster didn't link up with the new monster alpha as easily. There seemed to be some sort of subtle clash of mana happening within the cores of the two monsters—and it was far more noticeable for the glimmerspren that was forty meters away, compared to the one that was twenty meters away.

It didn't take her long to identify the cause of this clash of mana. It was the other monster alpha. From Alice's perspective, it looked like an invisible set of paired enchantments were fighting for dominance inside each monster's core.

Out of curiosity, Alice grabbed one of the ordinary monster test subjects and started jogging away from the monster-infested village. She made sure to avoid the range of the newly awakening monster alpha as well. She wanted to see what happened when a monster left the range of its alpha.

After it got a certain range away, the "paired enchantment" in the monster's core started to dissolve. Soon, the monster turned back into a normal monster. Whatever influence the original monster alpha had on its core also started to gradually disappear, and its accelerated mana absorption rate started to dissipate. Nothing else happened.

Alice set the monster down in a very obvious spot on a tree branch, so that she could continue to observe it, and then made her way back to the artificial monster alpha. It seemed more interesting than this now-mundane monster.

As the artificial alpha continued to evolve, the monster core started to form strands of mana that connected the monster core with the rest of its body more tightly. Alice was vaguely reminded of the nervous system of a human. The human nervous system was complicated, and Alice didn't know all the details—but she knew that human nerves branched out from the spinal cord and conveyed small electrical impulses around the human body. This was what enabled humans to move.

It seemed that monster cores had a similar function, except that electricity was replaced with mana. Nothing else seemed particularly remarkable about the monster's ascension, much to Alice's disappointment. She had been hoping for some insight about the way that the System's perk-creation and class seeds worked behind the scenes, but it seemed like this was the limit to how much information she could gather from this experiment.

Finally, about an hour after she started the experiment, the monster core flashed a couple of times and then stopped changing. The flashes of light caught Alice's attention, even if the monster's biology itself seemed to be out of useful information. She had seen multiple things flash with mana during her investigation of the

System. When she was observing a mana baptism, a successful one always resulted in several quick flashes of mana. Now, she had seen a monster's core do the exact same thing once it finished evolving into an alpha.

Alice still had no idea what that little flash of mana signified, or what it meant, but she was starting to suspect that it was linked to the success of any mana construct. Unfortunately, she had no way to investigate this hint in more detail right now.

She sighed and spent several more minutes observing the new monster alpha, hoping that it would do something else interesting. After another twenty minutes of observation, Alice finally gave up and killed her test subjects. Then she purified her mana types and checked her System notifications.

A moment later, Alice grinned.

The first System notification was the entire reason she had started this whole experiment chain.

You have leveled up!
Explorer of Magic: 83→85

Alice had finally reached level eighty-five in [Explorer of Magic].
Alice had also gotten some levels in her other classes as well.

You have leveled up!
Survivor: 68→69, Scholar: 62→66, Scientist: 66→68, Kinetic Manabinder: 51→52

Alice resisted the urge to rub her hands together in glee.
She had two new perks to choose.

Chapter 41

The first thing Alice did was look at her [Explorer of Magic] perks. She was nearly vibrating with excitement as she started to combine {Expanding Comprehension} with {Intuitive Magic Modeling}.

Then Alice froze. She forced herself to calm down. Even if she was mostly certain that she already had the correct idea, she should at least check her other options first.

She scanned the new perks she had unlocked after reaching level eighty-five. One looked all right—it would give her an extra three magic tendrils and slightly increase the effect of her magic stat. Alice *did* want to increase her combat abilities, but it wasn't a priority. She needed to learn how to deal with Alice mana. She checked her other possible perk combinations and then nodded to herself.

None of them were as good as the combination of {Expanding Comprehension} and {Intuitive Magic Modeling}.

Without further hesitation, Alice combined the perks.

Expanding Comprehension (Tier 2 perk, level 55 Explorer of Magic)
(level 50 Explorer of Magic perk + level 40 Explorer of Magic perk)
Perk costs: Infusion of Comprehension + Reset sacrificed to create this perk.

Once every two weeks, you may select one of your seeds. Over the course of the next hour, you will gradually expand your understanding of the seed, as well as the concepts associated with it. The clarity will be lower compared to directly using {Infusion of Comprehension}. In addition, the mana conversion ratio of the seed may improve by small amounts with each use of this perk. At maximum, an increase of 5% may occur. This perk may never improve the mana conversion ratio of a given seed by more than 50% in total.

Warning: You will be helpless during this time, so it is highly recommended you activate this perk only when your safety is assured and you are in an environment where you will not be disturbed.

Alice had gotten a great deal of use out of {Expanding Comprehension} in the past. It had given her a lot of inspiration and useful discoveries. Normally, Alice would have been very hesitant to lose it—but it was starting to feel incapable of coping with the problems she faced these days. Her System seed was too complex, and there were too many types of information Alice needed to untangle. {Expanding Comprehension} just wasn't suited for handling compound magic seeds. The perk needed an upgrade. She had high hopes for what the perk would achieve once combined with {Intuitive Magic Modeling}.

Intuitive Magic Modeling (Tier 2 perk, level 65 Explorer of Magic)
(level 5 Explorer of Magic perk + level 45 Explorer of Magic perk)
Perk costs: Magic Proficiency + Mana Construct Modeling sacrificed to create this perk.

You intuitively mentally model any form of mana within ten meters of you, whether they are complex mana constructs, forms of mana, or enchantments. You will know what kinds of mana they are made of and have an instinctive understanding of some of the simpler components of anything you model. In short, this will give you some level of understanding of what an enchantment or mana construct is, how it works, and what it does, although it won't feed you information beyond a certain level of complexity.

{Intuitive Magic Modeling} was only occasionally useful to Alice these days. She used it to help understand the effects of some enchantments that she came across on a day-to-day basis, and having a natural intuition that pointed her in the right direction was nice while doing research. The biggest problem with the perk was the final sentence: The perk would not feed her information beyond a certain level of complexity. Just like {Expanding Comprehension}, it was unable to keep up with her needs.

Alice took one final look at her two perks before she combined the two. She used her System seed to make sure that the translation for the perk made sense, and then started reading her new perk.

Magic Modeling (Tier 3 perk, level 85 Explorer of Magic)
(level 55 Explorer of Magic perk + level 65 Explorer of Magic perk)
Perk costs: Intuitive Magic Modeling + Expanding Comprehension sacrificed to create this perk.

You gain the ability to naturally understand types of mana that you come into contact with. Once per week, you may also create mental maps of any type of mana or mana-related phenomenon you come into contact with. Mental maps will create a comprehensive, detailed mental image of a type of mana that can be accurately tested in your mental library or analyzed for any details you wish to learn.

> Note: Creation of a mental map requires that you first interact with a type of mana or mana-related phenomenon, then spend time and mental energy focusing on it and thinking about it. The longer you spend working on a mental map, the more detailed and accurate it will become.

Alice resisted the urge to cackle in delight.

First of all, the limit on information complexity was gone. Instead, it had been replaced by a "mental map" feature. It sounded like it would take time to flesh out each mental map, but afterward she would have a detailed picture of any mana construct she wanted to investigate. She could work on her mental maps whenever she was in her {Dream Library} and then focus on other things when she was awake. Alice was very happy with the result of her perk combination.

The ability to enhance her magic seeds was also gone, but Alice didn't really care about that. She already had {Scholar of Magic} to help improve her magic seeds over time, and her magic stat was still increasing surprisingly quickly. While Alice was nowhere near the font of mana Ethan was, she was also four centuries younger. She would get there as time passed.

After that, Alice directed her new perk toward an object that had been puzzling her since the moment she saw it. She focused on her mana gem. After a few minutes of focus and effort, she felt a very fuzzy image of a mana gem form inside her thoughts. It looked like a low-resolution picture. She frowned before she realized that the longer she focused on the image, the clearer it became. Alice also realized that her mental map was very similar to a 3-D model from computer class—she could zoom in and manipulate her view as much as she wanted.

Of course, she would still need to focus on the map for a while before the image resolution reached a useful level. Based on her estimates, it would take twenty to thirty hours to finish—about three and a half days of focus in her dream library, roughly.

Once she was done, Alice would finally be able to figure out why her magic gem wasn't managing her Alice mana. She was close to a solution.

After that, Alice focused on her other perk selection—the [Scholar] perk.

She glanced at the new perks she had unlocked before she dismissed them. Then she turned her attention to her old perks. It was time for another perk combination. After several minutes of thought, Alice started thinking about combining {Scholar of Magic} with something.

> **Scholar of Magic**
> **Requirements: Scholar level 35 or higher, Intelligence 150 or higher, Magic 100 or higher, at least one magic seed is at a mana conversion ratio of 150% or higher, at least three magic seeds present**

> When reading a book, listening to a lecture, or interacting with schoolwork
> related to a certain kind of magic seed, if you have a correlating magic seed in
> your body at that time, you will be able to raise the mana conversion ratio of the
> seed beyond its limit.
> Note: This process is rather slow, and the speed will slow down more the higher
> the current mana conversion ratio of the related seed is.

While that was useful, it wasn't really *that* important. It was slow, and more importantly, mana quantity didn't seem to be the deciding factor in most of her battles. The number of tendrils she could command seemed like a much bigger limitation on her combat strength right now. Of course, Alice also recognized that mana quantity *would* be important if she increased her magic tendrils. If she had the same number of mana tendrils as Ethan, just fighting normally would drain her mana pool in less than a minute. Still, the perk was slow, and it would slow down more and more the stronger her magic seeds were. Was this really a perk she wanted to keep around long-term?

Alice couldn't help but think of Ethan. He had dumped thousands of Mariums of mana into the two monster alphas Alice had wanted for her experiments. And that was just the amount of mana Ethan felt comfortable spending while in the middle of uncontrolled territory, surrounded by monsters, and with potential [Assassins] lurking around every corner.

Ethan had always been very clear that he was putting safety before science. Which made it hard to imagine just how massive Ethan's mana reserves must be.

Alice sighed and rubbed her forehead in thought. If she combined {Scholar of Magic} with something, what would give her the best value? Was it worth sacrificing her slow but consistent magic seed growth for it?

Since [Scholar] was only at level sixty-six right now, Alice couldn't combine {Scholar of Magic} with a perk from a different class. After several more minutes of thought, Alice's eyes finally lit up. While it seemed a bit unorthodox, Alice thought that {Accelerated Thinking} and {Scholar of Magic} actually had a surprising amount of potential if they were combined.

Accelerated Thinking
Requirements: Scholar level 10 or higher, Intelligence 125 or greater

Slightly improves your thinking and processing speed.

{Accelerated Thinking} was a basic perk—which made sense, since it was from level fifteen. It wasn't even a proper level-fifteen perk—at the time, Alice remembered not finding anything she liked from the level-fifteen perks, so she had gone back to the level-ten [Scholar] perks to find something she wanted. Alice imagined that {Accelerated Thinking} paired with {Scholar of Magic} might enhance the rate she understood magic AND the rate at which she improved magic seeds or something like that. If the perk combination went well, she might not even lose her long-term mana capacity growth. She stuffed the two perks into the combination screen and then began the perk combination.

Alice felt the two perks start to combine, and a few moments later, a new perk appeared. Her shoulders tensed as she hoped for another useful perk—she needed all the help she could get right now. Alice used her half-built System seed to fix the perk's various grammatical and comprehensibility issues before she started reading.

Scholar of Thought and Magic
Tier 2 perk (level 65 Scholar) (level 35 Scholar perk + level 15 Scholar perk)
Perk costs: Scholar of Magic + Accelerated Thinking sacrificed to create this perk.

Your ability to understand magic is greatly expanded if you have a magic seed already related to the concept you are trying to understand. As your understanding grows, so too will your related magic seeds.

Alice relaxed.

Another upgrade to her understanding was an exceptional boon, especially given how absurdly complicated some of the topics she was trying to understand were. Combined with the understanding boost from her other new perk, {Magic Modeling}, Alice suspected that she would be able to do her research far more quickly and efficiently than before. The perk hadn't lost the ability to increase the size of her magic seeds, either. The perk wasn't anything exciting, but it helped her grow. That was all she needed out of this kind of perk.

With both of her new perks built, Alice focused her attention inward, toward her mana gem. She spent a few minutes nailing down its exact location before she continued using her mental map to build a perfect copy of it inside her mind.

Alice quickly confirmed that she could build her mental map of the mana gem far more quickly if she was also observing the real thing at the same time. She also realized that {Scholar of Thought and Magic} was surprisingly helpful when building a mental map. It seemed to help her perk build mental maps more quickly, even if Alice wasn't sure why that was the case.

As the mental map of the mana gem became clearer and clearer, Alice continued to observe it. After several minutes, Alice blinked in surprise. One of the facets of the mana gem seemed to boost her physical strength. Which, at least in Alice's mind, made no sense—she already understood where the System's boosts to physical abilities came from. Why was there more mana related to her physique inside of the mana gem?

As she focused, she realized that she wasn't looking at a copy of the mana muscles she had already figured out earlier. Instead, it seemed almost like the strange facet she was looking at boosted the effect of her [Strength] stat by 1 percent.

Alice stopped focusing on the other parts of the gem and instead started poking at that one facet of the mana gem. She quickly realized that [Strength] wasn't the only thing that the magic gem contained.

In addition to the 1 percent boost to [Strength], the little facet of the mana gem had four other components.

One of them gave her a 1 percent boost to the effect of her [Dexterity] stat.

Another gave her a 1 percent boost to her [Perception] stat.

The second-to-last component of the gem facet gave Alice a 15 percent boost to experience growth, but it only applied to the concept of fighting? Alice couldn't identify the last component yet, but the first four components sounded very familiar to her.

As Alice identified each part of the gem facet, she realized what she was looking at. She scanned her achievement list, and sure enough, she found what she was looking for after a few moments of searching.

Murderer (Rarity: 4)
You have slain another human being.
Effect of Strength, Dexterity, and Perception increased by 1%. Classes with some relationship to fighting other humans gain experience 15% faster.

The effects for this gem facet were *exactly* the same as the effects of the {Murderer} achievement that Alice had gotten all the way back in Cyra.

In short, the mana gem that Alice was looking at was where her achievements were stored?

Alice, admittedly, had never actually figured out where achievements were stored in the human body until now. Attributes were obviously stored in the respective muscles and nerves. Classes were represented by class seeds and stored in people's hearts or brains.

Now it appeared that she had finally found one of the missing pieces of the System.

Alice concentrated on the last aspect of the facet that she hadn't identified yet . . . and quickly realized it was the most complicated part of the whole thing.

As far as she could tell, the last component of the mana gem facet was further subdivided into two parts.

The first part was something like "containment" and restrained the other half of the facet component.

The other part of the gem facet was the magical manifestation of the concept of {Murder}.

For some reason, the last part of the mana gem facet was literally containing the concept of murder, preventing it from spilling out into the rest of her body. Just like a class seed. Alice grimaced.

She had finally figured out where achievements were stored, but she still had no idea why Alice mana wasn't being handled by her mana gem. If the gem was responsible for storing achievements, how was Alice mana related to the mana gem in the first place? Why were mana gems seemingly only present in people above level seventy-five? Instead of the long-awaited answers she had been hoping for, Alice felt even more confused as she looked over her new mental map.

Chapter 42

Alice continued to ponder the relationship between Alice mana and achievements as the group traveled. Every night, Alice worked on her mental map while she slept. She also took some time to discuss her new discoveries with Cecilia and Ethan, as well as a far more limited version with Allira. She wanted second opinions on what she had found and what it all meant. Alice also used {Shared Memories} to show Ethan and Cecilia what she was seeing, in hopes that they could provide her with new insights.

Allira, on the other hand, seemed disinterested in Alice's research. The more time Alice spent with her, the more Alice felt a certain sense of . . . distance. Allira was nice but never really engaged with the group on an emotional level. Alice vaguely recalled that the first time Ethan's mother had mentioned Allira, she had complained that Allira was friendly with everyone but never actually connected with people. Alice was beginning to see what Myra meant.

At the very least, Cecilia and Ethan were more than happy to weigh in on Alice's discoveries. On the second night after the monster alpha experiments, the three sat around the campfire and discussed Alice's mana gem in greater detail.

"I still don't know *why* the mana gem has achievements in it," said Alice. "It's obviously linked to Alice mana somehow, but the connection seems odd to me."

"Well, since all the mana is related to your achievements, and it's also directly linked to Alice mana, maybe it's linked to Immortality achievements?" Cecilia said thoughtfully. "It could work as a seed for Immortality or something."

"Seed for Immortality?" asked Alice. "What do you mean?"

"I should preface this by saying that I don't understand exactly how Immortality works," Cecilia said as she eyed Ethan. "Honored Immortal Ethan could probably tell you more about the actual process of turning into an Immortal. However, it is obvious that Immortals are biologically different from other people. They don't age, and they all have the ability to shrug off one lethal wound per week.

"The fact that Immortals ALL have this trait makes me think that it's something biological, which the System just lumps together with the achievement. You also said that the mana gem is only present in people above level seventy-five, which is basically the last hard part of the race to Immortality. Perhaps the mana gem is kind of like the fertile soil that your Immortality achievement will grow out of. Or maybe it's some sort of mixed magic and biology construct that grows into whatever characteristics Immortals have, kind of like how mana and muscles mix together to create System-enhanced muscles," said Cecilia.

Ethan frowned thoughtfully. "Cecilia's guess makes *some* sense. But I can't figure out why the mana gem would store other achievements in that case. If the mana gem is supposed to absorb all your Alice mana and serve as a building block for your Immortality achievement, why would it also absorb other achievements? After all, you only observed these mana gems in people above level seventy-five. Almost everyone alive on this planet has an achievement. Logically speaking, that *should* mean that everyone would have a mana gem, if it's built to deal with achievements. That particular bit of information is what's bothering me the most about these mana gems that you've found—why do they only appear after level eighty?"

Alice nodded.

To be honest, that was the most confusing part about the gems. If they truly contained achievements, why didn't everyone have them? Alice didn't think there were many people in this world who had no achievements at all, besides six-year-olds who had just gotten access to their status screen.

"You know, what if we're looking at this the wrong way?" asked Cecilia. "I remember you mentioning that only people above level seventy-five have these gems, but it's also true that reaching level seventy-five is impossible for most people. The average person reaches level fifty or sixty by the time they die of old age. To go further, you need at least decently high-rarity achievements that boost your leveling speed. Otherwise, the increasing cost of each level eventually stifles your progress. What if we're reversing cause and effect here? Maybe mana gems form once you get a certain rarity of achievement. In that case, people who have high-rarity achievements form mana gems, and those achievements also make them capable of reaching level seventy-five? After all, the number of people with the potential to reach level seventy-five is pretty low. This could be an issue with data collection and Alice's sample size, rather than a definite 'these gems appear after the first post–level-seventy-five perk.' Alice hasn't found a mana gem in anyone below level seventy-five YET, but that might be more of a probability issue."

Alice thought about that. It was actually a reasonable theory. Correlation and causation weren't the same thing, and Alice had gotten so lost in her thoughts and experiments that she had overlooked that. In fact, now that Cecilia brought it up,

Alice also realized that it was also possible everyone *did* have a mana gem. Perhaps they were just so tiny in normal people that they were impossible to see. Alice had already been having problems zooming in her vision enough to see most mana gems. If the rarity of someone's achievements determined the size of their mana gem, it made perfect sense for her to miss most people's mana gems.

Then Alice realized there was a problem with Cecilia's theory.

"I don't remember seeing my own mana gem before reaching level eighty, though," said Alice. "I got a rarity-ten achievement right after entering this world. If achievement rarity determines the size of a mana gem, I should have noticed it pretty fast after acquiring the perks that let me see all this."

Cecilia looked thoughtful. "Okay, that's a strong argument against my theory. That being said, the System also notes that you have increased support from the System, and while we've found a few corner cases where that seems to matter, it's hard to know what other impacts this achievement has on you. It's not inconceivable that the System works differently for *you* versus everyone else. You might be some kind of weird exception to how mana gems work."

Alice thought about it and nodded. While experiments and data based on herself were useful, Cecilia brought up a good point. The System clearly had *some* sort of difference in how it handled other people versus {Outworlders}. It was hard to say if data she collected from herself was useful when thinking about mana gems.

"Cecilia, can I take a look at your brain again?" Alice asked after a few moments. "I'd like to look for a mana gem again."

"Go for it," said Cecilia, extending an arm for Alice to grab.

Alice activated every single relevant perk that would let her see inside Cecilia's body, both from a mundane and a magical perspective. Then she started carefully scanning Cecilia's brain again to see if she could find a mana gem that she might have missed the first time. Once again, she found nothing.

Was it too small for her perks to pick out? Or was she missing something? Or did it not exist at all? Alice frowned in thought.

"Still didn't find it?" asked Cecilia. "You look disappointed."

Alice sighed and then nodded.

"Relax, Alice," said Cecilia. Alice realized that she had let her shoulders tense up unnaturally, and consciously relaxed her body.

"I remember seeing a phrase in your memories that fits well here. 'Rome wasn't built in a day,'" said Cecilia. "I believe in you."

Cecilia even said the last part in English, which made Alice smile. Cecilia was getting better and better at English. Had she been practicing behind Alice's back?

Hearing her friend try to cheer her up made Alice's mood a lot better.

"You're right," said Alice. She paused as another idea occurred to her. "Do you mind if I make a mental map of your brain next, Cecilia? I'm able to zoom in on images I've made mental maps of, which helps a lot."

"Go ahead. Actually, show me once you're done setting it up. I'm also curious."

Alice smiled before she returned to her tent and went to sleep. She might still have more questions than answers, but she was making progress. She just needed to wait for her perk cooldown.

With the help of Cecilia and Ethan, Alice knew that she would make progress before things got worse. She just needed to keep making progress every day until she got the information she needed.

Four days after the monster alpha experiment, Alice finished constructing the mental map of her mana gem. That was when Alice realized that her new perk was absolutely amazing.

Mental maps started out as nothing more than fuzzy images, but once Alice completed one, she realized that it was incredibly synergistic with {Dream Library}. In her dreams, she could create dozens of copies of an item and run it through whatever tests she wanted it to. She could use any perk on her mental maps, and it would activate as if the mana gem she had recorded was a snapshot frozen in time. She even got an intuitive understanding of how some bits of mana worked— and these little tidbits might have taken her months of study to figure out on her own. It was like saving a bunch of research time and having a perfect test subject rolled into one perk.

With the help of her new perk, she also started to figure out more of the mana gem and its workings.

First of all, Alice confirmed, beyond a shadow of a doubt, that the mana gem had every single one of her achievements stored inside it. The mana gem that she had found was basically a repository for achievements.

However, achievements were far from the only thing the mana gem stored.

In addition to achievements, Alice had found weird bundles of *concepts* floating around in the mana gem. These concepts didn't seem tied to anything. They didn't seem to be organized. They didn't strengthen the user. They didn't even seem like they were mana, or at least, not entirely. They were more like virtual images, in a way that Alice didn't quite understand.

The first of these concepts that Alice found in her mana gem was the concept of research. One moment, this virtual image made of mana looked like a mound of books. Another moment, it looked like a microscope, allowing her to glimpse at the unseen secrets of magic. Another moment, it felt like a perk, dissecting the parts of magic that were still unknown to her.

At first, Alice had assumed that this was some sort of alternate storage for class seeds. Maybe the System stuffed mana here until it got organized into another class, or something. After all, Alice found a little bit of [Laborer] mana sticking around in her mana gem, despite the fact that she had no class related to physical labor. Alice spent several moments trying to figure out where [Laborer] mana had come from in the first place before she remembered the bit of construction work she had done while living in Cyra.

After several more minutes of investigation, Alice realized that the mana gem wasn't a repository for unmade class seeds. This was because she kept coming back to the concept of research stored inside her mana gem.

As she continued to study and observe the mana gem, Alice started to realize something.

The concept of research, as defined by the mana inside her mana gem, looked rather odd. Besides the more generic research-related images she could see while investigating the bundle of concepts in her gem, she could also see constant, repeated images of *herself* doing research as well.

In addition to piles of books, microscopes, and perks, Alice could occasionally get glimpses of herself, viewed through the eyes of others. Once Alice started to pay attention, she recognized the library of the Magic Academy, where a little miniature image of Alice reading books could be seen. She was pretty sure that she could also figure out who this particular image came from. Alice distinctly remembered that, at least a few times, she had seen Arsi in the library, and the two had chatted after reading their respective books. The image in Alice's mana gem seemed to perfectly overlap with Arsi's position during a few of these encounters.

In short, this mana gem seemed to contain memories.

Alice also realized that the concept of researcher wasn't quite as nebulous as she had thought. The concept of researcher in the mana gem was kind of like the seed of a plant, rather than a mold a [Blacksmith] might pour metal into. Just like with trees, Alice could tell the concept she was looking at was based on the idea of research, but it was uniquely tailored to fit her, rather than being nebulous and universal. As she continued to investigate the mana gem, she started to understand what this concept actually meant.

As time passed, everyone in this world had formed certain ideas about what certain types of people behaved like. For example, when people pictured a [Swordsman], they generally pictured someone swinging their sword around, whether on a training field or on a battlefield. These collective ideas about what certain people acted like seemed to have eventually reconstructed themselves into a certain, more concrete, set of mana concepts. These concepts defined classes—but they *also* created achievements. Whenever someone became closer to a certain concept, it was like adding a giant pile of fertilizer to a class—thus allowing all related classes to grow more quickly. Alice had always wondered why achievements specified things such as "classes related to research will gain more experience" in their description. The answer was simple—achievements worked almost entirely off concepts rather than physical or biological constraints.

Since Alice had accomplished several feats of extraordinary research since coming to this world, people's ideas about what a "great researcher" looked like had intermingled with her own existence, allowing Alice to create a personalized connection between her vision of what it meant to be a researcher and the universal understanding, making it easier for her to grow her research-related classes.

Alice also realized something else.

The rest of the System was extremely distinct and well organized. Alice could state with certainty exactly what an attribute point was. She could write pages upon pages of notes discussing exactly what a class seed was. She could break things like attributes down into specific, well-defined, and understandable steps, from creation to integration.

However, classifying what an achievement was behind the scenes was hard, because achievements seemed to be *everything the System didn't know what to do with*. Achievements were basically the misc folder in an otherwise well-organized set of computer files.

Did someone have a distinct image of who *Alice* was, and the System needed to deal with the excess mana?

Make it into an achievement.

Has someone gotten closer to the concept of research, and they needed a way to bridge the gap between concept and human without warping the person's personality?

Make it into an achievement.

Was there some sort of weird mana fluctuation that the System needed to handle?

That was also an achievement.

Were people getting weaker because of old age? To prevent beliefs about old age from reinforcing a negative loop, the System had turned it into an achievement! Achievements were basically a dumping site where the System tossed absolutely everything that didn't fall under more normal categories, like classes or attributes.

Most achievements seemed to be related to these mana concepts that Alice had found, but a disturbing number of them just seemed like random nonsense as well. The achievements that had any sort of impact on leveling speed all had the strange concept-images that Alice had discovered. On the whole, achievements were a giant, disorganized mess.

The only other thing that Alice nailed down with certainty was that the mana gem was trying to connect to the System.

At least, she was pretty sure that was what she had found.

When Alice used her System seed to translate what the little facet of the gem she had found was *doing*, Alice essentially saw a constantly repeating message.

Error! Cannot connect to mainframe
Trying again.

This phrase repeated over . . . and over . . . and over . . . and over again. Every ten seconds, she saw the same thing cycling through her display mana. It was also a message Alice had seen before, almost word for word, when she was trying to learn about one of the other, smaller facets of the mana gem. In short, the achievement was trying to connect to the mainframe of the System for some reason.

Alice wasn't sure *why* the System needed to connect to the mana gem in her brain, but she suspected it was related to the reason that her Alice mana had never properly integrated into her mana gem.

Sadly, the System was gone.

Which meant that Alice had a much bigger task in front of her than she had imagined. Instead of just figuring out how one category of "things the System does" worked, Alice needed to untangle the mess of an achievement System and get it back in working order, or she might mess up and explode when she tried to fix her Alice mana.

At the very least, Alice was now pretty sure that part of Cecilia's speculation was right. There was a curious little bit of the mana gem near the bottom that looked like it was *supposed* to be doing something with Alice mana. It just . . . wasn't working. Alice could intuitively tell that it was like a jigsaw puzzle that was missing a piece. Alice mana fit perfectly into that missing puzzle piece. She just wasn't quite sure whether stuffing all the Alice mana into the same area would break everything. {Safety Analysis} was giving her "bad idea but not lethal" vibes, but Alice wasn't willing to risk it. This just seemed like something that would bite her in the butt if she poked it too hard.

The day after Alice discovered what a disorganized mess achievements were, Ethan and Allira informed her of something.

"We've almost reached the palace," said Ethan. "We're going to say hello and then move on. We just need to announce our presence before exiting the territory, or the [Queen] might think that we're avoiding her."

Allira sighed. "I wouldn't mind avoiding her," she said.

Ethan also rolled his eyes, but the two still led the group toward the city Alice could now see in the distance.

Chapter 43

As the group made their way through the streets of Sendria's capital city, Alice couldn't help but notice how dense the crowds were. Illvaria's capital was larger, but Sendria's capital, Zyndra, packed people inside its walls like sardines in a can.

It was also obvious that the city wasn't meant to handle this many people. The buildings weren't much taller than they were in Illvaria, and the buildings were a bit smaller. The streets were packed, and the city was overpopulated.

Why were there so many people packed into this city, when it couldn't accommodate them?

It only took a few more moments for Alice to realize why the city was so packed. Her realization was only reinforced when Allira started translating street signs for the rest of the group.

Refugee quarters—this way.

Those seeking aid with abnormal, class-related behavior—this way.

Urgent healing—this way.

Alice realized, belatedly, that the [Guards] standing outside the city hadn't been very inquisitive as the group moved past them. In Illvaria, Alice needed to answer detailed questionnaires under lie detection anytime she entered a city. Here, the [Guards] had just waved them through. There was still basic security, but it was very light. The line to enter the city had also been incredibly long.

The collapse of the System had hit Sendria far worse than Illvaria. Or perhaps Alice had simply been sheltered from the disaster due to her unique status as someone who might actually fix the problem. Here, Alice could see the evidence of Sendria's crumbling order playing out in real time.

Alice remembered Ethan and Allira indicating, in no uncertain terms, that the [Queen] of Sendria was usually quite unpleasant and had some issues with Illvaria. Alice had thought it was odd that the woman would let them pass through her country so easily if the two nations were rivals. Now, seeing Zyndra with her own eyes, it made much more sense. The survival of one's people was still what came first for any monarch. If Ethan had convinced the [Queen] that allowing the group to pass through Sendria would help her country, perhaps that had been enough to secure their passage.

The inhabitants of the inner part of the city were different from the bedraggled refugees in the outer district. As the group continued traveling toward the palace, Alice noticed that the people here seemed wealthier than those in Metsel. Even the [Soldiers] patrolling the streets seemed to have better funding available to them—they had more System-enchanted armor than their Illvarian counterparts.

Of course, while people had more System enchantments, they had fewer traditional enchantments. Alice only saw a few mages walking around, and there was little evidence of large numbers of [Enchanters] or magic healing. While Sendria looked more wealthy than Illvaria at first glance, it had far less magic available.

That was probably another reason Sendria was hit so much harder by the collapse of the System. Mages were a huge part of this world's military and economy. Illvaria was practically the magic capital of the Southern Continent. This made Illvarian society much more resilient against the enhanced monster swarms ravaging the countryside.

Finally, the group made it to the wall outside the palace. Much like the rest of the city, the palace seemed opulent, but the enchantments in its walls were far less dense than the palace of Illvaria. The walls of Sendria's palace only had three enchantments woven in. One enchantment seemed to be a wall fortification of some sort. The other two were based on light and heat. Alice suspected that the heat enchantment regulated the temperature inside the palace. She had no clue what the light-based enchantment was doing.

"Why do the enchantments on the palace seem so . . ." Alice struggled to figure out what word she wanted to use.

Casual?

Relaxed?

Harmless?

After seeing the military efficiency of Illvaria's palace, she had assumed that *every* palace in this world was a fortress of magic and perks. Sendria's palace looked like it was built for comfort rather than defense.

"Sendria spends a lot less on its military than Illvaria. That's because it's in a far safer position," said Ethan. "There is another Shil Confederacy member-nation to the north of Sendria, cutting off their border with the nomads. That country has to handle the nomad incursions, while Sendria doesn't have to worry about them. There is a country south of Sendria, so they don't have a direct border with the Mana Wastes. That means there are fewer powerful monsters that wander into the country. To the west, they have Illvaria as a neighbor—and we're too busy fending off the nomads and the Sigmusi to think about expanding east. Then to the east, all their neighbors are small and weak. Sendria only has a quarter of Illvaria's population, but two of the three nations to Sendria's east make even *that* tiny population seem massive." Ethan grimaced. "Well, technically there are four nations to the east of Sendria. But one of them is basically only a nation on technicality."

"I see," said Alice, frowning. If Sendria wasn't that worried about military invasion or conquest, their seemingly lax palace enchantments made more sense. Then Ethan's last words caught her attention.

"A nation that's only a nation by technicality?" asked Alice, frowning. How could a nation only be a nation on technicality?

The heavy mood of the group seemed to fade away as Ethan chuckled. He leaned a little closer to Alice so that his voice would carry less.

"About a hundred and fifty years ago, a [Farmer] moved here from the Central Continent. He's an Immortal who can outproduce a large village and grow all sorts of crops out of season, or in completely incorrect climates. He was single-handedly capable of feeding a large town on his own. For a while, he just lived his life—but eventually, he decided that he wanted to be more than just a [Farmer]. Thus, he founded a country—the nation of Superbia. A nation with a population of one person." Ethan's face became exceptionally flat. "Yes, that is what he named it. Superbia."

"Didn't the nation who owned his farmland object?" asked Alice. She had repeatedly heard that Immortals couldn't fight armies on their own. How did a single [Farmer] Immortal found a new country by himself?

"Well, they would have, but the [Farmer] was occupying a strip of barren land," said Ethan. "If the [Farmer] wasn't living there, the land would be worthless. The soil is atrocious, and there aren't any resources in the area—so the nearby nations didn't have a way to make it useful. The only real reason the land was valuable at all was because the Immortal [Farmer] lived there, and his perks made the land bountiful. Any of the three neighboring nations *could* kill the [Farmer] and take his land . . . but then what? They would own a strip of barren, worthless soil. That would cost them access to the [Farmer] and his crops. Is mustering a few hundred [Soldiers] and paying them to fight an Immortal worth taking over a strip of barren wasteland? Especially one that's smaller than most villages and has no people living on it?"

Alice didn't need to think about that question for long.

"No, it's a total waste of resources," she said. "I don't think anyone would bother. Realistically, the cost of putting together [Soldiers] to take the land back is not worth it."

"Exactly," said Ethan. "So, instead, they decided to work out a deal with the [Farmer]. He got to keep the nation of Superbia, a nation with a population of one. In exchange, they levied an extra tax on food he sold to nearby towns. Basically, he bribes them to acknowledge his nation's existence, and they don't invade him. Both sides are happy with the arrangement.

"Later, the population of Superbia expanded a bit, because he got married and had a few kids." Ethan rolled his eyes. "The population of Superbia is now five. The lady of Superbia is getting older, though, so the population will probably drop back to four in another decade or two. I've also heard that the [Prince] of Superbia wants to move out and keeps arguing with his father over it."

Allira snorted. "Not everyone wants to be the [Prince] of a random farmstead. I don't blame him."

Alice felt that the story was quite absurd.

A nation with a population of five?

The situation felt ridiculous.

"At least Superbia has one of the highest average levels among its population," said Cecilia as she chuckled.

Allira snickered. "You're not wrong. I don't know if there's another nation in the entire world with a population made of 20 percent Immortals. And one in five people of Superbia are capable of fighting dozens of people on their own. Per capita, the population of Superbia is also incredibly wealthy."

Ethan also chuckled.

"The Immortal [Farmer] who founded Superbia isn't a bad guy," said Ethan. "I'm half convinced he founded Superbia as a joke and then decided to keep it afloat for some levels in [King]. Levels in [King] might not do *much* for him, but there's no harm in having more secondary classes. He's one of my father's pen pals, and he also spent a few years unsuccessfully courting Doll a little over a century ago."

As the group relaxed and gossiped about the mighty nation of Superbia, they finally reached the gates of the palace.

"Halt!" said a [Guard], stopping the group as they chatted and laughed. "What business do you have with the palace? Do you have . . . ?" The [Guard]'s voice cut off midsentence as he noticed Allira. He stared.

The other nearby [Guard], a relatively average-looking woman with short, auburn hair, rolled her eyes. She whacked the other [Guard] on the side of his head, bringing him out of his daze.

The female [Guard] cleared her throat. "Who are you? Why are you here?" she asked, stepping in for the other distracted [Guard].

"I am Immortal Ethan of Illvaria. This is Immortal Allira, also of Illvaria," said Ethan, gesturing toward her. "This is my apprentice, Alice, and her friend Cecilia. The [Queen] should be expecting us."

The female [Soldier] paused for a moment, losing herself in thought. Then she nodded.

"The [Queen] did mention that we might have a few visitors. Can you wait for a moment, so that I can get someone to verify your identities? No offense, but the lady over there has so much [Charisma] that she can probably foil any lie detection I try to do."

Ethan nodded.

The two [Guards] gestured toward a few colleagues in the distance. Those colleagues came over to make sure the group didn't do anything funny, while the original two [Guards] disappeared into the palace. About five minutes later, a pompous-looking man with a plump belly exited the palace and observed the group. He scanned the group before giving them a respectful bow.

"Honored Immortals of Illvaria."

The female [Guard] and her companion looked relieved. "Thank you for your patience. Follow me."

The group walked into the palace, where Alice noticed that the walls were covered in gold ornaments, paintings, and other gaudy-looking art. The impression Alice got of the palace was that of someone flaunting their wealth. She missed the more obviously utilitarian and magically focused architecture of Illvaria. She hadn't realized how much of a blessing it was that she had ended up in the magic capital of the Southern Continent until now. Illvaria might have many shortcomings, but it was an amazing place to study magic. If she had ended up in Sendria instead, she probably would have had a much harder time establishing herself.

She dismissed those thoughts as the [Soldier] led them to an audience chamber.

They didn't need to wait for long before [Queen] Cendaria allowed them into the room.

The group of four walked into a throne room that sparkled with a variety of gems and a throne made of gold. Sitting atop the throne was a woman with wheat-colored hair, upraised, vibrant eyes, and a mischievous, totally mismatched smile that totally ruined her regal image. She was nearly as beautiful as Allira.

"Allira. Ethan. And Ethan's . . . two apprentices?" asked the [Queen], giving their group curious looks.

Ethan shook his head. "Cecilia is a friend of my apprentice. She is not my apprentice."

Cendaria nodded thoughtfully. Oddly enough, Alice noticed [Queen] Cendaria looking at *her* out of the corner of her eyes. Alice saw a veritable flood of perks pass through the [Queen]'s eyes. A few of them extended toward Alice, which she shut off using her perks. The [Queen]'s eyes widened, and then she looked thoughtful. A few moments later, Cendaria addressed her, nearly ignoring the rest of the group.

"I've seen several papers written in your name and heard that you've discovered quite a bit more than that. Are the rumors true?" asked [Queen] Cendaria.

"I did," said Alice, taken aback. Shouldn't conversations like this be Ethan's or Allira's job? "Why do you ask?"

"I was impressed by your papers. But more to the point . . . I wanted to ask you about things. Recently . . . a lot of disasters have fallen upon my people. Monster swarms ravaging the countryside as my [Soldiers] struggle to keep up and handle them. People are losing their minds as their class takes over. Almost 15 percent of the population in this city right now either survived a monster attack or are showing signs of class madness. The number keeps growing every week," said Cendaria. "What exactly is going on?"

Ethan shifted his body to shield Alice from view. He turned toward Alice and opened his mouth to speak . . . but closed it again. He looked thoughtfully at Alice and then back at [Queen] Cendaria. Alice couldn't quite figure out what the meaning of Ethan's glance was.

"That is the kind of information that you would need to speak with the [King] of Illvaria about, [Queen] Cendaria," Ethan said finally. "The relationship between our two countries isn't good enough that we would freely share valuable information."

Allira didn't say a word, but she glared at the [Queen] of Sendria. Alice could feel a hint of hostility in Allira's gaze, as if she particularly disliked the woman.

[Queen] Cendaria looked at Ethan and Allira before she sighed.

"I know that we've had our differences, and I acknowledge that a lot of it is my fault. But even if you dislike me, I don't want my people to die. I may be petty, rude, and obnoxious, but I became an Immortal [Queen] because I truly care about my people." [Queen] Cendaria sounded like she was forcing every single word out through gritted teeth. Alice could see just how little she liked saying this.

And yet, she did it anyway. Despite how much it must have rankled her pride, she was still willing to put her pride away when her people's lives were at stake.

That was . . . respectable. Despite everything Alice had heard about the woman, Cendaria didn't seem *too* bad. And she was right about one thing: The people of Sendria were clearly suffering right now. Alice sighed.

"I don't mind sharing a bit of information, Ethan," she said.

Ethan glanced doubtfully at Alice. "She's a [Queen] from a rival country. And not one that gets along well with Illvaria. You shouldn't just give away information for free to someone like her. You should at least make her pay something for the information," he said.

Alice shook her head.

Maybe she was being foolish. But the collapse of the System was a crisis that affected *everyone*. Just a few weeks ago, Alice and Ethan had run into a massive roadblock because they couldn't trust the Sigmusi to let them pass through their territory. Now, Alice felt like she was on the other side of that decision. Was it really right for her to let people die because of diplomatic tension?

Especially after [Queen] Cendaria had put aside her pride like this to get lifesaving information for her people?

"The entirety of humanity is experiencing a crisis right now," said Alice. "I think that means we should work together. At least until the crisis is over, we shouldn't be stockpiling information that could save lives. The more stable the rest of the world is, the longer I have to find a real solution."

Ethan and Allira gave Alice dubious glances, but after a moment, Ethan sighed and nodded.

Neither of Illvaria's two Immortals said another word—but neither of them moved to stop her.

Alice smiled. It might not be the correct choice, but a part of her felt like this was the only way forward.

Humanity was facing the crisis as a whole. They should work to resolve it as a whole.

Chapter 44

Alice spent the next few hours explaining what she had learned through her experiments.

Of course, Alice hid some information, especially information that touched upon the true nature of the System. But she told the [Queen] of Sendria a lot about simple safety measures she could use to help her people. She discussed how classes could influence people's minds, how [Willpower] seemed to help fight off this influence, and Alice also gave the [Queen] a sample of a ring that corrected [Farmer] mana. The [Queen] had called in her [Enchanter], who apparently had a rather unique ability—once per week, he was able to replicate an enchantment, given the correct materials. There were a lot of restrictions on what he could copy, but none of them prevented him from copying Alice's [Farmer] ring, which meant that it was possible to control at least some of the death and suffering in Sendria.

Alice didn't really have a good suggestion for how to handle the monster swarms, unfortunately. She had hoped that maybe Ethan or Allira would offer a few suggestions on that front, but the two of them didn't offer any advice. Alice wasn't sure whether that was because they weren't interested in helping the [Queen], or whether they had no good solutions to suggest. Either way, Alice certainly didn't have cheap and easy ways to strengthen the military of a nation.

After Alice and [Queen] Cendaria finished talking, the [Queen] promised to repay Alice's kindness in the future. Allira scoffed at the [Queen]'s promise but quietly admitted that she hadn't detected any lies. As the group rode out of Sendria's capital, Alice had mixed feelings about what she had seen.

Allira and Ethan had hinted that they still thought she had made a mistake by sharing so much so freely with [Queen] Cendaria. On an intellectual level, Alice understood where they were coming from. She was basically handing out important, valuable information to a country that Illvaria was on bad to neutral terms with. From a more ruthless perspective, it might be better if Sendria suffered. Alice was pretty tightly connected to Illvaria, since she had lived there for over a year and most of her close social connections lived in Illvaria.

But Alice still didn't think that sharing some of her information was wrong. The stronger humanity was, the better the odds that humanity would overcome this crisis. Alice was willing to help Illvaria more than other countries, but that didn't mean she was willing to leave people to die. In Alice's mind, science was about improving life for humanity as a whole—regardless of what country people lived in. While that didn't always pan out in reality, Alice wanted to at least try to live up to those ideals.

After they left the city, Alice spent some time filtering mana and tallying up her rewards as they rode into the Sendrian countryside. The first and most interesting reward was a few levels in [Legendary Organic Mage], but she had also gotten a level in [Scholar] and [Courtier].

You have leveled up!
Legendary Organic Mage: 1→7, Scholar: 66→67, Courtier: 2→3

Regrettably, [Legendary Organic Mage] was a secondary class instead of primary. If it had been a primary class, Alice suspected that she probably would have immediately jumped to level thirteen or fourteen. Not to mention, if it had been a primary class, she would have gotten new perk choices. Sadly, that wasn't how secondary classes worked.

Alice did start wondering whether it was worth ditching [Kinetic Manabinder] for [Legendary Organic Mage] as a primary class, but decided not to make the swap. Even if she was mostly relying on the Immortals in her group to keep her safe, that didn't mean she wanted to sideline one of her only two self-defense classes. Besides, Alice had gotten one new main class slot already—she had some hope that she would get another someday.

The level in [Courtier] meant nothing to Alice. She seriously doubted any perks from the class would be valuable to her, and didn't have any good ways to consistently level up, either. The level in [Scholar] was a bit disappointing as well—Alice had thought that presenting her research in front of a monarch would give her more than just one level. Alice was pretty sure she had already been close to level sixty-seven in [Scholar], so the rewards really felt lacking.

Maybe people in this world believed that [Scholars] were more inclined to mingle with their own circle or something? Alice suspected that the reason she only got one level was due to some sort of cultural difference in how people perceived [Scholars] in this world. Either way, there was nothing she could do to change that, so she accepted the single level and moved on.

Alice's final reward was quite a bit more exciting.

You have gained an achievement!
First Steps (I)→(III) (Rarity: 6→8)
You have taken the first steps toward resolving the aftermath of the collapse of the System. Even in the face of a seemingly hopeless task, you continue to find ways to mitigate the impact of the catastrophe. And, shockingly, you have started to find success in your actions. Not only that, but you have taken actions to spread your damage control methods far and wide, regardless of nationality.
+50%→100% growth speed for enchanter classes, +20%→40% growth speed for all classes, +50%→100% growth speed for healing classes.   You can improve up to five objects by increasing the number of enchanting instructions they can hold by one. Can be activated up to five times a month. To activate this perk, place the item in your storage perk and then focus on this achievement.   You may also repair a magic construct instead of increasing the number of enchantment instructions, but this is still subject to the five-object limitation. Mana constructs do not need to be placed in storage to be repaired, but you must be in close proximity to them and/or be touching them. (If the mana construct is in another person's body, you must also obtain permission from the owner before repairing anything.)

The {First Steps} achievement had improved significantly. Originally, the achievement had been a rarity-six achievement, but in one fell swoop, it had increased to rarity eight. The rewards for the improved achievement were substantial.

Previously, on top of the growth bonuses she got, the achievement had given Alice the option to improve five objects by a moderate amount, thus increasing the number of enchantment instructions they could hold.

Alice hadn't had much time to make use of this yet. This kind of effect was probably best reserved for when she tried to make an artifact, or perhaps some sort of specialized magic tool. The addition to this achievement made it far more usable, though. Instead of simply improving some enchantments, she could repair a mana construct instead.

Alice had one mana construct that she desperately needed to get working—her mana gem.

Alice still didn't understand everything the System did. However, it was obvious that mana gems were an important part of the last steps toward Immortality. They also somehow managed Alice mana, which was a gradual but terrifying threat to Alice's very personhood. In addition, all the achievements Alice had gained after the collapse of the System only gave about 50 percent of the benefits they were supposed to. Alice wanted both problems fixed.

Furthermore, the act of repairing a mana gem would give Alice some insight into how mana gems worked. Right now, one of the biggest issues Alice had when repairing the mana gem was the sheer complexity of her task. She didn't even know where to start—mana gems were too complicated to fix without some information that she couldn't get right now. But what if Alice could see a mana gem being repaired?

Even better, what if Alice created two different mental maps using her new perk?

One mental map would show the broken, uncorrected version of the mana gem. The other would show the corrected, fixed version. Alice could watch the repair process using her perks and then compare the fixed and unfixed versions. That would give her a *huge* amount of information to work with. Alice might not be able to learn everything from that, but she could certainly learn a lot. Maybe she would find a way to fix everyone's achievements and get another part of the System working again.

Alice smiled at the thought.

If she found a way to repair achievements, the biggest remaining problem to solve would be forming new class seeds. The group was already heading to an Immortal [Enchanter] who could help her solve that problem. In theory, Alice now had a way to solve every major part of the System. The only thing she would need to do afterward was find a way to propagate her repaired version of the System.

It was taking a great deal of time and effort, but everything was coming together.

Then Alice's good mood dissipated as she realized there were problems she hadn't accounted for. Even if she figured out how to rebuild the System, monster swarms were still rampaging unchecked throughout the world. There was also a small chance that the laws of physics might suddenly break and kill everyone tomorrow. Alice had been trying not to think about that because there wasn't much she could do to fix it, but there were still many things she needed to repair. She sighed and took a deep breath.

One step at a time. She still had a long way to go, but she was making progress.

As the group continued riding away from Sendria, Alice thought about the future. She dreamed of a world where the System would be restored and people would no longer need to fear monsters or the world suddenly breaking. As long as she kept working toward her goal, Alice knew that she could make it a reality.

She just hoped that she had enough time left before everyone died.

The next few days were uninteresting. The group mostly encountered abandoned villages, with the occasional inhabited village sprinkled in. There were also a few monsters, but Ethan and Allira quickly dealt with them. Alice spent most of her time focused on the mystery of mana gems. She spent every single moment she could going over the mental map of the mana gem, trying to see if there were any bits left that she still needed to flesh out, or if she could discover anything new.

On the third day, one day before Alice could create a new mental map, the group entered the lands of Superbia.

Alice had to admit, the greenery of Superbia was excellent—it was like walking into a jungle. The weather itself seemed to bend to the will of the Immortal who lived here. Even though it was still winter, in Superbia, it felt more like late spring or early summer.

Giant wheat stalks, nearly twice Alice's height, reached toward the sun as if they yearned to grasp the incandescent sphere in the sky. System mana covered every centimeter of soil, like a cradle enveloping a baby. In the distance, Alice could see giant trees, laden with so much fruit that the trunks were dragged toward the ground by the sheer weight of the produce. The largest tree of all appeared to be an apple tree that would have rivaled redwoods from Earth in height if it stood straight.

Alice didn't know much about apple trees, but she was pretty sure they weren't supposed to grow over a hundred meters tall. Even more bizarre, the tree was *moving*. Every few seconds, a branch dipped toward the earth. If Alice hadn't seen all the System mana, she might have thought she had stumbled upon a tree monster.

The group set exactly one foot into the field of wheat before Ethan gestured for them to stop. At the same time, a ripple of System mana rippled through the field.

"Hello?" called someone in the distance. Alice realized a moment later that the person who was speaking had been standing under the apple tree.

"Jonathan! It's me!" yelled Ethan. His voice carried far into the distance.

"Ah, Ethan!" yelled Jonathan. "Give me just a minute! Let me finish harvesting this apple tree!" Alice watched as the apple tree's branches continued to lower themselves to the ground, before another surge of rainbow mana caused the apples to detach themselves from the branches and drop toward a cloud of mana. Finally, all the apples on the tree were harvested, and Alice saw the cloud of distant mana begin making its way toward them.

A few moments later, she got her first good look at Jonathan, the Immortal [Farmer] who had founded a five-person country. He was a tall man. He had broad shoulders, a bushy beard, and rich brown hair. He was handsome, just like most Immortals, and had a somewhat mischievous gleam in his eyes that made Alice feel strangely relaxed. It was almost the same expression that a child might make after pulling off a successful prank.

"Ethan! It's been . . . what, three decades since we last met face-to-face?" asked Jonathan. "How have you been?"

"My past year has been quite interesting, especially the past few months," said Ethan. "For both good and bad reasons. On one hand, I have a very promising new apprentice"—Ethan gestured toward Alice—"on the other hand, the world seems to be falling apart."

Jonathan also grimaced. "The state of the world is indeed quite concerning." Jonathan sighed before he turned toward the others. "Allira," he said before giving her a courteous bow. "You're even more beautiful than when I last saw you."

"That is how stats work, Jonathan," Allira said as she rolled her eyes. But Alice noticed that the corner of Allira's lips were ever so slightly turned upward when she spoke—which surprised Alice. She hadn't seen Allira genuinely smile when interacting with people before.

Jonathan grinned before he gave Alice and Cecilia a courteous half bow.

"You're Ethan's apprentice, right? What's your name?"

"Alice."

"It's a pleasure to meet you. Good luck on your journey to Immortality."

Alice nodded. Finally, Jonathan turned toward Cecilia.

"I'm not sure who you are, but it's nice to meet you as well! I'm Jonathan, [King] of Superbia, the greatest nation on the planet," he said. The mischievous quirk in his lips became even more pronounced, and Alice realized why Ethan and Allira were so comfortable poking fun at the nation of Superbia.

As it turned out, Jonathan, the [King] of Superbia, was the person *most* comfortable with poking fun at the country. No wonder his acquaintances did the same thing.

Cecilia chuckled. "Nice to meet you. My name is Cecilia. I'm a [Merchant] and an [Enchanter]. But I'm mostly here as Alice's friend."

"Well, welcome to my home, and my country," said Jonathan. A small burst of rainbow mana exited his body, and Alice suddenly felt that Jonathan looked far more *dignified* than before. "Would you like to come in?"

CHAPTER 45

The group followed Jonathan through fields of giant crops as Alice admired the surroundings. She noticed that wheat and apples were nowhere near the only crops grown in Jonathan's country. There were also massive carrots, some kind of pepper, and several exotic plants.

Soon, they reached a large building at the center of the farm with incredibly strange architecture. It looked like a palace-themed farmhouse. The farmhouse was much, much smaller than an actual palace—it was three stories high, and probably had thirty rooms in total. However, it still had some of the traces of a real palace in it—layered enchantments, temperature regulation, and fancy decorations. On the other hand, the walls were made of regular wood, and someone had attached a barn to one side of the house.

Jonathan gestured toward the farmhouse and then winked cheerily.

"A stupendous palace, wouldn't you say, Lady Alice and Lady Cecilia?" he said. "It's the envy of other [Kings] and [Queens]. Truly, a marvel of magical engineering and architecture alike. It's also the very center of Superbia, the most powerful nation in the Shil Confederacy."

Cecilia giggled. Alice also chuckled softly as she looked at the farmhouse. Superbia felt . . . safe, somehow. The indications of monster attacks and the broken System felt almost nonexistent here, and Alice had never heard the [King] of a nation poke fun at his own country before. It felt fun in a way life hadn't been ever since the crisis began.

"It's definitely a mighty palace," Alice said as she fell into the same joking tone that Jonathan had used. Then she raised an eyebrow at Jonathan. "Out of curiosity, you don't . . . well . . ."

"Seem to take my glorious and powerful nation seriously?" asked Jonathan, before he wriggled his eyebrows at her. He grinned. "I get asked that question a lot, actually. I think a lot of people who come to meet with me expect to see a petty tyrant, lording over my random chunk of wasteland and holding a trumped-up opinion of myself." Jonathan shrugged.

"To be honest, I founded Superbia as a joke. I mean, it isn't *entirely* a joke. I do think that [King] and [Farmer] have some pretty good synergy. There's a reason I make so much money as a [Farmer]. But at the end of the day, my nation has five people in it. It's hard to take yourself too seriously when your nation has a weaker military than an average city's [Guard] station." Jonathan grinned. "Not that I can't ward off [Bandits] or monsters, mind you. I'm still an Immortal. But feel free to make whatever jokes about Superbia you want to. I do it myself all the time." Jonathan grinned mischievously again. "Of course, there is one other reason that I founded the nation of Superbia."

"Oh?" asked Alice, curious.

"My children," said Jonathan. "[Princes] and [Princesses] get some rather nice achievements for growing up. I suspect it's because most royal children experience a fair number of assassination attempts as they get older. Reaching the age of ten alive might not be an achievement for most people, but if you're a royal, you get a small achievement as a reward. My country may only be a country on technicality, but my children are still [Princes] and [Princesses]. Thus, they are qualified to receive those achievements. Those achievements aren't anything *too* special—but a free achievement for your kids is a free achievement, right?"

"Huh." Alice nodded to herself. She had to admit, that wasn't what she had been expecting, but it made sense, given Jonathan's attitude so far. If he just treated his "glorious nation" as a way to farm achievements and levels, it made sense that he was willing to poke fun at it. However, Alice also couldn't help but wonder if that messed with his leveling progress as a [King]. If everyone perceived his nation to be a joke, would that make it harder for Jonathan to gain levels as a ruler? Alice had a sneaking suspicion that the answer was yes, based on her understanding of the System.

As Alice ruminated on that idea, the group walked into the farmhouse.

Alice saw two men, one girl, and an older woman sitting in the house arguing with each other.

The youngest child was a girl. She had exceptionally pretty blond hair that resembled molten gold. She was probably eight or nine years old, and Alice guessed she was around level ten. She had bright blue eyes that sparkled with mischief and intelligence. She was sitting by the side as her older brother and her mother argued, and looked positively delighted to watch them yell at each other. When she saw Alice and the others enter, she held up her fingers in a shushing motion before she turned back toward her mother and brother.

The second-youngest child was around Alice's age. He had a bookish demeanor. Alice grinned when she recognized a little bit of [Scholar] mana floating around in his body. However, Alice's attention was quickly drawn to the last child of Jonathan's family.

The oldest man looked to be in his early twenties, and he was about level fifty. He had dark brown hair and green eyes and seemed to be at least reasonably attractive. However, the mana in his body was concerning.

For some reason, there seemed to be a fair amount of [Explorer] mana stuck in his body. He didn't have the [Explorer] class seed. In other words, he was suffering from class-mana poisoning. Alice frowned as she looked at him. She still didn't know how to create new class seeds yet. She couldn't help him right now.

The final member of the family was the older woman. She looked to be in her midforties and had graying hair and intelligent eyes. When she saw Alice and the others enter the room, she held up her hand toward the others, stopping the argument before Alice could make out their conversation. The oldest boy blinked in surprise, while the little girl gave them a disappointed gaze. It looked like she was sad the show had ended. She got up, dusted herself off, and then walked back over to her mother, who gently picked her back up.

"#@*$(&@#% @#(*$#@ @#$#@$?" the oldest child said as he looked at his mother.

"Illvarian . . . I think?" she said, turning toward Jonathan.

Jonathan nodded. "The guests speak Illvarian, Nerissa," he said. "Though the two older ones are Immortals and know most languages in the region."

Nerissa, Jonathan's wife, relaxed. "I speak Illvarian well enough," she said before shaking her head disapprovingly at her son. "Jacob here *should* know Illvarian, but whether he actually does is up for debate." Then she turned toward the bookish-looking boy and the little girl before she sighed. "As for Mimi and Stuart . . . Mimi probably won't understand a word. Stuart?"

"I can speak Illvarian quite well," said the bookish-looking boy. "I have the language skill at eighty."

The little girl looked at the group before she looked at her mother and then made the most dramatic sigh Alice had ever heard.

"*@#($* @#(*$#@$ @#(*$&@#(*$&#@ @)," she said.

"You'll live, Mimi," said Stuart as he snorted softly.

"@#*($@#(*!"

Stuart sighed, then dramatically rolled his eyes at his little sister. "I'll go take Mimi to play," he said. "She could use a little more exercise, anyway. Honestly, if she doesn't try to improve, I'm worried about what her future will be like."

"Go for it. Thank you, Stuart. @#*$(&@#$@. I love both of you," said the woman before she kissed both of them on the forehead. Stuart led Mimi away before Nerissa turned her attention toward Jonathan.

"As for *this* one, could you kindly explain why now is not the time?" she said, gesturing toward Jacob.

"Ahem . . . perhaps we should continue that conversation once the guests are settled?" Jonathan said.

The woman grumbled a few times before she sighed. "Fine." She turned toward Jacob. "Jacob, introduce yourself to the guests."

Jacob looked embarrassed, but after a moment, he nodded.

"Ahem. Nice you meet. Jacob," said the boy. Alice blinked.

Jacob's grammar in Illvarian was a bit questionable.

"I'm Alice," said Alice after a few moments. "Nice to meet you as well."

"I'm Cecilia," said Cecilia a moment later. "Nice to meet you . . . Your Highness?" She turned toward Jonathan. "What title should I be using here?"

Before Jonathan could answer, Jacob grimaced.

"I'm [Farmer]'s son. Not real royalty," he said. Cecilia looked questioningly at Jonathan, who shrugged.

"He's not wrong," said Jonathan.

"I understand. Nice to meet you, Jacob," said Cecilia.

Allira and Ethan eyed Jacob critically for a few moments before Ethan nodded. "I'm Ethan, the Illvarian Immortal of Spells and Seeds," he said.

"Allira, another Illvarian Immortal," said Allira. Then she turned back toward Jonathan. "He seems a bit silly, but at least he doesn't seem like a brat. His personality is all right." Alice tried to comprehend the idea of referring to a twenty-year-old man as a "brat," before she realized just how old most of the people in this room were. Ethan was around four centuries old, and Allira was nearly one hundred. She had no idea how old Jonathan was, but he was at least one hundred and fifty. To them, a twenty-year-old man really might seem like a brat.

Jonathan actually beamed at Allira's words. "He keeps trying to leave, but my wife isn't keen on it. Still, he's a fine young man," he said.

"Illvarian Immortals . . . then Murim know they?" asked Jacob. His eyes started to shine with expectation.

Allira and Ethan nodded, and Alice started to get a better understanding of Jacob's situation.

Jacob seemed to admire Murim. He also had a lot of [Explorer] magic stuck inside his body. He kept trying to leave . . .

He couldn't have picked a worse time. Normally, Alice felt that it wasn't a bad thing for children to find their own path. Admittedly, that was probably due to how she was raised. Her parents had always supported her in finding what she wanted to do in the future. Jacob was even older than her—it was definitely time for him to start finding his own path.

That is, it would have been a good thing if the System was up and running properly. Unfortunately, it was currently broken beyond repair.

Alice started to feel even more uneasy. Just a few minutes ago, she had been thinking that it was nice in Superbia because she couldn't see any signs of the collapse of the System. The moment she had entered the farmhouse, another problem had reared its ugly head.

Alice inched her way over to Ethan. "Ethan, can you put up a privacy perk?" she asked.

Immediately, a bubble of rainbow mana flickered into existence around them. "What did you want to talk about?"

"I have a question. How much do you trust Immortal Jonathan? Is it all right if I discuss more detailed parts of the collapse of the System, or should we only distribute standard information to him?"

"Immortal Jonathan is trustworthy. In his own words, he's just a simple [Farmer] who happens to be the [King] of the greatest nation on Luliv." Ethan rolled his eyes. "He's a good person."

Alice nodded.

"Then, second question. Do you think it's a good idea to tell Immortal Jonathan that his son is flooded with [Explorer] mana and Jacob does not have a class seed to handle it?"

Ethan paused. For a brief moment, his expression turned to horror as he looked at Jacob and Jonathan.

"Really?" Ethan asked. "Jacob is . . ." He then put a hand on his forehead. "No, I can see how that would have happened. That doesn't surprise me. Damn." Ethan sighed. "[Explorer], huh. I haven't visited Jonathan recently, but I did hear that his kid kept trying to leave the country. Why hasn't he picked up the damn class before now?"

Alice shrugged. "I don't know. It does seem like Jacob was arguing with his mother when we came in. If I had to guess, I imagine that his parents are afraid of him getting kidnapped by [Bandits] or something. It's hard to say. Either way, he never got the class when he had the chance, and things are going wrong now."

"So how in the world did the kid get access to [Explorer] mana *now*, after the collapse of the System?" Ethan sounded more numb and frustrated than genuinely curious. "What a mess."

Then, weirdly enough, Alice saw a hint of *respect* in Ethan's eyes. "Even though he picked a terrible time, at least the kid knows what he wants. Finding a way to sneak out and get some [Explorer] mana before Jonathan dragged him back home is pretty impressive, especially under the watch of an Immortal."

Alice sighed. Even if it normally might have been a bit of harmless fun, right now, it was a major threat to Jacob's sense of self.

Ethan sighed again.

"I don't think hiding it from Jonathan is a good idea." Ethan let the perk dissipate and then gestured toward Jonathan. "I trust him. Let's tell him everything and go from there."

Alice nodded, and the two made their way back toward Jonathan, who was still watching as Cecilia, Allira, and his wife chatted and the younger boy and the little girl played in the fields.

"Jonathan . . ." Ethan said hesitantly.

"Ethan?"

"I . . . or rather, my apprentice, has some news to share with you."

Jonathan looked at Ethan's face, and then Alice's, before his gaze hardened. "Not the good kind of news, I take it?"

"Sadly not."

Jonathan grimaced. "Well, let's hear it. The sooner I know, the sooner I can handle it. Is it a monster swarm heading this way?" Jonathan frowned. "If we evacuate my wife and kids to the nearest city, the two of us should be able to face it down, if you're willing to help out."

"Jonathan."

"If it's a bigger horde, I can abandon the farm for a while and just go somewhere else. My country doesn't really mean much to me, so I don't care if it's razed to the ground. I care about my family, and the country can always be rebuilt later."

"Jonathan."

"If there are a *lot* of problem monsters—"

"Jonathan," said Ethan. "It's not a monster horde. It's your son. Jacob. He's sick."

<h1 style="text-align:center">CHAPTER 46</h1>

Immortal Jonathan led Alice, Nerissa, Jacob, and Ethan to a side room, away from everyone else. Allira and Cecilia remained behind since the discussion was rather personal for Jonathan.

After the five sat down in a different room, Jonathan gave them a flat look. "All right, you have my attention. You said that Jacob is sick?" Jonathan's complicated gaze grew deeper as he glanced at his son. "I don't see him coughing or showing any other signs of illness. What do you mean?"

Jacob looked slightly baffled at Jonathan's words, while Nerissa seemed both worried and suspicious.

"I should start with my studies of the System," Alice said. "I've spent the last year using a unique blend of perks and achievements to investigate the System itself because I've always been deeply curious about what it is and how it works. I've learned a lot, but only one thing is relevant to our current discussion. The System operates on mana, the same as any other spell or enchantment."

Jonathan gave Alice a hard look.

That's . . . hard to swallow," said Jonathan. He sounded like he didn't believe her. Alice sighed.

"Well, if you use a lie-detection perk, you can at least confirm that I believe what I'm saying," said Alice. "From there—"

"I don't have any lie-detecting perks," said Jonathan.

"None of us do," said Nerissa. "We don't have much use for them. We live on a farm and sell crops for a living."

Huh?

Alice squinted at Jonathan's eyes and saw that he was telling the truth. She couldn't see any rainbow mana swirling around his eyes. Alice had assumed that most Immortals picked up a lie-detection perk and a privacy perk once they had a few years to spare on some secondary classes. They were just very convenient perks to have, after all. According to Ethan, Jonathan had moved here about a century and a half ago—meaning that Jonathan was probably about two centuries old. Why hadn't he bothered picking up a lie-detection perk yet? Alice decided not to think about this rather confusing fact and instead focused on what this changed. If Jonathan couldn't detect whether she was lying, it made her job a lot harder. Normally, the ubiquitous nature of lie-detection perks in this world made verifying her statements easy, since the other person *knew* that she wasn't lying.

"The System does indeed seem to be closer to a mana construct than a true deity," said Ethan. "I know it's hard to believe, but I wouldn't lie to you about something like this."

"You might not be willing to lie to me about something like this, but claiming the divine is made of mana is . . ." Jonathan massaged his temples. "I've been a devout believer of the Church of the System for almost two centuries."

Jacob and Nerissa both nodded, and Alice also clocked Jacob staring at her with a very slight hint of hostility in his eyes. He didn't seem to know what she was about to say, but he didn't look eager to hear it.

"It's not heresy if it's the truth, Jonathan. We aren't claiming that the System is malicious, or that it hasn't greatly aided humanity's development. If anything, the System seems to actively benefit humanity far more than we previously believed." Ethan shrugged. "It's just that it also runs off mana."

"Those claims sound similar to the Church of Mana's theological position," said Nerissa. "I've always thought their claims were quite bizarre, though. How can you say something that bestows blessings upon us and communicates with us uses magic just like the rest of us? Have you ever seen a mage that can do what the System does?"

Alice tried not to wince. She had never really believed in the System being divine to begin with, since she had been an atheist back on Earth. She had a very hard time wrapping her head around the inner turmoil a real theist would have when someone claimed their god wasn't divine.

"I know it's hard to believe, but look at the world around us," said Alice. "The monster swarms are behaving intelligently, they're using perks that they shouldn't have access to, people are suffering as their class mana spirals out of control. Everything related to the System is going wrong, all at once. As for communicating like the System . . ." Alice reached out a mana tendril to Nerissa and injected a bit of display and meaning mana into her. It was exactly enough to create a simple "Hello World" message, entirely via the same method the System's notifications used.

Nerissa looked as if she had seen a ghost. She glanced back and forth between Alice and the System message several times, while Jonathan and Jacob looked on in confusion. To help them understand what was going on, Alice gave them a fake System message as well.

Jonathan looked at Alice's custom System message for a few moments, before he rubbed his forehead and looked out the window.

"Damn. That's something I never thought I'd see. I've heard that people can't even see proper descriptions for new perks, but I didn't really think much of it until you pointed it out," Jonathan said before sighing. "I'm not one to disbelieve what's right in front of my eyes, I suppose. Do you have any other proof? I can accept that you can mimic System messages, but I can think of a few other ways to accomplish that using perks or alternate types of magic."

Alice sighed in relief. She had been expecting much worse when Jonathan had started disagreeing with their story. However, it seemed that Ethan's judgment was correct. Even though Immortal Jonathan and his family seemed to be devout believers in the Church of the System, they were still willing to hear her out. Alice could very much prove that she had been studying the System and could interact with it on a deeper level, at least.

"I *do* have a way to prove that I can interact with the System on a more fundamental level," said Alice after a moment. "I can't directly prove it runs on mana, since you don't seem to have any type of mana sense. But I can prove my abilities. Would that suffice for you?"

Nerissa paused for a few moments, as if thinking over Alice's suggestion. Finally, she nodded.

"If you can prove that you're able to interact with perks somehow, or some other aspect of the System, that would lend your story a lot of weight."

"Do you have any perks that affect your surroundings and that you don't mind me messing with? A few of my abilities let me shut down the mana perks run on," she said. Alice could also use {Shared Memories} to show Jonathan what she had seen during her experiments, of course. But Jonathan was neither a researcher nor a mage and might not know what he was looking at if she shared her memories with him. This seemed like a better way to prove her story.

"I'll use a perk that manipulates the weather by creating a few rain clouds. I usually use it to irrigate the farm."

Alice nodded. Jonathan closed his eyes. A few moments later, Alice saw a large burst of rainbow mana rip its way out of Jonathan's body.

Alice immediately cut the surge of rainbow mana down with a burst of the No_Magic mana that Alice could produce using her {No_Mana} perk, which Alice had recently renamed "antimagic mana" after gaining the ability to fix the System's broken grammar.

Jonathan glanced out the window, as if he were waiting for rain clouds to appear. Jacob and Nerissa were staring at Alice, but nobody spoke. After a few minutes of silence, Jonathan shook his head in surprise.

"Well, I'll be. You really stopped my perk from activating. You've made your point. I'll believe that the System is built off mana for now." Jonathan glanced at Alice again, and his expression turned thoughtful. "Are there limits to your ability to prevent perks from working?"

"I'd prefer not to talk about my combat abilities," said Alice. "I realize that I might not have made this clear from the beginning, but I'd also appreciate it if you didn't spread some of this information around. There are too many dangers that could potentially cause the world to shatter and kill everyone if people poke too hard at the underlying nature of reality."

Jonathan's eyes widened at Alice's words. "I apologize. My curiosity got the better of me, but asking was indeed disrespectful. It's probably not that relevant to this conversation any way. I promise not to spread your personal information to other people without your express consent. Back to the main topic. What's wrong with my boy?"

"The System does a lot of really important things with mana," said Alice. "Such as handling things like [Farmer] mana and turning them into magic seeds. Without the System's aid, mana seems to change people's thoughts and personalities by turning them into puppets of their class. Bit by bit, their free will is eroded and replaced by a burning desire to behave like a person of their profession. For example, a [Farmer] without the System's aid will start to farm mindlessly and endlessly. The System removes this impact on people's free will and converts it into class levels, turning a dangerous curse into something beneficial. But now, the System is unable to do its job properly."

"Ah, I see where this is going. I've heard that a lot of people were taken over by their classes recently, and that the [Willpower] stat helps mitigate this effect," said Jonathan. "I've even heard that eventually, if their condition gets bad enough, they stop sleeping, eating, or drinking on their own."

Alice nodded. It was nice to talk with people who could put together information quickly.

"How does this relate to me?" asked Jacob.

"You have a great deal of [Explorer] mana in your body, but no class seed," said Alice. "So all the [Explorer] mana in your body is now wiping away your sense of self and driving you to explore the world. I don't think the impact is that severe yet, but it can get worse very quickly if it's not taken care of. Especially if you give in to your desires and start exploring, since that will form more [Explorer] mana and form a problematic feedback loop."

Jonathan frowned. "Now that I think about it, for the past two weeks, Jacob was incessantly asking my wife and me if he can go exploring. You've always had a bit of wanderlust, but it has seemed far more impactful recently," said Jonathan as he turned toward Jacob. "Can you confirm whether your attitude toward exploration has been unusually heightened recently?"

Jacob seemed ready to object on sheer principle before he thought better of it. He furrowed his brows in thought before he reluctantly nodded. "I have been really interested in exploring recently. Far more than usual," said Jacob.

Jonathan grimaced. "So it's true," he said. Then, he relaxed. "At least he's not in immediate danger. " He turned toward Alice. "What's your solution? I doubt you would have brought it up if you didn't intend to help."

"The best thing to do is give Jacob an antimana ring. If he wears one, he won't break any nearby mana and convert it into [Explorer] mana, meaning that the dangerous mana won't build up and continue to corrode his mind. I can make one pretty quickly if I have the materials."

Jonathan relaxed a bit more when Alice mentioned her solution. It seemed like he had been afraid that the cure would be far more complicated.

"On the other hand, that's more of a temporary solution," said Alice. "He will still get hit by all the levels he *should* have gotten the moment the ring is taken off. But I don't actually know how to create a class seed yet. We were going to meet with someone who I hoped would help me figure this out, actually."

Jonathan frowned. "A temporary solution is far better than no solution at all, but you have no way to properly address the issue?"

"Unfortunately, I do not," said Alice. "I am working on it, though."

Nerissa looked anything but reassured by Alice's statement. Jonathan frowned as he looked at Jacob again. "How did you even *get* [Explorer] mana? Based on what Alice described, you would have needed to start exploring *after* the System broke down, but I don't recall you doing such a thing."

Jacob also looked confused. "That's a good question. I haven't done anything crazy behind your back. I mean, I did venture a bit out of the farm a few times to talk with some [Traders], but I've done that plenty of other times, and it has never created any [Explorer] mana."

"I wonder what it actually *means* to explore something," said Alice. "The exact ideas that people associate with exploring could have a pretty big impact on how classes work, so they are likely relevant to this case." Alice didn't know how to create class seeds yet, but she suspected that understanding what a class was supposed to be was probably part of it. "What distinguishes an [Explorer] from other similar professions? After all, Jacob is *mostly* filled with [Explorer] mana, although he does have other adjacent types of mana in his body as well."

"I've spoken with Murim about this a few times, actually," said Ethan. "[Explorers] are usually renowned for exploring unknown regions of territory. If you 'explore' a city that other people have already mapped out, you don't really get much XP for it. On the other hand, if you explore a region of wilderness that nobody has ever set foot in before, that's worth a bunch of levels. Regions that are poorly mapped out count for some growth, but not much. Most of the people who have set foot on the Western Continent and survived were [Explorers] who got a huge amount of experience for every meter of land they mapped out. If you escape alive, the continent is a golden opportunity to level [Explorer] classes. Of course, most people who tried became monster chow."

Alice turned toward Jacob, who still looked confused. She wasn't the best at reading people, but didn't think he was lying. "Are there any other ways to get [Explorer] levels?" asked Alice. "Any loopholes, or exceptional circumstances?"

"I do vaguely recall that there seem to be a few other circumstances where you can get levels in [Explorer]," Ethan said after a few moments of thought. "I know that people exploring southern Illvaria recently got [Explorer] levels just fine. Since the area was settled a century ago, that doesn't make sense—after all, while old maps are outdated, they are still largely accurate . . ."

"So maybe significant terrain alterations count as far as leveling goes?" asked Alice. "If people's understanding of an area is wrong or missing details, you can get [Explorer] mana from mapping it out?"

"Maybe. But even so, I don't recall there having been any major terrain modifications to my farm. Unless my perks count as major terrain modifications themselves? But I don't change up the farm much . . ." Jonathan looked even more confused than before. Alice also felt baffled.

Where had Jacob gotten so much [Explorer] mana? According to Alice's estimation, if the System were working properly, he probably had enough [Explorer] XP to gain seven or eight levels. The idea that nobody knew where he had gotten the XP from was disturbing.

Then Jonathan's gaze started to morph into an expression of horror.

"No, I know the problem. Two weeks ago, there was a monster horde that tried to run into my farmland. I ended up beating them back, but one of the two types of monsters was some kind of giant beetle that specialized in manipulating soil. They kept creating giant mounds of dirt and trying to bury me. The fields looked like someone had built an entire mountain around one of the edges—it was probably sixty meters high by the end of the fight, since they kept trying to add more soil to the mound and collapse it on top of me. They were way stronger than they should have been. It was highly unusual for monsters to be able to warp terrain that much, or at least rare before all this craziness started. I eventually removed it once I got the rest of the farm back in order, but that might have counted for altering the terrain?"

Alice grimaced.

"Probably?" she said. She was operating on pure guesswork here, but maybe that made sense. Alternately, perhaps Jacob had slipped away for a shorter trip to a different nearby area and had gotten some [Explorer] mana there. If terrain alterations also counted for leveling speed, it was much harder to determine what had happened. Alice sighed. "I don't know. Either way, the situation hasn't changed. We need to get Jacob an antimana ring, and I also need to figure out how to make actual class seeds. For that, we need to reach our destination."

Jonathan also frowned in thought at Alice's words. Until he turned toward Ethan.

"So the only way to fix this is with her?" he asked.

Ethan nodded. "My apprentice seems to be the best positioned person to solve this mess."

Jonathan grimaced as he looked at his farm before he finally sighed. "In that case, can my family come with you as you travel?"

Alice blinked in surprise.

CHAPTER 47

I'm sorry, what?" Alice asked as she scratched her head. Jonathan's suggestion had taken her by surprise. The idea of an Immortal family joining the group was outside of her expectations. "That seems rather sudden. What brought about this request?"

"I would also like to know that, Jonathan," said Nerissa.

Ethan nodded. "I was just planning to restock on food here and visit a friend, Jonathan, not recruit a new Immortal."

"First of all, the monster hordes are a potential threat," said Jonathan. "Even if I drove the last horde away, I didn't manage to exterminate it completely. I'm not a combat class, and I can feel the limitations that impose on my ability to protect my family. I don't want them to get killed because I'm not strong enough, and right now that seems like a distinct possibility."

Some of the surprise in Nerissa's eyes died out. Alice surmised that the situation really had been dire at the time for Nerissa's expression to change so drastically after Jonathan mentioned the previous monster horde.

Ethan winced. "I suppose that makes sense. If I had a family behind me and they couldn't protect themselves, I would also be worried. Still, is that the only reason? I don't mean to challenge your decision—I'm just wondering. Also, wouldn't this mean abandoning your country?"

"My five-person country that consists of a strip of wasteland that no one wants?" Jonathan rolled his eyes. "I can rebuild this farm anywhere I want in a week or two. My family is what I want to protect."

Alice agreed with that. When one person could manufacture enough food to feed a few towns and easily grow luxury crops from other climates, it was easy to accumulate wealth and establish good relations with neighbors. Jonathan might lose some benefits from his [King] class for a while, but exchanging protection for a few years of weakened production was probably a reasonable trade-off for him.

"Still, isn't moving with us dangerous?" asked Alice. "First of all, our group has a high chance of running into monsters as we travel. More importantly, however, traveling with us might end up increasing the level of [Explorer] mana you're exposed to. While we are theoretically traveling through well-known areas, we might run into more altered terrain if we get unlucky. Staying put seems less likely to cause this problem, at least."

Jacob's eyes shone for a moment as Alice mentioned that the group would be traveling, before his gaze dimmed as if it was dawning how dangerous it would be for him.

Jonathan shrugged. "If I don't move with your group, there are still potential ways to get [Explorer] mana—as shown by how Jacob ended up with [Explorer] mana despite never leaving the farm. Since that's the case, I'd rather travel with your group, since I know that Ethan and Allira are both combat-focused Immortals. If we run into a monster swarm that manages to bypass them and get at my family, that would be awful—but also incredibly unlikely. Two combat-focused Immortals is practically the best protection on the Southern Continent. Even some [Kings] on the Central Continent only have a few Immortals protecting them. Besides, if I travel with you, I can get a bit of [Explorer] mana . . . and I'm counting on that."

"Excuse me?" asked Alice. Jonathan *wanted* [Explorer] mana? That made no sense at all to her.

"Here's the thing," said Jonathan as he rested a hand on Jacob's shoulder. "My son really wants to leave. I haven't let him adventure out into the world *yet*, but that doesn't mean I never intend to let him go. I just want him to be a bit more prepared when it happens, and spend a few more years as a family together. But now my decision puts my kid in danger. Worse, if he had left to explore the world a few years ago, he would have had the [Explorer] class. He would have been safe. I don't want my decision to cost my child his life. You still need to find a way to actually create class seeds, right? You'll need test subjects. If I end up with a lot of [Explorer] mana, you can create an [Explorer] class seed on me first, right? With the condition that you prioritize my son the moment you have a way to create safe seeds. It'll be much, much harder to hurt me compared to the average test subject." Jonathan's eyes grew firmer, even as Alice's grew wider. "Are you willing to make that deal with me?"

"Dad . . ." Jacob's expression grew harsh. "I don't want you to put yourself in danger for me. I do want to explore, but that doesn't mean I don't care about you or Mom. I just don't want to be stuck on a farm for the rest of my life, either."

"As a father, it's my decision to put myself in danger to protect my kids," said Jonathan.

Jacob shook his head, but before he could speak up, Nerissa grabbed his hand and led him out of the room.

Alice glanced at Nerissa and Jacob as they left, and hesitated. She felt moved by Jonathan's words. Jonathan was an Immortal. He had forever to live, as long as he wasn't killed by an external force. Despite his Immortality, he was willing to put himself at risk to save his mortal son. Alice hadn't expected Jonathan to be willing to risk so much for his family.

Jacob had already made it clear that he didn't approve of Jonathan's decision, but it seemed like Nerissa approved. Otherwise, she wouldn't have led Jacob out of the room to let Jonathan argue his case in peace.

Then the moment passed. Alice pushed her emotions aside and shook her head like a rattle.

"I was intending to test everything on myself," said Alice. "I don't think it's a good idea to try things on someone else first. I can watch myself using my special perks and achievements to see if something goes wrong first. Besides, forcing someone else to be my test subject is wrong. I don't want to cross that line. There are other benefits to using myself as a test subject, too. I only test things on myself when I'm pretty sure they're safe, while I might subconsciously overlook greater risks if I'm using someone else as a lab rat instead."

"You might not have the option to be cautious anymore. Tell me, how much time do we have left before the System crisis spirals out of control?" asked Jonathan.

"I'm guessing less than a year," said Alice. "Actually, now that I think about it, the monsters rampaging around are probably a bigger problem than I've been giving them credit for being. As more people fall victim to class-mana madness and lose their sense of self, their sense of self-preservation will also become weaker. I imagine these two problems will compound and cause towns and cities to start to collapse rapidly once enough people get taken out by class-mana madness."

"And how long is this journey supposed to take?"

"Less than a month for the entire round trip, assuming that I learn quickly." Alice grimaced. "Though that doesn't factor in the time I'll need to actually learn how to make class seeds, so we'll see once we get there."

"Then I think it's all the more important you have a test subject you don't need to be quite as delicate with," said Jonathan. "Right now, you're planning on using yourself as a test subject—but if you mess up *once*, you might be stuck sick in bed for a week or two. When we're counting the weeks before everything falls apart, that means that one mistake on your end results in the destruction of the world. Besides, don't you think you'll feel more and more pressured as things get worse? When you see greater and greater piles of corpses and growing desperation, will you still test everything perfectly before taking risks? You seem like the type of person that tries to help other people when you can. I doubt you'll just sit by when people are dying. That's dangerous when we need you to be as calm and collected as possible. With me, you can be much more aggressive when trying new things out. After all, I am *very* sturdy."

That was a perspective Alice hadn't heard before—and Jonathan had a point. She hesitated. This was a big crossroad in her decision-making.

On one hand, Alice still felt that human experimentation was fundamentally *wrong*. The Society had gotten started on that path, and Alice was disgusted by the actions they had taken. She still remembered some of the test subjects that she and Ethan had rescued from the Society base. The people there, and the things they had been subjected to, still lived in Alice's nightmares. Even worse was the number of child test subjects, and test subjects that hadn't made it out alive.

On the other hand, this wasn't the same thing. Jonathan was volunteering to be a test subject, and as an Immortal [Farmer], his [Endurance] stat was far higher than the Society's test subjects' stats. Jonathan was also much stronger than her. The moment he didn't like what she was doing, he could knock her unconscious with a punch and then walk out, and there was nothing she could do to stop that. Times were also getting worse. Alice had developed some solutions to the catastrophe, but they were slow, hard to spread, and required special resources to create. If Alice refused to accept help from anyone else, there was still a possibility that the world would end. Alice didn't think that humans could live in this world without the System, and she wasn't replacing it fast enough to keep people alive.

Did she really have the option of denying a willing test subject?

"As a [Farmer], how resilient are you?" asked Alice.

"The two main stats that [Farmers] tend to improve are [Endurance] and [Strength]," said Jonathan. "They're the two most useful things for tilling the fields. I have over eight hundred [Endurance], once you factor in my multipliers and miscellaneous conditional perks. I just need to make sure I'm in the middle of farmland that I'm managing myself. Killing me, or even injuring me, is very, very hard."

Alice nodded thoughtfully but she was still hesitant.

The closest she had gotten to human experimentation before this was observing people undergo their mana baptisms. A project that was currently on hold because the collapse of the System was several orders of magnitude more important.

Deep in her heart, Alice still wanted to say no. But despite how much better it would make her feel, Alice also wasn't blind. Society was already collapsing, and this would increase her odds of finding a solution before everything fell apart.

Alice felt icky, but she also realized that saying no was impractical.

"I'll think about it," said Alice. That was the best she could do for now. She would leave this problem for future Alice to think about.

Jonathan nodded. "I'll let you think about it. But this is the best way."

Alice gritted her teeth and then turned toward Ethan.

"I believe it's time to leave," said Ethan thoughtfully. "I, for one, am not opposed to you joining us, Jonathan. You're a good man, and I'm happy to bring you along."

Jonathan nodded, and the group went to collect the rest of Jonathan's family.

Jonathan's family was not happy about leaving the farm. Since Jacob knew *why* they were leaving the farm, he seemed even more upset. Although whatever discussion he'd had with his mother had at least prevented him from speaking against Jonathan's decision. He still occasionally glared at Alice and Ethan, though.

This sharply contrasted with the little girl, Mimi, who asked why they were leaving their nice house for the dirty wilderness. Mimi seemed to perk up a bit when Alice gave Mimi her horse to ride—after all, the group had only brought four horses with them, and now that they were nine people, the horses were more of a way for the weaker members of the group to swap which muscles were sore instead of a way to speed up.

The middle child, Stuart, didn't seem to have much of a reaction either way. Thus, the group's size swelled considerably as they left Jonathan's farm. As the group stepped out of Jonathan's territory, Alice noticed a rather peculiar reaction from the farm itself.

The moment Jonathan stepped off the farm, it was as though a small tremor of rainbow mana radiated out of his feet. Then Alice rubbed her eyes, and she realized it wasn't a tremor that *left* Jonathan's feet. Instead, it was the reverse. As they moved farther away, all the rainbow mana in Jonathan's farm started to move toward his feet. One droplet of rainbow mana after another rushed toward his body, joining the nebulous cloud of mana inside him, and at the same time, the farm started to wither.

The verdant green crops started to die. Giant pieces of produce started to decay, dropping from the vines or branches that bore them. Every single plant on the farm started to disappear as the seconds passed.

The last to fall was the giant apple tree that had first caught Alice's attention. The branches and bark started to shrink and darken until eventually it collapsed under its own weight. Instead of a magnificent tree, it was now just a pile of ashy bark.

By the time ten minutes of travel had passed, the verdant farm filled with overripe produce, abundant water, and giant crops had disappeared. In its place was what Alice assumed must have been the farm's original appearance. It was a flat, gray wasteland with a scraggly, threadbare creek running through it. There were still a few weeds present in the farm's former territory, showing that it wasn't *impossible* to grow crops there—but the land was only a few steps away from looking like barren tundra.

No wonder nobody wanted to conquer this territory from Superbia. This kind of land was so worthless that most nations would probably forget it was even within their borders to begin with.

Mimi looked at the farm with big, sad eyes as the green wonderland vanished, and softly started crying as Jonathan's wife plucked her off the horse and cradled her in her arms. Mimi's muffled sobs continued to echo through the air as they moved.

"Sorry. She's very attached to our home," Nerissa said as the group kept walking.

"Where are we heading next, Ethan?" asked Alice, trying to distract Jonathan's family from the collapse of Superbia.

"This is the final country that we need to cross before reaching Morendia," said Ethan. "It's called Fendrallia. It's on the poorer side, since their territory has some pretty bad climate issues—the climate is cold, and the rainfall is pretty uneven. A lot of the country is tundra, with weird bits of frozen swamps mixed in. However, it does also have a good amount of iron, so their military has always had decent supplies. The country is a good one for [Blacksmiths]. They have a reasonably robust magic scene, too, although it's far behind Illvaria," said Ethan. "I would say their overall magical development is somewhere in the top twenty of the Southern Continent."

Alice nodded thoughtfully as the group made their way into Fendrallia.

Chapter 48

The air in Fendrallia was laced with a subtle, creeping chill that burrowed into Alice's bones as the group set foot in the country. The cold surprised her. After taking the {Extremophile} perk, Alice hadn't paid much attention to temperature. However, for the first time in months, she found herself bothered by the climate.

She glanced at Jonathan's family. They also looked uncomfortable.

"Ethan, could we get a bit of warmth?" Alice asked as her eyes flicked toward Jonathan's family.

Ethan winced. "I was distracted. Thank you for reminding me, Alice," he said. A burst of thermal mana drifted out of his body, and their surroundings started to warm up.

"Better?" asked Ethan.

Mimi nodded enthusiastically as she moved farther away from her mother, who had been serving as Mimi's makeshift heater.

"Good. Let's keep moving, then," said Ethan, and the group continued walking through the Fendrallian countryside.

The next thing that Alice noticed was the water. The land was becoming wetter and more swamplike, and a light fog blanketed the landscape, growing more dense the farther the group traveled. The fog was abnormal. It didn't just cut off vision—it also seemed to swallow sound. It wasn't too severe, but Alice noticed that sound wasn't traveling as far as it should have. Voices carried, but footsteps disappeared as if they were illusions. Which meant it might be fairly easy for something to sneak up on them.

In addition to the fog and the cold, there was a stench in the air. Alice turned toward the Immortals and realized she wasn't the only one to notice.

"I cannot identify this smell, but it is quite unpleasant," Ethan finally said.

Allira closed her eyes and started humming. The group waited patiently while Allira's music, colored with rainbow mana, drifted into their surroundings.

Finally, Allira's eyes snapped open.

"Ethan, do you have a way to filter the air?" she asked. "It shouldn't be a problem for us, but it might be for Jonathan's family, Cecilia, and your apprentice."

Alice shuddered and immediately scanned the air around them. Allira's wariness put Alice on alert. Was the stench some kind of dangerous chemical or poison?

Ethan's eyes widened. A burst of rainbow mana extended out of his left hand and started spreading outward. Wherever the rainbow mana went, the air seemed to ripple and bend, as if it were being funneled through an invisible filter. It looked similar to the ripples of heat cast by a hot campfire. As the magic finished its work and started to dissipate, the stench also began to fade.

Ethan grabbed Alice's hand. "Give me {Patient's Consent}." Alice was taken aback, but she nodded. A moment later, several pulses of organic mana pushed into her body. Ethan relaxed.

"You're fine. Let me go check Jonathan's family," he said before he made his way to the other half of the group.

As Ethan left, Alice turned toward Allira. "What's happening?" she asked. Allira was the one who had alerted the rest of the group, and Alice still wasn't entirely sure what was going on.

"It seems that some kind of poisonous gas is in the air," said Allira, frowning. "I don't actually know what it is, but one of my perks tells me it isn't safe. One of my scouts also started to meet with problems when I sent it forward. Since they don't need to breathe, I suspect that it can also harm through skin contact."

Alice wasn't sure what Allira meant by "scouts" but decided it must be something perk related. She wondered if Allira could summon them through her song illusions. The previous times Alice had seen Allira change reality by singing, her illusions hadn't seemed very sapient—but perhaps they could be with the right combination of perks? Alice decided not to dwell on it, and turned her attention back to the poison in the air.

"Is the poison magical?" asked Alice. But a moment later, she shook her head, realizing this was a silly question. If it was mana-related, she would have seen it with her mana sight. The only magic-related oddity Alice noticed in their surroundings was that the mana here was unusually dense.

"Jonathan's family is safe," said Ethan, shaking Alice out of her thoughts as he returned to the main group. "As for the mana here, it should still be low enough that Jonathan's family won't undergo a baptism, but we should keep an eye out. This place definitely didn't look like this originally. It's hard to say what monsters live here, or what other dangers we might run into."

Alice continued scanning the area, frowning. The area itself felt *wrong*. There wasn't any one geographical feature that stood out as incorrect. However, it was all unnaturally perfect. It looked like it had come straight out of a fairy tale. If Alice took a children's book and then looked up a picture of a treacherous bog, this was exactly what it would look like.

This was not promising news. Alice had already suspected that beliefs were influencing the landscape, since the region seemed very different from what Ethan had told her about it.

"This doesn't seem like it matches your description very well," said Alice, turning to Allira and Ethan.

"It's definitely different," Allira said. "I haven't been here in decades, but there is absolutely no way this place changed *that much* since then. This was either manipulated via the efforts of humans, or something else."

Alice doubted anyone would have spent the amount of money and manpower required to transform this area into a bog like this. Once again the power of belief was the only answer that made sense. Worse, Alice still had no idea how exactly this worked, or how to stop it. She was still very nervous about the idea that the laws of physics might just short-circuit and implode at any time. This was also the most obviously changed terrain she had discovered so far. Most other oddities she encountered, like the exploding trees back in Illvaria, had been less overt.

Taking a closer look at the swamp, Alice stepped back in surprise.

There was something new in the air. A type of mana construct that she had simply never noticed in the past. It was incredibly tiny—no bigger than a speck of dust floating in the air. It would have been almost impossible to spot, but it was faintly vibrating. Combined with its unusual density and the nearly homogenous mana type, Alice could *just* make out the presence of this tiny little thread. She squinted at her surroundings and realized that it wasn't alone. There were dozens of other little mana tethers—they were just as tiny, and just as nearly invisible, but now that she was looking for them, she could spot them if she paid close attention.

Altogether they formed something resembling a spiderweb that crisscrossed the entire swamp. It was made of pure mana, as well as . . . something else. Alice didn't know how to describe it, but it felt both inexplicably alien and inexplicably familiar at the same time.

"Hold on a moment," said Alice. The others froze while Alice inspected the strange thread.

After several minutes of observation, Alice was able to confirm a few things: First of all, the thread was vibrating at seemingly random intervals and the vibrations were infrequent.

Second, this was indeed not quite like the other unique types of mana that she had encountered so far. Alice had originally suspected that one of these threads might be another undiscovered variety, but in actuality, this little thread of mana wasn't unique in composition, only in structure.

Third, that probably meant it wasn't set up by some monster. After all, monsters didn't create mana structures like this.

Alice felt a rush of excitement and anxiety. Was this yet another piece of the System she had failed to understand before now? This swamp was the first place where Alice had encountered these threads, and if she had missed a critical piece of the System, she *needed* to know as soon as possible.

But that would mean going farther into the swamp.

Alice eyed the three Immortals and relaxed. She would never be willing to take this kind of risk on her own, but with three Immortals protecting her, it greatly reduced her chances of dying. Two of them were combat-focused, and Jonathan could likely survive a bomb detonating in his face.

Realizing she hadn't spoken for a few minutes, Alice popped her head up. "Do you think it would be possible to explore this bog?" Alice asked before she outlined her reasoning. She explained about the mana threads, and how they might be crucial to helping her understand this connection between beliefs and terrain that were creating new threats to humanity.

"If you've never seen these 'mana threads' before, then it's definitely worth investigating," said Ethan. "I was thinking of taking a detour around, but if it holds research value, we can push through instead. This swamp is right in the middle of the route we were originally planning to take but it wasn't here before. I don't know what we'll find. But I also doubt that anything here could harm us, even if we have a few noncombatants with us. Allira? What do you think?"

"Fine with me," said Allira confidently. "We're more than sufficient to deal with any reasonable threat."

Jonathan frowned then nodded. "If it'll help you learn more, I suppose that *is* the entire point of the trip. However, this would also mean that my family and I have to tag along. With how many monsters are in the area, I don't know if I can keep the noncombatants safe on my own if we try to split up. I don't know how I feel about that."

"At the end of the day, Alice's ability to learn more is what will determine how safe both you and your son are," said Ethan.

Jonathan paused before he sighed. "Fair point," he said.

If everyone was on board, they could gather some information before they departed.

"What do you see *inside* the bog, Allira?" asked Ethan. "Anything that will change our minds?"

"There are a lot of monsters lurking in the woods. Most of them look like ambush predators. Lots of camouflage, monsters hiding just below the surface of the water, and other threats with low mobility. If we watch our step, we should be able to avoid big fights."

"How about we go over instead?" Ethan asked. "I can pick up the group and fly us over the area for a few hours, find a spot to rest, and we could get back to moving. Still riskier than going around, but that should let Alice observe the area without exposing ourselves to real danger. If we see something more interesting, I can always drop down to the ground for a closer look. I can also temporarily fly ahead to scout where your shadows fail."

"That seems reasonable to me. Try doing a practice flight first, though—that way we'll know if there are any flying monsters we need to watch out for."

Ethan nodded, then his feet lifted off the ground. Alice, Allira, and Jonathan stayed behind as Ethan jerked through the air like a man launched out of a catapult. In seconds, he flew over the outermost reaches of the treacherous bog before he started to swerve left and right at breakneck speeds that would have killed a human from Earth. After several minutes of flying around, Ethan returned to the group.

"There aren't any airborne problems that I saw. We should be safe as long as we don't get too close to the ground. Alice, can you help me keep an eye out? With the number of perks and achievements you have dedicated to observing mana, your mana vision is better than mine. I'd never know if I missed something," said Ethan. Alice nodded. She had no problem serving as a backup scout.

Ethan's kinetic magic lifted up the entire group by their clothes. Alice kept an eye on their surroundings as they floated over the swamp. True to Ethan's word, soaring over the swamp seemed to insulate them from most of the danger on the ground. The group maintained a distance of about ten meters between themselves and the tops of the gnarled trees, which was close enough for Alice to observe the swamp's mana without getting attacked by the ambush predators on the ground. Even so, Alice was astounded by the wide variety of monsters she could see down there. With her mana sight, the various types of mana and camouflage monsters used to disguise themselves couldn't evade her vision, which meant Alice was being treated to an entire encyclopedia's worth of monsters lurking in the darkness, waiting for unwary prey to step in the wrong spot and get eaten.

As they went deeper into the bog, the mana threads became slightly easier to notice, too—because they were growing thicker. She had no clue what to make of that.

Nearly four hours passed before Ethan started to get tired. Allira found a clearing for the group to rest, and Ethan set everyone down to start setting up tents.

Everything was unpleasantly damp. More disturbing, the swamp seemed to literally squirm whenever she wasn't paying attention to it. It was like a sapient labyrinth that was actively trying to trap them. She was sure that if the group had tried to travel by land instead of air, they would have had a very hard time keeping their directions straight—which made her more wary of the swamp.

The threads of mana in the campsite were a bit thinner than they had been in the more monster-rich parts of the swamp, but Alice was still baffled by what it all meant.

Most unnerving of all, Alice could feel dozens of sets of eyes watching them from the shadows, and she could see flashes of monsters shuffling in the distance. Alice pointed out several of these spots to Ethan, who was happy to help get rid of any troublesome lurkers. But some spots didn't contain any monsters at all. Alice tried using {Enhanced Senses} to get a better idea of what she was feeling, but every single use of the perk just led to plants with unusually dense mana. It was as if the *swamp itself* was doing the watching. She shuddered.

The place really was creepy. Even though she had wanted to come in here, and she was getting all sorts of information about how human beliefs could *literally bring a swamp to life*, she was unnerved.

After Alice and Ethan cleaned up the surrounding monsters and ripped apart the plants that were watching them, the group settled down for the night, with Allira standing guard.

After falling asleep, Alice returned to her dream library. There, she had much less creepy things than the disturbing bog to worry about.

{Magic Modeling} had finally come off cooldown. That meant that she could run an experiment she had been thinking about.

Alice had already spent several days using {Magic Modeling} to map out every single nook and cranny of the mana gem in her brain. She also knew for a fact that there was something wrong with it—the gem was supposed to absorb all the Alice mana in her body, but it had failed to do so.

This had been a source of worry. It wasn't urgent, since she could handle a pretty sizable amount of Alice mana before it really started to influence her personality. Still, she wanted to resolve the issue sooner rather than later.

First, Alice examined {First Steps}, the achievement she had recently upgraded. It gave her two abilities: She could increase the number of enchanting instructions an object could hold by one, but Alice didn't really care about this as she hadn't been doing much enchanting recently.

What she did care about was the second option: She could use the achievement to repair mana constructs, such as the one in her brain.

Alice ran her idea through {Safety Analysis}, then activated the achievement to repair her mana gem.

All of a sudden, she felt the mana gem become *more*. Before, it had looked like a multifaceted, microscopic rainbow gemstone made of mana. But now it was beginning to look cleaner and more polished. Then it began to transform. For a brief moment, it tore itself to pieces. Then the entire thing unraveled into a ball of wires, chunks of mana, and flat edges that resembled plates. Several wires and cables started spreading from the messy pile of mana to the rest of her body, like a second set of nerves, while another part of the mana gem almost seemed as if it were trying to *catch* something. Some of the wires and plates started reassembling themselves into a structure that looked almost like a satellite dish. Parts of it opened and closed, and through a mechanism Alice utterly failed to comprehend, dragged in mana from nearby, like Charybdis, the sea monster from Greek mythology descending on helpless sailors. However, while it swallowed up nearby mana, it immediately spit it back out moments later, as if it weren't finding what it needed.

Alice had been expecting something to change, but this was *far* beyond anything she could have imagined. It looked like she had just summoned a demon inside of her, and if it weren't for {Safety Analysis} reassuring her that everything was fine, she might have screamed and started flinging mana at the abomination. She took a few seconds to steel her nerves before she got a grip and used {Magic Modeling} to create a snapshot of her mana gem while it got to work.

A few moments later, the fibers collapsed, almost as if they had never been there to begin with. Many of them recondensed back into the multifaceted gem she had seen before, though now, the Alice mana in her body had been dragged into the gem, resolving its unwanted influence on her personality. Several other bits of mana spread throughout her body had also been sucked up by the wires and cables.

Why had the mana gem turned into such a strange structure before returning to its original state? Alice spent a few more minutes poking through her achievements, their effects on her body, and her stats, before she realized that the mana gem *was* working now. Or, at the very least, her achievements were now working perfectly again.

One of the biggest things that had puzzled Alice after the collapse of the System was why achievements seemed half-broken. Post–System collapse, most achievements worked at somewhere between 40 and 60 percent of their full efficiency. But suddenly it was resolved—Alice was once again receiving the full benefit of all her achievements. Alice looked thoughtfully at her status screen. Perhaps the mana gem hadn't "broken" at all. She hypothesized that the little tendrils were never meant to be permanent. The process of these little wires slurping up mana in her body might just be the way the System normally dealt with the mana for getting a new achievement.

After several more minutes of contemplation, Alice decided to relax. For the moment, everything was operating as it should be. She would discover more as she scanned her perfect model of a mana gem at work. She decided to focus on that for now, spending several hours working on it. As the image became clearer, Alice paid particular attention to the structure of the mana gem, as well as the part that had turned into a strange satellite dish.

Suddenly it hit her. It was surprisingly simple once she knew what she was looking for. That part of the mana gem was acting as a relay between her and the System.

Based on that, as well as a few other bits of mana that looked like paired enchantments, Alice constructed a new theory about how mana gems worked.

The gems seemed to collect all sorts of miscellaneous mana—they were like giant, unsorted piles of chaos. This was probably by design—but it also meant that mana gems had a LOT of organizing and filtering to do. Mana could be compressed to incredible levels, but there were still limits to how much information could be stuffed inside.

Alice's hypothesis was that mana gems were meant to collect all unusual types of mana within someone's body, and send that information to the System. From there, the System would send a list of instructions back to the gem so it knew how to deal with everything. After all, the computing power inside the mainframe was several orders of magnitude higher than the computing power of the local version of the System.

If her theory was correct, the entire point of the mana gem was to collect everything and then ask the mainframe of the System: "Hey, what do I do with this?"

This would explain why achievements were underperforming, and why it couldn't manage her Alice mana. With the system down, her mana gem was getting zero instructions back, leaving the whole mess unsorted.

She was more than a little baffled by what {First Steps} had just done. Her mana gem wasn't actually broken at all—it was just missing access to the System. So why did her achievement get everything working anyway? Shouldn't her attempt to fix the mana gem result in nothing happening? Alice was glad that things had worked out, but she still had questions.

Either she was completely off base, or for a brief moment, her achievement had somehow actually simulated responses from the System itself. The first option seemed more likely. But whatever had happened, Alice caught a picture of it with {Magic Modeling} . . .

She felt a wave of excitement at the thought.

C H A P T E R   4 9

Alice spent the rest of the night working on her new image with {Magic Modeling}. The key to fixing achievements was right in front of her. Now all she had to do was buckle down and focus.

But even though Alice was excited to keep working, come morning, she was still dragged out of her dream library by Allira. After being gently shaken awake, Alice wanted to roll over and go back to sleep—until she looked at her surroundings. Her eyes widened.

The swamp was *different* from last night. The positions of the trees had shifted slightly. The fog that lay over the swamp like a blanket had become thicker and darker. The smell of rotting vegetation had grown stronger. And the tiny threads of mana she observed in the swamp had also shifted—their positions were *almost* the same, but since Alice had photographic memory now, she could definitely confirm it.

Alice frowned.

The impact of belief on reality and terrain was *much* stronger than she had anticipated. She didn't like it. She had thought that perhaps the laws of physics would only shift in subtle ways behind the scenes, but this was so . . . blatant. The trees were literally moving just to unnerve the party and make the swamp as close as possible to something out of a creepy fairytale.

As for the movement of the mana threads, she still had no clue what to make of that. Yet.

Alice eyed Allira with curiosity. Last night, Allira had kept watch over the group. Based on Alice's previous assumptions about how the swamp moved, it would not rearrange itself when someone was directly observing it. So, when had the swamp rearranged itself? Had her assumption been incorrect?

"Hey, Allira, you were on watch last night, right?" she asked.

"I was. Why?"

"What did it look like when the trees moved?"

"The trees never moved when I was watching them—only when I wasn't looking. But they didn't seem to care about my other senses, just the regular five," said

Allira. "If I could see them or hear them, they were still. But if I walked away, to the point where they were only visible to my more interesting perception perks, the trees grew feet and moved." Allira shrugged. "I thought they were monsters at first, so I blasted down a few of them. But the destroyed trees disappeared after I annihilated them. I only targeted that area before I realized something was off," said Allira as she indicated another part of the camp. "After that, I didn't destroy any more, out of fear that it might create some new threat."

Alice glanced at it, and after several rounds of checks, she blinked in surprise. Allira was right. Alice couldn't see a single trace of the decimated trees. She started asking herself new questions. Why was the influence of belief so much more *overt* in this area compared to others? Did it have to do with the concentration of mana? Or was it how strongly people believed that the swamp was sinister? Or was there a different variable entirely that changed the swamp?

Allira pointed in another direction. "I kept track of the way we came from and our destination. That's where we need to head, and that's the way to backtrack, if we need to."

"Alice, stop asking questions and come eat," Ethan said as he handed her a plate of steaming monster meat and scrambled eggs. He also had two loaves of bread on another plate, which he gave Alice a portion of.

Alice took the plate of food and stopped talking. She could pester Allira more when they were in the air.

"What's our travel speed looking like?" asked Jonathan, as Alice stuffed a forkful of eggs into her mouth.

"With any luck, we'll get through the swamp today. But with how much the geography of this area has been distorted, it's hard to say if our directions will need some revision." Ethan grinned, although it was tinged with a faint trace of annoyance. "We might end up losing some time with this route, so you better make the most of it, okay?" he said, indicating Alice.

Alice gave Ethan a thumbs-up as she stuffed a slice of bread into her mouth. Then her eyes lit up. The bread was *divine*.

Four minutes later, Alice finished eating her seventh slice of bread, and realized that she felt stuffed. She couldn't remember the last time she had eaten so much in one meal. Usually she just crammed food into her mouth and then moved on with her day. She didn't like eating enough to pay attention to it. One of her friends from Earth had always joked that if nutrient paste really existed, Alice would never eat a real meal again.

"I take it you like my bread?" asked Jonathan, pulling Alice's attention away from the food.

Alice was surprised before she put two and two together. Jonathan was a [Farmer], and he was known for growing large quantities of luxury crops. It made perfect sense for him to have a few perks that enhanced the flavor of his yield.

"The stuffed feeling will disappear pretty quickly. My bread has some useful boosts if you eat a lot of it, too—so you can eat more if you feel like it."

"Oh?"

"Eating enough produce from my farm can enhance a few stats for an hour or two." Jonathan shrugged. "Not a huge difference, but every bit helps. My bread gives [Endurance], as well as a bit of [Strength]."

Alice finished eating the final slice of bread and waited a few more minutes while the rest of the group finished their own breakfasts.

"Everyone ready to keep moving?" Ethan asked.

He was greeted with hesitant nods before he grinned.

"Splendid. Just like yesterday, try not to wriggle around too much. We have a lot of ground to cover, and the faster we move, the faster we can get to a real city. I'm looking forward to a nicer bed, and I'd prefer if we got there tonight instead of tomorrow," he said.

Then, just like yesterday, he picked up the group and started flying them above the marsh.

As the group lifted off, Alice noticed that the terrain they were flying through was a bit different from yesterday. Specifically, the area was now populated with new life forms.

Alice saw several flocks of ravens soaring through the air. At least, they appeared to be ravens. However, through Alice's mana sight, she could tell they were almost entirely constructed out of mana, much like Immortals. Even more confusing was the fact that they didn't appear to be monsters. As far as Alice could tell, they had no monster core. It was almost as if they had been born *from* mana. Each of them had a little thread of mana connecting it to something else in the area—a tree, another raven, a rock, or even a puddle of fetid water. There seemed to be no logic to it at all, but it got Alice thinking.

As far as she knew, mana couldn't give birth to independent life. There was no precedent for it. On the other hand, mana had shown that it behaved *very* differently without the System to stabilize it. Ethan and Allira had said this was a normal swamp at one point, but now it was a murky hellscape that rearranged itself to keep people trapped. Plus, ambush predators lurked in the shadows, and the swamp itself was watching them. All of that was natural behavior for mana now that the System had disappeared.

So, what if it *were* possible for mana to create living beings?

Alice ruminated on this idea as the group continued to fly. After some hesitation (and a check with Ethan to make sure she wasn't about to do something horrendously dumb), Alice tried to grab a few of the ravens with her kinetic magic to study.

However, it proved to be nearly impossible. Each time she tried, it felt like trying to drag an entire mountain along with them. The mana resistance of these creatures was ludicrous.

"It's no use," said Alice as she grunted in frustration.

"Let me try," said Ethan. One of his mana tendrils extended below the group and toward one of the ravens.

Ethan grunted, and nothing happened. He nearly dropped everybody out of shock, and Alice felt the world tilt unnervingly before Ethan regained control.

"What the . . . ?" asked Ethan. "I can't move them. I get the sense that even if I supercharged my magic tendrils, and threw every drop of mana in my kinetic seed at them, they *still* wouldn't move. What is wrong with these creatures?"

Alice frowned. Even an *Immortal* couldn't move the weird ravens? That was disturbing.

"Do you mind if I try to kill one of them by firing an object at it?" asked Alice. Her curiosity was fully piqued now. If the ravens were so mana-resistant that even an Immortal couldn't move them, what other odd biological traits did they have?

"Don't do it," said Ethan. "I don't know what these things are but I don't want to provoke them. If they can resist being dragged around by me, there's more to them than meets the eye." Alice realized that Ethan had a good point, so she fell silent.

"Maybe the ravens are like enchantments," said Cecilia as she looked at the woods.

Alice looked at her friend and tilted her head in confusion.

"Yesterday, you said that the swamp itself was 'watching' us, right? As in, the swamp is actively observing us in a way that implies sapience?"

"Probably. Why?"

"Beliefs changed the swamp into something unrecognizable. Maybe the ravens are also part of the body, rather than separate life forms. Sort of like a painting. If an artist paints a picture on a piece of paper or canvas, you can't pick up an image inside the painting and move it around. After all, it's just colored ink on a canvas. Maybe the ravens are literally part of the swamp and only *appear* to be separate?"

"I suppose it's possible," said Alice. "It would explain why they're so hard to move, at least. I don't have a better theory right now."

Cecilia grinned. "They're interesting, aren't they?"

After observing the odd ravens for several more minutes, Ethan tentatively decided that they weren't a threat to the group. Thus, they passed by them.

After the first raven sighting, the group ran into a new patch of ravens every hour or two. Just like the first, each flock of birds ignored them. Several hours of travel later, the group finally found something new—but not a good something.

"Is that smoke?" Allira asked, gesturing out in front of them.

There was, indeed, a thick pillar of smoke and smoke mana rising into the sky from a considerable distance away. Alice squinted and then frowned.

Most human mages formed one of the four basic magic seeds and used that as their core ability. A huge plume of smoke-related mana likely meant it had been created by monsters.

"Isn't that around where a major Fendrallian city is supposed to be?" asked Jonathan.

"Fuck," said Ethan.

The group spent the next hour flying closer to the plume of smoke. But the closer they got, the more Alice's heart sank.

The plume of smoke was, indeed, one of the former major cities of Fendrallia that seemed to have been destroyed a few days ago. Unlike the abandoned villages the group had encountered in Sendria, the city here clearly hadn't been evacuated.

From above they could see corpses littering the city. Tens of thousands of people—perhaps even more—all died, trapped. But even that wasn't the most concerning part of the whole encounter. The most concerning thing that Alice saw was the swamp.

It looked like the swamp had come to life and tried to take a giant bite out of the formerly human territory. City walls had been ripped apart by tree branches. Patches of fetid water were already starting to form at the bottoms of houses and streets. Ravens were feasting upon the dead, ripping apart their corpses and making the whole scene even more sickening.

It wasn't too hard to figure out what had happened here. If human belief could make a swamp rearrange its geography in an actively malicious way and make it create ravens that made no sense, human belief could empower a swamp to attack and destroy a city. It also spoke to just how bad things had gotten in the days after the collapse of the System. Human beliefs caused the environment to shift and change with their beliefs, and every single warped, twisted aspect of the swamp was born out of a primal, creeping terror. People had been scared of the swamp, and the swamp had grown stronger to match that fear. Alice didn't need to think too much to realize why people were terrified.

These people had lost their god. What could be scarier than that? It had been present in every aspect of their lives. The fact that monsters were using perks might not have been quite so obvious to them, but anyone who knew enough about perks might have still realized that monsters were using the System, while humans were suddenly cut off. To the people of the city, it might have even looked like their god had abandoned them and teamed up with monsters to destroy humanity.

She couldn't know exactly what thoughts had led this city and the swamp to total collapse, but she could speculate. Fear. Untethered human nature. The thought of these ideas being unleashed on the fabric of reality made her *very* uneasy about what they might find in other parts of Fendrallia. Alice took another look at the corpses below, and was overcome with sympathy for the people who had died here—and worry for what her group would encounter in the swamp.

Many people looked like they had been ripped apart by powerful monsters. The monsters they had seen so far were ambush predators. They were dangerous, but with Ethan's flight and Allira's scouting, they didn't pose much of a threat to the group. This was different. Ambush predators didn't charge into cities and rip apart people like this. In fact, ambush predators didn't tend to move very much at all, and certainly not in large groups.

Suddenly, the smoke mana in the air started to shift as if it, too, was alive.

Alice's stomach churned. She was learning about belief mana, but this discovery went far beyond her expectations.

"Let's keep away from the city," said Ethan, shuddering. "I don't like the look of that smoke. It might be poisonous. Besides, this place doesn't feel right."

Alice had the same feeling. And again the increasingly strong feeling that something was watching them took hold. This time, it wasn't just a swamp.

"The smoke is drifting toward us," said Allira, frowning. "I think it might be a monster."

"It doesn't have a core, though," said Alice.

"I don't like it," Ethan said as the group started to drift farther away from the city.

Luckily, the smoke didn't follow them for very long. But the unease in Alice's heart still grew stronger.

CHAPTER 50

The group's mood was solemn as they continued moving east. The ruined city had put everyone on edge. Even Alice, who had originally felt confident in resolving the crisis, now found her thoughts drifting toward worst-case scenarios.

She started wondering whether this swamp was truly unique. If scenes like this were happening all over the world, they had even less time than she thought. The problems caused by the collapse were speeding up.

Alice was starting to realize that she had underestimated the problems caused by beliefs impacting reality. She had originally assumed that the biggest danger was the collapse of the laws of physics causing any number of catastrophic extinction events, but it was now clear that this wasn't the only problem. The scary thing about mana influencing reality was that there were no brakes. Humans were already innately prone to believing things with only flimsy evidence to support it—such as flat-earthers and science-deniers back home. In this world, those odd beliefs could literally make the world flat if enough people bought into it.

Worse, the moment this information spread to more people, it would be like oil and fire. Beliefs change physics, people see this and assume the world is ending, the next thing you know you have a runaway reaction that could destroy cities or even countries in a few days. And the more people that witness this, the more they would also accept new "truths" plunging the world into a dangerous feedback loop.

Alice had thought she still had a lot of time to learn how to repair the System and figure out how to piece everything together. But after seeing the ruined city, she felt that time was running out.

Her thoughts were interrupted by Allira speaking up.

"Ethan, stop moving," she said.

Ethan halted the group in midair as Allira squinted at something in the distance.

A look of intense concentration appeared on her face. She started humming. It grew louder and louder until she suddenly stopped and sighed. "We need to detour south," she said. "There are odd monsters ahead. Normally, I wouldn't mind exterminating them, but after that city . . . I'm worried about picking a fight we can't win."

"How many are there?"

"Around four thousand. They move like a coordinated army, and I think they're watching us."

Ethan nodded. "Too many to deal with," he said. The group changed course and started flying southeast instead of directly east.

A few minutes passed before Allira frowned again. "They're following us," she said.

Immortals were incredible fighters. Even the weakest Immortal could usually fight several dozen people, and the strongest Immortals could usually fight up to a thousand average-level [Soldiers] and win. If they employed guerrilla warfare tactics, they could even become a nuisance for a proper army in the right circumstances. But no matter how strong they were, Immortals had limits. Four thousand monsters was far beyond what three Immortals could manage—especially since Jonathan wasn't combat-focused. The other members of their group were *not* capable of making up that difference in combat power.

"Are they gaining on us?" asked Alice.

"They are, but not quickly," said Allira.

Alice felt Ethan begin to increase speed. "I've been going at a pretty comfortable pace until now," he said. "I'm going to speed up. Allira, let me know if my actions interfere with any of your scouting abilities."

"Got it."

As they sped up, Alice watched their surroundings melt into an uncomfortable blur, and air resistance tore at her hair. A moment later, another of Ethan's perks sprang into existence to shield the group from the wind.

Out of the corner of her eye, Alice could see that Mimi and her brothers were starting to look pale. Cecilia didn't look much better. But at least the monster army was probably far behind them by now, she hoped.

A few minutes later, those hopes were shattered when she heard Allira swear. With the help of her perks, Allira's voice carried to Alice's ears, even with the ridiculous speed they were traveling at.

"They're still gaining on us," she said.

"How?" asked Ethan.

"They're speeding up, too. Go faster!" yelled Allira. "It's like they're using magic to *skip* chunks of distance every few seconds. I can see their bodies turning into smoke and then jumping closer to us as we fly. It looks kind of like dimensional magic."

Alice looked behind them and tried to confirm what Allira was saying. But at this distance she couldn't even see them.

After Allira urged him to speed up again, Ethan sighed. "I'm going to target flesh and bones instead of using our clothes to move us around. It'll hurt a little, but it's better than dropping someone!"

Alice watched Ethan's magic tendril drift toward her arms and ribs. A feeling gripped her, like someone had reached inside of her body and grabbed her organs. Then a jolt of pain radiated out from her ribs and her arms. It was so uncomfortable that Alice nearly vomited, but she managed to steady herself. She could see that the other non-Immortals in the group looked just as uncomfortable as she did, but they were also doing their best to restrain themselves. After a few seconds, some of the discomfort disappeared as Ethan shifted his magic tendrils to get a better grip on her. Alice glanced at Mimi, to make sure the most fragile member of the group wasn't about to die, and then relaxed. Mimi looked a bit pale, and it was obvious that she was going to have a painful set of bruises tomorrow—but the damage was far from life-threatening. {Extended Tissues} was also helping heal the other members of the group, even if it wasn't working very quickly.

Unfortunately, {Extended Tissues} didn't have the range to hit everyone. Cecilia, Mimi, and Jacob were in range, but Nerissa and Stuart were left to deal with the bruising on their own. Even after Ethan had readjusted his grip on them, they still looked deeply uncomfortable.

Alice tried to tell Ethan to move her closer to Mimi and the other fragile members of the group, but at this point, the wind was choking all the words out of her. She grew increasingly frustrated until she turned back toward her mana. Then Alice quickly realized that she was being silly.

She activated her knockoff System seed, and started using communication mana to force her words to be heard, even through the ridiculous amount of air resistance.

"Ethan, move me closer to the others!" Alice was finally able to say. "I can heal them! Focus on Jonathan's family! They're weaker!" Ethan nodded.

He readjusted her position slightly, and moments later, all of Jonathan's family was situated close enough to enjoy the benefits of {Extended Tissues}.

Meanwhile, Allira was at last starting to look slightly more relieved.

"The monsters are falling behind," she said, letting out a sigh. "Not very quickly, but we're losing them."

"Good."

Alice heard Jonathan also heave a sigh of relief. He leaned closer to Mimi and reached out to give her a firm hug. A moment later, Alice noticed Ethan readjusting his tendrils so that most of them hit Jonathan instead of Mimi—meaning Ethan was no longer disturbing her bones or organs. He still left a mana tendril nearby, to catch Mimi if Jonathan dropped her, but most of the damage was now being borne by the sturdiest member of the group.

"I don't know if I'll be able to keep this up for more than a few hours," said Ethan, as Mimi snuggled closer to her father. "Punching through the magic resistance of seven people, two of whom are Immortals, is incredibly hard."

Allira frowned. "I could sing a ship into existence. It would keep the wind resistance off us, and I can make it solid enough for your kinetic magic to interfere with it. As long as we stay in one of the cabins, it should keep air resistance to a minimum as well. Since it's still an illusion, it won't weigh much. However, it's going to eat through my perks and my mental energy like wildfire. If it's a short trip, I can manage. But don't expect me to be at full strength for a fight."

Ethan looked thoughtful. "That seems risky. If we run into another danger, we might be in an even worse situation than now."

"Your mana is running out though, isn't it? Maintaining this speed will be hard for you. If I create a ship, you'll still have to spend a bunch of mana lifting us up and moving us around, but it won't be quite as expensive as fighting through our mana resistance, at least. This way, both of us will still be running at nearly full strength, instead of having the burden of fighting be entirely on me if a new danger erupts. It also means both of us will be able to regenerate some of our energy expenditure. The only danger is if we get into a prolonged fight while low on energy."

Ethan finally nodded. "Do it. But it'll have to be quick. The monster swarm is catching up."

Allira cackled. "I can buy some time with my shadows." The group started to decelerate. Once they came to a stop, Allira started to hum again. Another cloud of rainbow mana started to form around her as she transitioned from humming to singing. The song was beautiful—but the impact on the surrounding marsh was horrifying.

All the shadows in the marsh started to tremble as though they were the organs and limbs of some unseen, long-forgotten creature made of darkness. Little strands of flesh and blood started to sprout from the scene, resembling some eldritch nightmare. Even though Alice knew Allira was an ally, for a brief moment, she felt deeply disturbed by what she was witnessing.

Alice finally understood why Allira was the Immortal of Song and Shadow. She had previously thought that "shadow" referred to illusions—but Allira didn't just manipulate illusions, that was clear now.

The meaty tendrils of shadows swarmed toward the horde of monsters. Alice heard enraged shrieks and bellows in the distance.

"That should buy us some time," said Allira, before she started humming again. This time the song was far less eerie and unnerving. A ship started to weave itself into existence before Alice's eyes, like threads of light squirming into place one at a time. It only took her a moment to recognize it. It was the same ship Ethan's mother had given them when they traveled back to Cyra. Alice heard the snarls and growls of monsters starting to get closer, despite Allira's shadow horrors holding them off. Nearly two minutes later, Allira relaxed as the final thread of light snapped into existence. She looked drained, as if she had just run a marathon, but she had a satisfied smile on her face.

"It's solid now, so get up on the deck," sang Allira, weaving the directions into her tune. Despite the ridiculous lyrics, it was still somehow beautiful. The group dashed onto the ship before it lifted off and started flying through the air, even faster than before. This time, the trip was far less uncomfortable.

"This is much better," said Alice.

Allira nodded. "I wish I had thought of this earlier. It really is much nicer, even if it consumes a lot of energy."

The group was calm for several minutes before Allira started to frown again.

"How odd," she said.

"Did something else happen?" asked Ethan.

"No matter how many of the swamp monsters my shadows kill, they just reappear after a while. I don't know if the monsters are returning to life somehow, or if they're just constantly being reinforced by new monsters teleporting in."

Alice rubbed her chin thoughtfully. Now that the army wasn't gaining on them, she had more time to think about their situation. She hadn't seen any actual monsters yet, but based on Allira's warning, they were probably just as strange as the rest of the swamp. "I wonder if the monsters are like the ravens we found earlier," she said. "They might seem to be alive, but in actuality they're more like enchantments, or extensions of the swamp itself."

If that was the case, they'd be quite a bit more difficult to deal with than *real* monsters. How could they beat an endlessly regenerating army? Perhaps they needed to destroy the swamp itself.

Which was easier said than done.

"If the monsters are literal parts of the swamp, that makes them harder to deal with," said Jonathan.

"If these monsters are somehow intrinsically linked to the swamp, then they probably can't leave it. In other words, we just need to escape fast enough," Ethan said.

It's a risky notion to stake the group's safety on, thought Alice. But it was also the best idea they had at the moment.

"I could try turning part of the swamp into my farm, and see if that helps?" asked Jonathan. "I have no idea how these monsters and their connection to the swamp works, but if I use my perks to transform an area into a farm instead of a swamp, maybe it would weaken them, or make them unwilling to follow us. Right?" he said as he turned toward Alice.

"It could be a viable short-term solution to our immediate situation," Alice said. "We should also try to see if there's a way to solve this issue more permanently after we leave. Perhaps we could try changing people's beliefs about the swamp?" she mused. "This warping of the underlying laws of physics, climate, and even reality is tied directly to them. I want to know what happens if we change those beliefs. If we make people *think* the threat of the swamp has been handled."

Ethan grimaced. "Sounds like we'd need an [Orator], or some similar kind of class to really tamp down the chaos."

Allira grinned toothily at Ethan. "Ethan, dear. Have you forgotten who I am? I might *specialize* in songs, but songs are also a form of storytelling. They're a good way to spread information," she said, turning to Alice. "You've been getting more and more overt in your discussions of how mana and the System work behind the scenes. If I understand you correctly, enough belief somehow makes mana itself change the world to match it, right?"

Alice hesitated, but she nodded. Allira's smile widened.

"Then I'll compose a new song while we fly. One about how we destroyed something called the 'heart of the swamp,' thus defeating it and condemning the monsters and strange terrain here to gradual destruction. We can incorporate some of your research into the song, to make it as logical and realistic as possible. That should make enough sense for people to *believe* that the swamp is weakened, yes? From there, the situation should be under control!"

"Can you really convince people that easily?" asked Alice.

Allira giggled. "Alice. We're *Immortals*. An Immortal slaying a monster is nothing new."

"Allira is right," Ethan said. "There are probably over a hundred stories of my father slaying some sort of powerful monster and saving a small town or village. Most of them are based on real events, though many have been exaggerated over the years. If we tell people around here that a group of Immortals fought off a deadly threat and the nearby towns are safe now, they'll probably believe it. After all, it would fit perfectly with what they've come to expect from Immortals."

"It would even be a good way to get into Fendrallia's good graces. Helping out a neighboring country would prove Illvaria's friendliness . . . and, in a twisted sort of way, might also prove that Illvaria is safe during this crisis. After all, if Illvaria can afford to send out two of its Immortals to help its neighbors, it surely isn't suffering as much as other countries, no? That would benefit us as a whole, if belief can change reality as much as you seem to think it can."

It made sense . . . and it also brought up a new aspect of the crisis that Alice hadn't really considered before. Public opinion. Making sure people understood the situation and believed it was being controlled would be a critical component to resolving it. Otherwise it would just keep creating new problems. Alice's heart sank as she realized that there was yet *another* dimension of the crisis that she needed to keep a handle on. But on the other hand, it also raised some interesting possibilities. If she could make parts of the crisis disappear by causing people to *believe* they were being dealt with, using this to her advantage might make handling things much easier.

Alice was lost in thought until she heard Allira curse again.

"There's another group of monsters catching up to us. Ethan, set us down. They're moving faster, but there are a lot less of them. I think they might be a specialized group of the first type of monster I saw—or perhaps a different type entirely. But this ship can't outrun them—my illusions are durable, but there is still a limit to how much force it can handle before the illusion implodes."

Ethan paused for a moment. "I have a few ideas for that. We can't kill them, but if they have low enough numbers, maybe we can trap them. How long until they arrive? And how many are there?"

"Ten minutes. About two hundred."

"Should be manageable," Ethan said as he started to lower the ship. Within a few minutes, the group was back on the ground, preparing for battle.

CHAPTER 51

Alice assessed her stock of enchanted items. She still had Doll's armor, a reasonable supply of bracelets filled with enchanted beads, and a few miscellaneous—likely useless—items in her storage perk. Nothing that would give her the edge she was looking for.

Alice scanned their surroundings, looking for some sort of trick that would make the fight easier. Around her, there was swamp, plants, a bit of fetid water, and little else. Nothing that she could use to contribute to a fight where Immortals were taking action.

Meanwhile, the others were finding much better ways to influence the battle. Ethan had already taken his father's old sword out of his storage perk, and Allira started singing. Just like the first time Alice had seen Allira sing, her voice began to change the surroundings. Houses made of stone and wood flickered in and out of existence as Allira's song crafted an illusion stronger than reality. Alice realized that this city Allira was singing into existence was different from the first time she had seen Allira use her abilities. This city was more populated than the previous one. It wasn't war-torn, either. Instead, it was filled with people happily going about their day, bustling to and from houses and marketplaces. Children played in the streets. It looked like a prosperous place.

Alice frowned. Last time, Allira had set up an illusion that actively attacked monsters. Now, Allira had summoned a seemingly peaceful city, which seemed useless. She was sure that Allira was up to something, but Alice had no idea what.

She turned her attention toward Jonathan who had taken a few seeds and a hoe out of his own storage perk and started to till the surrounding swamp. Normally, Alice would have assumed he was using a perk to prepare for battle, but there wasn't very much rainbow mana in his surroundings. The crops he planted were growing unnaturally quickly, and it looked almost like he was trying to build a palisade entirely out of corn. The moment he placed a corn seed into the ground, it grew at a rapid pace. Alice hoped Jonathan had something planned as well—perhaps a way to strengthen these corn stalks and turn it into a proper barricade against the monsters. She had no clue what Jonathan's build could do, so it was hard for her to guess what his actions meant.

Alice took a look at the rest of the group, and realized that the biggest danger on this battlefield would come from protecting the noncombatants. Jonathan's family members weren't good at fighting, and after being tossed around by Ethan's kinetic magic, they were even less capable of combat than usual. Cecilia was at least burying blast crystals around the clearing, which indicated she had some kind of plan to contribute. Alice wasn't sure how useful those would be, but it was worth a shot.

Then, Alice took stock of her perks and achievements, hoping to find something useful. With her use of {First Steps}, all her broken achievements had returned to normal. Alice wasn't sure how much it would help, but she was grateful for any advantage she could get right now. A moment later, Alice realized she had already done everything she could to prepare. She had her enchantments ready, and she knew what she could do on a battlefield. The rest would come down to staying aware of the group she was fighting with and not making any big mistakes.

Then the group waited. Even though Allira had made the approaching monster swarm sound imminent, Alice was surprised by how long it took to arrive. Even after she finished taking inventory and preparing herself for the fight, there was no sign of the enemy. It almost made Alice wonder if the monsters *knew* that they had stopped and prepared to fight, and so they were giving them time to grow anxious and afraid of the coming battle.

Then a harrowing thought struck her: *Perceiving the enemy as stronger would make them stronger!* That was one of the logical outcomes of the interaction between beliefs and mana right now—she had to keep her thoughts in line, or she might inadvertently strengthen her enemies. Alice focused and started thinking about how *weak* the monsters were compared to the Immortals. Ethan and Allira didn't seem very stressed—they looked annoyed, but they didn't look worried about winning. That meant that they were confident. Definitely.

Alice spent the next few minutes trying to make herself believe that the oncoming fight would be easy because their enemies were weak. She wasn't sure how much impact a single person's beliefs would have, but she didn't want to take the risk right now.

Finally, the first monsters arrived.

It was a horde of strange flying creatures that made her eyes hurt. Allira said that the monsters were odd, and she wasn't kidding. They looked like someone had taken a patch of fog, cut it into the shape of a monster, and then stuck the result in a blender for a few minutes. The smell of fetid swamp water wafted through the air, and Alice had the urge to cover her nose as the creatures drew closer. It was a truly horrendous assault on the senses.

Even more unnerving, Alice could see strands of mana that connected the monsters to the swamp itself, like they were puppets dancing on the end of a string. She was reminded of the way the swamp made her feel—like someone was constantly watching them, and shuddered. Clearly, it could do more than just watch.

Allira was the first to take action. Her strangely peaceful city changed just as abruptly as the melody coming from her mouth. As her song became more sharp and violent, all the illusory people in her city shimmered. Then they turned to the monster horde with empty, angry eyes, now resembling corpses, dragged out of their graves by pure, feral rage. Alice caught a glimpse of something *other* in them—a hint of something dark, hungry, and nameless. The illusory townsfolk looked more like monsters than the monsters did. The townsfolk grinned in unison at the enemy, and charged.

Several of the monsters switched targets and focused on the rampaging townsfolk, but most of them ignored the fakes. Instead, they glided toward the rest of the group.

Ethan made the next move. As Allira's creepy townspeople held off the first wave of attackers, his tendrils gathered up materials from their surroundings. Dead tree branches, stones, globs of mud, and other miscellaneous objects tore through the air and ripped apart the monsters in a barrage of deadly missiles.

The monsters responded more quickly than Alice expected. The mana threads began to shiver and a new set of threads tore out of the ground and launched toward Ethan's volley before freezing them in midair.

Ethan grimaced. "Alice, don't use the environment for combat. It isn't under our control!" he yelled. Instead, he started using Jonathan's corn as ammunition. The monsters charged straight at Ethan's barrage, but before any object could touch their bodies, they flashed with purple mana, and teleported away. Some were still caught in the attack, but most of them escaped.

Several of the monsters that got hit by Ethan's corn died, while the rest either teleported away or were seriously injured. Allira immediately redirected some of her villagers to finish off the ones that survived, who promptly began tearing them limb from limb.

Each time a monster died, the mana tether connecting it to the swamp brightened, while the mana in its immediate surroundings thinned. A new monster body would reappear in midair a few moments later, looking none the worse for wear. It was as if the monsters were draining the swamp of its mana in order to revive. Alice timed how long the whole process took, and felt her stomach tighten.

Ten seconds. It was ridiculously fast.

Of course, since each revival reduced the mana in the surrounding area, the swamp couldn't revive these fog monsters indefinitely. *Eventually* it would run out of mana. At least, as long as nobody started believing the monsters were unkillable—if that happened, Alice had no clue what the result would be. So *theoretically* the monster swarm was beatable, but Alice seriously doubted they had enough resources to outlast the mana reserves of an entire swamp. Let alone the fact that a much bigger army was still on its way.

Luckily, Alice wasn't completely helpless against this kind of tactic. Now that she had a rough idea how the monsters were revived, she used {Dimensional Camouflage} to open up a few new angles to attack from. She needed free access to the monsters without getting counterattacked, and she was determined to get it.

Pulling mana from her antimagic seed, Alice began to test something. She chose a nearby monster and flooded it with antimagic mana. But the monster didn't respond at all. It just kept charging at a nearby illusory villager. Alice had hoped that antimagic mana might corrode their bodies and turn them into dust. Unfortunately, it seemed like her idea had failed.

The monster clawed through the villager and turned toward its next nearest target—Alice herself. She sent a spray of bracelet beads into the creature, and it dropped dead. She waited for the creature to re-form or start reconstructing its body. Nothing happened. Instead, the threads of mana controlling the horrifying fog just hung in midair, as if they were searching for a connection that no longer existed.

Alice's eyes lit up as she realized what this meant. Antimagic mana might not be able to kill the monsters instantly, but it did cut off their revival mechanism. A moment later, the dead monster's mana thread started sinking back into the fetid water, then started to unravel. After ten seconds it had completely disappeared.

She had found a way to permanently kill the monsters. That would give the Immortals far more breathing room.

"Ethan!" she yelled. "Hit the ones I point out!" Alice targeted the denser clumps of monsters and used her portal setup to flood the area with antimagic mana. Each time she did so, she pointed out the monsters to Ethan and he quickly tore them to pieces with flying cobs of corn. A disconcerting number of the monsters still managed to survive, either by dodging or by turning their bodies into mist under the onslaught of attacks—but they couldn't teleport away or revive, removing some of their most frustrating abilities from the fight. Not to mention, Ethan was a competent fighter. Anytime one of the monsters dodged, he simply sent another spray of corn at them. Alice also assisted him from the side by tossing in her own bracelet beads whenever she had the focus for it.

Once they realized what Alice was doing, parts of the ground underneath her started to twist and shudder. Alice had a fraction of a moment to remember what the city they had found looked like before a tree root ripped out of the ground and tried to spear through her brain.

Right before Alice met a nasty end, Jonathan stepped in front of her. The tree root slammed into his outstretched arm and bounced off. Jonathan grimaced and rubbed his arm—but he didn't look hurt. He glared at the ground, and his muscles rippled. Rainbow mana flooded out of his body, and then the man pulled out a farming hoe and slammed it into the dirt. A storm of rainbow mana cascaded outward. Several nearby trees dissolved upon contact, leaving behind piles of fertilized, freshly tilled soil.

"Dealt with the trees," said Jonathan.

Alice relaxed as Jonathan guarded her from wave after wave of monsters. But by the fourth attack, the enemy started to adapt to her tactic. Since Alice could only cover one area at a time with her antimagic, the monsters spread out. Several of them also started targeting Jonathan's family, forcing the Immortals to divert more of their attention to keeping the noncombatants safe. Cecilia started putting her blast crystals to good use, disrupting the edges of the battlefield and allowing the others to pay more attention to the remaining monsters, but it was still a chaotic and dangerous fight.

On the bright side, Jonathan proved to be several times more useful than Alice had expected. His offensive abilities were weak, since his [Dexterity] seemed too low to land his blows. However, he was incredibly sturdy. More importantly, his [Farmer] abilities were perfectly suited to handle sneaky attacks from tree roots and terrain manipulation. Meanwhile, Ethan and Allira's illusions, summons, and projectiles destroyed every monster Alice could douse with antimagic mana. For a while, the combatants formed an uneasy, tenuous balance.

That was when Alice ran out of antimagic mana, and a crushing headache formed behind her eyeballs. Alice groaned.

"I'm out of antimagic!" she yelled, then took a few moments to survey her handiwork.

Nearly a hundred of the monsters had been killed. There were still over a hundred left, but the Immortals were having a much easier time maintaining the situation. She might not have ended the threat, but she certainly helped.

"Let us take it from here, then!" said Ethan. "Sit behind Jonathan and let him keep you safe!" Ethan started creating large, flat surfaces to physically push the monsters around. Meanwhile, Allira's townsfolk started work on a construction project. Tools flickered into existence as her people grabbed them and hacked, sawed, and hammered away.

After several seconds, Alice finally realized what Ethan and Allira were doing. Ethan was pushing monsters toward a group of cages that the townsfolk were constructing. Alice scratched her head in confusion. The cages were only illusions, and the monsters could teleport. How was this going to work?

Ethan and Allira had clearly also thought of this. Ethan created a giant fly swatter using several stalks of corn, and every time a monster teleported, he batted it into a cage right after it reappeared. Due to one of Allira's perks, the wooden cages would instantly form rainbow tethers connecting them to the fog monsters once the door to the cage was closed. There were still several fog monsters that teleported out before the rainbow tethers could latch on to them, but Ethan and Allira quickly worked to smack them back in.

By the time fifty were trapped, the monsters seemed to recognize the tide had turned against them. Breaking off their assault, they fled into the nearby woods. Ethan and Allira looked disappointed, but they didn't seem too inclined to chase them down.

Ethan sighed. "I wish we had more time to deal with all of them. They could still harass us during the rest of our journey. We're farther from the edge of the swamp than I thought we were, mostly because it's *grown* since the last time we were here. Who knows when they'll be back."

"We did what we could," said Allira. "If they come again, I'll feed more to my shadows."

Jonathan nodded in silent agreement.

Alice quickly tallied up their losses, and felt a bit of relief. The monsters that escaped were a hidden threat, but they hadn't lost anyone, either. Jonathan was the most injured, and they were essentially paper cuts. Even as Alice watched, the man's injuries were healing up, and they would probably be gone in a few minutes.

It wasn't a perfect conclusion to the battle, but it could have gone much, much worse. Alice just hoped that the monsters wouldn't be back.

You have leveled up!
Survivor: 69→71, Explorer of Magic: 85→86, Kinetic Manabinder: 52→54

C H A P T E R 5 2

After the battle, the group ran into an unexpected logistical problem. Allira couldn't sing the ship back into existence. Her music was now being used to maintain the cages for the swamp monsters and she was on the brink of exhaustion. Alice suspected that this would remain a problem until they reached a new settlement where they could get some proper monster cages built. For now, however, this meant that they were back to being carried by Ethan's raw kinetic magic. This was far less comfortable *and* slower, meaning that the horde of smoke monsters could reappear at any time for another round. Luckily, the monster horde did not reappear as the group fled. Still, as they continued to travel, hour after hour, Alice started to feel uneasy.

Just how big *was* this swamp? After over a day of flying over it, they still hadn't even seen the edge. Ethan and Allira had originally said that it might take a day or two of travel to pass through it, but they were well past the point where they should have at least started to approach the edge.

She started to wonder if they had somehow been steered off track. Had the swamp truly grown this much, or were they unknowingly walking in circles, unaware of how much they had been turned around? The swamp's conscious attempts to mislead travelers made it hard to trust her own sense of direction. She glanced at the swamp again and tried to see if she could spot any of the strange tethers that connected the monsters to the swamp itself. Since Alice had a massive set of perks dedicated to improving her mana vision, and she had seen these mana tethers, she suspected she would have an easier time picking the monsters out by their tether instead of by their actual physical forms.

As Alice thought about this, she noticed that another of the little threads of mana she had been investigating was vibrating *wildly* near her—but the moment she stopped thinking about the swamp and focused on the thread of mana, it stopped vibrating.

Alice frowned in confusion. The thread of mana looked kind of similar to the tethers that had connected the water/fog monsters to the swamp, now that she thought about it. Alice stared more closely at the thread of mana and then realized, with some surprise, that this time she could clearly tell where part of the thread of mana originated from. This one was connected directly to *her*.

Alice's eyes widened in surprise before she started to have a sneaking suspicion. It was just a hypothesis, but Alice thought she might have finally guessed what the mana threads were.

She spent a few minutes thinking about everything she knew about geography—how utterly ridiculous and illogical this swamp was and how little sense it made. Sure enough, the thread of mana started vibrating wildly as Alice thought about her knowledge of geography, and it stopped moving when Alice stopped thinking about her knowledge and how it compared to the reality in front of her eyes.

Alice would still need to run a few more tests, but she suspected that this little thread of mana literally represented the interaction between the beliefs of a sapient creature and the laws of reality.

If that was correct, it would also explain why the threads of mana were thicker near the center of the bog—this bog was utterly transformed by human belief, so, obviously, an awful lot of interaction between belief and mana must be happening here. Alice already knew that there must be *some* mechanism tying this all together—after all, beliefs didn't normally warp reality, but in this dimension, they did.

Little pieces of evidence slid together until Alice was mostly convinced that her guess was correct. She still wanted to verify it, but it seemed logical. Even if Alice couldn't understand the internal mechanisms that made these strings of mana operate, she felt that she was at least closer to understanding how the crisis was unfolding.

This brought another problem to mind: How did the System prevent beliefs from influencing reality? Was it a facet of communication mana? Was there a different type of mana that interacted with these strings of mana? The strings of mana seemed to vibrate whenever they were carrying beliefs and information from a person into the surrounding environment, so perhaps there was some kind of enchantment that prevented them from vibrating? Alice had no idea where to start. That was a real problem, because if there was one thing Alice had realized while they were traveling over the swamp, it was that human beliefs needed to stop warping the laws of physics. If beliefs kept constantly influencing reality, sooner or later everything would break behind the scenes. Past that point, Alice doubted that the world would remain stable.

She sighed. There was still so much work to do, and she was the only one who could do it. If she didn't solve these problems, nobody would. Not for the first time, Alice wished that Ethan or Cecilia had perks and achievements similar to hers. Having a full work colleague who had their own, specialized versions of Alice's tool kit would have made it thousands of times easier to fix all this. Instead, all she could do was use {Shared Memories} to try to brainstorm together. It was better than nothing, but far from what she wanted.

She sighed before she returned to her observation of the threads of mana in her surroundings. Now that she had a guess about what they were, she wanted as much information as she could find to prove or disprove her theory. After several minutes of observation and a few checks with {Safety Analysis}, Alice started trying to see if there were ways to interact with the threads of mana.

She first tried to cut off communication between humans and mana. She wanted to see if she could directly shut down the pathway between humans and mana entirely. That would be the easiest way to resolve the problem of human beliefs warping their surroundings, if her assumptions thus far were correct.

This had interesting results but was nowhere near a real success. The communication mana was, indeed, able to mess with the threads of weird mana—but it was not capable of stopping the vibrations of these threads, or doing much of anything. It COULD reduce the amplitude of these vibrations—but only to a limited extent.

At first, Alice thought that she was on the right path. She figured that with a bit more training, or more inventive use of her mana, maybe it was possible to snap off the communication between humans and mana entirely. After all, reducing the amplitude of each vibration was definitely progress.

But after some experimentation, Alice realized that communication mana was not as effective at shutting down the impact of human beliefs on reality as she had hoped. Whenever she tried to reduce the impact of human belief on a thread below a certain threshold, her communication mana would fail to take effect. Either she was missing something, or she needed a different kind of mana.

Alice tried using antimagic mana to outright destroy the thread of mana next, but the effects proved oddly temporary. When Alice poured antimagic mana onto a belief thread, it seemed to suppress the thread of mana for a short period of time. However, it didn't actually delete any of the information that the thread of mana was trying to exchange. The moment Alice stopped applying antimagic mana to the mana thread, all the information it had stored up would instantly ripple through it. It reminded Alice of the way levels worked. If she did a bunch of stuff in a no-mana zone, she wouldn't level up—but the moment she returned to a mana-dense area, she would get all the levels she'd missed out on.

Alice started trying out new things, but nothing worked. She failed to completely confirm or deny her suspicion about the nature of these mana threads, and also failed to come up with an actionable plan if her suspicion was correct. Eventually, she got frustrated and switched focus. If it was impossible for her to figure out the mana threads, she decided to focus on achievements instead. She still needed to finish fleshing out the connection between mana gems and achievements, and now was a great time to do so. Alice returned to her {Magic Modeling}, in order to squeeze out information about mana gems.

Hours passed as Alice sank into her thoughts. Soon, it was time for the group to rest again. They had yet to leave the swamp. This time, Jonathan kept watch while the rest of the group slept, since his [Endurance] drastically reduced his need for sleep. During their slumber, Alice used her dream library to keep working on {Magic Modeling}.

The next day, about six hours after daybreak, the group finally left the swamp. Alice felt a small urge to do a celebratory round of clapping as they finally reached the edge of the swamp. Before Alice could celebrate, however, she saw a wave of rainbow mana pour into the world, like a tidal wave of paint spilled by a careless child.

Unlike the last few times Alice had seen System mana return, this time it was fainter. Alice got the impression that it was *broken* when she saw it.

But even though it was broken, Alice still did her best to memorize every single thing that she could. For a moment, Alice deeply regretted that {Magic Modeling} was on cooldown right now. If it had been active, Alice could have gotten an image of a chunk of working System mana. Even if this wave of System mana felt disjointed, it would have given her more research material—and if this was the state of the System, Alice suspected she might not get to see another wave of System mana in *any* form unless she fixed the mainframe.

Sadly, there were no what-ifs in the world. All she could do was memorize every detail, soaking in every spot of color and mana like a sponge. With her photographic memory, she could sort out the details of what she had seen later—right now, she just tried to cram every single speck of data into her memories for future perusal. Moments later, the System mana dissipated, leaving nothing behind.

However, while Alice didn't get to investigate much, she had paid very close attention to one thing. She tried to check how the System handled the strings of mana she had been investigating for the past few days. In this respect, Alice wasn't disappointed. As she watched, she saw that some of the threads she had been observing earlier were *eaten* by the System.

It didn't look like the System had suppressed them with some mixture of communication mana and other types of mana. It didn't look like the System mana had *deleted* the mana threads, either. It was more like watching a whirlpool swallow a sinking ship. One moment, the little threads of weird mana were present, and the next moment, the System engulfed it and *integrated* them. Then it seemed almost as if the little threads of mana were a natural part of the System mana. It was so natural, so *obviously* part of normal System mana that Alice had a hard time picking out the little threads of mana again, even when she *knew what she was looking for.*

That was *very* interesting. Alice wasn't quite sure what to make of that yet, but if she could figure it out, she might have a way to handle the interaction between beliefs and the laws of physics.

Sadly, Alice had absolutely no idea what the System had actually done. Whatever had happened was far beyond her understanding, meaning that Alice might be stuck trying to find a knockoff version of the System's method for handling the strings of mana. The only upside was that Alice could now confirm the System did *something* to the threads of mana she had been investigating. In other words, they were important, even if her suspicion about their nature had yet to be confirmed.

After the tidal wave of System mana, the group resumed flying. Soon, they found a nearby village. Alice was surprised to see that the villagers were still present. It didn't even look like the villagers were getting ready to evacuate—although even from high above the village, she could see the villagers eyeing the swamp nervously. It seemed that they weren't unaware of the threat of the swamp expanding, but they were unwilling to leave their homes and their farms to rot as they fled. She could also see vibrating threads of mana tying the villagers and the swamp together, solidifying her suspicion that mana threads interacted with human beliefs somehow.

"This is a good place to start," Allira sang, weaving the words into the song keeping the monsters trapped. Alice frowned as she tried to parse the meaning of Allira's words before Allira's previous idea came back to her.

Allira had suggested spreading various stories related to "defeating the heart of the swamp." Despite the fact that the "heart of the swamp" didn't really exist, if people thought that the expansion of the swamp had been tied to a now-dead monster, the swamp truly would start to weaken and retract. Alice nodded and then glanced at the train of cages the group was carrying with them. She grinned.

"We can use the monsters we captured as props," said Alice. "Hmm . . . while we're at it, Allira, do you have a way to make the monsters wriggle around a bit and perhaps make some odd noises?"

"I could probably manage that with illusions, why?" sang Allira.

"Well, since human belief can probably influence these monsters, I'm thinking we should also spread a second rumor. We should make people think that the monsters get much weaker outside the swamp. Right now, it's entirely possible for the monsters that were created by the swamp to stroll out and attack various towns and cities. I'm hoping that you can make it look like the monsters are in pain." Alice shrugged. "It seems like a good precaution to add in."

Allira nodded. "I can do that," she sang. "While we're here, could one of you get some solid metal cages? My voice is getting tired."

"I'll do it," said Cecilia. "I'll go visit the local [Blacksmith]." As the group alighted on the ground, Cecilia dashed off. Moments later, Alice saw several villagers start pointing at them in shock. Ethan, Allira, and Jonathan were getting the most looks. Even though most of the villagers weren't able to tell that they were Immortals on the spot, the unusual dexterity and grace the three carried themselves with must have tipped them off that *something* was unusual about the three.

Allira smiled and took the lead as she stepped toward the village. Meanwhile, Alice tried not to think about what would happen next. Even if she knew it was rather important to control people's beliefs right now, lying didn't feel very good. Luckily, most of it would be left to Allira. Still, Alice felt a bit sour about the necessity of lying as the group stepped into the village.

CHAPTER 53

@*#$&%?" asked one of the villagers as a few outlying [Farmers] finally approached the group.

"@3%*#@ @#*$&#," Allira sang in fluent Fendrallian.

"Illvarian? Not speak well," said the villager. He stumbled over his words as he spoke and sounded almost . . . anxious as he spoke with Allira. "@*#$*&# @# %#@ @#$#@ @#$@ @#$#@#$ @#$# #$#@$@?"

"@#*($&#@ @#(*$&#(*@&#$ @#(*$*!" sang Allira, smiling brightly at the man. The man relaxed.

Alice started to wish that she spoke Fendrallian. Being unable to participate in the conversation was frustrating.

"Do you want me to translate?" asked Ethan.

"Yes, please," said Alice. "Knowing what she's saying might help me verify a few theories I've been thinking about, and give me more precise feedback on how a few aspects of reality interact with each other."

"The man started out by asking if we were Immortals, since our [Dexterity] and [Charisma] seemed so high." Ethan seemed a bit amused by that and shot Allira a glance. Allira rolled her eyes at Ethan. "Allira confirmed that three of us were Immortals. Then he asked if the conversation could be conducted in Fendrallian, since he's not very confident in his Illvarian. Allira said she was happy to speak in Fendrallian," he said.

"Now the villagers are asking why we're here, because their village isn't important enough to receive attention from a group of Immortals. They also mentioned that they don't recognize us, which they find odd, because they know the Fendrallian Immortals."

A moment later, Alice was distracted from Ethan's narration by Allira's voice, as Allira somehow managed to *laugh* while still singing. Ethan also chuckled.

"She said that we came to help out, because we'd heard that the swamp has had some issues recently. She also mentioned that we came from Illvaria and we're doing this before the swamp grows out of control."

Alice squinted at the belief mana threads in their surroundings. Now that they were farther away from the swamp, it was much harder to make out where the threads were or what they were doing—but she could still tell that a few of the larger strings of mana were vibrating wildly, especially the ones that seemed connected to the swamp. Even more proof that these threads of mana interacted with beliefs.

Alice also saw several villagers glance at the swamp. Their eyes shifted uneasily as they stared at it before one of them nodded and started talking again.

"The other villager said that the expansion of the swamp is unnatural, and how the swamp seems to be alive. He also mentioned that some people worry the swamp will overtake the village in a few weeks, just like the city that was destroyed a few days ago." Ethan frowned. "They're also talking about getting sick. I didn't notice anything related to *disease* in the swamp, but—Oh, never mind. They're talking about class-mana madness. Some of the people who have started to lose their minds have started forgetting to feed their children, and themselves."

From there, Ethan's expression turned unnatural as he stared at the man who was talking. He turned toward Alice. "I'm going to translate his next statement word for word, since it might have more important information for you.

"'The kids don't seem to notice that they're dying, either! They're clearly starving to death, but they just keep working for some reason! It's like they haven't even noticed how skinny they've become.'" The villager shuddered violently as he gazed into the distance. "'Recently, I've also started feeling odd as well. Like all I want to do is farm, and farm, and farm . . .'" The man seemed to get lost in thought for several seconds, almost as if he had been hypnotized, before he snapped out of it. "'I can't figure it out at all. I've been farming all my life, and I've *never* felt this way about farming before. There's a certain satisfaction in watching life sprout in your fields—but this isn't natural. It's almost like something is taking over my thoughts!'" The villager shuddered again. "'Recently, some of the villagers have been whispering that these events mean something else. That maybe something broke in the world itself, and this is the herald of the end. I don't know if I believe them or not, but times are bad. The swamp is expanding, people are changing, monsters are attacking villages . . .'" As Ethan directly translated the man's words, Alice started to feel alarm bells ring in her mind.

Human beliefs could influence the world. This was something she was now certain of. What would happen if a lot of people believed that the *world was ending*? Alice felt deeply worried. She needed to dispel this belief before it became worse. Luckily, Alice had a good idea of what was *actually* happening behind the scenes. Humans feared the unknown most of all. If she could just explain it all in terms that other people could accept, hopefully the talk of the end of the world would be silenced before it became a true threat.

Cecilia tapped Alice on the shoulder, and Alice realized she had gotten lost in her thoughts again. She returned her focus to Ethan's translations.

"'The [Innkeeper] keeps losing his train of thought for hours on end while he manages his inn. He's never been a distracted man, but falling into a routine for hours on end, and not even noticing what he's doing isn't right. He's also going mad. I've never heard of a monster that can slip into somebody's body and control it like a puppet before, but I can't think of any other reason why people would be acting this way!'" The man finally paused, before giving Allira a hopeful look. "'Have you come to fix everything?'"

Possession? That was another alarming belief. Alice felt a headache start to form. If the group hadn't stopped here, she wouldn't have realized just how many worrying beliefs could form in the average village. These needed to be addressed *immediately*, before the world broke in some sort of irrecoverable way.

Allira glanced at Alice. Obviously, Allira had been paying attention to Ethan's translations. Since Alice had started being a bit more open about some aspects of the collapse of the System with Allira, Allira also seemed to realize just how dangerous the situation was. She seemed to be asking Alice how to proceed. Alice took a deep breath and let it out.

"Tell them about our efforts to dispatch the heart of the swamp. Also, let them know that I'm willing to heal their getting lost in their work–related illness. You should also inform them that it's a reaction caused by bad mana—and that in the future, treating it will be even easier for me," said Alice. "Make sure they understand that it's a reaction caused by bad mana. It's close enough to the actual explanation, without needing me to get into a lot of technical details." Details that Alice wasn't sure it was a good idea to share with others. Alice also needed to make sure people were at least roughly correct in their understanding of how and why this strange disease had come about. Otherwise, there was no telling whether the rules behind this disease might suddenly change behind the scenes—rendering Alice's efforts to cure it pointless.

Allira gave Alice a thumbs-up and then turned her attention back to the villagers she had been speaking with. The group of people continued to converse, and after a few sentences, one of the villagers' eyes lit up.

Ethan grinned. "Allira has informed the villagers that the monstrous beast at the heart of the swamp has been slain, and the swamp should retreat over the next few days. She has also talked about the odd monsters in the swamp and how they have been captured for further study." Ethan pointed at the cages that Allira's illusions were still maintaining, before he chuckled. "The villagers seem far more excited about the prospect of curing their loved ones, though. They also confirmed that a [Blacksmith] can forge some more cages for the captured monsters and offered us free room and board at the inn if we help the [Innkeeper] with his class-mana madness."

About ten minutes later, Cecilia returned with a [Blacksmith]. The [Blacksmith] was a rather petite woman, with dark red hair and bright green eyes. She looked at the group with a strange sense of eagerness, and her eyes lit up when she saw

Alice and Allira. The two chattered in Fendrallian for several minutes before the [Blacksmith] ran off again. She returned a few minutes later with another woman, who seemed dazed. Alice only needed a quick check to confirm the woman the [Blacksmith] had brought over was a [Tailor] suffering from a very bad case of class-mana poisoning. Was the woman a friend of the [Blacksmith]? A lover? A sister? Alice had no idea. At the end of the day, it didn't matter. Alice used her filtration mana to resolve the woman's class-mana madness before the [Blacksmith] tried to give Alice a huge hug. Alice was caught off guard and tolerated the woman's quick embrace and grateful smile.

Alice wasn't much of a hugger, but even though she disliked being touched, she was still glad to see her actions had made the world a better place. The [Black-smith] followed up with another hug for Allira before she grabbed one of the monster cages from Allira's illusions and dashed off.

After the [Blacksmith], more villagers started to arrive. Several of them weren't capable of coming on their own, so their friends, neighbors, and family members guided them to Alice. After Alice saw the number of patients, she sighed. There were nearly four hundred people in the village, and over a quarter had bad enough class-mana poisoning that they needed guidance to come to Alice's healing session. Alice wasn't sure if part of that was due to the village's location, since it was near a swamp that basically served as a font of belief mana strings. However, it was worrying.

"Tell them to give me {Lesser Patient's Consent}," said Alice. Ethan translated for her, and the more lucid members of the group gave Alice a series of consent statements. Alice wasn't entirely sure whether {Lesser Patient's Consent} would work with her treatment of mana illness, but there was no harm in giving it a shot. Then she started treating people.

The next patient was a [Farmer]. Alice had an easy time cleaning up the mana in his body and filtering all of it back into [Farmer] mana. Just like when she corrected the mana in her own class seeds, Alice only needed a minute or two to convert everything into [Farmer] mana, unclog his other class seeds, and get everything straightened out. Partway through her treatment, as if he had realized what was happening, the man's eyes widened. It seemed that he had returned to some level of self-awareness. The [Farmer] sat as still as a rock, as if he was afraid that even breathing too loudly would cause Alice to make a mistake. Once she finished fixing his mana, he tried to give her a thank-you hug, which Ethan rejected after Alice sent him a pleading look. Alice was left wondering whether thank-you hugs were a common occurrence in Fendrallia. If so, this country was truly terrify-ing. The man seemed a little uncertain what to think of Alice's rejection of the hug, but after a few words from Allira and Ethan, he nodded and moved away so that the next patient could come to Alice.

Alice continued working her way through the villagers, over half of whom tried to give her a thank-you hug. Apparently, that *was* a cultural thing in

Fendrallia. As she worked, she started to reflect on her actions. She had done her best to find ways to spread knowledge of how to combat the collapse of the System. She had worked hard to control the crisis and try to help people. On the other hand, she also hadn't interacted with the people who were directly harmed by the crisis. She also hadn't found the time to do any form of mass healing before, despite having the capability to do so. Usually, she was more than willing to fix her own class mana, and she'd also healed a few close friends, such as Cecilia. She had always thought that it made the most sense to find a way to fix the crisis at its roots instead of treating a few people who would just get sick again afterward.

In a way, Alice still thought that was the correct approach to things. Part of Alice couldn't help but feel like mass healing people like this was a waste of time and mana.

The other part of her felt that she should have started doing this sooner. There was something to be said about using her magic to help people and seeing the results of her hard work right in front of her. Instead of seeing people's lives and health as abstract statistics and reports, this was the first time Alice could really *see* the impact she was making on the world. It was also comforting to take some time to handle a problem she actually knew how to solve. Most of her bigger projects were complicated and had several parts to them, most of which she had yet to figure out—but helping people deal with class mana wasn't about discovering and innovating anymore. All she had to do was follow the routine she had already established.

After getting through nearly two hundred patients, Alice was amused to see a few System notifications pop up.

You have leveled up!
Explorer of Magic: 86→87, Legendary Organic Mage: 7→8

Alice was also amused to see that [Legendary Organic Mage] had gained a level. Most people associated organic magic and healing with each other, which was probably why Alice had gotten that level. Still, the idea of getting levels in an [Organic Mage] class without using organic magic amused her.

Of course, the mana that her [Legendary Organic Mage] class seed absorbed seemed to be quite a bit less focused than usual, so Alice lost quite a bit more mana than usual during the filtration and conversion process. The progress in [Legendary Organic Mage] was still exciting, though. She hoped that the perks from a class with the word *legendary* in the name would be better than usual.

After Alice finished treating all the people in the village, the [Blacksmith] returned with several rainbow mana-infused cages, finally giving Allira's throat a rest. Alice scanned her System notifications again and dealt with the last wisps of mana, where she got two surprises.

First, after she purified her own mana, she had enough to level up [Legendary Organic Mage] one more time.

You have leveled up!
Legendary Organic Mage: 8→9

She was only one level away from getting a perk in [Legendary Organic Mage] now. However, much more interesting was the new achievement that she had gained during the treatment.

You have gained an achievement!
Distributing the Cure (I) (Rarity: 4)
You have treated the strange illness in the village of Frostriver. The villagers are grateful for your help!
+30% experience for healing and magic research–related classes, +5% Magic stat.

As Alice healed villagers, she had also observed the little strings of mana in the village reaching toward her and vibrating, carrying tiny bits of mana and something else. As these threads grew more numerous, and their vibrations grew more exaggerated, Alice had seen rainbow mana start to coalesce in the mana gem in her brain. Finally, she had gained her new achievement.

The achievement itself wasn't astounding, but Alice wasn't going to complain about a small XP boost and a minor improvement to her magic stat. Every little bit helped. Unfortunately, the new achievement was only giving Alice 50 percent of the benefits it was supposed to give, just like the other achievements she had received after the System broke. Alice would probably need to use {First Steps} again to fix it.

It got Alice thinking. If she treated a few more villagers, would she get a few more, similar achievements, or increase the rank of {Distributing the Cure}? If so, it might be a good way to boost her leveling speed. She would mention it to Ethan later.

Still, she pushed it to the back of her mind. She let herself smile and relax as the villagers thanked the group for healing them and dealing with the swamp. The group made their way into the inn to sleep shortly afterward. As she lay in bed that night, Alice had the easiest time falling asleep in days.

It was a day when she had made very little actual progress toward fixing the System as a whole, but she found herself in one of the best moods she'd had in weeks.

C H A P T E R 5 4

After the group woke up, they had a quick breakfast at the inn before they prepared to depart. To Alice's surprise, there were two elderly villagers waiting for them outside. One of them was an older man who looked to be in his sixties, with a gnarled back and hands. His body resembled the trunk of an old tree that had weathered many storms but had never broken under their weight. The other was an elderly woman who had a straight back and bright, clear eyes. Alice faintly remembered healing both yesterday.

The two of them seemed to be inspecting her in turn. After several heartbeats passed, the elderly man smiled and pushed a basket covered in red cloth into her hands. It was warm. Alice unwrapped the basket and found a few loaves of fresh bread.

"Thank you for help with village, Immortal apprentice," the man said in broken Illvarian. "Helped lots people. Try bread! Gratitude!"

Alice turned toward Ethan, and his eyes flashed rainbow. "You can eat it. It's safe," he said.

Alice pulled out one of the loaves of bread and took a hesitant bite before she nodded in approval. It wasn't as good as Immortal Jonathan's bread, but it still tasted nice. The insides were warm and soft, and the outside was crusty and tasted faintly of butter and some sort of savory herb. It reminded her of garlic bread.

"Thank you, elder," said Alice. The man clearly struggled with Illvarian, but Alice hoped he understood her words.

"No. Thank. Good help." The man gently smiled at her as Alice tried to parse his words for their actual meaning. "Would hug, but you hate. Bread instead."

As he retreated, the elderly woman stepped up. She handed Alice a little crown of flowers before patting Alice faintly on her shoulders.

"@#*$(@ @#(*$#@ @#$*() @#*$(#& @#$(*)@#$*(@)@#($)(@#$)@#($@(#)$ @#) ()(!@$!@&%@#$ %!(@#$*@!#(@ %&*#@$," she said. Unlike the man, the woman didn't even have a rudimentary understanding of Illvarian, so Alice had no idea what she had just said. She turned toward Ethan questioningly.

"She said her granddaughter made it, and she thanks you for healing her and her grandchildren," Ethan said. "She also says that her granddaughter insists that you're the princess of the healing mages, and that every princess needs a crown." Alice smiled awkwardly. Perhaps it was due to how she had been raised, but Alice had never gone through the wanting to be a princess phase. Still, she appreciated the sentiment behind the crown of flowers, even if it also made her feel odd. She carefully placed it on her head.

"Thank you," said Alice, with Ethan translating.

"@#*$(&@#$ @#*$(#! @#*$ @#*$* @(@#($ @#)(*#@$#@$!" The woman's face grew animated, and the wrinkles on her forehead seemed to shrink as she smiled at Alice.

Ethan paused and gave the crown of flowers a quick inspection before he shrugged. "You could preserve the flowers using organic magic, if you want a decent magic practice routine. It might even have some relevance to your current research. Altering things with magic without accidentally killing them is difficult, and even though Jonathan has volunteered to help you with experiments, flowers might still be a good starting point. Just a suggestion."

Alice vowed to squeeze in as much practice on the flowers as she could get. The old lady and the old man gave the group one more kind smile before they walked away.

Cecilia laughed. "You're the hero of a village, Alice. Just like the Immortals from stories and legends. You came to an unknown village, saved everyone, and then continued on your way. If my father was still around, maybe he would have told me stories about you, too." Cecilia's eyes seemed a little sad when she said that, but also a little happy. "I'm glad that we came here, even if it wasn't originally planned."

Ethan gave Alice a firm pat on the shoulders. "You did a good job. It's only one village, but you made a difference here. It might not be the most mana-efficient use of your time, but I'm glad you got to experience helping people this way." He gave Alice a lopsided grin. "If we're lucky, your actions might help feed into Allira's narrative, too, and help mitigate the dangers of the swamp."

After Ethan mentioned the swamp, Alice glanced back. She was surprised to see that the swamp had retreated a bit. It hadn't moved much—but the edge had clearly moved a bit farther away from the village. Some of the strings of mana connecting the village and the swamp had also shrunk. It was more tangible proof that her discoveries and her efforts were making a difference, even if it was a small one.

She admired the results of the group's efforts for a few more minutes before Allira gently placed a hand on her head.

"Ready to go?" asked Allira. "If you need to stay for a bit longer to gather more data, now is the time to tell me."

Alice hesitated. Then she sighed. "No. Let's go."

Allira started singing again, and a ship made of illusions and light sprang back into existence. The group boarded the ship before Ethan lifted it into the air.

"All right, we're going to fly for a bit longer this time. Hopefully we can find a place to buy new horses, since we left the old ones at the edge of the swamp. We'll see what we can find," said Ethan. "This kind of movement is a bit too much of a strain on my mana reserves, though, and so we're going to make shorter trips and stop whenever we need to. Alice, feel free to focus on research instead. No matter what, your priority is learning more." The group nodded, and then the ship shot forward.

Alice didn't spend very long thinking before she decided to do a few experiments. One of the nice things about traveling by ship was that she could experiment in peace. On horseback, she was more worried about not falling off her horse, but on the illusory ship, she could focus. As it just so happened, she hadn't had much time to investigate the monsters they'd captured in the swamp yet—and Alice thought they might be a gold mine of information.

She moved to the cages where the mana-born swamp monsters were kept and started running some tests on them.

The first thing she tried was placing one of the monsters into an artificial no-mana zone. Normal monsters suffocated if they didn't have access to mana, but mana-born seemed fundamentally different. She wanted to see how they reacted to a manaless environment.

As it turned out, the answer was . . . interesting. At first, the monster didn't react at all, leading Alice to feel rather disappointed. She had expected some sort of reaction, but standing around drooling was definitely not what she thought would happen. She supposed it wasn't *that* shocking—during the fight, the monsters hadn't instantly died when she cut them off from the surrounding mana. But even after five minutes of testing, the monsters didn't even react to their new environment.

It wasn't until nearly ten minutes that Alice noticed that things were not as simple as she had assumed. While the monster was still moving around in the manaless zone, after ten minutes, its movements started to become jerky. The monster resembled a rusted, worn-out automaton. It was still trying to react like a normal monster, but its joints and muscles weren't working properly anymore. Not only that, but its hand-eye coordination had collapsed. The mana-born monster resembled a fish out of water—it flopped and flailed but couldn't walk properly anymore. Strangest of all was the fact that it didn't even seem to notice.

Finally, after twenty minutes, the monster flopped over and stopped responding to its surroundings. It was like a puppet with no puppeteer. Alice hesitantly started poking it with a stick, to see if the monster was trying to fake its unresponsiveness as some kind of trick. The monster didn't respond.

Was it dead?

Alice waited for ten more minutes to see if anything changed, but the monster remained as stiff as a log. Finally, Alice tried releasing the antimana barrier.

A few minutes later, the mana-born creature started jerking around, as if it had come back to life. However, its movements weren't the same as before. It was still jerky, uncoordinated, and messy. It tried to snarl at her, but it could only manage uncoordinated flailing. It was like a broken wind-up doll.

She waited for several more minutes, but the monster never recovered. Its range of motion seemed damaged as a result of its time in a manaless environment.

Alice couldn't find any physical injuries on the monster, surmised that the time it had spent in a near-comatose state probably had left some kind of permanent damage behind. However, she was far more interested in the fact that the monster was still alive, despite spending nearly half an hour in a manaless zone. Any real monster would have died in that time. For some reason, even though they were born *from* mana, mana-born creatures were actually less reliant on mana to survive.

After that, Alice had a lovely idea, for a *much* more interesting test.

Instead of creating a zone with no mana at all, Alice tried doing something a bit more complicated.

The first thing she did was create a thin layer of antimagic mana shielding around herself and the monster. Within the room, there was now a small, bubble-shaped area that was perfectly clear of mana. Then Alice almost immediately began filling up that bubble with pure mana from her own magic seed, while maintaining a thin layer of antimagic mana to separate the inside and outside of the bubble.

Alice wasn't quite sure if this would work at all, but she was very curious to know what happened if she isolated the monster from the rest of the world's mana, but didn't cut off its supply of mana entirely.

The monster started to adopt similar problems to before. Its limbs grew clumsy and unresponsive, and it eventually collapsed, but its collapse wasn't total. Unlike the first monster, this one didn't resemble a corpse. Even more interesting was the fact that the tether connecting this monster to the distant swamp grew thinner and weaker as the seconds passed by. The monster itself kept reaching out some of its limbs toward Alice, in a doomed attempt to tear at her flesh. However, its movements were almost wholly uncoordinated.

At the same time, Alice noticed that the string of mana connecting her to this monster remained as strong as ever. In fact, it seemed as if the string had begun to vibrate more than before, as if the monster were latching on to a new set of beliefs to compensate for its lost connection to the swamp.

Alice started to wonder whether the monster actually had any natural behavior at all. Was the monster only moving the same way it had in the swamps because of *her* beliefs about how it moved and acted? Alice's threads of belief were clearly tied to the mana-born monster, so it might really have replaced the swamp with her. What would happen if Alice left the bubble and then someone with a completely different set of beliefs about how the monsters would act stepped into the bubble instead? Would that change the way the mana-born monster behaved? Even more interesting was the question of how far she could take these beliefs. What if she believed that the monster would grant anyone who ate its flesh godhood? Or what if she believed that the monster was a benevolent healer?

Alice kind of doubted that either of those beliefs would *actually* work, but it was definitely food for thought. She wanted to see how far she could push things.

Alice got an idea. Could belief program the monster to act a certain way? She left the room and found Cecilia.

"Cecilia!" she yelled. "I want to show you an interesting experiment! I managed to reprogram the mana-born monster a bit!"

"Reprogram?" asked Cecilia blinking in surprise. "What does that mean? I don't know that word."

Alice blushed as she realized that in her excitement, she had used the English word for "reprogram," since there was no corresponding word in Illvarian. She cleared her throat.

"I managed to get a really interesting result when I was messing with one of the mana-born monsters. I've been tinkering with it, and I've realized that they're kind of like wind-up dolls. You can manipulate the way they behave and act based on the way they interact with the mana in their surroundings. I got the monster to do a classical waltz. Could you take a look and see if your [Enchanter] perks give you any useful data about what's happening behind the scenes?"

Cecilia gave Alice a dubious look but shrugged and followed Alice back to the storage room. Alice made sure to remain outside of her isolated mana bubble, but ushered Cecilia into it. She noticed that in her absence, the monster had stopped moving around and had flopped over like a toy with no batteries. The moment Cecilia stepped into the mana bubble, Alice's theory proved to be correct. A new thread of mana formed between her and the mana-born monster, and the monster's legs started twitching again. The creature still looked kind of like it was suffering from nerve damage, but a moment later, two of its limbs started to coil up and try to perform a clumsy, erratic waltz. The other limbs on the monster's body tried to drag the rest of it forward, to rip Cecilia's face off and gnaw at her flesh—but the monster was trying to do a waltz at the same time. Alice grinned.

Cecilia seemed to have wholeheartedly believed Alice's words—and while that hadn't been enough to totally change the mana-born monster's behavior, it had clearly done something. She had confirmed that the strings of mana were related to human belief.

Chapter 55

Alice spent the next day poking at the mana-born monsters again. After her test with Cecilia, she explained what she had *actually* been testing and then got Jonathan's permission to have his children help her out. Mimi, in particular, was easy to fool, since she was still a child. Part of Alice felt bad for tricking a girl who wasn't even ten yet, but another part of her was grateful to finally have an easy way to test beliefs.

The first thing Alice confirmed was how much influence one person's beliefs could have on a mana-born monster. She quickly confirmed that the physical shapes of mana-born were *not* malleable. Even when Alice told Mimi all about the interesting one-eyed mana-born monster with forty legs she had been experimenting with and how the monster did funny hops when there was a carrot placed in front of it, the monster's form remained unchanged. It still looked like a monstrous patch of fog and fetid swamp water. It *did* try to hop when she put a carrot in front of it, though.

This result made Alice even more curious. She had always thought of fog as being rather shapable. In her mind, it would have made perfect sense for the monster to shape-shift into a one-eyed patch of fetid swamp gas after Mimi's beliefs were led in a certain direction. But the monster's form remained the same.

It seemed likely that mana-born monsters couldn't change shapes, regardless of what beliefs were fed into them. That also meant that there were limits to how much human beliefs could influence these monsters—which was an important thing to confirm, given how unstable Alice believed reality was. If there were limits to how much beliefs could impact reality, she wanted to know.

The second thing she confirmed was that, no matter what, none of the threads of mana and human belief could directly penetrate an enclosed layer of manaless space. However, even if she totally blocked these strings of mana from directly touching a test subject, somehow, *some* amount of belief was still getting through, even when she couldn't figure out how. Cutting off the threads of mana drastically reduced the impact human beliefs had upon the creature, but it didn't cut it off entirely.

Interestingly enough, this was *not* true if Alice removed all mana from the area the monster resided in instead of creating a multilayered set of mana-rich and manaless bubbles. If she cut off the mana-born monster from mana entirely, it was just like a robot with defective AI and rusty joints. This implied that mana itself was connected to all other mana in the area in some way that Alice couldn't detect. That was interesting, even though it was also a major pain in the neck.

She also confirmed that the impact of human beliefs upon mana-born monsters was quite long-lasting. The monster she had made do a waltz yesterday was still attempting to do a waltz today. Based on this, Alice had a new question. It was obvious that beliefs, aided by mana, could distort reality. But what happened if these "beliefs" were removed from an area entirely? If she somehow cut away every single thread of belief, would the area revert to its natural form? Or would the influence remain? This was a question she hadn't considered before, but it could be very relevant when she figured out her countermeasure against the unstable nature of reality. The best way to find the answer was to run more tests.

This time, Alice got all of Jonathan's children to believe that one of the mana-born monsters was jumping up and down for no reason, and she even told Ethan and Allira about her bunny-hopping mana-born monster. Then she set up the outer layer of a bubble of isolated mana that extended just outside the testing room—that way, beliefs would influence the monster before they saw it. When they entered the room, Alice was more than slightly relieved to find that the monster was jumping up and down.

After that, Alice shooed everyone out and tried throwing a bunch of antimana into the area to see if the monster kept hopping around after all the mana was purged. She also did her best to cut off any strings of mana and then watched the monster collapse like a dead fish. Then she flooded the area with mana again, *without* allowing any strings of human belief to reappear inside the bubble. The monster returned to doing random jumps a few minutes later.

Alice ran a similar test by convincing the others that she had found that one of the legs of a mana-born monster would turn into a marble and then float when she cut it off. (In reality, Alice just had a marble lying around in her storage perk.) After putting the marble through the same process, it continued to float, even though it had no logical reason to do so.

In other words, beliefs *permanently* altered things. They would not return to normal once the presence of mana was removed from the area—anything that was changed by mana would remain changed. This meant that the warped swamps and forests of the continent, the messed-up and mana-born monsters, wouldn't return to normal if she fixed the System. The people of this world would just have to learn to deal with them unless Alice found a solution for these problems as well.

She spent a while trying to figure out a countermeasure for this problem, but she couldn't think of one.

On the bright side, it seemed like Mimi got some sort of achievement for helping out, although she clammed up when Alice asked her about it. Alice assumed it was probably some sort of benefit for assisting in her research and decided not to ask any more about it. After all, it might have some sort of edge-case use in combat, and Alice didn't want to be rude.

Alternately, Mimi might have gotten an achievement for being easily misled. Something about the way Mimi started eyeing Alice didn't make it seem like Mimi would be easy to trick anymore . . .

Another few hours passed in relative calm. Alice was pulled out of the quagmire of fruitless experiments when the boat landed in a new town. This one was quite a bit larger than the village of Frostriver and had a population of about ten thousand. After the group touched down, they split into a few smaller groups. Ethan and Jonathan went to assess any horses that were available for purchase, since Ethan's mana reserves were starting to run dry. Meanwhile, Allira started singing about their heroic fight against the "Heart of the Swamp."

Alice started another healing session after Ethan helped set it up. There were far too many people for Alice to heal everyone, due to time and mana constraints, but she did still heal several dozen people before her mana bottomed out. It was nowhere near enough, but it was better than nothing.

Ethan returned with a new set of horses an hour later. The group left again—and this time, they didn't even stop to sleep. There was too much daylight left to waste.

The next few days were another blur of movement. Alice got very reacquainted with the smell of horses (unfortunately) and had less time than before for her practical experiments. After her experiments on the ship, Ethan did try to help her run a few experiments, but it was very difficult with the limited space and the constant motion of the horses. Eventually, Alice gave up and took the time to work on the second image she had formed via {Magic Modeling} instead.

By the time they reached Fendrallia's capital, Alice was almost done creating an image of a fully functional mana gem. Unfortunately, the moment the capital came into view was the moment things went horribly wrong.

Because even from a distance, Alice could see a thick plume of smoke rising into the sky.

"Is that Fendrallia's capital?" she asked.

"It should be," said Allira, lightly biting her lower lip in anxiety.

"Is it on fire?" asked Cecilia, sounding unnerved.

"I hope not, but I'm pretty sure it is," said Ethan.

"Let me scout," Allira said before she started humming. Alice noticed a few shadows in their surroundings start to ripple and elongate, like sinister, outstretched branches and limbs in a hungry forest. The shadows started making their way forward before they vanished into the distance.

"The capital is under attack," Allira said a few minutes later. "A swarm of monsters is storming the area."

"How are the defenders doing?" asked Ethan. Alice could see a glimmer of cold calculation start to enter his eyes.

"Not great, but not terrible," said Allira. "The walls are still intact, and they aren't overrun yet. However, the monster swarm is more numerous than the defenders, and they have a much greater number of magic users. It looks like Fendrallia is barely holding on." Allira's frown deepened. "I can see multiple swarms of monsters working together. There are over ten thousand monsters in total."

"Damn." Ethan curled his hands into fists. "How many defenders?"

"Eight thousand. A lot of them don't look very experienced, though. Half of them are proper troops, and the other half look like civilians with a few useful perks."

"That doesn't sound very promising," said Ethan.

"I say that we still try to help out," said Jonathan as he looked at the plume of smoke in the distance. "At the end of the day, we're still Immortals. But I'll defer to your judgment. I'm barely a combatant, after all, so most risks would be borne by you two if we step in."

Ethan nodded solemnly, and Alice saw some of the calculation in his gaze disappear. Ethan sighed.

"Fine. Let's go help the damn Fendrallians manage their monsters. Unless you object?" he asked as he turned toward Allira.

"No, I'm fine with helping out. I don't think we should wade directly into the thick of things, but as long as we sit near the edges of the battlefield, I don't mind tipping the scales a bit. It could also build some goodwill with Fendrallia, which might be relevant later," she said.

"Let's do that and see how things go."

With that, the group pushed their horses to speed up even more as they galloped toward the capital. As they drew closer, Alice started to see what had put the Immortals on edge. The capital was a *mess*.

Fendrallia's capital had originally been divided into two sections—the inner city and the outer city. The inner city was surrounded by a wall, while the outer city was outside the wall. Many portions of the outer city looked like they were made from poor materials, such as straw and bricks, and the construction was shoddy. Some of the houses didn't even have perks to support them, which was incredibly unusual in this world.

The houses made of straw and mud bricks were, almost without exception, ruined. It looked like monsters had broken into them and eaten the inhabitants— there were bloodstains and messy corpses strewn about the outer city, and the entire area was unusually low on mana. Several houses had also burned to cinders. Alice had no idea whether the defenders had set the houses alight to drive off the monsters, or the monsters had torched them using mana. Either way, it was clear that many monsters had eaten their fill here.

While the outer city seemed almost completely deserted, Alice still saw evidence of a few scattered groups of people surviving there. She could see a few chunks of System mana here and there, all of which were human-shaped. They were rare, though.

The inner city was still intact, but it was under siege. Some ant-based monsters were trying to climb up the walls. These monsters seemed to have the ability to manipulate stone, and they were using this to harass the defenders and to drill straight through the walls. Meanwhile, a swarm of vinebears was helping them out by causing moss and flowers to bloom in between the stones of the wall, weakening the mortar. There was also a flock of flying monsters in the skies, spraying the defenders with ice magic and also dropping temperatures in the area to freezing levels. The lower temperatures seemed to be bothering the humans almost as much as the actual icy projectiles.

Defenders at the top of the wall were desperately trying to keep the situation under control by shooting down the ant monsters and the vinebears with bows and kinetic projectiles, while mages from inside the city were trying to take out the flying monsters. To round out the picture, groups of people were pouring cauldrons of boiling water and sand onto the monsters at the base of the wall. At first, Alice thought that they were pouring boiling *oil* onto the monsters, but she quickly realized that oil was ridiculously expensive. The only place people would waste such a valuable substance as ammunition was in a movie.

Some of the people pouring boiling water onto the monsters were using perks to instantly heat up the water—which made Alice suspect they were [Chefs] rather than trained [Soldiers]. Other defenders were constantly repairing the holes in the wall at supernatural speeds, marking them as [Masons] instead of combatants. Both [Chefs] and [Masons] seemed underarmored and underequipped for the battle, and monstrous projectiles frequently dropped on them.

The mages seemed better equipped—they were wearing solid steel armor. Unfortunately, even that wasn't enough to keep them all alive. With how few of the other defenders of the wall were geared up, Alice quickly realized just how bad things were.

Alice grimaced as her group crept closer to the city under siege.

It wasn't long before the monsters spotted them. When some of the vinebears near the edge of the battlefield looked in their direction, their eyes lit up with ravenous greed. The creatures seemed to grow in size as Alice felt fear start to settle in her bones—before she immediately flooded the area with a little bit of antimagic mana, totally shutting off the fear magic the vinebears had been employing.

Ethan snorted, and before Allira could do anything, he sent a spray of wooden debris into the clump of vinebears. They went down in a swath of gurgles and bloody fur. Ethan stepped over their corpses and onto the edge of the battlefield.

Alice swallowed nervously before she followed suit.

Chapter 56

It wasn't long before the rest of the monster horde noticed their presence. The stone-controlling ants paid no heed to them—they continued swarming the wall and battling the defenders. The nearest vinebears proved far less focused. Several broke away from the wall and whirled toward the group with hungry expressions.

Allira started singing. Soft lyrics described a lost city and missiles that fell from the sky as an army brought ruin to families and businesses. The air around them rippled, and illusory buildings and corpses started to appear in the midst of the battlefield. Children and adults huddled in broken buildings as Sigmusi mages rained death upon them.

The vinebears seemed stunned by the disappearance of plant life in the area. To Alice's surprise, some of them started to retreat. This wasn't behavior that she was used to. Most monsters simply charged until they were dead.

For a moment, Alice was relieved. If the monsters started fleeing from this battlefield, it would be a good outcome. The city would be saved, and the group would be free to continue their journey. However, she realized she was too optimistic.

The vinebears weren't fleeing. They were *regrouping*. The moment the vinebears realized that Allira's illusion nullified their strongest weapon, they found a place where her illusions hadn't spread. Allira started slowly walking toward them as she tried to keep them in range—but the vinebears remained just out of reach. A moment later, one of the vinebears clambered over to one of the make-believe bricks on the ground. Then, as if it were an Olympic shot-put champion, it grabbed one of the rocks and awkwardly threw it at the group. Fortunately, its aim was atrocious—but Alice was still struck by how *different* these creatures were after the collapse of the System. To instantly swap to ranged weapons was something monsters of the past would never have been capable of doing. A moment later, one of Ethan's shrapnel pieces ripped through its throat, killing it instantly.

As the vinebear's missed projectile bounced off the ground, Alice moved over to inspect it. She noticed a small cluster of moss on the side of the rock that felt oddly sticky. It must have been how the bear-shaped monster had managed to throw it in the first place. Bears didn't have thumbs, so it had used magically enhanced moss to let it hurl the missile away. That was even more clever than she had first given the monsters credit for.

Alice took a closer look at the vinebears. Were the vinebears themselves intelligent, or was it just the monster alphas? If it were just the alphas, Alice might have a good way to assist on the battlefield. A few weeks ago, Alice had watched a monstrous glimmerspren evolve into an alpha. During that time, it looked almost as if the monster had formed a sort of paired enchantment between the monster alpha and all nearby glimmerspren. She had also observed the strings of belief mana that connected the mana-born and the strange swamp. Both of those were, at their heart, built upon connections and communication.

As it just so happened, Alice had access to antimagic mana, which was *great* at screwing up magical connections and communication.

Alice used {Dimensional Camouflage} in tandem with three of her magic tendrils to extend her range. Each portal was positioned right next to the vinebears, but thanks to {Dimensional Camouflage}, she didn't need to worry about getting counterattacked through the portals. Once her mana tendrils reached her targets, she started flooding the battlefield with antimagic mana.

The moment they were covered in antimagic mana, the vinebears closest to her portals looked like they had gone crazy. They started desperately running in different directions, trying and failing to use their magic on Allira's illusory city, and a few of them simply charged the group. It was as if they had lost their minds . . . or perhaps, their unusual intelligence. Ethan rapidly mowed down the closest vinebears.

Alice grinned. This tactic was surprisingly effective. However, she quickly noticed another problem. This tactic required flooding an area with antimagic mana, and Alice didn't have *that* much to spare. With a 171 [Magic] stat, 192 percent stat effectiveness, and 40 percent mana conversion ratio, she had about 131 Mariums of antimagic mana. Not a terrible amount, but not enough to flood the whole battlefield like this. Just to break down the [Intelligence] and [Strength] of a few dozen vinebears, she had spent nearly thirty Mariums. There were thousands of monsters in front of her. At this rate, she would run out of mana long before she made a substantial difference on the battlefield. Not to mention, the remaining vinebears were already starting to spread out, making her antimagic-mana tactic less effective.

Alice glanced toward the front of the group, where Ethan and Jonathan had blocked off another group of vinebears and eradicated them. She spent a moment observing Jonathan and noted that he was surprisingly effective in combat. He had none of the grace of a proper [Swordsman], but he had raw [Strength] and [Endurance]. Alice suspected that the man would seriously struggle against some types of enemies—fast, nimble opponents could probably dance circles around him. People with ranged attacks probably wouldn't have a hard time dealing with him, either, as long as they stayed out of range and whittled him down. However, when it came to these vinebears, after Allira had stripped away their most direct combat magic and Alice eliminated their tactical intelligence?

The man could almost ignore the scratches and bites of the vinebears, and his wild haymaker punches could shatter bones like they were brittle glass. Even if his aim could use some work, he still killed a vinebear with every other punch.

With three Immortals, the nearby vinebears had almost no chance to turn the battle around. The ones still under the command of their alpha retreated even farther away from Allira's illusory city while the nearby vinebears quickly turned into paste.

After the trapped vinebears were killed, Ethan immediately swapped to ranged attacks. Several died—but several others began using plants to form walls of vegetable matter and wood, blocking off Ethan's barrage. The other monsters started to notice the group as well and began to coordinate with the vinebears. Several flocks of flying birds broke away from the battlements and flew toward them.

To Alice's surprise, Cecilia and Jonathan's children joined the fight next. Jacob, Stuart, and Mimi pulled out bows and started firing at the monstrous fliers, while Cecilia launched a blast crystal into the air and detonated it in the middle of a flock of birds. Cecilia's aim wasn't great, so it only killed a few—but the loud noise and small shock wave sent the entire flock reeling. Jonathan's children also had poor aim, but they still managed to occasionally hit a monster. The volley of attacks might not have been very effective at killing monsters, but it made them wary.

Cecilia and Jonathan's children weren't anywhere near as strong as the Immortals, but they were working hard to keep some pressure off the core combatants.

Unfortunately, it was nowhere near enough. The first spray of icy shrapnel came ten seconds later, when the ice birds unleashed a volley at Ethan. Alice tried to deflect some of the frosty shrapnel, then wrinkled her lips in annoyance when her kinetic mana touched the missiles.

Something about these projectiles felt slippery when she tried to manipulate them. She had no clue how that was even possible, but it was very hard for her to touch them with her kinetic mana.

Ethan sent the wave of projectiles back at the birds, but that left Jonathan alone for a brief moment. During that time, a new group of vinebears charged through Allira's illusions and tried to dogpile him, backed up by more vinebear boulder throwers.

Alice started popping open portals near the ice-controlling birds and then ripping them apart with her enchanted bracelet beads. Unlike the icy projectiles she had failed to deflect, she ran into no problems once she stopped trying to defend the others and just leaned into her offensive abilities.

In this way, the group managed to create an uneasy stalemate with the monsters. They hadn't dragged over enough monsters to tilt the scales in favor of the city defenders, but they had taken some pressure off. The flying monsters, in particular, were important, because the mages on the walls were finally free to help knock down the stone-controlling giant ants.

However, Alice's group wasn't having an easy time, either. Some of the monsters displayed their access to perks, which threw wrenches into their combat plans more than once. Three minutes into the battle, Alice started sweating as an icicle teleported right next to her skull and nearly pulped her brain. Luckily, {Adrenaline Rush}, followed by {Reflection}, saved her before she met an untimely end. But the close call shook her out of complacency. Even with three Immortals here, if she got unlucky enough, she would die.

That was far from the only dangerous perk the monsters used. Five minutes into the battle, a vinebear that Alice thought was dead flashed with pseudo-System mana before it climbed back to its feet and gave Jonathan a solid punch, nearly knocking him into another pile of monsters. Ethan managed to wipe out the vinebears before they could trap Jonathan, but Jonathan seemed shaken after the incident.

Seven minutes into the battle, Alice nearly got brained by another icicle. Ethan responded by moving closer to her, making it easier for him to keep her safe. These constant wild cards made the battle far more difficult than it should have been. That got Alice thinking again.

Her mana reserves and number of magic tendrils were pitiful compared to Ethan's. Her comparative value on the battlefield, at least as a [Kinetic Mage], was negligible. Her greatest strength was the ability to come up with new, innovative tactics. How could she do that? The antimagic flooding worked, but it was too mana-intensive to make a big impact on the battlefield. Her enchantments were nowhere near good enough to make a huge difference here, and she didn't have time to make new ones. What could she do?

Alice gritted her teeth as she failed to come up with anything new. She activated another set of bracelet beads, killing another wave of ice birds. Then she saw something shift out of the corner of her eyes. Some of the stone ants were finally taking notice of them. They seemed annoyed by the fact that the ice birds and vinebears hadn't cleaned up their corner of the battlefield yet. Four hundred giant ants broke off from the assault on the wall and started stomping toward the group.

That was *not* good. The group was barely holding on as it was. If the stone ants joined the fray, they might be forced to retreat.

Just as Alice started sweating, Allira's singing took on a deeper, more urgent tone. Allira grunted in pain, and a surge of rainbow mana tore out of her body and into a nearby building. Then a giant maw made of shadows suddenly tore out of one of the ruined buildings in Allira's illusory city. It grinned at one of the densest clusters of stone ants before it surged forward and snapped shut with a resounding *crunch*. The sound had an unnerving note of finality to it.

Just like that, nearly a hundred stone ants disappeared. The remaining stone ants froze in their tracks, eyeing Ethan's group more warily. More importantly, they stopped moving to reinforce the birds and the bears.

Alice glanced at Allira and saw that the Immortal of Song and Shadow was panting heavily as she eyed their surroundings. Clearly, the shadowy maw, as well as maintaining the illusory city, had taken a lot out of her.

Allira noticed Alice glancing at her and gave a strained smile.

"Don't worry, I'm not out of perks quite yet," she said, shaking her head. "But I'm tired, so hopefully I don't need to pull that off again."

Seeing Allira so worn out was worrying. The monsters were still making progress in tearing through the walls, and the number of monsters heading toward them was increasing rapidly. Worse, after Allira's intervention, even more monsters started to take notice of their little group. Another five hundred stopped besieging the walls and whirled toward them. Alice felt the back of her neck prickle with fear as she realized that nearly a thousand monsters were now fixated on their group instead of the defenders of the wall. At this rate, the defenders would finally get a real break—but their group was about to be in deep trouble.

Alice flipped open her status screen to see if she could find *anything* that could help them. Flooding the area was a waste of her remaining antimagic mana. {Adrenaline Rush} had already been used, and she only had two uses of {Reflection} left for this battle. Alice resisted the urge to growl in frustration as she came up blank again.

Nothing she could think of was *enough*. Alice briefly thought about all the abilities Ethan had displayed during the fight with the [Assassin] and started to feel frustrated. Why wasn't he using any of them? Was she missing something?

Alice noticed that Allira was eyeing their surroundings. It didn't seem like she was just trying to keep track of potential threats—her eyes shone with a mixture of pity and hesitation. With a flash of realization, Alice understood why the Immortals were mostly sticking to normal combat. They were preparing to escape if anything went wrong. They were trying to help, but they valued their own lives and Alice's life more than this city. If things got dangerous, they would flee.

Leaving the city to die didn't sit right with her. Alice *needed* a way to keep that from happening.

She turned back toward the approaching army of monsters. Above them, ice birds soared like kites in the wind, preparing to unleash frozen hell. Vinebears tramped through the illusory city of Allira's creation, preparing to drag Jonathan to the ground and devour him even with the loss of their plant magic. Stone-manipulating ants strolled toward the group like death on six legs.

Alice finally got an idea.

Antimagic mana was useful, but it chewed through her mana reserves too quickly. But a big part of her antimagic mana was wasted. After all, she was flooding an area with antimagic mana, meaning most of her mana was spent covering empty air.

There were far too many monsters for Alice to target each individual monster with antimagic mana and sever their connection to their alpha, so optimizing her mana use was implausible. However, that didn't mean she was out of options.

What if she used communication mana to do the same thing? Or if she tried to use pure mana to destabilize monster communication? Or what if she used them as a sort of targeting system, to optimize antimagic mana use?

Alice closed her eyes and tried to push the invading monsters out of her thoughts. Ethan could keep her safe for a few seconds, or even a few minutes. She couldn't just stand around with her eyes closed forever, but she had time to concentrate when she needed it.

Then she put three magic tendrils in front of her face and started to experiment. What she wanted was simple—she wanted to use communication mana and pure mana to create a sort of monster-seeking missile composed of antimagic mana. If she succeeded, she could probably cut 90 percent of the cost for each monster she took out of the monstrous communication network. That would let her start doing real damage. If things went *really* well, the monsters might even start fighting each other. After all, monsters working together was a very new thing and only happened when monster alphas controlled their subordinates. Alice suspected that cooperation would fall apart the moment the alphas lost control of their minions.

She activated {Speed Experimentation} to give her as much experimentation time as possible. Time slowed down as Alice started assembling and disassembling different types of communication and mana-seeking antimagic missiles.

At first, the antimagic mana simply outright deleted the pure mana. The two types of mana were like matter and antimatter. But she kept trying. After a few failed experiments, she started creating multilayered communication-disrupting projectiles. The outer layer was made of pure mana, while communication mana acted as an insulating layer between the antimagic mana and the pure mana. For some reason, the antimagic mana was less reactive when it touched communication mana—meaning that it didn't instantly chew apart the missile and cause it to implode. It wasn't perfect—the antimagic mana still ate through the communication mana fast enough that a missile would only last five seconds before it lost all directional movement. But five seconds would be enough.

Alice tossed in some math mana to make sure these antimagic missiles were a bit better at calculating trajectories and targets, and spent another minute trying to get the whole mess functional. At the end, Alice had a slapdash, messy missile that would fall apart after less than ten seconds of travel time—but it was good enough.

Alice held her breath and then released a prototype monster core–seeking antimagic bullet.

The little speck of mana sailed lazily away from her face before it locked onto the nearest vinebear. In a flash, it sped toward the creature and then burst into a small cloud of antimagic mana a few meters in front of it.

The projectile hadn't quite made it to its target before it imploded. Still, Alice thought she was on the right path.

Alice spent the next few minutes refining her idea until, on her sixteenth try, another communication-sealing bullet flew out of her hands and hit a vinebear.

This time, the missile worked as intended. Right after the antimagic mana reached the creature, it found the little part of the monster core that resembled a dual enchantment and temporarily shut the whole thing off.

The vinebear froze, as if it had been struck by lightning. It raised its eyes toward a nearby stone ant, its expression still radiating confusion . . . and then it leaped at its fellow monster and took a massive bite out of its leg.

The stone ant reeled back before it ripped a cobblestone out of the ground and crushed the vinebear's skull. It didn't seem to think much about the odd incident, perhaps because it had realized Alice had done something to the vinebear first.

But even though it didn't cause a sudden collapse of the monster alliance, Alice still grinned.

It had worked.

CHAPTER 57

The next few minutes were a mindless slog of missile creation and release. Even though the mana costs were moderate, every single construct was very taxing on Alice's mind. Fortunately, her massive [Intelligence] stat made it easier to concentrate, even through the mindless repetition and paper-thin margin for error.

Still, it took a decent amount of time to make each essence missile. After creating her third, Alice started to question if she was having an impact at all. The biggest benefit of her disruption missiles, as far as she could tell, was that it created infighting in the monstrous horde. The monsters acting as an organized army created a big problem for the humans trying to fend them off. Each of Alice's missiles created a traitor in the monstrous horde that would attack its allies. If Alice could cause widespread chaos, that might throw the entire battlefield into a frenzy of monsters eating each other.

But she couldn't do that. Right now, it took Alice almost ten seconds to craft a single disruption missile, which was far from causing a major upheaval on the battlefield. Then Alice got a new idea.

Their biggest problem was the existence of perk-wielding monsters. Each of them had access to a wild card that could potentially put someone in danger or create a new variable on the battlefield. Alice's disruption missiles could make one monster start attacking nearby monsters of a different species. What if she only aimed her communication-disrupting missiles at monsters with perks?

Alice executed this idea immediately, leading to an immediate change on the battlefield. Not only was Alice removing the most unpredictable threats, but she was also turning them into threats for the monster horde instead. While many monsters had passive perks that provided minor boosts in combat strength, plenty of other monsters had active perks.

Whenever Alice hit a monster with an active perk, if that perk wasn't on cooldown, it could take down several nearby monsters and throw the area into disarray. It was an easy way to inflict the maximum amount of damage for minimal mana. She wasn't eliminating threats anywhere near as quickly as Ethan or Allira, but she was spending far less mana and no active perks to do so.

Alice started to lose herself in the flow of the fight as the group cut down monster after monster. Until, after several more minutes of movement, the group arrived at the wall itself.

Alice glanced at the defenders and saw that most were still struggling. However, things hadn't reached a breaking point. More importantly, it seemed like the monsters were starting to run out of steam.

While it hadn't originally occurred to her, Alice realized that monsters actually had a major shortcoming in protracted battles: They were utterly reliant on magic to keep functioning as effective combatants, and mana didn't regenerate very quickly. They were enemies that could do a terrifying amount of damage quickly, but they didn't have attributes the way humans did—meaning their physical bodies were actually a bit weaker than trained humans'.

The group's impact on the battlefield was also noticeable. The defenders on the wall nearest to them were actually having moments where they could take breaks, resupply, and reinforce other sections of the wall. As Alice observed the rest of the wall, she smiled. The battle was winnable.

"@#*$()#@! @*#$(# @#*$(#@?" one of the defenders called from the top of the wall, startling Alice out of her thoughts.

"@#*$#@ @#(*$@#)(!# !@#()%#@$*(!" yelled Allira. "But Illvarian would be better!"

"Illvarian?" asked the defender. "I speak semifluently! Thank you for assisting us! Who are you?"

"We are Immortal Ethan, Immortal Allira, and Immortal Jonathan," yelled Ethan as he sent another wave of shrapnel into the nearby monsters. "We're also bringing along my apprentice, one of her friends, and Jonathan's family."

The man frowned, as if he was scouring his memories to figure out why they were here. Finally, his eyes lit up.

"I remember now! A week ago, former [Commander] Hadlock mentioned an Illvarian Immortal might pass through our country. Sorry, with all the chaos, we forgot." The man tried to smile, although he looked more exhausted than happy. "It's good to see friendly faces here. Especially Immortals! System knows that if there was ever a time we needed Immortals, it's now."

"Former [Commander]?" asked Alice.

"He died yesterday on the wall. I got promoted this morning." The man grimaced. "He was a good man."

Ethan frowned as he glanced at the monsters again. "Sorry to hear that." He paused for a moment, giving the man on the wall a few seconds to control the faint grief in his expression. Then Ethan continued. "Any information you can share about the horde of monsters here?"

"Not much beyond what you can see. We first caught sight of them three days ago. They attacked two days ago. Luckily, they get just as tired as we do during each battle. They usually break off the attack when about half of them are running low on mana. That way they can still retaliate if we try to take advantage of their exhaustion. We still try every night. So during the daytime, they attack us, and at night, we attack them." The man grimaced. "The last few days have been hell, Honored Immortals."

"I can imagine," said Ethan. "The three of us, as well as our traveling companions, will hold down this corner of the battlefield. Is there anything your troops need that we could help with?"

"Well, I don't suppose you can find the actual alphas and assassinate them?" asked the man.

Allira laughed. "If we could track them down and assassinate them, we would have done so already. We're Immortals, not miracle workers."

"Damn. Figures." The man sounded frustrated and exhausted, but not angry. He sighed. "Well, if that's the case, you've already helped out quite a bit. Just taking some of the pressure off the wall is more than most would have done. If you have the spare perks and mana for it, we wouldn't mind it if you focus on the fliers. They're the biggest problem. The vinebears aren't much of a threat to the wall itself, and the stone ants can't destroy the wall very fast. But the damn ice birds keep ripping apart the archers and mages so we can't get rid of the ants."

"Got it," said Ethan as he eyed the other sections of the battlefield. "Allira, do you have anything that would work well in the air?"

Allira shook her head. "It's too far away from the shadows. I have a few perks that could cover the distance, but I'd rather not spend them unless I need to. They're emergency perks."

"Then don't spend them." Ethan glanced at the skies again. "Keep Alice safe. I'm heading up." Kinetic mana spread across his body before he floated toward the skies.

Alice watched her mentor transition to an aerial combatant and zoom into the skies, and she grimaced. She didn't think Ethan would do something he wasn't confident in, but she felt a bit worried when the first flock of ice birds dived toward him.

"Without Ethan, the rest of us will be much weaker," said Allira, pulling Alice out of her observation. "I think we should remain here, since we're at least partially protected by the [Archers] on the wall. We'll focus on keeping this part of the battlefield safe and let the defenders on the wall manage the rest of this mess."

Jonathan's shoulders relaxed, and Alice realized for the first time that he had been tense ever since they entered the battlefield.

"I have to admit, I'm not that eager to keep fighting, either," he said. "Even the vinebears are dangerous if I get overwhelmed. Being able to take hits and survive doesn't make up for my lack of reliable perks and experience."

Allira nodded sagely. The group settled down near the foot of the wall, constantly relieving the pressure on nearby wall defenders. Alice continued using her communication-blocking missiles to deal with perk-using monsters, while Allira's shadows nibbled away smaller groups of monsters and Jonathan punched down any vinebears in their vicinity. As the defenders on the wall got used to their presence, Alice noticed them transferring people away from their side of the wall and toward other areas. It seemed that the defenders had decided to leave this corner of the wall to their group entirely.

Alice had no problems with that. The group might not be enough to tilt the scales of the battle on their own, but they were still a powerful group of combatants, even with Ethan focused on the birds. The monsters also didn't seem that interested in pushing their group. Perhaps they had been intimidated by Allira and Ethan's show of force? With how intelligent monsters seemed these days, it was hard to guess what they were thinking.

Finally, after half an hour of constant fighting that felt like an eternity, something started to change.

Parts of the monster horde started to buckle under the pressure of constant losses and human retaliation. At first, it was hard to notice, since only a few monsters at the edges of the battlefield were retreating. Then larger groups of monsters started to break off from the assault and flee toward the woods. The defenders rained missiles as the monsters fled, but none of the melee combatants dared to follow them outside the safety of the walls. It certainly seemed like the monsters weren't fleeing in total disarray. They maintained organization far better than an equally sized human army would, especially while escaping the battlefield. Alice was both impressed and horrified by the level of coordination they maintained.

Fighting an enemy like this wasn't easy. The defenders were lucky they had held on this long. Worse, the monster horde didn't seem like it had given up. They were retreating to the woods to prepare for the next battle. Based on the newly appointed [Commander]'s words, the horde would return tomorrow.

Ethan drifted down from the sky while several defenders relaxed. Another few minutes passed as Alice saw [Soldiers] in urgent need of medical care get dragged off to healers and the defenders on the walls reorganized themselves. Then the [Commander] they had spoken with earlier reappeared.

"I've passed along word of your arrival. The gate is broken right now, so it might be hard for you to cross. You can wait a few minutes for our [Masons] to repair it, or fly over the wall if you prefer. Normally we have a no-flying policy, but you're free to ignore that law right now. After helping us, we can extend that much courtesy to you," the man said before he chuckled bitterly.

Ethan thought about it for a moment before he sighed. "We'll wait for the gate to open. It would be best to enter the city the normal way, I think." He turned toward the rest of the group and then spoke much more quietly. "I'm already below the amount of mana I prefer to keep reserved for emergencies, Let's conserve mana and perks as much as possible."

Alice didn't have any objections, and neither did the others. A few minutes later, the gate was repaired enough that it could open properly. As it creaked open, they made their way inside. Alice started to filter her mana while she walked, then grimaced. She was nearly out of mana, and trying to fix her class mana only gave her a headache. She decided to look at the rewards from the fight later and focused on the city they were walking into. She was appalled by what she saw.

Much like the capital of Sendria, signs directed people in different directions when they entered the capital. After Allira's translation, Alice learned that one of them was a directive for those who were suffering from class poisoning. Another one was for reporting monster sightings and problems in nearby villages. A third sign indicated the way for refugees in need of housing. The streets were nearly deserted of regular civilians, but they were filled with injured combatants and [Organic Mages].

As the group stepped into the city, the [Commander] ran over to them. His sides heaved unsteadily as he arrived.

"Honored Immortals and traveling companions. It's a pleasure to see you in the city, and . . ." He trailed off, and Alice got the distinct impression he was trying to remember what he was supposed to say. After pausing for an awkward period of silence, the man sighed and rubbed his forehead. "The [King] would like to see you. If you're interested in meeting him, he is available now."

"That's fine with me," said Ethan.

The group moved toward the palace. The first few times Alice had been in a palace, she had been a lot more interested and intimidated, but this time, she found herself feeling oddly tired. There wasn't much to Fendrallia's capital that she hadn't already seen elsewhere, apart from the scope of the damage caused by the monsters and class-mana madness. The palace looked like it was styled after Illvaria's palace, but with a considerably lower budget and less skilled [Enchanters] and [Architects]. The enchantments were weaker and lower in quantity, the building was supported by less System mana, and the decorations were simpler in design.

For a few moments, Alice felt that her life had become stranger than she had ever imagined. She was now comparing palace architecture between countries. Most people never entered even one palace, but Alice had now seen enough of them to start comparing them to each other.

The [King] of Fendrallia was a balding man in his late forties. He had a somewhat dignified appearance, despite the light reflecting off his bald head, and he had a firm look in his eyes.

When the group entered, the man gave them a deep bow.

"Thank you for assisting the city during our time of need, Immortals of Illvaria and Superbia. You didn't have any obligation to help, but you did anyway. We appreciate that."

"It was no problem. Helping other humans fend off monster swarms is natural during times of crisis," said Ethan.

The [King] simply sighed. "I wish that I had more information, but . . . well, things have been complicated recently. May we ask how long you are willing to stay?"

Alice frowned. Why was the [King] asking how long the group could stay? Alice had gotten the impression that Ethan intended to move on that night, or perhaps the next morning.

A moment later, the answer came to her. *He's hoping we'll stay longer so that the city's defenses can be further reinforced.* That made Alice think.

The group needed to keep moving. If Alice was ever going to have any hope of defusing this crisis and fixing it at its root, she needed to have access to every scrap of information she could get. That meant getting to their original destination as fast as possible so that she could finally start making class seeds.

On the other hand, was it right to refuse a [King] when he was asking them to help preserve the lives of his people? At the very least, it seemed incredibly cold to do so. Sure, Alice's actions might help save people later, and on a much larger scale—but at the same time, leaving now might doom the current inhabitants of this city. That made the decision far less clear-cut than she would have liked. It wasn't a case with an obvious no the way it was for human experimentation. It also wasn't an obvious yes, the way healing the village on the way to Fendrallia's capital had been. That had cost relatively little time, and the group had been preparing to rest for the night anyway.

Alice didn't like questions with ambiguous answers.

Before Alice could continue to ponder the matter, Ethan sighed and shook his head.

"My apologies, but we only intend to stay the night. We eliminated several hundred monsters already, and our mission is of utmost importance. However, we can fight again tomorrow as we're heading out, and we can carry messages to any other nearby cities. Do you have a message you wish to give?"

The [King] hesitated for a few moments as he looked at Ethan's face. It looked as if he was searching for a way to change Ethan's mind. Finally, the [King] sighed. He looked disappointed, but he nodded his head.

"Very well. I will have someone deliver a message to you tomorrow morning, which I request you carry to the nearest city with a functioning garrison or military. Would that be possible?"

"Yes."

The [King]'s forehead creased in worry, but he sighed and nodded. Less than a minute later, the group left the palace to find an inn for the night.

Chapter 58

The next morning, Alice's mana had regenerated enough for her to filter her class mana and deal with her System notifications. It was a good time to see how much she had progressed and pick up some new perks.

You have leveled up!
Scientist: 68→70, Scholar: 67→68, Explorer of Magic: 87→88, Kinetic Manabinder: 54→57, Careful Enchanter: 36→38

Her rewards for participating in the fight had been quite generous. Most likely, it was because Alice had experimented with different ways to use her mana during the fight, giving her a lot of progress in her research classes. She didn't get a new achievement, but she was still happy with her progress. More importantly, she had two new perks to choose, one for [Scientist] and one for [Kinetic Manabinder]. Alice scanned her status screen again and fell into thought.

If she had enough time, she might be able to get *three* new perks instead of two. [Legendary Organic Mage] was probably pretty close to level ten, and she was very interested in seeing what perks came out of that class. She was currently in the middle of a city besieged by monsters, so it would be easy to find injured people to heal. She had recovered a good chunk of her mana while in her dream library, so she could spare a bit to finish pushing the class to level ten.

She had also gotten very close to finishing her image in {Magic Modeling}, which was another positive note. She could finish it today, or tonight if she ended up busy during daytime hours.

After she finished filtering mana and checking her improvements, she started looking through her [Scientist] perks. The first thing to check was whether she wanted to combine perks or make a completely new perk.

{Mana Measurement} doesn't really need to be evolved into a new skill. It does exactly what it's supposed to. {Sample Collection} is basically just a storage perk, but

it's totally fine if it remains as a storage perk. Having a portable inventory I can bring with me is far too convenient to give up. {Safety Analysis} is far too useful to give up. {Shared Memory} has somewhat limited use, but it would be a shame to lose it. {Advanced Mana Measurement} is just an upgraded version of {Mana Measurement}, but I appreciate being able to measure mana near me. As for {For Science!}, the perk is far, far too useful to give up.

Alice scratched her head.

She wasn't willing to give up any of her [Scientist] perks. Perk combinations usually made perks better, but they also changed the very nature of the perk. Eventually, Alice sighed and decided to grab a new perk instead.

There were only two perk options, which was a bit low, so Alice gave both of them a careful read before she made a choice.

The first one was rather odd, but interesting.

Experimental Duplication
Requirements: Scientist level 70 or higher, Intelligence 150 or higher, enchanter class at level 35 or higher, have experimented on at least one hundred different types of material, have some interest in continued experiments on some form of physical object

You may spend mana to create copies of materials that you are currently experimenting on. This mana may be paid from any magic seed, but the closer the mana seed is in concept to whatever you are trying to duplicate, the lower the mana cost. (Cost of created material is based on weight and magical compatibility of item—items such as iron that can hold dozens of enchantment-related instructions cost far more per gram of matter than ordinary iron.)
Note: Creation of physical matter using mana is expensive! Proceed with caution!

The perk literally let her *create matter* out of mana. Considering the fact that Alice was still pretty sure mana obviated the laws of thermodynamics, that meant that she could theoretically create infinite matter if she had infinite time. Alice was more than a little amused by that idea, but at the same time, she suspected it wasn't that relevant to her current situation. She started trying to analyze the pros and cons.

The perk had some risk to it, because Alice had no idea how expensive matter creation was. If it took thousands of Mariums to create one gram of ordinary matter, the perk would be useless. She was nowhere near someone like Ethan's total mana capacity. However, if the cost was more reasonable, it gave Alice another way to address some of the material shortage problems that Illvaria had run into after the crisis started. For now, enchanting materials were being shipped north from Cyra, giving the country a source for System-enchantment materials. There was no guarantee this would continue, though. There was also a distinct possibility that some sort of rare material might be involved in creating artificial magic seeds. If that turned out to be the case, having a way to duplicate more might be a matter of life or death once Alice reached that point.

Alice was actually pretty interested in the perk when she thought of it like that, but it was also a very narrow use case for a scenario that might not happen.

The other one was even more odd, but also considerably more interesting.

Experimental Magic
Requirements: Scientist level 70 or higher, Intelligence 150 or higher, at least three different primary classes that are magic-related and above level 30, Magic stat of 150 or higher, at least three achievements of rarity 8 or greater

You gain a magic seed that is "experimental." It is always at 100% mana conversion ratio, and this total cannot be influenced by any other perks, achievements, etc.

This magic seed can change what type of mana it produces at any time. It can only produce noncompound types of mana.

Note: While this perk changes the type of mana PRODUCED, it does not change what is already present in the seed. This perk will prevent any conflicts between the present types of mana, but you still need to wait for more mana to be generated if you want to experiment with a new type of mana.

{Experimental Magic} was interesting. Alice had a long list of types of mana that she suspected System mana needed to work. Some were obvious, such as math mana and communication mana. However, some types of System mana were less obvious, leaving Alice clueless about what she was still missing.

This perk promised to fix that. It would let her experiment with more odd and unusual types of mana, and allow her more room to experiment with different types of mana combinations. It was very difficult to combine different types of mana if they weren't part of the same compound seed, but this would still give her some room for experimentation, at least. This perk promised to offer a whole new world of possibilities if Alice was clever about how she used it. It would also enhance her combat abilities. Alice had used up most of her antimagic mana and her dimensional mana during the battle yesterday. This seed would let her store a huge amount of extra antimagic and dimensional mana if she knew a fight was coming up.

Of course, using this perk for combat would also require that she prepare her mana reserves in advance. It still needed time to generate new types of mana. Alice still thought it had a lot of potential, though, despite that drawback.

The one and only reason she still found herself thinking about taking the first perk instead was fear. If she needed some sort of specific material to keep the world from collapsing, and she was stuck with {Experimental Magic} instead, Alice would hate herself.

But {Experimental Magic} would speed up some of her experiments. She wouldn't have to think carefully about some of her seed choices when {System's Ambition} came off cooldown, because she would already know exactly what building blocks she needed next. Most importantly, the {Experimental Magic} seed would have a lot of other utility. It seemed so incredibly useful that Alice didn't want to pass it up.

Alice spent a few minutes thinking about the choice before she finally chose {Experimental Magic}.

If she truly needed {Experimental Duplication}, she would be able to pick it up at level seventy-five. However, Alice thought it was too much of a waste to spend a perk on something she *might* need. She wasn't sure if she could even make it to the finish line in the first place. Restoring the System was a difficult and time-consuming journey. She needed to use every perk she could to speed up the process, and she would worry about what she was missing when she got there.

After choosing her new perk, Alice felt a new magic seed appear inside her mage core. When she focused on it, she had a feeling that the seed was asking her what type of mana to produce. For now, Alice set it to dimensional mana. It would be useful if they encountered the horde of monsters while exiting the city. When it was halfway full, she would swap it to antimagic mana.

After that, Alice focused on her next perk choice, for [Kinetic Manabinder]. It was the first time that she had a chance for perk combination for the class. Even more exciting was the fact that she had taken the apprentice version of this class before progressing it into a regular class. That meant she had far more options for perk combination available.

After much consideration, Alice finally settled on a few different options.

The first thing she ruled out was direct improvements to her combat power.

While Alice still wanted to be able to defend herself, for now, her strength was not her priority. She was strong enough to defend herself from most normal threats, but she was so far away from top-tier combat that a few perks wouldn't make a difference. She had a System to fix, and that didn't leave her much space to enhance her own strength, especially when she had already taken {Experimental Magic} to help bolster her weak combat strength.

Instead, Alice decided to focus on her enchanting skills. [Kinetic Manabinder] was a hybrid class that focused on both enchanting and kinetic combat. Since artificial magic seeds were created by Immortals focused on enchanting, Alice needed to boost her enchanting capabilities as much as possible.

When Alice focused on her enchanting-related perks, she found five options for perks she could combine: {Speed Analysis}, {Overclock}, {Kinetic Enchanting}, {Enhanced Focus}, and {Mana's Binding}.

Based on what results she could see, {Mana's Binding} combined well with all five other perks, and it seemed like one of the better building blocks for her perk combination. Alice decided to slot that in as the first ingredient for her combined perk.

Mana's Binding
Requirements: Kinetic Manabinder level 5 or higher
When creating an enchantment using kinetic energy, the enchantment will become much more resilient against wear and tear. This perk also makes your enchantments more resistant to damage from both internal and external factors. Finally, this perk helps improve the internal stability of kinetic enchantments.

It was a perk that had been with her for a long time, and it was still mildly helpful, but Alice honestly didn't *need* it anymore. It was more of a minor passive boost to her enchantments than anything else. At this point, she could do without it. Hopefully, combining it with another perk would elevate the perk to the point where it was useful again.

After that, Alice started figuring out which perks to exclude. {Overclock} boosted the speed at which she made enchantments, but that wasn't relevant to the quality of her work. Quality clearly mattered much more right now, since she was trying to find a way to replicate a feat usually restricted to Immortals.

{Kinetic Enchanting} was more of a way to buff whatever materials she was working on, rather than a direct boost to her enchanting, so it was also ignored. That left {Speed Analysis}, which let her do things with enchantments that weren't normally available to her, such as allowing her enchantments to detect velocity, and {Enhanced Focus}, which let her focus better while working on an enchantment. {Enhanced Focus} was more of a production-speed boost than a quality boost, but since it also helped her focus while working, it was an indirect quality boost.

Alice thought about it for a few more minutes, to make sure she was happy with her choice, and then decided to use {Speed Analysis} as the second component of her new perk. It fit her goals better.

Speed Analysis
Requirements: Kinetic Manabinder level 40, Intelligence 150 or higher, Perception 100 or higher, significant time spent trying to manipulate object speeds using enchantments
You may attach an additional advanced sensing function to any enchantments you make. This allows you to make objects sense how quickly or slowly an object is moving, what objects it is heading toward, and a variety of other, more precise functions. You can use this to trigger other, more conditional components of enchantments.

With her two selections made, Alice combined the perks.

<table>
<tr><td>

Speed Analysis and Manipulation (Tier 2 perk, level 55 Kinetic Manabinder)
(level 40 Kinetic Manabinder perk + level 5 Kinetic Manabinder perk)
Perk costs: Speed Analysis + Mana's Binding

</td></tr>
<tr><td>

All your enchantments become slightly connected to the concept of kinetic energy. This allows them to detect any kinetic energy in nearby objects and use that detection as trigger conditions for other parts of the perk, or directly warp the kinetic energy of nearby objects.

</td></tr>
</table>

Alice had been hoping that the perk combination would somehow make her general enchanting abilities stronger, or perhaps add in a few more things that let her close the distance between her enchantments and the enchantments of an Immortal. Instead, her enchantments were now innately connected to the concept of kinetic energy. Alice had never seen a perk explicitly refer to a concept before, and she had no idea what it meant in practice. Alice was obviously familiar with kinetic energy; she had learned about physics on Earth, and she was a [Kinetic Mage]. But why was the perk specifically mentioning the *concept* of kinetic energy, instead of just referring to it as kinetic energy? The System's description was less than helpful.

Alice frowned before she decided that if the System description was vague, she would just have to test it out herself.

She left the inn and grabbed a few raw enchanting materials from a nearby enchanting shop. After some tinkering, she confirmed that it was now possible to do a few interesting things with her enchantments.

Before, it had been somewhat difficult to make her enchantments sense the speed of other objects. Now, however, it was much, much easier to get the whole setup working. It also didn't cost any instruction slots anymore, meaning that she could add far more detailed if-then statements into her enchantments without needing to improve the quality of her materials.

However, that wasn't the interesting part. The interesting part was that some of the enchantments she could make were different than before. Specifically, it was as the perk noted—her enchanted objects could now interfere with the way velocity worked—or at least, that was what Alice thought was happening.

When she tried out an enchantment that slowed down objects in its area, rather than just spending mana to slow things down, it felt more like the enchantment created a small field of space where velocity *itself* was slowed down. It wasn't that objects had lost momentum—it was that reality itself had changed on a more fundamental level. Alice had a hard time putting it into more precise words than that, and she wasn't even sure when she would find a use for this property. However, Alice was faintly reminded of the way belief mana could change the laws of physics and reality. This perk seemed to borrow some of the same principles, albeit in a very limited way. She decided to keep the perk in mind and hope she found a use for it later.

With her two perk selections made, Alice closed her status screen and got to work healing people. She cured problems of both the class-mana variety and more mundane injuries. By the time she was low on mana, Alice had gotten the other thing she was hoping for.

You have leveled up!
Legendary Organic Mage: 9→10

After getting that final level, Alice started scanning the list of perks. She was pleasantly surprised by what she found. They weren't anything revolutionary for her current level, but they were exceptional for level-five perks.

The first perk was quite interesting.

Legendary Efficiency
Requirements: Legendary Organic Mage level 5 or higher, Intelligence 150 or higher, Magic 150 or higher, have a class at least partially related to combat at level 50 or higher
When using organic magic for *any* purpose (including feeding it to perks that transform mana into other effects), gain a 10% mana cost reduction (multiplicative with any other cost-reduction effects). Any attempt to mobilize and manipulate organic magic also becomes 10% faster. Any internal injuries or problems that would result from healing people with organic magic are mildly reduced in size and severity. (This effect will not occur if you are deliberately trying to harm someone with organic magic.)

The second and last parts of the perk weren't that unusual. Perks that made it easier to heal people were pretty normal, and perks that made it faster and easier to manipulate organic mana also weren't that uncommon. If the perk had only consisted of those two things, Alice wouldn't have found {Legendary Efficiency} to be very interesting.

However, in addition to those two effects, the perk also had a mana cost reduction. This was an effect Alice had never seen before. There were plenty of perks that made Alice use mana more *efficiently*, but they never actually reduced the cost of an action outright. They were just helping her make better use of the mana she was already spending, not dropping the cost in a way that totally defied the energy economy of mana costs.

At first glance, this might not seem that impressive, but when one actually thought about how energy conservation was supposed to work, it was obvious that this perk was bizarre. Alice couldn't help but wonder what would happen if she got twenty similar perks. Even if all of them were multiplicative and not additive, that still meant that she could spend 12 percent of the mana to do something that *should* cost far more mana. By that time, she would be outright breaking people's understanding of how much one Marium of mana could accomplish. That was an incredible effect.

Not to mention, this perk also applied to those that converted her organic mana into completely different effects, such as the perk that allowed her to convert mana into time dilation. The perk was odd, but incredible.

Alice was already pretty happy with her first perk, but her second was even more interesting.

<table>
<tr><td>

Legendary Muscle Enhancement
Requirements: Legendary Organic Mage level 5 or higher, have a class related to experimenting with mana at level 75 or higher, Magic stat 100 or higher, have used magic in combat at least ten times, have used weapons in combat at least ten times

</td></tr>
<tr><td>

You gain the ability to spend organic mana to massage your muscles.
This will slowly but permanently enhance the strength of the target. (This will increase the Strength stat of the target. Higher stats mean that it's harder and takes longer to raise the same stat more.) Cannot be performed on other people without their consent.

</td></tr>
</table>

This perk was rather promising. The effect itself wasn't actually that powerful—after all, Alice had a lot of competing uses for her organic mana, and adding in one that improved her [Strength] wasn't very useful. Her [Strength] was at a decent level, and she didn't have much of a use for more.

Even so, the implications were fascinating. Raising stats was far from easy. The further along people got, the less efficient raw stat training became. That was why Immortals typically didn't have truly insane stats—past a certain point, it started to take years or even decades just to raise a stat by one. Past a certain point, the only real way to get a major stat boost was to use either perks or achievements. While this perk didn't outright remove this issue, it did partially reduce the diminishing returns of raw stat training. In a way, it fit Alice's needs surprisingly well—or at least, it would if she actually used her [Strength] stat.

Unfortunately, Alice didn't really utilize it for much. When an actual fight broke out, Alice's first response was to use her magic. If she was trying to fight someone in physical combat, things had already gone horribly wrong.

Despite the perk's debatable value, Alice was still excited to see it. Even if she had no use for [Strength], it was still a hint about what kind of things she could expect to get from her [Legendary Organic Mage] class. If this was the kind of perk she got at level five, how much better would the level-ten and -fifteen perks be? Perhaps she could find a perk that let her boost her [Intelligence] over time, or her [Endurance].

Alice felt herself grinning at the thought. At the same time, she started wondering whether it was worthwhile to replace one of her main classes with the

[Legendary Organic Mage] class. If this was the kind of perk she could get from it when it was a secondary class, how much better would it be as a primary class?

Alice glanced through her primary classes before she sighed.

Even though a part of her wanted to throw out one of her primary classes and replace it with [Legendary Organic Mage], when she actually looked, it was hard to find a good class to remove. [Explorer of Magic] was obviously out of the question—the class was the core of her current setup. [Scientist] also had a lot of valuable perks that she was loath to lose. [Kinetic Manabinder] and [Careful Enchanter] were likely to be very relevant to Alice's attempts to create artificial magic seeds, so throwing them away would be foolish. [Scholar] provided her with her dream library, which Alice was incredibly reliant upon. Having a 50 percent boost to the amount of time she could research each day was too valuable to give up.

That left [Survivor], which Alice suspected [Legendary Organic Mage] would eventually replace. [Survivor] mostly offered {Adrenaline Rush}, {Enhanced Senses}, {Extended Tissues}, and {Dimensional Camouflage}. All four of those were useful to her current fighting style, but if [Legendary Organic Mage] got higher in level, it would probably provide its own replacements. Alice decided that if [Legendary Organic Mage] ever got higher in level than [Survivor], she would find a [Priest of the System] and swap around her primary classes. However, at least for now she had a hard time justifying the swap.

With her mind made up, Alice turned her attention back to her final perk option. This one had a lot of practical value.

<table>
<tr><td>

Healing Reserve
Requirements: Legendary Organic Mage level 5 or higher, Intelligence higher than 150, have healed at least thirty people, have cured at least five different types of illness or injury

</td></tr>
<tr><td>

You create a secondary energy storage that can ONLY store organic mana. Upon being stored in this energy reserve, the energy will become far less malleable than normal organic mana. It may only be used to heal others. Any attempt to misconstrue this healing into harm will fail, wasting the mana without accomplishing anything.
May only store 250 Mariums of organic mana before it runs out of storage capacity.

</td></tr>
</table>

This one was a simple, no-nonsense increase in the storage capacity of her organic magic seed. Specifically, it gave her an extra 250 Mariums of mana to work with. This mana would be incapable of doing many of the things that regular organic mana could do, such as enhancing muscles or harming enemies. Even with those restrictions, Alice found the perk rather interesting.

Alice's organic magic seed had increased to 85 percent recently, as a result of [Scholar of Magic]. Combined with her [Magic] stat of 171 and her stat effectiveness of 192 percent, that meant her organic seed stored about 277 Mariums of organic mana. This was with her unusually high magic stat, and a stat effectiveness ordinary people could only dream of. This perk nearly doubled her organic mana reserve.

Of course, the perk also had some notable weaknesses. The biggest issue was that it didn't improve as she improved. Even if Alice managed to triple her [Magic] stat in the future, this perk would still only give her 250 Mariums of storage. It also didn't increase her mana regeneration at all, unlike a real increase to her [Magic] stat. But those were minor weaknesses. Even a monster like Ethan couldn't treat 250 Mariums of mana like nothing. He might not care that much about an increase of only 250 Mariums, but it still gave Alice a number that even an *Immortal* would notice, albeit barely.

Alice didn't hesitate for long before deciding what she wanted. {Legendary Muscle Enhancement} and {Legendary Efficiency} were both excellent perks. They were so good that Alice wished she could take all three of them. But {Healing Reserve} was too good to pass up. So Alice grabbed {Healing Reserve}. A moment later, Alice felt a new space open inside her mana core. It was attached to her organic seed and felt strangely similar to an inflatable balloon with no helium inside.

Alice spent a few moments feeling it out before realizing she didn't need to do anything with it. If her magic seed was full, her excess organic mana would funnel itself into the extra space. Of course, Alice could also manually funnel her organic mana into the extra space if she wanted to, although she wasn't sure why she would bother.

Alice *did* decide to funnel a bit of organic mana into the perk, just to test how it worked. She found that the mana inside the extra storage space was a bit different than normal mana. It was as if the mana was filtered the moment it entered the empty balloon created by the perk. After inspecting it for a few more minutes, Alice shrugged and stopped paying attention to it. The perk worked as intended, and she didn't think she would learn how to do anything terribly interesting about the System by inspecting her new extra storage further.

After that, Alice went to find Ethan. She found the rest of the group already packing up again, so she joined them. Half an hour later, the group hopped back on their horses and left the city. Alice felt a bit nervous as she wondered whether the nearby monsters would attack them—but it seemed like they'd given up on attacking the city, or at least they were waiting until Alice's group moved on. She felt a weird mixture of thankfulness and sadness as she realized that the monsters might be waiting for them to leave. The monsters were even more intelligent than she had thought—they were waiting until the threat was gone so that they could resume their plans. Still, the group couldn't afford to stop and spend multiple days whittling down the monster horde. They would just have to hope the people here could hold out on their own.

With that sliver of uneasiness and resignation in her mind, the group rode out of the city. Soon, they approached the border between Fendrallia and Morendia. They had nearly reached their destination.

Chapter 59

As the group rode forward, Alice went back to working on her {Magic Model-ing} image of a mana gem. She spent the next three and a half hours in a daze before, at last, she put the finishing touch on her project. Alice grinned as the final bits of the mana-gem image slid into place. It was time to see what distin-guished a broken mana gem from a working one.

The first thing Alice noticed upon comparing the two images was that the working mana gem had incorporated her Alice mana in a rather odd way.

Alice had already known that the mana gem in her brain was somehow linked to achievements. After all, every single one of her achievements seemed to be stored in her mana gem, and using her achievement to fix her mana gem had immediately restored them all to 100 percent efficiency.

It was also obvious that a working mana gem did something with person mana, the strange type of mana that appeared after someone reached level seventy-five. After all, the mana gem had absorbed all her Alice mana the moment it started working properly again.

However, the working mana gem had processed Alice mana in a very different way than she'd expected it to. She had thought it would toss all her Alice mana into a new facet. Instead, it seemed like the mana gem had absorbed all her Alice mana and used it to create a core. It looked like a tiny, resplendent star in the center of her mana gem.

Of course, Alice could only see this when she zoomed in to a ridiculous level. Without the high-resolution images that {Magic Modeling} provided, Alice would have never noticed the little glowing mana core. It was so tiny that even once she knew what to look for, she couldn't find it with her regular vision.

Alice was very glad that she had taken {Magic Modeling}. She had no idea how she ever could have made this discovery without the perk.

As Alice continued to explore the image of a working mana gem, she discovered something else. Not only did Alice mana appear to be some sort of mini core for her mana gem, but it also had a lot of little threads of mana connecting it to the rest of the gem. Those threads strongly resembled the belief mana that Alice had analyzed while looking at mana-born monsters. Alice suspected that, somehow, belief mana was connecting Alice mana and the rest of the mana core.

Alice had no idea what to make of that. It was information she didn't have enough context to do anything with. However, it did make her consider something more deeply.

Alice mana was probably a form of mana generated by human beliefs. Alice still remembered that before she'd dealt with it, Alice mana had encouraged her to act based on how people thought of her. She felt a stronger urge to research things, less desire to socialize, and a stronger urge to obsess over things. While all these behaviors were quite normal for her, under the influence of Alice mana, her actions lacked the internal consistency and logic that usually guided her actions.

Strings of belief mana made things behave the way people *thought* they should behave, even if that overrode physics or the laws of reality. Class mana was very similar—if one had [Fisherman] mana and didn't have a class seed to absorb it, one would behave more and more like a stereotypical [Fisherman]. They would lose any other aspects of their personality in the process, essentially becoming a walking stereotype.

Class mana and Alice mana were surprisingly similar to each other and also seemed strongly connected to belief mana.

Alice had *also* realized, at an earlier point in time, that achievements were inherently linked to beliefs. There was no other way to explain why her achievement {Immortal's Apprentice at the Battle Against the Society} described her as a combat-oriented mage, even though she clearly wasn't. In fact, last time she had looked at her mana gem, she had theorized that achievements were like a dumping ground, where the System tossed weird chunks of mana that it didn't know what to do with.

Looking at the way the threads of belief mana connected Alice mana to the rest of the mana gem, Alice suspected there was more to the picture. It looked like the mana gem was built exclusively to regulate beliefs and how they interacted with people. The mana gem in her brain had collected a wide variety of beliefs related to her and then organized and controlled all of them. Each type of belief related to her was stored in a slightly different way, and all of them had slightly different forms, but they were all kind of the same thing. Achievements were a representation of beliefs about her, and so was Alice mana.

Class seeds were similar. They were built to absorb mana, which had beliefs mixed into it, and then turned those harmful forms of mana into something useful that didn't harm the host.

Why was there a division between the two? What made a mana gem different from a class gem?

Alice started thinking about this question as she analyzed the images of mana gems, but it didn't take her long before she realized the answer. Standardization.

Based on her understanding of the System, as well as what historical records Alice had of "updates" the System had made over the centuries, the System added new classes every so often. These classes were probably built whenever enough people recognized the existence of a new job, after which the System took those beliefs, standardized them, and created a new set of perks to suit that class's needs.

The achievements section of the mana gem seemed to be a place to toss belief mana that didn't have a job associated with it, or belief mana that didn't quite match any existing class seed.

For example, a healer who found the cure for an incurable disease and a regular healer were both healers. However, people would still think of the former very differently than the latter, adding a certain distinction to that person. That was probably how the System determined what was an achievement versus what belonged in a class seed.

Or at least, that was Alice's best explanation for why class mana and achievements seemed *almost* the same, but subtly different. She also thought that the dividing line between something that was a job and that wasn't a job seemed rather arbitrary. In fact, it was probably only based on what people believed counted as a job or not a job, making it weird and inconsistent. Just like the achievements section of her status screen.

This did still leave a major question unanswered: Why did mana gems only seem to appear after level seventy-five? Was it tied to the sudden creation of person mana?

Alice spent a while trying to find anything in the structure of the mana gem itself that would answer this question, but sadly, there was nothing to work with. The mana gem didn't exactly have a user's manual lying around in one corner. Therefore, Alice started to make crazy guesses.

Her first theory was that it was tied to the changes people experienced every twenty-five levels. Every twenty-five levels, perks changed their nature, and aging speed also dropped drastically. Most level seventy-fives took two or three years to age one year. They weren't quite Immortal yet, but they were clearly different from regular people. Level seventy-five was a major dividing line for biology in this world. Before level seventy-five, while people gained some resistance to aging speed, it was usually more of a life-span extension than a major difference. It was more like the distinction between life span for people on Earth who ate healthily and exercised often—it could make you live longer, but it didn't totally transform you.

Alice suspected that level seventy-five was *also* a dividing line between someone who was still human and someone who had started to step into Immortality. Perhaps the Alice mana that she had seen, as well as the belief mana and the mana gem, were some sort of preparation stage for this transition.

Alice also remembered that Ethan had told her all Immortals got a special achievement upon reaching Immortality. This achievement gave Immortals the ability to recover from lethal damage once a week, as well as a host of other, more specific bonuses. Ethan had never told Alice exactly what his achievement for Immortality gave him, since that directly pertained to his combat abilities. However, he had strongly hinted that Alice should expect huge bonuses to several attributes, a few unique abilities that were equivalent to level-one-hundred combined perks, and possibly a few weird but useful new abilities. That seemed to be what most Immortals got, according to what details Ethan had. He had admitted he wasn't 100 percent sure if that was how every Immortality achievement looked—but it was a good baseline for understanding.

With that in mind, perhaps Alice mana was also a building block for her Immortality achievement. As she grew more renowned and her other abilities improved, the Alice mana in her brain had grown more dense and well established, so perhaps once it reached a certain level, it would transform into a proper achievement—one that would grant her Immortality and make her stop aging forever.

That still left a few questions, like what specifically was required to form person mana and how mana gems could be created. Alice still wasn't 100 percent certain whether people below level seventy-five just had tiny mana gems she couldn't detect, or whether achievements were handled some other way before that point. But it felt like a reasonable start to an explanation, at least.

Alice shook her head. If her guess was correct, it also meant that trying to reach Immortality without the System might be problematic. While Alice had always thought of Immortality more as a side goal, she was still interested in it. Old age sounded horrible, and avoiding it forever sounded nice. If Alice wanted to get the messy mana gem, uncoordinated class mana, and Alice mana working together, she would probably need a rough idea how the System did that. Since the System was gone, that would be quite difficult.

Alice sighed and decided to deal with that problem when she got there. At least for now, she was still quite far away from Immortality, and she was already en route to figuring out how to restore the last big part of the System. She had made several useful inferences, and while she hadn't confirmed any of them, she was making progress. She would just have to keep an eye out for further clues and evidence. The most important thing in science was to keep an open mind. She would take her current hypotheses and do her best to disprove them. If they could survive rigorous scrutiny, they were likely correct. If she found an easy way to disprove them, they were clearly wrong.

Alice returned to the image of her working mana gem. There was one other thing she had wanted to check, and now was the perfect time to do so.

Alice knew that at least for a few seconds, right after using her achievement to fix her mana gem, the gem had somehow categorized and fixed all her achievements. Alice was hoping that her image of a working mana gem had captured this image—if so, she might have a good idea how to fix achievements manually, without relying on her achievement to do it for her. So she started scouring the image of a working mana gem again.

It took a lot more searching and analyzing, but after a while, Alice *did* find a little chunk of rainbow mana working on straightening out one of the facets of her mana gem. Since every single facet was an achievement, that meant one thing: Alice had, indeed, captured an image of the System at work fixing an achievement. She grinned.

She spent several more minutes trying to figure out what the System was doing, and after some analysis, she gained a basic understanding of the process. In order to fix an achievement, it looked like she first had to tell the System what an achievement *was*. Part of the rainbow mana captured in her {Magic Modeling} image looked like it was inspecting, sorting, and cataloging exactly what the achievement was, where it had come from, and what it did. Then it looked like the System made some sort of surgical alteration to the achievement, using a mixture of math mana, pure mana, filtration mana, and at least one other type of mana she was less familiar with. Somehow, these types of mana were straightening out the achievement, turning it from a chunk of partially controlled strings of belief mana and System mana into something a bit more . . . standard? Controlled?

Alice didn't have a good word for it, but it was obvious that something had been done to make the mana more stable. It hadn't totally changed the nature of the mana, but Alice suspected it was part of what let achievements function properly when the System was around.

Alice rubbed her chin thoughtfully.

She still only had a rough idea what was going on, but that was better than before, at least. The System probably had some sort of standard framework for how achievements were supposed to work. The surgical alteration process likely took achievements and converted them from raw, unprocessed mana into something usable by making them fit a template. Alice still wasn't entirely sure what that template was, but if she kept analyzing her image of a working mana gem, she could probably make some guesses. From there, she would just need to do some trial and error before she would learn how to fix achievements. She found herself smiling at the thought.

The two components of the System she still couldn't fix were achievements and class seeds. Now, she had a glimpse of how to fix achievements. There was still work to be done, but she had a foot in the door. They had also reached the border of Morendia, where she would learn how to fix class seeds.

"Ethan . . . do you mind if I take another look at your mana gem later?" Alice asked after signaling for him to move closer and dropping her voice to a whisper.

Ethan quickly set up his privacy perk and then gave Alice a glance. "Did you finally finish looking at your own gem, in both a working and broken condition?"

"Yes, I did," said Alice. "Do you want to see?"

Ethan nodded, so Alice used {Shared Memory} to give Ethan a review. She spent several minutes going over the two images, as well as explaining her own guesses about the nature of person mana and what she had found out about achievements so far.

After hearing her thoughts, Ethan started to look a bit nervous. "I'm not a researcher, but your results sound plausible. If so, reaching Immortality will be harder for you." Then he relaxed, and actually laughed. "But I suppose it's lucky that you're one of, if not *the* only person on the planet who can solve this problem. If I were to place an issue like this in front of Sujia, she would never fix it, even if she had two extra centuries to work with." Ethan grinned. "As for achievements, they aren't anywhere near as horrendously broken as classes, so we can probably treat that as a lower priority. I'll try to see if there's a way to get willing observation targets, but we can focus on other things first. For now, keep your eyes on the road. We've finally reached our destination."

While Alice had been lost in thought, the group had crossed the major river separating Fendrallia and Morendia. The monster-infested swamps and tundras were behind them, and Alice could make out the outline of another large city.

After several weeks of travel, the group had finally arrived at Morendia, the homeland of Demor. It was a place where Alice could learn to make artificial magic seeds and solve the last major problem caused by the collapse of the System. And with that, she would finally assemble all the knowledge she needed to save this dying world.

ABOUT THE AUTHOR

Acaswell is the author of the LitRPG series A Budding Scientist in a Fantasy World and Markets and Multiverses. He was born in Oregon and now resides in Colorado.